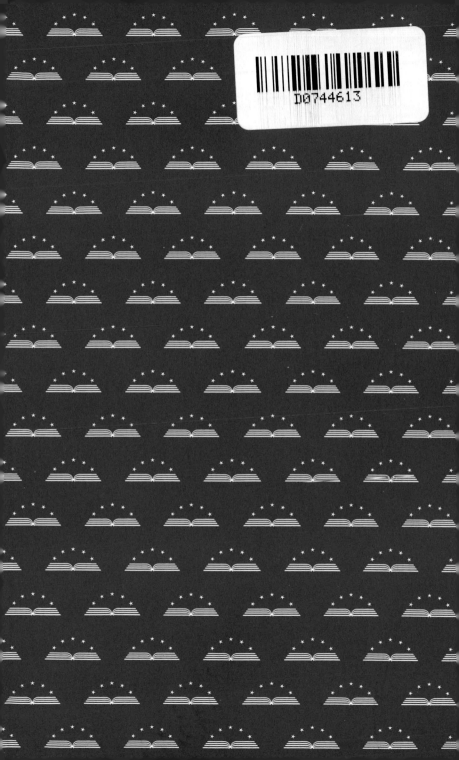

AMERICAN FANTASTIC TALES

AMERICAN FANTASTIC TALES

TERROR AND THE UNCANNY
FROM POE TO THE PULPS

Peter Straub, editor

THE LIBRARY OF AMERICA

Some of the material in this volume is reprinted with permission
of the holders of copyright and publication rights.
Acknowledgments are on page 736.

The paper used in this publication meets the
minimum requirements of the American National Standard for
Information Sciences—Permanence of Paper for Printed
Library Materials, ANSI Z39.48—1984.

Distributed to the trade in the United States
by Penguin Group (USA) Inc.
and in Canada by Penguin Books Canada Ltd.

Library of Congress Control Number: 2009927073
ISBN 978-1-59853-047-6

———

First Printing
The Library of America—196

Manufactured in the United States of America

Contents

Introduction

MOST YEARS, I set aside four or five days in mid-March to attend a gathering in Florida called The International Conference on the Fantastic in the Arts. It is the only occasion I know where writers and academics gather together in the absence of fans to discuss, among other things, precisely the kinds of stories to be found in the two volumes of *American Fantastic Tales*. (The other things have included fairy tales, anime, the films of George Romero and Hayao Miyazaki, Philip K. Dick, Joseph Cornell boxes, Doctor Who, and Tolkien. You get the idea.) During these conferences, for at least a couple of years now, John Clute (the only full-time professional critic and theorist in the field of science fiction and fantastic literature) has been using the occasion to evolve and refine an obvious-only-after-you-think-about-it theory: that fiction of this kind, at least in the form seen here, emerged as an expression of the universal sense of loss, grief, and terror produced by the gradual replacement of the Enlightenment's orderly, rational, reassuring world-view with the unstable and untrustworthy universe that came into being during the nineteenth and twentieth centuries.

For now, let us at least take note that loss, grief, and terror echo throughout the two volumes of *American Fantastic Tales*. If the fantastic story originates in such emotions, as I believe it does, it is constantly confessing its origins, and with helpless fervor. Gothic literature in general is inherently melancholy, and melancholy is generally its most cheerful aspect. If you consider Poe and Lovecraft to be "gothic" writers, as I certainly do, then in most of the cases here we are dealing with the gothic sensibility, the many avatars of which are riddled with isolation, loneliness, and dread.

A glance at the tables of contents of these volumes makes clear that apart from one or two stories that might be borderline science fiction, we are dealing almost entirely with the genre category called horror, which in fact allows a very great degree of latitude as to method, theme, tone and content. Anybody who picks up these volumes will probably already know that a couple of decades ago horror took a self-inflicted drubbing from which it is only now beginning to recover. It had been existing on only the most marginal, liminal fringes of respectability since the thirties, and three or four hundred misbegotten novels published in the eighties and early nineties—novels that tended to come garbed in a good deal of chrome, which was draped across jackets featuring drops of blood, houses whose façades looked like faces, and baleful, red-eyed children—dumped it firmly into the gutter. (Actually, I recommend the gutter very highly. The company entertains, and the view illuminates.) However, Henry James, no gutter-dweller, regularly visited the well of "dear old sacred terror," which spoke to him of "those most mysterious of mysteries, the mysteries which are at our own doors." Conflating the gothic and the fantastic through the medium of psychology, James's formulation describes a great many of the stories collected here.

The word "Tales" in our title goes a considerable distance toward clarifying the principles that helped guide the editorial process. From a tale one expects a bit of wildness, of exaggeration and dramatic effect. The tale has no inherent concern with decorum, balance, or harmony. In a tale, the completion of the railway involves a magical hammer, a bloody hacksaw, a man with one eye the color of curdled milk, an oath at midnight, and a ghastly specter glimpsed wandering through a downpour along the riverbank at midnight. (And that right there, sonny, is how we built the railway.) A tale may not display a great deal of structural, psychological, or narrative sophistication, though it might possess all three, but it seldom takes its eye off its primary goal, the creation of a particular emotional state in its reader. Depending on the tale, that state could be wonder, amazement, shock, terror, anger, anxiety, melancholia, or the momentary frisson of horror.

Although tales of this kind always keep their prospective readers in mind, they tend to resist easy accommodation with familiar narrative templates. Part of their appeal can lie in the unpredictability and unexpectedness of the plotting, the sheer strangeness of the characterization, and what can be experienced as the dreamlike, associational flow of events. In all of these ways, tales retain a connection to what I take to be their earliest ancestors: myth, folktale, and oral narratives that pass through a generation or two before being written down. The fantastic has a long, long history, and it existed as both a way of seeing and a way of representing what is seen centuries before it found expression in fiction. A friend of mine who was raised speaking the ancient language of his country, Irish, which we wrongly call Gaelic, told me that when a long-ago tale-teller wished to summon the children and silence the crowd, he would begin with a formula equivalent to, but more commanding than, our own "Once upon a time": *Long, long ago there lived an old man, and if you had known this old man, you wouldn't be alive today.* You can practically hear the wind blowing through that, almost smell the wood smoke and the burning tobacco.

Human beings across every culture I know about require such stories, stories with cool winds and wood smoke. They speak to something deep within us, the capacity to conceptualize, objectify, and find patterns, thereby to create the flow of events and perceptions that find perfect expression in fiction. We are built this way, we create stories by reflex, unstoppably. But this elegant system really works best when the elements of the emerging story, whether it is being written or being read, are taken as literal fact. Almost always, to respond to the particulars of the fantastic as if they were metaphorical or allegorical is to drain them of vitality. (The first of these two volumes does contain a story I take to be an allegory, Alice Brown's "Golden Baby," but it is so hypnotically bizarre that the obviousness of the allegory hardly gets in the way.)

In a story-driven species like ourselves the application of the fantastic as a mode is metaphoric in itself. When I was sixteen years old, I had the first literary insight of my life, that Edgar Allan Poe had created a shrinking room where a pendulum-like scimitar swung ever nearer the heart of man lashed to a bed because, in some central fashion, he saw the world in those terms. That he could project this internal condition into fiction was what made the story, despite its overheated language and absurdly convenient ending, so vivid, so immediately persuasive, so gripping. By grace of the imagination, his aching, fearful metaphor had moved firmly into the realm of the literal.

*

By way of introducing a theme found here in story after story, let us briefly consider the Puritans. One of their first acts of accommodation to a new continent was the establishment of churches that told them some people, the "elect," were saved, the others damned, and one could do nothing about these inflexible categories. Every human being was profoundly sinful by nature. Only harsh, unremitting discipline and hard work joylessly executed could result in the good.

These grim, suspicious people lived in small communities located at the edge of the original first-growth American climax forest. In every way, this seems to me of crucial importance. What did they see in that forest, in that teeming darkness? Everything, we might say, that was not themselves, everything that threatened them most profoundly. Nature was much worse than merely a force not to be trusted; nature was, inherently, wicked in its nature.

Two hundred years and more after the arrival of the Puritans, this message was still coming through loud and clear. Bad Nature, the belief that the natural world itself deludes, tempts, misleads, wishes to devour careless human beings, takes a commanding role here in the stories written by Nathaniel Hawthorne, Herman Melville, Harriet Prescott Spofford, Ralph Adams Cram, Robert E. Howard, and Clark Ashton Smith.

The essential aspect of this primal distrust of Nature is in its ultimate purpose, the surrender or collapse of the individual will. The theme of loss of will, of actual agency, haunts a surprising portion of the stories in this collection. For Americans of all decades, it seems, the loss of agency and selfhood, effected by whatever means, arouses a particularly resonant horror. Trance states, sleepwalking, mesmerism, obsession, possession, that variety of possession represented by literal invasion of wicked and ravenous forces, madness, spiritual infection, the evil potentiality of magnetism (dingbat pseudoscience pops up here a couple of times, especially as we move into the mid-nineteenth century), exotic curses, evil atmospheres, and the simple machinations of malign beings, all these states, conditions, and forces conspire against the healthy, purposive, functional human identity. To feel our character, our personality, and our personal, hard-won history fade from being is to be exposed to whatever lies beneath these comforting operational conveniences. What remains when the conscious and functioning self has been erased is mankind's fundamental condition-irrational, violent, guilt-wracked, despairing, and mad.

In Brockden Brown's "Somnambulism: A Fragment" and Poe's "Berenice," trance states represent erasure of the rational and functioning self; in Seabury Quinn's "The Case of Everard Maundy," the accursed words of a public speaker strip the will from members of his audience and tempt them into suicide. Similarly, words written in an evil or forbidden book have the power to distort and degrade the minds of all who read it. H. P. Lovecraft's *Necronomicon* by "the mad Arab Abdul Alhazred" stands as the most iconic example of what is a consistent marker throughout the history of the American fantastic. Here it becomes central to Robert W. Chambers' "The Repairer of Reputations" (Lovecraft got the idea from Chambers), Howard's "The Black Stone," and Lovecraft's "The Thing on the Doorstep."

The soul-destroying book has close thematic links to "the obscure shop," likely to disappear or change location, in which it or another soul-destroying object may be purchased. Robert Bloch's "The Cloak" provides a ripe example of the mysterious and occult shop. No less than the first story in this volume, Bloch's clever little vampire story concerns a fatal loss of the central, determinative self, which is in peril from the moment the vainglorious protagonist allows the object cited in the title to be draped over his shoulders. Had our Puritan forebears possessed any openness to the devices of fiction, they might have nodded their heads in recognition before going on their wintry way.

Peter Straub

CHARLES BROCKDEN BROWN

(1771–1810)

Somnambulism

A fragment

[The following fragment will require no other preface or commentary than an extract from the Vienna Gazette of June 14, 1784. "At Great Glogau, in Silesia, the attention of physicians, and of the people, has been excited by the case of a young man, whose behaviour indicates perfect health in all respects but one. He has a habit of rising in his sleep, and performing a great many actions with as much order and exactness as when awake. This habit for a long time showed itself in freaks and achievements merely innocent, or, at least, only troublesome and inconvenient, till about six weeks ago. At that period a shocking event took place about three leagues from the town, and in the neighbourhood where the youth's family resides. A young lady, travelling with her father by night, was shot dead upon the road, by some person unknown. The officers of justice took a good deal of pains to trace the author of the crime, and at length, by carefully comparing circumstances, a suspicion was fixed upon this youth. After an accurate scrutiny, by the tribunal of the circle, he has been declared author of the murder: but what renders the case truly extraordinary is, that there are good reasons for believing that the deed was perpetrated by the youth while asleep, and was entirely unknown to himself. The young woman was the object of his affection, and the journey in which she had engaged had given him the utmost anxiety for her safety."]

OUR guests were preparing to retire for the night, when somebody knocked loudly at the gate. The person was immediately admitted, and presented a letter to Mr. Davis. This letter was from a friend, in which he informed our guest of certain concerns of great importance, on which the letter-writer was extremely anxious to have a personal conference with his friend; but knowing that he intended to set out from —— four days previous to his writing, he was hindered from setting out

I

by the apprehension of missing him upon the way. Meanwhile, he had deemed it best to send a special messsage to quicken his motions, should he be able to find him.

The importance of this interview was such, that Mr. Davis declared his intention of setting out immediately. No solicitations could induce him to delay a moment. His daughter, convinced of the urgency of his motives, readily consented to brave the perils and discomforts of a nocturnal journey.

This event had not been anticipated by me. The shock that it produced in me was, to my own apprehension, a subject of surprise. I could not help perceiving that it was greater than the occasion would justify. The pleasures of this intercourse were, in a moment, to be ravished from me. I was to part from my new friend, and when we should again meet it was impossible to foresee. It was then that I recollected her expressions, that assured me that her choice was fixed upon another. If I saw her again, it would probably be as a wife. The claims of friendship, as well as those of love, would then be swallowed up by a superior and hateful obligation.

But, though betrothed, she was not wedded. That was yet to come; but why should it be considered as inevitable? Our dispositions and views must change with circumstances. Who was he that Constantia Davis had chosen? Was he born to outstrip all competitors in ardour and fidelity? We cannot fail of chusing that which appears to us most worthy of choice. He had hitherto been unrivalled; but was not this day destined to introduce to her one, to whose merits every competitor must yield? He that would resign this prize, without an arduous struggle, would, indeed, be of all wretches the most pusillanimous and feeble.

Why, said I, do I cavil at her present choice? I will maintain that it does honour to her discernment. She would not be that accomplished being which she seems, if she had acted otherwise. It would be sacrilege to question the rectitude of her conduct. The object of her choice was worthy. The engagement of her heart in his favour was unavoidable, because her experience had not hitherto produced one deserving to be placed in competition with him. As soon as his superior is found, his claims will be annihilated. Has not this propitious accident supplied the defects of her former observation? But soft! is she not betrothed? If she be, what have I to dread? The engagement is accompanied with certain conditions. Whether they be openly expressed or not, they necessarily limit it. Her vows are binding on condition that the present situation continues, and that another does not arise, previously to marriage, by whom claims those of the present lover will be justly superseded.

But how shall I contend with this unknown admirer? She is going whither it will not be possible for me to follow her. An interview of a few hours is not sufficient to accomplish the important purpose that I meditate; but even this is now at an end. I shall speedily be forgotten by her. I have done nothing that entitles me to a place in her remembrance. While my rival will be left at liberty to prosecute his suit, I shall be abandoned to solitude, and have no other employment than to ruminate on the bliss that has eluded my grasp. If scope were allowed to my exertions, I might hope that they would ultimately be crowned with success; but, as it is, I am manacled and powerless. The good would easily be reached, if my hands were at freedom: now that they are fettered, the attainment is impossible.

But is it true that such is my forlorn condition? What is it that irrecoverably binds me to this spot? There are seasons of respite from my present occupations, in which I commonly indulge myself in journeys. This lady's habitation is not at an immeasurable distance from mine. It may be easily comprised within the sphere of my excursions. Shall I want a motive or excuse for paying her a visit? Her father has claimed to be better acquainted with my uncle. The lady has intimated, that the sight of me, at any future period, will give her pleasure. This will furnish ample apology for visiting their house. But why should I delay my visit? Why not immediately attend them on their way? If not on their whole journey, at least for a part of it? A journey in darkness is not unaccompanied with peril. Whatever be the caution or knowledge of their guide, they cannot be supposed to surpass mine, who have trodden this part of the way so often, that my chamber floor is scarcely more familiar to me. Besides, there is danger, from which, I am persuaded, my attendance would be a sufficient, an indispensable safeguard.

I am unable to explain why I conceived this journey to be attended with uncommon danger. My mind was, at first, occupied with the remoter consequences of this untimely departure, but my thoughts gradually returned to the contemplation of its immediate effects. There were twenty miles to a ferry, by which the travellers designed to cross the river, and at which they expected to arrive at sun-rise the next morning. I have said that the intermediate way was plain and direct. Their guide professed to be thoroughly acquainted with it.—From what quarter, then, could danger be expected to arise? It was easy to enumerate and magnify possibilities; that a tree, or ridge, or stone unobserved might overturn the carriage; that their horse might fail, or be urged, by some accident, to flight, were far from being impossible. Still they were such as justified caution. My vigilance would, at least, contribute to their security. But I could not for a moment divest myself of the belief, that my aid was indispensable. As I pondered on this image my emotions arose to terror.

All men are, at times, influenced by inexplicable sentiments. Ideas haunt them in spite of all their efforts to discard them. Prepossessions are entertained, for which their reason is unable to discover any adequate cause. The strength of a belief, when it is destitute of any rational foundation, seems, of itself, to furnish a new ground for credulity. We first admit a powerful persuasion, and then, from reflecting on the insufficiency of the ground on which it is built, instead of being prompted to dismiss it, we become more forcibly attached to it.

I had received little of the education of design. I owed the formation of my character chiefly to accident. I shall not pretend to determine in what degree I was credulous or superstitious. A belief, for which I could not rationally account, I was sufficiently prone to consider as the work of some invisible agent; as an intimation from the great source of existence and knowledge. My imagination was vivid. My passions, when I allowed them sway, were incontroulable. My conduct, as my feelings, was characterised by precipitation and headlong energy.

On this occasion I was eloquent in my remonstrances. I could not suppress my opinion, that unseen danger lurked in their way. When called upon to state the reasons of my apprehensions, I could only enumerate possibilities of which they were already apprised, but which they regarded in their true light. I made bold enquiries into the importance of the motives that should induce them to expose themselves to the least hazard. They could not urge their horse beyond his real strength. They would be compelled to suspend their journey for some time the next day. A few hours were all that they could hope to save by their utmost expedition. Were a few hours of such infinite moment?

In these representations I was sensible that I had over-leaped the bounds of rigid decorum. It was not my place to weigh his motives and inducements. My age and situation, in this family, rendered silence and submission my peculiar province. I had hitherto confined myself within bounds of scrupulous propriety, but now I had suddenly lost sight of all regards but those which related to the safety of the travellers.

Mr. Davis regarded my vehemence with suspicion. He eyed me with more attention than I had hitherto received from him. The impression which this unexpected interference made upon him, I was, at the time, too much absorbed in other considerations to notice. It was afterwards plain that he suspected my zeal to originate in a passion for his daughter, which it was by no means proper for him to encourage. If this idea occurred to him, his humanity would not suffer it to generate indignation or resentment in his bosom. On the contrary, he treated my arguments with mildness, and assured me that I had over-rated the inconveniences and perils of the journey. Some regard was to be paid to his daughter's ease and health. He did not believe them to be materially endangered. They should make suitable provision of cloaks and caps against the inclemency of the air. Had not the occasion been extremely urgent, and of that urgency he alone could be the proper judge, he should certainly not consent to endure even these trivial inconveniences. "But you seem," continued he, "chiefly anxious for my daughter's sake. There is, without doubt, a large portion of gallantry in your fears. It is natural and venial in a young man to take infinite pains for the service of the ladies; but, my dear, what say you? I will refer this important question to your decision. Shall we go, or wait till the morning?"

"Go, by all means," replied she. "I confess the fears that have been expressed appear to be groundless. I am bound to our young friend for the concern he takes in our welfare, but certainly his imagination misleads him. I am not so much a girl as to be scared merely because it is dark."

I might have foreseen this decision; but what could I say? My fears and my repugnance were strong as ever.

The evil that was menaced was terrible. By remaining where they were till the next day they would escape it. Was no other method sufficient for their preservation? My attendance would effectually obviate the danger.

This scheme possessed irresistible attractions. I was thankful to the danger for suggesting it. In the fervour of my conceptions, I was willing to run to the world's end to show my devotion to the lady. I could sustain, with alacrity, the fatigue of many nights of travelling and watchfulness. I should unspeakably prefer them to warmth and ease, if I could thereby extort from this lady a single phrase of gratitude or approbation.

I proposed to them to bear them company, at least till the morning light. They would not listen to it. Half my purpose was indeed answered by the glistening eyes and affectionate looks of Miss Davis, but the remainder I was pertinaciously bent on likewise accomplishing. If Mr. Davis had not suspected my motives, he would probably have been less indisposed to compliance. As it was, however, his objections were insuperable. They earnestly insisted on my relinquishing my design. My uncle, also, not seeing any thing that justified extraordinary precautions, added his injunctions. I was conscious of my inability to show any sufficient grounds for my fears. As long as their representations rung in my ears, I allowed myself to be ashamed of my weakness, and conjured up a temporary persuasion that my attendance was, indeed, superfluous, and that I should show most wisdom in suffering them to depart alone.

But this persuasion was transient. They had no sooner placed themselves in their carriage, and exchanged the parting adieus, but my apprehensions returned upon me as forcibly as ever. No doubt part of my despondency flowed from the idea of separation, which, however auspicious it might prove to the lady, portended unspeakable discomforts to me. But this was not all. I was breathless with fear of some unknown and terrible disaster that awaited them. A hundred times I resolved to disregard their remonstrances, and hover near them till the morning. This might be done without exciting their displeasure. It was easy to keep aloof and be unseen by them. I should doubtless have pursued this method if my fears had assumed any definite and consistent form; if, in reality, I had been able distinctly to tell what it was that I feared. My guardianship would be of no use against the obvious sources of danger in the ruggedness and obscurity of the way. For that end I must have tendered them my services, which I knew would be refused, and, if pertinaciously obtruded on them, might justly excite displeasure. I was not insensible, too, of the obedience that was due to my uncle. My absence would be remarked. Some anger and much disquietude would have been the consequences with respect to him. And after all, what was this groundless and ridiculous persuasion that governed me? Had I profited nothing by experience of the effects of similar follies? Was I never to attend to the lessons of sobriety and truth? How ignominious to be thus the slave of a fortuitous and inexplicable impulse! To be the victim of terrors more chimerical than those which haunt the dreams of idiots and children! *They* can describe clearly, and attribute a real existence to the object of their terrors. Not so can I.

Influenced by these considerations, I shut the gate at which I had been standing, and turned towards the house. After a few steps I paused, turned, and listened to the distant sounds of the carriage. My courage was again on the point of yielding, and new efforts were requisite before I could resume my first resolutions.

I spent a drooping and melancholy evening. My imagination continually hovered over our departed guests. I recalled every circumstance of the road. I reflected by what means they were to pass that bridge, or extricate themselves from this slough. I imagined the possibility of their guide's forgetting the position of a certain oak that grew in the road. It was an ancient tree, whose boughs extended, on all sides, to an extraordinary distance. They seemed disposed by nature in that way in which they would produce the most ample circumference of shade. I could not recollect any other obstruction from which much was to be feared. This indeed was several miles distant, and its appearance was too remarkable not to have excited attention.

The family retired to sleep. My mind had been too power-fully excited to permit me to imitate their example. The incidents of the last two days passed over my fancy like a vision. The revolution was almost incredible which my mind had undergone, in consequence of these incidents. It was so abrupt and entire that my soul seemed to have passed into a new form. I pondered on every incident till the surrounding scenes disappeared, and I forgot my real situation. I mused upon the image of Miss Davis till my whole soul was dissolved in tenderness, and my eyes overflowed with tears. There insensibly arose a sort of persuasion that destiny had irreversably decreed that I should never see her more.

While engaged in this melancholy occupation, of which I cannot say how long it lasted, sleep overtook me as I sat. Scarcely a minute had elapsed during this period without conceiving the design, more or less strenuously, of sallying forth, with a view to overtake and guard the travellers; but this design was embarrassed with invincible objections, and was alternately formed and laid aside. At length, as I have said, I sunk into profound slumber, if that slumber can be termed profound, in which my fancy was incessantly employed in calling up the forms, into new combinations, which had constituted my waking reveries. —The images were fleeting and transient, but the events of the morrow recalled them to my remembrance with sufficient distinctness. The terrors which I had so deeply and unaccountably imbibed could not fail of retaining some portion of their influence, in spite of sleep.

In my dreams, the design which I could not bring myself to execute while awake I embraced without hesitation. I was summoned, methought, to defend this lady from the attacks of an assassin. My ideas were full of confusion and inaccuracy. All that I can recollect is, that my efforts had been unsuccessful to avert the stroke of the murderer. This, however, was not accomplished without drawing on his head a bloody retribution. I imagined myself engaged, for a long time, in pursuit of the guilty, and, at last, to have detected him in an artful disguise. I did not employ the usual preliminaries which honour prescribes, but, stimulated by rage, attacked him with a pistol, and terminated his career by a mortal wound.

I should not have described these phantoms had there not

been a remarkable coincidence between them and the real events of that night. In the morning, my uncle, whose custom it was to rise first in the family, found me quietly reposing in the chair in which I had fallen asleep. His summons roused and startled me. This posture was so unusual that I did not readily recover my recollection, and perceive in what circumstances I was placed.

I shook off the dreams of the night. Sleep had refreshed and invigorated my frame, as well as tranquillized my thoughts. I still mused on yesterday's adventures, but my reveries were more cheerful and benign. My fears and bodements were dispersed with the dark, and I went into the fields, not merely to perform the duties of the day, but to ruminate on plans for the future.

My golden visions, however, were soon converted into visions of despair. A messenger arrived before noon, intreating my presence, and that of my uncle, at the house of Dr. Inglefield, a gentleman who resided at the distance of three miles from our house. The messenger explained the intention of this request. It appeared that the terrors of the preceding evening had some mysterious connection with truth. By some deplorable accident, Miss Davis had been shot on the road, and was still lingering in dreadful agonies at the house of this physician. I was in a field near the road when the messenger approached the house. On observing me, he called me. His tale was meagre and imperfect, but the substance of it it was easy to gather. I stood for a moment motionless and aghast. As soon as I recovered my thoughts I set off full speed, and made not a moment's pause till I reached the house of Inglefield.

The circumstances of this mournful event, as I was able to collect them at different times, from the witnesses, were these. After they had parted from us, they proceeded on their way for some time without molestation. The clouds disappearing, the star-light enabled them with less difficulty to discern their path. They met not a human being till they came within less than three miles of the oak which I have before described. Here Miss Davis looked forward with some curiosity and said to her father, "Do you not see some one in the road before us? I saw him this moment move across from the fence on the right hand and stand still in the middle of the road."

"I see nothing, I must confess," said the father: "but that is no subject of wonder; your young eyes will of course see farther than my old ones."

"I see him clearly at this moment," rejoined the lady. "If he remain a short time where he is, or seems to be, we shall be able to ascertain his properties. Our horse's head will determine whether his substance be impassive or not."

The carriage slowly advancing, and the form remaining in the same spot, Mr. Davis at length percieved it, but was not allowed a clearer examination, for the person, having, as it seemed, ascertained the nature of the cavalcade, shot across the road, and disappeared. The behaviour of this unknown person furnished the travellers with a topic of abundant speculation.

Few possessed a firmer mind than Miss Davis; but whether she was assailed, on this occasion, with a mysterious foreboding of her destiny; whether the eloquence of my fears had not, in spite of resolution, infected her; or whether she imagined evils that my incautious temper might draw upon me, and which might originate in our late interview, certain it was that her spirits were visibly depressed. This accident made no sensible alteration in her. She was still disconsolate and incommunicative. All the efforts of her father were insufficient to inspire her with cheerfulness. He repeatedly questioned her as to the cause of this unwonted despondency. Her answer was, that her spirits were indeed depressed, but she believed that the circumstance was casual. She knew of nothing that could justify despondency. But such is humanity. Cheerfulness and dejection will take their turns in the best regulated bosoms, and come and go when they will, and not at the command of reason. This observation was succeeded by a pause. At length Mr. Davis said, "A thought has just occurred to me. The person whom we just now saw is young Althorpe."

Miss Davis was startled: "Why, my dear father, should you think so? It is too dark to judge, at this distance, by resemblance of figure. Ardent and rash as he appears to be, I should scarcely suspect him on this occasion. With all the fiery qualities of youth, unchastised by experience, untamed by adversity, he is capable no doubt of extravagant adventures, but what could induce him to act in this manner?"

"You know the fears that he expressed concerning the issue

of this night's journey. We know not what foundation he might have had for these fears. He told us of no danger that ought to deter us, but it is hard to conceive that he should have been thus vehement without cause. We know not what motives might have induced him to conceal from us the sources of his terror. And since he could not obtain our consent to his attending us, he has taken these means, perhaps, of effecting his purpose. The darkness might easily conceal him from our observation. He might have passed us without our noticing him, or he might have made a circuit in the woods we have just passed, and come out before us."

"That I own," replied the daughter, "is not improbable. If it be true, I shall be sorry for his own sake, but if there be any danger from which his attendance can secure us, I shall be well pleased for all our sakes. He will reflect with some satisfaction, perhaps, that he has done or intended us a service. It would be cruel to deny him a satisfaction so innocent."

"Pray, my dear, what think you of this young man? Does his ardour to serve us flow from a right source?"

"It flows, I have no doubt, from a double source. He has a kind heart, and delights to oblige others: but this is not all. He is likewise in love, and imagines that he cannot do too much for the object of his passion."

"Indeed!" exclaimed Mr. Davis, in some surprise. "You speak very positively. That is no more than it suspected; but how came you to know it with so much certainty?"

"The information came to me in the directest manner. He told me so himself."

"So ho! why, the impertinent young rogue!"

"Nay, my dear father, his behavior did not merit that epithet. He is rash and inconsiderate. That is the utmost amount of his guilt. A short absence will show him the true state of his feelings. It was unavoidable, in one of his character, to fall in love with the first woman whose appearance was in any degree specious. But attachments like these will be extinguished as easily as they are formed. I do not fear for him on this account."

"Have you reason to fear for him on any account?"

"Yes. The period of youth will soon pass away. Overweening and fickle, he will go on committing one mistake after another, incapable of repairing his errors, or of profiting by the daily lessons of experience. His genius will be merely an implement of mischief. His greater capacity will be evinced merely by the greater portion of unhappiness that, by means of it, will accrue to others or rebound upon himself."

"I see, my dear, that your spirits are low. Nothing else, surely, could suggest such melancholy presages. For my part, I question not, but he will one day be a fine fellow and a happy one. I like him exceedingly. I shall take pains to be acquainted with his future adventures, and do him all the good that I can."

"That intention," said his daughter, "is worthy of the goodness of your heart. He is no less an object of regard to me than to you. I trust I shall want neither the power nor inclination to contribute to his welfare. At present, however, his welfare will be best promoted by forgetting me. Hereafter, I shall solicit a renewal of intercourse."

"Speak lower," said the father. "If I mistake not, there is the same person again." He pointed to the field that skirted the road on the left hand. The young lady's better eyes enabled her to detect his mistake. It was the trunk of a cherry-tree that he had observed.

They proceeded in silence. Contrary to custom, the lady was buried in musing. Her father, whose temper and inclinations were moulded by those of his child, insensibly subsided into the same state.

The re-appearance of the same figure that had already excited their attention diverted them anew from their contemplations. "As I live," exclaimed Mr. Davis, "that thing, whatever it be, haunts us. I do not like it. This is strange conduct for young Althorpe to adopt. Instead of being our protector, the danger, against which he so pathetically warned us, may be, in some inscrutable way, connected with this personage. It is best to be upon our guard."

"Nay, my father," said the lady, "be not disturbed. What danger can be dreaded by two persons from one? This thing, I dare say, means us no harm. What is at present inexplicable might be obvious enough if we were better acquainted with this neighbourhood. It is not worth a thought. You see it is now gone." Mr. Davis looked again, but it was no longer discernible.

They were now approaching a wood. Mr. Davis called to the

guide to stop. His daughter enquired the reason of this command. She found it arose from his uncertainty as to the propriety of proceeding.

"I know not how it is," said he, "but I begin to be affected with the fears of young Althorpe. I am half resolved not to enter this wood.—That light yonder informs that a house is near. It may not be unadvisable to stop. I cannot think of delaying our journey till morning; but, by stopping a few minutes, we may possibly collect some useful information. Perhaps it will be expedient and practicable to procure the attendance of another person. I am not well pleased with myself for declining our young friend's offer."

To this proposal Miss Davis objected the inconveniences that calling at a farmer's house, at this time of night, when all were retired to rest, would probably occasion. "Besides," continued she, "the light which you saw is gone: a sufficient proof that it was nothing but a meteor."

At this moment they heard a noise, at a small distance behind them, as of shutting a gate. They called. Speedily an answer was returned in a tone of mildness. The person approached the chaise, and enquired who they were, whence they came, whither they were going, and, lastly, what they wanted.

Mr. Davis explained to this inquisitive person, in a few words, the nature of their situation, mentioned the appearance on the road, and questioned him, in his turn, as to what inconveniences were to be feared from prosecuting his journey. Satisfactory answers were returned to these enquiries.

"As to what you seed in the road," continued he, "I reckon it was nothing but a sheep or a cow. I am not more scary than some folks, but I never goes out a' nights without I sees some *sich* thing as that, that I takes for a man or woman, and am scared a little oftentimes, but not much. I'm sure after to find that it's not nothing but a cow, or hog, or tree, or something. If it wasn't some sich thing you seed, I reckon it was *Nick Handyside.*"

"Nick Handyside! who was he?"

"It was a fellow that went about the country a' nights. A shocking fool to be sure, that loved to plague and frighten people. Yes. Yes. It couldn't be nobody, he reckoned, but Nick.

Nick was a droll thing. He wondered they'd never heard of Nick. He reckoned they were strangers in these here parts."

"Very true, my friend. But who is Nick? Is he a reptile to be shunned, or trampled on?"

"Why I don't know how as that. Nick is an odd soul to be sure; but he don't do nobody no harm, as ever I heard, except by scaring them. He is easily skeart though, for that matter, himself. He loves to frighten folks, but he's shocking apt to be frightened himself. I reckon you took Nick for a ghost. That's a shocking good story, I declare. Yet it's happened hundreds and hundreds of times, I guess, and more."

When this circumstance was mentioned, my uncle, as well as myself, was astonished at our own negligence. While enumerating, on the preceding evening, the obstacles and inconveniences which the travellers were likely to encounter, we entirely and unaccountably overlooked one circumstance, from which inquietude might reasonably have been expected. Near the spot where they now were, lived a Mr. Handyside, whose only son was an idiot. He also merited the name of monster, if a projecting breast, a mis-shapen head, features horrid and distorted, and a voice that resembled nothing that was ever before heard, could entitle him to that appellation. This being, besides the natural deformity of his frame, wore looks and practised gesticulations that were, in an inconceivable degree, uncouth and hideous. He was mischievous, but his freaks were subjects of little apprehension to those who were accustomed to them, though they were frequently occasions of alarm to strangers. He particularly delighted in imposing on the ignorance of strangers and the timidity of women. He was a perpetual rover. Entirely bereft of reason, his sole employment consisted in sleeping, and eating, and roaming. He would frequently escape at night, and a thousand anecdotes could have been detailed respecting the tricks which Nick Handyside had played upon way-farers.

Other considerations, however, had, in this instance, so much engrossed our minds, that Nick Handyside had never been once thought of or mentioned. This was the more remarkable, as there had very lately happened an adventure, in which this person had acted a principal part. He had wandered from home, and got bewildered in a desolate tract, known by the name of Norwood. It was a region, rude, sterile, and lonely, bestrewn with rocks, and embarrassed with bushes.

He had remained for some days in this wilderness. Unable to extricate himself, and, at length, tormented with hunger, he manifested his distress by the most doleful shrieks. These were uttered with most vehemence, and heard at greatest distance, by night. At first, those who heard them were panic-struck; but, at length, they furnished a clue by which those who were in search of him were guided to the spot. Notwithstanding the recentness and singularity of this adventure, and the probability that our guests would suffer molestation from this cause, so strangely forgetful had we been, that no caution on this head had been given. This caution, indeed, as the event testified, would have been superfluous, and yet I cannot enough wonder that in hunting for some reason, by which I might justify my fears to them or to myself, I had totally overlooked this mischief-loving idiot.

After listening to an ample description of Nick, being warned to proceed with particular caution in a part of the road that was near at hand, and being assured that they had nothing to dread from human interference, they resumed their journey with new confidence.

Their attention was frequently excited by rustling leaves or stumbling footsteps, and the figure which they doubted not to belong to Nick Handyside, occasionally hovered in their sight. This appearance no longer inspired them with apprehension. They had been assured that a stern voice was sufficient to repulse him, when most importunate. This antic being treated all others as children. He took pleasure in the effects which the sight of his own deformity produced, and betokened his satisfaction by a laugh, which might have served as a model to the poet who has depicted the ghastly risibilities of Death. On this occasion, however, the monster behaved with unusual moderation. He never came near enough for his peculiarities to be distinguished by star-light. There was nothing fantastic in his motions, nor any thing surprising, but the celerity of his transitions. They were unaccompanied by those howls, which reminded you at one time of a troop of hungry wolves, and had, at another, something in them inexpressibly wild and melancholy. This monster possessed a certain species of dexterity. His talents, differently applied, would have excited rational admiration. He was fleet as a deer. He was patient, to an incredible degree, of watchfulness, and cold, and hunger. He had improved the flexibility of his voice, till his cries, always loud and rueful, were capable of being diversified without end. Instances had been known, in which the stoutest heart was appalled by them; and some, particularly in the case of women, in which they had been productive of consequences truly deplorable.

When the travellers had arrived at that part of the wood where, as they had been informed, it was needful to be particularly cautious, Mr. Davis, for their greater security, proposed to his daughter to alight. The exercise of walking, he thought, after so much time spent in a close carriage, would be salutary and pleasant. The young lady readily embraced the proposal. They forthwith alighted, and walked at a small distance before the chaise, which was now conducted by the servant. From this moment the spectre, which, till now, had been occasionally visible, entirely disappeared. This incident naturally led the conversation to this topic. So singular a specimen of the forms which human nature is found to assume could not fail of suggesting a variety of remarks.

They pictured to themselves many combinations of circumstances in which Handyside might be the agent, and in which the most momentous effects might flow from his agency, without its being possible for others to conjecture the true nature of the agent. The propensities of this being might contribute to realize, on an American road, many of those imaginary tokens and perils which abound in the wildest romance. He would be an admirable machine, in a plan whose purpose was to generate or foster, in a given subject, the frenzy of quixotism.—No theatre was better adapted than Norwood to such an exhibition. This part of the country had long been deserted by beasts of prey. Bears might still, perhaps, be found during a very rigorous season, but wolves which, when the country was a desert, were extremely numerous, had now, in consequence of increasing population, withdrawn to more savage haunts. Yet the voice of Handyside, varied with the force and skill of which he was known to be capable, would fill these shades with outcries as ferocious as those which are to be heard in Siamese or Abyssinian forests. The tale of his recent elopement had been told by the man with whom they had just parted, in a rustic but picturesque style.

"But why," said the lady, "did not our kind host inform us of this circumstance? He must surely have been well acquainted with the existence and habits of this Handyside. He must have perceived to how many groundless alarms our ignorance, in this respect, was likely to expose us. It is strange that he did not afford us the slightest intimation of it."

Mr. Davis was no less surprised at this omission. He was at a loss to conceive how this should be forgotten in the midst of those minute directions, in which every cause had been laboriously recollected from which he might incur danger or suffer obstruction.

This person, being no longer an object of terror, began to be regarded with a very lively curiosity. They even wished for his appearance and near approach, that they might carry away with them more definite conceptions of his figure. The lady declared she should be highly pleased by hearing his outcries, and consoled herself with the belief, that he would not allow them to pass the limits which he had prescribed to his wanderings, without greeting them with a strain or two. This wish had scarcely been uttered, when it was completely gratified.

The lady involuntarily started, and caught hold of her father's arm. Mr. Davis himself was disconcerted. A scream, dismally loud, and piercingly shrill, was uttered by one at less than twenty paces from them.

The monster had shown some skill in the choice of a spot suitable to his design. Neighbouring precipices, and a thick umbrage of oaks, on either side, contributed to prolong and to heighten his terrible notes. They were rendered more awful by the profound stillness that preceded and followed them. They were able speedily to quiet the trepidations which this hideous outcry, in spite of preparation and foresight, had produced, but they had not foreseen one of its unhappy consequences.

In a moment Mr. Davis was alarmed by the rapid sound of footsteps behind him. His presence of mind, on this occasion, probably saved himself and his daughter from instant destruction. He leaped out of the path, and, by a sudden exertion, at the same moment, threw the lady to some distance from the tract. The horse that drew the chaise rushed by them with the celerity of lightning. Affrighted at the sounds which had been uttered at a still less distance from the horse than from Mr. Davis, possibly with a malicious design to produce this very effect, he jerked the bridle from the hands that held it, and rushed forward with headlong speed. The man, before he could provide for his own safety, was beaten to the earth. He was considerably bruised by the fall, but presently recovered his feet, and went in pursuit of the horse.

This accident happened at about a hundred yards from the *oak*, against which so many cautions had been given. It was not possible, at any time, without considerable caution, to avoid it. It was not to be wondered at, therefore, that, in a few seconds, the carriage was shocked against the trunk, overturned, and dashed into a thousand fragments. The noise of the crash sufficiently informed them of this event. Had the horse been inclined to stop, a repetition, for the space of some minutes, of the same savage and terrible shrieks would have added tenfold to his consternation and to the speed of his flight. After this dismal strain had ended, Mr. Davis raised his daughter from the ground. She had suffered no material injury. As soon as they recovered from the confusion into which this accident had thrown them, they began to consult upon the measures proper to be taken upon this emergency. They were left alone. The servant had gone in pursuit of the flying horse. Whether he would be able to retake him was extremely dubious. Meanwhile they were surrounded by darkness. What was the distance of the next house could not be known. At that hour of the night they could not hope to be directed, by the far-seen taper, to any hospitable roof. The only alternative, therefore, was to remain where they were, uncertain of the fate of their companion, or to go forward with the utmost expedition.

They could not hesitate to embrace the latter. In a few minutes they arrived at the oak. The chaise appeared to have been dashed against a knotty projecture of the trunk, which was large enough for a person to be conveniently seated on it. Here they again paused.—Miss Davis desired to remain here a few minutes to recruit her exhausted strength. She proposed to her father to leave her here, and go forward in quest of the horse and the servant. He might return as speedily as he thought proper. She did not fear to be alone. The voice was still. Having accomplished his malicious purposes, the spectre had probably taken his final leave of them. At all events, if the report of the rustic was true, she had no personal injury to fear from him.

Through some deplorable infatuation, as he afterwards deemed it, Mr. Davis complied with her intreaties, and went in search of the missing. He had engaged in a most unpromising undertaking. The man and horse were by this time at a considerable distance. The former would, no doubt, shortly return. Whether his pursuit succeeded or miscarried, he would surely see the propriety of hastening his return with what tidings he could obtain, and to ascertain his master's situation. Add to this, the impropriety of leaving a woman, single and unarmed, to the machinations of this demoniac. He had scarcely parted with her when these reflections occurred to him. His resolution was changed. He turned back with the intention of immediately seeking her. At the same moment, he saw the flash and heard the discharge of a pistol. The light proceeded from the foot of the oak. His imagination was filled with horrible forebodings. He ran with all his speed to the spot. He called aloud upon the name of his daughter, but, alas! she was unable to answer him. He found her stretched at the foot of the tree, senseless, and weltering in her blood. He lifted her in his arms, and seated her against the trunk. He found himself stained with blood, flowing from a wound, which either the darkness of the night, or the confusion of his thoughts, hindered him from tracing. Overwhelmed with a catastrophe so dreadful and unexpected, he was divested of all presence of mind. The author of his calamity had vanished. No human being was at hand to succour him in his uttermost distress. He beat his head against the ground, tore away his venerable locks, and rent the air with his cries.

Fortunately there was a dwelling at no great distance from this scene. The discharge of a pistol produces a sound too loud not to be heard far and wide, in this lonely region. This house belonged to a physician. He was a man noted for his humanity and sympathy. He was roused, as well as most of his family, by a sound so uncommon. He rose instantly, and calling up his people proceeded with lights to the road. The lamentations of Mr. Davis directed them to the place. To the physician the scene was inexplicable. Who was the author of this distress; by whom the pistol was discharged; whether through some untoward chance or with design, he was as yet uninformed, nor could he gain any information from the incoherent despair of Mr. Davis.

Every measure that humanity and professional skill could suggest were employed on this occasion. The dying lady was removed to the house. The ball had lodged in her brain, and to extract it was impossible. Why should I dwell on the remaining incidents of this tale? She languished till the next morning, and then expired.

1805

WASHINGTON IRVING

(1783–1859)

The Adventure of the German Student

On a stormy night, in the tempestuous times of the French revolution, a young German was returning to his lodgings, at a late hour, across the old part of Paris. The lightning gleamed, and the loud claps of thunder rattled through the lofty, narrow streets—but I should first tell you something about this young German.

Gottfried Wolfgang was a young man of good family. He had studied for some time at Göttingen, but being of a visionary and enthusiastic character, he had wandered into those wild and speculative doctrines which have so often bewildered German students. His secluded life, his intense application, and the singular nature of his studies, had an effect on both mind and body. His health was impaired; his imagination diseased. He had been indulging in fanciful speculations on spiritual essences until, like Swedenborg, he had an ideal world of his own around him. He took up a notion, I do not know from what cause, that there was an evil influence hanging over him; an evil genius or spirit seeking to ensnare him and ensure his perdition. Such an idea working on his melancholy temperament produced the most gloomy effects. He became haggard and desponding. His friends discovered the mental malady preying upon him, and determined that the best cure was a change of scene; he was sent, therefore, to finish his studies amidst the splendours and gaieties of Paris.

Wolfgang arrived at Paris at the breaking out of the revolution. The popular delirium at first caught his enthusiastic mind, and he was captivated by the political and philosophical theories of the day: but the scenes of blood which followed shocked his sensitive nature; disgusted him with society and the world, and made him more than ever a recluse. He shut himself up in a solitary apartment in the *Pays Latin*, the quarter of students. There in a gloomy street not far from the monastic walls of the Sorbonne, he pursued his favourite speculations. Sometimes he spent hours together in the great libraries of Paris, those catacombs of departed authors, rummaging among their hoards of dusty and obsolete works in quest of food for his unhealthy appetite. He was, in a manner, a literary goul, feeding in the charnel house of decayed literature.

Wolfgang, though solitary and recluse, was of an ardent temperament, but for a time it operated merely upon his imagination. He was too shy and ignorant of the world to make any advances to the fair, but he was a passionate admirer of female beauty, and in his lonely chamber would often lose himself in reveries on forms and faces which he had seen, and his fancy would deck out images of loveliness far surpassing the reality.

While his mind was in this excited and sublimated state, a dream produced an extraordinary effect upon him. It was of a female face of transcendent beauty. So strong was the impression made, that he dreamt of it again and again. It haunted his thoughts by day, his slumbers by night; in fine, he became passionately enamoured of this shadow of a dream. This lasted so long, that it became one of those fixed ideas which haunt the minds of melancholy men, and are at times mistaken for madness.

Such was Gottfried Wolfgang, and such his situation at the time I mentioned. He was returning home late one stormy night, through some of the old and gloomy streets of the *Marais*, the ancient part of Paris. The loud claps of thunder rattled among the high houses of the narrow streets. He came to the Place de Grève, the square where public executions are performed. The lightning quivered about the pinnacles of the ancient Hôtel de Ville, and shed flickering gleams over the open space in front. As Wolfgang was crossing the square, he shrank back with horror at finding himself close by the guillotine. It was the height of the reign of terror, when this dreadful instrument of death stood ever ready, and its scaffold was continually running with the blood of the virtuous and the brave. It had that very day been actively employed in the work of carnage, and there it stood in grim array amidst a silent and sleeping city, waiting for fresh victims.

Wolfgang's heart sickened within him, and he was turning

shuddering from the horrible engine, when he beheld a shadowy form cowering as it were at the foot of the steps which led up to the scaffold. A succession of vivid flashes of lightning revealed it more distinctly. It was a female figure, dressed in black. She was seated on one of the lower steps of the scaffold, leaning forward, her face hid in her lap, and her long dishevelled tresses hanging to the ground, streaming with the rain which fell in torrents. Wolfgang paused. There was something awful in this solitary monument of wo. The female had the appearance of being above the common order. He knew the times to be full of vicissitude, and that many a fair head, which had once been pillowed on down, now wandered houseless. Perhaps this was some poor mourner whom the dreadful axe had rendered desolate, and who sat here heartbroken on the strand of existence, from which all that was dear to her had been launched into eternity.

He approached, and addressed her in the accents of sympathy. She raised her head and gazed wildly at him. What was his astonishment at beholding, by the bright glare of the lightning, the very face which had haunted him in his dreams. It was pale and disconsolate, but ravishingly beautiful.

Trembling with violent and conflicting emotions, Wolfgang again accosted her. He spoke something of her being exposed at such an hour of the night, and to the fury of such a storm, and offered to conduct her to her friends. She pointed to the guillotine with a gesture of dreadful signification.

"I have no friend on earth!" said she.

"But you have a home," said Wolfgang.

"Yes—in the grave!"

The heart of the student melted at the words.

"If a stranger dare make an offer," said he, "without danger of being misunderstood, I would offer my humble dwelling as a shelter; myself as a devoted friend. I am friendless myself in Paris, and a stranger in the land; but if my life could be of service, it is at your disposal, and should be sacrificed before harm or indignity should come to you."

There was an honest earnestness in the young man's manner that had its effect. His foreign accent, too, was in his favour; it showed him not to be a hackneyed inhabitant of Paris. Indeed there is an eloquence in true enthusiasm that is not to be doubted. The homeless stranger confided herself implicitly to the protection of the student.

He supported her faltering steps across the Pont Neuf, and by the place where the statue of Henry the Fourth had been overthrown by the populace. The storm had abated, and the thunder rumbled at a distance. All Paris was quiet; that great volcano of human passion slumbered for a while, to gather fresh strength for the next day's eruption. The student conducted his charge through the ancient streets of the *Pays Latin*, and by the dusky walls of the Sorbonne to the great, dingy hotel which he inhabited. The old portress who admitted them stared with surprise at the unusual sight of the melancholy Wolfgang with a female companion.

On entering his apartment, the student, for the first time, blushed at the scantiness and indifference of his dwelling. He had but one chamber—an old fashioned saloon—heavily carved and fantastically furnished with the remains of former magnificence, for it was one of those hotels in the quarter of the Luxembourg palace which had once belonged to nobility. It was lumbered with books and papers, and all the usual apparatus of a student, and his bed stood in a recess at one end.

When lights were brought, and Wolfgang had a better opportunity of contemplating the stranger, he was more than ever intoxicated by her beauty. Her face was pale, but of a dazzling fairness, set off by a profusion of raven hair that hung clustering about it. Her eyes were large and brilliant, with a singular expression approaching almost to wildness. As far as her black dress permitted her shape to be seen, it was of perfect symmetry. Her whole appearance was highly striking, though she was dressed in the simplest style. The only thing approaching to an ornament which she wore was a broad, black band round her neck, clasped by diamonds.

The perplexity now commenced with the student how to dispose of the helpless being thus thrown upon his protection. He thought of abandoning his chamber to her, and seeking shelter for himself elsewhere. Still he was so fascinated by her charms, there seemed to be such a spell upon his thoughts and senses, that he could not tear himself from her presence. Her manner, too, was singular and unaccountable. She spoke no more of the guillotine. Her grief had abated. The attentions of the student had first won her confidence, and then, apparently, her heart. She was evidently an enthusiast like himself, and enthusiasts soon understand each other.

In the infatuation of the moment Wolfgang avowed his passion for her. He told her the story of his mysterious dream, and how she had possessed his heart before he had even seen her. She was strangely affected by his recital, and acknowledged to have felt an impulse towards him equally unaccountable. It was the time for wild theory and wild actions. Old prejudices and superstitions were done away; every thing was under the sway of the "Goddess of Reason." Among other rubbish of the old times, the forms and ceremonies of marriage began to be considered superfluous bonds for honourable minds. Social compacts were the vogue. Wolfgang was too much of a theorist not to be tainted by the liberal doctrines of the day.

"Why should we separate?" said he: "our hearts are united; in the eye of reason and honour we are as one. What need is there of sordid forms to bind high souls together?"

The stranger listened with emotion: she had evidently received illumination at the same school.

"You have no home nor family," continued he; "let me be every thing to you, or rather let us be every thing to one another. If form is necessary, form shall be observed—there is my hand. I pledge myself to you for ever."

"For ever?" said the stranger, solemnly.

"For ever!" repeated Wolfgang.

The stranger clasped the hand extended to her: "Then I am yours," murmured she, and sank upon his bosom.

The next morning the student left his bride sleeping, and sallied forth at an early hour to seek more spacious apartments, suitable to the change in his situation. When he returned, he found the stranger lying with her head hanging over the bed, and one arm thrown over it. He spoke to her, but received no reply. He advanced to awaken her from her uneasy posture. On taking her hand, it was cold—there was no pulsation—her face was pallid and ghastly.—In a word—she was a corpse.

Horrified and frantic, he alarmed the house. A scene of confusion ensued. The police was summoned. As the officer of police entered the room, he started back on beholding the corpse.

"Great heaven!" cried he, "how did this woman come here?"

"Do you know any thing about her?" said Wolfgang, eagerly.

"Do I?" exclaimed the police officer: "she was guillotined yesterday!"

He stepped forward; undid the black collar round the neck of the corpse, and the head rolled on the floor!

The student burst into a frenzy. "The fiend! the fiend has gained possession of me!" shrieked he: "I am lost for ever!"

They tried to soothe him, but in vain. He was possessed with the frightful belief that an evil spirit had reanimated the dead body to ensnare him. He went distracted, and died in a madhouse.

———

Here the old gentleman with the haunted head finished his narrative.

"And is this really a fact?" said the inquisitive gentleman.

"A fact not to be doubted," replied the other. "I had it from the best authority. The student told it me himself. I saw him in a madhouse at Paris."

1824

EDGAR ALLAN POE

(1809–1849)

Berenice

*Dicebant mihi sodales, si sepulchrum amicae, visitarem,
curas meas aliquantulum fore levatas.—Ebn Zaiat*

M ISERY is manifold. The wretchedness of earth is multiform. Overreaching the wide horizon as the rainbow, its hues are as various as the hues of that arch,—as distinct too, yet as intimately blended. Overreaching the wide horizon as the rainbow! How is it that from beauty I have derived a type of unloveliness? —from the covenant of peace a simile of sorrow? But as, in ethics, evil is a consequence of good, so, in fact, out of joy is sorrow born. Either the memory of past bliss is the anguish of to-day, or the agonies which *are* have their origin in the ecstasies which *might have been.*

My baptismal name is Egæus; that of my family I will not mention. Yet there are no towers in the land more time-honored than my gloomy, gray, hereditary halls. Our line has been called a race of visionaries; and in many striking particulars—in the character of the family mansion—in the frescos of the chief saloon—in the tapestries of the dormitories—in the chiselling of some butresses in the armory—but more especially in the gallery of antique paintings—in the fashion of the library chamber— and, lastly, in the very peculiar nature of the library's contents, there is more than sufficient evidence to warrant the belief.

The recollections of my earliest years are connected with that chamber, and with its volumes—of which latter I will say no more. Here died my mother. Herein was I born. But it is mere idleness to say that I had not lived before—that the soul has no previous existence. You deny it?—let us not argue the matter. Convinced myself, I seek not to convince. There is, however, a remembrance of aërial forms—of spiritual and meaning eyes— of sounds, musical yet sad—a remembrance which will not be excluded; a memory like a shadow, vague, variable, indefinite, unsteady; and like a shadow, too, in the impossibility of my getting rid of it while the sunlight of my reason shall exist.

In that chamber was I born. Thus awaking from the long night of what seemed, but was not, nonentity, at once into the very regions of fairy-land—into a palace of imagination—into the wild dominions of monastic thought and erudition—it is not singular that I gazed around me with a startled and ardent eye —that I loitered away my boyhood in books, and dissipated my youth in reverie; but it *is* singular that as years rolled away, and the noon of manhood found me still in the mansion of my fathers—it *is* wonderful what stagnation there fell upon the springs of my life—wonderful how total an inversion took place in the character of my commonest thought. The realities of the world affected me as visions, and as visions only, while the wild ideas of the land of dreams became, in turn,—not the material of my everyday existence—but in very deed that existence utterly and solely in itself.

Berenice and I were cousins, and we grew up together in my paternal halls. Yet differently we grew—I ill of health and buried in gloom—she agile, graceful, and overflowing with energy— hers the ramble on the hill-side—mine the studies of the cloister —I living within my own heart, and addicted body and soul to the most intense and painful meditation—she roaming carelessly through life with no thought of the shadows in her path, or the silent flight of the raven-winged hours. Berenice!—I call upon her name—Berenice!—and from the gray ruins of memory a thousand tumultuous recollections are startled at the sound! Ah! vividly is her image before me now, as in the early days of her light-heartedness and joy! Oh! gorgeous yet fantastic beauty! Oh! sylph amid the shrubberies of Arnheim!—Oh! Naiad among its fountains!—and then—then all is mystery and terror, and a tale which should not be told. Disease—a fatal disease—fell like the simoom upon her frame, and, even while I gazed upon her, the spirit of change swept over her, pervading her mind, her habits, and her character, and, in a manner the most subtle and terrible, disturbing even the identity of her person! Alas! the destroyer came and went, and the victim— where was she? I knew her not—or knew her no longer as Berenice.

Among the numerous train of maladies superinduced by that fatal and primary one which effected a revolution of so horrible a kind in the moral and physical being of my cousin, may be mentioned as the most distressing and obstinate in its nature, a species of epilepsy not unfrequently terminating in *trance* itself—trance very nearly resembling positive dissolution, and from which her manner of recovery was, in most instances, startlingly abrupt. In the mean time my own disease— for I have been told that I should call it by no other appellation —my own disease, then, grew rapidly upon me, and assumed finally a monomaniac character of a novel and extraordinary form—hourly and momently gaining vigor—and at length obtaining over me the most incomprehensible ascendancy. This monomania, if I must so term it, consisted in a morbid irritability of those properties of the mind in metaphysical science termed the *attentive*. It is more than probable that I am not understood; but I fear, indeed, that it is in no manner possible to convey to the mind of the merely general reader, an adequate idea of that nervous *intensity of interest* with which, in my case, the powers of meditation (not to speak technically) busied and buried themselves, in the contemplation of even the most ordinary objects of the universe.

To muse for long unwearied hours with my attention riveted to some frivolous device on the margin, or in the typography of a book; to become absorbed for the better part of a summer's day in a quaint shadow falling aslant upon the tapestry, or upon the floor; to lose myself for an entire night in watching the steady flame of a lamp, or the embers of a fire; to dream away whole days over the perfume of a flower; to repeat monotonously some common word, until the sound, by dint of frequent repetition, ceased to convey any idea whatever to the mind; to lose all sense of motion or physical existence, by means of absolute bodily quiescence long and obstinately persevered in:—such were a few of the most common and least pernicious vagaries induced by a condition of the mental faculties, not, indeed, altogether unparalleled, but certainly bidding defiance to anything like analysis or explanation.

Yet let me not be misapprehended.—The undue, earnest, and morbid attention thus excited by objects in their own nature frivolous, must not be confounded in character with that ruminating propensity common to all mankind, and more especially indulged in by persons of ardent imagination. It was not even, as might be at first supposed, an extreme condition, or exaggeration of such propensity, but primarily and essentially distinct and different. In the one instance, the dreamer, or enthusiast, being interested by an object usually *not* frivolous, imperceptibly loses sight of this object in a wilderness of deductions and suggestions issuing therefrom, until, at the conclusion of a day dream *often replete with luxury*, he finds the *incitamentum* or first cause of his musings entirely vanished and forgotten. In my case the primary object was *invariably frivolous*, although assuming, through the medium of my distempered vision, a refracted and unreal importance. Few deductions, if any, were made; and those few pertinaciously returning in upon the original object as a centre. The meditations were *never* pleasurable; and, at the termination of the reverie, the first cause, so far from being out of sight, had attained that supernaturally exaggerated interest which was the prevailing feature of the disease. In a word, the powers of mind more particularly exercised were, with me, as I have said before, the *attentive*, and are, with the day-dreamer, the *speculative*.

My books, at this epoch, if they did not actually serve to irritate the disorder, partook, it will be perceived, largely, in their imaginative and inconsequential nature, of the characteristic qualities of the disorder itself. I well remember, among others, the treatise of the noble Italian Cœlius Secundus Curio "*de Amplitudine Beati Regni Dei*;" St. Austin's great work, the "City of God;" and Tertullian "*de Carne Christi*," in which the paradoxical sentence "*Mortuus est Dei filius; credibile est quia ineptum est; et sepultus resurrexit; certum est quia impossibile est*" occupied my undivided time, for many weeks of laborious and fruitless investigation.

Thus it will appear that, shaken from its balance only by trivial things, my reason bore resemblance to that ocean-crag spoken of by Ptolemy Hephestion, which steadily resisting the attacks of human violence, and the fiercer fury of the waters and the winds, trembled only to the touch of the flower called Asphodel. And although, to a careless thinker, it might appear a matter beyond doubt, that the alteration produced by her unhappy malady, in the *moral* condition of Berenice, would afford me many objects for the exercise of that intense and abnormal meditation whose nature I have been at some trouble in explaining, yet such was not in any degree the case. In the lucid intervals of my infirmity, her calamity, indeed, gave me pain, and, taking deeply to heart that total wreck of her fair and gentle life, I did not fail to ponder frequently and bitterly upon the wonder-working means by which so strange a revolution had been so suddenly brought to pass. But these reflections partook not of the idiosyncrasy of my disease, and were such as would have occurred, under similar circumstances, to the ordinary mass of mankind. True to its own character, my disorder revelled in the less important but more startling changes wrought in the *physical* frame of Berenice—in the singular and most appalling distortion of her personal identity.

During the brightest days of her unparalleled beauty, most surely I had never loved her. In the strange anomaly of my existence, feelings with me, *had never been* of the heart, and my passions *always were* of the mind. Through the gray of the early morning—among the trellissed shadows of the forest at noonday—and in the silence of my library at night, she had flitted by my eyes, and I had seen her—not as the living and breathing Berenice, but as the Berenice of a dream—not as a being of the earth, earthy, but as the abstraction of such a being—not as a thing to admire, but to analyze—not as an object of love, but as the theme of the most abstruse although desultory speculation. And *now*—now I shuddered in her presence, and grew pale at her approach; yet bitterly lamenting her fallen and desolate condition, I called to mind that she had loved me long, and, in an evil moment, I spoke to her of marriage.

And at length the period of our nuptials was approaching, when, upon an afternoon in the winter of the year,—one of those unseasonably warm, calm, and misty days which are the nurse of the beautiful Halcyon,*—I sat, (and sat, as I thought, alone,) in the inner apartment of the library. But uplifting my eyes I saw that Berenice stood before me.

Was it my own excited imagination—or the misty influence of the atmosphere—or the uncertain twilight of the chamber—or

*For as Jove, during the winter season, gives twice seven days of warmth, men have called this clement and temperate time the nurse of the beautiful Halcyon.—*Simonides.*

the gray draperies which fell around her figure—that caused in it so vacillating and indistinct an outline? I could not tell. She spoke no word, and I—not for worlds could I have uttered a syllable. An icy chill ran through my frame; a sense of insufferable anxiety oppressed me; a consuming curiosity pervaded my soul; and sinking back upon the chair, I remained for some time breathless and motionless, with my eyes riveted upon her person. Alas! its emaciation was excessive, and not one vestige of the former being, lurked in any single line of the contour. My burning glances at length fell upon the face.

The forehead was high, and very pale, and singularly placid; and the once jetty hair fell partially over it, and overshadowed the hollow temples with innumerable ringlets now of a vivid yellow, and jarring discordantly, in their fantastic character, with the reigning melancholy of the countenance. The eyes were lifeless, and lustreless, and seemingly pupil-less, and I shrank involuntarily from their glassy stare to the contemplation of the thin and shrunken lips. They parted; and in a smile of peculiar meaning, *the teeth* of the changed Berenice disclosed themselves slowly to my view. Would to God that I had never beheld them, or that, having done so, I had died!

The shutting of a door disturbed me, and, looking up, I found that my cousin had departed from the chamber. But from the disordered chamber of my brain, had not, alas! departed, and would not be driven away, the white and ghastly *spectrum* of the teeth. Not a speck on their surface—not a shade on their enamel—not an indenture in their edges—but what that brief period of her smile had sufficed to brand in upon my memory. I saw them now even more unequivocally than I beheld them *then*. The teeth!—the teeth!—they were here, and there, and every where, and visibly and palpably before me; long, narrow, and excessively white, with the pale lips writhing about them, as in the very moment of their first terrible development. Then came the full fury of my *monomania*, and I struggled in vain against its strange and irresistible influence. In the multiplied objects of the external world I had no thoughts but for the teeth. For these I longed with a phrenzied desire. All other matters and all different interests became absorbed in their single contemplation. They—they alone were present to the mental eye, and they, in their sole individuality, became the essence of my mental life. I held them in every light. I turned them in every attitude. I surveyed their characteristics. I dwelt upon their peculiarities. I pondered upon their conformation. I mused upon the alteration in their nature. I shuddered as I assigned to them in imagination a sensitive and sentient power, and even when unassisted by the lips, a capability of moral expression. Of Mad'selle Sallé it has been well said, "*que tous ses pas etaient des sentiments,*" and of Berenice I more seriously believed *que tous ses dents etaient des idées. Des idées!*—ah here was the idiotic thought that destroyed me! *Des idées!*—ah *therefore* it was that I coveted them so madly! I felt that their possession could alone ever restore me to peace, in giving me back to reason.

And the evening closed in upon me thus—and then the darkness came, and tarried, and went—and the day again dawned—and the mists of a second night were now gathering around—and still I sat motionless in that solitary room, and still I sat buried in meditation, and still the *phantasma* of the teeth maintained its terrible ascendancy as, with the most vivid and hideous distinctness, it floated about amid the changing lights and shadows of the chamber. At length there broke in upon my dreams a cry as of horror and dismay; and thereunto, after a pause, succeeded the sound of troubled voices, intermingled with many low moanings of sorrow, or of pain. I arose from my seat, and, throwing open one of the doors of the library, saw standing out in the antechamber a servant maiden, all in tears, who told me that Berenice was—no more. She had been seized with epilepsy in the early morning, and now, at the closing in of the night, the grave was ready for its tenant, and all the preparations for the burial were completed.

I found myself sitting in the library, and again sitting there alone. It seemed that I had newly awakened from a confused and exciting dream. I knew that it was now midnight, and I was well aware that since the setting of the sun Berenice had been interred. But of that dreary period which intervened I had no positive—at least no definite comprehension. Yet its memory was replete with horror—horror more horrible from being vague, and terror more terrible from ambiguity. It was a fearful page in the record of my existence, written all over with dim,

and hideous, and unintelligible recollections. I strived to de-
cypher them, but in vain; while ever and anon, like the spirit of
a departed sound, the shrill and piercing shriek of a female
voice seemed to be ringing in my ears. I had done a deed—
what was it? I asked myself the question aloud, and the whispering echoes of the chamber answered me, "*what was it?*"

On the table beside me burned a lamp, and near it lay a little
box. It was of no remarkable character, and I had seen it frequently before, for it was the property of the family physician;
but how came it *there*, upon my table, and why did I shudder
in regarding it? These things were in no manner to be accounted for, and my eyes at length dropped to the open pages
of a book, and to a sentence underscored therein. The words
were the singular but simple ones of the poet Ebn Zaiat. "*Dicebant mihi sodales si sepulchrum amicae visitarem, curas meas
aliquantulum fore levatas.*" Why then, as I perused them, did
the hairs of my head erect themselves on end, and the blood of
my body become congealed within my veins?

There came a light tap at the library door, and pale as the
tenant of a tomb, a menial entered upon tiptoe. His looks were
wild with terror, and he spoke to me in a voice tremulous, husky,
and very low. What said he?—some broken sentences I heard.
He told of a wild cry disturbing the silence of the night—of
the gathering together of the household—of a search in the direction of the sound;—and then his tones grew thrillingly distinct as he whispered me of a violated grave—of a disfigured
body enshrouded, yet still breathing, still palpitating, *still alive!*

He pointed to my garments;—they were muddy and clotted
with gore. I spoke not, and he took me gently by the hand;—
it was indented with the impress of human nails. He directed
my attention to some object against the wall;—I looked at it
for some minutes;—it was a spade. With a shriek I bounded to
the table, and grasped the box that lay upon it. But I could not
force it open; and in my tremor it slipped from my hands, and
fell heavily, and burst into pieces; and from it, with a rattling
sound, there rolled out some instruments of dental surgery, intermingled with thirty-two small, white and ivory-looking substances that were scattered to and fro about the floor.

1835

NATHANIEL HAWTHORNE
(1804–1864)

Young Goodman Brown

YOUNG GOODMAN BROWN came forth, at sunset, into the street of Salem village, but put his head back, after crossing the threshold, to exchange a parting kiss with his young wife. And Faith, as the wife was aptly named, thrust her own pretty head into the street, letting the wind play with the pink ribbons of her cap, while she called to Goodman Brown.

'Dearest heart,' whispered she, softly and rather sadly, when her lips were close to his ear, 'pr'y thee, put off your journey until sunrise, and sleep in your own bed to-night. A lone woman is troubled with such dreams and such thoughts, that she's afeard of herself, sometimes. Pray, tarry with me this night, dear husband, of all nights in the year!'

'My love and my Faith,' replied young Goodman Brown, 'of all nights in the year, this one night must I tarry away from thee. My journey, as thou callest it, forth and back again, must needs be done 'twixt now and sunrise. What, my sweet, pretty wife, dost thou doubt me already, and we but three months married!'

'Then, God bless you!' said Faith, with the pink ribbons, 'and may you find all well, when you come back.'

'Amen!' cried Goodman Brown. 'Say thy prayers, dear Faith, and go to bed at dusk, and no harm will come to thee.'

So they parted; and the young man pursued his way, until, being about to turn the corner by the meeting-house, he looked back, and saw the head of Faith still peeping after him, with a melancholy air, in spite of her pink ribbons.

'Poor little Faith!' thought he, for his heart smote him. 'What a wretch am I, to leave her on such an errand! She talks of dreams, too. Methought, as she spoke, there was trouble in her face, as if a dream had warned her what work is to be done to-night. But, no, no! 'twould kill her to think it. Well; she's a blessed angel on earth; and after this one night, I'll cling to her skirts and follow her to Heaven.'

With this excellent resolve for the future, Goodman Brown felt himself justified in making more haste on his present evil purpose. He had taken a dreary road, darkened by all the gloomiest trees of the forest, which barely stood aside to let the narrow path creep through, and closed immediately behind. It was all as lonely as could be; and there is this peculiarity in such a solitude, that the traveller knows not who may be concealed by the innumerable trunks and the thick boughs overhead; so that, with lonely footsteps, he may yet be passing through an unseen multitude.

'There may be a devilish Indian behind every tree,' said Goodman Brown, to himself; and he glanced fearfully behind him, as he added, 'What if the devil himself should be at my very elbow!'

His head being turned back, he passed a crook of the road, and looking forward again, beheld the figure of a man, in grave and decent attire, seated at the foot of an old tree. He arose, at Goodman Brown's approach, and walked onward, side by side with him.

'You are late, Goodman Brown,' said he. 'The clock of the Old South was striking as I came through Boston; and that is full fifteen minutes agone.'

'Faith kept me back awhile,' replied the young man, with a tremor in his voice, caused by the sudden appearance of his companion, though not wholly unexpected.

It was now deep dusk in the forest, and deepest in that part of it where these two were journeying. As nearly as could be discerned, the second traveller was about fifty years old, apparently in the same rank of life as Goodman Brown, and bearing a considerable resemblance to him, though perhaps more in expression than features. Still, they might have been taken for father and son. And yet, though the elder person was as simply clad as the younger, and as simple in manner too, he had an indescribable air of one who knew the world, and would not have felt abashed at the governor's dinner-table, or in King William's court, were it possible that his affairs should call him thither. But the only thing about him, that could be fixed upon as remarkable, was his staff, which bore the likeness of a great black snake, so curiously wrought, that it might almost be seen to twist and wriggle itself, like a living serpent. This, of course, must have been an ocular deception, assisted by the uncertain light.

'Come, Goodman Brown!' cried his fellow-traveller, 'this is a dull pace for the beginning of a journey. Take my staff, if you are so soon weary.'

'Friend,' said the other, exchanging his slow pace for a full stop, 'having kept covenant by meeting thee here, it is my purpose now to return whence I came. I have scruples, touching the matter thou wot'st of.'

'Sayest thou so?' replied he of the serpent, smiling apart. 'Let us walk on, nevertheless, reasoning as we go, and if I convince thee not, thou shalt turn back. We are but a little way in the forest, yet.'

'Too far, too far!' exclaimed the goodman, unconsciously resuming his walk. 'My father never went into the woods on such an errand, nor his father before him. We have been a race of honest men and good Christians, since the days of the martyrs. And shall I be the first of the name of Brown, that ever took this path, and kept—'

'Such company, thou wouldst say,' observed the elder person, interpreting his pause. 'Well said, Goodman Brown! I have been as well acquainted with your family as with ever a one among the Puritans; and that's no trifle to say. I helped your grandfather, the constable, when he lashed the Quaker woman so smartly through the streets of Salem. And it was I that brought your father a pitch-pine knot, kindled at my own hearth, to set fire to an Indian village, in King Philip's war. They were my good friends, both; and many a pleasant walk have we had along this path, and returned merrily after midnight. I would fain be friends with you, for their sake.'

'If it be as thou sayest,' replied Goodman Brown, 'I marvel they never spoke of these matters. Or, verily, I marvel not, seeing that the least rumor of the sort would have driven them from New-England. We are a people of prayer, and good works, to boot, and abide no such wickedness.'

'Wickedness or not,' said the traveller with the twisted staff, 'I have a very general acquaintance here in New-England. The deacons of many a church have drunk the communion wine with me; the selectmen, of divers towns, make me their chairman;

and a majority of the Great and General Court are firm sup-
porters of my interest. The governor and I, too—but these are
state-secrets.'

'Can this be so!' cried Goodman Brown, with a stare of
amazement at his undisturbed companion. 'Howbeit, I have
nothing to do with the governor and council; they have their
own ways, and are no rule for a simple husbandman, like me.
But, were I to go on with thee, how should I meet the eye of
that good old man, our minister, at Salem village? Oh, his voice
would make me tremble, both Sabbath-day and lecture-day!'

Thus far, the elder traveller had listened with due gravity,
but now burst into a fit of irrepressible mirth, shaking himself
so violently, that his snake-like staff actually seemed to wriggle
in sympathy.

'Ha! ha! ha!' shouted he, again and again; then composing
himself, 'Well, go on, Goodman Brown, go on; but pr'y thee,
don't kill me with laughing!'

'Well, then, to end the matter at once,' said Goodman
Brown, considerably nettled, 'there is my wife, Faith. It would
break her dear little heart; and I'd rather break my own!'

'Nay, if that be the case,' answered the other, 'e'en go thy
ways, Goodman Brown. I would not, for twenty old women
like the one hobbling before us, that Faith should come to any
harm.'

As he spoke, he pointed his staff at a female figure on the path,
in whom Goodman Brown recognized a very pious and exem-
plary dame, who had taught him his catechism, in youth, and
was still his moral and spiritual adviser, jointly with the minister and Deacon Gookin.

'A marvel, truly, that Goody Cloyse should be so far in the
wilderness, at night-fall!' said he. 'But, with your leave, friend,
I shall take a cut through the woods, until we have left this
Christian woman behind. Being a stranger to you, she might
ask whom I was consorting with, and whither I was going.'

'Be it so,' said his fellow-traveller. 'Betake you to the woods,
and let me keep the path.'

Accordingly, the young man turned aside, but took care to
watch his companion, who advanced softly along the road,
until he had come within a staff's length of the old dame. She,
meanwhile, was making the best of her way, with singular

speed for so aged a woman, and mumbling some indistinct words, a prayer, doubtless, as she went. The traveller put forth his staff, and touched her withered neck with what seemed the serpent's tail.

'The devil!' screamed the pious old lady.

'Then Goody Cloyse knows her old friend?' observed the traveller, confronting her, and leaning on his writhing stick.

'Ah, forsooth, and is it your worship, indeed?' cried the good dame. 'Yea, truly is it, and in the very image of my old gossip, Goodman Brown, the grandfather of the silly fellow that now is. But—would your worship believe it?—my broomstick hath strangely disappeared, stolen, as I suspect, by that unhanged witch, Goody Cory, and that, too, when I was all anointed with the juice of smallage and cinque-foil and wolf's-bane—'

'Mingled with fine wheat and the fat of a new-born babe,' said the shape of old Goodman Brown.

'Ah, your worship knows the receipt,' cried the old lady, cackling aloud. 'So, as I was saying, being all ready for the meeting, and no horse to ride on, I made up my mind to foot it; for they tell me, there is a nice young man to be taken into communion to-night. But now your good worship will lend me your arm, and we shall be there in a twinkling.'

'That can hardly be,' answered her friend. 'I may not spare you my arm, Goody Cloyse, but here is my staff, if you will.'

So saying, he threw it down at her feet, where, perhaps, it assumed life, being one of the rods which its owner had formerly lent to the Egyptian Magi. Of this fact, however, Goodman Brown could not take cognizance. He had cast up his eyes in astonishment, and looking down again, beheld neither Goody Cloyse nor the serpentine staff, but his fellow-traveller alone, who waited for him as calmly as if nothing had happened.

'That old woman taught me my catechism!' said the young man; and there was a world of meaning in this simple comment.

They continued to walk onward, while the elder traveller exhorted his companion to make good speed and persevere in the path, discoursing so aptly, that his arguments seemed rather to spring up in the bosom of his auditor, than to be suggested by himself. As they went, he plucked a branch of maple, to serve for a walking-stick, and began to strip it of the twigs and little boughs, which were wet with evening dew. The moment his fingers touched them, they became strangely withered and dried up, as with a week's sunshine. Thus the pair proceeded, at a good free pace, until suddenly, in a gloomy hollow of the road, Goodman Brown sat himself down on the stump of a tree, and refused to go any farther.

'Friend,' said he, stubbornly, 'my mind is made up. Not another step will I budge on this errand. What if a wretched old woman do choose to go to the devil, when I thought she was going to Heaven! Is that any reason why I should quit my dear Faith, and go after her?'

'You will think better of this, by-and-by,' said his acquaintance, composedly. 'Sit here and rest yourself awhile; and when you feel like moving again, there is my staff to help you along.'

Without more words, he threw his companion the maple stick, and was as speedily out of sight, as if he had vanished into the deepening gloom. The young man sat a few moments, by the road-side, applauding himself greatly, and thinking with how clear a conscience he should meet the minister, in his morning-walk, nor shrink from the eye of good old Deacon Gookin. And what calm sleep would be his, that very night, which was to have been spent so wickedly, but purely and sweetly now, in the arms of Faith! Amidst these pleasant and praiseworthy meditations, Goodman Brown heard the tramp of horses along the road, and deemed it advisable to conceal himself within the verge of the forest, conscious of the guilty purpose that had brought him thither, though now so happily turned from it.

On came the hoof-tramps and the voices of the riders, two grave old voices, conversing soberly as they drew near. These mingled sounds appeared to pass along the road, within a few yards of the young man's hiding-place; but owing, doubtless, to the depth of the gloom, at that particular spot, neither the travellers nor their steeds were visible. Though their figures brushed the small boughs by the way-side, it could not be seen that they intercepted, even for a moment, the faint gleam from the strip of bright sky, athwart which they must have passed. Goodman Brown alternately crouched and stood on tip-toe, pulling aside the branches, and thrusting forth his head as far as he durst, without discerning so much as a shadow. It vexed him the more, because he could have sworn, were such a thing possible, that he recognized the voices of the minister and Deacon Gookin, jogging along quietly, as they were wont to do, when bound to some ordination or ecclesiastical council. While yet within hearing, one of the riders stopped to pluck a switch.

'Of the two, reverend Sir,' said the voice like the deacon's, 'I had rather miss an ordination-dinner than to-night's meeting. They tell me that some of our community are to be here from Falmouth and beyond, and others from Connecticut and Rhode-Island; besides several of the Indian powows, who, after their fashion, know almost as much deviltry as the best of us. Moreover, there is a goodly young woman to be taken into communion.'

'Mighty well, Deacon Gookin!' replied the solemn old tones of the minister. 'Spur up, or we shall be late. Nothing can be done, you know, until I get on the ground.'

The hoofs clattered again, and the voices, talking so strangely in the empty air, passed on through the forest, where no church had ever been gathered, nor solitary Christian prayed. Whither, then, could these holy men be journeying, so deep into the heathen wilderness? Young Goodman Brown caught hold of a tree, for support, being ready to sink down on the ground, faint and overburthened with the heavy sickness of his heart. He looked up to the sky, doubting whether there really was a Heaven above him. Yet, there was the blue arch, and the stars brightening in it.

'With Heaven above, and Faith below, I will yet stand firm against the devil!' cried Goodman Brown.

While he still gazed upward, into the deep arch of the firmament and had lifted his hands to pray, a cloud, though no wind was stirring, hurried across the zenith, and hid the brightening stars. The blue sky was still visible, except directly overhead, where this black mass of cloud was sweeping swiftly northward. Aloft in the air, as if from the depths of the cloud, came a confused and doubtful sound of voices. Once, the listener fancied that he could distinguish the accents of town's-people of his own, men and women, both pious and ungodly, many of whom he had met at the communion-table, and had seen others rioting at the tavern. The next moment, so indistinct were the sounds, he doubted whether he had heard aught but the murmur of the

old forest, whispering without a wind. Then came a stronger
swell of those familiar tones, heard daily in the sunshine, at
Salem village, but never, until now, from a cloud of night.
There was one voice, of a young woman, uttering lamentations,
yet with an uncertain sorrow, and entreating for some favor,
which, perhaps, it would grieve her to obtain. And all the unseen multitude, both saints and sinners, seemed to encourage
her onward.

'Faith!' shouted Goodman Brown, in a voice of agony and
desperation; and the echoes of the forest mocked him, crying
—'Faith! Faith!' as if bewildered wretches were seeking her, all
through the wilderness.

The cry of grief, rage, and terror, was yet piercing the night,
when the unhappy husband held his breath for a response.
There was a scream, drowned immediately in a louder murmur
of voices, fading into far-off laughter, as the dark cloud swept
away, leaving the clear and silent sky above Goodman Brown.
But something fluttered lightly down through the air, and
caught on the branch of a tree. The young man seized it, and
beheld a pink ribbon.

'My Faith is gone!' cried he, after one stupefied moment.
'There is no good on earth; and sin is but a name. Come,
devil! for to thee is this world given.'

And maddened with despair, so that he laughed loud and
long, did Goodman Brown grasp his staff and set forth again,
at such a rate, that he seemed to fly along the forest-path,
rather than to walk or run. The road grew wilder and drearier,
and more faintly traced, and vanished at length, leaving in the
heart of the dark wilderness, still rushing onward, with the instinct that guides mortal man to evil. The whole forest was
peopled with frightful sounds; the creaking of the trees, the
howling of wild beasts, and the yell of Indians; while, sometimes, the wind tolled like a distant church-bell, and sometimes
gave a broad roar around the traveller, as if all Nature were
laughing him to scorn. But he was himself the chief horror of
the scene, and shrank not from its other horrors.

'Ha! ha! ha!' roared Goodman Brown, when the wind
laughed at him. 'Let us hear which will laugh loudest! Think not
to frighten me with your deviltry! Come witch, come wizard,

come Indian powow, come devil himself! and here comes Goodman Brown. You may as well fear him as he fear you!'

In truth, all through the haunted forest, there could be nothing more frightful than the figure of Goodman Brown. On he flew, among the black pines, brandishing his staff with frenzied gestures, now giving vent to an inspiration of horrid blasphemy, and now shouting forth such laughter, as set all the echoes of the forest laughing like demons around him. The fiend in his own shape is less hideous, than when he rages in the breast of man. Thus sped the demoniac on his course, until, quivering among the trees, he saw a red light before him, as when the felled trunks and branches of a clearing have been set on fire, and throw up their lurid blaze against the sky, at the hour of midnight. He paused, in a lull of the tempest that had driven him onward, and heard the swell of what seemed a hymn, rolling solemnly from a distance, with the weight of many voices. He knew the tune; it was a familiar one in the choir of the village meeting-house. The verse died heavily away, and was lengthened by a chorus, not of human voices, but of all the sounds of the benighted wilderness, pealing in awful harmony together. Goodman Brown cried out; and his cry was lost to his own ear, by its unison with the cry of the desert.

In the interval of silence, he stole forward, until the light glared full upon his eyes. At one extremity of an open space, hemmed in by the dark wall of the forest, arose a rock, bearing some rude, natural resemblance either to an altar or a pulpit, and surrounded by four blazing pines, their tops aflame, their stems untouched, like candles at an evening meeting. The mass of foliage, that had overgrown the summit of the rock, was all on fire, blazing high into the night, and fitfully illuminating the whole field. Each pendent twig and leafy festoon was in a blaze. As the red light arose and fell, a numerous congregation alternately shone forth, then disappeared in shadow, and again grew, as it were, out of the darkness, peopling the heart of the solitary woods at once.

'A grave and dark-clad company!' quoth Goodman Brown.

In truth, they were such. Among them, quivering to-and-fro, between gloom and splendor, appeared faces that would be seen, next day, at the council-board of the province, and others which, Sabbath after Sabbath, looked devoutly heavenward, and benignantly over the crowded pews, from the holiest pulpits in the land. Some affirm, that the lady of the governor was there. At least, there were high dames well known to her, and wives of honored husbands, and widows, a great multitude, and ancient maidens, all of excellent repute, and fair young girls, who trembled, lest their mothers should espy them. Either the sudden gleams of light, flashing over the obscure field, bedazzled Goodman Brown, or he recognized a score of the church-members of Salem village, famous for their especial sanctity. Good old Deacon Gookin had arrived, and waited at the skirts of that venerable saint, his revered pastor. But, irreverently consorting with these grave, reputable, and pious people, these elders of the church, these chaste dames and dewy virgins, there were men of dissolute lives and women of spotted fame, wretches given over to all mean and filthy vice, and suspected even of horrid crimes. It was strange to see, that the good shrank not from the wicked, nor were the sinners abashed by the saints. Scattered, also, among their pale-faced enemies, were the Indian priests, or powows, who had often scared their native forest with more hideous incantations than any known to English witchcraft.

'But, where is Faith?' thought Goodman Brown; and, as hope came into his heart, he trembled.

Another verse of the hymn arose, a slow and mournful strain, such as the pious love, but joined to words which expressed all that our nature can conceive of sin, and darkly hinted at far more. Unfathomable to mere mortals is the lore of fiends. Verse after verse was sung, and still the chorus of the desert swelled between, like the deepest tone of a mighty organ. And, with the final peal of that dreadful anthem, there came a sound, as if the roaring wind, the rushing streams, the howling beasts, and every other voice of the unconverted wilderness, were mingling and according with the voice of guilty man, in homage to the prince of all. The four blazing pines threw up a loftier flame, and obscurely discovered shapes and visages of horror on the smoke-wreaths, above the impious assembly. At the same moment, the fire on the rock shot redly forth, and formed a glowing arch above its base, where now appeared a figure. With reverence be it spoken, the figure bore no slight similitude, both in garb and manner, to some grave divine of the New-England churches.

'Bring forth the converts!' cried a voice, that echoed through the field and rolled into the forest.

At the word, Goodman Brown stept forth from the shadow of the trees, and approached the congregation, with whom he felt a loathful brotherhood, by the sympathy of all that was wicked in his heart. He could have well nigh sworn, that the shape of his own dead father beckoned him to advance, looking downward from a smoke-wreath, while a woman, with dim features of despair, threw out her hand to warn him back. Was it his mother? But he had no power to retreat one step, nor to resist, even in thought, when the minister and good old Deacon Gookin seized his arms, and led him to the blazing rock. Thither came also the slender form of a veiled female, led between Goody Cloyse, that pious teacher of the catechism, and Martha Carrier, who had received the devil's promise to be queen of hell. A rampant hag was she! And there stood the proselytes, beneath the canopy of fire.

'Welcome, my children,' said the dark figure, 'to the communion of your race! Ye have found, thus young, your nature and your destiny. My children, look behind you!'

They turned; and flashing forth, as it were, in a sheet of flame, the fiend-worshippers were seen; the smile of welcome gleamed darkly on every visage.

'There,' resumed the sable form, 'are all whom ye have reverenced from youth. Ye deemed them holier than yourselves, and shrank from your own sin, contrasting it with their lives of righteousness, and prayerful aspirations heavenward. Yet, here are they all, in my worshipping assembly! This night it shall be granted you to know their secret deeds; how hoary-bearded elders of the church have whispered wanton words to the young maids of their households; how many a woman, eager for widow's weeds, has given her husband a drink at bed-time, and let him sleep his last sleep in her bosom; how beardless youths have made haste to inherit their fathers' wealth; and how fair damsels—blush not, sweet ones!—have dug little graves in the garden, and bidden me, the sole guest, to an infant's funeral. By the sympathy of your human hearts for sin, ye shall scent out all the places—whether in church, bed-chamber, street, field, or forest—where crime has been committed, and shall exult to behold the whole earth one stain of guilt, one mighty blood-spot. Far more than this! It shall be yours to penetrate, in every bosom, the deep mystery of sin, the fountain of all wicked arts, and which inexhaustibly supplies more evil impulses than human power—than my power, at its utmost!— can make manifest in deeds. And now, my children, look upon each other.'

They did so; and, by the blaze of the hell-kindled torches, the wretched man beheld his Faith, and the wife her husband, trembling before that unhallowed altar.

'Lo! there ye stand, my children,' said the figure, in a deep and solemn tone, almost sad, with its despairing awfulness, as if his once angelic nature could yet mourn for our miserable race. 'Depending upon one another's hearts, ye had still hoped, that virtue were not all a dream. Now are ye undeceived! Evil is the nature of mankind. Evil must be your only happiness. Welcome, again, my children, to the communion of your race!'

"Welcome!' repeated the fiend-worshippers, in one cry of despair and triumph.

And there they stood, the only pair, as it seemed, who were yet hesitating on the verge of wickedness, in this dark world. A basin was hollowed, naturally, in the rock. Did it contain water, reddened by the lurid light? or was it blood? or, perchance, a liquid flame? Herein did the Shape of Evil dip his hand, and prepare to lay the mark of baptism upon their foreheads, that they might be partakers of the mystery of sin, more conscious of the secret guilt of others, both in deed and thought, than they could now be of their own. The husband cast one look at his pale wife, and Faith at him. What polluted wretches would the next glance shew them to each other, shuddering alike at what they disclosed and what they saw!

'Faith! Faith!' cried the husband. 'Look up to Heaven, and resist the Wicked One!'

Whether Faith obeyed, he knew not. Hardly had he spoken, when he found himself amid calm night and solitude, listening to a roar of the wind, which died heavily away through the forest. He staggered against the rock and felt it chill and damp, while a hanging twig, that had been all on fire, besprinkled his cheek with the coldest dew.

The next morning, young Goodman Brown came slowly into the street of Salem village, staring around him like a bewildered man. The good old minister was taking a walk along the grave-yard, to get an appetite for breakfast and meditate his sermon, and bestowed a blessing, as he passed, on Goodman Brown. He shrank from the venerable saint, as if to avoid an anathema. Old Deacon Gookin was at domestic worship, and the holy words of his prayer were heard through the open window. 'What God doth the wizard pray to?' quoth Goodman Brown. Goody Cloyse, that excellent old Christian, stood in the early sunshine, at her own lattice, catechising a little girl, who had brought her a pint of morning's milk. Goodman Brown snatched away the child, as from the grasp of the fiend himself. Turning the corner by the meeting-house, he spied the head of Faith, with the pink ribbons, gazing anxiously forth, and bursting into such joy at sight of him, that she skipt along the street, and almost kissed her husband before the whole village. But, Goodman Brown looked sternly and sadly into her face, and passed on without a greeting.

Had Goodman Brown fallen asleep in the forest, and only dreamed a wild dream of a witch-meeting?

Be it so, if you will. But, alas! it was a dream of evil omen for young Goodman Brown. A stern, a sad, a darkly meditative, a distrustful, if not a desperate man, did he become, from the night of that fearful dream. On the Sabbath-day, when the congregation were singing a holy psalm, he could not listen, because an anthem of sin rushed loudly upon his ear, and drowned all the blessed strain. When the minister spoke from the pulpit, with power and fervid eloquence, and, with his hand on the open Bible, of the sacred truths of our religion, and of saint-like lives and triumphant deaths, and of future bliss or misery unutterable, then did Goodman Brown turn pale, dreading, lest the roof should thunder down upon the gray blasphemer and his hearers. Often, awakening suddenly at midnight, he shrank from the bosom of Faith, and at morning or eventide, when the family knelt down at prayer, he scowled, and muttered to himself, and gazed sternly at his wife, and turned away. And when he had lived long, and was borne to his grave, a hoary corpse, followed by Faith, an aged woman, and children and grand-children, a goodly procession, besides neighbors, not a few, they carved no hopeful verse upon his tomb-stone; for his dying hour was gloom.

1835

HERMAN MELVILLE

(1819–1891)

The Tartarus of Maids

It lies not far from Woedolor Mountain in New England. Turning to the east, right out from among bright farms and sunny meadows, nodding in early June with odorous grasses, you enter ascendingly among bleak hills. These gradually close in upon a dusky pass, which, from the violent Gulf Stream of air unceasingly driving between its cloven walls of haggard rock, as well as from the tradition of a crazy spinster's hut having long ago stood somewhere hereabouts, is called the Mad Maid's Bellows'-pipe.

Winding along at the bottom of the gorge is a dangerously narrow wheel-road, occupying the bed of a former torrent. Following this road to its highest point, you stand as within a Dantean gateway. From the steepness of the walls here, their strangely ebon hue, and the sudden contraction of the gorge, this particular point is called the Black Notch. The ravine now expandingly descends into a great, purple, hopper-shaped hollow, far sunk among many Plutonian, shaggy-wooded mountains. By the country people this hollow is called the Devil's Dungeon. Sounds of torrents fall on all sides upon the ear. These rapid waters unite at last in one turbid brick-colored stream, boiling through a flume among enormous boulders. They call this strange-colored torrent Blood River. Gaining a dark precipice it wheels suddenly to the west, and makes one maniac spring of sixty feet into the arms of a stunted wood of gray-haired pines, between which it thence eddies on its further way down to the invisible lowlands.

Conspicuously crowning a rocky bluff high to one side, at the cataract's verge, is the ruin of an old saw-mill, built in those primitive times when vast pines and hemlocks superabounded throughout the neighboring region. The black-mossed bulk of those immense, rough-hewn, and spike-knotted logs, here and there tumbled all together, in long abandonment and

decay, or left in solitary, perilous projection over the cataract's
gloomy brink, impart to this rude wooden ruin not only much
of the aspect of one of rough-quarried stone, but also a sort of
feudal, Rhineland, and Thurmberg look, derived from the pin-
nacled wildness of the neighboring scenery.

Not far from the bottom of the Dungeon stands a large
white-washed building, relieved, like some great white sepulchre, against the sullen background of mountain-side firs, and
other hardy evergreens, inaccessibly rising in grim terraces for
some two thousand feet.

The building is a paper-mill.

Having embarked on a large scale in the seedsman's business
(so extensively and broadcast, indeed, that at length my seeds
were distributed through all the Eastern and Northern States,
and even fell into the far soil of Missouri and the Carolinas),
the demand for paper at my place became so great, that the expenditure soon amounted to a most important item in the
general account. It need hardly be hinted how paper comes
into use with seedsmen, as envelopes. These are mostly made of
yellowish paper, folded square; and when filled, are all but flat,
and being stamped, and superscribed with the nature of the
seeds contained, assume not a little the appearance of business-
letters ready for the mail. Of these small envelopes I used an incredible quantity—several hundreds of thousands in a year. For
a time I had purchased my paper from the wholesale dealers in
a neighboring town. For economy's sake, and partly for the
adventure of the trip, I now resolved to cross the mountains,
some sixty miles, and order my future paper at the Devil's
Dungeon paper-mill.

The sleighing being uncommonly fine toward the end of
January, and promising to hold so for no small period, in spite
of the bitter cold I started one gray Friday noon in my pung,
well fitted with buffalo and wolf robes; and, spending one
night on the road, next noon came in sight of Woedolor
Mountain.

The far summit fairly smoked with frost; white vapors curled
up from its white-wooded top, as from a chimney. The intense
congelation made the whole country look like one petrifac-
tion. The steel shoes of my pung craunched and gritted over
the vitreous, chippy snow, as if it had been broken glass. The

forests here and there skirting the route, feeling the same all-stiffening influence, their inmost fibres penetrated with the cold, strangely groaned—not in the swaying branches merely, but likewise in the vertical trunk—as the fitful gusts remorselessly swept through them. Brittle with excessive frost, many colossal tough-grained maples, snapped in twain like pipe-stems, cumbered the unfeeling earth.

Flaked all over with frozen sweat, white as a milky ram, his nostrils at each breath sending forth two horn-shaped shoots of heated respiration, Black, my good horse, but six years old, started at a sudden turn, where, right across the track—not ten minutes fallen—an old distorted hemlock lay, darkly undulatory as an anaconda.

Gaining the Bellows'-pipe, the violent blast, dead from behind, all but shoved my high-backed pung up-hill. The gust shrieked through the shivered pass, as if laden with lost spirits bound to the unhappy world. Ere gaining the summit, Black, my horse, as if exasperated by the cutting wind, slung out with his strong hind legs, tore the light pung straight up-hill, and sweeping grazingly through the narrow notch, sped downward madly past the ruined saw-mill. Into the Devil's Dungeon horse and cataract rushed together.

With might and main, quitting my seat and robes, and standing backward, with one foot braced against the dash-board, I rasped and churned the bit, and stopped him just in time to avoid collision, at a turn, with the bleak nozzle of a rock, couchant like a lion in the way—a road-side rock.

At first I could not discover the paper-mill.

The whole hollow gleamed with the white, except, here and there, where a pinnacle of granite showed one wind-swept angle bare. The mountains stood pinned in shrouds—a pass of Alpine corpses. Where stands the mill? Suddenly a whirling, humming sound broke upon my ear. I looked, and there, like an arrested avalanche, lay the large whitewashed factory. It was subordinately surrounded by a cluster of other and smaller buildings, some of which, from their cheap, blank air, great length, gregarious windows, and comfortless expression, no doubt were boarding-houses of the operatives. A snow-white hamlet amidst the snows. Various rude, irregular squares and courts resulted from the somewhat picturesque clusterings of these buildings, owing to the broken, rocky nature of the ground, which forbade all method in their relative arrangement. Several narrow lanes and alleys, too, partly blocked with snow fallen from the roof, cut up the hamlet in all directions.

When, turning from the traveled highway, jingling with bells of numerous farmers—who, availing themselves of the fine sleighing, were dragging their wood to market—and frequently diversified with swift cutters dashing from inn to inn of the scattered villages—when, I say, turning from that bustling main-road, I by degrees wound into the Mad Maid's Bellows'-pipe, and saw the grim Black Notch beyond, then something latent, as well as something obvious in the time and scene, strangely brought back to my mind my first sight of dark and grimy Temple-Bar. And when Black, my horse, went darting through the Notch, perilously grazing its rocky wall, I remembered being in a runaway London omnibus, which in much the same sort of style, though by no means at an equal rate, dashed through the ancient arch of Wren. Though the two objects did by no means completely correspond, yet this partial inadequacy but served to tinge the similitude not less with the vividness than the disorder of a dream. So that, when upon reining up at the protruding rock I at last caught sight of the quaint groupings of the factory-buildings, and with the traveled highway and the Notch behind, found myself all alone, silently and privily stealing through deep-cloven passages into this sequestered spot, and saw the long, high-gabled main factory edifice, with a rude tower—for hoisting heavy boxes—at one end, standing among its crowded outbuildings and boarding-houses, as the Temple Church amidst the surrounding offices and dormitories, and when the marvelous retirement of this mysterious mountain nook fastened its whole spell upon me, then, what memory lacked, all tributary imagination furnished, and I said to myself, "This is the very counterpart of the Paradise of Bachelors, but snowed upon, and frost-painted to a sepulchre."

Dismounting, and warily picking my way down the dangerous declivity—horse and man both sliding now and then upon the icy ledges—at length I drove, or the blast drove me, into the largest square, before one side of the main edifice. Piercingly and shrilly the shotted blast blew by the corner; and redly and demoniacally boiled Blood River at one side. A long wood-pile, of many scores of cords, all glittering in mail of crusted ice, stood crosswise in the square. A row of horse-posts, their north sides plastered with adhesive snow, flanked the factory wall. The bleak frost packed and paved the square as with some ringing metal.

The inverted similitude recurred—"The sweet, tranquil Temple garden, with the Thames bordering its green beds," strangely meditated I.

But where are the gay bachelors?

Then, as I and my horse stood shivering in the wind-spray, a girl ran from a neighboring dormitory door, and throwing her thin apron over her bare head, made for the opposite building.

"One moment, my girl; is there no shed hereabouts which I may drive into?"

Pausing, she turned upon me a face pale with work, and blue with cold; an eye supernatural with unrelated misery.

"Nay," faltered I, "I mistook you. Go on; I want nothing."

Leading my horse close to the door from which she had come, I knocked. Another pale, blue girl appeared, shivering in the doorway as, to prevent the blast, she jealously held the door ajar.

"Nay, I mistake again. In God's name shut the door. But hold, is there no man about?"

That moment a dark-complexioned well-wrapped personage passed, making for the factory door, and spying him coming, the girl rapidly closed the other one.

"Is there no horse-shed here, Sir?"

"Yonder, to the wood-shed," he replied, and disappeared inside the factory.

With much ado I managed to wedge in horse and pung between the scattered piles of wood all sawn and split. Then, blanketing my horse, and piling my buffalo on the blanket's top, and tucking in its edges well around the breast-band and breeching, so that the wind might not strip him bare, I tied him fast, and ran lamely for the factory door, stiff with frost, and cumbered with my driver's dread-naught.

Immediately I found myself standing in a spacious place, in-tolerably lighted by long rows of windows, focusing inward the snowy scene without.

At rows of blank-looking counters sat rows of blank-looking girls, with blank, white folders in their blank hands, all blankly folding blank paper.

In one corner stood some huge frame of ponderous iron, with a vertical thing like a piston periodically rising and falling upon a heavy wooden block. Before it—its tame minister— stood a tall girl, feeding the iron animal with half-quires of rose-hued note paper, which, at every downward dab of the piston-like machine, received in the corner the impress of a wreath of roses. I looked from the rosy paper to the pallid cheek, but said nothing.

Seated before a long apparatus, strung with long, slender strings like any harp, another girl was feeding it with foolscap sheets, which, so soon as they curiously traveled from her on the cords, were withdrawn at the opposite end of the machine by a second girl. They came to the first girl blank; they went to the second girl ruled.

I looked upon the first girl's brow, and saw it was young and fair; I looked upon the second girl's brow, and saw it was ruled and wrinkled. Then, as I still looked, the two—for some small variety to the monotony—changed places; and where had stood the young, fair brow, now stood the ruled and wrinkled one.

Perched high upon a narrow platform, and still higher upon a high stool crowning it, sat another figure serving some other iron animal; while below the platform sat her mate in some sort of reciprocal attendance.

Not a syllable was breathed. Nothing was heard but the low, steady, overruling hum of the iron animals. The human voice was banished from the spot. Machinery—that vaunted slave of humanity—here stood menially served by human beings, who served mutely and cringingly as the slave serves the Sultan. The girls did not so much seem accessory wheels to the general machinery as mere cogs to the wheels.

All this scene around me was instantaneously taken in at one sweeping glance—even before I had proceeded to unwind the heavy fur tippet from around my neck. But as soon as this fell from me the dark-complexioned man, standing close by, raised a sudden cry, and seizing my arm, dragged me out into the open air, and without pausing for a word instantly caught up some congealed snow and began rubbing both my cheeks.

"Two white spots like the whites of your eyes," he said; "man, your cheeks are frozen."

"That may well be," muttered I; "'tis some wonder the frost of the Devil's Dungeon strikes in no deeper. Rub away."

Soon a horrible, tearing pain caught at my reviving cheeks. Two gaunt blood-hounds, one on each side, seemed mumbling them. I seemed Actæon.

Presently, when all was over, I re-entered the factory, made known my business, concluded it satisfactorily, and then begged to be conducted throughout the place to view it.

"Cupid is the boy for that," said the dark-complexioned man. "Cupid!" and by this odd fancy-name calling a dimpled, red-cheeked, spirited-looking, forward little fellow, who was rather impudently, I thought, gliding about among the passive-looking girls—like a gold fish through hueless waves—yet doing nothing in particular that I could see, the man bade him lead the stranger through the edifice.

"Come first and see the water-wheel," said this lively lad, with the air of boyishly-brisk importance.

Quitting the folding-room, we crossed some damp, cold boards, and stood beneath a great wet shed, incessantly showering with foam, like the green barnacled bow of some East Indiaman in a gale. Round and round here went the enormous revolutions of the dark colossal water-wheel, grim with its one immutable purpose.

"This sets our whole machinery a-going, Sir; in every part of all these buildings; where the girls work and all."

I looked, and saw that the turbid waters of Blood River had not changed their hue by coming under the use of man.

"You make only blank paper; no printing of any sort, I suppose? All blank paper, don't you?"

"Certainly; what else should a paper-factory make?"

The lad here looked at me as if suspicious of my common-sense.

"Oh, to be sure!" said I, confused and stammering; "it only struck me as so strange that red waters should turn out pale chee—paper, I mean."

He took me up a wet and rickety stair to a great light room, furnished with no visible thing but rude, manger-like receptacles running all round its sides; and up to these mangers, like so many mares haltered to the rack, stood rows of girls. Before each was vertically thrust up a long, glittering scythe, immovably fixed at bottom to the manger-edge. The curve of the scythe, and its having no snath to it, made it look exactly like a sword. To and fro, across the sharp edge, the girls forever dragged long strips of rags, washed white, picked from baskets at one side; thus ripping asunder every seam, and converting the tatters almost into lint. The air swam with the fine, poisonous particles, which from all sides darted, subtilely, as motes in sun-beams, into the lungs.

"This is the rag-room," coughed the boy.

"You find it rather stifling here," coughed I, in answer; "but the girls don't cough."

"Oh, they are used to it."

"Where do you get such hosts of rags?" picking up a handful from a basket.

"Some from the country round about; some from far over sea—Leghorn and London."

"'Tis not unlikely, then," murmured I, "that among these heaps of rags there may be some old shirts, gathered from the dormitories of the Paradise of Bachelors. But the buttons are all dropped off. Pray, my lad, do you ever find any bachelor's buttons hereabouts?"

"None grow in this part of the country. The Devil's Dungeon is no place for flowers."

"Oh! you mean the *flowers* so called—the Bachelor's Buttons?"

"And was not that what you asked about? Or did you mean the gold bosom-buttons of our boss, Old Bach, as our whispering girls all call him?"

"The man, then, I saw below is a bachelor, is he?"

"Oh, yes, he's a Bach."

"The edges of those swords, they are turned outward from the girls, if I see right; but their rags and fingers fly so, I can not distinctly see."

"Turned outward."

Yes, murmured I to myself; I see it now; turned outward;

and each erected sword is so borne, edge-outward, before each girl. If my reading fails me not, just so, of old, condemned state-prisoners went from the hall of judgment to their doom: an officer before, bearing a sword, its edge turned outward, in significance of their fatal sentence. So, through consumptive pallors of this blank, raggy life, go these white girls to death.

"Those scythes look very sharp," again turning toward the boy.

"Yes; they have to keep them so. Look!"

That moment two of the girls, dropping their rags, plied each a whet-stone up and down the sword-blade. My unaccustomed blood curdled at the sharp shriek of the tormented steel.

Their own executioners; themselves whetting the very swords that slay them; meditated I.

"What makes those girls so sheet-white, my lad?"

"Why"—with a roguish twinkle, pure ignorant drollery, not knowing heartlessness—"I suppose the handling of such white bits of sheets all the time makes them so sheety."

"Let us leave the rag-room now, my lad."

More tragical and more inscrutably mysterious than any mystic sight, human or machine, throughout the factory, was the strange innocence of cruel-heartedness in this usage-hardened boy.

"And now," said he, cheerily, "I suppose you want to see our great machine, which cost us twelve thousand dollars only last autumn. That's the machine that makes the paper, too. This way, Sir."

Following him, I crossed a large, bespattered place, with two great round vats in it, full of a white, wet, woolly-looking stuff, not unlike the albuminous part of an egg, soft-boiled.

"There," said Cupid, tapping the vats carelessly, "these are the first beginnings of the paper; this white pulp you see. Look how it swims bubbling round and round, moved by the paddle here. From hence it pours from both vats into that one common channel yonder, and so goes, mixed up and leisurely, to the great machine. And now for that."

He led me into a room, stifling with a strange, blood-like, abdominal heat, as if here, true enough, were being finally developed the germinous particles lately seen.

Before me, rolled out like some long Eastern manuscript, lay stretched one continuous length of iron frame-work—multitudinous and mystical, with all sorts of rollers, wheels, and cylinders, in slowly-measured and unceasing motion.

"Here first comes the pulp now," said Cupid, pointing to the nighest end of the machine. "See; first it pours out and spreads itself upon this wide, sloping board; and then—look—slides, thin and quivering beneath the first roller there. Follow on now, and see it as it slides from under that to the next cylinder. There; see how it has become just a very little less pulpy now. One step more, and it grows still more to some slight consistence. Still another cylinder, and it is so knitted—though as yet mere dragon-fly wing—that it forms an air-bridge here, like a suspended cobweb, between two more separated rollers; and flowing over the last one, and under again, and doubling about there out of sight for a minute among all those mixed cylinders you indistinctly see, it reappears here, looking now at last a little less like pulp and more like paper, but still quite delicate and defective yet awhile. But—a little further onward, Sir, if you please—here now, at this further point, it puts on something of a real look, as if it might turn out to be something you might possibly handle in the end. But it's not yet done, Sir. Good way to travel yet, and plenty more of cylinders must roll it."

"Bless my soul!" said I, amazed at the elongation, interminable convolutions, and deliberate slowness of the machine; "it must take a long time for the pulp to pass from end to end, and come out paper."

"Oh! not so long," smiled the precocious lad, with a superior and patronizing air; "only nine minutes. But look; you may try it for yourself. Have you a bit of paper? Ah! here's a bit on the floor. Now mark that with any word you please, and let me dab it on here, and well see how long before it comes out at the other end."

"Well, let me see," said I, taking out my pencil; "come, I'll mark it with your name."

Bidding me take out my watch, Cupid adroitly dropped the inscribed slip on an exposed part of the incipient mass.

Instantly my eye marked the second-hand on my dial-plate.

Slowly I followed the slip, inch by inch; sometimes pausing for full half a minute as it disappeared beneath inscrutable groups of the lower cylinders, but only gradually to emerge again; and so, on, and on, and on—inch by inch; now in open sight, sliding along like a freckle on the quivering sheet; and then again wholly vanished; and so, on, and on, and on—inch by inch; all the time the main sheet growing more and more to final firmness—when, suddenly, I saw a sort of paper-fall, not wholly unlike a water-fall; a scissory sound smote my ear, as of some cord being snapped; and down dropped an unfolded sheet of perfect foolscap, with my "Cupid" half faded out of it, and still moist and warm.

My travels were at an end, for here was the end of the machine.

"Well, how long was it?" said Cupid.

"Nine minutes to a second," replied I, watch in hand.

"I told you so."

For a moment a curious emotion filled me, not wholly unlike that which one might experience at the fulfillment of some mysterious prophecy. But how absurd, thought I again; the thing is a mere machine, the essence of which is unvarying punctuality and precision.

Previously absorbed by the wheels and cylinders, my attention was now directed to a sad-looking woman standing by.

"That is rather an elderly person so silently tending the machine-end here. She would not seem wholly used to it either."

"Oh," knowingly whispered Cupid, through the din, "she only came last week. She was a nurse formerly. But the business is poor in these parts, and she's left it. But look at the paper she is piling there."

"Ay, foolscap," handling the piles of moist, warm sheets, which continually were being delivered into the woman's waiting hands. "Don't you turn out any thing but foolscap at this machine?"

"Oh, sometimes, but not often, we turn out finer work—cream-laid and royal sheets, we call them. But foolscap being in chief demand, we turn out foolscap most."

It was very curious. Looking at that blank paper continually dropping, dropping, dropping, my mind ran on in wonderings of those strange uses to which those thousand sheets eventually would be put. All sorts of writings would be writ on those now vacant things—sermons, lawyers' briefs, physicians' prescriptions, love-letters, marriage certificates, bills of divorce, registers of births, death-warrants, and so on, without end. Then, recurring back to them as they here lay all blank, I could not but bethink me of that celebrated comparison of John Locke, who, in demonstration of his theory that man had no innate ideas, compared the human mind at birth to a sheet of blank paper; something destined to be scribbled on, but what sort of characters no soul might tell.

Pacing slowly to and fro along the involved machine, still humming with its play, I was struck as well by the inevitability as the evolvement-power in all its motions.

"Does that thin cobweb there," said I, pointing to the sheet in its more imperfect stage, "does that never tear or break? It is marvelous fragile, and yet this machine it passes through is so mighty."

"It never is known to tear a hair's point."

"Does it never stop—get clogged?"

"No. It *must* go. The machinery makes it go just *so*; just that very way, and at that very pace you there plainly *see* it go. The pulp can't help going."

Something of awe now stole over me, as I gazed upon this inflexible iron animal. Always, more or less, machinery of this ponderous, elaborate sort strikes, in some moods, strange dread into the human heart, as some living, panting Behemoth might. But what made the thing I saw so specially terrible to me was the metallic necessity, the unbudging fatality which governed it. Though, here and there, I could not follow the thin, gauzy vail of pulp in the course of its more mysterious or entirely invisible advance, yet it was indubitable that, at those points where it eluded me, it still marched on in unvarying docility to the autocratic cunning of the machine. A fascination fastened on me. I stood spell-bound and wandering in my soul. Before my eyes —there, passing in slow procession along the wheeling cylinders, I seemed to see, glued to the pallid incipience of the pulp, the yet more pallid faces of all the pallid girls I had eyed that heavy day. Slowly, mournfully, beseechingly, yet unresistingly, they gleamed along, their agony dimly outlined on the imperfect paper, like the print of the tormented face on the handkerchief of Saint Veronica.

"Halloa! the heat of the room is too much for you," cried Cupid, staring at me.

"No—I am rather chill, if any thing."

"Come out, Sir—out—out," and, with the protecting air of a careful father, the precocious lad hurried me outside.

In a few moments, feeling revived a little, I went into the folding-room—the first room I had entered, and where the desk for transacting business stood, surrounded by the blank counters and blank girls engaged at them.

"Cupid here has led me a strange tour," said I to the dark-complexioned man before mentioned, whom I had ere this discovered not only to be an old bachelor, but also the principal proprietor. "Yours is a most wonderful factory. Your great machine is a miracle of inscrutable intricacy."

"Yes, all our visitors think it so. But we don't have many. We arc in a very out-of-the-way corner here. Few inhabitants, too. Most of our girls come from far-off villages."

"The girls," echoed I, glancing round at their silent forms. "Why is it, Sir, that in most factories, female operatives, of whatever age, are indiscriminately called girls, never women?"

"Oh! as to that—why, I suppose, the fact of their being generally unmarried—that's the reason, I should think. But it never struck me before. For our factory here, we will not have married women; they are apt to be off-and-on too much. We want none but steady workers: twelve hours to the day, day after day, through the three hundred and sixty-five days, excepting Sundays, Thanksgiving, and Fast-days. That's our rule. And so, having no married women, what females we have are rightly enough called girls."

"Then these are all maids," said I, while some pained homage to their pale virginity made me involuntarily bow.

"All maids."

Again the strange emotion filled me.

"Your cheeks look whitish yet, Sir," said the man, gazing at me narrowly. "You must be careful going home. Do they pain you at all now? It's a bad sign, if they do."

"No doubt, Sir," answered I, "when once I have got out of the Devil's Dungeon, I shall feel them mending."

"Ah, yes; the winter air in valleys, or gorges, or any sunken place, is far colder and more bitter than elsewhere. You would hardly believe it now, but it is colder here than at the top of Woedolor Mountain."

"I dare say it is, Sir. But time presses me; I must depart."

With that, remuffling myself in dread-naught and tippet, thrusting my hands into my huge seal-skin mittens, I sallied out into the nipping air, and found poor Black, my horse, all cringing and doubled up with the cold.

Soon, wrapped in furs and meditations, I ascended from the Devil's Dungeon.

At the Black Notch I paused, and once more bethought me of Temple-Bar. Then, shooting through the pass, all alone with inscrutable nature, I exclaimed—Oh! Paradise of Bachelors! and oh! Tartarus of Maids!

1855

FITZ-JAMES O'BRIEN

(1828–1862)

What Was It?
A Mystery

It is, I confess, with considerable diffidence that I approach the strange narrative which I am about to relate. The events which I purpose detailing are of so extraordinary and unheard-of a character that I am quite prepared to meet with an unusual amount of incredulity and scorn. I accept all such beforehand. I have, I trust, the literary courage to face unbelief. I have, after mature consideration, resolved to narrate, in as simple and straightforward a manner as I can compass, some facts that passed under my observation in the month of July last, and which, in the annals of the mysteries of physical science, are wholly unparalleled.

I live at No. — Twenty-sixth Street, in this city. The house is in some respects a curious one. It has enjoyed for the last two years the reputation of being haunted. It is a large and stately residence, surrounded by what was once a garden, but which is now only a green inclosure used for bleaching clothes. The dry basin of what has been a fountain, and a few fruit-trees, ragged and unpruned, indicate that this spot, in past days, was a pleasant, shady retreat, filled with fruits and flowers and the sweet murmur of waters.

The house is very spacious. A hall of noble size leads to a vast spiral staircase winding through its centre; while the various apartments are of imposing dimensions. It was built some fifteen or twenty years since by Mr. A——, the well-known New York merchant, who five years ago threw the commercial world into convulsions by a stupendous bank fraud. Mr. A——, as every one knows, escaped to Europe, and died not long after of a broken heart. Almost immediately after the news of his decease reached this country, and was verified, the report spread in Twenty-sixth Street that No. — was haunted. Legal

63

measures had dispossessed the widow of its former owner, and it was inhabited merely by a care-taker and his wife, placed there by the house-agent into whose hands it had passed for purposes of renting or sale. These people declared that they were troubled with unnatural noises. Doors were opened without any visible agency. The remnants of furniture scattered through the various rooms were, during the night, piled one upon the other by unknown hands. Invisible feet passed up and down the stairs in broad daylight, accompanied by the rustle of unseen silk dresses and the gliding of viewless hands along the massive balusters. The care-taker and his wife declared they would live there no longer. The house-agent laughed, dismissed them, and put others in their place. The noises and supernatural manifestations continued. The neighborhood caught up the story, and the house remained untenanted for three years. Several parties negotiated for it; but somehow, always before the bargain was closed, they heard the unpleasant rumors, and declined to treat any further.

It was in this state of things that my landlady—who at that time kept a boarding-house in Bleecker Street, and who wished to move farther up town—conceived the bold idea of renting No. — Twenty-sixth Street. Happening to have in her house rather a plucky and philosophical set of boarders, she laid her scheme before us, stating candidly every thing she had heard respecting the ghostly qualities of the establishment to which she wished to remove us. With the exception of one or two timid persons—a sea-captain and a returned Californian, who immediately gave notice that they would leave—every one of Mrs. Moffat's guests declared that they would accompany her in her chivalric incursion into the abode of spirits.

Our removal was effected in the month of May, and we were all charmed with our new residence. The portion of Twenty-sixth Street where our house is situated—between Seventh and Eighth Avenues—is one of the pleasantest localities in New York. The gardens back of the houses, running down nearly to the Hudson, form, in the summer time, a perfect avenue of verdure. The air is pure and invigorating, sweeping, as it does, straight across the river from the Weehawken heights, and even the ragged garden which surrounded the house on two sides, although displaying on washing-days rather too much clothesline, still gave us a piece of green sward to look at, and a cool retreat in the summer evenings, where we smoked our cigars in the dusk, and watched the fire-flies flashing their dark-lanterns in the long grass.

Of course we had no sooner established ourselves at No. — than we began to expect the ghosts. We absolutely awaited their advent with eagerness. Our dinner conversation was supernatural. One of the boarders, who had purchased Mrs. Crowe's "Night Side of Nature" for his own private delectation, was regarded as a public enemy by the entire household for not having bought twenty copies. The man led a life of supreme wretchedness while he was perusing the volume. A system of espionage was established, of which he was the victim. If he incautiously laid the book down for an instant and left the room, it was immediately seized and read aloud in secret places to a select few. I found myself a person of immense importance, it having leaked out that I was tolerably well versed in the history of supernaturalism, and had once written a story, entitled "The Pot of Tulips," for *Harper's Monthly*, the foundation of which was a ghost. If a table or a wainscot panel happened to warp when we were assembled in the large drawing-room, there was an instant silence, and every one was prepared for an immediate clanking of chains and a spectral form.

After a month of psychological excitement, it was with the utmost dissatisfaction that we were forced to acknowledge that nothing in the remotest degree approaching the supernatural had manifested itself. Once the black butler asseverated that his candle had been blown out by some invisible agency while in the act of undressing himself for the night; but as I had more than once discovered this colored gentleman in a condition when one candle must have appeared to him like two, I thought it possible that, by going a step farther in his potations, he might have reversed this phenomenon, and seen no candle at all where he ought to have beheld one.

Things were in this state when an incident took place so awful and inexplicable in its character that my reason fairly reels at the bare memory of the occurrence. It was the 10th of July. After dinner was over I repaired, with my friend Dr. Hammond, to the garden to smoke my evening pipe. Independent of certain mental sympathies which existed between the Doctor and myself, we were linked together by a secret vice. We both smoked opium. We knew each other's secret, and respected it. We enjoyed together that wonderful expansion of thought; that marvelous intensifying of the perceptive faculties; that boundless feeling of existence when we seem to have points of contact with the whole universe; in short, that unimaginable spiritual bliss, which I would not surrender for a throne, and which I hope you, reader, will never—never taste.

Those hours of opium happiness which the Doctor and I spent together in secret were regulated with a scientific accuracy. We did not blindly smoke the drug of Paradise, and leave our dreams to chance. While smoking we carefully steered our conversation through the brightest and calmest channels of thought. We talked of the East, and endeavored to recall the magical panorama of its glowing scenery. We criticised the most sensuous poets, those who painted life ruddy with health, brimming with passion, happy in the possession of youth, and strength, and beauty. If we talked of Shakspeare's "Midsummer Night's Dream," we lingered over Ariel and avoided Caliban. Like the Gebers, we turned our faces to the East, and saw only the sunny side of the world.

This skillful coloring of our train of thought produced in our subsequent visions a corresponding tone. The splendors of Arabian fairy-land dyed our dreams. We paced that narrow strip of grass with the tread and port of kings. The song of the *Rana arborea* while he clung to the bark of the ragged plum-tree sounded like the strains of divine orchestras. Houses, walls, and streets melted like rain-clouds, and vistas of unimaginable glory stretched away before us. It was a rapturous companionship. We each of us enjoyed the vast delight more perfectly because, even in our most ecstatic moments, we were ever conscious of each other's presence. Our pleasures, while individual, were still twin, vibrating and moving in musical accord.

On the evening in question, the 10th of July, the Doctor and myself found ourselves in an unusually metaphysical mood. We lit our large meerschaums, filled with fine Turkish tobacco, in the core of which burned a little black nut of opium, that, like the nut in the fairy tale, held within its narrow limits wonders beyond the reach of kings; we paced to and fro, conversing. A strange perversity dominated the currents of our thought. They would *not* flow through the sun-lit channels into which we strove to divert them. For some unaccountable reason they constantly diverged into dark and lonesome beds, where a continual gloom brooded. It was in vain that, after our old fashion, we flung ourselves on the shores of the East, and talked of its gay bazaars, of the splendors of the time of Haroun, of harems and golden palaces. Black afreets continually arose from the depths of our talk, and expanded, like the one the fisherman released from the copper vessel, until they blotted every thing bright from our vision. Insensibly we yielded to the occult force that swayed us, and indulged in gloomy speculation. We had talked some time upon the proneness of the human mind to mysticism and the almost universal love of the Terrible, when Hammond suddenly said to me:

"What do you consider to be the greatest element of Terror?"

The question, I own, puzzled me. That many things were terrible, I knew. Stumbling over a corpse in the dark; beholding, as I once did, a woman floating down a deep and rapid river, with wildly-lifted arms and awful, upturned face, uttering, as she sank, shrieks that rent one's heart, while we, the spectators, stood frozen at a window which overhung the river at a height of sixty feet, unable to make the slightest effort to save her, but dumbly watching her last supreme agony and her disappearance. A shattered wreck, with no life visible, encountered floating listlessly on the ocean, is a terrible object, for it suggests huge terror, the proportions of which are vailed. But it now struck me for the first time that there must be one great and ruling embodiment of fear, a King of Terrors to which all others must succumb. What might it be? To what train of circumstances would it owe its existence?

"I confess, Hammond," I replied to my friend, "I never considered the subject before. That there must be one Something more terrible than any other thing, I feel. I can not attempt, however, even the most vague definition."

"I am somewhat like you, Harry," he answered. "I feel my capacity to experience a terror greater than any thing yet conceived by the human mind. Something combining in fearful and unnatural amalgamation hitherto supposed incompatible elements. The calling of the voices in Brockden Brown's novel of 'Wieland' is awful; so is the picture of the Dweller of the Threshold in Bulwer's 'Zanoni;' but," he added, shaking his head gloomily, "there is something more horrible still than these."

"Look here, Hammond," I rejoined; "let us drop this kind of talk for Heaven's sake. We shall suffer for it, depend on it."

"I don't know what's the matter with me to-night," he replied, "but my brain is running upon all sorts of weird and awful thoughts. I feel as if I could write a story like Hoffman to-night, if I were only master of a literary style."

"Well, if we are going to be Hoffmanesque in our talk I'm off to bed. Opium and nightmares should never be brought together. How sultry it is! Good-night, Hammond."

"Goodnight, Harry. Pleasant dreams to you."

"To you, gloomy wretch, afreets, ghouls, and enchanters."

We parted, and each sought his respective chamber. I undressed quickly and got into bed, taking with me, according to my usual custom, a book, over which I generally read myself to sleep. I opened the volume as soon as I had laid my head upon the pillow, and instantly flung it to the other side of the room. It was Goudon's "History of Monsters"—a curious French work, which I had lately imported from Paris, but which, in the state of mind I was then in, was any thing but an agreeable companion. I resolved to go to sleep at once; so turning down my gas until nothing but a little blue point of light glimmered on the top of the tube, I composed myself to rest once more.

The room was in total darkness. The atom of gas that still remained lighted did not illuminate a distance of three inches round the burner. I desperately drew my arm across my eyes, as if to shut out even the darkness, and tried to think of nothing. It was in vain. The confounded themes touched on by Hammond in the garden kept obtruding themselves on my brain. I battled against them. I erected ramparts of would-be blankness of intellect to keep them out. They still crowded upon me. While I was lying still as a corpse, hoping that by a perfect physical inaction I would hasten mental repose, an awful incident occurred. A Something dropped, as it seemed, from the ceiling, plumb upon my chest, and the next instant I

felt two bony hands encircling my throat, endeavoring to
choke me.

I am no coward, and am possessed of considerable physical
strength. The suddenness of the attack instead of stunning me
strung every nerve to its highest tension. My body acted from
instinct, before my brain had time to realize the terrors of my
position. In an instant I wound two muscular arms around the
creature, and squeezed it, with all the strength of despair,
against my chest. In a few seconds the bony hands that had fastened on my throat loosened their hold, and I was free to
breathe once more. Then commenced a struggle of awful intensity. Immersed in the most profound darkness, totally ignorant of the nature of the Thing by which I was so suddenly
attacked, finding my grasp slipping every moment by reason, it
seemed to me, of the entire nakedness of my assailant, bitten
with sharp teeth in the shoulder, neck, and chest, having every
moment to protect my throat against a pair of sinewy, agile
hands, which my utmost efforts could not confine—these were
a combination of circumstances to combat which required all
the strength and skill and courage that I possessed.

At last, after a silent, deadly, exhausting struggle, I got my
assailant under by a series of incredible efforts of strength.
Once pinned, with my knee on what I made out to be its chest,
I knew that I was victor. I rested for a moment to breathe. I
heard the creature beneath me panting in the darkness, and
felt the violent throbbing of a heart. It was apparently as exhausted as I was, that was one comfort. At this moment I remembered that I usually placed under my pillow, before going
to bed, a large, yellow silk pocket-handkerchief, for use during
the night. I felt for it instantly; it was there. In a few seconds
more I had, after a fashion, pinioned the creature's arms.

I now felt tolerably secure. There was nothing more to be
done but to turn on the gas, and, having first seen what my
midnight assailant was like, arouse the household. I will confess to being actuated by a certain pride in not giving the alarm
before; I wished to make the capture alone and unaided.

Never loosing my hold for an instant, I slipped from the bed
to the floor, dragging my captive with me. I had but a few steps
to make to reach the gas-burner; these I made with the greatest

caution, holding the creature in a grip like a vice. At last I got within arm's-length of the tiny speck of blue light, which told me where the gas-burner lay. Quick as lightning I released my grasp with one hand and let on the full flood of light. Then I turned to look at my captive.

I can not even attempt to give any definition of my sensations the instant after I turned on the gas. I suppose I must have shrieked with terror, for in less than a minute afterward my room was crowded with the inmates of the house. I shudder now as I think of that awful moment. *I saw nothing!* Yes; I had one arm firmly clasped round a breathing, panting, corporeal shape, my other hand gripped with all its strength a throat as warm, and apparently fleshly, as my own; and yet, with this living substance in my grasp, with its body pressed against my own, and all in the bright glare of a large jet of gas, I absolutely beheld nothing! Not even an outline—a vapor!

I do not, even at this hour, realize the situation in which I found myself. I can not recall the astounding incident thoroughly. Imagination in vain tries to compass the awful paradox.

It breathed. I felt its warm breath upon my cheek. It struggled fiercely. It had hands. They clutched me. Its skin was smooth, just like my own. There it lay, pressed close up against me, solid as stone—and yet utterly invisible!

I wonder that I did not faint or go mad on the instant. Some wonderful instinct must have sustained me; for, absolutely, in place of loosening my hold on the terrible Enigma, I seemed to gain an additional strength in my moment of horror, and tightened my grasp with such wonderful force that I felt the creature shivering with agony.

Just then Hammond entered my room at the head of the household. As soon as he beheld my face—which, I suppose, must have been an awful sight to look at—he hastened forward, crying,

"Great Heaven, Harry! what has happened?"

"Hammond! Hammond!" I cried, "come here. Oh! this is awful! I have been attacked in bed by something or other, which I have hold of; but I can't see it—I can't see it!"

Hammond, doubtless struck by the unfeigned horror expressed in my countenance, made one or two steps forward with an anxious yet puzzled expression. A very audible titter burst from the remainder of my visitors. This suppressed laughter made me furious. To laugh at a human being in my position! It was the worst species of cruelty. *Now*, I can understand why the appearance of a man struggling violently, as it would seem, with an airy nothing, and calling for assistance against a vision, should have appeared ludicrous. *Then*, so great was my rage against the mocking crowd that had I the power I would have stricken them dead where they stood.

"Hammond! Hammond!" I cried again, despairingly, "for God's sake come to me. I can hold the—the Thing but a short while longer. It is overpowering me. Help me. Help me!"

"Harry," whispered Hammond, approaching me, "you have been smoking too much opium."

"I swear to you Hammond that this is no vision," I answered, in the same low tone. "Don't you see how it shakes my whole frame with its struggles? If you don't believe me convince yourself. Feel it—touch it."

Hammond advanced and laid his hand in the spot I indicated. A wild cry of horror burst from him. He had felt it!

In a moment he had discovered somewhere in my room a long piece of cord, and was the next instant winding it, and knotting it about the body of the unseen being that I clasped in my arms.

"Harry," he said, in a hoarse, agitated voice, for, though he preserved his presence of mind, he was deeply moved, "Harry, it's all safe now. You may let go, old fellow, if you're tired. The Thing can't move."

I was utterly exhausted, and I gladly loosed my hold.

Hammond stood holding the ends of the cord that bound the Invisible, twisted round his hand, while before him, self-supporting, as it were, he beheld a rope laced and interlaced, and stretching tightly around a vacant space. I never saw a man look so thoroughly stricken with awe. Nevertheless his face expressed all the courage and determination which I knew him to possess. His lips, although white, were set firmly, and one could perceive at a glance that, although stricken with fear, he was not daunted.

The confusion that ensued among the guests of the house, who were witnesses of this extraordinary scene between Hammond and myself—who beheld the pantomime of binding this struggling Something—who beheld me almost sinking from physical exhaustion when my task of jailer was over—the confusion and terror that took possession of the by-standers, when they saw all this, was beyond description. Many of the weaker ones fled from the apartment. The few who remained behind clustered near the door, and could not be induced to approach Hammond and his Charge. Still incredulity broke out through their terror. They had not the courage to satisfy themselves, and yet they doubted. It was in vain that I begged of some of the men to come near and convince themselves by touch of the existence of a living being in that room which was invisible. They were incredulous, but did not dare to undeceive themselves. How could a solid, living, breathing body be invisible? they asked. My reply was this. I gave a sign to Hammond, and both of us—conquering our fearful repugnance to touching the invisible creature—lifted it from the ground, manacled as it was, and took it to my bed. Its weight was about that of a boy of fourteen.

"Now my friends," I said, as Hammond and myself held the creature suspended over the bed, "I can give you self-evident proof that here is a solid, ponderable body which, nevertheless, you can not see. Be good enough to watch the surface of the bed attentively."

I was astonished at my own courage in treating this strange event so calmly; but I had recovered from my first terror, and felt a sort of scientific pride in the affair which dominated every other feeling.

The eyes of the by-standers were immediately fixed on my bed. At a given signal Hammond and I let the creature fall. There was the dull sound of a heavy body alighting on a soft mass. The timbers of the bed creaked. A deep impression marked itself distinctly on the pillow, and on the bed itself. The crowd who witnessed this gave a sort of low, universal cry, and rushed from the room. Hammond and I were left alone with our Mystery.

We remained silent for some time, listening to the low, irregular breathing of the creature on the bed, and watching the rustle of the bedclothes as it impotently struggled to free itself from confinement. Then Hammond spoke.

"Harry, this is awful."

"Ay, awful."

"But not unaccountable."

"Not unaccountable! What do you mean? Such a thing has never occurred since the birth of the world. I know not what to think, Hammond. God grant that I am not mad, and that this is not an insane fantasy!"

"Let us reason a little, Harry. Here is a solid body which we touch, but which we can not see. The fact is so unusual that it strikes us with terror. Is there no parallel, though, for such a phenomenon? Take a piece of pure glass. It is tangible and transparent. A certain chemical coarseness is all that prevents its being so entirely transparent as to be totally invisible. It is not *theoretically impossible*, mind you, to fabricate a glass which shall not reflect a single ray of light—a glass so pure and homogeneous in its atoms that the rays from the sun shall pass through it as they do through the air, refracted but not reflected. We do not see the air, and yet we feel it."

"That's all very well, Hammond, but these are inanimate substances. Glass does not breathe, air does not breathe. *This* thing has a heart that palpitates. A will that moves it. Lungs that play and inspire and respire."

"You forget the strange phenomena of which we have so often heard of late," answered the Doctor, gravely. "At the meetings called 'spirit circles,' invisible hands have been thrust into the hands of those persons round the table—warm, fleshly hands that seemed to pulsate with mortal life."

"What? Do you think, then, that this thing is—"

"I don't know what it is," was the solemn reply; "but please the gods I will, with your assistance, thoroughly investigate it."

We watched together, smoking many pipes, all night long by the bedside of the unearthly being that tossed and panted until it was apparently wearied out. Then we learned by the low, regular breathing that it slept.

The next morning the house was all astir. The boarders congregated on the landing outside my room, and Hammond and myself were lions. We had to answer a thousand questions as to the state of our extraordinary prisoner, for as yet not one person in the house except ourselves could be induced to set foot in the apartment.

The creature was awake. This was evidenced by the convulsive manner in which the bed-clothes were moved in its efforts to escape. There was something truly terrible in beholding, as it were, those second-hand indications of the terrible writhings and agonized struggles for liberty, which themselves were invisible.

Hammond and myself had racked our brains during the long night to discover some means by which we might realize the shape and general appearance of the Enigma. As well as we could make out by passing our hands over the creature's form, its outlines and lineaments were human. There was a mouth; a round, smooth head without hair; a nose, which, however, was little elevated above the cheeks; and its hands and feet felt like those of a boy. At first we thought of placing the being on a smooth surface and tracing its outline with chalk, as shoe-makers trace the outline of the foot. This plan was given up as being of no value. Such an outline would give not the slightest idea of its conformation.

A happy thought struck me. We would take a cast of it in plaster of Paris. This would give us the solid figure, and satisfy all our wishes. But how to do it? The movements of the creature would disturb the setting of the plastic covering, and distort the mould. Another thought. Why not give it chloroform? It had respiratory organs—that was evident by its breathing. Once reduced to a state of insensibility, we could do with it what we would. Doctor X—— was sent for; and after the worthy physician had recovered from the first shock of amazement, he proceeded to administer the chloroform. In three minutes afterward we were enabled to remove the fetters from the creature's body, and a well-known modeler of this city was busily engaged in covering the invisible form with the moist clay. In five minutes more we had a mould, and before evening a rough *fac-simile* of the Mystery. It was shaped like a man. Distorted, uncouth, and horrible, but still a man. It was small, not over four feet and some inches in height, and its limbs betrayed a muscular development that was unparalleled. Its face surpassed in hideousness any thing I had ever seen. Gustave Doré, or Callot, or Tony Johannot never conceived any thing so horrible. There is a face in one of the latter's illustrations to " *Un voyage ou il vous plaira,*" which somewhat approaches the countenance of this creature, but does not equal it. It was the physiognomy of what I should have fancied a ghoul to be. It looked as if it was capable of feeding on human flesh.

Having satisfied our curiosity, and bound every one in the house over to secrecy, it became a question what was to be done with our Enigma? It was impossible that we should keep such a horror in our house; it was equally impossible that such an awful being should be let loose upon the world. I confess that I would have gladly voted for the creature's destruction. But who would shoulder the responsibility? Who would undertake the execution of this horrible semblance of a human being? Day after day this question was deliberated gravely. The boarders all left the house. Mrs. Moffat was in despair, and threatened Hammond and myself with all sorts of legal penalties if we did not remove the Horror. Our answer was, "We will go if you like, but we decline taking this creature with us. Remove it yourself if you please. It appeared in your house. On you the responsibility rests." To this there was, of course, no answer. Mrs. Moffat could not obtain for love or money a person who would even approach the Mystery.

The most singular part of the transaction was, that we were entirely ignorant of what the creature habitually fed on. Every thing in the way of nutriment that we could think of was placed before it, but was never touched. It was awful to stand by, day after day, and see the clothes lost and hear the hard breathing, and know that it was starving.

Ten, twelve days, a fortnight passed, and it still lived. The pulsations of the heart, however, were daily growing fainter, and had now nearly ceased altogether. It was evident that the creature was dying for want of sustenance. While this terrible life-struggle was going on I felt miserable. I could not sleep of nights. Horrible as the creature was, it was pitiful to think of the pangs it was suffering.

At last it died. Hammond and I found it cold and stiff one morning in the bed. The heart had ceased to beat, the lungs to inspire. We hastened to bury it in the garden. It was a strange funeral, the dropping of that viewless corpse into the damp hole. The cast of its form I gave to Doctor X——, who keeps it in his museum in Tenth Street.

As I am on the eve of a long journey from which I may not return, I have drawn up this narrative of an event the most singular that has ever come to my knowledge.

HARRY ESCOTT.

[NOTE.—It is rumored that the proprietors of a well-known museum in this city have made arrangements with Dr. X—— to exhibit to the public the singular cast which Mr. Escott deposited with him. So extraordinary a history can not fail to attract universal attention.]

1859

BRET HARTE

(1836–1902)

The Legend of Monte del Diablo

THE cautious reader will detect a lack of authenticity in the following pages. I am not a cautious reader myself, yet I confess with some concern to the absence of much documentary evidence in support of the singular incident I am about to relate. Disjointed memoranda, the proceedings of ayuntamientos and early departmental juntas, with other records of a primitive and superstitious people, have been my inadequate authorities. It is but just to state, however, that though this particular story lacks corroboration, in ransacking the Spanish archives of Upper California I have met with many more surprising and incredible stories, attested and supported to a degree that would have placed this legend beyond a cavil or doubt. I have, also, never lost faith in the legend myself, and in so doing have profited much from the examples of divers grant-claimants, who have often jostled me in their more practical researches, and who have my sincere sympathy at the skepticism of a modern hard-headed and practical world.

For many years after Father Junipero Serro first rang his bell in the wilderness of Upper California, the spirit which animated that adventurous priest did not wane. The conversion of the heathen went on rapidly in the establishment of missions throughout the land. So sedulously did the good Fathers set about their work, that around their isolated chapels there presently arose adobe huts, whose mud-plastered and savage tenants partook regularly of the provisions, and occasionally of the Sacrament, of their pious hosts. Nay, so great was their progress, that one zealous Padre is reported to have administered the Lord's Supper one Sabbath morning to "over three hundred heathen salvages." It was not to be wondered that the Enemy of Souls, being greatly incensed thereat, and alarmed at his decreasing popularity, should have grievously tempted and embarrassed these holy Fathers, as we shall presently see.

Yet they were happy, peaceful days for California. The vagrant keels of prying Commerce had not as yet ruffled the lordly gravity of her bays. No torn and ragged gulch betrayed the suspicion of golden treasure. The wild oats drooped idly in the morning heat or wrestled with the afternoon breezes. Deer and antelope dotted the plain. The watercourses brawled in their familiar channels, nor dreamed of ever shifting their regular tide. The wonders of the Yosemite and Calaveras were as yet unrecorded. The holy Fathers noted little of the landscape beyond the barbaric prodigality with which the quick soil repaid the sowing. A new conversion, the advent of a saint's day, or the baptism of an Indian baby, was at once the chronicle and marvel of their day.

At this blissful epoch there lived at the Mission of San Pablo Father José Antonio Haro, a worthy brother of the Society of Jesus. He was of tall and cadaverous aspect. A somewhat romantic history had given a poetic interest to his lugubrious visage. While a youth, pursuing his studies at famous Salamanca, he had become enamored of the charms of Doña Carmen de Torrencevara, as that lady passed to her matutinal devotions. Untoward circumstances, hastened, perhaps, by a wealthier suitor, brought this amour to a disastrous issue, and Father José entered a monastery, taking upon himself the vows of celibacy. It was here that his natural fervor and poetic enthusiasm conceived expression as a missionary. A longing to convert the uncivilized heathen succeeded his frivolous earthly passion, and a desire to explore and develop unknown fastnesses continually possessed him. In his flashing eye and sombre exterior was detected a singular commingling of the discreet Las Casas and the impetuous Balboa.

Fixed by this pious zeal, Father José went forward in the van of Christian pioneers. On reaching Mexico he obtained authority to establish the Mission of San Pablo. Like the good Junipero, accompanied only by an acolyte and muleteer, he unsaddled his mules in a dusky cañon, and rang his bell in the wilderness. The savages—a peaceful, inoffensive, and inferior race—presently flocked around him. The nearest military post was far away, which contributed much to the security of these pious pilgrims, who found their open trustfulness and amiability better fitted to repress hostility than the presence of an

armed, suspicious, and brawling soldiery. So the good Father
José said matins and prime, mass and vespers, in the heart of
sin and heathenism, taking no heed to himself, but looking
only to the welfare of the Holy Church. Conversions soon followed, and on the 7th of July, 1760, the first Indian baby was
baptized,—an event which, as Father José piously records, "ex-
ceeds the richnesse of gold or precious jewels or the chancing
upon the Ophir of Solomon." I quote this incident as best
suited to show the ingenious blending of poetry and piety
which distinguished Father José's record.

The Mission of San Pablo progressed and prospered, until
the pious founder thereof, like the infidel Alexander, might
have wept that there were no more heathen worlds to conquer.
But his ardent and enthusiastic spirit could not long brook an
idleness that seemed begotten of sin; and one pleasant August
morning in the year of grace 1770 Father José issued from the
outer court of the mission building, equipped to explore the
field for new missionary labors.

Nothing could exceed the quiet gravity and unpretentious-
ness of the little cavalcade. First rode a stout muleteer, leading
a pack-mule laden with the provisions of the party, together
with a few cheap crucifixes and hawks' bells. After him came
the devout Padre José, bearing his breviary and cross, with a
black serapa thrown around his shoulders; while on either side
trotted a dusky convert, anxious to show a proper sense of his
regeneration by acting as guide into the wilds of his heathen
brethren. Their new condition was agreeably shown by the
absence of the usual mud-plaster, which in their unconverted
state they assumed to keep away vermin and cold. The
morning was bright and propitious. Before their departure,
mass had been said in the chapel, and the protection of St.
Ignatius invoked against all contingent evils, but especially
against bears, which, like the fiery dragons of old, seemed to
cherish unconquerable hostility to the Holy Church.

As they wound through the cañon, charming birds dis-
ported upon boughs and sprays, and sober quails piped from
the alders; the willowy watercourses gave a musical utterance,
and the long grass whispered on the hillside. On entering the
deeper defiles, above them towered dark green masses of pine,
and occasionally the madroño shook its bright scarlet berries.

As they toiled up many a steep ascent, Father José sometimes picked up fragments of scoria, which spake to his imagination of direful volcanoes and impending earthquakes. To the less scientific mind of the muleteer Ignacio they had even a more terrifying significance; and he once or twice snuffed the air suspiciously, and declared that it smelt of sulphur. So the first day of their journey wore away, and at night they encamped without having met a single heathen face.

It was on this night that the Enemy of Souls appeared to Ignacio in an appalling form. He had retired to a secluded part of the camp and had sunk upon his knees in prayerful meditation, when he looked up and perceived the Arch-Fiend in the likeness of a monstrous bear. The Evil One was seated on his hind legs immediately before him, with his fore paws joined together just below his black muzzle. Wisely conceiving this remarkable attitude to be in mockery and derision of his devotions, the worthy muleteer was transported with fury. Seizing an arquebus, he instantly closed his eyes and fired. When he had recovered from the effects of the terrific discharge, the apparition had disappeared. Father José, awakened by the report, reached the spot only in time to chide the muleteer for wasting powder and ball in a contest with one whom a single ave would have been sufficient to utterly discomfit. What further reliance he placed on Ignacio's story is not known; but, in commemoration of a worthy Californian custom, the place was called "La Cañada de la Tentacion del Pio Muletero," or "The Glen of the Temptation of the Pious Muleteer," a name which it retains to this day.

The next morning the party, issuing from a narrow gorge, came upon a long valley, sear and burnt with the shadeless heat. Its lower extremity was lost in a fading line of low hills, which, gathering might and volume toward the upper end of the valley, upheaved a stupendous bulwark against the breezy north. The peak of this awful spur was just touched by a fleecy cloud that shifted to and fro like a banneret. Father José gazed at it with mingled awe and admiration. By a singular coincidence, the muleteer Ignacio uttered the simple ejaculation "Diablo!"

As they penetrated the valley, they soon began to miss the agreeable life and companionable echoes of the cañon they had quitted. Huge fissures in the parched soil seemed to gape as with thirsty mouths. A few squirrels darted from the earth and disappeared as mysteriously before the jingly mules. A gray wolf trotted leisurely along just ahead. But whichever way Father José turned, the mountain always asserted itself and arrested his wandering eye. Out of the dry and arid valley it seemed to spring into cooler and bracing life. Deep cavernous shadows dwelt along its base; rocky fastnesses appeared midway of its elevation; and on either side huge black hills diverged like massy roots from a central trunk. His lively fancy pictured these hills peopled with a majestic and intelligent race of savages; and looking into futurity, he already saw a monstrous cross crowning the dome-like summit. Far different were the sensations of the muleteer, who saw in those awful solitudes only fiery dragons, colossal bears, and breakneck trails. The converts, Concepcion and Incarnacion, trotting modestly beside the Padre, recognized, perhaps, some manifestation of their former weird mythology.

At nightfall they reached the base of the mountain. Here Father José unpacked his mules, said vespers, and, formally ringing his bell, called upon the Gentiles within hearing to come and accept the holy faith. The echoes of the black frowning hills around him caught up the pious invitation and repeated it at intervals; but no Gentiles appeared that night. Nor were the devotions of the muleteer again disturbed, although he afterward asserted that, when the Father's exhortation was ended, a mocking peal of laughter came from the mountain. Nothing daunted by these intimations of the near hostility of the Evil One, Father José declared his intention to ascend the mountain at early dawn, and before the sun rose the next morning he was leading the way.

The ascent was in many places difficult and dangerous. Huge fragments of rock often lay across the trail, and after a few hours' climbing they were forced to leave their mules in a little gully and continue the ascent afoot. Unaccustomed to such exertion, Father José often stopped to wipe the perspiration from his thin cheeks. As the day wore on a strange silence oppressed them. Except the occasional pattering of a squirrel, or a rustling in the chimisal bushes, there were no signs of life. The half-human print of a bear's foot sometimes appeared before them, at which Ignacio always crossed himself piously. The eye was sometimes cheated by a dripping from the rocks, which on closer inspection proved to be a resinous oily liquid with an abominable sulphurous smell. When they were within a short distance of the summit, the discreet Ignacio, selecting a sheltered nook for the camp, slipped aside and busied himself in preparations for the evening, leaving the holy Father to continue the ascent alone. Never was there a more thoughtless act of prudence, never a more imprudent piece of caution. Without noticing the desertion, buried in pious reflection, Father José pushed mechanically on, and, reaching the summit, cast himself down and gazed upon the prospect.

Below him lay a succession of valleys opening into each other like gentle lakes, until they were lost to the southward. Westerly the distant range hid the bosky cañada which sheltered the Mission of San Pablo. In the farther distance the Pacific Ocean stretched away, bearing a cloud of fog upon its bosom, which crept through the entrance of the bay, and rolled thickly between him and the northeastward; the same fog hid the base of the mountain and the view beyond. Still from time to time the fleecy veil parted, and timidly disclosed charming glimpses of mighty rivers, mountain defiles, and rolling plains, sear with ripened oats and bathed in the glow of the setting sun. As father José gazed, he was penetrated with a pious longing. Already his imagination, filled with enthusiastic conceptions, beheld all that vast expanse gathered under the mild sway of the holy faith and peopled with zealous converts. Each little knoll in fancy became crowned with a chapel; from each dark cañon gleamed the white walls of a mission building. Growing bolder in his enthusiasm and looking farther into futurity, he beheld a new Spain rising on these savage shores. He already saw the spires of stately cathedrals, the domes of palaces, vineyards, gardens, and groves. Convents, half hid among the hills, peeping from plantations of branching limes, and long processions of chanting nuns wound through the defiles. So completely was the good Father's conception of the future confounded with the past, that even in their choral strain the well-remembered accents of Carmen struck his ear. He was busied in these fanciful imaginings, when suddenly over that extended prospect the faint distant tolling of a bell rang sadly out and died. It was the Angelus. Father José listened with superstitious exaltation.

The Mission of San Pablo was far away, and the sound must have been some miraculous omen. But never before, to his enthusiastic sense, did the sweet seriousness of this angelic symbol come with such strange significance. With the last faint peal his glowing fancy seemed to cool; the fog closed in below him, and the good Father remembered he had not had his supper. He had risen and was wrapping his serapa around him, when he perceived for the first time that he was not alone.

Nearly opposite, and where should have been the faithless Ignacio, a grave and decorous figure was seated. His appearance was that of an elderly hidalgo, dressed in mourning, with mustaches of iron-gray carefully waxed and twisted round a pair of lantern-jaws. The monstrous hat and prodigious feather, the enormous ruff and exaggerated trunk-hose, contrasted with a frame shriveled and wizened, all belonged to a century previous. Yet Father José was not astonished. His adventurous life and poetic imagination, continually on the lookout for the marvelous, gave him a certain advantage over the practical and material-minded. He instantly detected the diabolical quality of his visitant, and was prepared. With equal coolness and courtesy he met the cavalier's obeisance.

"I ask your pardon, Sir Priest," said the stranger, "for disturbing your meditations. Pleasant they must have been, and right fanciful, I imagine, when occasioned by so fair a prospect.

"Worldly, perhaps, Sir Devil,—for such I take you to be," said the holy Father, as the stranger bowed his black plumes to the ground; "worldly, perhaps; for it hath pleased Heaven to retain even in our regenerated state much that pertaineth to the flesh, yet still, I trust, not without some speculation for the welfare of the Holy Church. In dwelling upon yon fair expanse, mine eyes have been graciously opened with prophetic inspiration, and the promise of the heathen as an inheritance hath marvelously recurred to me. For there can be none lack such diligence in the true faith but may see that even the conversion of these pitiful salvages hath a meaning. As the blessed St. Ignatius discreetly observes," continued Father José, clearing his throat and slightly elevating his voice, " 'the heathen is given to the warriors of Christ, even as the pearls of rare discovery which gladden the hearts of shipmen.' Nay, I might say"—

But here the stranger, who had been wrinkling his brows

and twisting his mustaches with well-bred patience, took advantage of an oratorical pause.

"It grieves me, Sir Priest, to interrupt the current of your eloquence as discourteously as I have already broken your meditations; but the day already waneth to night. I have a matter of serious import to make with you, could I entreat your cautious consideration a few moments."

Father José hesitated. The temptation was great, and the prospect of acquiring some knowledge of the Great Enemy's plans not the least trifling object. And, if the truth must be told, there was a certain decorum about the stranger that interested the Padre. Though well aware of the Protean shapes the Arch-Fiend could assume, and though free from the weaknesses of the flesh, Father José was not above the temptations of the spirit. Had the Devil appeared, as in the case of the pious St. Anthony, in the likeness of a comely damsel, the good Father, with his certain experience of the deceitful sex, would have whisked her away in the saying of a paternoster. But there was, added to the security of age, a grave sadness about the stranger, —a thoughtful consciousness, as of being at a great moral disadvantage, which at once decided him on a magnanimous course of conduct.

The stranger then proceeded to inform him that he had been diligently observing the holy Father's triumphs in the valley. That, far from being greatly exercised thereat, he had been only grieved to see so enthusiastic and chivalrous an antagonist wasting his zeal in a hopeless work. For, he observed, the issue of the great battle of Good and Evil had been otherwise settled, as he would presently show him. "It wants but a few moments of night," he continued, "and over this interval of twilight, as you know, I have been given complete control. Look to the west."

As the Padre turned, the stranger took his enormous hat from his head and waved it three times before him. At each sweep of the prodigious feather the fog grew thinner, until it melted impalpably away, and the former landscape returned, yet warm with the glowing sun. As Father José gazed a strain of martial music arose from the valley, and issuing from a deep cañon the good Father beheld a long cavalcade of gallant cavaliers, habited like his companion. As they swept down the plain, they were joined by like processions, that slowly defiled from every ravine and cañon of the mysterious mountain. From time to time the peal of a trumpet swelled fitfully upon the breeze; the cross of Santiago glittered, and the royal banners of Castile and Aragon waved over the moving column. So they moved on solemnly toward the sea, where, in the distance, Father José saw stately caravels, bearing the same familiar banner, awaiting them. The good Padre gazed with conflicting emotions, and the serious voice of the stranger broke the silence.

"Thou hast beheld, Sir Priest, the fading footprints of adventurous Castile. Thou hast seen the declining glory of old Spain,—declining as yonder brilliant sun. The sceptre she hath wrested from the heathen is fast dropping from her decrepit and fleshless grasp. The children she hath fostered shall know her no longer. The soil she hath acquired shall be lost to her as irrevocably as she herself hath thrust the Moor from her own Granada."

The stranger paused, and his voice seemed broken by emotion; at the same time, Father José, whose sympathizing heart yearned toward the departing banners, cried in poignant accents,—

"Farewell, ye gallant cavaliers and Christian soldiers! Farewell, thou, Nuñes de Balboa! thou, Alonzo de Ojeda! and thou, most venerable Las Casas! farewell, and may Heaven prosper still the seed ye left behind!"

Then turning to the stranger, Father José beheld him gravely draw his pocket-handkerchief from the basket-hilt of his rapier and apply it decorously to his eyes.

"Pardon this weakness, Sir Priest," said the cavalier apologetically; "but these worthy gentlemen were ancient friends of mine, and have done me many a delicate service,—much more, perchance, than these poor sables may signify," he added, with a grim gesture toward the mourning suit he wore.

Father José was too much preoccupied in reflection to notice the equivocal nature of this tribute, and, after a few moments' silence, said, as if continuing his thought,—

"But the seed they have planted shall thrive and prosper on this fruitful soil."

As if answering the interrogatory, the stranger turned to the opposite direction, and, again waving his hat, said, in the same serious tone, "Look to the east!"

The Father turned, and, as the fog broke away before the waving plume, he saw that the sun was rising. Issuing with its bright beams through the passes of the snowy mountains beyond appeared a strange and motley crew. Instead of the dark and romantic visages of his last phantom train, the Father beheld with strange concern the blue eyes and flaxen hair of a Saxon race. In place of martial airs and musical utterance, there rose upon the ear a strange din of harsh gutturals and singular sibilation. Instead of the decorous tread and stately mien of the cavaliers of the former vision, they came pushing, bustling, panting, and swaggering. And as they passed, the good Father noticed that giant trees were prostrated as with the breath of a tornado, and the bowels of the earth were torn and rent as with a convulsion. And Father José looked in vain for holy cross or Christian symbol; there was but one that seemed an ensign, and he crossed himself with holy horror as he perceived it bore the effigy of a bear.

"Who are these swaggering Ishmaelites?" he asked, with something of asperity in his tone.

The stranger was gravely silent.

"What do they here, with neither cross nor holy symbol?" he again demanded.

"Have you the courage to see, Sir Priest?" responded the stranger quietly.

Father José felt his crucifix, as a lonely traveler might his rapier, and assented.

"Step under the shadow of my plume," said the stranger.

Father José stepped beside him and they instantly sank through the earth.

When he opened his eyes, which had remained closed in prayerful meditation during his rapid descent, he found himself in a vast vault, bespangled overhead with luminous points like the starred firmament. It was also lighted by a yellow glow that seemed to proceed from a mighty sea or lake that occupied the centre of the chamber. Around this subterranean sea dusky figures flitted, bearing ladles filled with the yellow fluid, which they had replenished from its depths. From this lake diverging streams of the same mysterious flood penetrated like mighty rivers the cavernous distance. As they walked by the banks of this glittering Styx, Father José perceived how the liquid stream at certain places became solid. The ground was strewn with glittering flakes. One of these the Padre picked up and curiously examined. It was virgin gold.

An expression of discomfiture overcast the good Father's face at this discovery; but there was trace neither of malice nor satisfaction in the stranger's air, which was still of serious and fateful contemplation. When Father José recovered his equanimity, he said bitterly,—

"This, then, Sir Devil, is your work! This is your deceitful lure for the weak souls of sinful nations! So would you replace the Christian grace of Holy Spain!"

"This is what must be," returned the stranger gloomily. "But listen, Sir Priest. It lies with you to avert the issue for a time. Leave me here in peace. Go back to Castile, and take with you your bells, your images, and your missions. Continue here, and you only precipitate results. Stay! promise me you will do this, and you shall not lack that which will render your old age an ornament and a blessing;" and the stranger motioned significantly to the lake.

It was here, the legend discreetly relates, that the Devil showed—as he always shows sooner or later—his cloven hoof. The worthy Padre, sorely perplexed by this threefold vision, and, if the truth must be told, a little nettled at this wresting away of the glory of holy Spanish discovery, had shown some hesitation. But the unlucky bribe of the Enemy of Souls touched his Castilian spirit. Starting back in deep disgust, he brandished his crucifix in the face of the unmasked Fiend, and in a voice that made the dusky vault resound cried,—

"Avaunt thee, Sathanas! Diabolus, I defy thee! What! wouldst thou bribe me,—me, a brother of the Sacred Society of the Holy Jesus, Licentiate of Cordova and Inquisitor of Guadalaxara? Thinkest thou to buy me with thy sordid treasure? Avaunt!"

What might have been the issue of this rupture, and how complete might have been the triumph of the holy Father over the Arch-Fiend, who was recoiling aghast at these sacred titles and the flourishing symbol, we can never know, for at that moment the crucifix slipped through his fingers.

Scarcely had it touched the ground before Devil and holy Father simultaneously cast themselves toward it. In the struggle they clinched, and the pious José, who was as much the superior of his antagonist in bodily as in spiritual strength, was about to treat the Great Adversary to a back somersault, when he suddenly felt the long nails of the stranger piercing his flesh. A new fear seized his heart, a numbing chillness crept through his body, and he struggled to free himself, but in vain. A strange roaring was in his ears; the lake and cavern danced before his eyes and vanished, and with a loud cry he sank senseless to the ground.

When he recovered his consciousness, he was aware of a gentle swaying motion of his body. He opened his eyes, and saw it was high noon, and that he was being carried in a litter through the valley. He felt stiff, and looking down, perceived that his arm was tightly bandaged to his side.

He closed his eyes, and, after a few words of thankful prayer, thought how miraculously he had been preserved, and made a vow of candlesticks to the blessed Saint José. He then called in a faint voice, and presently the penitent Ignacio stood beside him.

The joy the poor fellow felt at his patron's returning consciousness for some time choked his utterance. He could only ejaculate, "A miracle! Blessed Saint José, he lives!" and kiss the Padre's bandaged hand. Father José, more intent on his last night's experience, waited for his emotion to subside, and asked where he had been found.

"On the mountain, your Reverence, but a few varas from where he attacked you."

"How?—you saw him then?" asked the Padre in unfeigned astonishment,

"Saw him, your Reverence! Mother of God! I should think I did! And your Reverence shall see him too, if he ever comes again within range of Ignacio's arquebus."

"What mean you, Ignacio?" said the Padre, sitting bolt-upright in his litter.

"Why, the bear, your Reverence,—the bear, holy Father, who attacked your worshipful person while you were meditating on the top of yonder mountain."

"Ah!" said the holy Father, lying down again. "Chut, child! I would be at peace."

When he reached the mission he was tenderly cared for, and in a few weeks was enabled to resume those duties from which, as will be seen, not even the machinations of the Evil One could divert him. The news of his physical disaster spread over the country, and a letter to the Bishop of Guadalaxara contained a confidential and detailed account of the good Father's spiritual temptation. But in some way the story leaked out; and long after José was gathered to his fathers, his mysterious encounter formed the theme of thrilling and whispered narrative. The mountain was generally shunned. It is true that Señor Joaquin Pedrillo afterward located a grant near the base of the mountain; but as Señora Pedrillo was known to be a termagant half-breed, the señor was not supposed to be over-fastidious.

Such is the legend of Monte del Diablo. As I said before, it may seem to lack essential corroboration. The discrepancy between the Father's narrative and the actual climax has given rise to some skepticism on the part of ingenious quibblers. All such I would simply refer to that part of the report of Señor Julio Serro, Sub-Prefect of San Pablo, before whom attest of the above was made. Touching this matter, the worthy Prefect observes, "That although the body of Father José doth show evidence of grievous conflict in the flesh, yet that is no proof that the Enemy of Souls, who could assume the figure of a decorous elderly caballero, could not at the same time transform himself into a bear for his own vile purposes."

1863

HARRIET PRESCOTT SPOFFORD

(1835–1921)

The Moonstone Mass

THERE was a certain weakness possessed by my ancestors, though in nowise peculiar to them, and of which, in common with other more or less undesirable traits, I have come into the inheritance.

It was the fear of dying in poverty. That, too, in the face of a goodly share of pelf stored in stocks, and lands, and copper-bottomed clippers, or what stood for copper-bottomed clippers, or rather sailed for them, in the clumsy commerce of their times.

There was one old fellow in particular—his portrait is hanging over the hall stove to-day, leaning forward, somewhat blistered by the profuse heat and wasted fuel there, and as if as long as such an outrageous expenditure of caloric was going on he meant to have the full benefit of it—who is said to have frequently shed tears over the probable price of his dinner, and on the next day to have sent home a silver dish to eat it from at a hundred times the cost. I find the inconsistencies of this individual constantly cropping out in myself; and although I could by no possibility be called a niggard, yet I confess that even now my prodigalities make me shiver.

Some years ago I was the proprietor of the old family estate, unencumbered by any thing except timber, that is worth its weight in gold yet, as you might say; alone in the world, save for an unloved relative; and with a sufficiently comfortable income, as I have since discovered, to meet all reasonable wants. I had, moreover, promised me in marriage the hand of a woman without a peer, and which, I believe now, might have been mine on any day when I saw fit to claim it.

That I loved Eleanor tenderly and truly you can not doubt; that I desired to bring her home, to see her flitting here and there in my dark old house, illuminating it with her youth and beauty, sitting at the head of my table that sparkled with its gold and silver heir-looms, making my days and nights like one delightful dream, was just as true.

And yet I hesitated. I looked over my bank-book—I cast up my accounts. I have enough for one, I said; I am not sure that it is enough for two. Eleanor, daintily nurtured, requires as dainty care for all time to come; moreover, it is not two alone to be considered, for should children come, there is their education, their maintenance, their future provision and portion to be found. All this would impoverish us, and unless we ended by becoming mere dependents, we had, to my excited vision, only the cold charity of the world and the work-house to which to look forward. I do not believe that Eleanor thought me right in so much of the matter as I saw fit to explain, but in maiden pride her lips perforce were sealed. She laughed though, when I confessed my work-house fear, and said that for her part she was thankful there was such a refuge at all, standing as it did on its knoll in the midst of green fields, and shaded by broad-limbed oaks—she had always envied the old women sitting there by their evening fireside, and mumbling over their small affairs to one another. But all her words seemed merely idle badinage—so I delayed. I said—when this ship sails in, when that dividend is declared, when I see how this speculation turns out—the days were long that added up the count of years, the nights were dreary; but I believed that I was actuated by principle, and took pride to myself for my strength and self-denial.

Moreover, old Paul, my great-uncle on my mother's side, and the millionaire of the family, was a bitter misogynist, and regarded women and marriage and household cares as the three remediless mistakes of an overruling Providence. He knew of my engagement to Eleanor, but so long as it remained in that stage he had nothing to say. Let me once marry, and my share of his million would be best represented by a cipher. However, he was not a man to adore, and he could not live forever.

Still, with all my own effort, I amassed wealth but slowly, according to my standard; my various ventures had various luck; and one day my old Uncle Paul, always intensely interested in the subject, both scientifically and from a commercial point of view, too old and feeble to go himself, but fain to send a proxy, and desirous of money in the family, made me an offer of that portion of his wealth on my return which would be mine on his demise, funded safely subject to my order, provided I made one of those who sought the discovery of the Northwest Passage.

I went to town, canvassed the matter with the experts—I had always an adventurous streak, as old Paul well knew—and having given many hours to the pursuit of the smaller sciences, had a turn for danger and discovery as well. And when the *Albatross* sailed—in spite of Eleanor's shivering remonstrance and prayers and tears, in spite of the grave looks of my friends —I was one of those that clustered on her deck, prepared for either fate. They—my companions—it is true, were led by nobler lights; but as for me, it was much as I told Eleanor—my affairs were so regulated that they would go on uninterrupt-edly in my absence; I should be no worse off for going, and if I returned, letting alone the renown of the thing, my Uncle Paul's donation was to be appropriated; every thing then was assured, and we stood possessed of lucky lives. If I had any keen or eager desire of search, any purpose to aid the growth of the world or to penetrate the secrets of its formation, as in-deed I think I must have had, I did not at that time know any thing about it. But I was to learn that death and stillness have no kingdom on this globe, and that even in the extremest bit-terness of cold and ice perpetual interchange and motion is taking place. So we went, all sails set on favorable winds, bounding over blue sea, skirting frowning coasts, and ever pushing our way up into the dark mystery of the North.

I shall not delay here to tell of Danish posts and the hospi-tality of summer settlements in their long afternoon of arctic daylight; nor will I weary you with any description of the suc-culence of the radishes that grew under the panes of glass in the Governor's scrap of moss and soil, scarcely of more size than a lady's parlor fernery, and which seemed to our dry mouths full of all the earth's cool juices—but advance, as we ourselves hastened to do, while that chill and crystalline sun shone, up into the ice-cased dens and caverns of the Pole. By the time that the long, blue twilight fell, when the rough and rasping cold sheathed all the atmosphere, and the great stars pricked themselves out on the heavens like spears' points, the *Albatross* was hauled up for winter-quarters, banked and boarded, heaved high on fields of ice; and all her inmates, during the wintry dark, led the life that prepared them for further exploits in higher latitudes the coming year, learning the dialects of the Esquimaux, the tricks of the seal and walrus, making long explorations with the dogs and Glipnu, their master, breaking ourselves in for business that had no play about it.

Then, at last, the August suns set us free again; inlets of tumultuous water traversed the great ice-floes; the *Albatross*, refitted, ruffled all her plumage and spread her wings once more for the North—for the secret that sat there domineering all its substance.

It was a year since we had heard from home; but who staid to think of that while our keel spurned into foam the sheets of steely seas, and day by day brought us nearer to the hidden things we sought? For myself I confess that, now so close to the end as it seemed, curiosity and research absorbed every other faculty; Eleanor might be mouldering back to the parent earth—I could not stay to meditate on such a possibility; my Uncle Paul's donation might enrich itself with gold-dust instead of the gathered dust of idle days—it was nothing to me. I had but one thought, one ambition, one desire in those days —the discovery of the clear seas and open passage. I endured all our hardships as if they had been luxuries: I made light of scurvy, banqueted off train-oil, and met that cold for which there is no language framed, and which might be a new element; or which, rather, had seemed in that long night like the vast void of ether beyond the uttermost star, where was neither air nor light nor heat, but only bitter negation and emptiness. I was hardly conscious of my body; I was only a concentrated search in myself.

The recent explorers had announced here, in the neighborhood of where our third summer at last found us, the existence of an immense space of clear water. One even declared that he had seen it.

My Uncle Paul had pronounced the declaration false, and the sight an impossibility. The North he believed to be the breeder of icebergs, an ever-welling fountain of cold; the great glaciers there forever form, forever fall; the ice-packs line the gorges from year to year unchanging; peaks of volcanic rock drop their frozen mantles like a scale only to display the fresher one beneath. The whole region, said he, is Plutonic, blasted by a primordial convulsion of the great forces of creation; and though it may be a few miles nearer to the central fires of the earth, allowing that there are such things, yet that would not in itself detract from the frigid power of its sunless solitudes, the more especially when it is remembered that the spinning of the earth, while in its first plastic material, which gave it greater circumference and thinness of shell at its equator, must have thickened the shell correspondingly at the poles; and the character of all the waste and wilderness there only signifies the impenetrable wall between its surface and centre, through which wall no heat could enter or escape. The great rivers, like the White and the Mackenzie, emptying to the north of the continents, so far from being enough in themselves to form any body of ever fresh and flowing water, can only pierce the opposing ice-fields in narrow streams and bays and inlets as they seek the Atlantic and the Pacific seas. And as for the theory of the currents of water heated in the tropics and carried by the rotary motion of the planet to the Pole, where they rise and melt the ice-floes into this great supposititious sea, it is simply an absurdity on the face of it, he argued, when you remember that warm water being in its nature specifically lighter than cold it would have risen to the surface long before it reached there. No, thought my Uncle Paul, who took nothing for granted; it is as I said, an absurdity on the face of it; my nephew shall prove it, and I stake half the earnings of my life upon it.

To tell the truth, I thought much the same as he did; and now that such a mere trifle of distance intervened, between me and the proof, I was full of a feverish impatience that almost amounted to insanity.

We had proceeded but a few days, coasting the crushing capes of rock that every where seemed to run out in a diablerie of tusks and horns to drive us from the region that they warded, now cruising through a runlet of blue water just wide enough for our keel, with silver reaches of frost stretching away into a ghastly horizon—now plunging upon tossing seas, the sun wheeling round and round, and never sinking from the strange, weird sky above us, when again to our look-out a glimmer in the low horizon told its awful tale—a sort of smoky lustre like that which might ascend from an army of spirits—the fierce and fatal spirits tented on the terrible field of the ice-floe.

We were alone, our single little ship speeding ever upward in the midst of that untraveled desolation. We spoke seldom to one another, oppressed with the sense of our situation. It was a loneliness that seemed more than a death in life, a solitude that was supernatural. Here and now it was clear water; ten hours later and we were caught in the teeth of the cold, wedged in the ice that had advanced upon us and surrounded us, fettered by another winter in latitudes where human life had never before been supported.

We found, before the hands of the dial had taught us the lapse of a week, that this would be something not to be endured. The sun sank lower every day behind the crags and silvery horns; the heavens grew to wear a hue of violet, almost black, and yet unbearably dazzling; as the notes of our voices fell upon the atmosphere they assumed a metallic tone, as if the air itself had become frozen from the beginning of the world and they tinkled against it; our sufferings had mounted in their intensity till they were too great to be resisted.

It was decided at length—when the one long day had given place to its answering night, and in the jet-black heavens the stars, like knobs of silver, sparkled so large and close upon us that we might have grasped them in our hands—that I should take a sledge with Glipnu and his dogs, and see if there were any path to the westward by which, if the *Albatross* were forsaken, those of her crew that remained might follow it, and find an escape to safety. Our path was on a frozen sea; if we discovered land we did not know that the foot of man had ever trodden it; we could hope to find no *caché* of snow-buried food—neither fish nor game lived in this desert of ice that was so devoid of life in any shape as to seem dead itself. But, well provisioned, furred to the eyes, and essaying to nurse some hopefulness of heart, we set out on our way through this Valley of Death, relieving one another, and traveling day and night.

Still night and day to the west rose the black coast, one interminable height; to the east extended the sheets of unbroken ice; sometimes a huge glacier hung pendulous from the precipice; once we saw, by the starlight, a white, foaming, rushing river arrested and transformed to ice in its flight down that steep. A south wind began to blow behind us; we traveled on the ice; three days, perhaps, as days are measured among

men, had passed, when we found that we made double progress, for the ice traveled too; the whole field, carried by some
northward-bearing current, was afloat; it began to be crossed
and cut by a thousand crevasses; the cakes, an acre each, tilted
up and down, and made wide waves with their ponderous
plashing in the black body of the sea; we could hear them
grinding distantly in the clear dark against the coast, against
each other. There was no retreat—there was no advance; we
were on the ice, and the ice was breaking up. Suddenly we
rounded a tongue of the primeval rock, and recoiled before a
narrow gulf—one sharp shadow, as deep as despair, as full of
aguish fears. It was just wide enough for the sledge to span.
Glipnu made the dogs leap; we could be no worse off if they
drowned. They touched the opposite block; it careened; it
went under; the sledge went with it; I was left alone where I
had stood. Two dogs broke loose, and scrambled up beside me;
Glipnu and the others I never saw again. I sank upon the ice;
the dogs crouched beside me; sometimes I think they saved
my brain from total ruin, for without them I could not have
withstood the enormity of that loneliness, a loneliness that it
was impossible should be broken—floating on and on with that
vast journeying company of spectral ice. I had food enough to
support life for several days to come, in the pouch at my belt;
the dogs and I shared it—for, last as long as it would, when it
should be gone there was only death before us—no reprieve—
sooner or later that; as well sooner as later—the living terrors
of this icy hell were all about us, and death could be no worse.

Still the south wind blew, the rapid current carried us, the
dark skies grew deep and darker, the lanes and avenues
between the stars were crowded with forebodings—for the air
seemed full of a new power, a strange and invisible influence,
as if a king of unknown terrors here held his awful state. Sometimes the dogs stood up and growled and bristled their shaggy
hides; I, prostrate on the ice, in all my frame was stung with a
universal tingle. I was no longer myself. At this moment my
blood seemed to sing and bubble in my veins; I grew giddy with
a sort of delirious and inexplicable ecstasy; with another moment unutterable horror seized me; I was plunged and
weighed down with a black and suffocating load, while evil
things seemed to flap their wings in my face, to breathe in my

mouth, to draw my soul out of my body and carry it careering through the frozen realm of that murky heaven, to restore it with a shock of agony. Once as I lay there, still floating, floating northward, out of the dim dark rim of the water-world, a lance of piercing light shot up the zenith; it divided the heavens like a knife; they opened out in one blaze, and the fire fell sheetingly down before my face—cold fire, curdingly cold—light robbed of heat, and set free in a preternatural anarchy of the elements; its fringes swung to and fro before my face, pricked it with flaming spiculæ, dissolving in a thousand colors that spread every where over the low field, flashing, flickering, creeping, reflecting, gathering again in one long serpentine line of glory that wavered in slow convolutions across the cuts and crevasses of the ice, wreathed ever nearer, and, lifting its head at last, became nothing in the darkness but two great eyes like glowing coals, with which it stared me to a stound, till I threw myself face down to hide me in the ice; and the whining, bristling dogs cowered backward, and were dead.

I should have supposed myself to be in the region of the magnetic pole of the sphere, if I did not know that I had long since left it behind me. My pocket-compass had become entirely useless, and every scrap of metal that I had about me had become a loadstone. The very ice, as if it were congealed from water that held large quantities of iron in solution; iron escaping from whatever solid land there was beneath or around, the Plutonic rock that such a region could have alone veined and seamed with metal. The very ice appeared to have a magnetic quality; it held me so that I changed my position upon it with difficulty, and, as if it established a battery by the aid of the singular atmosphere above it, frequently sent thrills quivering through and through me till my flesh seemed about to resolve into all the jarring atoms of its original constitution; and again soothed me, with a velvet touch, into a state which, if it were not sleep, was at least haunted by visions that I dare not believe to have been realities, and from which I always awoke with a start to find myself still floating, floating. My watch had long since ceased to beat. I felt an odd persuasion that I had died when that stood still, and only this slavery of the magnet, of the cold, this power that locked every thing in invisible fetters and let nothing loose again, held my soul still in the bonds of my body. Another idea, also, took possession of me, for my mind was open to whatever visitant chose to enter, since utter despair of safety or release had left it vacant of a hope or fear. These enormous days and nights, swinging in their arc six months long, were the pendulum that dealt time in another measure than that dealt by the sunlight of lower zones; they told the time of what interminable years, the years of what vast generations far beyond the span that covered the age of the primeval men of Scripture—they measured time on this gigantic and enduring scale for what wonderful and mighty beings, old as the everlasting hills, as destitute as they of mortal sympathy, cold and inscrutable, handling the two-edged javelins of frost and magnetism, and served by all the unknown polar agencies. I fancied that I saw their far-reaching cohorts, marshaling and manœuvring at times in the field of an horizon that was boundless, the glitter of their spears and casques, the sheen of their white banners; and again, sitting in fearful circle with their phantasmagoria they shut and hemmed me in and watched me writhe like a worm before them.

I had a fancy that the perpetual play of magnetic impulses here gradually disintegrated myself to any further fear, I cowered beneath the stare of those dead and icy eyes. Slowly we rounded, and ever rounded; the inside, on which my place was, moving less slowly than the outer circle of the sheeted mass in its viscid flow; and as we moved, by some fate my eye was caught by the substance on which this figure sat. It was no figure at all now, but a bare jag of rock rising in the centre of this solid whirlpool, and carrying on its summit something which held a light that not one of these icy freaks, pranking in the dress of gems and flowers, had found it possible to assume. It was a thing so real, so genuine, my breath became suspended; my heart ceased to beat; my brain, that had been a lump of ice, seemed to move in its skull; hope, that had deserted me, suddenly sprung up like a second life within me; the old passion was not dead, if I was. It rose stronger than life or death or than myself. If I could but snatch that mass of moonstone, that inestimable wealth! It was nothing deceptive, I declared to myself. What more natural home could it have than this region, thrown up here by the old Plutonic powers of the planet, as the same substance in smaller shape was thrown up on the peaks of the Mount St. Gothard, when the Alpine aiguilles first sprang into the day? There it rested, limpid with its milky pearl, casting out flakes of flame and azure, of red and leaf-green light, and holding yet a sparkle of silver in the reflections and refractions of its inner axis—the splendid Turk's-eye of the lapidaries, the cousin of the water-opal and the girasole, the precious essence of feldspar. Could I break it, I would find clusters of great hemitrope crystals. Could I obtain it, I should have a jewel in that mass of moonstone such as the world never saw! The throne of Jemschid could not cast a shadow beside it.

Then the bitterness of my fate overwhelmed me. Here, with this treasure of a kingdom, this jewel that could not be priced, this wealth beyond an Emperor's—and here only to die! My stolid apathy vanished, old thoughts dominated once more, old habits, old desires. I thought of Eleanor then in her warm, sunny home, the blossoms that bloomed around her, the birds that sang, the cheerful evening fires, the longing thoughts for one who never came, who never was to come. But I would! I cried, where human voice had never cried before. I would return! I would take this treasure with me! I would not be defrauded! Should not I, a man, conquer this inanimate blind matter? I reached out my hands to seize it. Slowly it receded—slowly, and less slowly; or was the motion of the ice still carrying me onward? Had we encircled this apex? and were we driving out into the open and uncovered North, and so down the seas and out to the open main of black water again? If so—if I could live through it—I must have this thing!

I rose, and as well as I could, with my cramped and stiffened limbs, I moved to go back for it. It was useless; the current that carried us was growing invincible, the gaping gulfs of the outer seas were sucking us toward them. I fell; I scrambled to my feet; I would still have gone back, but, as I attempted it, the ice whereon I was inclined ever so slightly, tipped more boldly, gave way, and rose in a billow, broke, and piled over on another mass beneath. Then the cavern was behind us, and I comprehended that this ice-stream, having doubled its central point, now in its outward movement encountered the still incoming body, and was to pile above and pass over it, the whole expanse bending, cracking, breaking, crowding, and compressing, till its rearing tumult made bergs more mountainous than the offshot glaciers of the Greenland continent, that should ride safely down to crumble in the surging seas below. As block after block of the rent ice rose in the air, lighted by the blue and bristling aurora-points, toppled and mounted higher, it seemed to me that now indeed I was battling with those elemental agencies in the dreadful fight I had desired—one man against the might of matter. I sprang from that block to another; I gained my balance on a third, climbing, shouldering, leaping, struggling, holding with my hands, catching with my feet, crawling, stumbling, tottering, rising high and higher with the mountain ever making underneath; a power unknown to my foes coming to my aid, a blessed rushing warmth that glowed on all the surface of my skin, that set the blood to racing in my veins, that made my heart beat with newer hope, sink with newer despair, rise buoyant with new determination. Except when the shaft of light pierced the shivering sky I could not see or guess the height that I had gained. I was vaguely aware of chasms that were bottomless, of precipices that opened on them, of pinnacles rising round me in aerial spires, when suddenly the shelf, on which I must have stood, yielded, as if it were pushed by great hands, swept down a steep incline like an avalanche, stopped half-way, but sent me flying on, sliding, glancing, like a shooting-star, down, down the slippery side, breathless, dizzy, smitten with blistering pain by awful winds that whistled by me, far out upon the level ice below that tilted up and down again with the great resonant plash of open water, and conscious for a moment that I lay at last upon a fragment that the mass behind urged on, I knew and I remembered nothing more.

Faces were bending over me when I opened my eyes again, rough, uncouth, and bearded faces, but no monsters of the pole. Whalemen rather, smelling richly of train-oil, but I could recall nothing in all my life one fraction so beautiful as they; the angels on whom I hope to open my eyes when Death has really taken me will scarcely seem sights more blest than did those rude whalers of the North Pacific Sea. The North Pacific Sea—for it was there that I was found, explain it how you may—whether the *Albatross* had pierced farther to the west than her sailing-master knew, and had lost her reckoning with a disordered compass-needle under new stars—or whether I had really been the sport of the demoniac beings of the ice, tossed by them from zone to zone in a dozen hours. The whalers, real creatures enough, had discovered me on a block of ice, they said; nor could I, in their opinion, have been many days undergoing my dreadful experience, for there was still food in my wallet when they opened it. They would never believe a word of my story, and so far from regarding me as one who had proved the Northwest Passage in my own person, they considered me a mere idle maniac, as uncomfortable a thing to have on shipboard as a ghost or a dead body, wrecked and unable to account for myself, and gladly transferred me to a homeward-bound Russian man-of-war, whose officers afforded me more polite but quite as decided skepticism. I have never to this day found any one who believed my story when I told it—so you can take it for what it is worth. Even my Uncle Paul flouted it, and absolutely refused to surrender the sum on whose expectation I had taken ship; while my old ancestor, who hung peeling over the hall fire, dropped from his frame in disgust at the idea of one of his hard-cash descendants turning romancer. But all I know is that the *Albatross* never sailed into port again, and that if I open my knife to-day and lay it on the table it will wheel about till the tip of its blade points full at the North Star.

I have never found any one to believe me, did I say? Yes, there is one—Eleanor never doubted a word of my narration, never asked me if cold and suffering had not shaken my reason. But then, after the first recital, she has never been willing to hear another word about it, and if I ever allude to my lost treasure or the possibility of instituting search for it, she asks me if I need more lessons to be content with the treasure that I have, and gathers up her work and gently leaves the room. So that, now I speak of it so seldom, if I had not told the thing to you it might come to pass that I should forget altogether the existence of my mass of moonstone. My mass of moonshine, old Paul calls it. I let him have his say; he can not have that nor any thing else much longer; but when all is done I recall Galileo and I mutter to myself, "*Per si muove*—it *was* a mass of moonstone! With these eyes I saw it, with these hands I touched it, with this heart I longed for it, with this will I mean to have it yet!"

1868

W. C. MORROW

(1854–1923)

His Unconquerable Enemy

I WAS summoned from Calcutta to the heart of India to perform a difficult surgical operation on one of the women of a
great rajah's household. I found the rajah a man of a noble
character, but possessed, as I afterwards discovered, of a sense
of cruelty purely Oriental and in contrast to the indolence of
his disposition. He was so grateful for the success that attended my mission that he urged me to remain a guest at the
palace as long as it might please me to stay, and I thankfully accepted the invitation.

One of the male servants early attracted my notice for his
marvellous capacity of malice. His name was Neranya, and I
am certain that there must have been a large proportion of
Malay blood in his veins, for, unlike the Indians (from whom
he differed also in complexion), he was extremely alert, active,
nervous, and sensitive. A redeeming circumstance was his love
for his master. Once his violent temper led him to the commission of an atrocious crime,—the fatal stabbing of a dwarf. In
punishment for this the rajah ordered that Neranya's right arm
(the offending one) be severed from his body. The sentence
was executed in a bungling fashion by a stupid fellow armed
with an axe, and I, being a surgeon, was compelled, in order to
save Neranya's life, to perform an amputation of the stump,
leaving not a vestige of the limb remaining.

After this he developed an augmented fiendishness. His love
for the rajah was changed to hate, and in his mad anger he flung
discretion to the winds. Driven once to frenzy by the rajah's
scornful treatment, he sprang upon the rajah with a knife, but,
fortunately, was seized and disarmed. To his unspeakable dismay
the rajah sentenced him for this offence to suffer amputation
of the remaining arm. It was done as in the former instance.
This had the effect of putting a temporary curb on Neranya's
spirit, or, rather, of changing the outward manifestations of his

diabolism. Being armless, he was at first largely at the mercy of those who ministered to his needs,—a duty which I undertook to see was properly discharged, for I felt an interest in this strangely distorted nature. His sense of helplessness, combined with a damnable scheme for revenge which he had secretly formed, caused Neranya to change his fierce, impetuous, and unruly conduct into a smooth, quiet, insinuating bearing, which he carried so artfully as to deceive those with whom he was brought in contact, including the rajah himself.

Neranya, being exceedingly quick, intelligent, and dexterous, and having an unconquerable will, turned his attention to the cultivating of an enlarged usefulness of his legs, feet, and toes, with so excellent effect that in time he was able to perform wonderful feats with those members. Thus his capability, especially for destructive mischief, was considerably restored.

One morning the rajah's only son, a young man of an uncommonly amiable and noble disposition, was found dead in bed. His murder was a most atrocious one, his body being mutilated in a shocking manner, but in my eyes the most significant of all the mutilations was the entire removal and disappearance of the young prince's arms.

The death of the young man nearly brought the rajah to the grave. It was not, therefore, until I had nursed him back to health that I began a systematic inquiry into the murder. I said nothing of my own discoveries and conclusions until after the rajah and his officers had failed and my work had been done; then I submitted to him a written report, making a close analysis of all the circumstances and closing by charging the crime to Neranya. The rajah, convinced by my proof and argument, at once ordered Neranya to be put to death, this to be accomplished slowly and with frightful tortures. The sentence was so cruel and revolting that it filled me with horror, and I implored that the wretch be shot. Finally, through a sense of gratitude to me, the rajah relaxed. When Neranya was charged with the crime he denied it, of course, but, seeing that the rajah was convinced, he threw aside all restraint, and, dancing, laughing, and shrieking in the most horrible manner, confessed his guilt, gloated over it, and reviled the rajah to his teeth, —this, knowing that some fearful death awaited him.

The rajah decided upon the details of the matter that night, and in the morning he informed me of his decision. It was that Neranya's life should be spared, but that both of his legs should be broken with hammers, and that then I should amputate the limbs at the trunk! Appended to this horrible sentence was a provision that the maimed wretch should be kept and tortured at regular intervals by such means as afterwards might be devised.

Sickened to the heart by the awful duty set out for me, I nevertheless performed it with success, and I care to say nothing more about that part of the tragedy. Neranya escaped death very narrowly and was a long time in recovering his wonted vitality. During all these weeks the rajah neither saw him nor made inquiries concerning him, but when, as in duty bound, I made official report that the man had recovered his strength, the rajah's eyes brightened, and he emerged with deadly activity from the stupor into which he so long had been plunged.

The rajah's palace was a noble structure, but it is necessary here to describe only the grand hall. It was an immense chamber, with a floor of polished, inlaid stone and a lofty, arched ceiling. A soft light stole into it through stained glass set in the roof and in high windows on one side. In the middle of the room was a rich fountain, which threw up a tall, slender column of water, with smaller and shorter jets grouped around it. Across one end of the hall, half-way to the ceiling, was a balcony, which communicated with the upper story of a wing, and from which a flight of stone stairs descended to the floor of the hall. During the hot summers this room was delightfully cool; it was the rajah's favorite lounging-place, and when the nights were hot he had his cot taken thither, and there he slept.

This hall was chosen for Neranya's permanent prison; here was he to stay so long as he might live, with never a glimpse of the shining world or the glorious heavens. To one of his nervous, discontented nature such confinement was worse than death. At the rajah's order there was constructed for him a small pen of open iron-work, circular, and about four feet in diameter, elevated on four slender iron posts, ten feet above the floor, and placed between the balcony and the fountain. Such was Neranya's prison. The pen was about four feet in depth, and the pen-top was left open for the convenience of the servants whose duty it should be to care for him. These precautions for his safe confinement were taken at my suggestion, for, although the man was now deprived of all four of his limbs, I still feared that he might develop some extraordinary, unheard-of power for mischief. It was provided that the attendants should reach his cage by means of a movable ladder.

All these arrangements having been made and Neranya hoisted into his cage, the rajah emerged upon the balcony to see him for the first time since the last amputation. Neranya had been lying panting and helpless on the floor of his cage, but when his quick ear caught the sound of the rajah's footfall he squirmed about until he had brought the back of his head against the railing, elevating his eyes above his chest, and enabling him to peer through the open-work of the cage. Thus the two deadly enemies faced each other. The rajah's stern face paled at sight of the hideous, shapeless thing which met his gaze; but he soon recovered, and the old hard, cruel, sinister look returned. Neranya's black hair and beard had grown long, and they added to the natural ferocity of his aspect. His eyes blazed upon the rajah with a terrible light, his lips parted, and he gasped for breath; his face was ashen with rage and despair, and his thin, distended nostrils quivered.

The rajah folded his arms and gazed down from the balcony upon the frightful wreck that he had made. Oh, the dreadful pathos of that picture; the inhumanity of it; the deep and dismal tragedy of it! Who might look into the wild, despairing heart of the prisoner and see and understand the frightful turmoil there; the surging, choking passion; unbridled but impotent ferocity; frantic thirst for a vengeance that should be deeper than hell! Neranya gazed, his shapeless body heaving, his eyes aflame; and then, in a strong, clear voice, which rang throughout the great hall, with rapid speech he hurled at the rajah the most insulting defiance, the most awful curses. He cursed the womb that had conceived him, the food that should nourish him, the wealth that had brought him power; cursed him in the name of Buddha and all the wise men; cursed by the sun, the moon, and the stars; by the continents, mountains, oceans, and rivers; by all things living; cursed his head, his heart, his entrails; cursed in a whirlwind of unmentionable words; heaped unimaginable insults and contumely upon him; called him a knave, a beast, a fool, a liar, an infamous and unspeakable coward.

The rajah heard it all calmly, without the movement of a muscle, without the slightest change of countenance; and when the poor wretch had exhausted his strength and fallen helpless and silent to the floor, the rajah, with a grim, cold smile, turned and strode away.

The days passed. The rajah, not deterred by Neranya's curses often heaped upon him, spent even more time than formerly in the great hall, and slept there oftener at night; and finally Neranya wearied of cursing and defying him, and fell into a sullen silence. The man was a study for me, and I observed every change in his fleeting moods. Generally his condition was that of miserable despair, which he attempted bravely to conceal. Even the boon of suicide had been denied him, for when he would wriggle into an erect position the rail of his pen was a foot above his head, so that he could not clamber over and break his skull on the stone floor beneath; and when he had tried to starve himself the attendants forced food down his throat; so that he abandoned such attempts. At times his eyes would blaze and his breath would come in gasps, for imaginary vengeance was working within him; but steadily he became quieter and more tractable, and was pleasant and responsive when I would converse with him. Whatever might have been the tortures which the rajah had decided on, none as yet had been ordered; and although Neranya knew that they were in contemplation, he never referred to them or complained of his lot.

The awful climax of this situation was reached one night, and even after this lapse of years I cannot approach its description without a shudder.

It was a hot night, and the rajah had gone to sleep in the great hall, lying on a high cot placed on the main floor just underneath the edge of the balcony. I had been unable to sleep in my own apartment, and so I had stolen into the great hall through the heavily curtained entrance at the end farthest from the balcony. As I entered I heard a peculiar, soft sound above the patter of the fountain. Neranya's cage was partly concealed from my view by the spraying water, but I suspected that the unusual sound came from him. Stealing a little to one side, and crouching against the dark hangings of the wall, I could see him in the faint light which dimly illuminated the

hall, and then I discovered that my surmise was correct—Neranya was quietly at work. Curious to learn more, and knowing
that only mischief could have been inspiring him, I sank into a
thick robe on the floor and watched him.

To my great astonishment Neranya was tearing off with his
teeth the bag which served as his outer garment. He did it cautiously, casting sharp glances frequently at the rajah, who,
sleeping soundly on his cot below, breathed heavily. After
starting a strip with his teeth, Neranya, by the same means,
would attach it to the railing of his cage and then wriggle away,
much after the manner of a caterpillar's crawling, and this would
cause the strip to be torn out the full length of his garment. He
repeated this operation with incredible patience and skill until
his entire garment had been torn into strips. Two or three of
these he tied end to end with his teeth, lips, and tongue, tight-
ening the knots by placing one end of the strip under his body
and drawing the other taut with his teeth. In this way he made
a line several feet long, one end of which he made fast to the
rail with his mouth. It then began to dawn upon me that he was
going to make an insane attempt—impossible of achievement
without hands, feet, arms, or legs—to escape from his cage! For
what purpose? The rajah was asleep in the hall—ah! I caught
my breath. Oh, the desperate, insane thirst for revenge which
could have unhinged so clear and firm a mind! Even though
he should accomplish the impossible feat of climbing over the
railing of his cage that he might fall to the floor below (for how
could he slide down the rope?), he would be in all probability
killed or stunned; and even if he should escape these dangers it
would be impossible for him to clamber upon the cot without
rousing the rajah, and impossible even though the rajah were
dead! Amazed at the man's daring, and convinced that his sufferings and brooding had destroyed his reason, nevertheless I
watched him with breathless interest.

With other strips tied together he made a short swing across
one side of his cage. He caught the long line in his teeth at a
point not far from the rail; then, wriggling with great effort to
an upright position, his back braced against the rail, he put his
chin over the swing and worked toward one end. He tightened
the grasp of his chin on the swing, and with tremendous exertion, working the lower end of his spine against the railing, he

began gradually to ascend the side of his cage. The labor was so great that he was compelled to pause at intervals, and his breathing was hard and painful; and even while thus resting he was in a position of terrible strain, and his pushing against the swing caused it to press hard against his windpipe and nearly strangle him.

After amazing effort he had elevated the lower end of his body until it protruded above the railing, the top of which was now across the lower end of his abdomen. Gradually he worked his body over, going backward, until there was sufficient excess of weight on the outer side of the rail; and then, with a quick lurch, he raised his head and shoulders and swung into a horizontal position on top of the rail. Of course, he would have fallen to the floor below had it not been for the line which he held in his teeth. With so great nicety had he estimated the distance between his mouth and the point where the rope was fastened to the rail, that the line tightened and checked him just as he reached the horizontal position on the rail. If one had told me beforehand that such a feat as I had just seen this man accomplish was possible, I should have thought him a fool.

Neranya was now balanced on his stomach across the top of the rail, and he eased his position by bending his spine and hanging down on either side as much as possible. Having rested thus for some minutes, he began cautiously to slide off backward, slowly paying out the line through his teeth, finding almost a fatal difficulty in passing the knots. Now, it is quite possible that the line would have escaped altogether from his teeth laterally when he would slightly relax his hold to let it slip, had it not been for a very ingenious plan to which he had resorted. This consisted in his having made a turn of the line around his neck before he attacked the swing, thus securing a threefold control of the line,—one by his teeth, another by friction against his neck, and a third by his ability to compress it between his cheek and shoulder. It was quite evident now that the minutest details of a most elaborate plan had been carefully worked out by him before beginning the task, and that possibly weeks of difficult theoretical study had been consumed in the mental preparation. As I observed him I was reminded of certain hitherto unaccountable things which he had

been doing for some weeks past—going through certain hitherto inexplicable motions, undoubtedly for the purpose of
training his muscles for the immeasurably arduous labor which
he was now performing.

A stupendous and seemingly impossible part of his task had
been accomplished. Could he reach the floor in safety? Gradually he worked himself backward over the rail, in imminent
danger of falling; but his nerve never wavered, and I could see
a wonderful light in his eyes. With something of a lurch, his body
fell against the outer side of the railing, to which he was hanging
by his chin, the line still held firmly in his teeth. Slowly he
slipped his chin from the rail, and then hung suspended by the
line in his teeth. By almost imperceptible degrees, with infinite
caution, he descended the line, and, finally, his unwieldy body
rolled upon the floor, safe and unhurt!

What miracle would this superhuman monster next accomplish? I was quick and strong, and was ready and able to intercept any dangerous act; but not until danger appeared would I
interfere with this extraordinary scene.

I must confess to astonishment upon having observed that
Neranya, instead of proceeding directly toward the sleeping
rajah, took quite another direction. Then it was only escape, after
all, that the wretch contemplated, and not the murder of the
rajah. But how could he escape? The only possible way to reach
the outer air without great risk was by ascending the stairs to
the balcony and leaving by the corridor which opened upon it,
and thus fall into the hands of some British soldiers quartered
thereabout, who might conceive the idea of hiding him; but
surely it was impossible for Neranya to ascend that long flight
of stairs! Nevertheless, he made directly for them, his method of
progression this: He lay upon his back, with the lower end of
his body toward the stairs; then bowed his spine upward, thus
drawing his head and shoulders a little forward; straightened,
and then pushed the lower end of his body forward a space
equal to that through which he had drawn his head; repeating
this again and again, each time, while bending his spine, pre-
venting his head from slipping by pressing it against the floor.
His progress was laborious and slow, but sensible; and, finally,
he arrived at the foot of the stairs.

It was manifest that his insane purpose was to ascend them.

The desire for freedom must have been strong within him! Wriggling to an upright position against the newel-post, he looked up at the great height which he had to climb and sighed; but there was no dimming of the light in his eyes. How could he accomplish the impossible task?

His solution of the problem was very simple, though daring and perilous as all the rest. While leaning against the newel-post he let himself fall diagonally upon the bottom step, where he lay partly hanging over, but safe, on his side. Turning upon his back, he wriggled forward along the step to the rail and raised himself to an upright position against it as he had against the newel-post, fell as before, and landed on the second step. In this manner, with inconceivable labor, he accomplished the ascent of the entire flight of stairs.

It being apparent to me that the rajah was not the object of Neranya's movements, the anxiety which I had felt on that account was now entirely dissipated. The things which already he had accomplished were entirely beyond the nimblest imagination. The sympathy which I had always felt for the wretched man was now greatly quickened; and as infinitesimally small as I knew his chances for escape to be, I nevertheless hoped that he would succeed. Any assistance from me, however, was out of the question; and it never should be known that I had witnessed the escape.

Neranya was now upon the balcony, and I could dimly see him wriggling along toward the door which led out upon the balcony. Finally he stopped and wriggled to an upright position against the rail, which had wide openings between the balusters. His back was toward me, but he slowly turned and faced me and the hall. At that great distance I could not distinguish his features, but the slowness with which he had worked, even before he had fully accomplished the ascent of the stairs, was evidence all too eloquent of his extreme exhaustion. Nothing but a most desperate resolution could have sustained him thus far, but he had drawn upon the last remnant of his strength. He looked around the hall with a sweeping glance, and then down upon the rajah, who was sleeping immediately beneath him, over twenty feet below. He looked long and earnestly, sinking lower, and lower, and lower upon the rail. Suddenly, to my inconceivable astonishment and dismay, he toppled through and shot downward from his lofty height! I held my breath, expecting to see him crushed upon the stone floor beneath; but instead of that he fell full upon the rajah's breast, driving him through the cot to the floor. I sprang forward with a loud cry for help, and was instantly at the scene of the catastrophe. With indescribable horror I saw that Neranya's teeth were buried in the rajah's throat! I tore the wretch away, but the blood was pouring from the rajah's arteries, his chest was crushed in, and he was gasping in the agony of death. People came running in, terrified. I turned to Neranya. He lay upon his back, his face hideously smeared with blood. Murder, and not escape, had been his intentions from the beginning; and he had employed the only method by which there was ever a possibility of accomplishing it. I knelt beside him, and saw that he too was dying; his back had been broken by the fall. He smiled sweetly into my face, and a triumphant look of accomplished revenge sat upon his face even in death.

1889

SARAH ORNE JEWETT

(1849–1909)

In Dark New England Days

I.

THE last of the neighbors was going home; officious Mrs. Peter Downs had lingered late and sought for additional house-work with which to prolong her stay. She had talked incessantly, and buzzed like a busy bee as she helped to put away the best crockery after the funeral supper, while the sisters Betsey and Hannah Knowles grew every moment more forbidding and unwilling to speak. They lighted a solitary small oil lamp at last, as if for Sunday evening idleness, and put it on the side table in the kitchen.

"We ain't intending to make a late evening of it," announced Betsey, the elder, standing before Mrs. Downs in an expectant, final way, making an irresistible opportunity for saying good-night. "I'm sure we're more than obleeged to ye,—ain't we, Hannah?—but I don't feel 's if we ought to keep ye longer. We ain't going to do no more to-night, but set down a spell and kind of collect ourselves, and then make for bed."

Susan Downs offered one more plea. "I'd stop all night with ye an' welcome; 't is gettin' late—an' dark," she added plaintively; but the sisters shook their heads quickly, while Hannah said that they might as well get used to staying alone, since they would have to do it first or last. In spite of herself Mrs. Downs was obliged to put on her funeral best bonnet and shawl and start on her homeward way.

"Closed-mouthed old maids!" she grumbled as the door shut behind her all too soon and denied her the light of the lamp along the footpath. Suddenly there was a bright ray from the window, as if some one had pushed back the curtain and stood with the lamp close to the sash. "That's Hannah," said the retreating guest. "She'd told me somethin' about things, I know, if it hadn't 'a' been for Betsey. Catch me workin' myself to pieces again for 'em." But, however grudgingly this was said, Mrs. Downs's conscience told her that the industry of the past two days had been somewhat selfish on her part; she had hoped that in the excitement of this unexpected funeral season she might for once be taken into the sisters' confidence. More than this, she knew that they were certain of her motive, and had deliberately refused the expected satisfaction. "'T ain't as if I was one o' them curious busy-bodies anyway," she said to herself pityingly; "they might 'a' neighbored with somebody for once, I do believe." Everybody would have a question ready for her the next day, for it was known that she had been slaving herself devotedly since the news had come of old Captain Knowles's sudden death in his bed from a stroke, the last of three which had in the course of a year or two changed him from a strong old man to a feeble, chair-bound cripple.

Mrs. Downs stepped bravely along the dark country road; she could see a light in her own kitchen window half a mile away, and did not stop to notice either the penetrating dampness, or the shadowy woods at her right. It was a cloudy night, but there was a dim light over the open fields. She had a disposition of mind towards the exciting circumstances of death and burial, and was in request at such times among her neighbors; in this she was like a city person who prefers tragedy to comedy, but not having the semblance within her reach, she made the most of looking on at real griefs and departures.

Some one was walking towards her in the road; suddenly she heard footsteps. The figure stopped, then it came forward again.

"Oh, 't is you, ain't it?" with a tone of disappointment. "I cal'lated you'd stop all night, 't had got to be so late, an' I was just going over to the Knowles gals'; well, to kind o' ask how they be, an'"—Mr. Peter Downs was evidently counting on his visit.

"They never passed me the compliment," replied the wife. "I declare I didn't covet the walk home; I'm most beat out, bein' on foot so much. I was 'most put out with 'em for letten' of me see quite so plain that my room was better than my company. But I don't know 's I blame 'em; they want to look an' see what they've got, an' kind of git by theirselves, I expect. 'T was natural."

Mrs. Downs knew that her husband would resent her first statements, being a sensitive and grumbling man. She had formed a pacific habit of suiting her remarks to his point of view, to save an outburst. He contented himself with calling the Knowles girls hoggish, and put a direct question as to whether they had let fall any words about their situation, but Martha Downs was obliged to answer in the negative.

"Was Enoch Holt there after the folks come back from the grave?"

"He wa'n't; they never give him no encouragement neither."

"He appeared well, I must say," continued Peter Downs. "He took his place next but one behind us in the procession, 'long of Melinda Dutch, an' walked to an' from with her, give her his arm, and then I never see him after we got back; but I thought he might be somewhere in the house, an' I was out about the barn an' so on."

"They was civil to him. I was by when he come, just steppin' out of the bedroom after we'd finished layin' the old Cap'n into his coffin. Hannah looked real pleased when she see Enoch, as if she hadn't really expected him, but Betsey stuck out her hand 's if 't was an eend o' board, an' drawed her face solemner 'n ever. There, they had natural feelin's. He was their own father when all was said, the Cap'n was, an' I don't know but he was clever to 'em in his way, 'ceptin' when he disappointed Hannah about her marryin' Jake Good'in. She l'arned to respect the old Cap'n's foresight, too."

"Sakes alive, Marthy, how you do knock folks down with one hand an' set 'em up with t' other," chuckled Mr. Downs. They next discussed the Captain's appearance as he lay in state in the front room, a subject which, with its endless ramifications, would keep the whole neighborhood interested for weeks to come.

An hour later the twinkling light in the Downs house suddenly disappeared. As Martha Downs took a last look out of doors through her bedroom window she could see no other light; the neighbors had all gone to bed. It was a little past nine, and the night was damp and still.

II.

The Captain Knowles place was eastward from the Downs's, and a short turn in the road and the piece of hard-wood growth hid one house from the other. At this unwontedly late hour the elderly sisters were still sitting in their warm kitchen; there were bright coals under the singing tea-kettle which hung from the crane by three or four long pothooks. Betsey Knowles objected when her sister offered to put on more wood.

"Father never liked to leave no great of a fire, even though he slept right here in the bedroom. He said this floor was one that would light an' catch easy, you r'member."

"Another winter we can move down and take the bedroom ourselves—'t will be warmer for us," suggested Hannah; but Betsey shook her head doubtfully. The thought of their old father's grave, unwatched and undefended in the outermost dark field, filled their hearts with a strange tenderness. They had been his dutiful, patient slaves, and it seemed like disloyalty to have abandoned the poor shape; to be sitting there disregarding the thousand requirements and services of the past. More than all, they were facing a free future; they were their own mistresses at last, though past sixty years of age. Hannah was still a child at heart. She chased away a dread suspicion, when Betsey forbade the wood, lest this elder sister, who favored their father's looks, might take his place as stern ruler of the household.

"Betsey," said the younger sister suddenly, "we'll have us a cook stove, won't we, next winter? I expect we're going to have something to do with?"

Betsey did not answer; it was impossible to say whether she truly felt grief or only assumed it. She had been sober and silent for the most part since she routed neighbor Downs, though she answered her sister's prattling questions with patience and sympathy. Now, she rose from her chair and went to one of the windows, and, pushing back the sash curtain, pulled the wooden shutter across and hasped it.

"I ain't going to bed just yet," she explained. "I've been a-waiting to make sure nobody was coming in. I don't know 's there 'll be any better time to look in the chest and see what we've got to depend on. We never 'll get no chance to do it by day."

Hannah looked frightened for a moment, then nodded, and turned to the opposite window and pulled that shutter with much difficulty; it had always caught and hitched and been provoking—a warped piece of red oak, when even-grained white pine would have saved strength and patience to three generations of the Knowles race. Then the sisters crossed the kitchen and opened the bedroom door. Hannah shivered a little as the colder air struck her, and her heart beat loudly. Perhaps it was the same with Betsey.

The bedroom was clean and orderly for the funeral guests. Instead of the blue homespun there was a beautifully quilted white coverlet which had been part of their mother's wedding furnishing, and this made the bedstead with its four low posts look unfamiliar and awesome. The lamplight shone through the kitchen door behind them, not very bright at best, but Betsey reached under the bed, and with all the strength she could muster pulled out the end of a great sea chest. The sisters tugged together and pushed, and made the most of their strength before they finally brought it through the narrow door into the kitchen. The solemnity of the deed made them both whisper as they talked, and Hannah did not dare to say what was in her timid heart—that she would rather brave discovery by daylight than such a feeling of being disapprovingly watched now, in the dead of night. There came a slight sound outside the house which made her look anxiously at Betsey, but Betsey remained tranquil.

"It's nothing but a stick falling down the woodpile," she answered in a contemptuous whisper, and the younger woman was reassured.

Betsey reached deep into her pocket and found a great key which was worn smooth and bright like silver, and never had been trusted willingly into even her own careful hands. Hannah held the lamp, and the two thin figures bent eagerly over the lid as it opened. Their shadows were waving about the low walls, and looked like strange shapes bowing and dancing behind them.

The chest was stoutly timbered, as if it were built in some ship-yard, and there were heavy wrought-iron hinges and a large escutcheon for the keyhole that the ship's blacksmith might have hammered out. On the top somebody had scratched deeply the crossed lines for a game of fox and geese, which had a trivial, irreverent look, and might have been the unforgiven fault of some idle ship's boy. The sisters had hardly dared look at the chest or to signify their knowledge of its existence, at unwary times. They had swept carefully about it year after year, and wondered if it were indeed full of gold as the neighbors used to hint; but no matter how much found a way in, little had found the way out. They had been hampered all their lives for money, and in consequence had developed a wonderful facility for spinning and weaving, mending and making. Their small farm was an early example of intensive farming; they were allowed to use its products in a niggardly way, but the money that was paid for wool, for hay, for wood, and for summer crops had all gone into the chest. The old captain was a hard master; he rarely commended and often blamed. Hannah trembled before him, but Betsey faced him sturdily, being amazingly like him, with a feminine difference; as like as a ruled person can be to a ruler, for the discipline of life had taught the man to aggress, the woman only to defend. In the chest was a fabled sum of prize-money, besides these slender earnings of many years; all the sisters' hard work and self-sacrifice were there in money and a mysterious largess besides. All their lives they had been looking forward to this hour of ownership.

There was a solemn hush in the house; the two sisters were safe from their neighbors, and there was no fear of interruption at such an hour in that hard-working community, tired with a day's work that had been early begun. If any one came knocking at the door, both door and windows were securely fastened.

The eager sisters bent above the chest, they held their breath and talked in softest whispers. With stealthy tread a man came out of the woods near by.

He stopped to listen, came nearer, stopped again, and then crept close to the old house. He stepped upon the banking, next the window with the warped shutter; there was a knothole in it high above the women's heads, towards the top. As they leaned over the chest, an eager eye watched them. If they had turned that way suspiciously, the eye might have caught the flicker of the lamp and betrayed itself. No, they were too busy: the eye at the shutter watched and watched.

There was a certain feeling of relief in the sisters' minds because the contents of the chest were so commonplace at first sight. There were some old belongings dating back to their father's early days of seafaring. They unfolded a waistcoat pattern or two of figured stuff which they had seen him fold and put away again and again. Once he had given Betsey a gay China silk handkerchief, and here were two more like it. They had not known what a store of treasures might be waiting for them, but the reality so far was disappointing; there was much spare room to begin with, and the wares within looked pinched and few. There were bundles of papers, old receipts, some letters in two not very thick bundles, some old account books with worn edges, and a blackened silver can which looked very small in comparison with their anticipation, being an heirloom and jealously hoarded and secreted by the old man. The women began to feel as if his lean angry figure were bending with them over the sea chest.

They opened a package wrapped in many layers of old soft paper—a worked piece of Indian muslin, and an embroidered red scarf which they had never seen before. "He must have brought them home to mother," said Betsey with a great outburst of feeling. "He never was the same man again; he never would let nobody else have them when he found she was dead, poor old father!"

Hannah looked wistfully at the treasures. She rebuked herself for selfishness, but she thought of her pinched girlhood and the delight these things would have been. Ah yes! it was too late now for many things besides the sprigged muslin. "If I was young as I was once there's lots o' things I'd like to do now I'm free," said Hannah with a gentle sigh; but her sister checked her anxiously—it was fitting that they should preserve a semblance of mourning even to themselves.

The lamp stood in a kitchen chair at the chest's end and shone full across their faces. Betsey looked intent and sober as she turned over the old man's treasures. Under the India mull was an antique pair of buff trousers, a waistcoat of strange old-fashioned foreign stuff, and a blue coat with brass buttons, brought home from over seas, as the women knew, for their father's wedding clothes. They had seen him carry them out at long intervals to hang them in the spring sunshine; he had been very feeble the last time, and Hannah remembered that she had longed to take them from his shaking hands.

"I declare for 't I wish't we had laid him out in 'em, 'stead o' the robe," she whispered; but Betsey made no answer. She was kneeling still, but held herself upright and looked away. It was evident that she was lost in her own thoughts.

"I can't find nothing else by eyesight," she muttered. "This chest never 'd be so heavy with them old clothes. Stop! Hold that light down, Hannah; there's a place underneath here. Them papers in the till takes a shallow part. Oh, my gracious! See here, will ye? Hold the light, hold the light!"

There was a hidden drawer in the chest's side—a long, deep place, and it was full of gold pieces. Hannah had seated herself in the chair to be out of her sister's way. She held the lamp with one hand and gathered her apron on her lap with the other, while Betsey, exultant and hawk-eyed, took out handful after handful of heavy coins, letting them jingle and chink, letting them shine in the lamp's rays, letting them roll across the floor—guineas, dollars, doubloons, old French and Spanish and English gold!

Now, now! Look! The eye at the window!

At last they have found it all; the bag of silver, the great roll of bank bills, and the heavy weight of gold—the prize-money that had been like Robinson Crusoe's in the cave. They were rich women that night; their faces grew young again as they sat side by side and exulted while the old kitchen grew cold. There was nothing they might not do within the range of their timid ambitions; they were women of fortune now and their own mistresses. They were beginning at last to live.

The watcher outside was cramped and chilled. He let himself down softly from the high step of the winter banking, and crept toward the barn, where he might bury himself in the hay and think. His fingers were quick to find the peg that opened the little barn door; the beasts within were startled and stumbled to their feet, then went back to their slumbers. The night wore on; the light spring rain began to fall, and the sound of it on the house roof close down upon the sisters' bed lulled them quickly to sleep. Twelve, one, two o'clock passed by.

They had put back the money and the clothes and the minor goods and treasures and pulled the chest back into the bedroom so that it was out of sight from the kitchen; the bedroom door was always shut by day. The younger sister wished to carry the money to their own room, but Betsey disdained such precaution. The money had always been safe in the old chest, and there it should stay. The next week they would go to Riverport and put it into the bank; it was no use to lose the interest any longer. Because their father had lost some invested money in his early youth, it did not follow that every bank was faithless. Betsey's self-assertion was amazing, but they still whispered to each other as they got ready for bed. With strange forgetfulness Betsey had laid the chest key on the white coverlet in the bedroom and left it there.

III.

In August of that year the whole countryside turned out to go to court.

The sisters had been rich for one night; in the morning they waked to find themselves poor with a bitter pang of poverty of which they had never dreamed. They had said little, but they grew suddenly pinched and old. They could not tell how much money they had lost, except that Hannah's lap was full of gold, a weight she could not lift nor carry. After a few days of stolid misery they had gone to the chief lawyer of their neighborhood to accuse Enoch Holt of the robbery. They dressed in their best and walked solemnly side by side across the fields and along the road, the shortest way to the man of law. Enoch Holt's daughter saw them go as she stood in her doorway, and felt a cold shiver run through her frame as if in foreboding. Her father was not at home; he had left for Boston late on the afternoon of Captain Knowles's funeral. He had had notice the day before of the coming in of a ship in which he owned a thirty-second; there was talk of selling the ship, and the owners' agent had summoned him. He had taken pains to go to the funeral, because he and the old captain had been on bad terms ever since they had bought a piece of woodland together, and the captain declared himself wronged at the settling of accounts. He was growing feeble even then, and had left the business to the younger man. Enoch Holt was not a trusted man, yet he had never before been openly accused of dishonesty. He was not a professor of religion, but foremost on the secular side of church matters. Most of the men in that region were hard men; it was difficult to get money, and there was little real comfort in a community where the sterner, stingier, forbidding side of New England life was well exemplified.

The proper steps had been taken by the officers of the law, and in answer to the writ Enoch Holt appeared, much shocked and very indignant, and was released on bail which covered the sum his shipping interest had brought him. The weeks had dragged by; June and July were long in passing, and here was court day at last, and all the townsfolk hastening by high-roads and by-roads to the court-house. The Knowles girls themselves had risen at break of day and walked the distance steadfastly, like two of the three Fates: who would make the third, to cut the thread for their enemy's disaster? Public opinion was divided. There were many voices ready to speak on the accused man's side; a sharp-looking acquaintance left his business in Boston to swear that Holt was in his office before noon on the day following the robbery, and that he had spent most of the night in Boston, as proved by several minor details of their interview. As for Holt's young married daughter, she was a favorite with the townsfolk, and her husband was away at sea overdue these last few weeks. She sat on one of the hard court benches with a young child in her arms, born since its father sailed; they had been more or less unlucky, the Holt family, though Enoch himself was a man of brag and bluster.

All the hot August morning, until the noon recess, and all the hot August afternoon, fly-teased and wretched with the heavy air, the crowd of neighbors listened to the trial. There was not much evidence brought; everybody knew that Enoch Holt left the funeral procession hurriedly, and went away on horseback towards Boston. His daughter knew no more than this. The Boston man gave his testimony impatiently, and one or two persons insisted that they saw the accused on his way at nightfall, several miles from home.

As the testimony came out, it all tended to prove his innocence, though public opinion was to the contrary. The Knowles
sisters looked more stern and gray hour by hour; their
vengeance was not to be satisfied; their accusation had been
listened to and found wanting, but their instinctive knowledge
of the matter counted for nothing. They must have been
watched through the knot-hole of the shutter; nobody had
noticed it until, some years before, Enoch Holt himself had
spoken of the light's shining through on a winter's night as he
came towards the house. The chief proof was that nobody else
could have done the deed. But why linger over *pros* and *cons*?
The jury returned directly with a verdict of "not proven," and
the tired audience left the court-house.

But not until Hannah Knowles with angry eyes had risen to
her feet.

The sterner elder sister tried to pull her back; every one said
that they should have looked to Betsey to say the awful words
that followed, not to her gentler companion. It was Hannah,
broken and disappointed, who cried in a strange high voice as
Enoch Holt was passing by without a look:

"You stole it, you thief! You know it in your heart!"

The startled man faltered, then he faced the women. The
people who stood near seemed made of eyes as they stared to
see what he would say.

"I swear by my right hand I never touched it."

"Curse your right hand, then!" cried Hannah Knowles,
growing tall and thin like a white flame drawing upward.
"Curse your right hand, yours and all your folks' that follow
you! May I live to see the day!"

The people drew back, while for a moment accused and ac-
cuser stood face to face. Then Holt's flushed face turned white,
and he shrank from the fire in those wild eyes, and walked
away clumsily down the courtroom. Nobody followed him,
nobody shook hands with him, or told the acquitted man that
they were glad of his release. Half an hour later, Betsey and
Hannah Knowles took their homeward way, to begin their
hard round of work again. The horizon that had widened with
such glory for one night, had closed round them again like an
iron wall.

Betsey was alarmed and excited by her sister's uncharacteristic behavior, and she looked at her anxiously from time to time. Hannah had become the harder-faced of the two. Her disappointment was the keener, for she had kept more of the unsatisfied desires of her girlhood until that dreary morning when they found the sea-chest rifled and the treasure gone.

Betsey said inconsequently that it was a pity she did not have that black silk gown that would stand alone. They had planned for it over the open chest, and Hannah's was to be a handsome green. They might have worn them to court. But even the pathetic facetiousness of her elder sister did not bring a smile to Hannah Knowles's face, and the next day one was at the loom and the other at the wheel again. The neighbors talked about the curse with horror; in their minds a fabric of sad fate was spun from the bitter words.

The Knowles sisters never had worn silk gowns and they never would. Sometimes Hannah or Betsey would stealthily look over the chest in one or the other's absence. One day when Betsey was very old and her mind had grown feeble, she tied her own India silk handkerchief about her neck, but they never used the other two. They aired the wedding suit once every spring as long as they lived. They were both too old and forlorn to make up the India mull. Nobody knows how many times they took everything out of the heavy old clamped box, and peered into every nook and corner to see if there was not a single gold piece left. They never answered any one who made bold to speak of their misfortune.

IV.

Enoch Holt had been a seafaring man in his early days, and there was news that the owners of a Salem ship in which he held a small interest wished him to go out as super-cargo. He was brisk and well in health, and his son-in-law, an honest but an unlucky fellow, had done less well than usual, so that nobody was surprised when Enoch made ready for his voyage. It was nearly a year after the theft, and nothing had come so near to restoring him to public favor as his apparent lack of ready money. He openly said that he put great hope in his adventure to the Spice Islands, and when he said farewell one Sunday to some members of the dispersing congregation, more than one person wished him heartily a pleasant voyage and safe return. He had an insinuating tone of voice and an imploring look that day, and this fact, with his probable long absence and the dangers of the deep, won him much sympathy. It is a shameful thing to accuse a man wrongfully, and Enoch Holt had behaved well since the trial; and, what is more, had shown no accession to his means of living. So away he went, with a fair amount of good wishes, though one or two persons assured remonstrating listeners that they thought it likely Enoch would make a good voyage, better than common, and show himself forwarded when he came to port. Soon after his departure, Mrs. Peter Downs and an intimate acquaintance discussed the ever-exciting subject of the Knowles robbery over a friendly cup of tea.

They were in the Downs kitchen, and quite by themselves. Peter Downs himself had been drawn as a juror, and had been for two days at the county town. Mrs. Downs was giving herself to social interests in his absence, and Mrs. Forder, an asthmatic but very companionable person, had arrived by two o'clock that afternoon with her knitting work, sure of being welcome. The two old friends had first talked over varied subjects of immediate concern, but when supper was nearly finished, they fell back upon the lost Knowles gold, as has been already said.

"They got a dreadful blow, poor gals," wheezed Mrs. Forder, with compassion. " 'T was harder for them than for most folks; they'd had a long stent with the ol' gentleman; very arbitrary, very arbitrary."

"Yes," answered Mrs. Downs, pushing back her tea-cup, then lifting it again to see if it was quite empty. "Yes, it took holt o' Hannah, the most. I should 'a' said Betsey was a good deal the most set in her ways an' would 'a' been most tore up, but 't wa'n't so."

"Lucky that Holt's folks sets on the other aisle in the meetin'-house, I do consider, so 't they needn't face each other sure as Sabbath comes round."

"I see Hannah an' him come face to face two Sabbaths afore Enoch left. So happened he dallied to have a word 'long o' Deacon Good'in, an' him an' Hannah stepped front of each other 'fore they knowed what they 's about. I sh'd thought her eyes 'd looked right through him. No one of 'em took the word; Enoch he slinked off pretty quick."

"I see 'em too," said Mrs. Forder; "made my blood run cold."

"Nothin' ain't come of the curse yit,"—Mrs. Downs lowered the tone of her voice,—"least, folks says so. It kind o' worries pore Phœbe Holt—Mis' Dow, I would say. She was narved all up at the time o' the trial, an' when her next baby come into the world, first thin' she made out t' ask me was whether it seemed likely, an' she gived me a pleadin' look as if I'd got to tell her what she hadn't heart to ask. 'Yes, dear,' says I, 'put up his little hands to me kind of wonted'; an' she turned a look on me like another creatur', so pleased an' contented."

"I s'pose you don't see no great of the Knowles gals?" inquired Mrs. Forder, who lived two miles away in the other direction.

"They stepped to the door yisterday when I was passin' by, an' I went in an' set a spell long of 'em," replied the hostess. "They'd got pestered with that ol' loom o' theirn. 'Fore I thought, says I, ''T is all worn out, Betsey,' says I. 'Why on airth don't ye git somebody to git some o' your own wood an' season it well so 't won't warp, same 's mine done, an' build ye a new one?' But Betsey muttered an' twitched away; 't wa'n't like her, but they're dis'p'inted at every turn, I s'pose, an' feel poor where they've got the same 's ever to do with. Hannah's a-coughin' this spring 's if somethin' ailed her. I asked her if she had bad feelin's in her pipes, an' she said yis, she had, but not to speak of 't before Betsey. I'm goin' to fix her up some hoarhound an' elecampane quick 's the ground 's nice an' warm an' roots livens up a grain more. They're limp an' wizened 'long to the fust of the spring. Them would be service'ble, simmered away to a syrup 'long o' molasses; now don't you think so, Mis' Forder?"

"Excellent," replied the wheezing dame. "I covet a portion myself, now you speak. Nothin' cures my complaint, but a new remedy takes holt clever sometimes, an' eases me for a spell." And she gave a plaintive sigh, and began to knit again.

Mrs. Downs rose and pushed the supper-table to the wall and drew her chair nearer to the stove. The April nights were chilly.

"The folks is late comin' after me," said Mrs. Forder, ostentatiously. "I may 's well confess that I told 'em if they was late

with the work they might let go o' fetchin' o' me an' I'd walk
home in the mornin'; take it easy when I was fresh. Course I
mean ef 't wouldn't put you out: I knowed you was all alone,
an' I kind o' wanted a change."

"Them words was in my mind to utter while we was to
table," avowed Mrs. Downs, hospitably. "I ain't reelly afeared,
but 't is sort o' creepy fastenin' up an' goin' to bed alone. Nobody can't help hearkin', an' every common noise starts you. I
never used to give nothin' a thought till the Knowleses was
robbed, though."

"'Twas mysterious, I do maintain," acknowledged Mrs.
Forder. "Comes over me sometimes p'raps 't wasn't Enoch;
he'd 'a' branched out more in course o' time. I'm waitin' to
see if he does extry well to sea 'fore I let my mind come to bear
on his bein' clean handed."

"Plenty thought 't was the ole Cap'n come back for it an'
sperited it away. Enough said that 't wasn't no honest gains;
most on 't was prize-money o' slave ships, an' all kinds o' devil's
gold was mixed in. I s'pose you've heard that said?"

"Time an' again," responded Mrs. Forder; "an' the worst
on 't was simple old Pappy Flanders went an' told the Knowles
gals themselves that folks thought the ole Cap'n come back
an' got it, and Hannah done wrong to cuss Enoch Holt an' his
ginerations after him the way she done."

"I think it took holt on her ter'ble after all she'd gone
through," said Mrs. Downs, compassionately. "He ain't near
so simple as he is ugly, Pappy Flanders ain't. I've seen him set
here an' read the paper sober 's anybody when I've been goin'
about my mornin's work in the shed-room, an' when I'd come
in to look about he'd twist it with his hands an' roll his eyes an'
begin to git off some o' his gable. I think them wanderin'
cheap-wits likes the fun on 't an' 'scapes stiddy work, an' gits
the rovin' habit so fixed, it sp'iles 'em."

"My gran'ther was to the South Seas in his young days," related Mrs. Forder, impressively, "an' he said cussin' was common there. I mean sober spitin' with a cuss. He seen one o'
them black folks git a gredge against another an' go an' set
down an' look stiddy at him in his hut an' cuss him in his mind
an' set there an' watch, watch, until the other kind o' took sick
an' died, all in a fortnight, I believe he said; 't would make

your blood run cold to hear gran'ther describe it, 't would so. He never done nothin' but set an' look, an' folks would give him somethin' to eat now an' then, as if they thought 't was all right, an' the other one 'd try to go an' come, an' at last he hived away altogether an' died. I don't know what you'd call it that ailed him. There 's suthin' in cussin' that 's bad for folks, now I tell ye, Mis Downs."

"Hannah's eyes always makes me creepy now," Mrs. Downs confessed uneasily. "They don't look pleadin' an' childish same 's they used to. Seems to me as if she'd had the worst on 't."

"We ain't seen the end on 't yit," said Mrs. Forder, impressively. "I feel it within me, Marthy Downs, an' it 's a terrible thing to have happened right amon'st us in Christian times. If we live long enough we're goin' to have plenty to talk over in our old age that 's come o' that cuss. Some seed 's shy o' sproutin' till a spring when the s'ile 's jest right to breed it."

"There 's lobeely now," agreed Mrs. Downs, pleased to descend to prosaic and familiar levels. "They ain't a good crop one year in six, and then you find it in a place where you never observed none to grow afore, like 's not; ain't it so, reelly?" And she rose to clear the table, pleased with the certainty of a guest that night. Their conversation was not reassuring to the heart of a timid woman, alone in an isolated farmhouse on a dark spring evening, especially so near the anniversary of old Captain Knowles's death.

V.

Later in these rural lives by many years two aged women were crossing a wide field together, following a footpath such as one often finds between widely separated homes of the New England country. Along these lightly traced thoroughfares, the children go to play, and lovers to plead, and older people to companion one another in work and pleasure, in sickness and sorrow; generation after generation comes and goes again by these country by-ways.

The footpath led from Mrs. Forder's to another farmhouse half a mile beyond, where there had been a wedding. Mrs. Downs was there, and in the June weather she had been easily persuaded to go home to tea with Mrs. Forder with the promise of being driven home later in the evening. Mrs. Downs's husband had been dead three years, and her friend's large family was scattered from the old nest; they were lonely at times in their later years, these old friends, and found it very pleasant now to have a walk together. Thin little Mrs. Forder, with all her wheezing, was the stronger and more active of the two; Mrs. Downs had grown heavier and weaker with advancing years.

They paced along the footpath slowly, Mrs. Downs rolling in her gait like a sailor, and availing herself of every pretext to stop and look at herbs in the pasture ground they crossed, and at the growing grass in the mowing fields. They discussed the wedding minutely, and then where the way grew wider they walked side by side instead of following each other, and their voices sank to the low tone that betokens confidence.

"You don't say that you really put faith in all them old stories?"

"It ain't accident altogether, noways you can fix it in your mind," maintained Mrs. Downs. "Needn't tell me that cussin' don't do neither good nor harm. I shouldn't want to marry amon'st the Holts if I was young ag'in! I r'member when this young man was born that 's married to-day, an' the fust thing his poor mother wanted to know was about his hands bein' right. I said yes they was, but las' year he was twenty year old and come home from the frontier with one o' them hands— his right one—shot off in a fight. They say 't happened to sights o' other fellows, an' their laigs gone too, but I count 'em over on my fingers, them Holts, an' he 's the third. May say that 't was all an accident his mother's gittin' throwed out o' her waggin comin' home from meetin', an' her wrist not bein' set good, an' she, bein' run down at the time, 'most lost it altogether, but thar' it is, stiffened up an' no good to her. There was the second. An' Enoch Holt hisself come home from the Chiny seas, made a good passage an' a sight o' money in the pepper trade, jest 's we expected, an' goin' to build him a new house, an' the frame gives a kind o' lurch when they was raisin' of it an' surges over on to him an' nips him under. 'Which arm?' says everybody along the road when they was comin' an' goin' with the doctor. 'Right one—got to lose it,' says the doctor to 'em, an' next time Enoch Holt got out to meetin' he stood up in the house o' God with the hymn-book in his left hand, an' no right hand to turn his leaf with. He knowed what we was all a-thinkin'."

"Well," said Mrs. Forder, very short-breathed with climbing the long slope of the pasture hill, "I don't know but I'd as soon be them as the Knowles gals. Hannah never knowed no peace again after she spoke them words in the co't-house. They come back an' harnted her, an' you know, Miss Downs, better 'n I do, being door-neighbors as one may say, how they lived their lives out like wild beasts into a lair."

"They used to go out some by night to git the air," pursued Mrs. Downs with interest. "I used to open the door an' step right in, an' I used to take their yarn an' stuff 'long o' mine an' sell 'em, an' do for the poor stray creatur 's long 's they'd let me. They'd be grateful for a mess o' early pease or potatoes as ever you see, an' Peter he allays favored 'em with pork, fresh an' salt, when we slaughtered. The old Cap'n kept 'em child'n long as he lived, an' then they was too old to l'arn different. I allays liked Hannah the best till that change struck her. Betsey she held out to the last jest about the same. I don't know, now I come to think of it, but what she felt it the most o' the two."

"They'd never let me 's much as git a look at 'em," complained Mrs. Forder. "Folks got awful stories a-goin' one time. I've heard it said, an' it allays creeped me cold all over, that there was somethin' come an' lived with 'em—a kind o' black shadder, a cobweb kind o' a man-shape that followed 'em about the house an' made a third to them; but they got hardened to it theirselves, only they was afraid 't would follow if they went anywheres from home. You don't believe no such piece o' nonsense?—But there, I've asked ye times enough before."

"They'd got shadders enough, poor creatur's," said Mrs. Downs with reserve. "Wasn't no kind o' need to make 'em up no spooks, as I know on. Well, here's these young folks a-startin'; I wish 'em well, I'm sure. She likes him with his one hand better than most gals likes them as has a good sound pair. They looked prime happy; I hope no curse won't foller 'em."

The friends stopped again—poor, short-winded bodies—on the crest of the low hill and turned to look at the wide landscape, bewildered by the marvelous beauty and the sudden flood of golden sunset light that poured out of the western sky. They could not remember that they had ever observed the wide view before; it was like a revelation or an outlook towards the celestial country, the sight of their own green farms and the countryside that bounded them. It was a pleasant country indeed, their own New England: their petty thoughts and vain imaginings seemed futile and unrelated to so fair a scene of things. But the figure of a man who was crossing the meadow below looked like a malicious black insect. It was an old man, it was Enoch Holt; time had worn and bent him enough to have satisfied his bitterest foe. The women could see his empty coat-sleeve flutter as he walked slowly and unexpectantly in that glorious evening light.

1890

CHARLOTTE PERKINS GILMAN
(1860–1935)

The Yellow Wall Paper

IT is very seldom that mere ordinary people like John and myself secure ancestral halls for the summer.

A colonial mansion, a hereditary estate, I would say a
haunted house, and reach the height of romantic felicity,—but
that would be asking too much of fate!

Still I will proudly declare that there is something queer
about it.

Else, why should it be let so cheaply? And why have stood so
long untenanted?

John laughs at me, of course, but one expects that in
marriage.

John is practical in the extreme. He has no patience with faith,
an intense horror of superstition, and he scoffs openly at any talk
of things not to be felt and seen and put down in figures.

John is a physician, and *perhaps*—(I would not say it to a living
soul, of course, but this is dead paper and a great relief to my
mind)—*perhaps* that is one reason I do not get well faster.

You see, he does not believe I am sick!

And what can one do?

If a physician of high standing, and one's own husband, as-
sures friends and relatives that there is really nothing the
matter with one but temporary nervous depression,—a slight
hysterical tendency,—what is one to do?

My brother is also a physician, and also of high standing,
and he says the same thing.

So I take phosphates or phosphites,—whichever it is,—and
tonics, and journeys, and air, and exercise, and am absolutely
forbidden to "work" until I am well again.

Personally I disagree with their ideas.

Personally I believe that congenial work, with excitement and
change, would do me good.

But what is one to do?

I did write for a while in spite of them; but it *does* exhaust me a good deal—having to be so sly about it, or else meet with heavy opposition.

I sometimes fancy that in my condition if I had less opposition and more society and stimulus—but John says the very worst thing I can do is to think about my condition, and I confess it always makes me feel bad.

So I will let it alone and talk about the house.

The most beautiful place! It is quite alone, standing well back from the road, quite three miles from the village. It makes me think of English places that you read about, for there are hedges and walls and gates that lock, and lots of separate little houses for the gardeners and people.

There is a *delicious* garden! I never saw such a garden—large and shady, full of box-bordered paths, and lined with long grape-covered arbors with seats under them.

There were greenhouses, too, but they are all broken now.

There was some legal trouble, I believe, something about the heirs and co-heirs; anyhow, the place has been empty for years.

That spoils my ghostliness, I am afraid; but I don't care— there is something strange about the house—I can feel it.

I even said so to John one moonlight evening, but he said what I felt was a *draught* and shut the window.

I get unreasonably angry with John sometimes. I'm sure I never used to be so sensitive. I think it is due to this nervous condition.

But John says if I feel so I shall neglect proper self-control; so I take pains to control myself,—before him, at least,—and that makes me very tired.

I don't like our room a bit. I wanted one downstairs that opened on the piazza and had roses all over the window, and such pretty, old-fashioned chintz hangings! but John would not hear of it.

He said there was only one window and not room for two beds, and no near room for him if he took another.

He is very careful and loving, and hardly lets me stir without special direction.

I have a schedule prescription for each hour in the day; he takes all care from me, and so I feel basely ungrateful not to value it more.

He said we came here solely on my account, that I was to have perfect rest and all the air I could get. "Your exercise depends on your strength, my dear," said he, "and your food somewhat on your appetite; but air you can absorb all the time." So we took the nursery, at the top of the house.

It is a big, airy room, the whole floor nearly, with windows that look all ways, and air and sunshine galore. It was nursery first and then playground and gymnasium, I should judge; for the windows are barred for little children, and there are rings and things in the walls.

The paint and paper look as if a boys' school had used it. It is stripped off—the paper—in great patches all around the head of my bed, about as far as I can reach, and in a great place on the other side of the room low down. I never saw a worse paper in my life.

One of those sprawling flamboyant patterns committing every artistic sin.

It is dull enough to confuse the eye in following, pronounced enough to constantly irritate, and provoke study, and when you follow the lame, uncertain curves for a little distance they suddenly commit suicide—plunge off at outrageous angles, destroy themselves in unheard-of contradictions.

The color is repellant, almost revolting; a smouldering, unclean yellow, strangely faded by the slow-turning sunlight.

It is a dull yet lurid orange in some places, a sickly sulphur tint in others.

No wonder the children hated it! I should hate it myself if I had to live in this room long.

There comes John, and I must put this away,—he hates to have me write a word.

We have been here two weeks, and I haven't felt like writing before, since that first day.

I am sitting by the window now, up in this atrocious nursery, and there is nothing to hinder my writing as much as I please, save lack of strength.

John is away all day, and even some nights when his cases are serious.

I am glad my case is not serious!

But these nervous troubles are dreadfully depressing.

John does not know how much I really suffer. He knows there is no *reason* to suffer, and that satisfies him.

Of course it is only nervousness. It does weigh on me so not to do my duty in any way!

I meant to be such a help to John, such a real rest and comfort, and here I am a comparative burden already!

Nobody would believe what an effort it is to do what little I am able—to dress and entertain, and order things.

It is fortunate Mary is so good with the baby. Such a dear baby!

And yet I *cannot* be with him, it makes me so nervous.

I suppose John never was nervous in his life. He laughs at me so about this wall paper!

At first he meant to repaper the room, but afterwards he said that I was letting it get the better of me, and that nothing was worse for a nervous patient than to give way to such fancies.

He said that after the wall paper was changed it would be the heavy bedstead, and then the barred windows, and then that gate at the head of the stairs, and so on.

"You know the place is doing you good," he said, "and really, dear, I don't care to renovate the house just for a three months' rental."

"Then do let us go downstairs," I said, "there are such pretty rooms there."

Then he took me in his arms and called me a blessed little goose, and said he would go down cellar if I wished, and have it whitewashed into the bargain.

But he is right enough about the beds and windows and things.

It is as airy and comfortable a room as any one need wish, and, of course, I would not be so silly as to make him uncomfortable just for a whim.

I'm really getting quite fond of the big room, all but that horrid paper.

Out of one window I can see the garden, those mysterious

deep-shaded arbors, the riotous old-fashioned flowers, and bushes and gnarly trees.

Out of another I get a lovely view of the bay and a little private wharf belonging to the estate. There is a beautiful shaded lane that runs down there from the house. I always fancy I see people walking in these numerous paths and arbors, but John has cautioned me not to give way to fancy in the least. He says that with my imaginative power and habit of story-making a nervous weakness like mine is sure to lead to all manner of excited fancies, and that I ought to use my will and good sense to check the tendency. So I try.

I think sometimes that if I were only well enough to write a little it would relieve the press of ideas and rest me.

But I find I get pretty tired when I try.

It is so discouraging not to have any advice and companionship about my work. When I get really well John says we will ask Cousin Henry and Julia down for a long visit; but he says he would as soon put fire-works in my pillow-case as to let me have those stimulating people about now.

I wish I could get well faster.

But I must not think about that. This paper looks to me as if it *knew* what a vicious influence it had!

There is a recurrent spot where the pattern lolls like a broken neck and two bulbous eyes stare at you upside-down.

I got positively angry with the impertinence of it and the everlastingness. Up and down and sideways they crawl, and those absurd, unblinking eyes are everywhere. There is one place where two breadths didn't match, and the eyes go all up and down the line, one a little higher than the other.

I never saw so much expression in an inanimate thing before, and we all know how much expression they have! I used to lie awake as a child and get more entertainment and terror out of blank walls and plain furniture than most children could find in a toy-store.

I remember what a kindly wink the knobs of our big old bureau used to have, and there was one chair that always seemed like a strong friend.

I used to feel that if any of the other things looked too fierce I could always hop into that chair and be safe.

The furniture in this room is no worse than inharmonious,

however, for we had to bring it all from downstairs. I suppose when this was used as a playroom they had to take the nursery things out, and no wonder! I never saw such ravages as the children have made here.

The wall paper, as I said before, is torn off in spots, and it sticketh closer than a brother—they must have had perseverance as well as hatred.

Then the floor is scratched and gouged and splintered, the plaster itself is dug out here and there, and this great heavy bed, which is all we found in the room, looks as if it had been through the wars.

But I don't mind it a bit—only the paper.

There comes John's sister. Such a dear girl as she is, and so careful of me! I must not let her find me writing.

She is a perfect, an enthusiastic housekeeper, and hopes for no better profession. I verily believe she thinks it is the writing which made me sick!

But I can write when she is out, and see her a long way off from these windows.

There is one that commands the road, a lovely, shaded, winding road, and one that just looks off over the country. A lovely country, too, full of great elms and velvet meadows.

This wall paper has a kind of sub-pattern in a different shade, a particularly irritating one, for you can only see it in certain lights, and not clearly then.

But in the places where it isn't faded, and where the sun is just so, I can see a strange, provoking, formless sort of figure, that seems to sulk about behind that silly and conspicuous front design.

There's sister on the stairs!

Well, the Fourth of July is over! The people are all gone and I am tired out. John thought it might do me good to see a little company, so we just had mother and Nellie and the children down for a week.

Of course I didn't do a thing. Jennie sees to everything now.

But it tired me all the same.

John says if I don't pick up faster he shall send me to Weir Mitchell in the fall.

But I don't want to go there at all. I had a friend who was in his hands once, and she says he is just like John and my brother, only more so!

Besides, it is such an undertaking to go so far.

I don't feel as if it was worth while to turn my hand over for anything, and I'm getting dreadfully fretful and querulous.

I cry at nothing, and cry most of the time.

Of course I don't when John is here, or anybody else, but when I am alone.

And I am alone a good deal just now. John is kept in town very often by serious cases, and Jennie is good and lets me alone when I want her to.

So I walk a little in the garden or down that lovely lane, sit on the porch under the roses, and lie down up here a good deal.

I'm getting really fond of the room in spite of the wall paper. Perhaps *because* of the wall paper.

It dwells in my mind so!

I lie here on this great immovable bed—it is nailed down, I believe—and follow that pattern about by the hour. It is as good as gymnastics, I assure you. I start, we'll say, at the bottom, down in the corner over there where it has not been touched, and I determine for the thousandth time that I *will* follow that pointless pattern to some sort of a conclusion.

I know a little of the principles of design, and I know this thing was not arranged on any laws of radiation, or alternation, or repetition, or symmetry, or anything else that I ever heard of.

It is repeated, of course, by the breadths, but not otherwise.

Looked at in one way, each breadth stands alone, the bloated curves and flourishes—a kind of "debased Romanesque" with *delirium tremens*—go waddling up and down in isolated columns of fatuity.

But, on the other hand, they connect diagonally, and the sprawling outlines run off in great slanting waves of optic horror, like a lot of wallowing seaweeds in full chase.

The whole thing goes horizontally, too, at least it seems so, and I exhaust myself in trying to distinguish the order of its going in that direction.

They have used a horizontal breadth for a frieze, and that adds wonderfully to the confusion.

There is one end of the room where it is almost intact, and there, when the cross-lights fade and the low sun shines directly upon it, I can almost fancy radiation, after all,—the interminable grotesques seem to form around a common centre and rush off in head-long plunges of equal distraction.

It makes me tired to follow it. I will take a nap, I guess.

I don't know why I should write this.

I don't want to.

I don't feel able.

And I know John would think it absurd. But I *must* say what I feel and think in some way—it is such a relief!

But the effort is getting to be greater than the relief.

Half the time now I am awfully lazy, and lie down ever so much.

John says I mustn't lose my strength, and has me take cod-liver oil and lots of tonics and things, to say nothing of ale and wine and rare meat.

Dear John! He loves me very dearly, and hates to have me sick. I tried to have a real earnest reasonable talk with him the other day, and tell him how I wished he would let me go and make a visit to Cousin Henry and Julia.

But he said I wasn't able to go, nor able to stand it after I got there; and I did not make out a very good case for myself, for I was crying before I had finished.

It is getting to be a great effort for me to think straight. Just this nervous weakness, I suppose.

And dear John gathered me up in his arms, and just carried me upstairs and laid me on the bed, and sat by me and read to me till he tired my head.

He said I was his darling and his comfort and all he had, and that I must take care of myself for his sake, and keep well.

He says no one but myself can help me out of it, that I must use my will and self-control and not let my silly fancies run away with me.

There's one comfort, the baby is well and happy, and does not have to occupy this nursery with the horrid wall paper.

If we had not used it that blessed child would have! What a fortunate escape! Why, I wouldn't have a child of mine, an impressionable little thing, live in such a room for worlds.

I never thought of it before, but it is lucky that John kept me here, after all. I can stand it so much easier than a baby, you see.

Of course I never mention it to them any more,—I am too wise,—but I keep watch of it all the same.

There are things in that paper that nobody knows but me, or ever will.

Behind that outside pattern the dim shapes get clearer every day.

It is always the same shape, only very numerous.

And it is like a woman stooping down and creeping about behind that pattern. I don't like it a bit. I wonder—I begin to think—I wish John would take me away from here!

It is so hard to talk with John about my case, because he is so wise, and because he loves me so.

But I tried it last night.

It was moonlight. The moon shines in all around, just as the sun does.

I hate to see it sometimes, it creeps so slowly, and always comes in by one window or another.

John was asleep and I hated to waken him, so I kept still and watched the moonlight on that undulating wall paper till I felt creepy.

The faint figure behind seemed to shake the pattern, just as if she wanted to get out.

I got up softly and went to feel and see if the paper *did* move, and when I came back John was awake.

"What is it, little girl?" he said. "Don't go walking about like that—you'll get cold."

I thought it was a good time to talk, so I told him that I really was not gaining here, and that I wished he would take me away.

"Why, darling!" said he, "our lease will be up in three weeks, and I can't see how to leave before.

"The repairs are not done at home, and I cannot possibly leave town just now. Of course if you were in any danger I could and would, but you really are better, dear, whether you can see it or not. I am a doctor, dear, and I know. You are gaining flesh and color, your appetite is better. I feel really much easier about you."

"I don't weigh a bit more," said I, "nor as much; and my appetite may be better in the evening, when you are here, but it is worse in the morning, when you are away."

"Bless her little heart!" said he with a big hug; "she shall be as sick as she pleases. But now let's improve the shining hours by going to sleep, and talk about it in the morning."

"And you won't go away?" I asked gloomily.

"Why, how can I, dear? It is only three weeks more and then we will take a nice little trip of a few days while Jennie is getting the house ready. Really, dear, you are better!"

"Better in body, perhaps"—I began, and stopped short, for he sat up straight and looked at me with such a stern, reproachful look that I could not say another word.

"My darling," said he, "I beg of you, for my sake and for our child's sake, as well as for your own, that you will never for one instant let that idea enter your mind! There is nothing so dangerous, so fascinating, to a temperament like yours. It is a false and foolish fancy. Can you not trust me as a physician when I tell you so?"

So of course I said no more on that score, and we went to sleep before long. He thought I was asleep first, but I wasn't,— I lay there for hours trying to decide whether that front pattern and the back pattern really did move together or separately.

On a pattern like this, by daylight, there is a lack of sequence, a defiance of law, that is a constant irritant to a normal mind.

The color is hideous enough, and unreliable enough, and infuriating enough, but the pattern is torturing.

You think you have mastered it, but just as you get well under way in following, it turns a back somersault, and there you are. It slaps you in the face, knocks you down, and tramples upon you. It is like a bad dream.

The outside pattern is a florid arabesque, reminding one of a fungus. If you can imagine a toadstool in joints, an interminable string of toadstools, budding and sprouting in endless convolutions,—why, that is something like it.

That is, sometimes!

There is one marked peculiarity about this paper, a thing nobody seems to notice but myself, and that is that it changes as the light changes.

When the sun shoots in through the east window—I always watch for that first long, straight ray—it changes so quickly that I never can quite believe it.

That is why I watch it always.

By moonlight—the moon shines in all night when there is a moon—I wouldn't know it was the same paper.

At night in any kind of light, in twilight, candlelight, lamplight, and worst of all by moonlight, it becomes bars! The outside pattern, I mean, and the woman behind it is as plain as can be.

I didn't realize for a long time what the thing was that showed behind,—that dim sub-pattern,—but now I am quite sure it is a woman.

By daylight she is subdued, quiet. I fancy it is the pattern that keeps her so still. It is so puzzling. It keeps me quiet by the hour.

I lie down ever so much now. John says it is good for me, and to sleep all I can.

Indeed, he started the habit by making me lie down for an hour after each meal.

It is a very bad habit, I am convinced, for, you see, I don't sleep.

And that cultivates deceit, for I don't tell them I'm awake,—oh, no!

The fact is, I am getting a little afraid of John.

He seems very queer sometimes, and even Jennie has an inexplicable look.

It strikes me occasionally, just as a scientific hypothesis, that perhaps it is the paper!

I have watched John when he did not know I was looking, and come into the room suddenly on the most innocent excuses, and I've caught him several times *looking at the paper!* And Jennie too. I caught Jennie with her hand on it once.

She didn't know I was in the room, and when I asked her in a quiet, a very quiet voice, with the most restrained manner possible, what she was doing with the paper she turned around as if she had been caught stealing, and looked quite angry— asked me why I should frighten her so!

Then she said that the paper stained everything it touched, that she had found yellow smooches on all my clothes and John's, and she wished we would be more careful!

Did not that sound innocent? But I know she was studying that pattern, and I am determined that nobody shall find it out but myself!

*

Life is very much more exciting now than it used to be. You see I have something more to expect, to look forward to, to watch. I really do eat better, and am more quiet than I was.

John is so pleased to see me improve! He laughed a little the other day, and said I seemed to be flourishing in spite of my wall paper.

I turned it off with a laugh. I had no intention of telling him it was *because* of the wall paper—he would make fun of me. He might even want to take me away.

I don't want to leave now until I have found it out. There is a week more, and I think that will be enough.

I'm feeling ever so much better! I don't sleep much at night, for it is so interesting to watch developments; but I sleep a good deal in the daytime.

In the daytime it is tiresome and perplexing.

There are always new shoots on the fungus, and new shades of yellow all over it. I cannot keep count of them, though I have tried conscientiously.

It is the strangest yellow, that wall paper! It makes me think of all the yellow things I ever saw—not beautiful ones like buttercups, but old foul, bad yellow things.

But there is something else about that paper—the smell! I noticed it the moment we came into the room, but with so much air and sun it was not bad. Now we have had a week of fog and rain, and whether the windows are open or not the smell is here.

It creeps all over the house.

I find it hovering in the dining-room, skulking in the parlor, hiding in the hall, lying in wait for me on the stairs.

It gets into my hair.

Even when I go to ride, if I turn my head suddenly and surprise it—there is that smell!

Such a peculiar odor, too! I have spent hours in trying to analyze it, to find what it smelled like.

It is not bad—at first, and very gentle, but quite the subtlest, most enduring odor I ever met.

In this damp weather it is awful. I wake up in the night and find it hanging over me.

It used to disturb me at first. I thought seriously of burning the house—to reach the smell.

But now I am used to it. The only thing I can think of that it is like is the *color* of the paper—a yellow smell!

There is a very funny mark on this wall, low down, near the mopboard. A streak that runs around the room. It goes behind every piece of furniture, except the bed, a long, straight, even *smooch*, as if it had been rubbed over and over.

I wonder how it was done and who did it, and what they did it for. Round and round and round—round and round and round—it makes me dizzy!

I really have discovered something at last.

Through watching so much at night, when it changes so, I have finally found out.

The front pattern *does* move—and no wonder! The woman behind shakes it!

Sometimes I think there are a great many women behind, and sometimes only one, and she crawls around fast, and her crawling shakes it all over.

Then in the very bright spots she keeps still, and in the very shady spots she just takes hold of the bars and shakes them hard.

And she is all the time trying to climb through. But nobody could climb through that pattern—it strangles so; I think that is why it has so many heads.

They get through, and then the pattern strangles them off and turns them upside-down, and makes their eyes white!

If those heads were covered or taken off it would not be half so bad.

I think that woman gets out in the daytime!

And I'll tell you why—privately—I've seen her!

I can see her out of every one of my windows!

It is the same woman, I know, for she is always creeping, and most women do not creep by daylight.

I see her in that long shaded lane, creeping up and down. I see her in those dark grape arbors, creeping all around the garden.

I see her on that long road under the trees, creeping along, and when a carriage comes she hides under the blackberry vines.

I don't blame her a bit. It must be very humiliating to be caught creeping by daylight!

I always lock the door when I creep by daylight. I can't do it at night, for I know John would suspect something at once.

And John is so queer, now, that I don't want to irritate him. I wish he would take another room! Besides, I don't want anybody to get that woman out at night but myself.

I often wonder if I could see her out of all the windows at once.

But, turn as fast as I can, I can only see out of one at one time.

And though I always see her she *may* be able to creep faster than I can turn!

I have watched her sometimes away off in the open country, creeping as fast as a cloud shadow in a high wind.

If only that top pattern could be gotten off from the under one! I mean to try it, little by little.

I have found out another funny thing, but I shan't tell it this time! It does not do to trust people too much.

There are only two more days to get this paper off, and I believe John is beginning to notice. I don't like the look in his eyes.

And I heard him ask Jennie a lot of professional questions about me. She had a very good report to give.

She said I slept a good deal in the daytime.

John knows I don't sleep very well at night, for all I'm so quiet!

He asked me all sorts of questions, too, and pretended to be very loving and kind.

As if I couldn't see through him!

Still, I don't wonder he acts so, sleeping under this paper for three months.

It only interests me, but I feel sure John and Jennie are secretly affected by it.

Hurrah! This is the last day, but it is enough. John is to stay in town over night, and won't be out until this evening.

Jennie wanted to sleep with me—the sly thing! but I told her I should undoubtedly rest better for a night all alone.

That was clever, for really I wasn't alone a bit! As soon as it was moonlight, and that poor thing began to crawl and shake the pattern, I got up and ran to help her.

I pulled and she shook, I shook and she pulled, and before morning we had peeled off yards of that paper.

A strip about as high as my head and half around the room.

And then when the sun came and that awful pattern began to laugh at me I declared I would finish it to-day!

We go away to-morrow, and they are moving all my furniture down again to leave things as they were before.

Jennie looked at the wall in amazement, but I told her merrily that I did it out of pure spite at the vicious thing.

She laughed and said she wouldn't mind doing it herself, but I must not get tired.

How she betrayed herself that time!

But I am here, and no person touches this paper but me— not *alive*!

She tried to get me out of the room—it was too patent! But I said it was so quiet and empty and clean now that I believed I would lie down again and sleep all I could; and not to wake me even for dinner—I would call when I woke.

So now she is gone, and the servants are gone, and the things are gone, and there is nothing left but that great bedstead nailed down, with the canvas mattress we found on it.

We shall sleep downstairs to-night, and take the boat home to-morrow.

I quite enjoy the room, now it is bare again.

How those children did tear about here!

This bedstead is fairly gnawed!

But I must get to work.

I have locked the door and thrown the key down into the front path.

I don't want to go out, and I don't want to have anybody come in, till John comes.

I want to astonish him.

I've got a rope up here that even Jennie did not find. If that woman does get out, and tries to get away, I can tie her!

But I forgot I could not reach far without anything to stand on!

This bed will *not* move!

I tried to lift and push it until I was lame, and then I got so angry I bit off a little piece at one corner—but it hurt my teeth.

Then I peeled off all the paper I could reach standing on the floor. It sticks horribly and the pattern just enjoys it! All those strangled heads and bulbous eyes and waddling fungus growths just shriek with derision!

I am getting angry enough to do something desperate. To jump out of the window would be admirable exercise, but the bars are too strong even to try.

Besides, I wouldn't do it. Of course not. I know well enough that a step like that is improper and might be misconstrued.

I don't like to *look* out of the windows even—there are so many of those creeping women, and they creep so fast.

I wonder if they all come out of that wall paper, as I did?

But I am securely fastened now by my well-hidden rope—you don't get *me* out in the road there!

I suppose I shall have to get back behind the pattern when it comes night, and that is hard!

It is so pleasant to be out in this great room and creep around as I please!

I don't want to go outside. I won't, even if Jennie asks me to.

For outside you have to creep on the ground, and everything is green instead of yellow.

But here I can creep smoothly on the floor, and my shoulder just fits in that long smooch around the wall, so I cannot lose my way.

Why, there's John at the door!

It is no use, young man, you can't open it!

How he does call and pound!

Now he's crying for an axe.

It would be a shame to break down that beautiful door!

"John, dear!" said I in the gentlest voice, "the key is down by the front steps, under a plantain leaf!"

That silenced him for a few moments.

Then he said—very quietly indeed, "Open the door, my darling!"

"I can't," said I. "The key is down by the front door, under a plantain leaf!"

And then I said it again, several times, very gently and

slowly, and said it so often that he had to go and see, and he got it, of course, and came in. He stopped short by the door.

"What is the matter?" he cried.

"For God's sake, what are you doing?"

I kept on creeping just the same, but I looked at him over my shoulder.

"I've got out at last," said I, "in spite of you and Jane! And I've pulled off most of the paper, so you can't put me back!"

Now why should that man have fainted? But he did, and right across my path by the wall, so that I had to creep over him every time!

1892

STEPHEN CRANE
(1871–1900)

The Black Dog

THERE was a ceaseless rumble in the air as the heavy raindrops battered upon the laurel-thickets and the matted moss and haggard rocks beneath. Four water-soaked men made their difficult ways through the drenched forest. The little man stopped and shook an angry finger at where night was stealthily following them. "Cursed be fate and her children and her children's children! We are everlastingly lost!" he cried. The panting procession halted under some dripping, drooping hemlocks and swore in wrathful astonishment.

"It will rain for forty days and forty nights," said the pudgy man, moaningly, "and I feel like a wet loaf of bread, now. We shall never find our way out of this wilderness until I am made into a porridge."

In desperation, they started again to drag their listless bodies through the watery bushes. After a time, the clouds withdrew from above them and great winds came from concealment and went sweeping and swirling among the trees. Night also came very near and menaced the wanderers with darkness. The little man had determination in his legs. He scrambled among the thickets and made desperate attempts to find a path or road. As he climbed a hillock, he espied a small clearing upon which sat desolation and a venerable house, wept over by wind-waved pines.

"Ho," he cried, "here's a house."

His companions straggled painfully after him as he fought the thickets between him and the cabin. At their approach, the wind frenziedly opposed them and skirled madly in the trees. The little man boldly confronted the weird glances from the crannies of the cabin and rapped on the door. A score of timbers answered with groans and, within, something fell to the floor with a clang.

"Ho," said the little man. He stepped back a few paces.

Somebody in a distant part started and walked across the floor toward the door with an ominous step. A slate-colored man appeared. He was dressed in a ragged shirt and trousers, the latter stuffed into his boots. Large tears were falling from his eyes.

"How-d'-do, my friend?" said the little man, affably.

"My ol' uncle, Jim Crocker, he's sick ter death," replied the slate-colored person.

"Ho," said the little man. "Is that so?"

The latter's clothing clung desperately to him and water sogged in his boots. He stood patiently on one foot for a time.

"Can you put us up here until to-morrow?" he asked, finally.

"Yes," said the slate-colored man.

The party passed into a little unwashed room, inhabited by a stove, a stairway, a few precarious chairs and a misshapen table.

"I'll fry yer some po'k and make yer some coffee," said the slate-colored man to his guests.

"Go ahead, old boy," cried the little man cheerfully from where he sat on the table, smoking his pipe and dangling his legs.

"My ol' uncle, Jim Crocker, he's sick ter death," said the slate-colored man.

"Think he'll die?" asked the pudgy man, gently.

"No!"

"No?"

"He won't die! He's an ol' man, but he won't die, yit! The black dorg hain't been around yit!"

"The black dog?" said the little man, feebly. He struggled with himself for a moment.

"What's the black dog?" he asked at last.

"He's a sperrit," said the slate-colored man in a voice of sombre hue.

"Oh, he is? Well?"

"He hants these parts, he does, an' when people are goin' ter die, he comes an' sets an' howls."

"Ho," said the little man. He looked out of the window and saw night making a million shadows.

The little man moved his legs nervously.

"I don't believe in these things," said he, addressing the slate-colored man, who was scuffling with a side of pork.

"Wot things?" came incoherently from the combatant.

"Oh, these-er-phantoms and ghosts and what not. All rot, I say."

"That's because you have merely a stomach and no soul," grunted the pudgy man.

"Ho, old pudgkins!" replied the little man. His back curved with passion. A tempest of wrath was in the pudgy man's eye. The final epithet used by the little man was a carefully-studied insult, always brought forth at a crisis. They quarrelled.

"All right, pudgkins, bring on your phantom," cried the little man in conclusion.

His stout companion's wrath was too huge for words. The little man smiled triumphantly. He had staked his opponent's reputation.

The visitors sat silent. The slate-colored man moved about in a small personal atmosphere of gloom.

Suddenly, a strange cry came to their ears from somewhere. It was a low, trembling call which made the little man quake privately in his shoes. The slate-colored man bounded at the stairway, and disappeared with a flash of legs through a hole in the ceiling. The party below heard two voices in conversation, one belonging to the slate-colored man, and the other in the quavering tones of age. Directly the slate-colored man reappeared from above and said: "The ol' man is took bad for his supper."

He hurriedly prepared a mixture with hot water, salt and beef. Beef-tea, it might be called. He disappeared again. Once more the party below heard, vaguely, talking over their heads. The voice of age arose to a shriek.

"Open the window, fool! Do you think I can live in the smell of your soup?"

Mutterings by the slate-colored man and the creaking of a window were heard.

The slate-colored man stumbled down the stairs, and said with intense gloom, "The black dorg'll be along soon."

The little man started, and the pudgy man sneered at him. They ate a supper and then sat waiting. The pudgy man listened so palpably that the little man wished to kill him. The wood-fire became excited and sputtered frantically. Without, a thousand spirits of the winds had become entangled in the pine branches and were lowly pleading to be loosened. The slate-colored man tiptoed across the room and lit a timid candle. The men sat waiting.

The phantom dog lay cuddled to a round bundle, asleep down the roadway against the windward side of an old shanty. The spectre's master had moved to Pike County. But the dog lingered as a friend might linger at the tomb of a friend. His fur was like a suit of old clothes. His jowls hung and flopped, exposing his teeth. Yellow famine was in his eyes. The wind-rocked shanty groaned and muttered, but the dog slept. Suddenly, however, he got up and shambled to the roadway. He cast a long glance from his hungry, despairing eyes in the direction of the venerable house. The breeze came full to his nostrils. He threw back his head and gave a long, low howl and started intently up the road. Maybe he smelled a dead man.

The group around the fire in the venerable house were listening and waiting. The atmosphere of the room was tense. The slate-colored man's face was twitching and his drabbed hands were gripped together. The little man was continually looking behind his chair. Upon the countenance of the pudgy man appeared conceit for an approaching triumph over the little man, mingled with apprehension for his own safety. Five pipes glowed as rivals of the timid candle. Profound silence drooped heavily over them. Finally the slate-colored man spoke.

"My ol' uncle, Jim Crocker, he's sick ter death."

The four men started and then shrank back in their chairs.

"Damn it!" replied the little man, vaguely.

Again there was a long silence. Suddenly it was broken by a wild cry from the room above. It was a shriek that struck upon them with appalling swiftness, like a flash of lightning. The walls whirled and the floor rumbled. It brought the men together with a rush. They huddled in a heap and stared at the white terror in each other's faces. The slate-colored man grasped the candle and flared it above his head. "The black dorg," he howled, and plunged at the stairway. The maddened four men followed frantically, for it is better to be in the presence of the awful than only within hearing.

Their ears still quivering with the shriek, they bounded through the hole in the ceiling, and into the sick room.

With quilts drawn closely to his shrunken breast for a shield, his bony hand gripping the cover, an old man lay, with glazing eyes fixed on the open window. His throat gurgled and a froth appeared at his mouth.

From the outer darkness came a strange, unnatural wail, burdened with weight of death and each note filled with foreboding. It was the song of the spectral dog.

"God!" screamed the little man. He ran to the open window. He could see nothing at first save the pine-trees, engaged in a furious combat tossing back and forth and struggling. The moon was peeping cautiously over the rims of some black clouds. But the chant of the phantom guided the little man's eyes, and he at length perceived its shadowy form on the ground under the window. He fell away gasping at the sight. The pudgy man crouched in a corner, chattering insanely. The slate-colored man, in his fear, crooked his legs and looked like a hideous Chinese idol. The man upon the bed was turned to stone, save the froth, which pulsated.

In the final struggle, terror will fight the inevitable. The little man roared maniacal curses, and, rushing again to the window, began to throw various articles at the spectre.

A mug, a plate, a knife, a fork, all crashed or clanged on the ground, but the song of the spectre continued. The bowl of beef-tea followed. As it struck the ground the phantom ceased its cry.

The men in the chamber sank limply against the walls, with the unearthly wail still ringing in their ears and the fear unfaded from their eyes. They waited again.

The little man felt his nerves vibrate. Destruction was better than another wait. He grasped a candle and, going to the window, held it over his head and looked out.

"Ho!" he said.

His companions crawled to the window and peered out with him.

"He's eatin' the beef-tea," said the slate-colored man, faintly.

"The damn dog was hungry," said the pudgy man.

"There's your phantom," said the little man to the pudgy man.

On the bed, the old man lay dead. Without, the spectre was wagging its tail.

1892

KATE CHOPIN

(1850–1904)

Ma'ame Pélagie

I.

WHEN the war began, there stood on Côte Joyeuse an imposing mansion of red brick, shaped like the Pantheon. A grove of majestic live-oaks surrounded it.

Thirty years later, only the thick walls were standing, with the dull red brick showing here and there through a matted growth of clinging vines. The huge round pillars were intact; so to some extent was the stone flagging of hall and portico. There had been no home so stately along the whole stretch of Côte Joyeuse. Every one knew that, as they knew it had cost Philippe Valmêt sixty thousand dollars to build, away back in 1840. No one was in danger of forgetting that fact, so long as his daughter Pélagie survived. She was a queenly, white-haired woman of fifty. "Ma'ame Pélagie," they called her, though she was unmarried, as was her sister Pauline, a child in Ma'ame Pélagie's eyes; a child of thirty-five.

The two lived alone in a three-roomed cabin, almost within the shadow of the ruin. They lived for a dream, for Ma'ame Pélagie's dream, which was to rebuild the old home.

It would be pitiful to tell how their days were spent to accomplish this end; how the dollars had been saved for thirty years and the picayunes hoarded; and yet, not half enough gathered! But Ma'ame Pélagie felt sure of twenty years of life before her, and counted upon as many more for her sister. And what could not come to pass in twenty—in forty—years?

Often, of pleasant afternoons, the two would drink their black coffee, seated upon the stone-flagged portico whose canopy was the blue sky of Louisiana. They loved to sit there in the silence, with only each other and the sheeny, prying lizards for company, talking of the old times and planning for the new;

while light breezes stirred the tattered vines high up among the columns, where owls nested.

"We can never hope to have all just as it was, Pauline," Ma'ame Pélagie would say; "perhaps the marble pillars of the salon will have to be replaced by wooden ones, and the crystal candelabra left out. Should you be willing, Pauline?"

"Oh, yes, Sesoeur, I shall be willing." It was always, "Yes, Sesoeur," or "No, Sesoeur," "Just as you please, Sesoeur," with poor little Mam'selle Pauline. For what did she remember of that old life and that old splendor? Only a faint gleam here and there; the half-consciousness of a young, uneventful existence; and then a great crash. That meant the nearness of war; the revolt of slaves; confusion ending in fire and flame through which she was borne safely in the strong arms of Pélagie, and carried to the log cabin which was still their home. Their brother, Léandre, had known more of it all than Pauline, and not so much as Pélagie. He had left the management of the big plantation with all its memories and traditions to his older sister, and had gone away to dwell in cities. That was many years ago. Now, Léandre's business called him frequently and upon long journeys from home, and his motherless daughter was coming to stay with her aunts at Côte Joyeuse.

They talked about it, sipping their coffee on the ruined portico. Mam'selle Pauline was terribly excited; the flush that throbbed into her pale, nervous face showed it; and she locked her thin fingers in and out incessantly.

"But what shall we do with La Petite, Sesoeur? Where shall we put her? How shall we amuse her? Ah, Seigneur!"

"She will sleep upon a cot in the room next to ours," responded Ma'ame Pélagie, "and live as we do. She knows how we live, and why we live; her father has told her. She knows we have money and could squander it if we chose. Do not fret, Pauline; let us hope La Petite is a true Valmêt."

Then Ma'ame Pélagie rose with stately deliberation and went to saddle her horse, for she had yet to make her last daily round through the fields; and Mam'selle Pauline threaded her way slowly among the tangled grasses toward the cabin.

The coming of La Petite, bringing with her as she did the pungent atmosphere of an outside and dimly known world, was a shock to these two, living their dream-life. The girl was quite as tall as her aunt Pélagie, with dark eyes that reflected joy as a still pool reflects the light of stars; and her rounded cheek was tinged like the pink crèpe myrtle. Mam'selle Pauline kissed her and trembled. Ma'ame Pélagie looked into her eyes with a searching gaze, which seemed to seek a likeness of the past in the living present.

And they made room between them for this young life.

II.

La Petite had determined upon trying to fit herself to the strange, narrow existence which she knew awaited her at Côte Joyeuse. It went well enough at first. Sometimes she followed Ma'ame Pélagie into the fields to note how the cotton was opening, ripe and white; or to count the ears of corn upon the hardy stalks. But oftener she was with her aunt Pauline, assisting in household offices, chattering of her brief past, or walking with the older woman arm-in-arm under the trailing moss of the giant oaks.

Mam'selle Pauline's steps grew very buoyant that summer, and her eyes were sometimes as bright as a bird's, unless La Petite were away from her side, when they would lose all other light but one of uneasy expectancy. The girl seemed to love her well in return, and called her endearingly Tan'tante. But as the time went by, La Petite became very quiet,—not listless, but thoughtful, and slow in her movements. Then her cheeks began to pale, till they were tinged like the creamy plumes of the white crèpe myrtle that grew in the ruin.

One day when she sat within its shadow, between her aunts, holding a hand of each, she said: "Tante Pélagie, I must tell you something, you and Tan'tante." She spoke low, but clearly and firmly. "I love you both,—please remember that I love you both. But I must go away from you. I can't live any longer here at Côte Joyeuse."

A spasm passed through Mam'selle Pauline's delicate frame. La Petite could feel the twitch of it in the wiry fingers that were intertwined with her own. Ma'ame Pélagie remained unchanged and motionless. No human eye could penetrate so deep as to see the satisfaction which her soul felt. She said: "What do you mean, Petite? Your father has sent you to us, and I am sure it is his wish that you remain."

"My father loves me, tante Pélagie, and such will not be his wish when he knows. Oh!" she continued with a restless movement, "it is as though a weight were pressing me backward here. I must live another life; the life I lived before. I want to know things that are happening from day to day over the world, and hear them talked about. I want my music, my books, my companions. If I had known no other life but this one of privation, I suppose it would be different. If I had to live this life, I should make the best of it. But I do not have to; and you know, tante Pélagie, you do not need to. It seems to me," she added in a whisper, "that it is a sin against myself. Ah, Tan'tante!—what is the matter with Tan'tante?"

It was nothing; only a slight feeling of faintness, that would soon pass. She entreated them to take no notice; but they brought her some water and fanned her with a palmetto leaf.

But that night, in the stillness of the room, Mam'selle Pauline sobbed and would not be comforted. Ma'ame Pélagie took her in her arms.

"Pauline, my little sister Pauline," she entreated, "I never have seen you like this before. Do you no longer love me? Have we not been happy together, you and I?"

"Oh, yes, Sesoeur."

"Is it because La Petite is going away?"

"Yes, Sesoeur."

"Then she is dearer to you than I!" spoke Ma'ame Pélagie with sharp resentment. "Than I, who held you and warmed you in my arms the day you were born; than I, your mother, father, sister, everything that could cherish you. Pauline, don't tell me that."

Mam'selle Pauline tried to talk through her sobs.

"I can't explain it to you, Sesoeur. I don't understand it myself. I love you as I have always loved you; next to God. But if La Petite goes away I shall die. I can't understand,—help me, Sesoeur. She seems—she seems like a saviour; like one who had come and taken me by the hand and was leading me somewhere —somewhere I want to go."

Ma'ame Pélagie had been sitting beside the bed in her

peignoir and slippers. She held the hand of her sister who lay there, and smoothed down the woman's soft brown hair. She said not a word, and the silence was broken only by Ma'mselle Pauline's continued sobs. Once Ma'ame Pélagie arose to drink of orange-flower water, which she gave to her sister, as she would have offered it to a nervous, fretful child. Almost an hour passed before Ma'ame Pélagie spoke again. Then she said:—

"Pauline, you must cease that sobbing, now, and sleep. You will make yourself ill. La Petite will not go away. Do you hear me? Do you understand? She will stay, I promise you."

Mam'selle Pauline could not clearly comprehend, but she had great faith in the word of her sister, and soothed by the promise and the touch of Ma'ame Pélagie's strong, gentle hand, she fell asleep.

III.

Ma'ame Pélagie, when she saw that her sister slept, arose noiselessly and stepped outside upon the low-roofed narrow gallery. She did not linger there, but with a step that was hurried and agitated, she crossed the distance that divided her cabin from the ruin.

The night was not a dark one, for the sky was clear and the moon resplendent. But light or dark would have made no difference to Ma'ame Pélagie. It was not the first time she had stolen away to the ruin at night-time, when the whole plantation slept; but she never before had been there with a heart so nearly broken. She was going there for the last time to dream her dreams; to see the visions that hitherto had crowded her days and nights, and to bid them farewell.

There was the first of them, awaiting her upon the very portal; a robust old white-haired man, chiding her for returning home so late. There are guests to be entertained. Does she not know it? Guests from the city and from the near plantations. Yes, she knows it is late. She had been abroad with Félix, and they did not notice how the time was speeding. Félix is there; he will explain it all. He is there beside her, but she does not want to hear what he will tell her father.

Ma'ame Pélagie had sunk upon the bench where she and

her sister so often came to sit. Turning, she gazed in through
the gaping chasm of the window at her side. The interior of
the ruin is ablaze. Not with the moonlight, for that is faint
beside the other one—the sparkle from the crystal candelabra,
which negroes, moving noiselessly and respectfully about, are
lighting, one after the other. How the gleam of them reflects
and glances from the polished marble pillars!

The room holds a number of guests. There is old Monsieur
Lucien Santien, leaning against one of the pillars, and laughing
at something which Monsieur Lafirme is telling him, till his fat
shoulders shake. His son Jules is with him—Jules, who wants
to marry her. She laughs. She wonders if Félix has told her
father yet. There is young Jerome Lafirme playing at checkers
upon the sofa with Léandre. Little Pauline stands annoying
them and disturbing the game. Léandre reproves her. She
begins to cry, and old black Clémentine, her nurse, who is not
far off, limps across the room to pick her up and carry her
away. How sensitive the little one is! But she trots about and
takes care of herself better than she did a year or two ago,
when she fell upon the stone hall floor and raised a great
"bobo" on her forehead. Pélagie was hurt and angry enough
about it; and she ordered rugs and buffalo robes to be brought
and laid thick upon the tiles, till the little one's steps were
surer.

"Il ne faut pas faire mal à Pauline." She was saying it
aloud—"faire mal à Pauline."

But she gazes beyond the salon, back into the big dining
hall, where the white crêpe myrtle grows. Ha! how low that
bat has circled. It has struck Ma'ame Pélagie full on the breast.
She does not know it. She is beyond there in the dining hall,
where her father sits with a group of friends over their wine. As
usual they are talking politics. How tiresome! She has heard
them say "la guerre" oftener than once. La guerre. Bah! She and
Félix have something pleasanter to talk about, out under the
oaks, or back in the shadow of the oleanders.

But they were right! The sound of a cannon, shot at Sumter,
has rolled across the Southern States, and its echo is heard
along the whole stretch of Côte Joyeuse.

Yet Pélagie does not believe it. Not till La Ricaneuse stands before her with bare, black arms akimbo, uttering a volley of vile abuse and of brazen impudence. Pélagie wants to kill her. But yet she will not believe. Not till Félix comes to her in the chamber above the dining hall—there where that trumpet vine hangs—comes to say good-by to her. The hurt which the big brass buttons of his new gray uniform pressed into the tender flesh of her bosom has never left it. She sits upon the sofa, and he beside her, both speechless with pain. That room would not have been altered. Even the sofa would have been there in the same spot, and Ma'ame Pélagie had meant all along, for thirty years, all along, to lie there upon it some day when the time came to die.

But there is no time to weep, with the enemy at the door. The door has been no barrier. They are clattering through the halls now, drinking the wines, shattering the crystal and glass, slashing the portraits.

One of them stands before her and tells her to leave the house. She slaps his face. How the stigma stands out red as blood upon his blanched cheek!

Now there is a roar of fire and the flames are bearing down upon her motionless figure. She wants to show them how a daughter of Louisiana can perish before her conquerors. But little Pauline clings to her knees in an agony of terror. Little Pauline must be saved.

"Il ne faut pas faire mal à Pauline."

Again she is saying it aloud—"faire mal à Pauline."

The night was nearly spent; Ma'ame Pélagie had glided from the bench upon which she had rested, and for hours lay prone upon the stone flagging, motionless. When she dragged herself to her feet it was to walk like one in a dream. About the great, solemn pillars, one after the other, she reached her arms, and pressed her cheek and her lips upon the senseless brick.

"Adieu, adieu!" whispered Ma'ame Pélagie.

There was no longer the moon to guide her steps across the familiar pathway to the cabin. The brightest light in the sky was Venus, that swung low in the east. The bats had ceased to beat their wings about the ruin. Even the mockingbird that had warbled for hours in the old mulberry-tree had sung himself asleep. That darkest hour before the day was mantling the earth. Ma'ame Pélagie hurried through the wet, clinging grass, beating aside the heavy moss that swept across her face, walking on toward the cabin—toward Pauline. Not once did she look back upon the ruin that brooded like a huge monster—a black spot in the darkness that enveloped it.

IV.

Little more than a year later the transformation which the old Valmêt place had undergone was the talk and wonder of Côte Joyeuse. One would have looked in vain for the ruin; it was no longer there; neither was the log cabin. But out in the open, where the sun shone upon it, and the breezes blew about it, was a shapely structure fashioned from woods that the forests of the State had furnished. It rested upon a solid foundation of brick.

Upon a corner of the pleasant gallery sat Léandre smoking his afternoon cigar, and chatting with neighbors who had called. This was to be his *pied à terre* now; the home where his sisters and his daughter dwelt. The laughter of young people was heard out under the trees, and within the house where La Petite was playing upon the piano. With the enthusiasm of a young artist she drew from the keys strains that seemed marvelously beautiful to Mam'selle Pauline, who stood enraptured near her. Mam'selle Pauline had been touched by the re-creation of Valmêt. Her cheek was as full and almost as flushed as La Petite's. The years were falling away from her.

Ma'ame Pélagie had been conversing with her brother and his friends. Then she turned and walked away; stopping to listen awhile to the music which La Petite was making. But it was only for a moment. She went on around the curve of the veranda, where she found herself alone. She stayed there, erect, holding to the banister rail and looking out calmly in the distance across the fields.

She was dressed in black, with the white kerchief she always wore folded across her bosom. Her thick, glossy hair rose like a silver diadem from her brow. In her deep, dark eyes smouldered the light of fires that would never flame. She had grown very old. Years instead of months seemed to have passed over her since the night she bade farewell to her visions.

Poor Ma'ame Pélagie! How could it be different! While the outward pressure of a young and joyous existence had forced her footsteps into the light, her soul had stayed in the shadow of the ruin.

1893

JOHN KENDRICK BANGS

(1862–1922)

Thurlow's Christmas Story

I

(Being the Statement of Henry Thurlow, Author,
to George Currier, Editor of the "Idler,"
a Weekly Journal of Human Interest.)

I HAVE always maintained, my dear Currier, that if a man wishes to be considered sane, and has any particular regard for his reputation as a truth-teller, he would better keep silent as to the singular experiences that enter into his life. I have had many such experiences myself; but I have rarely confided them in detail, or otherwise, to those about me, because I know that even the most trustful of my friends would regard them merely as the outcome of an imagination unrestrained by conscience, or of a gradually weakening mind subject to hallucinations. I know them to be true, but until Mr. Edison or some other modern wizard has invented a search-light strong enough to lay bare the secrets of the mind and conscience of man, I cannot prove to others that they are not pure fabrications, or at least the conjurings of a diseased fancy. For instance, no man would believe me if I were to state to him the plain and indisputable fact that one night last month, on my way up to bed shortly after midnight, having been neither smoking nor drinking, I saw confronting me upon the stairs, with the moonlight streaming through the windows back of me, lighting up its face, a figure in which I recognized my very self in every form and feature. I might describe the chill of terror that struck to the very marrow of my bones, and wellnigh forced me to stagger backward down the stairs, as I noticed in the face of this confronting figure every indication of all the bad qualities which I know myself to possess, of every evil instinct which by no easy effort I have repressed heretofore, and realized that that *thing* was, as far as I knew, entirely independent of my true self, in which I hope at least the moral has made an honest fight against the immoral always. I might describe this chill, I say, as vividly as I felt it at that moment, but it would be of no use to do so, because, however realistic it might prove as a bit of description, no man would believe that the incident really happened; and yet it did happen as truly as I write, and it has happened a dozen times since, and I am certain that it will happen many times again, though I would give all that I possess to be assured that never again should that disquieting creation of mind or matter, whichever it may be, cross my path. The experience has made me afraid almost to be alone, and I have found myself unconsciously and uneasily glancing at my face in mirrors, in the plate-glass of show-windows on the shopping streets of the city, fearful lest I should find some of those evil traits which I have struggled to keep under, and have kept under so far, cropping out there where all the world, all *my* world, can see and wonder at, having known me always as a man of right doing and right feeling. Many a time in the night the thought has come to me with prostrating force, what if that thing were to be seen and recognized by others, myself and yet not my whole self, my unworthy self unrestrained and yet recognizable as Henry Thurlow.

I have also kept silent as to that strange condition of affairs which has tortured me in my sleep for the past year and a half; no one but myself has until this writing known that for that period of time I have had a continuous, logical dream-life; a life so vivid and so dreadfully real to me that I have found myself at times wondering which of the two lives I was living and which I was dreaming; a life in which that other wicked self has dominated, and forced me to a career of shame and horror; a life which, being taken up every time I sleep where it ceased with the awakening from a previous sleep, has made me fear to close my eyes in forgetfulness when others are near at hand, lest, sleeping, I shall let fall some speech that, striking on their ears, shall lead them to believe that in secret there is some wicked mystery connected with my life. It would be of no use for me to tell these things. It would merely serve to make my family and my friends uneasy about me if they were told in their awful detail, and so I have kept silent about them. To you alone, and now for the first time, have I hinted as to the troubles which have oppressed me for many days, and to you they are confided only because of the demand you have made that I explain to you the extraordinary complication in which the Christmas story sent you last week has involved me. You know that I am a man of dignity; that I am not a school-boy and a lover of childish tricks; and knowing that, your friendship, at least, should have restrained your tongue and pen when, through the former, on Wednesday, you accused me of perpetrating a trifling, and to you excessively embarrassing, practical joke—a charge which, at the moment, I was too overcome to refute; and through the latter, on Thursday, you reiterated the accusation, coupled with a demand for an explanation of my conduct satisfactory to yourself, or my immediate resignation from the staff of the *Idler*. To explain is difficult, for I am certain that you will find the explanation too improbable for credence, but explain I must. The alternative, that of resigning from your staff, affects not only my own welfare, but that of my children, who must be provided for; and if my post with you is taken from me, then are all resources gone. I have not the courage to face dismissal, for I have not sufficient confidence in my powers to please elsewhere to make me easy in my mind, or, if I could please elsewhere, the certainty of finding the immediate employment of my talents which is necessary to me, in view of the at present overcrowded condition of the literary field.

To explain, then, my seeming jest at your expense, hopeless as it appears to be, is my task; and to do so as completely as I can, let me go back to the very beginning.

In August you informed me that you would expect me to provide, as I have heretofore been in the habit of doing, a story for the Christmas issue of the *Idler*; that a certain position in the make-up was reserved for me, and that you had already taken steps to advertise the fact that the story would appear. I undertook the commission, and upon seven different occasions set about putting the narrative into shape. I found great difficulty, however, in doing so. For some reason or other I could not concentrate my mind upon the work. No sooner would I start in on one story than a better one, in my estimation, would suggest itself to me; and all the labor expended on the story already begun would be cast aside, and the new story set in motion. Ideas were plenty enough, but to put them properly upon paper seemed beyond my powers. One story, however, I did finish; but after it had come back to me from my typewriter I read it, and was filled with consternation to discover that it was nothing more nor less than a mass of jumbled sentences, conveying no idea to the mind—a story which had seemed to me in the writing to be coherent had returned to me as a mere bit of incoherence—formless, without ideas—a bit of raving. It was then that I went to you and told you, as you remember, that I was worn out, and needed a month of absolute rest, which you granted. I left my work wholly, and went into the wilderness, where I could be entirely free from everything suggesting labor, and where no summons back to town could reach me. I fished and hunted. I slept; and although, as I have already said, in my sleep I found myself leading a life that was not only not to my taste, but horrible to me in many particulars, I was able at the end of my vacation to come back to town greatly refreshed, and, as far as my feelings went, ready to undertake any amount of work. For two or three days after my return I was busy with other things. On the fourth day after my arrival you came to me, and said that the story must be finished at the very latest by October 15th, and I assured you that you should have it by that time. That night I set about it. I mapped it out, incident by incident, and before starting up to bed had actually written some twelve or fifteen hundred words of the opening chapter—it was to be told in four chapters. When I had gone thus far I experienced a slight return of one of my nervous chills, and, on consulting my watch, discovered that it was after midnight, which was a sufficient explanation of my nervousness: I was merely tired. I arranged my manuscripts on my table so that I might easily take up the work the following morning. I locked up the windows and doors, turned out the lights, and proceeded up-stairs to my room.

It was then that I first came face to face with myself—that other self, in which I recognized, developed to the full, every bit of my capacity for an evil life.

Conceive of the situation if you can. Imagine the horror of it, and then ask yourself if it was likely that when next morning came I could by any possibility bring myself to my work-table in fit condition to prepare for you anything at all worthy of publication in the *Idler*. I tried. I implore you to believe that I did not hold lightly the responsibilities of the commission you had intrusted to my hands. You must know that if any of your writers has a full appreciation of the difficulties which are strewn along the path of an editor, I, who have myself had an editorial experience, have it, and so would not, in the nature of things, do anything to add to your troubles. You cannot but believe that I have made an honest effort to fulfil my promise to you. But it was useless, and for a week after that visitation was it useless for me to attempt the work. At the end of the week I felt better, and again I started in, and the story developed satisfactorily until—*it* came again. That figure which was my own figure, that face which was the evil counterpart of my own countenance, again rose up before me, and once more was I plunged into hopelessness.

Thus matters went on until the 14th day of October, when I received your peremptory message that the story must be forthcoming the following day. Needless to tell you that it was not forthcoming; but what I must tell you, since you do not know it, is that on the evening of the 15th day of October a strange thing happened to me, and in the narration of that incident, which I almost despair of your believing, lies my explanation of the discovery of October 16th, which has placed my position with you in peril.

At half-past seven o'clock on the evening of October 15th I was sitting in my library trying to write. I was alone. My wife and children had gone away on a visit to Massachusetts for a week. I had just finished my cigar, and had taken my pen in hand, when my front-door bell rang. Our maid, who is usually prompt in answering summonses of this nature, apparently did not hear the bell, for she did not respond to its clanging. Again the bell rang, and still did it remain unanswered, until finally, at the third ringing, I went to the door myself. On opening it I saw standing before me a man of, I should say, fifty odd years of age, tall, slender, pale-faced, and clad in sombre black. He was entirely unknown to me. I had never seen him before, but he had about him such an air of pleasantness and wholesomeness that I instinctively felt glad to see him, without knowing why or whence he had come.

"Does Mr. Thurlow live here?" he asked.

You must excuse me for going into what may seem to you to

be petty details, but by a perfectly circumstantial account of all that happened that evening alone can I hope to give a semblance of truth to my story, and that it must be truthful I realize as painfully as you do.

"I am Mr. Thurlow," I replied.

"Henry Thurlow, the author?" he said, with a surprised look upon his face.

"Yes," said I; and then, impelled by the strange appearance of surprise on the man's countenance, I added, "don't I look like an author?"

He laughed, and candidly admitted that I was not the kind of looking man he had expected to find from reading my books, and then he entered the house in response to my invitation that he do so. I ushered him into my library, and, after asking him to be seated, inquired as to his business with me.

His answer was gratifying at least. He replied that he had been a reader of my writings for a number of years, and that for some time past he had had a great desire, not to say curiosity, to meet me and tell me how much he had enjoyed certain of my stories.

"I'm a great devourer of books, Mr. Thurlow," he said, "and I have taken the keenest delight in reading your verses and humorous sketches. I may go further, and say to you that you have helped me over many a hard place in my life by your work. At times when I have felt myself worn out with my business, or face to face with some knotty problem in my career, I have found much relief in picking up and reading your books at random. They have helped me to forget my weariness or my knotty problems for the time being; and to-day, finding myself in this town, I resolved to call upon you this evening and thank you for all that you have done for me."

Thereupon we became involved in a general discussion of literary men and their works, and I found that my visitor certainly did have a pretty thorough knowledge of what has been produced by the writers of to-day. I was quite won over to him by his simplicity, as well as attracted to him by his kindly opinion of my own efforts, and I did my best to entertain him, showing him a few of my little literary treasures in the way of autograph letters, photographs, and presentation copies of well-known books from the authors themselves. From this we drifted naturally and easily into a talk on the methods of work adopted by literary men. He asked me many questions as to my own methods; and when I had in a measure outlined to him the manner of life which I had adopted, telling him of my days at home, how little detail office-work I had, he seemed much interested with the picture—indeed, I painted the picture of my daily routine in almost too perfect colors, for, when I had finished, he observed quietly that I appeared to him to lead the ideal life, and added that he supposed I knew very little unhappiness.

The remark recalled to me the dreadful reality, that through some perversity of fate I was doomed to visitations of an uncanny order which were practically destroying my usefulness in my profession and my sole financial resource.

"Well," I replied, as my mind reverted to the unpleasant predicament in which I found myself, "I can't say that I know little unhappiness. As a matter of fact, I know a great deal of that undesirable thing. At the present moment I am very much embarrassed through my absolute inability to fulfil a contract into which I have entered, and which should have been filled this morning. I was due to-day with a Christmas story. The presses are waiting for it, and I am utterly unable to write it."

He appeared deeply concerned at the confession. I had hoped, indeed, that he might be sufficiently concerned to take his departure, that I might make one more effort to write the promised story. His solicitude, however, showed itself in another way. Instead of leaving me, he ventured the hope that he might aid me.

"What kind of a story is it to be?" he asked.

"Oh, the usual ghostly tale," I said, "with a dash of the Christmas flavor thrown in here and there to make it suitable to the season."

"Ah," he observed. "And you find your vein worked out?"

It was a direct and perhaps an impertinent question; but I thought it best to answer it, and to answer it as well without giving him any clew as to the real facts. I could not very well take an entire stranger into my confidence, and describe to him the extraordinary encounters I was having with an uncanny other self. He would not have believed the truth, hence I told him an untruth, and assented to his proposition.

"Yes," I replied, "the vein is worked out. I have written ghost stories for years now, serious and comic, and I am to-day at the end of my tether—compelled to move forward and yet held back."

"That accounts for it," he said, simply. "When I first saw you to-night at the door I could not believe that the author who had provided me with so much merriment could be so pale and worn and seemingly mirthless. Pardon me, Mr. Thurlow, for my lack of consideration when I told you that you did not appear as I had expected to find you."

I smiled my forgiveness, and he continued:

"It may be," he said, with a show of hesitation—"it may be that I have come not altogether inopportunely. Perhaps I can help you."

I smiled again. "I should be most grateful if you could," I said.

"But you doubt my ability to do so?" he put in. "Oh—well —yes—of course you do; and why shouldn't you? Nevertheless, I have noticed this: At times when I have been baffled in my work a mere hint from another, from one who knew nothing of my work, has carried me on to a solution of my problem. I have read most of your writings, and I have thought over some of them many a time, and I have even had ideas for stories, which, in my own conceit, I have imagined were good enough for you, and I have wished that I possessed your facility with the pen that I might make of them myself what I thought you would make of them had they been ideas of your own."

The old gentleman's pallid face reddened as he said this, and while I was hopeless as to anything of value resulting from his ideas, I could not resist the temptation to hear what he had to say further, his manner was so deliciously simple, and his desire to aid me so manifest. He rattled on with suggestions for a half-hour. Some of them were good, but none were new. Some were irresistibly funny, and did me good because they made me laugh, and I hadn't laughed naturally for a period so long that it made me shudder to think of it, fearing lest I should forget how to be mirthful. Finally I grew tired of his persistence, and, with a very ill-concealed impatience, told him plainly that I could do nothing with his suggestions, thanking him, however, for the spirit of kindliness which had prompted him to offer them. He appeared somewhat hurt, but immediately desisted, and when nine o'clock came he rose up to go. As he walked to the door he seemed to be undergoing some mental struggle, to which, with a sudden resolve, he finally succumbed, for, after having picked up his hat and stick and donned his overcoat, he turned to me and said:

"Mr. Thurlow, I don't want to offend you. On the contrary, it is my dearest wish to assist you. You have helped me, as I have told you. Why may I not help you?"

"I assure you, sir—" I began, when he interrupted me.

"One moment, please," he said, putting his hand into the inside pocket of his black coat and extracting from it an envelope addressed to me. "Let me finish: it is the whim of one who has an affection for you. For ten years I have secretly been at work myself on a story. It is a short one, but it has seemed good to me. I had a double object in seeking you out to-night. I wanted not only to see you, but to read my story to you. No one knows that I have written it; I had intended it as a surprise to my—to my friends. I had hoped to have it published somewhere, and I had come here to seek your advice in the matter. It is a story which I have written and rewritten and rewritten time and time again in my leisure moments during the ten years past, as I have told you. It is not likely that I shall ever write another. I am proud of having done it, but I should be prouder yet if it—if it could in some way help you. I leave it with you, sir, to print or to destroy; and if you print it, to see it in type will be enough for me; to see your name signed to it will be a matter of pride to me. No one will ever be the wiser, for, as I say, no one knows I have written it, and I promise you that no one shall know of it if you decide to do as I not only suggest but ask you to do. No one would believe me after it has appeared as *yours*, even if I should forget my promise and claim it as my own. Take it. It is yours. You are entitled to it as a slight measure of repayment for the debt of gratitude I owe you."

He pressed the manuscript into my hands, and before I could reply had opened the door and disappeared into the darkness of the street. I rushed to the sidewalk and shouted out to him to return, but I might as well have saved my breath and spared the neighborhood, for there was no answer. Holding his story in my hand, I re-entered the house and walked back into my library, where, sitting and reflecting upon the curious interview, I realized for the first time that I was in entire ignorance as to my visitor's name and address.

I opened the envelope hoping to find them, but they were not there. The envelope contained merely a finely written manuscript of thirty odd pages, unsigned.

And then I read the story. When I began it was with a half-smile upon my lips, and with a feeling that I was wasting my time. The smile soon faded, however; after reading the first paragraph there was no question of wasted time. The story was a masterpiece. It is needless to say to you that I am not a man of enthusiasms. It is difficult to arouse that emotion in my breast, but upon this occasion I yielded to a force too great for me to resist. I have read the tales of Hoffmann and of Poe, the wondrous romances of De La Motte Fouque, the unfortunately little-known tales of the lamented Fitz-James O'Brien, the weird tales of writers of all tongues have been thoroughly sifted by me in the course of my reading, and I say to you now that in the whole of my life I never read one story, one paragraph, one line, that could approach in vivid delineation, in weirdness of conception, in anything, in any quality which goes to make up the truly great story, that story which came into my hands as I have told you. I read it once and was amazed. I read it a second time and was—tempted. It was mine. The writer himself had authorized me to treat it as if it were my own; had voluntarily sacrificed his own claim to its authorship that he might relieve me of my very pressing embarrassment. Not only this; he had almost intimated that in putting my name to his work I should be doing him a favor. Why not do so, then, I asked myself; and immediately my better self rejected the idea as impossible. How could I put out as my own another man's work and retain my self-respect? I resolved on another and better course—to send you the story in lieu of my own with a full statement of the circumstances under which it had come into my possession, when that demon rose up out of the floor at my side, this time more evil of aspect than before, more commanding in its manner. With a groan I shrank back into the cushions of my chair, and by passing my hands over my eyes tried to obliterate forever the offending sight; but it was useless. The uncanny thing approached me, and as truly as I write sat upon the edge of my couch, where for the first time it addressed me.

"Fool!" it said, "how can you hesitate? Here is your position: you have made a contract which must be filled; you are already behind, and in a hopeless mental state. Even granting that between this and to-morrow morning you could put together the necessary number of words to fill the space allotted to you, what kind of a thing do you think that story would make? It would be a mere raving like that other precious effort of August. The public, if by some odd chance it ever reached them, would think your mind was utterly gone; your reputation would go with that verdict. On the other hand, if you do not have the story ready by to-morrow, your hold on the *Idler* will be destroyed. They have their announcements printed, and your name and portrait appear among those of the prominent contributors. Do you suppose the editor and publisher will look leniently upon your failure?"

"Considering my past record, yes," I replied. "I have never yet broken a promise to them."

"Which is precisely the reason why they will be severe with you. You, who have been regarded as one of the few men who can do almost any kind of literary work at will—you, of whom it is said that your 'brains are on tap'—will they be lenient with *you*? Bah! Can't you see that the very fact of your invariable readiness heretofore is going to make your present unreadiness a thing incomprehensible?"

"Then what shall I do?" I asked. "If I can't, I can't, that is all."

"You can. There is the story in your hands. Think what it will do for you. It is one of the immortal stories—"

"You have read it, then?" I asked.

"Haven't you?"

"Yes—but—"

"It is the same," it said, with a leer and a contemptuous shrug. "You and I are inseparable. Aren't you glad?" it added, with a laugh that grated on every fibre of my being. I was too overwhelmed to reply, and it resumed: "It is one of the immortal stories. We agree to that. Published over your name, your name will live. The stuff you write yourself will give you present glory; but when you have been dead ten years people won't remember your name even—unless I get control of you, and in that case there is a very pretty though hardly a literary record in store for you."

Again it laughed harshly, and I buried my face in the pillows of my couch, hoping to find relief there from this dreadful vision.

"Curious," it said. "What you call your decent self doesn't dare look me in the eye! What a mistake people make who say that the man who won't look you in the eye is not to be trusted! As if mere brazenness were a sign of honesty; really, the theory of decency is the most amusing thing in the world. But come, time is growing short. Take that story. The writer gave it to you. Begged you to use it as your own. It is yours. It will make your reputation, and save you with your publishers. How can you hesitate?"

"I shall not use it!" I cried, desperately.

"You must—consider your children. Suppose you lose your connection with these publishers of yours?"

"But it would be a crime."

"Not a bit of it. Whom do you rob? A man who voluntarily came to you, and gave you that of which you rob him. Think of it as it is—and act, only act quickly. It is now midnight."

The tempter rose up and walked to the other end of the room, whence, while he pretended to be looking over a few of my books and pictures, I was aware he was eying me closely, and gradually compelling me by sheer force of will to do a thing which I abhorred. And I—I struggled weakly against the temptation, but gradually, little by little, I yielded, and finally succumbed altogether. Springing to my feet, I rushed to the table, seized my pen, and signed my name to the story.

"There!" I said. "It is done. I have saved my position and made my reputation, and am now a thief!"

"As well as a fool," said the other, calmly. "You don't mean to say you are going to send that manuscript in as it is?"

"Good Lord!" I cried. "What under heaven have you been trying to make me do for the last half hour?"

"Act like a sane being," said the demon. "If you send that

manuscript to Currier he'll know in a minute it isn't yours. He knows you haven't an amanuensis, and that handwriting isn't yours. Copy it."

"True!" I answered. "I haven't much of a mind for details to-night. I will do as you say."

I did so. I got out my pad and pen and ink, and for three hours diligently applied myself to the task of copying the story. When it was finished I went over it carefully, made a few minor corrections, signed it, put it in an envelope, addressed it to you, stamped it, and went out to the mail-box on the corner, where I dropped it into the slot, and returned home. When I had returned to my library my visitor was still there.

"Well," it said, "I wish you'd hurry and complete this affair. I am tired, and wish to go."

"You can't go too soon to please me," said I, gathering up the original manuscripts of the story and preparing to put them away in my desk.

"Probably not," it sneered. "I'll be glad to go too, but I can't go until that manuscript is destroyed. As long as it exists there is evidence of your having appropriated the work of another. Why, can't you see that? Burn it!"

"I can't see my way clear in crime!" I retorted. "It is not in my line."

Nevertheless, realizing the value of his advice, I thrust the pages one by one into the blazing log fire, and watched them as they flared and flamed and grew to ashes. As the last page disappeared in the embers the demon vanished. I was alone, and throwing myself down for a moment's reflection upon my couch, was soon lost in sleep.

It was noon when I again opened my eyes, and, ten minutes after I awakened, your telegraphic summons reached me.

"Come down at once," was what you said, and I went; and then came the terrible *dénouement*, and yet a *dénouement* which was pleasing to me since it relieved my conscience. You handed me the envelope containing the story.

"Did you send that?" was your question.

"I did—last night, or rather early this morning. I mailed it about three o'clock," I replied.

"I demand an explanation of your conduct," said you.

"Of what?" I asked.

"Look at your so-called story and see. If this is a practical joke, Thurlow, it's a damned poor one."

I opened the envelope and took from it the sheets I had sent you—twenty-four of them.

They were every one of them as blank as when they left the paper-mill!

You know the rest. You know that I tried to speak; that my utterance failed me; and that, finding myself unable at the time to control my emotions, I turned and rushed madly from the office, leaving the mystery unexplained. You know that you wrote demanding a satisfactory explanation of the situation or my resignation from your staff.

This, Currier, is my explanation. It is all I have. It is absolute truth. I beg you to believe it, for if you do not, then is my condition a hopeless one. You will ask me perhaps for a *résumé* of the story which I thought I had sent you.

It is my crowning misfortune that upon that point my mind is an absolute blank. I cannot remember it in form or in substance. I have racked my brains for some recollection of some small portion of it to help to make my explanation more credible, but, alas! it will not come back to me. If I were dishonest I might fake up a story to suit the purpose, but I am not dishonest. I came near to doing an unworthy act; I did do an unworthy thing, but by some mysterious provision of fate my conscience is cleared of that.

Be sympathetic, Currier, or, if you cannot, be lenient with me this time. *Believe, believe, believe*, I implore you. Pray let me hear from you at once.

(Signed)   HENRY THURLOW.

II

(Being a Note from George Currier,
Editor of the "Idler," to Henry Thurlow, Author.)

Your explanation has come to hand. As an explanation it isn't worth the paper it is written on, but we are all agreed here that it is probably the best bit of fiction you ever wrote. It is accepted for the Christmas issue. Enclosed please find check for one hundred dollars.

Dawson suggests that you take another month up in the Adirondacks. You might put in your time writing up some account of that dream-life you are leading while you are there. It seems to me there are possibilities in the idea. The concern will pay all expenses. What do you say?

(Signed)   Yours ever,   G. C.

1894

ROBERT W. CHAMBERS

(1865–1933)

"*Along the shore the cloud waves break,*
The twin suns sink behind the lake,
The shadows lengthen
                          In Carcosa.

"*Strange is the night where black stars rise*
And strange moons circle through the skies,
But stranger still is
                          Lost Carcosa.

"*Songs that the Hyades shall sing.*
Where flap the tatters of the King,
Must die unheard in
                          Dim Carcosa.

"*Song of my soul, my voice is dead,*
Die thou, unsung, as tears unshed
Shall dry and die in
                          Lost Carcosa."

—Cassilda's song in "The King in Yellow,"
                          act i., scene 2.

The Repairer of Reputations

I

"*Ne raillons pas les fous; leur folie dure plus longtemps que la nôtre. . . .*
Voilà toute la différence."

TOWARDS the end of the year 1920 the government of the
United States had practically completed the programme
adopted during the last months of President Winthrop's
administration. The country was apparently tranquil. Everybody knows how the Tariff and Labor questions were settled.
The war with Germany, incident on that country's seizure of
the Samoan Islands, had left no visible scars upon the republic,
and the temporary occupation of Norfolk by the invading army

177

had been forgotten in the joy over repeated naval victories and the subsequent ridiculous plight of General Von Gartenlaube's forces in the State of New Jersey. The Cuban and Hawaiian investments had paid one hundred per cent., and the territory of Samoa was well worth its cost as a coaling station. The country was in a superb state of defence. Every coast city had been well supplied with land fortifications; the army, under the parental eye of the general staff, organized according to the Prussian system, had been increased to three hundred thousand men, with a territorial reserve of a million; and six magnificent squadrons of cruisers and battle-ships patrolled the six stations of the navigable seas, leaving a steam reserve amply fitted to control home waters. The gentlemen from the West had at last been constrained to acknowledge that a college for the training of diplomats was as necessary as law schools are for the training of barristers; consequently we were no longer represented abroad by incompetent patriots. The nation was prosperous. Chicago, for a moment paralyzed after a second great fire, had risen from its ruins, white and imperial, and more beautiful than the white city which had been built for its plaything in 1893. Everywhere good architecture was replacing bad, and even in New York a sudden craving for decency had swept away a great portion of the existing horrors. Streets had been widened, properly paved, and lighted, trees had been planted, squares laid out, elevated structures demolished, and underground roads built to replace them. The new government buildings and barracks were fine bits of architecture, and the long system of stone quays which completely surrounded the island had been turned into parks, which proved a godsend to the population. The subsidizing of the state theatre and state opera brought its own reward. The United States National Academy of Design was much like European institutions of the same kind. Nobody envied the Secretary of Fine Arts either his cabinet position or his portfolio. The Secretary of Forestry and Game Preservation had a much easier time, thanks to the new system of National Mounted Police. We had profited well by the latest treaties with France and England; the exclusion of foreign-born Jews as a measure of national self-preservation, the settlement of the new independent negro state of Suanee, the checking of immigration, the new laws concerning naturalization, and the gradual centralization of power in the executive all contributed to national calm and prosperity. When the government solved the Indian problem and squadrons of Indian cavalry scouts in native costume were substituted for the pitiable organizations tacked on to the tail of skeletonized regiments by a former Secretary of War, the nation drew a long sigh of relief. When, after the colossal Congress of Religions, bigotry and intolerance were laid in their graves, and kindness and charity began to draw warring sects together, many thought the millennium had arrived, at least in the new world, which, after all, is a world by itself.

But self-preservation is the first law, and the United States had to look on in helpless sorrow as Germany, Italy, Spain, and Belgium writhed in the throes of anarchy, while Russia, watching from the Caucasus, stooped and bound them one by one.

In the city of New York the summer of 1910 was signalized by the dismantling of the Elevated Railroads. The summer of 1911 will live in the memories of New York people for many a cycle; the Dodge statue was removed in that year. In the following winter began that agitation for the repeal of the laws prohibiting suicide, which bore its final fruit in the month of April, 1920, when the first Government Lethal Chamber was opened on Washington Square.

I had walked down that day from Dr. Archer's house on Madison Avenue, where I had been as a mere formality. Ever since that fall from my horse, four years before, I had been troubled at times with pains in the back of my head and neck, but now for months they had been absent, and the doctor sent me away that day saying there was nothing more to be cured in me. It was hardly worth his fee to be told that; I knew it myself. Still I did not grudge him the money. What I minded was the mistake which he made at first. When they picked me up from the pavement where I lay unconscious, and somebody had mercifully sent a bullet through my horse's head, I was carried to Dr. Archer, and he, pronouncing my brain affected, placed me in his private asylum, where I was obliged to endure treatment for insanity. At last he decided that I was well, and I, knowing that my mind had always been as sound as his, if not sounder, "paid my tuition," as he jokingly called it, and left. I told him, smiling, that I would get even with him for his mistake, and he laughed heartily, and asked me to call once in a while. I did so, hoping for a chance to even up accounts, but he gave me none, and I told him I would wait.

The fall from my horse had fortunately left no evil results; on the contrary, it had changed my whole character for the better. From a lazy young man about town, I had become active, energetic, temperate, and, above all—oh, above all else—ambitious. There was only one thing which troubled me: I laughed at my own uneasiness, and yet it troubled me.

During my convalescence I had bought and read for the first time "The King in Yellow." I remember after finishing the first act that it occurred to me that I had better stop. I started up and flung the book into the fireplace; the volume struck the barred grate and fell open on the hearth in the fire-light. If I had not caught a glimpse of the opening words in the second act I should never have finished it, but as I stooped to pick it up my eyes became riveted to the open page, and with a cry of terror, or perhaps it was of joy so poignant that I suffered in every nerve, I snatched the thing from the hearth and crept shaking to my bedroom, where I read it and reread it, and wept and laughed and trembled with a horror which at times assails me yet. This is the thing that troubles me, for I cannot forget Carcosa, where black stars hang in the heavens, where the shadows of men's thoughts lengthen in the afternoon, when the twin suns sink into the Lake of Hali, and my mind will bear forever the memory of the Pallid Mask. I pray God will curse the writer, as the writer has cursed the world with this beautiful, stupendous creation, terrible in its simplicity, irresistible in its truth—a world which now trembles before the King in Yellow. When the French government seized the translated copies which had just arrived in Paris, London, of course, became eager to read it. It is well known how the book spread like an infectious disease, from city to city, from continent to continent, barred out here, confiscated there, denounced by press and pulpit, censured even by the most advanced of literary anarchists. No definite principles had been violated in those wicked pages, no doctrine promulgated, no convictions outraged. It could not be judged by any known standard, yet, although it was acknowledged that the supreme note of art had been struck in "The King in Yellow," all felt that human nature could not bear the strain nor thrive on words in which the essence of purest poison lurked. The very banality and innocence of the first act only allowed the blow to fall afterwards with more awful effect.

It was, I remember, the 13th day of April, 1920, that the first Government Lethal Chamber was established on the south side of Washington Square, between Wooster Street and South Fifth Avenue. The block, which had formerly consisted of a lot of shabby old buildings, used as cafés and restaurants for foreigners, had been acquired by the government in the winter of 1913. The French and Italian cafés and restaurants were torn down; the whole block was enclosed by a gilded iron railing, and converted into a lovely garden, with lawns, flowers, and fountains. In the centre of the garden stood a small, white building, severely classical in architecture, and surrounded by thickets of flowers. Six Ionic columns supported the roof, and the single door was of bronze. A splendid marble group of "The Fates" stood before the door, the work of a young American sculptor, Boris Yvain, who had died in Paris when only twenty-three years old.

The inauguration ceremonies were in progress as I crossed University Place and entered the square. I threaded my way through the silent throng of spectators, but was stopped at Fourth Street by a cordon of police. A regiment of United States Lancers were drawn up in a hollow square around the Lethal Chamber. On a raised tribune facing Washington Park stood the Governor of New York, and behind him were grouped the Mayor of Greater New York, the Inspector-General of Police, the commandant of the State troops, Colonel Livingston (military aid to the President of the United States), General Blount (commanding at Governor's Island), Major-General Hamilton (commanding the garrison of Greater New York), Admiral Buffby (of the fleet in the North River), Surgeon-General Lanceford, the staff of the National Free Hospital, Senators Wyse and Franklin, of New York, and the Commissioner of Public Works. The tribune was surrounded by a squadron of hussars of the National Guard.

The Governor was finishing his reply to the short speech of the Surgeon-General. I heard him say: "The laws prohibiting suicide and providing punishment for any attempt at self-destruction have been repealed. The government has seen fit to acknowledge the right of man to end an existence which may have become intolerable to him, through physical suffering or mental despair. It is believed that the community will be benefited by the removal of such people from their midst. Since the passage of this law, the number of suicides in the United States has not increased. Now that the government has determined to establish a Lethal Chamber in every city, town, and village in the country, it remains to be seen whether or not that class of human creatures from whose desponding ranks new victims of self-destruction fall daily will accept the relief thus provided." He paused, and turned to the white Lethal Chamber. The silence in the street was absolute. "There a painless death awaits him who can no longer bear the sorrows of this life. If death is welcome, let him seek it there." Then, quickly turning to the military aid of the President's household, he said, "I declare the Lethal Chamber open"; and again facing the vast crowd, he cried, in a clear voice: "Citizens of New York and of the United States of America, through me the government declares the Lethal Chamber to be open."

The solemn hush was broken by a sharp cry of command, the squadron of hussars filed after the Governor's carriage, the lancers wheeled and formed along Fifth Avenue to wait for the commandant of the garrison, and the mounted police followed them. I left the crowd to gape and stare at the white marble death-chamber, and, crossing South Fifth Avenue, walked along the western side of that thoroughfare to Bleecker Street. Then I turned to the right and stopped before a dingy shop which bore the sign,

HAWBERK, ARMORER.

I glanced in at the door-way and saw Hawberk busy in his little shop at the end of the hall. He looked up, and, catching sight of me, cried, in his deep, hearty voice, "Come in, Mr. Castaigne!" Constance, his daughter, rose to meet me as I crossed the threshold, and held out her pretty hand, but I saw the blush of disappointment on her cheeks, and knew that it was another Castaigne she had expected, my cousin Louis. I smiled at her confusion and complimented her on the banner which she was embroidering from a colored plate. Old Hawberk sat riveting the worn greaves of some ancient suit of armor, and the ting! ting! ting! of his little hammer sounded pleasantly in the quaint shop. Presently he dropped his hammer and fussed about for a moment with a tiny wrench. The soft clash of the mail sent a thrill of pleasure through me. I loved to hear the music of steel brushing against steel, the mellow shock of the mallet on thigh-pieces, and the jingle of chain armor. That was the only reason I went to see Hawberk. He had never interested me personally, nor did Constance, except for the fact of her being in love with Louis. This did occupy my attention, and sometimes even kept me awake at night. But I knew in my heart that all would come right, and that I should arrange their future as I expected to arrange that of my kind doctor, John Archer. However, I should never have troubled myself about visiting them just then had it not been, as I say, that the music of the tinkling hammer had for me this strong fascination. I would sit for hours, listening and listening, and when a stray sunbeam struck the inlaid steel, the sensation it gave me was almost too keen to endure. My eyes would become fixed, dilating with a pleasure that stretched every nerve almost to breaking, until some movement of the old armorer cut off the ray of sunlight, then, still thrilling secretly, I leaned back and listened again to the sound of the polishing rag—swish! swish! —rubbing rust from the rivets.

Constance worked with the embroidery over her knees, now and then pausing to examine more closely the pattern in the colored plate from the Metropolitan Museum.

"Who is this for?" I asked.

Hawberk explained that in addition to the treasures of armor in the Metropolitan Museum, of which he had been appointed armorer, he also had charge of several collections belonging to rich amateurs. This was the missing greave of a famous suit which a client of his had traced to a little shop in Paris on the Quai d'Orsay. He, Hawberk, had negotiated for and secured the greave, and now the suit was complete. He laid down his hammer and read me the history of the suit, traced since 1450 from owner to owner until it was acquired by Thomas Stainbridge. When his superb collection was sold, this client of Hawberk's bought the suit, and since then the search for the missing greave had been pushed until it was, almost by accident, located in Paris.

"Did you continue the search so persistently without any certainty of the greave being still in existence?" I demanded.

"Of course," he replied, coolly.

Then for the first time I took a personal interest in Hawberk.

"It was worth something to you," I ventured.

"No," he replied, laughing, "my pleasure in finding it was my reward."

"Have you no ambition to be rich?" I asked, smiling.

"My one ambition is to be the best armorer in the world," he answered, gravely.

Constance asked me if I had seen the ceremonies at the Lethal Chamber. She herself had noticed cavalry passing up Broadway that morning, and had wished to see the inauguration, but her father wanted the banner finished, and she had stayed at his request.

"Did you see your cousin, Mr. Castaigne, there?" she asked, with the slightest tremor of her soft eyelashes.

"No," I replied, carelessly. "Louis' regiment is manœuvring out in Westchester County." I rose and picked up my hat and cane.

"Are you going up-stairs to see the lunatic again?" laughed old Hawberk. If Hawberk knew how I loathe that word "lunatic," he would never use it in my presence. It rouses certain feelings within me which I do not care to explain. However, I answered him quietly:

"I think I shall drop in and see Mr. Wilde for a moment or two."

"Poor fellow," said Constance, with a shake of her head, "it must be hard to live alone year after year, poor, crippled, and almost demented. It is very good of you, Mr. Castaigne, to visit him as often as you do."

"I think he is vicious," observed Hawberk, beginning again with his hammer. I listened to the golden tinkle on the greave-plates; when he had finished I replied:

"No, he is not vicious, nor is he in the least demented. His mind is a wonder chamber, from which he can extract treasures that you and I would give years of our lives to acquire."

Hawberk laughed.

I continued, a little impatiently: "He knows history as no one else could know it. Nothing, however trivial, escapes his search, and his memory is so absolute, so precise in details, that were it known in New York that such a man existed the people could not honor him enough."

"Nonsense!" muttered Hawberk, searching on the floor for a fallen rivet.

"Is it nonsense," I asked, managing to suppress what I felt— "is it nonsense when he says that the tassets and cuissards of the enamelled suit of armor commonly known as the 'Prince's Emblazoned' can be found among a mass of rusty theatrical properties, broken stoves, and rag-picker's refuse in a garret in Pell Street?"

Hawberk's hammer fell to the ground, but he picked it up and asked, with a great deal of calm, how I knew that the tassets and left cuissard were missing from the "Prince's Emblazoned."

"I did not know until Mr. Wilde mentioned it to me the other day. He said they were in the garret of 998 Pell Street."

"Nonsense!" he cried; but I noticed his hand trembling under his leathern apron.

"Is this nonsense, too?" I asked, pleasantly. "Is it nonsense when Mr. Wilde continually speaks of you as the Marquis of Avonshire, and of Miss Constance—"

I did not finish, for Constance had started to her feet with terror written on every feature. Hawberk looked at me and slowly smoothed his leathern apron. "That is impossible," he observed. "Mr. Wilde may know a great many things—"

"About armor, for instance, and the 'Prince's Emblazoned,'" I interposed, smiling.

"Yes," he continued, slowly, "about armor also—maybe— but he is wrong in regard to the Marquis of Avonshire, who, as you know, killed his wife's traducer years ago, and went to Australia, where he did not long survive his wife."

"Mr. Wilde is wrong," murmured Constance. Her lips were blanched, but her voice was sweet and calm.

"Let us agree, if you please, that in this one circumstance Mr. Wilde is wrong," I said.

II

I climbed the three dilapidated flights of stairs which I had so often climbed before, and knocked at a small door at the end of the corridor. Mr. Wilde opened the door and I walked in.

When he had double-locked the door and pushed a heavy chest against it, he came and sat down beside me, peering up into my face with his little, light-colored eyes. Half a dozen new scratches covered his nose and cheeks, and the silver wires which supported his artificial ears had become displaced. I thought I had never seen him so hideously fascinating. He had no ears. The artificial ones, which now stood out at an angle from the fine wire, were his one weakness. They were made of wax and painted a shell pink; but the rest of his face was yellow. He might better have revelled in the luxury of some artificial fingers for his left hand, which was absolutely fingerless, but it seemed to cause him no inconvenience, and he was satisfied with his wax ears. He was very small, scarcely higher than a child of ten, but his arms were magnificently developed, and his thighs as thick as any athlete's. Still, the most remarkable thing about Mr. Wilde was that a man of his marvellous intelligence and knowledge should have such a head. It was flat and pointed, like the heads of many of those unfortunates whom people imprison in asylums for the weak-minded. Many called him insane, but I knew him to be as sane as I was.

I do not deny that he was eccentric; the mania he had for keeping that cat and teasing her until she flew at his face like a demon was certainly eccentric. I never could understand why he kept the creature, nor what pleasure he found in shutting himself up in his room with the surly, vicious beast. I remember once glancing up from the manuscript I was studying by the light of some tallow dips and seeing Mr. Wilde squatting motionless on his high chair, his eyes fairly blazing with excitement, while the cat, which had risen from her place before the stove, came creeping across the floor right at him. Before I could move she flattened her belly to the ground, crouched, trembled, and sprang into his face. Howling and foaming, they rolled over and over on the floor, scratching and clawing, until the cat screamed and fled under the cabinet, and Mr. Wilde turned over on his back, his limbs contracting and curling up like the legs of a dying spider. He *was* eccentric.

Mr. Wilde had climbed into his high chair, and, after studying my face, picked up a dog's-eared ledger and opened it.

"Henry B. Matthews," he read, "book-keeper with Whysot Whysot & Company, dealers in church ornaments. Called April 3d. Reputation damaged on the race-track. Known as a welcher. Reputation to be repaired by August 1st. Retainer, Five Dollars." He turned the page and ran his fingerless knuckles down the closely written columns.

"P. Greene Dusenberry, Minister of the Gospel, Fairbeach, New Jersey. Reputation damaged in the Bowery. To be repaired as soon as possible. Retainer, $100."

He coughed and added, "Called, April 6th."

"Then you are not in need of money, Mr. Wilde," I inquired.

"Listen"—he coughed again.

"Mrs. C. Hamilton Chester, of Chester Park, New York City, called April 7th. Reputation damaged at Dieppe, France. To be repaired by October 1st. Retainer, $500.

"Note.—C. Hamilton Chester, Captain U.S.S. *Avalanche*, ordered home from South Sea Squadron October 1st."

"Well," I said, "the profession of a Repairer of Reputations is lucrative."

His colorless eyes sought mine. "I only wanted to demonstrate that I was correct. You said it was impossible to succeed as a Repairer of Reputations; that even if I did succeed in certain cases, it would cost me more than I would gain by it. To-day I have five hundred men in my employ, who are poorly paid, but who pursue the work with an enthusiasm which possibly may be born of fear. These men enter every shade and grade of society; some even are pillars of the most exclusive social temples; others are the prop and pride of the financial world; still others hold undisputed sway among the 'Fancy and the Talent.' I choose them at my leisure from those who reply to my advertisements. It is easy enough—they are all cowards. I could treble the number in twenty days if I wished. So, you see, those who have in their keeping the reputations of their fellow-citizens, *I* have in my pay."

"They may turn on you," I suggested.

He rubbed his thumb over his cropped ears and adjusted the wax substitutes. "I think not," he murmured, thoughtfully, "I seldom have to apply the whip, and then only once. Besides, they like their wages."

"How do you apply the whip?" I demanded.

His face for a moment was awful to look upon. His eyes dwindled to a pair of green sparks.

"I invite them to come and have a little chat with me," he said, in a soft voice.

A knock at the door interrupted him, and his face resumed its amiable expression.

"Who is it?" he inquired.

"Mr. Steylette," was the answer.

"Come to-morrow," replied Mr. Wilde.

"Impossible," began the other; but was silenced by a sort of bark from Mr. Wilde.

"Come to-morrow," he repeated.

We heard somebody move away from the door and turn the corner by the stair-way.

"Who is that?" I asked.

"Arnold Steylette, owner and editor-in-chief of the great New York daily."

He drummed on the ledger with his fingerless hand, adding, "I pay him very badly, but he thinks it a good bargain."

"Arnold Steylette!" I repeated, amazed.

"Yes," said Mr. Wilde, with a self-satisfied cough.

The cat, which had entered the room as he spoke, hesitated, looked up at him, and snarled. He climbed down from the chair, and, squatting on the floor, took the creature into his arms and caressed her. The cat ceased snarling and presently began a loud purring, which seemed to increase in timbre as he stroked her.

"Where are the notes?" I asked. He pointed to the table, and for the hundredth time I picked up the bundle of manuscript entitled

"THE IMPERIAL DYNASTY OF AMERICA."

One by one I studied the well-worn pages, worn only by my own handling, and, although I knew all by heart, from the beginning, "When from Carcosa, the Hyades, Hastur, and Aldebaran," to "Castaigne, Louis de Calvados, born December 19, 1887," I read it with an eager, rapt attention, pausing to repeat parts of it aloud, and dwelling especially on "Hildred de Calvados, only son of Hildred Castaigne and Edythe Landes Castaigne, first in succession," etc., etc.

When I finished, Mr. Wilde nodded and coughed.

"Speaking of your legitimate ambition," he said, "how do Constance and Louis get along?"

"She loves him," I replied, simply.

The cat on his knee suddenly turned and struck at his eyes, and he flung her off and climbed on to the chair opposite me.

"And Dr. Archer? But that's a matter you can settle any time you wish," he added.

"Yes," I replied, "Dr. Archer can wait, but it is time I saw my cousin Louis."

"It is time," he repeated. Then he took another ledger from the table and ran over the leaves rapidly.

"We are now in communication with ten thousand men," he muttered. "We can count on one hundred thousand within the first twenty-eight hours, and in forty-eight hours the State will rise *en masse*. The country follows the State, and the portion that will not, I mean California and the Northwest, might better never have been inhabited. I shall not send them the Yellow Sign."

The blood rushed to my head, but I only answered, "A new broom sweeps clean."

"The ambition of Cæsar and of Napoleon pales before that which could not rest until it had seized the minds of men and controlled even their unborn thoughts," said Mr. Wilde.

"You are speaking of the King in Yellow," I groaned, with a shudder.

"He is a king whom emperors have served."

"I am content to serve him," I replied.

Mr. Wilde sat rubbing his ears with his crippled hand. "Perhaps Constance does not love him," he suggested.

I started to reply, but a sudden burst of military music from the street below drowned my voice. The Twentieth Dragoon Regiment, formerly in garrison at Mount St. Vincent, was returning from the manœuvres in Westchester County to its new

barracks on East Washington Square. It was my cousin's regiment. They were a fine lot of fellows, in their pale-blue, tight-
fitting jackets, jaunty busbies, and white riding-breeches, with
the double yellow stripe, into which their limbs seemed
moulded. Every other squadron was armed with lances, from
the metal points of which fluttered yellow-and-white pennons.
The band passed, playing the regimental march, then came the
colonel and staff, the horses crowding and trampling, while
their heads bobbed in unison, and the pennons fluttered from
their lance points. The troopers, who rode with the beautiful
English seat, looked brown as berries from their bloodless campaign among the farms of Westchester, and the music of their
sabres against the stirrups, and the jingle of spurs and carbines
was delightful to me. I saw Louis riding with his squadron. He
was as handsome an officer as I have ever seen. Mr. Wilde, who
had mounted a chair by the window, saw him, too, but said
nothing. Louis turned and looked straight at Hawberk's shop
as he passed, and I could see the flush on his brown cheeks. I
think Constance must have been at the window. When the last
troopers had clattered by, and the last pennons vanished into
South Fifth Avenue, Mr. Wilde clambered out of his chair and
dragged the chest away from the door.

"Yes," he said, "it is time that you saw your cousin Louis."

He unlocked the door and I picked up my hat and stick and
stepped into the corridor. The stairs were dark. Groping about,
I set my foot on something soft, which snarled and spit, and I
aimed a murderous blow at the cat, but my cane shivered to
splinters against the balustrade, and the beast scurried back
into Mr. Wilde's room.

Passing Hawberk's door again, I saw him still at work on the
armor, but I did not stop, and, stepping out into Bleecker
Street, I followed it to Wooster, skirted the grounds of the
Lethal Chamber, and, crossing Washington Park, went straight
to my rooms in the Benedick. Here I lunched comfortably, read
the *Herald* and the *Meteor*, and finally went to the steel safe in
my bedroom and set the time combination. The three and
three-quarter minutes which it is necessary to wait, while the
time lock is opening, are to me golden moments. From the instant I set the combination to the moment when I grasp the
knobs and swing back the solid steel doors, I live in an ecstacy

of expectation. Those moments must be like moments passed in paradise. I know what I am to find at the end of the time limit. I know what the massive safe holds secure for me, for me alone, and the exquisite pleasure of waiting is hardly enhanced when the safe opens and I lift, from its velvet crown, a diadem of purest gold, blazing with diamonds. I do this every day, and yet the joy of waiting and at last touching again the diadem only seems to increase as the days pass. It is a diadem fit for a king among kings, an emperor among emperors. The King in Yellow might scorn it, but it shall be worn by his royal servant.

I held it in my arms until the alarm on the safe rang harshly, and then tenderly, proudly I replaced it and shut the steel doors. I walked slowly back into my study, which faces Washington Square, and leaned on the window-sill. The afternoon sun poured into my windows, and a gentle breeze stirred the branches of the elms and maples in the park, now covered with buds and tender foliage. A flock of pigeons circled about the tower of the Memorial Church; sometimes alighting on the purple-tiled roof, sometimes wheeling downward to the lotos fountain in front of the marble arch. The gardeners were busy with the flower-beds around the fountain, and the freshly turned earth smelled sweet and spicy. A lawn-mower, drawn by a fat, white horse, clinked across the greensward, and watering-carts poured showers of spray over the asphalt drives. Around the statue of Peter Stuyvesant, which in 1906 had replaced the monstrosity supposed to represent Garibaldi, children played in the spring sunshine, and nurse girls wheeled elaborate baby-carriages with a reckless disregard for the pasty-faced occupants, which could probably be explained by the presence of half a dozen trim dragoon troopers languidly lolling on the benches. Through the trees the Washington Memorial Arch glistened like silver in the sunshine, and beyond, on the eastern extremity of the square, the gray-stone barracks of the dragoons and the white-granite artillery stables were alive with color and motion.

I looked at the Lethal Chamber on the corner of the square opposite. A few curious people still lingered about the gilded iron railing, but inside the grounds the paths were deserted. I watched the fountains ripple and sparkle; the sparrows had already found this new bathing nook, and the basins were crowded with the dusty-feathered little things. Two or three white peacocks picked their way across the lawns, and a drab-colored pigeon sat so motionless on the arm of one of the Fates that it seemed to be a part of the sculptured stone.

As I was turning carelessly away, a slight commotion in the group of curious loiterers around the gates attracted my attention. A young man had entered, and was advancing with nervous strides along the gravel path which leads to the bronze doors of the Lethal Chamber. He paused a moment before the Fates, and as he raised his head to those three mysterious faces, the pigeon rose from its sculptured perch, circled about for a moment, and wheeled to the east. The young man pressed his hands to his face, and then, with an undefinable gesture, sprang up the marble steps, the bronze doors closed behind him, and half an hour later the loiterers slouched away and the frightened pigeon returned to its perch in the arms of Fate.

I put on my hat and went out into the park for a little walk before dinner. As I crossed the central driveway a group of officers passed, and one of them called out, "Hello, Hildred!" and came back to shake hands with me. It was my cousin Louis, who stood smiling and tapping his spurred heels with his riding-whip.

"Just back from Westchester," he said; "been doing the bucolic; milk and curds, you know; dairy-maids in sunbonnets, who say 'haeow' and 'I don't think' when you tell them they are pretty. I'm nearly dead for a square meal at Delmonico's. What's the news?"

"There is none," I replied, pleasantly. "I saw your regiment coming in this morning."

"Did you? I didn't see you. Where were you?"

"In Mr. Wilde's window."

"Oh, hell!" he began, impatiently, "that man is stark mad! I don't understand why you—"

He saw how annoyed I felt by this outburst, and begged my pardon.

"Really, old chap," he said, "I don't mean to run down a man you like, but for the life of me I can't see what the deuce you find in common with Mr. Wilde. He's not well bred, to put it generously; he's hideously deformed; his head is the head of a criminally insane person. You know yourself he's been in an asylum—"

"So have I," I interrupted, calmly.

Louis looked startled and confused for a moment, but recovered and slapped me heartily on the shoulder.

"You were completely cured," he began; but I stopped him again.

"I suppose you mean that I was simply acknowledged never to have been insane."

"Of course that—that's what I meant," he laughed.

I disliked his laugh, because I knew it was forced; but I nodded gayly and asked him where he was going. Louis looked after his brother officers, who had now almost reached Broadway.

"We had intended to sample a Brunswick cocktail, but, to tell you the truth, I was anxious for an excuse to go and see Hawberk instead. Come along; I'll make you my excuse."

We found old Hawberk, neatly attired in a fresh spring suit, standing at the door of his shop and sniffing the air.

"I had just decided to take Constance for a little stroll before dinner," he replied to the impetuous volley of questions from Louis. "We thought of walking on the park terrace along the North River."

At that moment Constance appeared and grew pale and rosy by turns as Louis bent over her small, gloved fingers. I tried to excuse myself, alleging an engagement up-town, but Louis and Constance would not listen, and I saw I was expected to remain and engage old Hawberk's attention. After all, it would be just as well if I kept my eye on Louis, I thought, and, when they hailed a Spring Street electric-car, I got in after them and took my seat beside the armorer.

The beautiful line of parks and granite terraces overlooking the wharves along the North River, which were built in 1910 and finished in the autumn of 1917, had become one of the most popular promenades in the metropolis. They extended from the Battery to One Hundred and Ninetieth Street, overlooking the noble river, and affording a fine view of the Jersey shore and the Highlands opposite. Cafés and restaurants were scattered here and there among the trees, and twice a week military bands from the garrison played in the kiosques on the parapets.

We sat down in the sunshine on the bench at the foot of the equestrian statue of General Sheridan. Constance tipped her sunshade to shield her eyes, and she and Louis began a murmuring conversation which was impossible to catch. Old Hawberk, leaning on his ivory-headed cane, lighted an excellent cigar, the mate to which I politely refused, and smiled at vacancy. The sun hung low above the Staten Island woods, and the bay was dyed with golden hues reflected from the sunwarmed sails of the shipping in the harbor.

Brigs, schooners, yachts, clumsy ferry-boats, their decks swarming with people, railroad transports carrying lines of brown, blue, and white freight-cars, stately Sound steamers, *déclassé* tramp steamers, coasters, dredgers, scows, and everywhere pervading the entire bay impudent little tugs puffing and whistling officiously—these were the craft which churned the sunlit waters as far as the eye could reach. In calm contrast to the hurry of sailing vessel and steamer, a silent fleet of white war-ships lay motionless in midstream.

Constance's merry laugh aroused me from my reverie.

"What *are* you staring at?" she inquired.

"Nothing—the fleet." I smiled.

Then Louis told us what the vessels were, pointing out each by its relative position to the old red fort on Governor's Island.

"That little cigar-shaped thing is a torpedo-boat," he explained; "there are four more lying close together. They are the *Tarpon*, the *Falcon*, the *Sea Fox*, and the *Octopus*. The gunboats just above are the *Princeton*, the *Champlain*, the *Still Water*, and the *Erie*. Next to them lie the cruisers *Farragut* and *Los Angeles*, and above them the battle-ships *California* and *Dakota*, and the *Washington*, which is the flagship. Those two squatty-looking chunks of metal which are anchored there off Castle William are the double-turreted monitors *Terrible* and *Magnificent*; behind them lies the ram *Osceola*."

Constance looked at him with deep approval in her beautiful eyes. "What loads of things you know for a soldier," she said, and we all joined in the laugh which followed.

Presently Louis rose with a nod to us and offered his arm to Constance, and they strolled away along the river-wall. Hawberk watched them for a moment, and then turned to me.

"Mr. Wilde was right," he said. "I have found the missing

tassets and left cuissard of the 'Prince's Emblazoned,' in a vile old junk garret in Pell Street."

"998?" I inquired, with a smile.

"Yes."

"Mr. Wilde is a very intelligent man," I observed.

"I want to give him the credit of this most important discovery," continued Hawberk. "And I intend it shall be known that he is entitled to the fame of it."

"He won't thank you for that," I answered, sharply; "please say nothing about it."

"Do you know what it is worth?" said Hawberk.

"No—fifty dollars, perhaps."

"It is valued at five hundred, but the owner of the 'Prince's Emblazoned' will give two thousand dollars to the person who completes his suit; that reward also belongs to Mr. Wilde."

"He doesn't want it! He refuses it!" I answered, angrily. "What do you know about Mr. Wilde? He doesn't need the money. He is rich—or will be—richer than any living man except myself. What will we care for money then—what will we care, he and I, when—when—"

"When what?" demanded Hawberk, astonished.

"You will see," I replied, on my guard again.

He looked at me narrowly, much as Dr. Archer used to, and I knew he thought I was mentally unsound. Perhaps it was fortunate for him that he did not use the word lunatic just then.

"No," I replied to his unspoken thought, "I am not mentally weak; my mind is as healthy as Mr. Wilde's. I do not care to explain just yet what I have on hand, but it is an investment which will pay more than mere gold, silver, and precious stones. It will secure the happiness and prosperity of a continent—yes, a hemisphere!"

"Oh," said Hawberk.

"And eventually," I continued, more quietly, "it will secure the happiness of the whole world."

"And incidentally your own happiness and prosperity as well as Mr. Wilde's?"

"Exactly." I smiled, but I could have throttled him for taking that tone.

He looked at me in silence for a while, and then said, very

gently: "Why don't you give up your books and studies, Mr. Castaigne, and take a tramp among the mountains somewhere or other? You used to be fond of fishing. Take a cast or two at the trout in the Rangelys."

"I don't care for fishing any more," I answered, without a shade of annoyance in my voice.

"You used to be fond of everything," he continued— "athletics, yachting, shooting, riding—"

"I have never cared to ride since my fall," I said, quietly.

"Ah, yes, your fall," he repeated, looking away from me.

I thought this nonsense had gone far enough, so I turned the conversation back to Mr. Wilde; but he was scanning my face again in a manner highly offensive to me.

"Mr. Wilde," he repeated; "do you know what he did this afternoon? He came down-stairs and nailed a sign over the hall door next to mine; it read:

MR. WILDE,
REPAIRER OF REPUTATIONS.
3d Bell.

Do you know what a Repairer of Reputations can be?"

"I do," I replied, suppressing the rage within.

"Oh," he said again.

Louis and Constance came strolling by and stopped to ask if we would join them. Hawberk looked at his watch. At the same moment a puff of smoke shot from the casemates of Castle William, and the boom of the sunset gun rolled across the water and was re-echoed from the Highlands opposite. The flag came running down from the flag-pole, the bugles sounded on the white decks of the war-ships, and the first electric light sparkled out from the Jersey shore.

As I turned into the city with Hawberk I heard Constance murmur something to Louis which I did not understand; but Louis whispered "My darling!" in reply; and again, walking ahead with Hawberk through the square, I heard a murmur of "sweetheart!" and "my own Constance!" and I knew the time had nearly arrived when I should speak of important matters with my cousin Louis.

III

One morning early in May I stood before the steel safe in my bedroom, trying on the golden jewelled crown. The diamonds flashed fire as I turned to the mirror, and the heavy beaten gold burned like a halo about my head. I remembered Camilla's agonized scream and the awful words echoing through the dim streets of Carcosa. They were the last lines in the first act, and I dared not think of what followed—dared not, even in the spring sunshine, there in my own room, surrounded with familiar objects, reassured by the bustle from the street and the voices of the servants in the hall-way outside. For those poisoned words had dropped slowly into my heart, as death-sweat drops upon a bed-sheet and is absorbed. Trembling, I put the diadem from my head and wiped my forehead, but I thought of Hastur and of my own rightful ambition, and I remembered Mr. Wilde as I had last left him, his face all torn and bloody from the claws of that devil's creature, and what he said—ah, what he said! The alarm-bell in the safe began to whir harshly, and I knew my time was up; but I would not heed it, and, replacing the flashing circlet upon my head, I turned defiantly to the mirror. I stood for a long time absorbed in the changing expression of my own eyes. The mirror reflected a face which was like my own, but whiter, and so thin that I hardly recognized it. And all the time I kept repeating between my clinched teeth, "The day has come! the day has come!" while the alarm in the safe whirred and clamored, and the diamonds sparkled and flamed above my brow. I heard a door open, but did not heed it. It was only when I saw two faces in the mirror; it was only when another face rose over my shoulder, and two other eyes met mine. I wheeled like a flash and seized a long knife from my dressing-table, and my cousin sprang back very pale, crying: "Hildred! for God's sake!" Then, as my hand fell, he said: "It is I, Louis; don't you know me?" I stood silent. I could not have spoken for my life. He walked up to me and took the knife from my hand.

"What is all this?" he inquired, in a gentle voice. "Are you ill?"

"No," I replied. But I doubt if he heard me.

"Come, come, old fellow," he cried, "take off that brass

crown and toddle into the study. Are you going to a masquerade? What's all this theatrical tinsel anyway?"

I was glad he thought the crown was made of brass and
paste, yet I didn't like him any the better for thinking so. I let
him take it from my hand, knowing it was best to humor him.
He tossed the splendid diadem in the air, and, catching it,
turned to me smiling.

"It's dear at fifty cents," he said. "What's it for?"

I did not answer, but took the circlet from his hands, and,
placing it in the safe, shut the massive steel door. The alarm
ceased its infernal din at once. He watched me curiously, but
did not seem to notice the sudden ceasing of the alarm. He did,
however, speak of the safe as a biscuit-box. Fearing lest he might
examine the combination, I led the way into my study. Louis
threw himself on the sofa and flicked at flies with his eternal
riding-whip. He wore his fatigue uniform, with the braided
jacket and jaunty cap, and I noticed that his riding-boots were
all splashed with red mud.

"Where have you been?" I inquired.

"Jumping mud creeks in Jersey," he said. "I haven't had time
to change yet; I was rather in a hurry to see you. Haven't you
got a glass of something? I'm dead tired; been in the saddle
twenty-four hours."

I gave him some brandy from my medicinal store, which he
drank with a grimace.

"Damned bad stuff," he observed. "I'll give you an address
where they sell brandy that is brandy."

"It's good enough for my needs," I said, indifferently. "I use
it to rub my chest with." He stared and flicked at another fly.

"See here, old fellow," he began, "I've got something to suggest to you. It's four years now that you've shut yourself up here
like an owl, never going anywhere, never taking any healthy exercise, never doing a damn thing but poring over those books
up there on the mantel-piece."

He glanced along the row of shelves. "Napoleon, Napoleon,
Napoleon!" he read. "For Heaven's sake, have you nothing
but Napoleons there?"

"I wish they were bound in gold," I said. "But wait—yes,
there is another book, 'The King in Yellow.'" I looked him
steadily in the eye.

"Have you never read it?" I asked.

"I? No, thank God! I don't want to be driven crazy."

I saw he regretted his speech as soon as he had uttered it. There is only one word which I loathe more than I do lunatic, and that word is crazy. But I controlled myself and asked him why he thought "The King in Yellow" dangerous.

"Oh, I don't know," he said, hastily. "I only remember the excitement it created and the denunciations from pulpit and press. I believe the author shot himself after bringing forth this monstrosity, didn't he?"

"I understand he is still alive," I answered.

"That's probably true," he muttered; "bullets couldn't kill a fiend like that."

"It is a book of great truths," I said.

"Yes," he replied, "of 'truths' which send men frantic and blast their lives. I don't care if the thing is, as they say, the very supreme essence of art. It's a crime to have written it, and I for one shall never open its pages."

"Is that what you have come to tell me?" I asked.

"No," he said, "I came to tell you that I am going to be married."

I believe for a moment my heart ceased to beat, but I kept my eyes on his face.

"Yes," he continued, smiling happily, "married to the sweetest girl on earth."

"Constance Hawberk," I said, mechanically.

"How did you know?" he cried, astonished. "I didn't know it myself until that evening last April, when we strolled down to the embankment before dinner."

"When is it to be?" I asked.

"It was to have been next September; but an hour ago a despatch came, ordering our regiment to the Presidio, San Francisco. We leave at noon to-morrow. To-morrow," he repeated. "Just think, Hildred, tomorrow I shall be the happiest fellow that ever drew breath in this jolly world, for Constance will go with me."

I offered him my hand in congratulation, and he seized and shook it like the good-natured fool he was—or pretended to be.

"I am going to get my squadron as a wedding present," he rattled on. "Captain and Mrs. Louis Castaigne—eh, Hildred?"

Then he told me where it was to be and who were to be there, and made me promise to come and be best man. I set my teeth and listened to his boyish chatter without showing what I felt, but—

I was getting to the limit of my endurance, and when he jumped up, and, switching his spurs till they jingled, said he must go, I did not detain him.

"There's one thing I want to ask of you," I said, quietly.

"Out with it—it's promised," he laughed.

"I want you to meet me for a quarter of an hour's talk to-night."

"Of course, if you wish," he said, somewhat puzzled. "Where?"

"Anywhere—in the park there."

"What time, Hildred?"

"Midnight."

"What in the name of—" he began, but checked himself and laughingly assented. I watched him go down the stairs and hurry away, his sabre banging at every stride. He turned into Bleecker Street, and I knew he was going to see Constance. I gave him ten minutes to disappear and then followed in his footsteps, taking with me the jewelled crown and the silken robe embroidered with the Yellow Sign. When I turned into Bleecker Street and entered the doorway which bore the sign,

MR. WILDE,
REPAIRER OF REPUTATIONS,
3d Bell,

I saw old Hawberk moving about in his shop, and imagined I heard Constance's voice in the parlor; but I avoided them both and hurried up the trembling stair-ways to Mr. Wilde's apartment. I knocked, and entered without ceremony. Mr. Wilde lay groaning on the floor, his face covered with blood, his clothes torn to shreds. Drops of blood were scattered about over the carpet, which had also been ripped and frayed in the evidently recent struggle.

"It's that cursed cat," he said, ceasing his groans and turning his colorless eyes to me; "she attacked me while I was asleep. I believe she will kill me yet."

This was too much, so I went into the kitchen and, seizing a hatchet from the pantry, started to find the infernal beast and settle her then and there. My search was fruitless, and after a while I gave it up and came back to find Mr. Wilde squatting on his high chair by the table. He had washed his face and changed his clothes. The great furrows which the cat's claws had ploughed up in his face he had filled with collodion, and a rag hid the wound in his throat. I told him I should kill the cat when I came across her, but he only shook his head and turned to the open ledger before him. He read name after name of the people who had come to him in regard to their reputation, and the sums he had amassed were startling.

"I put on the screws now and then," he explained.

"One day or other some of these people will assassinate you," I insisted.

"Do you think so?" he said, rubbing his mutilated ears.

It was useless to argue with him, so I took down the manuscript entitled Imperial Dynasty of America for the last time I should ever take it down in Mr. Wilde's study. I read it through, thrilling and trembling with pleasure. When I had finished, Mr. Wilde took the manuscript, and, turning to the dark passage which leads from his study to his bedchamber, called out, in a loud voice, "Vance." Then for the first time I noticed a man crouching there in the shadow. How I had overlooked him during my search for the cat I cannot imagine.

"Vance, come in!" cried Mr. Wilde.

The figure rose and crept towards us, and I shall never forget the face that he raised to mine as the light from the window illuminated it.

"Vance, this is Mr. Castaigne," said Mr. Wilde. Before he had finished speaking, the man threw himself on the ground before the table, crying and gasping, "Oh, God! Oh, my God! Help me! Forgive me— Oh, Mr. Castaigne, keep that man away! You cannot, you cannot mean it! You are different—save me! I am broken down—I was in a madhouse, and now—when all was coming right—when I had forgotten the King—the King in Yellow, and—but I shall go mad again—I shall go mad—"

His voice died into a choking rattle, for Mr. Wilde had leaped on him, and his right hand encircled the man's throat. When Vance fell in a heap on the floor, Mr. Wilde clambered nimbly into his chair again, and, rubbing his mangled ears with the stump of his hand, turned to me and asked me for the ledger. I reached it down from the shelf and he opened it. After a moment's searching among the beautifully written pages, he coughed complacently and pointed to the name Vance.

"Vance," he read, aloud—"Osgood Oswald Vance." At the sound of his name the man on the floor raised his head and turned a convulsed face to Mr. Wilde. His eyes were injected with blood, his lips tumefied. "Called April 28th," continued Mr. Wilde. "Occupation, cashier in the Seaforth National Bank; has served a term for forgery at Sing Sing, whence he was transferred to the Asylum for the Criminal Insane. Pardoned by the Governor of New York, and discharged from the Asylum January 19, 1918. Reputation damaged at Sheepshead Bay. Rumors that he lives beyond his income. Reputation to be repaired at once. Retainer, $1500.

"Note.—Has embezzled sums amounting to $30,000 since March 20, 1919. Excellent family, and secured present position through uncle's influence. Father, President of Seaforth Bank."

I looked at the man on the floor.

"Get up, Vance," said Mr. Wilde, in a gentle voice. Vance rose as if hypnotized. "He will do as we suggest now," observed Mr. Wilde, and, opening the manuscript, he read the entire history of the Imperial Dynasty of America. Then, in a kind and soothing murmur, he ran over the important points with Vance, who stood like one stunned. His eyes were so blank and vacant that I imagined he had become half-witted, and remarked it to Mr. Wilde, who replied that it was of no consequence anyway. Very patiently we pointed out to Vance what his share in the affair would be, and he seemed to understand after a while. Mr. Wilde explained the manuscript, using several volumes on Heraldry to substantiate the result of his researches. He mentioned the establishment of the Dynasty in Carcosa, the lakes which connected Hastur, Aldebaran, and the mystery of the Hyades. He spoke of Cassilda and Camilla, and sounded the cloudy depths of Demhe and the Lake of Hali. "The scalloped tatters of the King in Yellow must hide Yhtill forever," he muttered, but I do not believe Vance heard him. Then by degrees he led Vance along the ramifications of the imperial family to Uoht and Thale, from Naotalba and Phantom of Truth to Aldones, and then, tossing aside his manuscript and notes, he began the wonderful story of the Last King. Fascinated and thrilled, I watched him. He threw up his head, his long arms were stretched out in a magnificent gesture of pride and power, and his eyes blazed deep in their sockets like two emeralds. Vance listened, stupefied. As for me, when at last Mr. Wilde had finished, and, pointing to me, cried, "The cousin of the King," my head swam with excitement.

Controlling myself with a superhuman effort, I explained to Vance why I alone was worthy of the crown, and why my cousin must be exiled or die. I made him understand that my cousin must never marry, even after renouncing all his claims, and how that, least of all, he should marry the daughter of the Marquis of Avonshire and bring England into the question. I showed him a list of thousands of names which Mr. Wilde had drawn up; every man whose name was there had received the Yellow Sign, which no living human being dared disregard. The city, the State, the whole land, were ready to rise and tremble before the Pallid Mask.

The time had come, the people should know the son of Hastur, and the whole world bow to the black stars which hang in the sky over Carcosa.

Vance leaned on the table, his head buried in his hands. Mr. Wilde drew a rough sketch on the margin of yesterday's *Herald* with a bit of lead-pencil. It was a plan of Hawberk's rooms. Then he wrote out the order and affixed the seal, and, shaking like a palsied man, I signed my first writ of execution with my name Hildred-Rex.

Mr. Wilde clambered to the floor and, unlocking the cabinet, took a long, square box from the first shelf. This he brought to the table and opened. A new knife lay in the tissue-paper inside, and I picked it up and handed it to Vance, along with the order and the plan of Hawberk's apartment. Then Mr. Wilde told Vance he could go; and he went, shambling like an outcast of the slums.

I sat for a while watching the daylight fade behind the square tower of the Judson Memorial Church, and finally, gathering up the manuscript and notes, took my hat and started for the door.

Mr. Wilde watched me in silence. When I had stepped into the hall I looked back; Mr. Wilde's small eyes were still fixed on me. Behind him the shadows gathered in the fading light. Then I closed the door behind me and went out into the darkening streets.

I had eaten nothing since breakfast, but I was not hungry. A wretched, half-starved creature, who stood looking across the street at the Lethal Chamber, noticed me and came up to tell me a tale of misery. I gave him money—I don't know why—and he went away without thanking me. An hour later another outcast approached and whined his story. I had a blank bit of paper in my pocket, on which was traced the Yellow Sign, and I handed it to him. He looked at it stupidly for a moment, and then, with an uncertain glance at me, folded it with what seemed to me exaggerated care and placed it in his bosom.

The electric lights were sparkling among the trees, and the new moon shone in the sky above the Lethal Chamber. It was tiresome waiting in the square; I wandered from the marble arch to the artillery stables, and back again to the lotos fountain. The flowers and grass exhaled a fragrance which troubled me. The jet of the fountain played in the moonlight, and the musical splash of falling drops reminded me of the tinkle of chained mail in Hawberk's shop. But it was not so fascinating, and the dull sparkle of the moonlight on the water brought no such sensations of exquisite pleasure as when the sunshine played over the polished steel of a corselet on Hawberk's knee. I watched the bats darting and turning above the water plants in the fountain basin, but their rapid, jerky flight set my nerves on edge, and I went away again to walk aimlessly to and fro among the trees.

The artillery stables were dark, but in the cavalry barracks the officers' windows were brilliantly lighted, and the sally-port was constantly filled with troopers in fatigue, carrying straw and harness and baskets filled with tin dishes.

Twice the mounted sentry at the gates was changed while I wandered up and down the asphalt walk. I looked at my watch. It was nearly time. The lights in the barracks went out one by one, the barred gate was closed, and every minute or two an officer passed in through the side wicket, leaving a rattle of accoutrements and a jingle of spurs on the night air. The square had become very silent. The last homeless loiterer had been driven away by the gray-coated park policeman, the car tracks along Wooster Street were deserted, and the only sound which broke the stillness was the stamping of the sentry's horse and the ring of his sabre against the saddle pommel. In the barracks the officers' quarters were still lighted, and military servants passed and repassed before the bay-windows. Twelve o'clock sounded from the new spire of St. Francis Xavier, and at the last stroke of the sad-toned bell a figure passed through the wicket beside the portcullis, returned the salute of the sentry, and, crossing the street, entered the square and advanced towards the Benedick apartment house.

"Louis," I called.

The man pivoted on his spurred heels and came straight towards me.

"Is that you, Hildred?"

"Yes, you are on time."

I took his offered hand and we strolled towards the Lethal Chamber.

He rattled on about his wedding and the graces of Constance and their future prospects, calling my attention to his captain's shoulder-straps and the triple gold arabesque on his sleeve and fatigue cap. I believe I listened as much to the music of his spurs and sabre as I did to his boyish babble, and at last we stood under the elms on the Fourth Street corner of the square opposite the Lethal Chamber. Then he laughed and asked me what I wanted with him. I motioned him to a seat on a bench under the electric light, and sat down beside him. He looked at me curiously, with that same searching glance which I hate and fear so in doctors. I felt the insult of his look, but he did not know it, and I carefully concealed my feelings.

"Well, old chap," he inquired, "what can I do for you?"

I drew from my pocket the manuscript and notes of the Imperial Dynasty of America, and, looking him in the eye, said:

"I will tell you. On your word as a soldier, promise me to read this manuscript from beginning to end without asking me a question. Promise me to read these notes in the same way, and promise me to listen to what I have to tell later."

"I promise, if you wish it," he said, pleasantly. "Give me the paper, Hildred."

He began to read, raising his eyebrows with a puzzled,

whimsical air, which made me tremble with suppressed anger. As he advanced, his eyebrows contracted, and his lips seemed to form the word "rubbish."

Then he looked slightly bored, but apparently for my sake read, with an attempt at interest, which presently ceased to be an effort. He started when, in the closely written pages he came to his own name, and when he came to mine he lowered the paper and looked sharply at me for a moment. But he kept his word, and resumed his reading, and I let the half-formed question die on his lips unanswered. When he came to the end and read the signature of Mr. Wilde, he folded the paper carefully and returned it to me. I handed him the notes, and he settled back, pushing his fatigue cap up to his forehead with a boyish gesture which I remembered so well in school. I watched his face as he read, and when he finished I took the notes, with the manuscript, and placed them in my pocket. Then I unfolded a scroll marked with the Yellow Sign. He saw the sign, but he did not seem to recognize it, and I called his attention to it somewhat sharply.

"Well," he said, "I see it. What is it?"

"It is the Yellow Sign," I said, angrily.

"Oh, that's it, is it?" said Louis, in that flattering voice which Dr. Archer used to employ with me, and would probably have employed again, had I not settled his affair for him.

I kept my rage down and answered as steadily as possible, "Listen, you have engaged your word?"

"I am listening, old chap," he replied, soothingly.

I began to speak very calmly: "Dr. Archer, having by some means become possessed of the secret of the Imperial Succession, attempted to deprive me of my right, alleging that, because of a fall from my horse four years ago, I had become mentally deficient. He presumed to place me under restraint in his own house in hopes of either driving me insane or poisoning me. I have not forgotten it. I visited him last night and the interview was final."

Louis turned quite pale, but did not move. I resumed, triumphantly: "There are yet three people to be interviewed in the interests of Mr. Wilde and myself. They are my cousin Louis, Mr. Hawberk, and his daughter Constance."

Louis sprang to his feet, and I arose also, and flung the paper marked with the Yellow Sign to the ground.

"Oh, I don't need that to tell you what I have to say," I cried, with a laugh of triumph. "You must renounce the crown to me—do you hear, to *me*?"

Louis looked at me with a startled air, but, recovering himself, said kindly, "Of course I renounce the—what is it I must renounce?"

"The crown," I said, angrily.

"Of course," he answered, "I renounce it. Come, old chap, I'll walk back to your rooms with you."

"Don't try any of your doctor's tricks on me," I cried, trembling with fury. "Don't act as if you think I am insane."

"What nonsense!" he replied. "Come, it's getting late, Hildred."

"No," I shouted, "you must listen. You cannot marry; I forbid it. Do you hear? I forbid it. You shall renounce the crown, and in reward I grant you exile; but if you refuse you shall die."

He tried to calm me, but I was roused at last, and, drawing my long knife, barred his way.

Then I told him how they would find Dr. Archer in the cellar with his throat open, and I laughed in his face when I thought of Vance and his knife, and the order signed by me.

"Ah, you are the King," I cried, "but I shall be King. Who are you to keep me from empire over all the habitable earth! I was born the cousin of a king, but I shall be King!"

Louis stood white and rigid before me. Suddenly a man came running up Fourth Street, entered the gate of the Lethal Temple, traversed the path to the bronze doors at full speed, and plunged into the death-chamber with the cry of one demented, and I laughed until I wept tears, for I had recognized Vance, and knew that Hawberk and his daughter were no longer in my way.

"Go," I cried to Louis, "you have ceased to be a menace. You will never marry Constance now, and if you marry any one else in your exile, I will visit you as I did my doctor last night. Mr. Wilde takes charge of you to-morrow." Then I turned and darted into South Fifth Avenue, and with a cry of terror Louis dropped his belt and sabre and followed me like the wind. I heard him close behind me at the corner of Bleecker Street, and I dashed into the door-way under Hawberk's sign. He cried, "Halt, or I fire!" but when he saw that I flew up the stairs leaving Hawberk's shop below, he left me, and I heard him hammering and shouting at their door as though it were possible to arouse the dead.

Mr. Wilde's door was open, and I entered, crying: "It is done, it is done! Let the nations rise and look upon their King!" but I could not find Mr. Wilde, so I went to the cabinet and took the splendid diadem from its case. Then I drew on the white silk robe, embroidered with the Yellow Sign, and placed the crown upon my head. At last I was King, King by my right in Hastur, King because I knew the mystery of the Hyades, and my mind had sounded the depths of the Lake of Hali. I was King! The first gray pencillings of dawn would raise a tempest which would shake two hemispheres. Then as I stood, my every nerve pitched to the highest tension, faint with the joy and splendor of my thought, without, in the dark passage, a man groaned.

I seized the tallow dip and sprang to the door. The cat passed me like a demon, and the tallow dip went out, but my long knife flew swifter than she, and I heard her screech, and I knew that my knife had found her. For a moment I listened to her tumbling and thumping about in the darkness, and then, when her frenzy ceased, I lighted a lamp and raised it over my head. Mr. Wilde lay on the floor with his throat torn open. At first I thought he was dead, but as I looked a green sparkle came into his sunken eyes, his mutilated hand trembled, and then a spasm stretched his mouth from ear to ear. For a moment my terror and despair gave place to hope, but as I bent over him his eyeballs rolled clean around in his head, and he died. Then, while I stood transfixed with rage and despair, seeing my crown, my empire, every hope and every ambition, my very life, lying prostrate there with the dead master, *they* came, seized me from behind and bound me until my veins stood out like cords, and my voice failed with the paroxysms of my frenzied screams. But I still raged, bleeding and infuriated, among them, and more than one policeman felt my sharp teeth. Then when I could no longer move they came nearer; I saw old Hawberk, and behind him my cousin Louis' ghastly face, and farther away, in the corner, a woman, Constance, weeping softly.

"Ah! I see it now!" I shrieked. "You have seized the throne and the empire. Woe! woe to you who are crowned with the crown of the King in Yellow!"

[EDITOR'S NOTE.—Mr. Castaigne died yesterday in the Asylum for Criminal Insane.]

1895

RALPH ADAMS CRAM

The Dead Valley

I HAVE a friend, Olof Ehrensvärd, a Swede by birth, who yet, by reason of a strange and melancholy mischance of his early boyhood, has thrown his lot with that of the New World. It is a curious story of a headstrong boy and a proud and relentless family: the details do not matter here, but they are sufficient to weave a web of romance around the tall yellow-bearded man with the sad eyes and the voice that gives itself perfectly to plaintive little Swedish songs remembered out of childhood. In the winter evenings we play chess together, he and I, and after some close, fierce battle has been fought to a finish—usually with my own defeat—we fill our pipes again, and Ehrensvärd tells me stories of the far, half-remembered days in the fatherland, before he went to sea: stories that grow very strange and incredible as the night deepens and the fire falls together, but stories that, nevertheless, I fully believe.

One of them made a strong impression on me, so I set it down here, only regretting that I cannot reproduce the curiously perfect English and the delicate accent which to me increased the fascination of the tale. Yet, as best I can remember it, here it is.

"I never told you how Nils and I went over the hills to Hallsberg, and how we found the Dead Valley, did I? Well, this is the way it happened. I must have been about twelve years old, and Nils Sjöberg, whose father's estate joined ours, was a few months younger. We were inseparable just at that time, and whatever we did, we did together.

"Once a week it was market day in Engelholm, and Nils and I went always there to see the strange sights that the market gathered from all the surrounding country. One day we quite lost our hearts, for an old man from across the Elfborg had brought a little dog to sell, that seemed to us the most beautiful dog in all the world. He was a round, woolly puppy, so funny that Nils and I sat down on the ground and laughed at him, until he came and played with us in so jolly a way that we felt that there was only one really desirable thing in life, and that was the little dog of the old man from across the hills. But alas! we had not half money enough wherewith to buy him, so we were forced to beg the old man not to sell him before the next market day, promising that we would bring the money for him then. He gave us his word, and we ran home very fast and implored our mothers to give us money for the little dog.

"We got the money, but we could not wait for the next market day. Suppose the puppy should be sold! The thought frightened us so that we begged and implored that we might be allowed to go over the hills to Hallsberg where the old man lived, and get the little dog ourselves, and at last they told us we might go. By starting early in the morning we should reach Hallsberg by three o'clock, and it was arranged that we should stay there that night with Nils's aunt, and, leaving by noon the next day, be home again by sunset.

"Soon after sunrise we were on our way, after having received minute instructions as to just what we should do in all possible and impossible circumstances, and finally a repeated injunction that we should start for home at the same hour the next day, so that we might get safely back before nightfall.

"For us, it was magnificent sport, and we started off with our rifles, full of the sense of our very great importance: yet the journey was simple enough, along a good road, across the big hills we knew so well, for Nils and I had shot over half the territory this side of the dividing ridge of the Elfborg. Back of Engelholm lay a long valley, from which rose the low mountains, and we had to cross this, and then follow the road along the side of the hills for three or four miles, before a narrow path branched off to the left, leading up through the pass.

"Nothing occurred of interest on the way over, and we reached Hallsberg in due season, found to our inexpressible joy that the little dog was not sold, secured him, and so went to the house of Nils's aunt to spend the night.

"Why we did not leave early on the following day, I can't quite remember; at all events, I know we stopped at a shooting range just outside of the town, where most attractive pasteboard pigs were sliding slowly through painted foliage, serving so as beautiful marks. The result was that we did not get fairly started for home until afternoon, and as we found ourselves at last pushing up the side of the mountain with the sun dangerously near their summits, I think we were a little scared at the prospect of the examination and possible punishment that awaited us when we got home at midnight.

"Therefore we hurried as fast as possible up the mountain side, while the blue dusk closed in about us, and the light died in the purple sky. At first we had talked hilariously, and the little dog had leaped ahead of us with the utmost joy. Latterly, however, a curious oppression came on us; we did not speak or even whistle, while the dog fell behind, following us with hesitation in every muscle.

"We had passed through the foothills and the low spurs of the mountains, and were almost at the top of the main range, when life seemed to go out of everything, leaving the world dead, so suddenly silent the forest became, so stagnant the air. Instinctively we halted to listen.

"Perfect silence,—the crushing silence of deep forests at night; and more, for always, even in the most impenetrable fastnesses of the wooded mountains, is the multitudinous murmur of little lives, awakened by the darkness, exaggerated and intensified by the stillness of the air and the great dark: but here and now the silence seemed unbroken even by the turn of a leaf, the movement of a twig, the note of night bird or insect. I could hear the blood beat through my veins; and the crushing of the grass under our feet as we advanced with hesitating steps sounded like the falling of trees.

"And the air was stagnant,—dead. The atmosphere seemed to lie upon the body like the weight of sea on a diver who has ventured too far into its awful depths. What we usually call silence seems so only in relation to the din of ordinary experience. This was silence in the absolute, and it crushed the mind while it intensified the senses, bringing down the awful weight of inextinguishable fear.

"I know that Nils and I stared towards each other in abject terror, listening to our quick, heavy breathing, that sounded to our acute senses like the fitful rush of waters. And the poor little dog we were leading justified our terror. The black oppression seemed to crush him even as it did us. He lay close on the ground, moaning feebly, and dragging himself painfully and slowly closer to Nils's feet. I think this exhibition of utter animal fear was the last touch, and must inevitably have blasted our reason—mine anyway; but just then, as we stood quaking on the bounds of madness, came a sound, so awful, so ghastly, so horrible, that it seemed to rouse us from the dead spell that was on us.

"In the depth of the silence came a cry, beginning as a low, sorrowful moan, rising to a tremulous shriek, culminating in a yell that seemed to tear the night in sunder and rend the world as by a cataclysm. So fearful was it that I could not believe it had actual existence: it passed previous experience, the powers of belief, and for a moment I thought it the result of my own animal terror, an hallucination born of tottering reason.

"A glance at Nils dispelled this thought in a flash. In the pale light of the high stars he was the embodiment of all possible human fear, quaking with an ague, his jaw fallen, his tongue out, his eyes protruding like those of a hanged man. Without a word we fled, the panic of fear giving us strength, and together, the little dog caught close in Nils's arms, we sped down the side of the cursed mountains,—anywhere, goal was of no account: we had but one impulse—to get away from that place.

"So under the black trees and the far white stars that flashed through the still leaves overhead, we leaped down the mountain side, regardless of path or landmark, straight through the tangled underbrush, across mountain streams, through fens and copses, anywhere, so only that our course was downward.

"How long we ran thus, I have no idea, but by and by the forest fell behind, and we found ourselves among the foothills, and fell exhausted on the dry short grass, panting like tired dogs.

"It was lighter here in the open, and presently we looked around to see where we were, and how we were to strike out in order to find the path that would lead us home. We looked in vain for a familiar sign. Behind us rose the great wall of black forest on the flank of the mountain: before us lay the undulating mounds of low foothills, unbroken by trees or rocks, and beyond, only the fall of black sky bright with multitudinous stars that turned its velvet depth to a luminous gray.

"As I remember, we did not speak to each other once: the terror was too heavy on us for that, but by and by we rose simultaneously and started out across the hills.

"Still the same silence, the same dead, motionless air—air that was at once sultry and chilling: a heavy heat struck through with an icy chill that felt almost like the burning of frozen steel. Still carrying the helpless dog, Nils pressed on through the hills, and I followed close behind. At last, in front of us, rose a slope of moor touching the white stars. We climbed it wearily, reached the top, and found ourselves gazing down into a great, smooth valley, filled half way to the brim with—what?

"As far as the eye could see stretched a level plain of ashy white, faintly phosphorescent, a sea of velvet fog that lay like motionless water, or rather like a floor of alabaster, so dense did it appear, so seemingly capable of sustaining weight. If it were possible, I think that sea of dead white mist struck even greater terror into my soul than the heavy silence or the deadly cry—so ominous was it, so utterly unreal, so phantasmal, so impossible, as it lay there like a dead ocean under the steady stars. Yet through that mist *we must go!* there seemed no other way home, and, shattered with abject fear, mad with the one desire to get back, we started down the slope to where the sea of milky mist ceased, sharp and distinct around the stems of the rough grass.

"I put one foot into the ghostly fog. A chill as of death struck through me, stopping my heart, and I threw myself backward on the slope. At that instant came again the shriek, close, close, right in our ears, in ourselves, and far out across that damnable sea I saw the cold fog lift like a water-spout and toss itself high in writhing convolutions towards the sky. The stars began to grow dim as thick vapor swept across them, and in the growing dark I saw a great, watery moon lift itself slowly above the palpitating sea, vast and vague in the gathering mist.

"This was enough: we turned and fled along the margin of the white sea that throbbed now with fitful motion below us, rising, rising, slowly and steadily, driving us higher and higher up the side of the foothills.

"It was a race for life; that we knew. How we kept it up I cannot understand, but we did, and at last we saw the white sea fall behind us as we staggered up the end of the valley, and then down into a region that we knew, and so into the old path. The last thing I remember was hearing a strange voice, that of

Nils, but horribly changed, stammer brokenly, 'The dog is dead!' and then the whole world turned around twice, slowly and resistlessly, and consciousness went out with a crash.

"It was some three weeks later, as I remember, that I awoke in my own room, and found my mother sitting beside the bed. I could not think very well at first, but as I slowly grew strong again, vague flashes of recollection began to come to me, and little by little the whole sequence of events of that awful night in the Dead Valley came back. All that I could gain from what was told me was that three weeks before I had been found in my own bed, raging sick, and that my illness grew fast into brain fever. I tried to speak of the dread things that had happened to me, but I saw at once that no one looked on them save as the hauntings of a dying frenzy, and so I closed my mouth and kept my own counsel.

"I must see Nils, however, and so I asked for him. My mother told me that he also had been ill with a strange fever, but that he was now quite well again. Presently they brought him in, and when we were alone I began to speak to him of the night on the mountain. I shall never forget the shock that struck me down on my pillow when the boy denied everything: denied having gone with me, ever having heard the cry, having seen the valley, or feeling the deadly chill of the ghostly fog. Nothing would shake his determined ignorance, and in spite of myself I was forced to admit that his denials came from no policy of concealment, but from blank oblivion.

"My weakened brain was in a turmoil. Was it all but the floating phantasm of delirium? Or had the horror of the real thing blotted Nils's mind into blankness so far as the events of the night in the Dead Valley were concerned? The latter explanation seemed the only one, else how explain the sudden illness which in a night had struck us both down? I said nothing more, either to Nils or to my own people, but waited, with a growing determination that, once well again, I would find that valley if it really existed.

"It was some weeks before I was really well enough to go, but finally, late in September, I chose a bright, warm, still day, the last smile of the dying summer, and started early in the morning along the path that led to Hallsberg. I was sure I knew where the trail struck off to the right, down which we had come from the valley of dead water, for a great tree grew by the Hallsberg path at the point where, with a sense of salvation, we had found the home road. Presently I saw it to the right, a little distance ahead.

"I think the bright sunlight and the clear air had worked as a tonic to me, for by the time I came to the foot of the great pine, I had quite lost faith in the verity of the vision that haunted me, believing at last that it was indeed but the nightmare of madness. Nevertheless, I turned sharply to the right, at the base of the tree, into a narrow path that led through a dense thicket. As I did so I tripped over something. A swarm of flies sung into the air around me, and looking down I saw the matted fleece, with the poor little bones thrusting through, of the dog we had bought in Hallsberg.

"Then my courage went out with a puff, and I knew that it all was true, and that now I was frightened. Pride and the desire for adventure urged me on, however, and I pressed into the close thicket that barred my way. The path was hardly visible: merely the worn road of some small beasts, for, though it showed in the crisp grass, the bushes above grew thick and hardly penetrable. The land rose slowly, and rising grew clearer, until at last I came out on a great slope of hill, unbroken by trees or shrubs, very like my memory of that rise of land we had topped in order that we might find the dead valley and the icy fog. I looked at the sun; it was bright and clear, and all around insects were humming in the autumn air, and birds were darting to and fro. Surely there was no danger, not until nightfall at least; so I began to whistle, and with a rush mounted the last crest of brown hill.

"There lay the Dead Valley! A great oval basin, almost as smooth and regular as though made by man. On all sides the grass crept over the brink of the encircling hills, dusty green on the crests, then fading into ashy brown, and so to a deadly white, this last color forming a thin ring, running in a long line around the slope. And then? Nothing. Bare, brown, hard earth, glittering with grains of alkali, but otherwise dead and barren. Not a tuft of grass, not a stick of brushwood, not even a stone, but only the vast expanse of beaten clay.

"In the midst of the basin, perhaps a mile and a half away, the level expanse was broken by a great dead tree, rising leafless and gaunt into the air. Without a moment's hesitation I started down into the valley and made for this goal. Every particle of fear seemed to have left me, and even the valley itself did not look so very terrifying. At all events, I was driven by an overwhelming curiosity, and there seemed to be but one thing in the world to do,—to get to that Tree! As I trudged along over the hard earth, I noticed that the multitudinous voices of birds and insects had died away. No bee or butterfly hovered through the air, no insects leaped or crept over the dull earth. The very air itself was stagnant.

"As I drew near the skeleton tree, I noticed the glint of sunlight on a kind of white mound around its roots, and I wondered curiously. It was not until I had come close that I saw its nature.

"All around the roots and barkless trunk was heaped a wilderness of little bones. Tiny skulls of rodents and of birds, thousands of them, rising about the dead tree and streaming off for several yards in all directions, until the dreadful pile ended in isolated skulls and scattered skeletons. Here and there a larger bone appeared,—the thigh of a sheep, the hoofs of a horse, and to one side, grinning slowly, a human skull.

"I stood quite still, staring with all my eyes, when suddenly the dense silence was broken by a faint, forlorn cry high over my head. I looked up and saw a great falcon turning and sailing downward just over the tree. In a moment more she fell motionless on the bleaching bones.

"Horror struck me, and I rushed for home, my brain whirling, a strange numbness growing in me. I ran steadily, on and on. At last I glanced up. Where was the rise of hill? I looked around wildly. Close before me was the dead tree with its pile of bones. I had circled it round and round, and the valley wall was still a mile and a half away.

"I stood dazed and frozen. The sun was sinking, red and dull, towards the line of hills. In the east the dark was growing fast. Was there still time? *Time!* It was not *that* I wanted, it was *will!* My feet seemed clogged as in a nightmare. I could hardly drag them over the barren earth. And then I felt the slow chill creeping through me. I looked down. Out of the earth a thin mist was rising, collecting in little pools that grew ever larger until they joined here and there, their currents swirling slowly like thin blue smoke. The western hills halved the copper sun.

When it was dark I should hear that shriek again, and then I should die. I knew that, and with every remaining atom of will I staggered towards the red west through the writhing mist that crept clammily around my ankles, retarding my steps.

"And as I fought my way off from the Tree, the horror grew, until at last I thought I was going to die. The silence pursued me like dumb ghosts, the still air held my breath, the hellish fog caught at my feet like cold hands.

"But I won! though not a moment too soon. As I crawled on my hands and knees up the brown slope, I heard, far away and high in the air, the cry that already had almost bereft me of reason. It was faint and vague, but unmistakable in its horrible intensity. I glanced behind. The fog was dense and pallid, heaving undulously up the brown slope. The sky was gold under the setting sun, but below was the ashy gray of death. I stood for a moment on the brink of this sea of hell, and then leaped down the slope. The sunset opened before me, the night closed behind, and as I crawled home weak and tired, darkness shut down on the Dead Valley."

1895

MADELINE YALE WYNNE

(1847–1918)

The Little Room

'How would it do for a smoking-room?'

'Just the very place! only, you know, Roger, you must not think of smoking in the house. I am almost afraid that having just a plain, common man around, let alone a smoking man, will upset Aunt Hannah. She is New England—Vermont New England—boiled down.'

'You leave Aunt Hannah to me; I'll find her tender side. I'm going to ask her about the old sea-captain and the yellow calico.'

'Not yellow calico—blue chintz.'

'Well, yellow *shell* then.'

'No, no! don't mix it up so; you won't know yourself what to expect, and that's half the fun.'

'Now you tell me again exactly what to expect; to tell the truth, I didn't half hear about it the other day; I was wool-gathering. It was something queer that happened when you were a child, wasn't it?'

'Something that began to happen long before that, and kept happening, and may happen again; but I hope not.'

'What was it?'

'I wonder if the other people in the car can hear us?'

'I fancy not; we don't hear them—not consecutively, at least.'

'Well, mother was born in Vermont, you know; she was the only child by a second marriage. Aunt Hannah and Aunt Maria are only half-aunts to me, you know.'

'I hope they are half as nice as you are.'

'Roger, be still; they certainly will hear us.'

'Well, don't you want them to know we are married?'

'Yes, but not just married. There's all the difference in the world.'

'You are afraid we look too happy!'

'No; only I want my happiness all to myself.'

'Well, the little room?'

'My aunts brought mother up; they were nearly twenty years older than she. I might say Hiram and they brought her up. You see, Hiram was bound out to my grandfather when he was a boy, and when grandfather died Hiram said he "s'posed he went with the farm, long o' the critters," and he has been there ever since. He was my mother's only refuge from the decorum of my aunts. They are simply workers. They make me think of the Maine woman who wanted her epitaph to be: "She was a *hard* working woman."'

'They must be almost beyond their working-days. How old are they?'

'Seventy, or thereabouts; but they will die standing; or, at least, on a Saturday night, after all the house-work is done up. They were rather strict with mother, and I think she had a lonely childhood. The house is almost a mile away from any neighbors, and off on top of what they call Stony Hill. It is bleak enough up there, even in summer.

'When mamma was about ten years old they sent her to cousins in Brooklyn, who had children of their own, and knew more about bringing them up. She staid there till she was married; she didn't go to Vermont in all that time, and of course hadn't seen her sisters, for they never would leave home for a day. They couldn't even be induced to go to Brooklyn to her wedding, so she and father took their wedding trip up there.'

'And that's why we are going up there on our own?'

'Don't, Roger; you have no idea how loud you speak.'

'You never say so except when I am going to say that one little word.'

'Well, don't say it, then, or say it very, very quietly.'

'Well, what was the queer thing?'

'When they got to the house, mother wanted to take father right off into the little room; she had been telling him about it, just as I am going to tell you, and she had said that of all the rooms, that one was the only one that seemed pleasant to her. She described the furniture and the books and paper and everything, and said it was on the north side, between the front and back room. Well, when they went to look for it, there was no little room there; there was only a shallow china-closet. She asked her sisters when the house had been altered and a closet made of the room that used to be there. They both said the house was exactly as it had been built—that they had never made any changes, except to tear down the old wood-shed and build a smaller one.

'Father and mother laughed a good deal over it, and when anything was lost they would always say it must be in the little room, and any exaggerated statement was called "little-roomy." When I was a child I thought that was a regular English phrase, I heard it so often.

'Well, they talked it over, and finally they concluded that my mother had been a very imaginative sort of a child, and had read in some book about such a little room, or perhaps even dreamed it, and then had "made believe," as children do, till she herself had really thought the room was there.'

'Why, of course, that might easily happen.'

'Yes, but you haven't heard the queer part yet; you wait and see if you can explain the rest as easily.

'They staid at the farm two weeks, and then went to New York to live. When I was eight years old my father was killed in the war, and mother was broken-hearted. She never was quite strong afterwards, and that summer we decided to go up to the farm for three months.

'I was a restless sort of a child, and the journey seemed very long to me; and finally, to pass the time, mamma told me the story of the little room, and how it was all in her own imagination, and how there really was only a china-closet there.

'She told it with all the particulars; and even to me, who knew beforehand that the room wasn't there, it seemed just as real as could be. She said it was on the north side, between the front and back rooms; that it was very small, and they sometimes called it an entry. There was a door also that opened out-of-doors, and that one was painted green, and was cut in the middle like the old Dutch doors, so that it could be used for a window by opening the top part only. Directly opposite the door was a lounge or couch; it was covered with blue chintz—India chintz—some that had been brought over by an old Salem sea-captain as a "venture." He had given it to Hannah when she was a young girl. She was sent to Salem for two years to school. Grandfather originally came from Salem.'

'I thought there wasn't any room or chintz.'

'*That is just it.* They had decided that mother had imagined it all, and yet you see how exactly everything was painted in her mind, for she had even remembered that Hiram had told her that Hannah could have married the sea-captain if she had wanted to!

'The India cotton was the regular blue stamped chintz, with the peacock figure on it. The head and body of the bird were in profile, while the tail was full front view behind it. It had seemed to take mamma's fancy, and she drew it for me on a piece of paper as she talked. Doesn't it seem strange to you that she could have made all that up, or even dreamed it?

'At the foot of the lounge were some hanging shelves with some old books on them. All the books were leather-colored except one; that was bright red, and was called the *Ladies' Album*. It made a bright break between the other thicker books.

'On the lower shelf was a beautiful pink sea-shell, lying on a mat made of balls of red shaded worsted. This shell was greatly coveted by mother, but she was only allowed to play with it when she had been particularly good. Hiram had shown her how to hold it close to her ear and hear the roar of the sea in it.

'I know you will like Hiram, Roger; he is quite a character in his way.

'Mamma said she remembered, or *thought* she remembered, having been sick once, and she had to lie quietly for some days on the lounge; then was the time she had become so familiar with everything in the room, and she had been allowed to have the shell to play with all the time. She had had her toast brought to her in there, with make-believe tea. It was one of her pleasant memories of her childhood; it was the first time she had been of any importance to anybody, even herself.

'Right at the head of the lounge was a light-stand, as they called it, and on it was a very brightly polished brass candle-stick and a brass tray, with snuffers. That is all I remember of her describing, except that there was a braided rag rug on the floor, and on the wall was a beautiful flowered paper—roses and morning-glories in a wreath on a light blue ground. The same paper was in the front room.'

'And all this never existed except in her imagination?'

'She said that when she and father went up there, there wasn't any little room at all like it anywhere in the house; there was a china-closet where she had believed the room to be.'

'And your aunts said there had never been any such room.'

'That is what they said.'

'Wasn't there any blue chintz in the house with a peacock figure?'

'Not a scrap, and Aunt Hannah said there had never been any that she could remember; and Aunt Maria just echoed her—she always does that. You see, Aunt Hannah is an up-and-down New England woman. She looks just like herself; I mean, just like her character. Her joints move up and down or backward and forward in a plain square fashion. I don't believe she ever leaned on anything in her life, or sat in an easy-chair. But Maria is different; she is rounder and softer; she hasn't any ideas of her own; she never had any. I don't believe she would think it right or becoming to have one that differed from Aunt Hannah's, so what would be the use of having any? She is an echo, that's all.

'When mamma and I got there, of course I was all excitement to see the china-closet, and I had a sort of feeling that it would be the little room after all. So I ran ahead and threw open the door, crying, "Come and see the little room."'

'And Roger,' said Mrs. Grant, laying her hand in his, 'there really was a little room there, exactly as mother had remembered it. There was the lounge, the peacock chintz, the green door, the shell, the morning-glory, and rose paper, *everything exactly as she had described it to me.*'

'What in the world did the sisters say about it?'

'Wait a minute and I will tell you. My mother was in the front hall still talking with Aunt Hannah. She didn't hear me at first, but I ran out there and dragged her through the front room, saying, "The room *is* here—it is all right."'

'It seemed for a minute as if my mother would faint. She clung to me in terror. I can remember now how strained her eyes looked and how pale she was.

'I called out to Aunt Hannah and asked her when they had had the closet taken away and the little room built; for in my excitement I thought that that was what had been done.

' "That little room has always been there," said Aunt Hannah, "ever since the house was built."

' "But mamma said there wasn't any little room here, only a china-closet, when she was here with papa," said I.

' "No, there has never been any china-closet there; it has always been just as it is now," said Aunt Hannah.

'Then mother spoke; her voice sounded weak and far off. She said, slowly, and with an effort, "Maria, don't you remember that you told me that there had *never been any little room here?* and Hannah said so too, and then I said I must have dreamed it?"

' "No, I don't remember anything of the kind," said Maria, without the slightest emotion. "I don't remember you ever said anything about any china-closet. The house has never been altered; you used to play in this room when you were a child, don't you remember?"

' "I know it," said mother, in that queer slow voice that made me feel frightened. "Hannah, don't you remember my finding the china-closet here, with the gilt-edged china on the shelves, and then *you* said that the *china-closet* had always been here?"

' "No," said Hannah, pleasantly but unemotionally—"no, I don't think you ever asked me about any china-closet, and we haven't any gilt-edged china that I know of."

'And that was the strangest thing about it. We never could make them remember that there had ever been any question about it. You would think they could remember how surprised mother had been before, unless she had imagined the whole thing. Oh, it was so queer! They were always pleasant about it, but they didn't seem to feel any interest or curiosity. It was always this answer: "The house is just as it was built; there have never been any changes, so far as we know."

'And my mother was in an agony of perplexity. How cold their gray eyes looked to me! There was no reading anything in them. It just seemed to break my mother down, this queer thing. Many times that summer, in the middle of the night, I have seen her get up and take a candle and creep softly downstairs. I could hear the steps creak under her weight. Then she would go through the front room and peer into the darkness, holding her thin hand between the candle and her eyes. She seemed to think the little room might vanish. Then she would come back to bed and toss about all night, or lie still and shiver; it used to frighten me.

'She grew pale and thin, and she had a little cough; then she did not like to be left alone. Sometimes she would make errands in order to send me to the little room for something—a book, or her fan, or her handkerchief; but she would never sit there or let me stay in there long, and sometimes she wouldn't let me go in there for days together. Oh, it was pitiful!'

'Well, don't talk any more about it, Margaret, if it makes you feel so,' said Mr. Grant.

'Oh yes, I want you to know all about it, and there isn't much more—no more about the room.

'Mother never got well, and she died that autumn. She used often to sigh, and say, with a wan little laugh, "There is one thing I am glad of, Margaret: your father knows now all about the little room." I think she was afraid I distrusted her. Of course, in a child's way, I thought there was something queer about it, but I did not brood over it. I was too young then, and took it as a part of her illness. But, Roger, do you know, it really did affect me. I almost hate to go there after talking about it; I somehow feel as if it might, you know, be a china-closet again.'

'That's an absurd idea.'

'I know it; of course it can't be. I saw the room, and there isn't any china-closet there, and no gilt-edged china in the house, either.'

And then she whispered: 'But, Roger, you may hold my hand as you do now, if you will, when we go to look for the little room.'

'And you won't mind Aunt Hannah's gray eyes?'

'I won't mind *anything*.'

It was dusk when Mr. and Mrs. Grant went into the gate under the two old Lombardy poplars and walked up the narrow path to the door, where they were met by the two aunts.

Hannah gave Mrs. Grant a frigid but not unfriendly kiss; and Maria seemed for a moment to tremble on the verge of an emotion, but she glanced at Hannah, and then gave her greeting in exactly the same repressed and non-committal way.

Supper was waiting for them. On the table was the *gilt-edged china*. Mrs. Grant didn't notice it immediately, till she saw her husband smiling at her over his teacup; then she felt fidgety, and couldn't eat. She was nervous, and kept wondering what was behind her, whether it would be a little room or a closet.

After supper she offered to help about the dishes, but, mercy! she might as well have offered to help bring the seasons round; Maria and Hannah couldn't be helped.

So she and her husband went to find the little room, or closet, or whatever was to be there.

Aunt Maria followed them, carrying the lamp, which she set down, and then went back to the dish-washing.

Margaret looked at her husband. He kissed her, for she seemed troubled; and then, hand in hand, they opened the door. It opened into a *china-closet*. The shelves were neatly draped with scalloped paper; on them was the gilt-edged china, with the dishes missing that had been used at the supper, and which at that moment were being carefully washed and wiped by the two aunts.

Margaret's husband dropped her hand and looked at her. She was trembling a little, and turned to him for help, for some explanation, but in an instant she knew that something was wrong. A cloud had come between them; he was hurt; he was antagonized.

He paused for an appreciable instant, and then said, kindly enough, but in a voice that cut her deeply:

'I am glad this ridiculous thing is ended; don't let us speak of it again.'

'Ended!' said she. 'How ended?' And somehow her voice sounded to her as her mother's voice had when she stood there and questioned her sisters about the little room. She seemed to have to drag her words out. She spoke slowly: 'It seems to me to have only just begun in my case. It was just so with mother when she—'

'I really wish, Margaret, you would let it drop. I don't like to hear you speak of your mother in connection with it. It—' He hesitated, for was not this their wedding-day? 'It doesn't seem quite the thing, quite delicate, you know, to use her name in the matter.'

She saw it all now: *he didn't believe her.* She felt a chill sense of withering under his glance.

'Come,' he added, 'let us go out, or into the dining-room, somewhere, anywhere, only drop this nonsense.'

He went out; he did not take her hand now—he was vexed, baffled, hurt. Had he not given her his sympathy, his attention, his belief—and his hand?—and she was fooling him. What did it mean?—she so truthful, so free from morbidness—a thing he hated. He walked up and down under the poplars, trying to get into the mood to go and join her in the house.

Margaret heard him go out; then she turned and shook the shelves; she reached her hand behind them and tried to push the boards away; she ran out of the house on to the north side and tried to find in the darkness, with her hands, a door, or some steps leading to one. She tore her dress on the old rose-trees, she fell and rose and stumbled, then she sat down on the ground and tried to think. What could she think—was she dreaming?

She went into the house and out into the kitchen, and begged Aunt Maria to tell her about the little room—what had become of it, when had they built the closet, when had they bought the gilt-edged china?

They went on washing dishes and drying them on the spotless towels with methodical exactness; and as they worked they said that there had never been any little room, so far as they knew; the china-closet had always been there, and the gilt-edged china had belonged to their mother, it had always been in the house.

'No, I don't remember that your mother ever asked about any little room,' said Hannah. 'She didn't seem very well that summer, but she never asked about any changes in the house; there hadn't ever been any changes.'

There it was again: not a sign of interest, curiosity, or annoyance, not a spark of memory.

She went out to Hiram. He was telling Mr. Grant about the farm. She had meant to ask him about the room, but her lips were sealed before her husband.

Months afterwards, when time had lessened the sharpness of their feelings, they learned to speculate reasonably about the phenomenon, which Mr. Grant had accepted as something not to be scoffed away, not to be treated as a poor joke, but to be put aside as something inexplicable on any ordinary theory.

Margaret alone in her heart knew that her mother's words carried a deeper significance than she had dreamed of at the time. 'One thing I am glad of, your father knows now,' and she wondered if Roger or she would ever know.

Five years later they were going to Europe. The packing was done; the children were lying asleep, with their travelling things ready to be slipped on for an early start.

Roger had a foreign appointment. They were not to be back in America for some years. She had meant to go up to say good-by to her aunts; but a mother of three children intends to do a great many things that never get done. One thing she had done that very day, and as she paused for a moment between the writing of two notes that must be posted before she went to bed, she said:

'Roger, you remember Rita Lash? Well, she and Cousin Nan go up to the Adirondacks every autumn. They are clever girls, and I have intrusted to them something I want done very much.'

'They are the girls to do it, then, every inch of them.'

'I know it, and they are going to.'

'Well?'

'Why, you see, Roger, that little room—'

'Oh—'

'Yes, I was a coward not to go myself, but I didn't find time, because I hadn't the courage.'

'Oh! *that* was it, was it?'

'Yes, just that. They are going, and they will write us about it.'

'Want to bet?'

'No; I only want to know.'

Rita Lash and Cousin Nan planned to go to Vermont on their way to the Adirondacks. They found they would have three hours between trains, which would give them time to drive up to the Keys farm, and they could still get to the camp that night. But, at the last minute, Rita was prevented from going. Nan had to go to meet the Adirondack party, and she promised to telegraph her when she arrived at the camp. Imagine Rita's amusement when she received this message: 'Safely arrived; went to the Keys farm; it is a little room.'

Rita was amused, because she did not in the least think Nan had been there. She thought it was a hoax; but it put it into her mind to carry the joke further by really stopping herself when she went up, as she meant to do the next week.

She did stop over. She introduced herself to the two maiden ladies, who seemed familiar, as they had been described by Mrs. Grant.

They were, if not cordial, at least not disconcerted at her visit, and willingly showed her over the house. As they did not speak of any other stranger's having been to see them lately, she became confirmed in her belief that Nan had not been there.

In the north room she saw the roses and morning-glory paper on the wall, and also the door that should open into—what?

She asked if she might open it.

'Certainly,' said Hannah; and Maria echoed, 'Certainly.'

She opened it, and found the china-closet. She experienced a certain relief; she at least was not under any spell. Mrs. Grant left it a china-closet; she found it the same. Good.

But she tried to induce the old sisters to remember that there had at various times been certain questions relating to a confusion as to whether the closet had always been a closet. It was no use; their stony eyes gave no sign.

Then she thought of the story of the sea-captain, and said, 'Miss Keys, did you ever have a lounge covered with India chintz, with a figure of a peacock on it, given to you in Salem by a sea-captain, who brought it from India?'

'I dun'no' as I ever did,' said Hannah. That was all. She thought Maria's cheeks were a little flushed, but her eyes were like a stone wall.

She went on that night to the Adirondacks. When Nan and she were alone in their room she said, 'By-the-way, Nan, what did you see at the farm-house? and how did you like Maria and Hannah?'

Nan didn't mistrust that Rita had been there, and she began excitedly to tell her all about her visit. Rita could almost have believed Nan had been there if she hadn't known it was not so. She let her go on for some time, enjoying her enthusiasm, and the impressive way in which she described her opening the door and finding the 'little room.' Then Rita said: 'Now, Nan, that is enough fibbing. I went to the farm myself on my way up yesterday, and there is *no* little room, and there *never* has been any; it is a china-closet, just as Mrs. Grant saw it last.'

She was pretending to be busy unpacking her trunk, and did not look up for a moment; but as Nan did not say anything, she glanced at her over her shoulder. Nan was actually pale, and it was hard to say whether she was most angry or frightened. There was something of both in her look. And then Rita began to explain how her telegram had put her in the spirit of going up there alone. She hadn't meant to cut Nan out. She only thought— Then Nan broke in: 'It isn't that; I am sure you can't think it is that. But I went myself, and you did not go; you can't have been there, for *it is a little room.*'

Oh, what a night they had! They couldn't sleep. They talked and argued, and then kept still for a while, only to break out again, it was so absurd. They both maintained that they had been there, but both felt sure the other one was either crazy or obstinate beyond reason. They were wretched; it was perfectly ridiculous, two friends at odds over such a thing; but there it was—'little room,' 'china-closet,'—'china-closet,' 'little room.'

The next morning Nan was tacking up some tarlatan at a window to keep the midges out. Rita offered to help her, as she had done for the past ten years. Nan's 'No, thanks,' cut her to the heart.

'Nan,' said she, 'come right down from that step-ladder and pack your satchel. The stage leaves in just twenty minutes. We can catch the afternoon express train, and we will go together to the farm. I am either going there or going home. You better go with me.'

Nan didn't say a word. She gathered up the hammer and tacks, and was ready to start when the stage came round.

It meant for them thirty miles of staging and six hours of train, besides crossing the lake; but what of that, compared with having a lie lying round loose between them! Europe would have seemed easy to accomplish, if it would settle the question.

At the little junction in Vermont they found a farmer with a wagon full of meal-bags. They asked him if he could not take them up to the old Keys farm and bring them back in time for the return train, due in two hours.

They had planned to call it a sketching trip, so they said, 'We have been there before, we are artists, and we might find some views worth taking; and we want also to make a short call upon the Misses Keys.'

'Did ye calculate to paint the old *house* in the picture?'

They said it was possible they might do so. They wanted to see it, anyway.

'Waal, I guess you are too late. The *house* burnt down last night, and everything in it.'

1895

GERTRUDE ATHERTON

(1857–1948)

The Striding Place

WEIGALL, continental and detached, tired early of grouse-shooting. To stand propped against a sod fence while his host's workmen routed up the birds with long poles and drove them towards the waiting guns, made him feel himself a parody on the ancestors who had roamed the moors and forests of this West Riding of Yorkshire in hot pursuit of game worth the killing. But when in England in August he always accepted whatever proffered for the season, and invited his host to shoot pheasants on his estates in the South. The amusements of life, he argued, should be accepted with the same philosophy as its ills.

It had been a bad day. A heavy rain had made the moor so spongy that it fairly sprang beneath the feet. Whether or not the grouse had haunts of their own, wherein they were immune from rheumatism, the bag had been small. The women, too, were an unusually dull lot, with the exception of a new-minded *débutante* who bothered Weigall at dinner by demanding the verbal restoration of the vague paintings on the vaulted roof above them.

But it was no one of these things that sat on Weigall's mind as, when the other men went up to bed, he let himself out of the castle and sauntered down to the river. His intimate friend, the companion of his boyhood, the chum of his college days, his fellow-traveller in many lands, the man for whom he possessed stronger affection than for all men, had mysteriously disappeared two days ago, and his track might have sprung to the upper air for all trace he had left behind him. He had been a guest on the adjoining estate during the past week, shooting with the fervor of the true sportsman, making love in the intervals to Adeline Cavan, and apparently in the best of spirits. As far as was known there was nothing to lower his mental mercury, for his rent-roll was a large one, Miss Cavan blushed whenever he looked at her, and, being one of the best shots in England, he was never happier than in August. The suicide theory was preposterous, all agreed, and there was as little reason to believe him murdered. Nevertheless, he had walked out of March Abbey two nights ago without hat or overcoat, and had not been seen since.

The country was being patrolled night and day. A hundred keepers and workmen were beating the woods and poking the bogs on the moors, but as yet not so much as a handkerchief had been found.

Weigall did not believe for a moment that Wyatt Gifford was dead, and although it was impossible not to be affected by the general uneasiness, he was disposed to be more angry than frightened. At Cambridge Gifford had been an incorrigible practical joker, and by no means had outgrown the habit; it would be like him to cut across the country in his evening clothes, board a cattle-train, and amuse himself touching up the picture of the sensation in West Riding.

However, Weigall's affection for his friend was too deep to companion with tranquillity in the present state of doubt, and, instead of going to bed early with the other men, he determined to walk until ready for sleep. He went down to the river and followed the path through the woods. There was no moon, but the stars sprinkled their cold light upon the pretty belt of water flowing placidly past wood and ruin, between green masses of overhanging rocks or sloping banks tangled with tree and shrub, leaping occasionally over stones with the harsh notes of an angry scold, to recover its equanimity the moment the way was clear again.

It was very dark in the depths where Weigall trod. He smiled as he recalled a remark of Gifford's: "An English wood is like a good many other things in life—very promising at a distance, but a hollow mockery when you get within. You see daylight on both sides, and the sun freckles the very bracken. Our woods need the night to make them seem what they ought to be—what they once were, before our ancestors' descendants demanded so much more money, in these so much more various days."

Weigall strolled along, smoking, and thinking of his friend, his pranks—many of which had done more credit to his imagination than this—and recalling conversations that had lasted the night through. Just before the end of the London season they had walked the streets one hot night after a party, discussing the various theories of the soul's destiny. That afternoon they had met at the coffin of a college friend whose mind had been a blank for the past three years. Some months previously they had called at the asylum to see him. His expression had been senile, his face imprinted with the record of debauchery. In death the face was placid, intelligent, without ignoble lineation—the face of the man they had known at college. Weigall and Gifford had had no time to comment there, and the afternoon and evening were full; but, coming forth from the house of festivity together, they had reverted almost at once to the topic.

"I cherish the theory," Gifford had said, "that the soul sometimes lingers in the body after death. During madness, of course, it is an impotent prisoner, albeit a conscious one. Fancy its agony, and its horror! What more natural than that, when the life-spark goes out, the tortured soul should take possession of the vacant skull and triumph once more for a few hours while old friends look their last? It has had time to repent while compelled to crouch and behold the result of its work, and it has shrived itself into a state of comparative purity. If I had my way, I should stay inside my bones until the coffin had gone into its niche, that I might obviate for my poor old comrade the tragic impersonality of death. And I should like to see justice done to it, as it were—to see it lowered among its ancestors with the ceremony and solemnity that are its due. I am afraid that if I dissevered myself too quickly, I should yield to curiosity and hasten to investigate the mysteries of space."

"You believe in the soul as an independent entity, then—that it and the vital principle are not one and the same?"

"Absolutely. The body and soul are twins, life comrades—sometimes friends, sometimes enemies, but always loyal in the last instance. Some day, when I am tired of the world, I shall go to India and become a mahatma, solely for the pleasure of receiving proof during life of this independent relationship."

"Suppose you were not sealed up properly, and returned after one of your astral flights to find your earthly part unfit for habitation? It is an experiment I don't think I should care to try, unless even juggling with soul and flesh had palled."

"That would not be an uninteresting predicament. I should rather enjoy experimenting with broken machinery."

The high wild roar of water smote suddenly upon Weigall's ear and checked his memories. He left the wood and walked out on the huge slippery stones which nearly close the River Wharfe at this point, and watched the waters boil down into the narrow pass with their furious untiring energy. The black quiet of the woods rose high on either side. The stars seemed colder and whiter just above. On either hand the perspective of the river might have run into a rayless cavern. There was no lonelier spot in England, nor one which had the right to claim so many ghosts, if ghosts there were.

Weigall was not a coward, but he recalled uncomfortably the tales of those that had been done to death in the Strid.* Wordsworth's Boy of Egremond had been disposed of by the practical Whitaker; but countless others, more venturesome than wise, had gone down into that narrow boiling course, never to appear in the still pool a few yards beyond. Below the great rocks which form the walls of the Strid was believed to be a natural vault, on to whose shelves the dead were drawn. The spot had an ugly fascination. Weigall stood, visioning skeletons, uncoffined and green, the home of the eyeless things which had devoured all that had covered and filled that rattling symbol of man's mortality; then fell to wondering if any one had attempted to leap the Strid of late. It was covered with slime; he had never seen it look so treacherous.

He shuddered and turned away, impelled, despite his manhood, to flee the spot. As he did so, something tossing in the foam below the fall—something as white, yet independent of it—caught his eye and arrested his step. Then he saw that it was describing a contrary motion to the rushing water—an upward backward motion. Weigall stood rigid, breathless; he fancied he heard the crackling of his hair. Was that a hand? It

*"This striding place is called the 'Strid,'
    A name which it took of yore;
  A thousand years hath it borne the name,
    And it shall a thousand more."

thrust itself still higher above the boiling foam, turned side-wise, and four frantic fingers were distinctly visible against the black rock beyond.

Weigall's superstitious terror left him. A man was there, struggling to free himself from the suction beneath the Strid, swept down, doubtless, but a moment before his arrival, perhaps as he stood with his back to the current.

He stepped as close to the edge as he dared. The hand doubled as if in imprecation, shaking savagely in the face of that force which leaves its creatures to immutable law; then spread wide again, clutching, expanding, crying for help as audibly as the human voice.

Weigall dashed to the nearest tree, dragged and twisted off a branch with his strong arms, and returned as swiftly to the Strid. The hand was in the same place, still gesticulating as wildly; the body was undoubtedly caught in the rocks below, perhaps already half-way along one of those hideous shelves. Weigall let himself down upon a lower rock, braced his shoulder against the mass beside him, then, leaning out over the water, thrust the branch into the hand. The fingers clutched it convulsively. Weigall tugged powerfully, his own feet dragged perilously near the edge. For a moment he produced no impression, then an arm shot above the waters.

The blood sprang to Weigall's head; he was choked with the impression that the Strid had him in her roaring hold, and he saw nothing. Then the mist cleared. The hand and arm were nearer, although the rest of the body was still concealed by the foam. Weigall peered out with distended eyes. The meagre light revealed in the cuffs links of a peculiar device. The fingers clutching the branch were as familiar.

Weigall forgot the slippery stones, the terrible death if he stepped too far. He pulled with passionate will and muscle. Memories flung themselves into the hot light of his brain, trooping rapidly upon each other's heels, as in the thought of the drowning. Most of the pleasures of his life, good and bad, were identified in some way with this friend. Scenes of college days, of travel, where they had deliberately sought adventure and stood between one another and death upon more occasions than one, of hours of delightful companionship among the treasures of art, and others in the pursuit of pleasure, flashed like the changing particles of a kaleidoscope. Weigall had loved several women; but he would have flouted in these moments the thought that he had ever loved any woman as he loved Wyatt Gifford. There were so many charming women in the world, and in the thirty-two years of his life he had never known another man to whom he had cared to give his intimate friendship.

He threw himself on his face. His wrists were cracking, the skin was torn from his hands. The fingers still gripped the stick. There was life in them yet.

Suddenly something gave way. The hand swung about, tearing the branch from Weigall's grasp. The body had been liberated and flung outward, though still submerged by the foam and spray.

Weigall scrambled to his feet and sprang along the rocks, knowing that the danger from suction was over and that Gifford must be carried straight to the quiet pool. Gifford was a fish in the water and could live under it longer than most men. If he survived this, it would not be the first time that his pluck and science had saved him from drowning.

Weigall reached the pool. A man in his evening clothes floated on it, his face turned towards a projecting rock over which his arm had fallen, upholding the body. The hand that had held the branch hung limply over the rock, its white reflection visible in the black water. Weigall plunged into the shallow pool, lifted Gifford in his arms and returned to the bank. He laid the body down and threw off his coat that he might be the freer to practise the methods of resuscitation. He was glad of the moment's respite. The valiant life in the man might have been exhausted in that last struggle. He had not dared to look at his face, to put his ear to the heart. The hesitation lasted but a moment. There was no time to lose.

He turned to his prostrate friend. As he did so, something strange and disagreeable smote his senses. For a half-moment he did not appreciate its nature. Then his teeth clacked together, his feet, his outstretched arms pointed towards the woods. But he sprang to the side of the man and bent down and peered into his face. There was no face.

1896

EMMA FRANCIS DAWSON

(1851–1926)

An Itinerant House

"Eternal longing with eternal pain,
Want without hope, and memory saddening all,
All congregated failure and despair
Shall wander there through some old maze of wrong."

"His *wife?*" cried Felipa.

"Yes," I answered, unwillingly; for until the steamer brought Mrs. Anson I believed in this Mexican woman's right to that name. l felt sorry for the bright eyes and kind heart that had cheered Anson's lodgers through weary months of early days in San Francisco.

She burst into tears. None of us knew how to comfort her. Dering spoke first: "Beauty always wins friends."

Between her sobs she repeated one of the pithy sayings of her language: "It is as easy to find a lover as to keep a friend, but as hard to find a friend as to keep a lover."

"Yes," said Volz, "a new friendship is like a new string to your guitar—you are not sure what its tone may prove, nor how soon it may break."

"But at least its falsity is learned at once," she sobbed.

"Is it possible," I asked, "that you had no suspicion?"

"None. He told me—" She ended in a fresh gust of tears.

"The old story," muttered Dering. "Marryatt's skipper was right in thinking everything that once happened would come again somewhere."

Anson came. He had left the new-comer at the Niantic, on pretense of putting his house in order. Felipa turned on him before we could go.

"Is this true?" she cried.

Without reply he went to the window and stood looking out. She sprang toward him, with rage distorting her face.

"Coward!" she screamed, in fierce scorn.

Then she fell senseless. Two doctors were called. One said

she was dead. The other, at first doubtful, vainly tried hot sealing-wax and other tests. After thirty-six hours her funeral was planned. Yet Dering, once medical student, had seen an electric current used in such a case in Vienna, and wanted to try it. That night, he, Volz, and I offered to watch. When all was still, Dering, who had smuggled in the simple things needed, began his weird work.

"Is it not too late?" I asked.

"Every corpse," said he, "can be thus excited soon after death, for a brief time only, and but once. If the body is not lifeless, the electric current has power at any time."

Volz, too nervous to stay near, stood in the door open to the dark hall. It was a dreadful sight. The dead woman's breast rose and fell; smiles and frowns flitted across her face.

"The body begins to react finely," cried Dering, making Volz open the windows, while I wrapped hot blankets round Felipa, and he instilled clear coffee and brandy.

"It seems like sacrilege! Let her alone!" I exclaimed. "Better dead than alive!"

"My God! say not that!" cried Volz; "the nerve which hears is last to die. She may know all we say."

"Musical bosh!" I muttered.

"Perhaps not," said Dering; "in magnetic sleep that nerve can be roused."

The night seemed endless. The room gained an uncanny look, the macaws on the gaudy, old-fashioned wall-paper seemed fluttering and changing places. Volz crouched in a heap near the door. Dering stood by Felipa, watching closely. I paced the shadowy room, looked at the gleam of the moon on the bay, listened to the soughing wind in the gum-trees mocking the sea, and tried to recall more cheerful scenes, but always bent under the weight of that fearful test going on beside me. Where was her soul? Beyond the stars, in the room with us, or "like trodden snowdrift melting in the dark?" Volz came behind, startling me by grasping my elbow.

"Shall I not play?" he whispered. "Familiar music is remembrance changed to sound—it brings the past as perfume does. Gypsy music in her ear would be like holding wild flowers to her nostrils."

"Ask Dering," I said; "he will know best."

I heard him urging Dering.

"She has gypsy blood," he said; "their music will rouse her."
Dering unwillingly agreed. "But nothing abrupt—begin low," said he.

Vaguely uneasy, I turned to object; but Volz had gone for his violin. Far off arose a soft, wavering, sleepy strain, like a wind blowing over a field of poppies. He passed, in slow, dramatic style, through the hall, playing on the way. As he came in, oddly sustained notes trembled like sighs and sobs; these were by degrees subdued, though with spasmodic outbursts, amid a grand movement as of phantom shapes through cloud-land. One heart-rending phrase recurring as of one of the shadowy host striving to break loose, but beaten back by impalpable throngs, numberless grace-notes trailing their sparks like fire-works. No music of our intervals and our rhythms, but per-plexing in its charm like a draught that maddens. Time, space, our very identities, were consumed in this white heat of sound. I held my breath. I caught his arm.

"It is too bold and distracting," I cried. "It is enough to kill us! Do you expect to torment her back? How can it affect us so?"

"Because," he answered, laying down his violin and wiping his brow, "in the gypsy minor scale the fourth and seventh are augmented. The sixth is diminished. The frequent augmenta-tion of the fourth makes that sense of unrest."

"Bah! Technical terms make it no plainer," I said, returning to the window.

He played a whispered, merry discordance, resolving into click of castanets, laugh, and dance of a gypsy camp. Out of the whirl of flying steps and tremolo of tambourines rose a tender voice, asking, denying, sighing, imploring, passing into an over-ruling, long-drawn call that vibrated in widening rings to reach the farthest horizon—nay, beyond land or sea, "east of the sun, west of the moon." With a rush returned the wild jol-lity of men's bass laughter, women's shrill reply, the stir of the gypsy camp. This dropped behind vague, rolling measures of clouds and chaos, where to and fro floated grotesque goblins of grace-notes like the fancies of a madman; struggling, rising, falling, vain-reaching strains; fierce cries like commands. The music seemed another vital essence thrilling us with its own emotion.

"No more, no more!" I cried, half gasping, and grasping Volz's arm. "What is it, Dering?"

He had staggered from the bed and was trying to see his watch. "It is just forty-four hours!" he said, pointing to Felipa.

Her eyes were open! We were alarmed as if doing wrong and silently watched her. Fifteen minutes later her lips formed one word:

"Idiots!"

Half an hour after she flung the violin from bed to floor, but would not speak. People began to stir about the house. The prosaic sounds jarred on our strained nerves. We felt brought from another sphere. Volz and I were going, but Felipa's upraised hand kept us. She sat up, looking a ghastly vision. Turning first toward me she quoted my words:

" 'Better dead than alive!' True. You knew I would be glad to die. What right had you to bring me back? God's curses on you! I was dead. Then came agony. I heard your voices. I thought we were all in hell. Then I found how by your evil cunning I was to be forced to live. It was like an awful nightmare. I shall not forget you, nor you me. These very walls shall remember—here, where I have been so tortured no one shall have peace! Fools! Leave me! Never come in this room again!"

We went, all talking at once, Dering angry at her mood; Volz, sorry he had not reached a soothing *pianissimo* passage; I, owning we had no right to make the test. We saw her but once more, when with a threatening nod toward us she left the house.

From that time a gloom settled over the place. Mrs. Anson proved a hard-faced, cold-hearted, Cape Cod woman, a scold and drudge, who hated us as much as we disliked her. Homesick and unhappy, she soon went East and died. Within a year, Anson was found dead where he had gone hunting in the Saucelito woods, supposed a suicide; Dering was hung by the Vigilantes, and the rest were scattered on the four winds. Volz and I were last to go. The night before we sailed, he for Australia, I for New York, he said:

"I am sorry for those who come after us in this house."

"Not knowing of any tragedy here," I said, "they will not feel its influence."

"They must feel it," he insisted; "it is written in the Proverbs, 'Evil shall not depart from his house.' "

Some years later, I was among passengers embarking at New York for California, when there was a cry of "Man overboard!" In the confusion of his rescue, among heartless and pitiful talk, I overheard one man declare that the drowned might be revived.

"Oh, yes!" cried a well-known voice behind me. "But they might not thank you."

I turned—to find Volz! He was coming out with Wynne, the actor. Enjoying our comradeship on the voyage, on reaching San Francisco we took rooms together, on Bush Street, in an old house with a large garden. Volz became leader of the orchestra, and Wynne, leading man at the same theatre. Lest my folks, a Maine deacon's family, should think I was on the road to ruin, I told in letters home only of the city missionary in the house.

Volz was hard worked. Wynne was not much liked. My business went wrong. It rained for many weeks; to this we laid the discomfort that grew to weigh on us. Volz wreaked his sense of it on his violin, adding to the torment of Wynne and myself, for to lonesome anxious souls "the demon in music" shows horns and cloven foot in the trying sounds of practice. One Sunday Volz played the "Witches Dance," the "Dream," and "The long, long weary day."

"I can bear it no longer!" said Wynne. "I feel like the haunted Matthias in 'The Bells.' If I could feel so when acting such parts, it would make my fortune. But I feel it only here."

"I think," said Volz, "it is the *gloria fonda* bush near the window; the scent is too strong." He dashed off Strauss' fretful, conflicting "Hurry and Delay."

"There, there! It is too much," said I. "You express my feelings."

He looked doubtful. "Put it in words," said he.

"How can I?" I said. "When our firm sent me abroad, I went sight-seeing among old palaces, whose Gobelin tapestries framed in their walls were faded to gray phantoms of pictures, but out of some the thrilling eyes followed me till I could not stay in their range. My feeling here is the uneasy one of being watched."

"Ha!" said Volz. "You remind me of Heine, when he wrote

from Livorno. He knew no Italian, but the old palaces whispered secrets unheard by day. The moon was interpreter, knew the lapidary style, translated to dialect of his heart."

"'Strange effects after the moon,'" mused Wynne. "That gives new meaning to Kent's threat: 'I'll make a sop o' the moonshine of you!'"

Volz went on: "Heine wrote: 'The stones here speak to me, and I know their mute language. Also, they seem deeply to feel what I think. So a broken column of the old Roman times, an old tower of Lombardy, a weather-beaten Gothic piece of a pillar understands me well. But I am a ruin myself, wandering among ruins.'"

"Perhaps, like Poe's hero," said I, "'I have imbibed shadows of fallen columns at Balbec, and Tadmor, and Persepolis, until my very soul has become a ruin.'"

"But I, too," said Wynne, "feel the unrest of Tannhauser:

> 'Alas! what seek I here, or anywhere,
> Whose way of life is like the crumbled stair
> That winds and winds about a ruined tower,
> And leads no whither.'"

"I am oppressed," Volz owned, "as if some one in my presence was suffering deeply."

"I feel," said Wynne, "as if the scene was not set right for the performance now going on. There is a hitch and drag somewhere—scene-shifters on a strike. Happy are you poets and musicians, who can express what is vague."

Volz laughed. "As in Liszt's oratorio of 'Christus,'" said he, "where a sharp, ear-piercing *sostenuto* on the piccolo-flute shows the shining of the star of Bethlehem." He turned to me. "Schubert's 'Wanderer' always recalls to me a house you and I know to be under a ban."

"Haunted?" asked Wynne. "Of all speculative theories, St. Martin's sends the most cold thrills up one's back. He said none of the dead come back, but some stay."

"What we Germans call *gebannt*—tied to one spot," said Volz. "But this is no ghost, only a proof of what a German psychologist holds, that the magnetic man is a spirit."

"Go on, 'and tell quaint lies'—I like them," said Wynne.

I told in brief outline, with no names, the tale Volz and I

knew, while we strolled to Telegraph Hill, passing five streets
blocked by the roving houses common to San Francisco.

Wynne said: "They seem to have minds of their own, with
their entrances and exits in a *moving* drama."

"Sort of 'Poor Jo's,'" said I.

"Castles in chess," said Volz.

"Io-like," said Wynne, "with a gad in their hearts that forever drives them on."

A few foreign sailors lounged on the hill top, looking at the
view. The wind blew such a gale we did not stay. The steps we
had known, cut in the side, were gone. Where the old house
used to be, goats were browsing.

"Perchance we do inhabit it but now," mockingly cried
Wynne; "methinks it must be so."

"Then," said Volz, thoughtfully, "it might be what Germans
call 'far-working'—acted in distance—that affects us."

"What do you mean?" I asked. "Do you know anything of
her now?"

"I know she went to Mexico," said he; "that is all."

"What is 'far-working?'" asked Wynne. "If I could act in the
distance, and here too—'what larks!'"

"Yes—'if,'" said I. "Think how all our lives turn on that
pivot. Suppose Hawthorne's offer to join Wilkes' exploring expedition had been taken!"

"Only to wills that know no 'if' is 'far-working' possible,"
said Volz. "Substance or space can no more hinder this force
than the one of mineral magnetism. Passavent joins it with pictures falling, or watches stopping at the time of a death. In
sleep-walking, some kinds of illness, or nearness of death, the
nervous ether is not so closely allied to its material conductors,
the nerves, and may be loosened to act from afar, the surest
where blood or feeling makes attraction or repulsion."

Wynne in the two voices of the play repeated:

> "VICTOR.—Where is the gentleman?
> CHISPE.—As the old song says:
> > 'His body is in Segovia,
> > His soul is in Madrid.'"

We could learn about the house we were in only that five
families had moved in and out during the last year. Wynne

resolved to shake off the gloom that wrapped us. In struggles to defy it, he on the strength of a thousand-dollar benefit, made one payment on the house and began repairs.

On an off-night he was vainly trying to study a new part. Volz advised the relief to his nerves of reciting the dream scene from "The Bells," reminding him he had compared it with his restlessness there. Wynne denied it.

"Yes," said Volz, "where the mesmerizer forces Matthias to confess."

But Wynne refused, as if vexed, till Volz offered to show in music his own mood, and I agreed to read some rhymes about mine. Volz was long tuning his violin.

"I feel," he said, "as if the passers-by would hear a secret. Music is such a subtle expression of emotion—like flower-odor rolls far and affects the stranger. Hearken! In Heine's 'Reise-bilder,' as the cross was thrown ringing on the banquet table of the gods, they grew dumb and pale, and even paler till they melted in mist. So shall you at the long-drawn wail of my violin grow breathless, and fade from each other's sight."

The music closed round us, and we waited in its deep solitude. One brief, sad phrase fell from airy heights to lowest depths into a sea of sound, whose harmonious eddies as they widened breathed of passion and pain, now swooning, now reviving, with odd pauses and sighs that rose to cries of despair, but the tormenting first strain recurring fainter and fainter, as if drowning, drowning, drowned—yet floating back for repeated last plaint, as if not to be quelled, and closing, as it began, the whole.

As I read the name of my verses, Volz murmured: "*Les Nuits Blanches.* No. 4. Stephen Heller."

SLEEPLESS NIGHTS.

Against the garden's mossy paling
    I lean, and wish the night away,
Whose faint, unequal shadows trailing
    Seem but a dream of those of day.

Sleep burdens blossom, bud, and leaf,
    My soul alone aspires, dilates,

Yearns to forget its care and grief—
　　No bath of sleep its pain abates.

How dread these dreams of wide-eyed nights!
　　What is, and is not, both I rue,
My wild thoughts fly like wand'ring kites,
　　No peace falls with this balmy dew.

Through slumb'rous stillness, scarcely stirred
　　By sudden trembles, as when shifts
O'er placid pool some skimming bird,
　　Its Lethean bowl a poppy lifts.

If one deep draught my doubts could solve,
　　The world might bubble down its brim,
Like Cleopatra's pearl dissolve,
　　With all my dreams within its rim.

What should I know but calm repose?
　　How feel, recalling this lost sphere?
Alas! the fabled poppy shows
　　Upon its bleeding heart—a tear!

Wynne unwillingly began to recite: "'I fear nothing, but dreams are dreams—'"

He stammered, could not go on, and fell to the floor. We got him to bed. He never spoke sanely after. His wild fancies appalled us watching him all night.

"Avaunt Sathanas! That's not my cue," he muttered. "A full house to-night. How could Talma forget how the crowd looked, and fancy it a pack of skeletons? Tell Volz to keep the violins playing through this scene, it works me up as well as thrills the audience. Oh, what tiresome nights I have lately, always dreaming of scenes where rival women move, as in 'Court and Stage,' where, all masked, the king makes love to Frances Stewart before the queen's face! How do I try to cure it? 'And being thus frighted, swear a prayer or two and sleep again.' Madame, you're late; you've too little rouge; you'll look ghastly. We're not called yet; let's rehearse our scene. Now, then, I enter left, pass to the window. You cry 'is this true?' and faint. All crowd about. Quick curtain."

Volz and I looked at each other.

"Can our magnetism make his senses so sharp that he knows what is in our minds?" he asked me.

"Nonsense!" I said. "Memory, laudanum, and whisky."

"There," Wynne went on, "the orchestra is stopping. They've rung up the curtain. Don't hold me. The stage waits, yet how can I go outside my door to step on dead bodies? Street and sidewalk are knee-deep with them. They rise and curse me for disturbing them. I lift my cane to strike. It turns to a snake, whose slimy body writhes in my hand. Trying to hold it from biting me, my nails cut my palm till blood streams to drown the snake."

He awed us not alone from having no control of his thoughts, but because there came now and then a strange influx of emotion as if other souls passed in and out of his body.

"Is this hell?" he groaned. "What blank darkness! Where am I? What is that infernal music haunting me through all space? If I could only escape it I need not go back to earth—to that room where I feel choked, where the very wall paper frets me with its flaunting birds flying to and fro, mocking my fettered state. 'Here, here in the very den of the wolf!' Hallo, Benvolio, call-boy's hunting you. Romeo's gone on.

'See where he steals—
Locked in some gloomy covert under key
Of cautionary silence, with his arms
Threaded, like these cross-boughs, in sorrow's knot.'

What is this dread that weighs like a nightmare? 'I do not fear; like Macbeth, I only inhabit trembling.' 'For one of them—she is in hell already, and burns, poor soul! For the other'—Ah! must I die here, alone in the woods, felled by a coward, Indian-like, from behind a tree? None of the boys will know. 'I just now come from a whole world of mad women that had almost—what, is she dead?' Poor Felipa!"

"Did you tell him her name?" I asked Volz.

"No," said he. "Can one man's madness be another's real life?"

"Blood was spilt—the avenger's wing hovered above my house," raved Wynne. "What are these lights, hundreds of them—serpent's eyes? Is it the audience—coiled, many-headed monster, following me round the world? Why do they hiss? I've played this part a hundred times. 'Taught by Rage, and Hunger, and Despair?' Do they, full-fed, well-clothed, light-hearted, know how to judge me? 'A plague on both your houses!' What is that flame? Fire that consumes my vitals—spon-ta-neous combustion! It is then possible. Water! water!"

The doctor said there had been some great strain on Wynne's mind. He sank fast, though we did all we could. Toward morning I turned to Volz with the words:

"He is dead."

The city missionary was passing the open door. He grimly muttered:

"Better dead than alive!"

"My God! say not that!" cried Volz. "The nerve which hears is last to die. He may know——"

He faltered. We stood aghast. The room grew suddenly familiar. I tore off a strip of the gray tint on the walls. Under it we found the old paper with its bright macaws.

"Ah, ha!" Volz said; "will you now deny my theory of 'far-working?'"

Dazed, I could barely murmur: "Then people *can* be affected by it!"

"Certainly," said he, "as rubbed glasses gain electric power."

Within a week we sailed—he for Brazil, I for New York.

Several years after, at Sacramento, Arne, an artist I had known abroad, found me on the overland train, and on reaching San Francisco urged me to go where he lodged.

"I am low-spirited here," he said; "I don't know why."

I stopped short on the crowded wharf. "Where do you live?" I asked.

"Far up Market Street," said he.

"What sort of a house?" I insisted.

"Oh—nothing modern—over a store," he answered.

Reassured, I went with him. He lived in a jumble of easels, portfolios, paint, canvas, bits of statuary, casts, carvings, foils, red curtains, Chinese goatskins, woodcuts, photographs, sketches, and unfinished pictures. On the wall hung a scene from "The Wandering Jew," as we saw it at the Adelphi, in London, where in the Arctic regions he sees visions foreshadowing the future of his race. Under it was quoted:

———"All in my mind is confused, nor can I dissever
The mould of the visible world from the shape of my
thought in me—
The Inward and Outward are fused, and through them
murmur forever
The sorrow whose sound is the wind and the roar of the
limitless sea."

"Do you remember," Arne asked, "when we saw that play? Both younger and more hopeful. How has the world used you? As for me, I have done nothing since I came here but that sketch, finished months ago. I have not lost ambition, but I feel fettered."

"Absinthe?—opium?—tobacco?" I hinted.

"Neither," he answered. "I try to work, but visions, widely different from what I will, crowd on me, as on the Jew in the play. Not the unconscious brain action all thinkers know, but a dictation from without. No rush of creative impulses, but a dragging sense of something else I ought to paint."

"Briefly," I said, "you are a 'Haunted Man.'"

"Haunted by a willful design," said he. "I feel as if something had happened somewhere which I *must* show."

"What is it like?" I asked.

"I wish I could tell you," he replied. "But only odd bits change places, like looking in a kaleidoscope; yet all cluster around one centre."

One day, looking over his portfolios, I found an old *Temple Bar*, which he said he kept for this passage—which he read to me—from T. A. Trollope's "Artist's Tragedy:"

"The old walls and ceilings and floors must be saturated with the exhalations of human emotions! These lintels, doorways, and stairs have become, by long use and homeliness, dear to human hearts, and have become so intimately blended a portion of the mental furniture of human lives, that they have contributed their part to the formation of human characters. Such facts and considerations have gone to the fashioning of the mental habitudes of all of us. If all could have been recorded! If emotion had the property of photographing itself on the surfaces of the walls which had witnessed it! Even if only passion, when translated into acts, could have done so! Ah, what palimpsests! What deciphering of tangled records! What skillful separation of successive layers of 'passionography!'"

"I know a room," said Arne, "thronged with acts that elbow me from my work and fill me with unrest."

I looked at him in mute surprise.

"I suppose," he went on, "such things do not interest you."

"No—yes," I stammered. "I have marked in traveling how lonely houses change their expression as you come near, pass, and leave them. Some frown, others smile. The Bible buildings had life of their own and human diseases; the priests cursed or blessed them as men."

"Houses seem to remember," said he. "Some rooms oppress us with a sense of lives that have been lived in them."

"That," I said, "is like Draper's theory of shadows on walls always staying. He shows how after a breath passes over a coin or key, its spectral outline remains for months after the substance is removed. But can the mist of circumstance sweeping over us make our vacant places hold any trace of us?"

"Why not? Who can deny it? Why do you look at me so?" he asked.

I could not tell him the sad tale. I hesitated; then said: "I was thinking of Volz, a friend I had, who not only believed in what Bulwer calls 'a power akin to mesmerism and superior to it, once called Magic, and that it might reach over the dead, so far as their experience on earth,' but also in animal magnetism from any distance."

Arne grew queerly excited. "If Time and Space exist but in our thoughts, why should it not be true?" said he. "Macdonald's lover cries, 'That which has been is, and the Past can never cease. She is mine, and I shall find her—what matters it when, or where, or how?'" He sighed. "In Acapulco, a year ago, I saw a woman who has been before me ever since—the centre of the circling, changing, crude fancies that trouble me."

"Did you know her?" I asked.

'No, nor anything about her, not even her name. It is like a spell. I must paint her before anything else, but I cannot yet decide how. I feel sure she has played a tragic part in some life-drama."

"Swinburne's queen of panthers," I hinted.

"Yes. But I was not in love. Love I must forego. I am not a man with an income."

"I know you are not a nincompoop!" I said, always trying to

change such themes by a jest. I could not tell him I knew a place which had the influence he talked of. I could not re-visit that house.

Soon after he told me he had begun his picture, but would not show it. He complained that one figure kept its back toward him. He worked on it till he fell ill. Even then he hid it. "Only a layer of passionography," he said.

I grew restless. I thought his mood affected mine. It was a torment as well as a puzzle to me that his whole talk should be of the influence of houses, rooms, even personal property that had known other owners. Once I asked him if he had anything like the brown coat Sheridan swore drew ill-luck to him.

"Sometimes I think," he answered, "it is this special brown paint artists prize which affects me. It is made from the best asphaltum, and that can be got only from Egyptian mummy-cloths. Very likely dust of the mummies is ground in it. I ought to feel their ill-will."

One day I went to Saucelito. In the still woods I forgot my unrest till coming to the stream where, as I suddenly remembered, Anson was found dead, a dread took me which I tried to lose by putting into rhyme. Turning my pockets at night, I crumpled the page I had written on, and threw it on the floor.

In uneasy sleep I dreamed I was again in Paris, not where I liked to recall being, but at "Bullier's," and in war-time. The bald, spectacled leader of the orchestra, leaning back, shamming sleep, while a dancing, stamping, screaming crowd wave tri-colored flags, and call for the "Chant du Depart." Three thousand voices in a rushing roar that makes the twenty thousand lights waver, in spasmodic but steady chorus:

> "Les departs—parts—parts!
> Les departs—parts—parts!
> Les departs—parts—parts!"

Roused, I supposed by passing rioters, I did not try to sleep again, but rose to write a letter for the early mail. As I struck a light I saw, smoothed out on the table, the wrinkled page I had cast aside. The ink was yet wet on two lines added to each verse. A chill crept over me as I read:

FOREST MURMURS.

Across the woodland bridge I pass,
　　And sway its three long, narrow planks,
To mark how gliding waters glass
　　Bright blossoms doubled ranks on ranks;
And how through tangle of the ferns
Floats incense from veiled flower-urns,
What would the babbling brook reveal?
What may these trembling depths conceal?
Dread secret of the dense woods, held
With restless shudders horror-spelled!

How shift the shadows of the wood,
　　As if it tossed in troubled sleep!
Strange whispers, vaguely understood,
　　Above, below, around me creep;
While in the sombre-shadowed stream
Great scarlet splashes far down gleam,
The odd-reflected, stately shapes
Of cardinals in crimson capes;
Not those—but spectral pools of blood
That stain these sands through strongest flood!

Like blare of trumpets through black nights—
　　Or sunset clouds before a storm—
Are these red phantom water-sprites
　　That mock me with fantastic form;
With flitting of the last year's bird
Fled ripples that its low flight stirred—
How should these rushing waters learn
Aught but the bend of this year's fern?
The lonesome wood, with bated breath,
Hints of a hidden blow—and death!

I could not stay alone. I ran to Arne's room. As I knocked,
the falling of some light thing within made me think he was
stirring. I went in. He sat in the moonlight, back to me before
his easel. The picture on it might be the one he kept secret. I
would not look. I went to his side and touched him. He had
been dead for hours! I turned the unseen canvas to the wall.

Next day I packed and planned to go East. I paid the land-lady not to send Arne's body to the morgue, and watched it that night, when a sudden memory swept over me like a tidal wave. There was a likeness in the room to one where I had before watched the dead. Yes—there were the windows, there the doors—just here stood the bed, in the same spot I sat. What wildness was in the air of San Francisco!

To put such crazy thoughts to flight I would look at Arne's last work. Yet I wavered, and more than once turned away after laying my hand on it. At last I snatched it, placed it on the easel and lighted the nearest gas-burner before looking at it. Then—great heavens! How had this vision come to Arne? It was the scene where Felipa cursed us. Every detail of the room reproduced, even the gay birds on the wall-paper, and her flower-pots. The figures and faces of Dering and Volz were true as hers, and in the figure with averted face which Arne had said kept its back to him, I knew—myself! What strange in-sight had he gained by looking at Felipa? It was like the man who trembled before the unknown portrait of the Marquise de Brinvilliers.

How long I gazed at the picture I do not know. I heard, without heeding, the doorbell ring and steps along the hall. Voices. Some one looking at rooms. The landlady, saying this room was to let, but unwilling to show it, forced to own its last tenant lay there dead. This seemed no shock to the stranger.

"Well," said her shrill tones, "poor as he was he's better dead than alive!"

The door opened as a well-known voice cried: "My God! say not that! The nerve which hears is last to die—"

Volz stood before me! Awe-struck, we looked at each other in silence. Then he waved his hand to and fro before his eyes.

"Is this a dream?" he said. "There," pointing to the bed; "you"—to me; "the same words—the very room! Is it our fate?"

I pointed to the picture and to Arne. "The last work of this man, who thought it a fancy sketch?"

While Volz stood dumb and motionless before it, the land-lady spoke:

"Then you know the place. Can you tell what ails it? There

have been suicides in this room. No one prospers in the house. My cousin, who is a house-mover, warned me against taking it. He says before the store was put under it here it stood on Bush Street, and before that on Telegraph Hill."

Volz clutched my arm. "It is 'The Flying Dutchman' of a house!" he cried, and drew me fast down stairs and out into a dense fog which made the world seem a tale that was told, blotting out all but our two slanting forms, bent as by what poor Wynne would have called "a blast from hell," hurrying blindly away. I heard the voice of Volz as if from afar: "The magnetic man *is* a spirit!"

1897

MARY WILKINS FREEMAN

(1852–1930)

Luella Miller

CLOSE to the village street stood the one-story house in which Luella Miller, who had an evil name in the village, had dwelt. She had been dead for years, yet there were those in the village who, in spite of the clearer light which comes on a vantage-point from a long-past danger, half believed in the tale which they had heard from their childhood. In their hearts, although they scarcely would have owned it, was a survival of the wild horror and frenzied fear of their ancestors who had dwelt in the same age with Luella Miller. Young people even would stare with a shudder at the old house as they passed, and children never played around it as was their wont around an untenanted building. Not a window in the old Miller house was broken: the panes reflected the morning sunlight in patches of emerald and blue, and the latch of the sagging front door was never lifted, although no bolt secured it. Since Luella Miller had been carried out of it, the house had had no tenant except one friendless old soul who had no choice between that and the far-off shelter of the open sky. This old woman, who had survived her kindred and friends, lived in the house one week, then one morning no smoke came out of the chimney, and a body of neighbours, a score strong, entered and found her dead in her bed. There were dark whispers as to the cause of her death, and there were those who testified to an expression of fear so exalted that it showed forth the state of the departing soul upon the dead face. The old woman had been hale and hearty when she entered the house, and in seven days she was dead; it seemed that she had fallen a victim to some uncanny power. The minister talked in the pulpit with covert severity against the sin of superstition; still the belief prevailed. Not a soul in the village but would have chosen the almshouse rather than that dwelling. No vagrant, if he heard the tale, would seek shelter beneath that old roof, unhallowed by nearly half a century of superstitious fear.

There was only one person in the village who had actually known Luella Miller. That person was a woman well over eighty, but a marvel of vitality and unextinct youth. Straight as an arrow, with the spring of one recently let loose from the bow of life, she moved about the streets, and she always went to church, rain or shine. She had never married, and had lived alone for years in a house across the road from Luella Miller's.

This woman had none of the garrulousness of age, but never in all her life had she ever held her tongue for any will save her own, and she never spared the truth when she essayed to present it. She it was who bore testimony to the life, evil, though possibly wittingly or designedly so, of Luella Miller, and to her personal appearance. When this old woman spoke—and she had the gift of description, although her thoughts were clothed in the rude vernacular of her native village—one could seem to see Luella Miller as she had really looked. According to this woman, Lydia Anderson by name, Luella Miller had been a beauty of a type rather unusual in New England. She had been a slight, pliant sort of creature, as ready with a strong yielding to fate and as unbreakable as a willow. She had glimmering lengths of straight, fair hair, which she wore softly looped round a long, lovely face. She had blue eyes full of soft pleading, little slender, clinging hands, and a wonderful grace of motion and attitude.

"Luella Miller used to sit in a way nobody else could if they sat up and studied a week of Sundays," said Lydia Anderson, "and it was a sight to see her walk. If one of them willows over there on the edge of the brook could start up and get its roots free of the ground, and move off, it would go just the way Luella Miller used to. She had a green shot silk she used to wear, too, and a hat with green ribbon streamers, and a lace veil blowing across her face and out sideways, and a green ribbon flyin' from her waist. That was what she came out bride in when she married Erastus Miller. Her name before she was married was Hill. There was always a sight of 'l's' in her name, married or single. Erastus Miller was good lookin', too, better lookin' than Luella. Sometimes I used to think that Luella wa'n't so handsome after all. Erastus just about worshiped her.

I used to know him pretty well. He lived next door to me, and we went to school together. Folks used to say he was waitin' on me, but he wa'n't. I never thought he was except once or twice when he said things that some girls might have suspected meant somethin'. That was before Luella came here to teach the district school. It was funny how she came to get it, for folks said she hadn't any education, and that one of the big girls, Lottie Henderson, used to do all the teachin' for her, while she sat back and did embroidery work on a cambric pocket-handkerchief. Lottie Henderson was a real smart girl, a splendid scholar, and she just set her eyes by Luella, as all the girls did. Lottie would have made a real smart woman, but she died when Luella had been here about a year—just faded away and died: nobody knew what ailed her. She dragged herself to that schoolhouse and helped Luella teach till the very last minute. The committee all knew how Luella didn't do much of the work herself, but they winked at it. It wa'n't long after Lottie died that Erastus married her. I always thought he hurried it up because she wa'n't fit to teach. One of the big boys used to help her after Lottie died, but he hadn't much government, and the school didn't do very well, and Luella might have had to give it up, for the committee couldn't have shut their eyes to things much longer. The boy that helped her was a real honest, innocent sort of fellow, and he was a good scholar, too. Folks said he overstudied, and that was the reason he was took crazy the year after Luella married, but I don't know. And I don't know what made Erastus Miller go into consumption of the blood the year after he was married: consumption wa'n't in his family. He just grew weaker and weaker, and went almost bent double when he tried to wait on Luella, and he spoke feeble, like an old man. He worked terrible hard till the last trying to save up a little to leave Luella. I've seen him out in the worst storms on a wood-sled—he used to cut and sell wood—and he was hunched up on top lookin' more dead than alive. Once I couldn't stand it: I went over and helped him pitch some wood on the cart—I was always strong in my arms. I wouldn't stop for all he told me to, and I guess he was glad enough for the help. That was only a week before he died. He fell on the kitchen floor while he was gettin' breakfast. He always got the breakfast and let Luella lay abed. He did all

the sweepin' and the washin' and the ironin' and most of the
cookin'. He couldn't bear to have Luella lift her finger, and she
let him do for her. She lived like a queen for all the work
she did. She didn't even do her sewin'. She said it made her
shoulder ache to sew, and poor Erastus's sister Lily used to do
all her sewin'. She wa'n't able to, either; she was never strong
in her back, but she did it beautifully. She had to, to suit Luella,
she was so dreadful particular. I never saw anythin' like the
fagottin' and hemstitchin' that Lily Miller did for Luella. She
made all Luella's weddin' outfit, and that green silk dress, after
Maria Babbit cut it. Maria she cut it for nothin', and she did a
lot more cuttin' and fittin' for nothin' for Luella, too. Lily
Miller went to live with Luella after Erastus died. She gave up
her home, though she was real attached to it and wa'n't a mite
afraid to stay alone. She rented it and she went to live with
Luella right away after the funeral."

Then this old woman, Lydia Anderson, who remembered
Luella Miller, would go on to relate the story of Lily Miller. It
seemed that on the removal of Lily Miller to the house of her
dead brother, to live with his widow, the village people first
began to talk. This Lily Miller had been hardly past her first
youth, and a most robust and blooming woman, rosy-cheeked,
with curls of strong, black hair overshadowing round, candid
temples and bright dark eyes. It was not six months after she
had taken up her residence with her sister-in-law that her rosy
colour faded and her pretty curves became wan hollows. White
shadows began to show in the black rings of her hair, and the
light died out of her eyes, her features sharpened, and there
were pathetic lines at her mouth, which yet wore always an expression of utter sweetness and even happiness. She was devoted to her sister; there was no doubt that she loved her with
her whole heart, and was perfectly content in her service. It
was her sole anxiety lest she should die and leave her alone.

"The way Lily Miller used to talk about Luella was enough
to make you mad and enough to make you cry," said Lydia
Anderson. "I've been in there sometimes toward the last when
she was too feeble to cook and carried her some blanc-mange
or custard—somethin' I thought she might relish, and she'd
thank me, and when I asked her how she was, say she felt
better than she did yesterday, and asked me if I didn't think

she looked better, dreadful pitiful, and say poor Luella had an awful time takin' care of her and doin' the work—she wa'n't strong enough to do anythin'—when all the time Luella wa'n't liftin' her finger and poor Lily didn't get any care except what the neighbours gave her, and Luella eat up everythin' that was carried in for Lily. I had it real straight that she did. Luella used to just sit and cry and do nothin'. She did act real fond of Lily, and she pined away considerable, too. There was those that thought she'd go into a decline herself. But after Lily died, her Aunt Abby Mixter came, and then Luella picked up and grew as fat and rosy as ever. But poor Aunt Abby begun to droop just the way Lily had, and I guess somebody wrote to her married daughter, Mrs. Sam Abbot, who lived in Barre, for she wrote her mother that she must leave right away and come and make her a visit, but Aunt Abby wouldn't go. I can see her now. She was a real good-lookin' woman, tall and large, with a big, square face and a high forehead that looked of itself kind of benevolent and good. She just tended out on Luella as if she had been a baby, and when her married daughter sent for her she wouldn't stir one inch. She'd always thought a lot of her daughter, too, but she said Luella needed her and her married daughter didn't. Her daughter kept writin' and writin', but it didn't do any good. Finally she came, and when she saw how bad her mother looked, she broke down and cried and all but went on her knees to have her come away. She spoke her mind out to Luella, too. She told her that she'd killed her husband and everybody that had anythin' to do with her, and she'd thank her to leave her mother alone. Luella went into hysterics, and Aunt Abby was so frightened that she called me after her daughter went. Mrs. Sam Abbot she went away fairly cryin' out loud in the buggy, the neighbours heard her, and well she might, for she never saw her mother again alive. I went in that night when Aunt Abby called for me, standin' in the door with her little green-checked shawl over her head. I can see her now. 'Do come over here, Miss Anderson,' she sung out, kind of gasping for breath. I didn't stop for anythin'. I put over as fast as I could, and when I got there, there was Luella laughin' and cryin' all together, and Aunt Abby trying to hush her, and all the time she herself was white as a sheet and shakin' so she could hardly stand. 'For the land sakes, Mrs. Mixter,' says I, 'you look worse than she does. You ain't fit to be up out of your bed.'

"'Oh, there ain't anythin' the matter with me,' says she. Then she went on talkin' to Luella. 'There, there, don't, don't, poor little lamb,' says she. 'Aunt Abby is here. She ain't goin' away and leave you. Don't, poor little lamb.'

"'Do leave her with me, Mrs. Mixter, and you get back to bed,' says I, for Aunt Abby had been layin' down considerable lately, though somehow she contrived to do the work.

"'I'm well enough,' says she. 'Don't you think she had better have the doctor, Miss Anderson?'

"'The doctor,' says I, 'I think *you* had better have the doctor. I think you need him much worse than some folks I could mention.' And I looked right straight at Luella Miller laughin' and cryin' and goin' on as if she was the centre of all creation. All the time she was actin' so—seemed as if she was too sick to sense anythin'—she was keepin' a sharp lookout as to how we took it out of the corner of one eye. I see her. You could never cheat me about Luella Miller. Finally I got real mad and I run home and I got a bottle of valerian I had, and I poured some boilin' hot water on a handful of catnip, and I mixed up that catnip tea with most half a wineglass of valerian, and I went with it over to Luella's. I marched right up to Luella, a-holdin' out of that cup, all smokin'. 'Now,' says I, 'Luella Miller, '*you swallar this!*'

"'What is—what is it, oh, what is it?' she sort of screeches out. Then she goes off a-laughin' enough to kill.

"'Poor lamb, poor little lamb,' says Aunt Abby, standin' over her, all kind of tottery, and tryin' to bathe her head with camphor.

"'*You swaller this right down,*' says I. And I didn't waste any ceremony. I just took hold of Luella Miller's chin and I tipped her head back, and I caught her mouth open with laughin', and I clapped that cup to her lips, and I fairly hollered at her: 'Swaller, swaller, swaller!' and she gulped it right down. She had to, and I guess it did her good. Anyhow, she stopped cryin' and laughin' and let me put her to bed, and she went to sleep like a baby inside of half an hour. That was more than poor Aunt Abby did. She lay awake all that night and I stayed with her, though she tried not to have me; said she wa'n't sick enough for watchers. But I stayed, and I made some good cornmeal gruel and I fed her a teaspoon every little while all night long. It seemed to me as if she was jest dyin' from bein' all wore out. In the mornin' as soon as it was light I run over to the Bisbees and sent Johnny Bisbee for the doctor. I told him to tell the doctor to hurry, and he come pretty quick. Poor Aunt Abby didn't seem to know much of anythin' when he got there. You couldn't hardly tell she breathed, she was so used up. When the doctor had gone, Luella came into the room lookin' like a baby in her ruffled nightgown. I can see her now. Her eyes were as blue and her face all pink and white like a blossom, and she looked at Aunt Abby in the bed sort of innocent and surprised. 'Why,' says she, 'Aunt Abby ain't got up yet?'

" 'No, she ain't,' says I, pretty short.

" 'I thought I didn't smell the coffee,' says Luella.

" 'Coffee,' says I. 'I guess if you have coffee this mornin' you'll make it yourself.'

" 'I never made the coffee in all my life,' says she, dreadful astonished. 'Erastus always made the coffee as long as he lived, and then Lily she made it, and then Aunt Abby made it. I don't believe I *can* make the coffee, Miss Anderson.'

" 'You can make it or go without, jest as you please,' says I.

" 'Ain't Aunt Abby goin' to get up?' says she.

" 'I guess she won't get up,' says I, 'sick as she is.' I was gettin' madder and madder. There was somethin' about that little pink-and-white thing standin' there and talkin' about coffee, when she had killed so many better folks than she was, and had jest killed another, that made me feel 'most as if I wished somebody would up and kill her before she had a chance to do any more harm.

" 'Is Aunt Abby sick?' says Luella, as if she was sort of aggrieved and injured.

" 'Yes,' says I, 'she's sick, and she's goin' to die, and then you'll be left alone, and you'll have to do for yourself and wait on yourself, or do without things.' I don't know but I was sort of hard, but it was the truth, and if I was any harder than Luella Miller had been I'll give up. I ain't never been sorry that I said it. Well, Luella, she up and had hysterics again at that, and I jest let her have 'em. All I did was to bundle her into the room on the other side of the entry where Aunt Abby couldn't hear her, if she wa'n't past it—I don't know but she was—and set her down hard in a chair and told her not to come back into the other room, and she minded. She had her hysterics in there till she got tired. When she found out that nobody was comin' to coddle her and do for her she stopped. At least I suppose she did. I had all I could do with poor Aunt Abby tryin' to keep the breath of life in her. The doctor had told me that she was dreadful low, and give me some very strong medicine to give to her in drops real often, and told me real particular about the nourishment. Well, I did as he told me real faithful till she wa'n't able to swaller any longer. Then I had her daughter sent for. I had begun to realize that she wouldn't last any time at all. I hadn't realized it before, though I spoke to Luella the way I did. The doctor he came, and Mrs. Sam Abbot, but when she got there it was too late; her mother was dead. Aunt Abby's daughter just give one look at her mother layin' there, then she turned sort of sharp and sudden and looked at me.

" 'Where is she?' says she, and I knew she meant Luella.

" 'She's out in the kitchen,' says I. 'She's too nervous to see folks die. She's afraid it will make her sick.'

"The Doctor he speaks up then. He was a young man. Old Doctor Park had died the year before, and this was a young fellow just out of college. 'Mrs. Miller is not strong,' says he, kind of severe, 'and she is quite right in not agitating herself.'

" 'You are another, young man; she's got her pretty claw on you,' thinks I, but I didn't say anythin' to him. I just said over to Mrs. Sam Abbot that Luella was in the kitchen, and Mrs. Sam Abbot she went out there, and I went, too, and I never heard anythin' like the way she talked to Luella Miller. I felt pretty hard to Luella myself, but this was more than I ever would have dared to say. Luella she was too scared to go into hysterics. She jest flopped. She seemed to jest shrink away to nothin' in that kitchen chair, with Mrs. Sam Abbot standin' over her and talkin' and tellin' her the truth. I guess the truth was most too much for her and no mistake, because Luella presently actually did faint away, and there wa'n't any sham about it, the way I always suspected there was about them hysterics. She fainted dead away and we had to lay her flat on the floor, and the Doctor he came runnin' out and he said somethin' about a weak heart dreadful fierce to Mrs. Sam Abbot, but she wa'n't a mite scared. She faced him jest as white as even Luella was layin' there lookin' like death and the Doctor feelin' of her pulse.

" 'Weak heart,' says she, 'weak heart; weak fiddlesticks! There ain't nothin' weak about that woman. She's got strength enough to hang onto other folks till she kills 'em. Weak? It was my poor mother that was weak: this woman killed her as sure as if she had taken a knife to her.'

"But the Doctor he didn't pay much attention. He was bendin' over Luella layin' there with her yellow hair all streamin' and her pretty pink-and-white face all pale, and her blue eyes like stars gone out, and he was holdin' onto her hand and smoothin' her forehead, and tellin' me to get the brandy in Aunt Abby's room, and I was sure as I wanted to be that Luella had got somebody else to hang onto, now Aunt Abby was gone, and I thought of poor Erastus Miller, and I sort of pitied the poor young Doctor, led away by a pretty face, and I made up my mind I'd see what I could do.

"I waited till Aunt Abby had been dead and buried about a month, and the Doctor was goin' to see Luella steady and folks were beginnin' to talk; then one evenin', when I knew the Doctor had been called out of town and wouldn't be round, I went over to Luella's. I found her all dressed up in a blue muslin with white polka dots on it, and her hair curled jest as pretty, and there wa'n't a young girl in the place could compare with her. There was somethin' about Luella Miller seemed to draw the heart right out of you, but she didn't draw it out of *me*. She was settin' rocking in the chair by her sittin'-room window, and Maria Brown had gone home. Maria Brown had been in to help her, or rather to do the work, for Luella wa'n't helped when she didn't do anythin'. Maria Brown was real capable and she didn't have any ties; she wa'n't married, and lived alone, so she'd offered. I couldn't see why she should do the work any more than Luella; she wa'n't any too strong; but she seemed to think she could and Luella seemed to think so, too, so she went over and did all the work—washed, and ironed, and baked, while Luella sat and rocked. Maria didn't live long afterward. She began to fade away just the same fashion the others had. Well, she was warned, but she acted real mad when folks said anythin': said Luella was a poor, abused woman, too delicate to help herself, and they'd ought to be ashamed, and if she died helpin' them that couldn't help themselves she would—and she did.

" 'I s'pose Maria has gone home,' says I to Luella, when I had gone in and sat down opposite her.

" 'Yes, Maria went half an hour ago, after she had got supper and washed the dishes,' says Luella, in her pretty way.

" 'I suppose she has got a lot of work to do in her own house to-night,' says I, kind of bitter, but that was all thrown away on Luella Miller. It seemed to her right that other folks that wa'n't any better able than she was herself should wait on her, and she couldn't get it through her head that anybody should think it *wa'n't* right.

" 'Yes,' says Luella, real sweet and pretty, 'yes, she said she had to do her washin' to-night. She has let it go for a fortnight along of comin' over here.'

" 'Why don't she stay home and do her washin' instead of comin' over here and doin' *your* work, when you are just as well able, and enough sight more so, than she is to do it?' says I.

"Then Luella she looked at me like a baby who has a rattle shook at it. She sort of laughed as innocent as you please. 'Oh, I can't do the work myself, Miss Anderson,' says she. 'I never did. Maria *has* to do it.'

"Then I spoke out: 'Has to do it!' says I. 'Has to do it!' She don't have to do it, either. Maria Brown has her own home and enough to live on. She ain't beholden to you to come over here and slave for you and kill herself.'

"Luella she jest set and stared at me for all the world like a doll-baby that was so abused that it was comin' to life.

" 'Yes,' says I, 'she's killin' herself. She's goin' to die just the way Erastus did, and Lily, and your Aunt Abby. You're killin' her jest as you did them. I don't know what there is about you, but you seem to bring a curse,' says I. 'You kill everybody that is fool enough to care anythin' about you and do for you.'

"She stared at me and she was pretty pale.

" 'And Maria ain't the only one you're goin' to kill,' says I.

'You're goin' to kill Doctor Malcom before you're done with him.'

"Then a red colour came flamin' all over her face. 'I ain't goin' to kill him, either,' says she, and she begun to cry.

"'Yes, you *be*!' says I. Then I spoke as I had never spoke before. You see, I felt it on account of Erastus. I told her that she hadn't any business to think of another man after she'd been married to one that had died for her: that she was a dreadful woman; and she was, that's true enough, but sometimes I have wondered lately if she knew it—if she wa'n't like a baby with scissors in its hand cuttin' everybody without knowin' what it was doin'.

"Luella she kept gettin' paler and paler, and she never took her eyes off my face. There was somethin' awful about the way she looked at me and never spoke one word. After awhile I quit talkin' and I went home. I watched that night, but her lamp went out before nine o'clock, and when Doctor Malcom came drivin' past and sort of slowed up he see there wa'n't any light and he drove along. I saw her sort of shy out of meetin' the next Sunday, too, so he shouldn't go home with her, and I begun to think mebbe she did have some conscience after all. It was only a week after that that Maria Brown died—sort of sudden at the last, though everybody had seen it was comin'. Well, then there was a good deal of feelin' and pretty dark whispers. Folks said the days of witchcraft had come again, and they were pretty shy of Luella. She acted sort of offish to the Doctor and he didn't go there, and there wa'n't anybody to do anythin' for her. I don't know how she *did* get along. I wouldn't go in there and offer to help her—not because I was afraid of dyin' like the rest, but I thought she was just as well able to do her own work as I was to do it for her, and I thought it was about time that she did it and stopped killin' other folks. But it wa'n't very long before folks began to say that Luella herself was goin' into a decline jest the way her husband, and Lily, and Aunt Abby and the others had, and I saw myself that she looked pretty bad. I used to see her goin' past from the store with a bundle as if she could hardly crawl, but I remembered how Erastus used to wait and 'tend when he couldn't hardly put one foot before the other, and I didn't go out to help her.

"But at last one afternoon I saw the Doctor come drivin' up like mad with his medicine chest, and Mrs. Babbit came in after supper and said that Luella was real sick.

" 'I'd offer to go in and nurse her,' says she, 'but I've got my children to consider, and mebbe it ain't true what they say, but it's queer how many folks that have done for her have died.'

"I didn't say anythin', but I considered how she had been Erastus's wife and how he had set his eyes by her, and I made up my mind to go in the next mornin', unless she was better, and see what I could do; but the next mornin' I see her at the window, and pretty soon she came steppin' out as spry as you please, and a little while afterward Mrs. Babbit came in and told me that the Doctor had got a girl from out of town, a Sarah Jones, to come there, and she said she was pretty sure that the Doctor was goin' to marry Luella.

"I saw him kiss her in the door that night myself, and I knew it was true. The woman came that afternoon, and the way she flew around was a caution. I don't believe Luella had swept since Maria died. She swept and dusted, and washed and ironed; wet clothes and dusters and carpets were flyin' over there all day, and every time Luella set her foot out when the Doctor wa'n't there there was that Sarah Jones helpin' of her up and down the steps, as if she hadn't learned to walk.

"Well, everybody knew that Luella and the Doctor were goin' to be married, but it wa'n't long before they began to talk about his lookin' so poorly, jest as they had about the others; and they talked about Sarah Jones, too.

"Well, the Doctor did die, and he wanted to be married first, so as to leave what little he had to Luella, but he died before the minister could get there, and Sarah Jones died a week afterward.

"Well, that wound up everything for Luella Miller. Not another soul in the whole town would lift a finger for her. There got to be a sort of panic. Then she began to droop in good earnest. She used to have to go to the store herself, for Mrs. Babbit was afraid to let Tommy go for her, and I've seen her goin' past and stoppin' every two or three steps to rest. Well, I stood it as long as I could, but one day I see her comin' with her arms full and stoppin' to lean against the Babbit fence, and I run out and took her bundles and carried them to her house.

Then I went home and never spoke one word to her though she called after me dreadful kind of pitiful. Well, that night I was taken sick with a chill, and I was sick as I wanted to be for two weeks. Mrs. Babbit had seen me run out to help Luella and she came in and told me I was goin' to die on account of it. I didn't know whether I was or not, but I considered I had done right by Erastus's wife.

"That last two weeks Luella she had a dreadful hard time, I guess. She was pretty sick, and as near as I could make out nobody dared go near her. I don't know as she was really needin' anythin' very much, for there was enough to eat in her house and it was warm weather, and she made out to cook a little flour gruel every day, I know, but I guess she had a hard time, she that had been so petted and done for all her life.

"When I got so I could go out, I went over there one morning. Mrs. Babbit had just come in to say she hadn't seen any smoke and she didn't know but it was somebody's duty to go in, but she couldn't help thinkin' of her children, and I got right up, though I hadn't been out of the house for two weeks, and I went in there, and Luella she was layin' on the bed, and she was dyin'.

"She lasted all that day and into the night. But I sat there after the new doctor had gone away. Nobody else dared to go there. It was about midnight that I left her for a minute to run home and get some medicine I had been takin', for I begun to feel rather bad.

"It was a full moon that night, and just as I started out of my door to cross the street back to Luella's, I stopped short, for I saw something."

Lydia Anderson at this juncture always said with a certain defiance that she did not expect to be believed, and then proceeded in a hushed voice:

"I saw what I saw, and I know I saw it, and I will swear on my death bed that I saw it. I saw Luella Miller and Erastus Miller, and Lily, and Aunt Abby, and Maria, and the Doctor, and Sarah, all goin' out of her door, and all but Luella shone white in the moonlight, and they were all helpin' her along till she seemed to fairly fly in the midst of them. Then it all disappeared. I stood a minute with my heart poundin', then I went over there. I thought of goin' for Mrs. Babbit, but I thought she'd be afraid. So I went alone, though I knew what had happened. Luella was layin' real peaceful, dead on her bed."

This was the story that the old woman, Lydia Anderson, told, but the sequel was told by the people who survived her, and this is the tale which has become folklore in the village.

Lydia Anderson died when she was eighty-seven. She had continued wonderfully hale and hearty for one of her years until about two weeks before her death.

One bright moonlight evening she was sitting beside a window in her parlour when she made a sudden exclamation, and was out of the house and across the street before the neighbour who was taking care of her could stop her. She followed as fast as possible and found Lydia Anderson stretched on the ground before the door of Luella Miller's deserted house, and she was quite dead.

The next night there was a red gleam of fire athwart the moonlight and the old house of Luella Miller was burned to the ground. Nothing is now left of it except a few old cellar stones and a lilac bush, and in summer a helpless trail of morning glories among the weeds, which might be considered emblematic of Luella herself.

1902

FRANK NORRIS

(1870–1902)

Grettir at Thorhall-stead

I—Glamr

THORHALL the bonder had been to the great Thingvalla, or annual fair of Iceland, to engage a shepherd, and was now returning. It had been a good two-days' journey home, for his shaggy little pony, though sure footed, was slow. For the better part of three hours on the evening of the second day he had been picking his way cautiously among the great boulders of black basalt that encumbered the path. At length, on the summit of a low hill, he brought the little animal to a standstill and paused a moment, looking off to the northward, a smile of satisfaction spreading over his broad, sober face. For he had just passed the white stone that marked the boundary of his own land. Below him opened the little valley named the Vale of Shadows, and in its midst, overshadowed by a single Norway pine, black, wind-distorted, was the stone farmhouse, the byre, Thorhall's home.

Only an Icelander could have found pleasure in that prospect. It was dreary beyond expression. Save only for the deformed pine, tortured and warped by its unending battle with the wintry gales, no other tree relieved the monotony of the landscape. To the west, mountains barred the horizon—volcanic mountains, gashed, cragged, basaltic, and still blackened with primeval fires. Bare of vegetation they were—somber, solitary, empty of life. To the eastward, low, rolling sand dunes, sprinkled thinly with gorse, bore down to the sea. They shut off a view of the shore, but farther on the horizon showed itself, a bitter, inhospitable waste of gray water, blotted by fogs and murk and sudden squalls. Though the shore was invisible, it none the less asserted itself. With the rushing of the wind was mingled the prolonged, everlasting thunder of the surf, while the taint of salt, of decaying kelp, of fish, of seaweed, of all the pungent aromas of the sea, pervaded the air on every hand.

Black gulls, sharply defined against the gray sky, slanted in long tacking flights hither and thither over sea and land. The raucous bark of the seal hunting mackerel off the shore made itself occasionally heard. Otherwise there was no sign of life. Veils of fine rain, half fog, drove across the scene between ocean and mountain. The wind blew incessantly from off the sea with a steady and uninterrupted murmur.

Thorhall rode on, inclining his head against the gusts and driving wind. Soon he had come to the farmhouse. The servants led the pony to the stables and in the doorway Thorhall found his wife waiting for him. They embraced one another and—for they were pious folk—thanked God for the bonder's safe journey and speedy return. Before the roaring fire of drift that evening Thorhall told his wife of all that had passed at the Thingvalla, of the wrestling, and of the stallion fights.

"And did you find a shepherd to your liking?" asked his wife.

"Yes; a great fellow with white teeth and black hair. Rather surly, I believe, but strong as a troll. He promised to be with me by the beginning of the Winter night. His name is Glamr."

But the Summer passed, the sun dipped below the horizon not to reappear for six months, the Winter night drew on, snow buried all the landscape, hurricanes sharp as boar-spears descended upon the Vale of Shadows; in their beds the dwellers in the byre heard the grind and growl of the great bergs careering onward through the ocean, and many a night the howl of hunger-driven wolves startled Thorhall from his sleep; yet Glamr did not come.

Then at length and of a sudden he appeared; and Thorhall on a certain evening, called hastily by a frightened servant, beheld the great figure of him in the midst of the kitchen floor, his eyebrows frosted yet scowling, his white teeth snapping with cold, while in a great hoarse voice, like the grumble of a bear, he called for meat and drink.

From thenceforward Glamr became a member of Thorhall's household. Yet seldom was he found in the byre. By day he was away with the sheep; by night he slept in the stables. The servants were afraid of him, though he rarely addressed them a word. He was not only feared, but disliked. This aversion was partly explained by Glamr's own peculiar disposition—gloomy, solitary, uncanny, and partly by a fact that came to light within the first month of his coming to the Vale of Shadows.

He was an unbeliever. Never did his broad bulk darken the lich-gate of the kirk; the knolling of matin and vesper-bell put him in a season of even deeper gloom than usual. It was noticed that he could not bear to look upon a cross; the priest he abhorred as a pestilence. On holy days he kept far from home, absenting himself upon one pretext or another, withdrawing up into the chasms and gorges of the hills.

So passed the first months of the Winter.

Christmas Day came, and Christmas Night. It was bitter, bitter cold. Snow had fallen since second cockcrow the day before, and as night closed in such a gale as had not been known for years gathered from off the Northern Ocean and whirled shrieking over the Vale of Shadows. All day long Glamr was in the hills with the sheep, and even above the roaring of the wind his bell-toned voice had occasionally been heard as he called and shouted to his charges. At candle-lighting time he had not returned. The bonder and his family busked themselves to attend the Christmas mass.

Some two hours later they were returning. The wind was going down, but even yet shreds of torn seaweed and scud of foam, swept up by the breath of the gale, drove landward across the valley. The clouds overhead were breaking up, and between their galloping courses one saw the sky, the stars glittering like hoar frost.

The bonder's party drew near the farmhouse, and the servants, going before with lanthorns and pine torches, undid the fastenings of the gate. The wind lapsed suddenly, and in the stillness between two gusts the plunge of the surf made itself heard.

Then all at once Thorhall and his wife stopped and her hand clutched quickly at his wrist.

"Hark! what was that?"

What, indeed? Was it an echo of the storm sounding hollow and faint from some thunder-split crag far off there in those hills toward which all eyes were suddenly turned; was it the cry of a wolf, the clamor of a falcon, or was it the horrid scream of human agony and fury, vibrating to a hoarse and bell-like note that sounded familiar in their ears?

"Glamr! Where is Glamr?" shouted Thorhall, as he entered

the byre. But those few servants who had been left in charge of the house reported he had not yet returned.

Night passed and no Glamr; and in the morning the search-party set out toward the hills. Half way up the slope, the sheep —a few of them—were found, scattered, half buried in drifts; then a dog, dead and frozen hard as wood. From it led a track up into the higher mountains, a strange track indeed, not human certainly, yet whether of wolf or bear no one could determine. Some had started to follow when a lad who had looked behind the shoulder of a great rock raised a cry.

There was the body of Glamr. The shepherd was stretched upon his back, dead, rigid. The open eyes were glazed, the face livid; the tongue protruding from the mouth had been bitten through in the last agony. All about the snow was trampled down, and the bare bushes crushed and flattened out. Even the massive boulder near which the body had been found was moved a little from its place. A fearful struggle had been wrought out here, yet upon the body of Glamr was no trace of a wound, no mark of claw or hand. Only among his footprints was mingled that strange track that had been noticed before, and as before it led straight up toward the high part of the mountains.

The young men raised the body of the shepherd and the party moved off toward the kirk and the graveyard. Even though Glamr had shunned the mass, the priest might be prevailed upon to bury him in consecrated ground. But soon the young men had to pause to rest. The body was unexpectedly heavy. Once again, after stopping to breathe, they raised the bier upon their shoulders. Soon another helper was summoned, then another; even Thorhall aided. Ten strong men though they were, they staggered and trembled under that unearthly weight. Even in that icy air the perspiration streamed from them. Heavier and still heavier grew the burden; it bore them to the earth. Their knees bowed out from under them, their backs bent. They were obliged to give over.

Later in the day they returned with oxen and a sledge. They repaired to the spot where the body had been left; then stared at each other with paling faces. In the snow at their feet there was the impression made by the great frame of the shepherd. But that was all; the body was gone, nor was there any footprint in the snow other than they themselves had made.

A cairn was erected over the spot, and for many a long day the strange death of the shepherd of the Vale of Shadows was the talk of the country side. But about a month or so after the death of Glamr a strange sense of uneasiness seemed to invade the household of the byre. By degrees it took possession of first one and then another of the servants and family. No one spoke about this. It was not a thing that could be reduced to words, and for the matter of that, each one believed that he or she was the only one affected. This one thought himself sick; that one believed herself merely nervous. But nevertheless a certain perplexity, a certain disturbance of spirit was in the air.

One evening Thorhall and his wife met accidentally in the passage between the main body of the house and the dairy. They paused and looked at each other for no reason that they could imagine. Thus they stood for several seconds.

"Well," said Thorhall at length, "what is it?"

"Ay," responded his wife. "Ay, what *is* it?"

"Nothing," he replied; and she, echoing his words, also answered "Nothing."

Then they laughed nervously, yet still looking fixedly into each other's eyes for all that.

"I believe," said Thorhall the next day, "that I am to be sick. I cannot tell—I feel no pain—no fever—and yet——"

"And I, too," declared his wife. "I am—no, not sick—but distressed. I—I am troubled. I cannot tell what it is. I sometimes think I am *afraid*."

A week later, on a certain evening just after curfew, the whole family was aroused by a wild shriek as of some one in mortal terror. Thorhall and his wife rushed into the dairy whence the cry came and found one of the maids in a fit upon the floor.

When she recovered she cried out that she had seen at one of the windows the face of Glamr.

II—Grettir

The cold, bright Icelandic Summer shone over Thorhall's byre and the Vale of Shadows. There was no cloud in the sky. The void and lonely ocean was indigo blue. But still the prospect was barren, inhospitable. Only a few pallid flowers, hardy bluebells and buttercups, appeared here and there on the sand dunes in the hollows beneath the gorse and bracken. In the lower hills, on the far side of the valley, a tenuous skim of verdure appeared. At times a ptarmigan fluttered in and out of the crevices of these hills searching for blueberries; at times on the surfaces of the waste of dunes a sandpiper uttered its shrill and feeble piping. Always, as ever, the wind blew from off the ocean; always, as ever, the solitary pine by the farmhouse writhed and tossed its gaunt arms; always the gorse and bracken billowed and weltered under it. The sand drifted like snow, encroaching forever upon the cultivated patches around the house. Always the surf—surge on surge—boomed and thundered on the shore, casting up broken kelp and jetsam of wreck. Always, always forever and forever, the monotony remained. The bleakness, the wild, solitary stretches of sea and sky and land turned to the eye their staring emptiness. At long intervals the figure of a servant, a herdsman or at times Thorhall himself moved—a speck of black on the illimitable gray of nature—across the landscape. Ponies, shagged, half wild, their eyes hidden under tangled forelocks, sometimes wandered down upon the shore —their thick hair roughing in the wind—to snuff at the salty seaweeds. The males sometimes fought here on the shore, their hoofs thudding on the resounding beach, their screams mingling with the incessant roar of the breakers.

Once even, at Easter-tide, during a gale, an empty galley drove ashore, a *snekr* with dragon prow, the broken oars dangling from the thole-pins; and in the waist of her a Viking chieftain, dead, the salt rime rusting on his helmet.

With the advent of Summer the mysterious trouble at the farmhouse in the Vale of Shadows disappeared. But the fall equinox drew on, the nights became longer; soon the daylight lasted but a few hours and the sun set before it could be said to have actually risen.

As the Winter darkness descended upon the farmhouse the trouble recommenced. During the night the tread of footsteps could be heard making the rounds of the byre. The fumbling of unseen fingers could be distinguished at the locks. The low eaves of the house were seized in the grip of strong hands and wrenched and pulled till the rafters creaked. Outhouses were plucked apart and destroyed, fences uprooted. After nightfall no one dared venture abroad.

Thorhall had engaged a new shepherd, one Thorgaut, a young man, who professed himself fearless of the haunted sheep-walks and farmyard. He was as popular as Glamr had been disliked. He made love to the housemaids, helped in the butter-making and rode the children on his back. As to the Vampire, he snapped his fingers and asked only to meet him in the open.

The snow came in August, and was followed by sleet and icy rains and blotting sea-fogs. As the time went on the nightly manifestations increased. Windows were broken in; iron bars shaken and wrenched; sheep and even horses killed.

At length one night a terrible commotion broke out in the stables—the shrill squealing of the horses and the tramping and bellowing of cows, mingled with deep tones of a dreadful voice. Thorhall and his people rushed out. They found that the stable door had been riven and splintered, and they entered the stable itself across the wreckage. The cattle were goring each other, and across the stone partition between the stalls was the body of Thorgaut, the shepherd, his head upon one side, his feet on the other, and his spine snapped in twain.

It chanced that about this time Grettir, well known and well beloved throughout all Iceland, came into that part of the country and one eventide drew rein at Thorhall's farmhouse. This was before Grettir had been hunted from the island by the implacable Thorbjorn, called The Hook, and driven to an asylum and practical captivity upon the rock of Drangey.

He was at this time in the prime of his youth and of a noble appearance. His shoulders were broad, his arms long, his eye a bright blue and his flaxen hair braided like a Viking's. For cloak he wore a bearskin, while as for weapons he carried nothing but a short sword.

Thorhall, as may be easily understood, welcomed the famous outlaw, but warned him of Glamr.

Grettir, however, was not to be dissuaded from remaining overnight at the byre.

"Vampire or troll, troll or vampire, here bide I till daybreak," he declared.

Yet despite the bonder's fears the night passed quietly. No sound broke the stillness but the murmur of the distant surf, no footfall sounded around the house, no fingers came groping at the doors.

"I have never slept easier," announced Grettir in the morning.

"Good; and Heaven be praised," declared the bonder fervently.

They walked together toward the stables, Thorhall instructing Grettir as to the road he should follow that day. As they drew near, Grettir whistled for his horse, but no answering whicker responded.

"How is this?" he muttered, frowning.

Thorhall and the outlaw hurried into the building, and Grettir, who was in the advance, stopped stock-still in the midst of the floor and swore a great oath.

His horse lay prone in the straw of his stall, his eyeballs protruding, the foam stiff upon his lips. He was dead. Grettir approached and examined him. Between shoulder and withers, the back—as if it had been a wheat-straw—was broken.

"Never mind," cried the bonder eagerly, "I have another animal for you, a piebald stallion of Norway stock, just the beast for your weight. Here is your saddle. On with it. Up you go and a speedy journey to you."

"Never!" exclaimed Grettir, his blue eyes flashing. "Here will I stay till I meet Glamr face to face. No man did me an injury that he did not rue it. I sleep at the byre another night."

Dark as a wolf's mouth, silent as his footfalls, the night closed down. There was no moon as yet, but the heavens were bright. Steadily as the blast of some great huntsman's horn, the wind held from the northeast. The sand skimming over the dunes and low hills near the coast was caught up and carried landward and drifted in at crevice and door-chink of the farm-house. A young seal—lost, no doubt, from the herd that had all day been feeding in the offing—barked and barked incessantly from a rock in the breakers. In the pine tree by the house a huge night-bird, owl or hawk, stirred occasionally with a prolonged note. By and by the weather grew colder, the ground began to freeze and crack. Inside in the main hall of the house, covered by his bearskin cloak, Grettir lay wakeful and watching.

He reclined in such a manner—his head pillowed on his arm—that he could see the door. At the other end of the hall the fire of drift was dying down upon the flags. On the other side of the partition, in the next room, lay the bonder, alternately dozing and waking.

The time passed heavily, slowly. From far off toward the shore could be heard the lost seal raising from time to time his hoarse, sobbing bark.

Then at length a dog howled, and an instant after the bonder spoke aloud. He had risen from his bed and stood in the door of his room.

"Hark! Did you not hear something?"

"I hear the barking of the seal," said Grettir, "the baying of the hound, the cry of the night-bird, and the break of the surges; nothing else."

"No. This was a footstep. There. Listen!"

A heavy footfall sounded crunching in the snow from without and close by. It passed around and in front of the house; and the wooden shutter of a window of the hall was plucked at and shaken. Then an outhouse was attacked—a shed where in Summer time the calves were fed. Grettir could hear the snap and rasp of splintering boards.

"It has a strong arm," he muttered.

Once more the tread encircled the house. In a very short time it sounded again in the front of the byre.

"It has a long stride," said Grettir.

The tread ceased. For a long moment there was silence, while the scurrying sand rattled delicately against the house like minute hailstones. Suddenly a corner eave was seized. Something tugged at it, wrenching, and the thatch gave with the long swish of rent linen.

"It has a tall figure," said Grettir.

For nearly a quarter of an hour these different sounds continued, now distinct, now confused, now distant, now near at hand. Suddenly from overhead there came a jar and a crash, and Grettir felt the dust from the rafters descend upon his face; the Vampire was on the roof. But soon he leaped down and now the footsteps came straight to the door of the hall. The door itself was gripped with colossal strength. In the crescent-shaped openings of the upper panels a hand appeared, black against the faint outside light, groping, picking. It seized upon the edge of the board in the lower bend of the crescent and pulled. The board gave way, ripped to the very door-sill; then an arm followed the hand, reaching for one of the two iron bars with which the door was fenced. Evidently it could not find these, for the effort was soon abandoned and another panel was split and torn away. The cross-panel followed, the nails shrieking as they were drawn from out the wood. Then at last the door, shattered to its very hinges, gave way, leaving only the bars set in the stone sockets of the jamb, and against the square of gray light of the entrance stood, silhouetted, the figure of a monster. Stood but for a moment, for almost at once the bars were pulled out.

The Vampire was within the house, the light from the smoldering logs illuminating the face.

Glamr's face was livid. The pupils of the eyes were white, the hair matted and thick. The whole figure was monstrously enlarged, bulked like a *jotun*, and the vast hands, white as those of the drowned, swung heavily at his sides.

Once in the hall, he stood for a long moment looking from side to side, then moved slowly forward, reaching his great arms overhead, feeling and fumbling with the roof-beams with his fingers, and guiding himself thus from beam to beam.

Grettir, watching, alert, never moved, but lay in his place, his eyes fixed upon the monster.

But at length Glamr made out the form stretched upon the couch and came up and laid hold of a flap of the bearskin under Grettir's shoulders and tugged at it. But Grettir, bracing his feet against the foot-board of the couch, held back with all his strength. Glamr seized the flap in both hands and set his might to the pull, till the tough hide fetched away, and he staggered back, the corner of skin still in his grip. He looked at it stupidly, wondering, bewildered.

Then suddenly the bonder, listening from within his bolted door, heard the muffled crashing shock of the onset. The rafters cracked, the byre shook, the shutters rocked in their grooves, and Grettir, eyes alight, hair flying like a torch, thews rigid as iron, leaped to the attack.

Down upon the hero's arms came the numbing, crushing grip of the dead man's might. One instant of that inhuman embrace and Grettir knew that now peril of his life was toward. Never in all his days of battle and strength had such colossal might risen to match his own. Back bore the wrestlers, back, back toward the sides of the hall. Benches ironed to the wall were overturned, wrenched like paper from their fastenings. The great table crashed and splintered beneath their weight. The floor split with their tramping, and the fire was scattered upon the hearth. Now forward, now back, from side to side and from end to end of the wrecked hall drove the fight. Great of build though the fighters were, huge of bone, big of muscle, they yet leaped and writhed with the agility, the rapidity of young lambs.

But fear was not in Grettir. Never in his life had he been afraid. Only anger shook him, and fine, above-board fury, and the iron will to beat his enemy.

All at once Grettir, his arms gripped about the Vampire's middle, his head beneath the armpit, realized that the creature was dragging him toward the door. He fought back from this till the effort sent the blood surging in his ears, for he knew well that ill as the fight had fared within the house it must go worse without. But it was all one that he braced his feet against the broken benches, the wreck of the table, the every unevenness of the floor. The Vampire had gripped him close and dragged and clutched and heaved at his body, so that the white nails drove into his flesh, and the embrace of those arms of steel shut in the ribs till the breath gushed from the nostrils in long gasps of agony.

And now they swayed and grappled in the doorway. Grettir's back was bent like a bow, and Grettir's arms at fullest stretch strained to their sockets, till it seemed as though the very tendons must tear from off the bones. And ever the foul thing above him drew him farther and yet farther from out the entrance-way of the house.

"God save you, Grettir!" cried the bonder, "God save you, brave man and true. Never was such fight as this in all Iceland. Are you spent, Grettir?"

Muffled under the arms of his foe, the voice of Grettir shouted: "Stand from us. I am much spent, but I fear not."

Then with the words, feeling the half-sunk stone of the threshold beneath his feet, he bowed his knees, and with his shoulder against the Vampire's breast drove, not, as hitherto, back, but forward, and that with all the power of limb and loin.

The Vampire reeled from the attack. His shoulder crashed against the outer door-case, and with that gigantic shock the roof burst asunder. Down crushed and roared the frozen thatch, and then in that hideous ruin of splintering rafters, grinding stones and wreck of panel and beam the Vampire fell backward and prone to the ground, while Grettir toppled down upon him till his face was against the dead man's face, his eye to his dead eye, his forehead against his front, and the gray bristle of his beard between his teeth.

The moon was bright outside, and all at once, lighted by her rays, Grettir for the first time saw the Vampire's face.

Then the soul of him shrank and sank, and the fear that all his days he had not known leaped to life in his heart. Terror of that glare of the dead man's gaze caught him by the throat, till his grip relaxed, and his strength dwindled away and he crouched there motionless but for his trembling, looking, looking into those blind, white, dead eyes.

And then the Vampire began to speak:

"Eagerly hast thou striven to match thyself with me, and ill hast thou done this night. Now thou art weak with the fear and the rigor of this fight, yet never henceforth shalt thou be stronger than at this moment. Till now thou hast won much fame by great deeds, yet henceforth ill-luck shall follow thee and woe and man-slayings and untoward fortune. Outlawed shalt thou be, and thy lot shall be cast in lands far from thine home. Alone shalt thou dwell, and in that loneliness, this weird I lay upon thee: Ever to see these eyes with thine eyes, till the terror of the Dark shall come upon thee and the fear of night, and the twain shall drag thee to thy death and thy undoing."

As the voice ceased, Grettir's wits and strength returned, and suddenly seizing the hair of the creature in one hand and his short sword in the other, he hewed off the head.

But within the heart of him he knew that the Vampire had said true words, and as he stood looking down upon the great body of his enemy and saw the glazed and fish-like eyes beneath the lids, he could for one instant look ahead to the days of his life yet to be, to the ill-fortune that should dog him from henceforth, and knew that at the gathering of each night's dusk the eyes of Glamr would look into his.

Thorhall came out when the fight was done, praising God for the issue, and he and Grettir together burned the body and, wrapping the ashes in a skin, buried them in a far corner of the sheep-walks.

In the morning Thorhall gave Grettir the piebald horse and new clothes and set him a mile on his road. They rode through the Vale of Shadows and kissed each other farewell on the shore where the road led away toward Waterdale.

The clouds had gathered again during the dawn and the rain was falling, driven landward by the incessant wind. The seals again barked and hunted in the offing, and the rough-haired ponies once more wandered about on the beach snuffing at the kelp and seaweed.

Long time Thorhall stood on the ridge watching the figure of Grettir grow small and indistinct in the waste of north country and under the blur of the rain. Then at last he turned back to the byre.

But Grettir after these things rode on to Biarg, to his mother's house, and sat at home through the winter.

1903

LAFCADIO HEARN

(1850–1904)

Yuki-Onna

In a village of Musashi Province, there lived two woodcutters: Mosaku and Minokichi. At the time of which I am speaking, Mosaku was an old man; and Minokichi, his apprentice, was a lad of eighteen years. Every day they went together to a forest situated about five miles from their village. On the way to that forest there is a wide river to cross; and there is a ferry-boat. Several times a bridge was built where the ferry is; but the bridge was each time carried away by a flood. No common bridge can resist the current there when the river rises.

Mosaku and Minokichi were on their way home, one very cold evening, when a great snowstorm overtook them. They reached the ferry; and they found that the boatman had gone away, leaving his boat on the other side of the river. It was no day for swimming; and the woodcutters took shelter in the ferryman's hut,—thinking themselves lucky to find any shelter at all. There was no brazier in the hut, nor any place in which to make a fire: it was only a two-mat* hut, with a single door, but no window. Mosaku and Minokichi fastened the door, and lay down to rest, with their straw rain-coats over them. At first they did not feel very cold; and they thought that the storm would soon be over.

The old man almost immediately fell asleep; but the boy, Minokichi, lay awake a long time, listening to the awful wind, and the continual slashing of the snow against the door. The river was roaring; and the hut swayed and creaked like a junk at sea. It was a terrible storm; and the air was every moment becoming colder; and Minokichi shivered under his raincoat. But at last, in spite of the cold, he too fell asleep.

He was awakened by a showering of snow in his face. The

---

*That is to say, with a floor-surface of about six feet square.

door of the hut had been forced open; and, by the snow-light (*yuki-akari*), he saw a woman in the room,—a woman all in white. She was bending above Mosaku, and blowing her breath upon him;—and her breath was like a bright white smoke. Almost in the same moment she turned to Minokichi, and stooped over him. He tried to cry out, but found that he could not utter any sound. The white woman bent down over him, lower and lower, until her face almost touched him; and he saw that she was very beautiful,—though her eyes made him afraid. For a little time she continued to look at him;—then she smiled, and she whispered:—"I intended to treat you like the other man. But I cannot help feeling some pity for you,—because you are so young. . . . You are a pretty boy, Minokichi; and I will not hurt you now. But, if you ever tell anybody —even your own mother—about what you have seen this night, I shall know it; and then I will kill you. . . . Remember what I say!"

With these words, she turned from him, and passed through the doorway. Then he found himself able to move; and he sprang up, and looked out. But the woman was nowhere to be seen; and the snow was driving furiously into the hut. Minokichi closed the door, and secured it by fixing several billets of wood against it. He wondered if the wind had blown it open; —he thought that he might have been only dreaming, and might have mistaken the gleam of the snow-light in the doorway for the figure of a white woman: but he could not be sure. He called to Mosaku, and was frightened because the old man did not answer. He put out his hand in the dark, and touched Mosaku's face, and found that it was ice! Mosaku was stark and dead. . . .

By dawn the storm was over; and when the ferryman returned to his station, a little after sunrise, he found Minokichi lying senseless beside the frozen body of Mosaku. Minokichi was promptly cared for, and soon came to himself; but he remained a long time ill from the effects of the cold of that terrible night. He had been greatly frightened also by the old man's death; but he said nothing about the vision of the woman in white. As soon as he got well again, he returned to his calling, —going alone every morning to the forest, and coming back

at nightfall with his bundles of wood, which his mother helped
him to sell.

One evening, in the winter of the following year, as he was
on his way home, he overtook a girl who happened to be traveling by the same road. She was a tall, slim girl, very good-
looking; and she answered Minokichi's greeting in a voice as
pleasant to the ear as the voice of a song-bird. Then he walked
beside her; and they began to talk. The girl said that her name
was O-Yuki;* that she had lately lost both of her parents; and
that she was going to Yedo, where she happened to have some
poor relations, who might help her to find a situation as servant. Minokichi soon felt charmed by this strange girl; and the
more that he looked at her, the handsomer she appeared to be.
He asked her whether she was yet betrothed; and she answered, laughingly, that she was free. Then, in her turn, she
asked Minokichi whether he was married, or pledged to marry;
and he told her that, although he had only a widowed mother
to support, the question of an "honorable daughter-in-law"
had not yet been considered, as he was very young. . . . After
these confidences, they walked on for a long while without
speaking; but, as the proverb declares, *Ki ga aréba, mé mo
kuchi hodo ni mono wo iu:* "When the wish is there, the eyes
can say as much as the mouth." By the time they reached the
village, they had become very much pleased with each other;
and then Minokichi asked O-Yuki to rest awhile at his house.
After some shy hesitation, she went there with him; and his
mother made her welcome, and prepared a warm meal for her.
O-Yuki behaved so nicely that Minokichi's mother took a sudden fancy to her, and persuaded her to delay her journey to
Yedo. And the natural end of the matter was that Yuki never
went to Yedo at all. She remained in the house, as an "honorable daughter-in-law."

O-Yuki proved a very good daughter-in-law. When Minokichi's mother came to die,—some five years later,—her last
words were words of affection and praise for the wife of her

---

*This name, signifying "Snow," is not uncommon. On the subject of Japa-
nese female names, see my paper in the volume entitled *Shadowings.*

son. And O-Yuki bore Minokichi ten children, boys and girls,—handsome children all of them, and very fair of skin.

The country-folk thought O-Yuki a wonderful person, by nature different from themselves. Most of the peasant-women age early; but O-Yuki, even after having become the mother of ten children, looked as young and fresh as on the day when she had first come to the village.

One night, after the children had gone to sleep, O-Yuki was sewing by the light of a paper lamp; and Minokichi, watching her, said:—

"To see you sewing there, with the light on your face, makes me think of a strange thing that happened when I was a lad of eighteen. I then saw somebody as beautiful and white as you are now—indeed, she was very like you." . . .

Without lifting her eyes from her work, O-Yuki responded:—

"Tell me about her. . . . Where did you see her?"

Then Minokichi told her about the terrible night in the ferryman's hut,—and about the White Woman that had stooped above him, smiling and whispering,—and about the silent death of old Mosaku. And he said:—

"Asleep or awake, that was the only time that I saw a being as beautiful as you. Of course, she was not a human being; and I was afraid of her,—very much afraid,—but she was so white! . . . Indeed, I have never been sure whether it was a dream that I saw, or the Woman of the Snow." . . .

O-Yuki flung down her sewing, and arose, and bowed above Minokichi where he sat, and shrieked into his face:—

"It was I—I—I! Yuki it was! And I told you then that I would kill you if you ever said one word about it! . . . But for those children asleep there, I would kill you this moment! And now you had better take very, very good care of them; for if ever they have reason to complain of you, I will treat you as you deserve!" . . .

Even as she screamed, her voice became thin, like a crying of wind;—then she melted into a bright white mist that spired to the roof-beams, and shuddered away through the smoke-hole. . . . Never again was she seen.

1904

F. MARION CRAWFORD

(1854–1909)

For the Blood Is the Life

WE had dined at sunset on the broad roof of the old tower, because it was cooler there during the great heat of summer. Besides, the little kitchen was built at one corner of the great square platform, which made it more convenient than if the dishes had to be carried down the steep stone steps, broken in places and everywhere worn with age. The tower was one of those built all down the west coast of Calabria by the Emperor Charles V. early in the sixteenth century, to keep off the Barbary pirates, when the unbelievers were allied with Francis I. against the Emperor and the Church. They have gone to ruin, a few still stand intact, and mine is one of the largest. How it came into my possession ten years ago, and why I spend a part of each year in it, are matters which do not concern this tale. The tower stands in one of the loneliest spots in Southern Italy, at the extremity of a curving rocky promontory, which forms a small but safe natural harbour at the southern extremity of the Gulf of Policastro, and just north of Cape Scalea, the birthplace of Judas Iscariot, according to the old local legend. The tower stands alone on this hooked spur of the rock, and there is not a house to be seen within three miles of it. When I go there I take a couple of sailors, one of whom is a fair cook, and when I am away it is in charge of a gnome-like little being who was once a miner and who attached himself to me long ago.

My friend, who sometimes visits me in my summer solitude, is an artist by profession, a Scandinavian by birth, and a cosmopolitan by force of circumstances. We had dined at sunset; the sunset glow had reddened and faded again, and the evening purple steeped the vast chain of the mountains that embrace the deep gulf to eastward and rear themselves higher and higher toward the south. It was hot, and we sat at the landward corner of the platform, waiting for the night breeze to come down from the lower hills. The colour sank out of the air, there was a little interval of deep-grey twilight, and a lamp sent a yellow streak from the open door of the kitchen, where the men were getting their supper.

Then the moon rose suddenly above the crest of the promontory, flooding the platform and lighting up every little spur of rock and knoll of grass below us, down to the edge of the motionless water. My friend lighted his pipe and sat looking at a spot on the hillside. I knew that he was looking at it, and for a long time past I had wondered whether he would ever see anything there that would fix his attention. I knew that spot well. It was clear that he was interested at last, though it was a long time before he spoke. Like most painters, he trusts to his own eyesight, as a lion trusts his strength and a stag his speed, and he is always disturbed when he cannot reconcile what he sees with what he believes that he ought to see.

"It's strange," he said. "Do you see that little mound just on this side of the boulder?"

"Yes," I said, and I guessed what was coming.

"It looks like a grave," observed Holger.

"Very true. It does look like a grave."

"Yes," continued my friend, his eyes still fixed on the spot. "But the strange thing is that I see the body lying on the top of it. Of course," continued Holger, turning his head on one side as artists do, "it must be an effect of light. In the first place, it is not a grave at all. Secondly, if it were, the body would be inside and not outside. Therefore, it's an effect of the moonlight. Don't you see it?"

"Perfectly; I always see it on moonlight nights."

"It doesn't seem to interest you much," said Holger.

"On the contrary, it does interest me, though I am used to it. You're not so far wrong, either. The mound is really a grave."

"Nonsense!" cried Holger, incredulously. "I suppose you'll tell me what I see lying on it is really a corpse!"

"No," I answered, "it's not. I know, because I have taken the trouble to go down and see."

"Then what is it?" asked Holger.

"It's nothing."

"You mean that it's an effect of light, I suppose?"

"Perhaps it is. But the inexplicable part of the matter is that it makes no difference whether the moon is rising or setting, or waxing or waning. If there's any moonlight at all, from east or west or overhead, so long as it shines on the grave you can see the outline of the body on top."

Holger stirred up his pipe with the point of his knife, and then used his finger for a stopper. When the tobacco burned well he rose from his chair.

"If you don't mind," he said, "I'll go down and take a look at it."

He left me, crossed the roof, and disappeared down the dark steps. I did not move, but sat looking down until he came out of the tower below. I heard him humming an old Danish song as he crossed the open space in the bright moonlight, going straight to the mysterious mound. When he was ten paces from it, Holger stopped short, made two steps forward, and then three or four backward, and then stopped again. I know what that meant. He had reached the spot where the Thing ceased to be visible—where, as he would have said, the effect of light changed.

Then he went on till he reached the mound and stood upon it. I could see the Thing still, but it was no longer lying down; it was on its knees now, winding its white arms round Holger's body and looking up into his face. A cool breeze stirred my hair at that moment, as the night wind began to come down from the hills, but it felt like a breath from another world.

The Thing seemed to be trying to climb to its feet, helping itself up by Holger's body while he stood upright, quite unconscious of it and apparently looking toward the tower, which is very picturesque when the moonlight falls upon it on that side.

"Come along!" I shouted. "Don't stay there all night!"

It seemed to me that he moved reluctantly as he stepped from the mound, or else with difficulty. That was it. The Thing's arms were still round his waist, but its feet could not leave the grave. As he came slowly forward it was drawn and lengthened like a wreath of mist, thin and white, till I saw distinctly that Holger shook himself, as a man does who feels a chill. At the same instant a little wail of pain came to me on the breeze—it might have been the cry of the small owl that lives among the rocks—and the misty presence floated swiftly back from Holger's advancing figure and lay once more at its length upon the mound.

Again I felt the cool breeze in my hair, and this time an icy thrill of dread ran down my spine. I remembered very well that I had once gone down there alone in the moonlight; that presently, being near, I had seen nothing; that, like Holger, I had gone and had stood upon the mound; and I remembered how, when I came back, sure that there was nothing there, I had felt the sudden conviction that there was something after all if I would only look behind me. I remembered the strong temptation to look back, a temptation I had resisted as unworthy of a man of sense, until, to get rid of it, I had shaken myself just as Holger did.

And now I knew that those white, misty arms had been round me too; I knew it in a flash, and I shuddered as I remembered that I had heard the night owl then too. But it had not been the night owl. It was the cry of the Thing.

I refilled my pipe and poured out a cup of strong southern wine; in less than a minute Holger was seated beside me again.

"Of course there's nothing there," he said, "but it's creepy, all the same. Do you know, when I was coming back I was so sure that there was something behind me that I wanted to turn round and look? It was an effort not to."

He laughed a little, knocked the ashes out of his pipe, and poured himself out some wine. For a while neither of us spoke, and the moon rose higher, and we both looked at the Thing that lay on the mound.

"You might make a story about that," said Holger after a long time.

"There is one," I answered. "If you're not sleepy, I'll tell it to you."

"Go ahead," said Holger, who likes stories.

Old Alario was dying up there in the village behind the hill. You remember him, I have no doubt. They say that he made his money by selling sham jewellery in South America, and escaped with his gains when he was found out. Like all those fellows, if they bring anything back with them, he at once set to work to enlarge his house, and as there are no masons here, he sent all the way to Paola for two workmen. They were a rough-looking pair of scoundrels—a Neapolitan who had lost one eye and a Sicilian with an old scar half an inch deep across his left cheek. I often saw them, for on Sundays they used to come down here and fish off the rocks. When Alario caught the fever that killed him the masons were still at work. As he had agreed that part of their pay should be their board and lodging, he made them sleep in the house. His wife was dead, and he had an only son called Angelo, who was a much better sort than himself. Angelo was to marry the daughter of the richest man in the village, and, strange to say, though the marriage was arranged by their parents, the young people were said to be in love with each other.

For that matter, the whole village was in love with Angelo, and among the rest a wild, good-looking creature called Cristina, who was more like a gipsy than any girl I ever saw about here. She had very red lips and very black eyes, she was built like a greyhound, and had the tongue of the devil. But Angelo did not care a straw for her. He was rather a simple-minded fellow, quite different from his old scoundrel of a father, and under what I should call normal circumstances I really believe that he would never have looked at any girl except the nice plump little creature, with a fat dowry, whom his father meant him to marry. But things turned up which were neither normal nor natural.

On the other hand, a very handsome young shepherd from the hills above Maratea was in love with Cristina, who seems to have been quite indifferent to him. Cristina had no regular means of subsistence, but she was a good girl and willing to do any work or go on errands to any distance for the sake of a loaf of bread or a mess of beans, and permission to sleep under cover. She was especially glad when she could get something to do about the house of Angelo's father. There is no doctor in the village, and when the neighbours saw that old Alario was dying they sent Cristina to Scalea to fetch one. That was late in the afternoon, and if they had waited so long, it was because the dying miser refused to allow any such extravagance while he was able to speak. But while Cristina was gone matters grew rapidly worse, the priest was brought to the bedside, and when he had done what he could he gave it as his opinion to the by-standers that the old man was dead, and left the house.

You know these people. They have a physical horror of death. Until the priest spoke, the room had been full of people. The words were hardly out of his mouth before it was empty. It was night now. They hurried down the dark steps and out into the street.

Angelo, as I have said, was away, Cristina had not come back —the simple woman-servant who had nursed the sick man fled with the rest, and the body was left alone in the flickering light of the earthen oil lamp.

Five minutes later two men looked in cautiously and crept forward toward the bed. They were the one-eyed Neapolitan mason and his Sicilian companion. They knew what they wanted. In a moment they had dragged from under the bed a small but heavy iron-bound box, and long before any one thought of coming back to the dead man they had left the house and the village under cover of the darkness. It was easy enough, for Alario's house is the last toward the gorge which leads down here, and the thieves merely went out by the back door, got over the stone wall, and had nothing to risk after that except the possibility of meeting some belated countryman, which was very small indeed, since few of the people use that path. They had a mattock and shovel, and they made their way here without accident.

I am telling you this story as it must have happened, for, of course, there were no witnesses to this part of it. The men brought the box down by the gorge, intending to bury it until they should be able to come back and take it away in a boat. They must have been clever enough to guess that some of the money would be in paper notes, for they would otherwise have buried it on the beach in the wet sand, where it would have been much safer. But the paper would have rotted if they had been obliged to leave it there long, so they dug their hole down there, close to that boulder. Yes, just where the mound is now.

Cristina did not find the doctor in Scalea, for he had been sent for from a place up the valley, halfway to San Domenico. If she had found him, he would have come on his mule by the upper road, which is smoother but much longer. But Cristina took the short cut by the rocks, which passes about fifty feet above the mound, and goes round that corner. The men were digging when she passed, and she heard them at work. It would not have been like her to go by without finding out what the noise was, for she was never afraid of anything in her life, and, besides, the fishermen sometimes come ashore here at night to get a stone for an anchor or to gather sticks to make a little fire. The night was dark, and Cristina probably came close to the two men before she could see what they were doing. She knew them, of course, and they knew her, and understood instantly that they were in her power. There was only one thing to be done for their safety, and they did it. They knocked her on the head, they dug the hole deep, and they buried her quickly with the iron-bound chest. They must have understood that their only chance of escaping suspicion lay in getting back to the village before their absence was noticed, for they returned immediately, and were found half an hour later gossiping quietly with the man who was making Alario's coffin. He was a crony of theirs, and had been working at the repairs in the old man's house. So far as I have been able to make out, the only persons who were supposed to know where Alario kept his treasure were Angelo and the one woman-servant I have mentioned. Angelo was away; it was the woman who discovered the theft.

It is easy enough to understand why no one else knew where the money was. The old man kept his door locked and the key in his pocket when he was out, and did not let the woman enter to clean the place unless he was there himself. The whole village knew that he had money somewhere, however, and the masons had probably discovered the whereabouts of the chest by climbing in at the window in his absence. If the old man had not been delirious until he lost consciousness, he would have been in frightful agony of mind for his riches. The faithful woman-servant forgot their existence only for a few moments when she fled with the rest, overcome by the horror of death. Twenty minutes had not passed before she returned with the two hideous old hags who are always called in to prepare the dead for burial. Even then she had not at first the courage to go near the bed with them, but she made a pretence of dropping something, went down on her knees as if to find it, and looked under the bedstead. The walls of the room were newly whitewashed down to the floor, and she saw at a glance that the chest was gone. It had been there in the afternoon, it had therefore been stolen in the short interval since she had left the room.

There are no carabineers stationed in the village; there is not so much as a municipal watchman, for there is no municipality. There never was such a place, I believe. Scalea is supposed to look after it in some mysterious way, and it takes a couple of hours to get anybody from there. As the old woman had lived in the village all her life, it did not even occur to her to apply to any civil authority for help. She simply set up a howl and ran through the village in the dark, screaming out that her dead master's house had been robbed. Many of the people looked out, but at first no one seemed inclined to help her. Most of them, judging her by themselves, whispered to each other that she had probably stolen the money herself. The first man to move was the father of the girl whom Angelo was to marry; having collected his household, all of whom felt a personal interest in the wealth which was to have come into the family, he declared it to be his opinion that the chest had been stolen by the two journeyman masons who lodged in the house. He headed a search for them, which naturally began in Alario's house and ended in the carpenter's workshop, where the thieves were found discussing a measure of wine with the carpenter over the half-finished coffin, by the light of one earthen lamp filled with oil and tallow. The search party at once accused the delinquents of the crime, and threatened to lock them up in the cellar till the carabineers could be fetched from Scalea. The two men looked at each other for one moment, and then without the slightest hesitation they put out the single light, seized the unfinished coffin between them, and using it as a sort of battering ram, dashed upon their assailants in the dark. In a few moments they were beyond pursuit.

That is the end of the first part of the story. The treasure had disappeared, and as no trace of it could be found the people naturally supposed that the thieves had succeeded in carrying it off. The old man was buried, and when Angelo came back at last he had to borrow money to pay for the miserable funeral, and had some difficulty in doing so. He hardly needed to be told that in losing his inheritance he had lost his bride. In this part of the world marriages are made on strictly business

principles, and if the promised cash is not forthcoming on the
appointed day the bride or the bridegroom whose parents
have failed to produce it may as well take themselves off, for
there will be no wedding. Poor Angelo knew that well enough.
His father had been possessed of hardly any land, and now that
the hard cash which he had brought from South America was
gone, there was nothing left but debts for the building materials that were to have been used for enlarging and improving
the old house. Angelo was beggared, and the nice plump little
creature who was to have been his turned up her nose at him
in the most approved fashion. As for Cristina, it was several
days before she was missed, for no one remembered that she
had been sent to Scalea for the doctor, who had never come.
She often disappeared in the same way for days together, when
she could find a little work here and there at the distant farms
among the hills. But when she did not come back at all, people
began to wonder, and at last made up their minds that she had
connived with the masons and had escaped with them.

I paused and emptied my glass.

*"That sort of thing could not happen anywhere else," observed
Holger, filling his everlasting pipe again. "It is wonderful what a
natural charm there is about murder and sudden death in a romantic country like this. Deeds that would be simply brutal and
disgusting anywhere else become dramatic and mysterious
because this is Italy and we are living in a genuine tower of
Charles V. built against genuine Barbary pirates."*

*"There's something in that," I admitted. Holger is the most ro-
mantic man in the world inside of himself, but he always thinks
it necessary to explain why he feels anything.*

*"I suppose they found the poor girl's body with the box," he said
presently.*

*"As it seems to interest you," I answered, "I'll tell you the rest of
the story."*

*The moon had risen high by this time; the outline of the Thing
on the mound was clearer to our eyes than before.*

The village very soon settled down to its small, dull life. No
one missed old Alario, who had been away so much on his
voyages to South America that he had never been a familiar

figure in his native place. Angelo lived in the half-finished house, and because he had no money to pay the old woman-servant she would not stay with him, but once in a long time she would come and wash a shirt for him for old acquaintance' sake. Besides the house, he had inherited a small patch of ground at some distance from the village; he tried to cultivate it, but he had no heart in the work, for he knew he could never pay the taxes on it and on the house, which would certainly be confiscated by the Government, or seized for the debt of the building material, which the man who had supplied it refused to take back.

Angelo was very unhappy. So long as his father had been alive and rich, every girl in the village had been in love with him; but that was all changed now. It had been pleasant to be admired and courted, and invited to drink wine by fathers who had girls to marry. It was hard to be stared at coldly, and some-times laughed at because he had been robbed of his inheri-tance. He cooked his miserable meals for himself, and from being sad became melancholy and morose.

At twilight, when the day's work was done, instead of hanging about in the open space before the church with young fellows of his own age, he took to wandering in lonely places on the outskirts of the village till it was quite dark. Then he slunk home and went to bed to save the expense of a light. But in those lonely twilight hours he began to have strange waking dreams. He was not always alone, for often when he sat on the stump of a tree, where the narrow path turns down the gorge, he was sure that a woman came up noiselessly over the rough stones, as if her feet were bare; and she stood under a clump of chestnut trees only half a dozen yards down the path, and beckoned to him without speaking. Though she was in the shadow he knew that her lips were red, and that when they parted a little and smiled at him she showed two small sharp teeth. He knew this at first rather than saw it, and he knew that it was Cristina, and that she was dead. Yet he was not afraid; he only wondered whether it was a dream, for he thought that if he had been awake he should have been frightened.

Besides, the dead woman had red lips, and that could only happen in a dream. Whenever he went near the gorge after sunset she was already there waiting for him, or else she very

soon appeared, and he began to be sure that she came a little
nearer to him every day. At first he had only been sure of her
blood-red mouth, but now each feature grew distinct, and the
pale face looked at him with deep and hungry eyes.

It was the eyes that grew dim. Little by little he came to
know that some day the dream would not end when he turned
away to go home, but would lead him down the gorge out of
which the vision rose. She was nearer now when she beckoned
to him. Her cheeks were not livid like those of the dead, but
pale with starvation, with the furious and unappeased physical
hunger of her eyes that devoured him. They feasted on his soul
and cast a spell over him, and at last they were close to his own
and held him. He could not tell whether her breath was as hot
as fire or as cold as ice; he could not tell whether her red lips
burned his or froze them, or whether her five fingers on his
wrists seared scorching scars or bit his flesh like frost; he could
not tell whether he was awake or asleep, whether she was alive
or dead, but he knew that she loved him, she alone of all creatures, earthly or unearthly, and her spell had power over him.

When the moon rose high that night the shadow of that
Thing was not alone down there upon the mound.

Angelo awoke in the cool dawn, drenched with dew and
chilled through flesh, and blood, and bone. He opened his
eyes to the faint grey light, and saw the stars still shining overhead. He was very weak, and his heart was beating so slowly
that he was almost like a man fainting. Slowly he turned his
head on the mound, as on a pillow, but the other face was not
there. Fear seized him suddenly, a fear unspeakable and unknown; he sprang to his feet and fled up the gorge, and he
never looked behind him until he reached the door of the
house on the outskirts of the village. Drearily he went to his
work that day, and wearily the hours dragged themselves after
the sun, till at last he touched the sea and sank, and the great
sharp hills above Maratea turned purple against the dove-
coloured eastern sky.

Angelo shouldered his heavy hoe and left the field. He felt
less tired now than in the morning when he had begun to
work, but he promised himself that he would go home without lingering by the gorge, and eat the best supper he could

get himself, and sleep all night in his bed like a Christian man. Not again would he be tempted down the narrow way by a shadow with red lips and icy breath; not again would he dream that dream of terror and delight. He was near the village now; it was half an hour since the sun had set, and the cracked church bell sent little discordant echoes across the rocks and ravines to tell all good people that the day was done. Angelo stood still a moment where the path forked, where it led toward the village on the left, and down to the gorge on the right, where a clump of chestnut trees overhung the narrow way. He stood still a minute, lifting his battered hat from his head and gazing at the fast-fading sea westward, and his lips moved as he silently repeated the familiar evening prayer. His lips moved, but the words that followed them in his brain lost their meaning and turned into others, and ended in a name that he spoke aloud— Cristina! With the name, the tension of his will relaxed suddenly, reality went out and the dream took him again, and bore him on swiftly and surely like a man walking in his sleep, down, down, by the steep path in the gathering darkness. And as she glided beside him, Cristina whispered strange, sweet things in his ear, which somehow, if he had been awake, he knew that he could not quite have understood; but now they were the most wonderful words he had ever heard in his life. And she kissed him also, but not upon his mouth. He felt her sharp kisses upon his white throat, and he knew that her lips were red. So the wild dream sped on through twilight and darkness and moonrise, and all the glory of the summer's night. But in the chilly dawn he lay as one half dead upon the mound down there, recalling and not recalling, drained of his blood, yet strangely longing to give those red lips more. Then came the fear, the awful nameless panic, the mortal horror that guards the confines of the world we see not, neither know of as we know of other things, but which we feel when its icy chill freezes our bones and stirs our hair with the touch of a ghostly hand. Once more Angelo sprang from the mound and fled up the gorge in the breaking day, but his step was less sure this time, and he panted for breath as he ran; and when he came to the bright spring of water that rises halfway up the hillside, he dropped upon his knees and hands and plunged his whole face in and drank as he had never drunk before—for it was the thirst of the wounded man who has lain bleeding all night long upon the battle-field.

She had him fast now, and he could not escape her, but would come to her every evening at dusk until she had drained him of his last drop of blood. It was in vain that when the day was done he tried to take another turning and to go home by a path that did not lead near the gorge. It was in vain that he made promises to himself each morning at dawn when he climbed the lonely way up from the shore to the village. It was all in vain, for when the sun sank burning into the sea, and the cool-ness of the evening stole out as from a hiding-place to delight the weary world, his feet turned toward the old way, and she was waiting for him in the shadow under the chestnut trees; and then all happened as before, and she fell to kissing his white throat even as she flitted lightly down the way, winding one arm about him. And as his blood failed, she grew more hungry and more thirsty every day, and every day when he awoke in the early dawn it was harder to rouse himself to the effort of climbing the steep path to the village; and when he went to his work his feet dragged painfully, and there was hardly strength in his arms to wield the heavy hoe. He scarcely spoke to any one now, but the people said he was "consuming him-self" for love of the girl he was to have married when he lost his inheritance; and they laughed heartily at the thought, for this is not a very romantic country. At this time, Antonio, the man who stays here to look after the tower, returned from a visit to his people, who live near Salerno. He had been away all the time since before Alario's death and knew nothing of what had happened. He has told me that he came back late in the afternoon and shut himself up in the tower to eat and sleep, for he was very tired. It was past midnight when he awoke, and when he looked out the waning moon was rising over the shoulder of the hill. He looked out toward the mound, and he saw something, and he did not sleep again that night. When he went out again in the morning it was broad daylight, and there was nothing to be seen on the mound but loose stones and driven sand. Yet he did not go very near it; he went straight up the path to the village and directly to the house of the old priest.

"I have seen an evil thing this night," he said; "I have seen how the dead drink the blood of the living. And the blood is the life."

"Tell me what you have seen," said the priest in reply.

Antonio told him everything he had seen.

"You must bring your book and your holy water to-night," he added. "I will be here before sunset to go down with you, and if it pleases your reverence to sup with me while we wait, I will make ready."

"I will come," the priest answered, "for I have read in old books of these strange beings which are neither quick nor dead, and which lie ever fresh in their graves, stealing out in the dusk to taste life and blood."

Antonio cannot read, but he was glad to see that the priest understood the business; for, of course, the books must have instructed him as to the best means of quieting the half-living Thing for ever.

So Antonio went away to his work, which consists largely in sitting on the shady side of the tower, when he is not perched upon a rock with a fishing-line catching nothing. But on that day he went twice to look at the mound in the bright sunlight, and he searched round and round it for some hole through which the being might get in and out; but he found none. When the sun began to sink and the air was cooler in the shadows, he went up to fetch the old priest, carrying a little wicker basket with him; and in this they placed a bottle of holy water, and the basin, and sprinkler, and the stole which the priest would need; and they came down and waited in the door of the tower till it should be dark. But while the light still lingered very grey and faint, they saw something moving, just there, two figures, a man's that walked, and a woman's that flitted beside him, and while her head lay on his shoulder she kissed his throat. The priest has told me that, too, and that his teeth chattered and he grasped Antonio's arm. The vision passed and disappeared into the shadow. Then Antonio got the leathern flask of strong liquor, which he kept for great occasions, and poured such a draught as made the old man feel almost young again; and he got the lantern, and his pick and shovel, and gave the priest his stole to put on and the holy water to carry, and they went out together toward the spot

where the work was to be done. Antonio says that in spite of
the rum his own knees shook together, and the priest stumbled over his Latin. For when they were yet a few yards from
the mound the flickering light of the lantern fell upon Angelo's white face, unconscious as if in sleep, and on his up-
turned throat, over which a very thin red line of blood trickled
down into his collar; and the flickering light of the lantern
played upon another face that looked up from the feast—upon
two deep, dead eyes that saw in spite of death—upon parted
lips redder than life itself —upon two gleaming teeth on which
glistened a rosy drop. Then the priest, good old man, shut his
eyes tight and showered holy water before him, and his cracked
voice rose almost to a scream; and then Antonio, who is no
coward after all, raised his pick in one hand and the lantern in
the other, as he sprang forward, not knowing what the end
should be; and then he swears that he heard a woman's cry,
and the Thing was gone, and Angelo lay alone on the mound
unconscious, with the red line on his throat and the beads of
deathly sweat on his cold forehead. They lifted him, half-dead
as he was, and laid him on the ground close by; then Antonio
went to work, and the priest helped him, though he was old
and could not do much; and they dug deep, and at last Antonio, standing in the grave, stooped down with his lantern to
see what he might see.

His hair used to be dark brown, with grizzled streaks about
the temples; in less than a month from that day he was as grey
as a badger. He was a miner when he was young, and most of
these fellows have seen ugly sights now and then, when accidents have happened, but he had never seen what he saw that
night—that Thing which is neither alive nor dead, that Thing
that will abide neither above ground nor in the grave. Antonio
had brought something with him which the priest had not noticed. He had made it that afternoon—a sharp stake shaped
from a piece of tough old driftwood. He had it with him now,
and he had his heavy pick, and he had taken the lantern down
into the grave. I don't think any power on earth could make
him speak of what happened then, and the old priest was too
frightened to look in. He says he heard Antonio breathing like
a wild beast, and moving as if he were fighting with something
almost as strong as himself; and he heard an evil sound also,

with blows, as of something violently driven through flesh and bone; and then the most awful sound of all—a woman's shriek, the unearthly scream of a woman neither dead nor alive, but buried deep for many days. And he, the poor old priest, could only rock himself as he knelt there in the sand, crying aloud his prayers and exorcisms to drown these dreadful sounds. Then suddenly a small iron-bound chest was thrown up and rolled over against the old man's knee, and in a moment more Antonio was beside him, his face as white as tallow in the flickering light of the lantern, shovelling the sand and pebbles into the grave with furious haste, and looking over the edge till the pit was half full; and the priest said that there was much fresh blood on Antonio's hands and on his clothes.

I had come to the end of my story. Holger finished his wine and leaned back in his chair.

"So Angelo got his own again," he said. "Did he marry the prim and plump young person to whom he had been betrothed?"

"No; he had been badly frightened. He went to South America, and has not been heard of since."

"And that poor thing's body is there still, I suppose," said Holger. "Is it quite dead yet, I wonder?"

I wonder, too. But whether it be dead or alive, I should hardly care to see it, even in broad daylight. Antonio is as grey as a badger, and he has never been quite the same man since that night.

1905

AMBROSE BIERCE

(1842–1914?)

The Moonlit Road

I

STATEMENT OF JOEL HETMAN, JR.

I AM the most unfortunate of men. Rich, respected, fairly well educated and of sound health—with many other advantages usually valued by those having them and coveted by those who have them not—I sometimes think that I should be less unhappy if they had been denied me, for then the contrast between my outer and my inner life would not be continually demanding a painful attention. In the stress of privation and the need of effort I might sometimes forget the somber secret ever baffling the conjecture that it compels.

I am the only child of Joel and Julia Hetman. The one was a well-to-do country gentleman, the other a beautiful and accomplished woman to whom he was passionately attached with what I now know to have been a jealous and exacting devotion. The family home was a few miles from Nashville, Tennessee, a large, irregularly built dwelling of no particular order of architecture, a little way off the road, in a park of trees and shrubbery.

At the time of which I write I was nineteen years old, a student at Yale. One day I received a telegram from my father of such urgency that in compliance with its unexplained demand I left at once for home. At the railway station in Nashville a distant relative awaited me to apprise me of the reason for my recall: my mother had been barbarously murdered—why and by whom none could conjecture, but the circumstances were these:

My father had gone to Nashville, intending to return the next afternoon. Something prevented his accomplishing the business in hand, so he returned on the same night, arriving just before the dawn. In his testimony before the coroner he explained that having no latchkey and not caring to disturb the sleeping servants, he had, with no clearly defined intention, gone round to the rear of the house. As he turned an angle of the building, he heard a sound as of a door gently closed, and saw in the darkness, indistinctly, the figure of a man, which instantly disappeared among the trees of the lawn. A hasty pursuit and brief search of the grounds in the belief that the trespasser was some one secretly visiting a servant proving fruitless, he entered at the unlocked door and mounted the stairs to my mother's chamber. Its door was open, and stepping into black darkness he fell headlong over some heavy object on the floor. I may spare myself the details; it was my poor mother, dead of strangulation by human hands!

Nothing had been taken from the house, the servants had heard no sound, and excepting those terrible finger-marks upon the dead woman's throat—dear God! that I might forget them!—no trace of the assassin was ever found.

I gave up my studies and remained with my father, who, naturally, was greatly changed. Always of a sedate, taciturn disposition, he now fell into so deep a dejection that nothing could hold his attention, yet anything—a footfall, the sudden closing of a door—aroused in him a fitful interest; one might have called it an apprehension. At any small surprise of the senses he would start visibly and sometimes turn pale, then relapse into a melancholy apathy deeper than before. I suppose he was what is called a "nervous wreck." As to me, I was younger then than now—there is much in that. Youth is Gilead, in which is balm for every wound. Ah, that I might again dwell in that enchanted land! Unacquainted with grief, I knew not how to appraise my bereavement; I could not rightly estimate the strength of the stroke.

One night, a few months after the dreadful event, my father and I walked home from the city. The full moon was about three hours above the eastern horizon; the entire countryside had the solemn stillness of a summer night; our footfalls and the ceaseless song of the katydids were the only sound aloof. Black shadows of bordering trees lay athwart the road, which, in the short reaches between, gleamed a ghostly white. As we approached the gate to our dwelling, whose front was in shadow, and in which no light shone, my father suddenly stopped and clutched my arm, saying, hardly above his breath:

"God! God! what is that?"

"I hear nothing," I replied.

"But see—see!" he said, pointing along the road, directly ahead.

I said: "Nothing is there. Come, father, let us go in—you are ill."

He had released my arm and was standing rigid and motionless in the center of the illuminated roadway, staring like one bereft of sense. His face in the moonlight showed a pallor and fixity inexpressibly distressing. I pulled gently at his sleeve, but he had forgotten my existence. Presently he began to retire backward, step by step, never for an instant removing his eyes from what he saw, or thought he saw. I turned half round to follow, but stood irresolute. I do not recall any feeling of fear, unless a sudden chill was its physical manifestation. It seemed as if an icy wind had touched my face and enfolded my body from head to foot; I could feel the stir of it in my hair.

At that moment my attention was drawn to a light that suddenly streamed from an upper window of the house: one of the servants, awakened by what mysterious premonition of evil who can say, and in obedience to an impulse that she was never able to name, had lit a lamp. When I turned to look for my father he was gone, and in all the years that have passed no whisper of his fate has come across the borderland of conjecture from the realm of the unknown.

II
STATEMENT OF CASPAR GRATTAN

To-day I am said to live; to-morrow, here in this room, will lie a senseless shape of clay that all too long was I. If anyone lift the cloth from the face of that unpleasant thing it will be in gratification of a mere morbid curiosity. Some, doubtless, will go further and inquire, "Who was he?" In this writing I supply the only answer that I am able to make—Caspar Grattan. Surely, that should be enough. The name has served my small need for more than twenty years of a life of unknown length. True,

I gave it to myself, but lacking another I had the right. In this world one must have a name; it prevents confusion, even when it does not establish identity. Some, though, are known by numbers, which also seem inadequate distinctions.

One day, for illustration, I was passing along a street of a city, far from here, when I met two men in uniform, one of whom, half pausing and looking curiously into my face, said to his companion, "That man looks like 767." Something in the number seemed familiar and horrible. Moved by an uncontrollable impulse, I sprang into a side street and ran until I fell exhausted in a country lane.

I have never forgotten that number, and always it comes to memory attended by gibbering obscenity, peals of joyless laughter, the clang of iron doors. So I say a name, even if self-bestowed, is better than a number. In the register of the potter's field I shall soon have both. What wealth!

Of him who shall find this paper I must beg a little consideration. It is not the history of my life; the knowledge to write that is denied me. This is only a record of broken and apparently unrelated memories, some of them as distinct and sequent as brilliant beads upon a thread, others remote and strange, having the character of crimson dreams with interspaces blank and black—witch-fires glowing still and red in a great desolation.

Standing upon the shore of eternity, I turn for a last look landward over the course by which I came. There are twenty years of footprints fairly distinct, the impressions of bleeding feet. They lead through poverty and pain, devious and unsure, as of one staggering beneath a burden—

Remote, unfriended, melancholy, slow.

Ah, the poet's prophecy of Me—how admirable, how dreadfully admirable!

Backward beyond the beginning of this *via dolorosa*—this epic of suffering with episodes of sin—I see nothing clearly; it comes out of a cloud. I know that it spans only twenty years, yet I am an old man.

One does not remember one's birth—one has to be told. But with me it was different; life came to me full-handed and dowered me with all my faculties and powers. Of a previous existence I know no more than others, for all have stammering intimations that may be memories and may be dreams. I know only that my first consciousness was of maturity in body and mind—a consciousness accepted without surprise or conjecture. I merely found myself walking in a forest, half-clad, footsore, unutterably weary and hungry. Seeing a farmhouse, I approached and asked for food, which was given me by one who inquired my name. I did not know, yet knew that all had names. Greatly embarrassed, I retreated, and night coming on, lay down in the forest and slept.

The next day I entered a large town which I shall not name. Nor shall I recount further incidents of the life that is now to end—a life of wandering, always and everywhere haunted by an overmastering sense of crime in punishment of wrong and of terror in punishment of crime. Let me see if I can reduce it to narrative.

I seem once to have lived near a great city, a prosperous planter, married to a woman whom I loved and distrusted. We had, it sometimes seems, one child, a youth of brilliant parts and promise. He is at all times a vague figure, never clearly drawn, frequently altogether out of the picture.

One luckless evening it occurred to me to test my wife's fidelity in a vulgar, commonplace way familiar to everyone who has acquaintance with the literature of fact and fiction. I went to the city, telling my wife that I should be absent until the following afternoon. But I returned before daybreak and went to the rear of the house, purposing to enter by a door with which I had secretly so tampered that it would seem to lock, yet not actually fasten. As I approached it, I heard it gently open and close, and saw a man steal away into the darkness. With murder in my heart, I sprang after him, but he had vanished without even the bad luck of identification. Sometimes now I cannot even persuade myself that it was a human being.

Crazed with jealousy and rage, blind and bestial with all the elemental passions of insulted manhood, I entered the house and sprang up the stairs to the door of my wife's chamber. It was closed, but having tampered with its lock also, I easily entered and despite the black darkness soon stood by the side of her bed. My groping hands told me that although disarranged it was unoccupied.

"She is below," I thought, "and terrified by my entrance has evaded me in the darkness of the hall."

With the purpose of seeking her I turned to leave the room, but took a wrong direction—the right one! My foot struck her, cowering in a corner of the room. Instantly my hands were at her throat, stifling a shriek, my knees were upon her struggling body; and there in the darkness, without a word of accusation or reproach, I strangled her till she died!

There ends the dream. I have related it in the past tense, but the present would be the fitter form, for again and again the somber tragedy reenacts itself in my consciousness—over and over I lay the plan, I suffer the confirmation, I redress the wrong. Then all is blank; and afterward the rains beat against the grimy window-panes, or the snows fall upon my scant attire, the wheels rattle in the squalid streets where my life lies in poverty and mean employment. If there is ever sunshine I do not recall it; if there are birds they do not sing.

There is another dream, another vision of the night. I stand among the shadows in a moonlit road. I am aware of another presence, but whose I cannot rightly determine. In the shadow of a great dwelling I catch the gleam of white garments; then the figure of a woman confronts me in the road—my murdered wife! There is death in the face; there are marks upon the throat. The eyes are fixed on mine with an infinite gravity which is not reproach, nor hate, nor menace, nor anything less terrible than recognition. Before this awful apparition I retreat in terror—a terror that is upon me as I write. I can no longer rightly shape the words. See! they—

Now I am calm, but truly there is no more to tell: the incident ends where it began—in darkness and in doubt.

Yes, I am again in control of myself: "the captain of my soul." But that is not respite; it is another stage and phase of expiation. My penance, constant in degree, is mutable in kind: one of its variants is tranquillity. After all, it is only a life-sentence. "To Hell for life"—that is a foolish penalty: the culprit chooses the duration of his punishment. To-day my term expires.

To each and all, the peace that was not mine.

III
STATEMENT OF THE LATE JULIA HETMAN,
THROUGH THE MEDIUM BAYROLLES

I had retired early and fallen almost immediately into a peaceful sleep, from which I awoke with that indefinable sense of peril which is, I think, a common experience in that other, earlier life. Of its unmeaning character, too, I was entirely persuaded, yet that did not banish it. My husband, Joel Hetman, was away from home; the servants slept in another part of the house. But these were familiar conditions; they had never before distressed me. Nevertheless, the strange terror grew so insupportable that conquering my reluctance to move I sat up and lit the lamp at my bedside. Contrary to my expectation this gave me no relief; the light seemed rather an added danger, for I reflected that it would shine out under the door, disclosing my presence to whatever evil thing might lurk outside. You that are still in the flesh, subject to horrors of the imagination, think what a monstrous fear that must be which seeks in darkness security from malevolent existences of the night. That is to spring to close quarters with an unseen enemy—the strategy of despair!

Extinguishing the lamp I pulled the bed-clothing about my head and lay trembling and silent, unable to shriek, forgetful to pray. In this pitiable state I must have lain for what you call hours—with us there are no hours, there is no time.

At last it came—a soft, irregular sound of footfalls on the stairs! They were slow, hesitant, uncertain, as of something that did not see its way; to my disordered reason all the more terrifying for that, as the approach of some blind and mindless malevolence to which is no appeal. I even thought that I must have left the hall lamp burning and the groping of this creature proved it a monster of the night. This was foolish and inconsistent with my previous dread of the light, but what would you have? Fear has no brains; it is an idiot. The dismal witness that it bears and the cowardly counsel that it whispers are unrelated. We know this well, we who have passed into the Realm of Terror, who skulk in eternal dusk among the scenes of our former lives, invisible even to ourselves and one another, yet hiding forlorn in lonely places; yearning for speech with our loved ones, yet dumb, and as fearful of them as they of us. Sometimes the disability is removed, the law suspended: by the deathless power of love or hate we break the spell—we are seen by those whom we would warn, console, or punish. What form we seem to them to bear we know not; we know only that we terrify even those whom we most wish to comfort, and from whom we most crave tenderness and sympathy.

Forgive, I pray you, this inconsequent digression by what was once a woman. You who consult us in this imperfect way —you do not understand. You ask foolish questions about things unknown and things forbidden. Much that we know and could impart in our speech is meaningless in yours. We must communicate with you through a stammering intelligence in that small fraction of our language that you yourselves can speak. You think that we are of another world. No, we have knowledge of no world but yours, though for us it holds no sunlight, no warmth, no music, no laughter, no song of birds, nor any companionship. O God! what a thing it is to be a ghost, cowering and shivering in an altered world, a prey to apprehension and despair!

No, I did not die of fright: the Thing turned and went away. I heard it go down the stairs, hurriedly, I thought, as if itself in sudden fear. Then I rose to call for help. Hardly had my shaking hand found the doorknob when—merciful heaven!—I heard it returning. Its footfalls as it remounted the stairs were rapid, heavy and loud; they shook the house. I fled to an angle of the wall and crouched upon the floor. I tried to pray. I tried to call the name of my dear husband. Then I heard the door thrown open. There was an interval of unconsciousness, and when I revived I felt a strangling clutch upon my throat—felt my arms feebly beating against something that bore me backward—felt my tongue thrusting itself from between my teeth! And then I passed into this life.

No, I have no knowledge of what it was. The sum of what we knew at death is the measure of what we know afterward of all that went before. Of this existence we know many things, but no new light falls upon any page of that; in memory is written all of it that we can read. Here are no heights of truth overlooking the confused landscape of that dubitable domain. We still dwell in the Valley of the Shadow, lurk in its desolate places, peering from brambles and thickets at its mad, malign inhabitants. How should we have new knowledge of that fading past?

What I am about to relate happened on a night. We know when it is night, for then you retire to your houses and we can venture from our places of concealment to move unafraid about our old homes, to look in at the windows, even to enter and gaze upon your faces as you sleep. I had lingered long near the dwelling where I had been so cruelly changed to what I am, as we do while any that we love or hate remain. Vainly I had sought some method of manifestation, some way to make my continued existence and my great love and poignant pity understood by my husband and son. Always if they slept they would wake, or if in my desperation I dared approach them when they were awake, would turn toward me the terrible eyes of the living, frightening me by the glances that I sought from the purpose that I held.

On this night I had searched for them without success, fearing to find them; they were nowhere in the house, nor about the moonlit lawn. For, although the sun is lost to us for-ever, the moon, full-orbed or slender, remains to us. Sometimes it shines by night, sometimes by day, but always it rises and sets, as in that other life.

I left the lawn and moved in the white light and silence along the road, aimless and sorrowing. Suddenly I heard the voice of my poor husband in exclamations of astonishment, with that of my son in reassurance and dissuasion; and there by the shadow of a group of trees they stood—near, so near! Their faces were toward me, the eyes of the elder man fixed upon mine. He saw me—at last, at last, he saw me! In the consciousness of that, my terror fled as a cruel dream. The death-spell was bro-ken: Love had conquered Law! Mad with exultation I shouted —I *must* have shouted, "He sees, he sees: he will understand!" Then, controlling myself, I moved forward, smiling and con-sciously beautiful, to offer myself to his arms, to comfort him with endearments, and, with my son's hand in mine, to speak words that should restore the broken bonds between the living and the dead.

Alas! alas! his face went white with fear, his eyes were as

those of a hunted animal. He backed away from me, as I advanced, and at last turned and fled into the wood—whither, it is not given to me to know.

To my poor boy, left doubly desolate, I have never been able to impart a sense of my presence. Soon he, too, must pass to this Life Invisible and be lost to me forever.

1907

EDWARD LUCAS WHITE
(1866–1934)

Lukundoo

"IT stands to reason," said Twombly, "that a man must accept the evidence of his own eyes, and when eyes and ears agree, there can be no doubt. He has to believe what he has both seen and heard."

"Not always," put in Singleton, softly.

Every man turned toward Singleton. Twombly was standing on the hearth-rug, his back to the grate, his legs spread out, with his habitual air of dominating the room. Singleton, as usual, was as much as possible effaced in a corner. But when Singleton spoke he said something. We faced him in that flattering spontaneity of expectant silence which invites utterance.

"I was thinking," he said, after an interval, "of something I both saw and heard in Africa."

Now, if there was one thing we had found impossible it had been to elicit from Singleton anything definite about his African experiences. As with the Alpinist in the story, who could tell only that he went up and came down, the sum of Singleton's revelations had been that he went there and came away. His words now riveted our attention at once. Twombly faded from the hearth-rug, but not one of us could ever recall having seen him go. The room readjusted itself, focused on Singleton, and there was some hasty and furtive lighting of fresh cigars. Singleton lit one also, but it went out immediately, and he never relit it.

I

We were in the Great Forest, exploring for pigmies. Van Rieten had a theory that the dwarfs found by Stanley and others were a mere cross-breed between ordinary negroes and the real pigmies. He hoped to discover a race of men three feet tall at most, or shorter. We had found no trace of any such beings.

Natives were few; game scarce; food, except game, there was none; and the deepest, dankest, drippingest forest all about. We were the only novelty in the country, no native we met had even seen a white man before, most had never heard of white men. All of a sudden, late one afternoon, there came into our camp an Englishman, and pretty well used up he was, too. We had heard no rumor of him; he had not only heard of us but had made an amazing five-day march to reach us. His guide and two bearers were nearly as done up as he. Even though he was in tatters and had five days' beard on, you could see he was naturally dapper and neat and the sort of man to shave daily. He was small, but wiry. His face was the sort of British face from which emotion has been so carefully banished that a foreigner is apt to think the wearer of the face incapable of any sort of feeling; the kind of face which, if it has any expression at all, expresses principally the resolution to go through the world decorously, without intruding upon or annoying anyone.

His name was Etcham. He introduced himself modestly, and ate with us so deliberately that we should never have suspected, if our bearers had not had it from his bearers, that he had had but three meals in the five days, and those small. After we had lit up he told us why he had come.

"My chief is ve'y seedy," he said between puffs. "He is bound to go out if he keeps this way. I thought perhaps. . . ."

He spoke quietly in a soft, even tone, but I could see little beads of sweat oozing out on his upper lip under his stubby mustache, and there was a tingle of repressed emotion in his tone, a veiled eagerness in his eye, a palpitating inward solicitude in his demeanor that moved me at once. Van Rieten had no sentiment in him; if he was moved he did not show it. But he listened. I was surprised at that. He was just the man to refuse at once. But he listened to Etcham's halting, diffident hints. He even asked questions.

"Who is your chief?"

"Stone," Etcham lisped.

That electrified both of us.

"Ralph Stone?" we ejaculated together.

Etcham nodded.

For some minutes Van Rieten and I were silent. Van Rieten had never seen him, but I had been a classmate of Stone's, and

Van Rieten and I had discussed him over many a camp-fire. We had heard of him two years before, south of Luebo in the Balunda country, which had been ringing with his theatrical strife against a Balunda witch-doctor, ending in the sorcerer's complete discomfiture and the abasement of his tribe before Stone. They had even broken the fetish-man's whistle and given Stone the pieces. It had been like the triumph of Elijah over the prophets of Baal, only more real to the Balunda.

We had thought of Stone as far off, if still in Africa at all, and here he turned up ahead of us and probably forestalling our quest.

II

Etcham's naming of Stone brought back to us all his tantalizing story, his fascinating parents, their tragic death; the brilliance of his college days; the dazzle of his millions; the promise of his young manhood; his wide notoriety, so nearly real fame; his romantic elopement with the meteoric authoress whose sudden cascade of fiction had made her so great a name so young, whose beauty and charm were so much heralded; the frightful scandal of the breach-of-promise suit that followed; his bride's devotion through it all; their sudden quarrel after it was all over; their divorce; the too much advertised announcement of his approaching marriage to the plaintiff in the breach-of-promise suit; his precipitate remarriage to his divorced bride; their second quarrel and second divorce; his departure from his native land; his advent in the dark continent. The sense of all this rushed over me and I believe Van Rieten felt it, too, as he sat silent.

Then he asked:

"Where is Werner?"

"Dead," said Etcham. "He died before I joined Stone."

"You were not with Stone above Luebo?"

"No," said Etcham, "I joined him at Stanley Falls."

"Who is with him?" Van Rieten asked.

"Only his Zanzibar servants and the bearers," Etcham replied.

"What sort of bearers?" Van Rieten demanded.

"Mang-Battu men," Etcham responded simply.

Now that impressed both Van Rieten and myself greatly. It

bore out Stone's reputation as a notable leader of men. For up to that time no one had been able to use Mang-Battu as bearers outside of their own country, or to hold them for long or difficult expeditions.

"Were you long among the Mang-Battu?" was Van Rieten's next question.

"Some weeks," said Etcham. "Stone was interested in them and made up a fair-sized vocabulary of their words and phrases. He had a theory that they are an offshoot of the Balunda and he found much confirmation in their customs."

"What do you live on?" Van Rieten inquired.

"Game, mostly," Etcham lisped.

"How long has Stone been laid up?" Van Rieten next asked.

"More than a month," Etcham answered.

"And you have been hunting for the camp!" Van Rieten exclaimed.

Etcham's face, burnt and flayed as it was, showed a flush.

"I missed some easy shots," he admitted ruefully. "I've not felt ve'y fit myself."

"What's the matter with your chief?" Van Rieten inquired.

"Something like carbuncles," Etcham replied.

"He ought to get over a carbuncle or two," Van Rieten declared.

"They are not carbuncles," Etcham explained. "Nor one or two. He has had dozens, sometimes five at once. If they had been carbuncles he would have been dead long ago. But in some ways they are not so bad, though in others they are worse."

"How do you mean?" Van Rieten queried.

"Well," Etcham hesitated, "they do not seem to inflame so deep nor so wide as carbuncles, nor to be so painful, nor to cause so much fever. But then they seem to be part of a disease that affects his mind. He let me help him dress the first, but the others he has hidden most carefully, from me and from the men. He keeps his tent when they puff up, and will not let me change the dressings or be with him at all."

"Have you plenty of dressings?" Van Rieten asked.

"We have some," said Etcham doubtfully. "But he won't use them; he washes out the dressings and uses them over and over."

"How is he treating the swellings?" Van Rieten inquired.

"He slices them off clear down to flesh level, with his razor."

"What?" Van Rieten shouted.

Etcham made no answer but looked him steadily in the eyes.

"I beg pardon," Van Rieten hastened to say. "You startled me. They can't be carbuncles. He'd have been dead long ago."

"I thought I had said they are not carbuncles," Etcham lisped.

"But the man must be crazy!" Van Rieten exclaimed.

"Just so," said Etcham. "He is beyond my advice or control."

"How many has he treated that way?" Van Rieten demanded.

"Two, to my knowledge," Etcham said.

"Two?" Van Rieten queried.

Etcham flushed again.

"I saw him," he confessed, "through a crack in the hut. I felt impelled to keep a watch on him, as if he was not responsible."

"I should think not," Van Rieten agreed. "And you saw him do that twice?"

"I conjecture," said Etcham, "that he did the like with all the rest."

"How many has he had?" Van Rieten asked.

"Dozens," Etcham lisped.

"Does he eat?" Van Rieten inquired.

"Like a wolf," said Etcham. "More than any two bearers."

"Can he walk?" Van Rieten asked.

"He crawls a bit, groaning," said Etcham simply.

"Little fever, you say," Van Rieten ruminated.

"Enough and too much," Etcham declared.

"Has he been delirious?" Van Rieten asked.

"Only twice," Etcham replied; "once when the first swelling broke, and once later. He would not let anyone come near him then. But we could hear him talking, talking steadily, and it scared the natives."

"Was he talking their patter in delirium?" Van Rieten demanded.

"No," said Etcham, "but he was talking some similar lingo. Hamed Burghash said he was talking Balunda. I know too little Balunda. I do not learn languages readily. Stone learned more Mang-Battu in a week than I could have learned in a year. But I seemed to hear words like Mang-Battu words. Anyhow the Mang-Battu bearers were scared."

"Scared?" Van Rieten repeated, questioningly.

"So were the Zanzibar men, even Hamed Burghash, and so was I," said Etcham, "only for a different reason. He talked in two voices."

"In two voices," Van Rieten reflected.

"Yes," said Etcham, more excitedly than he had yet spoken. "In two voices, like a conversation. One was his own, one a small, thin, bleaty voice like nothing I ever heard. I seemed to make out, among the sounds the deep voice made, something like Mang-Battu words I knew, as *nedru*, *metebaba*, and *nedo*, their terms for 'head,' 'shoulder,' 'thigh,' and perhaps *kudra* and *nekere* ('speak' and 'whistle'); and among the noises of the shrill voice *matomipa*, *angunzi*, and *kamomami* ('kill,' 'death,' and 'hate'). Hamed Burghash said he also heard those words. He knew Mang-Battu far better than I."

"What did the bearers say?" Van Rieten asked.

"They said, '*Lukundoo, Lukundoo!*'" Etcham replied. "I did not know that word; Hamed Burghash said it was Mang-Battu for 'leopard.'"

"It's Mang-Battu for 'witchcraft,'" said Van Rieten.

"I don't wonder they thought so," said Etcham. "It was enough to make one believe in sorcery to listen to those two voices."

"One voice answering the other?" Van Rieten asked perfunctorily.

Etcham's face went gray under his tan.

"Sometimes both at once," he answered huskily.

"Both at once!" Van Rieten ejaculated.

"It sounded that way to the men, too," said Etcham. "And that was not all."

He stopped and looked helplessly at us for a moment.

"Could a man talk and whistle at the same time?" he asked.

"How do you mean?" Van Rieten queried.

"We could hear Stone talking away, his big, deep-chested baritone rumbling along, and through it all we could hear a high, shrill whistle, the oddest, wheezy sound. You know, no matter how shrilly a grown man may whistle, the note has a different quality from the whistle of a boy or a woman or little girl. They sound more treble, somehow. Well, if you can imagine the smallest girl who could whistle keeping it up tunelessly right along, that whistle was like that, only even more piercing, and it sounded right through Stone's bass tones."

"And you didn't go to him?" Van Rieten cried.

"He is not given to threats," Etcham disclaimed. "But he had threatened, not volubly, nor like a sick man, but quietly and firmly, that if any man of us (he lumped me in with the men), came near him while he was in his trouble, that man should die. And it was not so much his words as his manner. It was like a monarch commanding respected privacy for a death-bed. One simply could not transgress."

"I see," said Van Rieten shortly.

"He's ve'y seedy," Etcham repeated helplessly. "I thought perhaps. . . ."

His absorbing affection for Stone, his real love for him, shone out through his envelope of conventional training. Worship of Stone was plainly his master passion.

Like many competent men, Van Rieten had a streak of hard selfishness in him. It came to the surface then. He said we carried our lives in our hands from day to day just as genuinely as Stone; that he did not forget the ties of blood and calling between any two explorers, but that there was no sense in imperiling one party for a very problematical benefit to a man probably beyond any help; that it was enough of a task to hunt for one party; that if two were united, providing food would be more than doubly difficult; that the risk of starvation was too great. Deflecting our march seven full days' journey (he complimented Etcham on his marching powers) might ruin our expedition entirely.

III

Van Rieten had logic on his side and he had a way with him. Etcham sat there apologetic and deferential, like a fourth-form schoolboy before a head master. Van Rieten wound up.

"I am after pigmies, at the risk of my life. After pigmies I go."

"Perhaps, then, these will interest you," said Etcham, very quietly.

He took two objects out of the sidepocket of his blouse, and handed them to Van Rieten. They were round, bigger than big plums, and smaller than small peaches, about the right size to enclose in an average hand. They were black, and at first I did not see what they were.

"Pigmies!" Van Rieten exclaimed. "Pigmies, indeed! Why, they wouldn't be two feet high! Do you mean to claim that these are adult heads?"

"I claim nothing," Etcham answered evenly. "You can see for yourself."

Van Rieten passed one of the heads to me. The sun was just setting and I examined it closely. A dried head it was, perfectly preserved, and the flesh as hard as Argentine jerked beef. A bit of a vertebra stuck out where the muscles of the vanished neck had shriveled into folds. The puny chin was sharp on a projecting jaw, the minute teeth white and even between the retracted lips, the tiny nose was flat, the little forehead retreating, there were inconsiderable clumps of stunted wool on the Lilliputian cranium. There was nothing babyish, childish or youthful about the head, rather it was mature to senility.

"Where did these come from?" Van Rieten inquired.

"I do not know," Etcham replied precisely. "I found them among Stone's effects while rummaging for medicines or drugs or anything that could help me to help him. I do not know where he got them. But I'll swear he did not have them when we entered this district."

"Are you sure?" Van Rieten queried, his eyes big and fixed on Etcham's.

"Ve'y sure," lisped Etcham.

"But how could he have come by them without your knowledge?" Van Rieten demurred.

"Sometimes we were apart ten days at a time hunting," said Etcham. "Stone is not a talking man. He gave me no account of his doings and Hamed Burghash keeps a still tongue and a tight hold on the men."

"You have examined these heads?" Van Rieten asked.

"Minutely," said Etcham.

Van Rieten took out his notebook. He was a methodical chap. He tore out a leaf, folded it and divided it equally into three pieces. He gave one to me and one to Etcham.

"Just for a test of my impressions," he said, "I want each of us to write separately just what he is most reminded of by these heads. Then I want to compare the writings."

I handed Etcham a pencil and he wrote. Then he handed the pencil back to me and I wrote.

"Read the three," said Van Rieten, handing me his piece.

Van Rieten had written:

"An old Balunda witch-doctor."

Etcham had written:

"An old Mang-Battu fetish-man."

I had written:

"An old Katongo magician."

"There!" Van Rieten exclaimed. "Look at that! There is nothing Wagabi or Batwa or Wambuttu or Wabotu about these heads. Nor anything pigmy either."

"I thought as much," said Etcham.

"And you say he did not have them before?"

"To a certainty he did not," Etcham asserted.

"It is worth following up," said Van Rieten. "I'll go with you. And first of all, I'll do my best to save Stone."

He put out his hand and Etcham clasped it silently. He was grateful all over.

IV

Nothing but Etcham's fever of solicitude could have taken him in five days over the track. It took him eight days to retrace with full knowledge of it and our party to help. We could not have done it in seven, and Etcham urged us on, in a repressed fury of anxiety, no mere fever of duty to his chief, but a real ardor of devotion, a glow of personal adoration for Stone which blazed under his dry conventional exterior and showed in spite of him.

We found Stone well cared for. Etcham had seen to a good, high thorn *zareeba* round the camp, the huts were well built and thatched and Stone's was as good as their resources would permit. Hamed Burghash was not named after two Seyyids for nothing. He had in him the making of a sultan. He had kept the Mang-Battu together, not a man had slipped off, and he had kept them in order. Also he was a deft nurse and a faithful servant.

The two other Zanzabaris had done some creditable hunting. Though all were hungry, the camp was far from starvation.

Stone was on a canvas cot and there was a sort of collapsible camp-stool-table, like a Turkish tabouret, by the cot. It had a water-bottle and some vials on it and Stone's watch, also his razor in its case.

Stone was clean and not emaciated, but he was far gone; not unconscious, but in a daze; past commanding or resisting anyone. He did not seem to see us enter or to know we were there. I should have recognized him anywhere. His boyish dash and grace had vanished utterly, of course. But his head was even more leonine; his hair was still abundant, yellow and wavy; the close, crisped blond beard he had grown during his illness did not alter him. He was big and big-chested yet. His eyes were dull and he mumbled and babbled mere meaningless syllables, not words.

Etcham helped Van Rieten to uncover him and look him over. He was in good muscle for a man so long bedridden. There were no scars on him except about his knees, shoulders and chest. On each knee and above it he had a full score of roundish cicatrices, and a dozen or more on each shoulder, all in front. Two or three were open wounds and four or five barely healed. He had no fresh swellings except two, one on each side, on his pectoral muscles, the one on the left being higher up and farther out than the other. They did not look like boils or carbuncles, but as if something blunt and hard were being pushed up through the fairly healthy flesh and skin, not much inflamed.

"I should not lance those," said Van Rieten, and Etcham assented.

They made Stone as comfortable as they could, and just before sunset we looked in at him again. He was lying on his back, and his chest showed big and massive yet, but he lay as if in a stupor. We left Etcham with him and went into the next hut, which Etcham had resigned to us. The jungle noises were no different there than anywhere else for months past, and I was soon fast asleep.

V

Sometime in the pitch dark I found myself awake and listening. I could hear two voices, one Stone's, the other sibilant and wheezy. I knew Stone's voice after all the years that had passed since I heard it last. The other was like nothing I remembered. It had less volume than the wail of a new-born baby, yet there was an insistent carrying power to it, like the shrilling of an insect. As I listened I heard Van Rieten breathing near me in the dark, then he heard me and realized that I was listening, too. Like Etcham I knew little Balunda, but I could make out a word or two. The voices alternated with intervals of silence between.

Then suddenly both sounded at once and fast, Stone's baritone basso, full as if he were in perfect health, and that incredibly stridulous falsetto, both jabbering at once like the voices of two people quarreling and trying to talk each other down.

"I can't stand this," said Van Rieten. "Let's have a look at him."

He had one of those cylindrical electric night-candles. He fumbled about for it, touched the button and beckoned me to come with him. Outside of the hut he motioned me to stand still, and instinctively turned off the light, as if seeing made listening difficult.

Except for a faint glow from the embers of the bearers' fire we were in complete darkness, little starlight struggled through the trees, the river made but a faint murmur. We could hear the two voices together and then suddenly the creaking voice changed into a razor-edged, slicing whistle, indescribably cutting, continuing right through Stone's grumbling torrent of croaking words.

"Good God!" exclaimed Van Rieten.

Abruptly he turned on the light.

We found Etcham utterly asleep, exhausted by his long anxiety and the exertions of his phenomenal march and relaxed completely now that the load was in a sense shifted from his shoulders to Van Rieten's. Even the light on his face did not wake him.

The whistle had ceased and the two voices now sounded together. Both came from Stone's cot, where the concentrated white ray showed him lying just as we had left him, except that he had tossed his arms above his head and had torn the coverings and bandages from his chest.

The swelling on his right breast had broken. Van Rieten aimed the center line of the light at it and we saw it plainly. From his flesh, grown out of it, there protruded a head, such a head as the dried specimens Etcham had shown us, as if it were a miniature of the head of a Balunda fetishman. It was black, shining black as the blackest African skin; it rolled the whites of its wicked, wee eyes and showed its microscopic teeth between lips repulsively negroid in their red fullness, even in so diminutive a face. It had crisp, fuzzy wool on its minikin skull, it turned malignantly from side to side and chittered incessantly in that inconceivable falsetto. Stone babbled brokenly against its patter.

Van Rieten turned from Stone and waked Etcham, with some difficulty. When he was awake and saw it all, Etcham stared and said not one word.

"You saw him slice off two swellings?" Van Rieten asked.

Etcham nodded, chokingly.

"Did he bleed much?" Van Rieten demanded.

"Ve'y little," Etcham replied.

"You hold his arms," said Van Rieten to Etcham.

He took up Stone's razor and handed me the light. Stone showed no sign of seeing the light or of knowing we were there. But the little head mewled and screeched at us.

Van Rieten's hand was steady, and the sweep of the razor even and true. Stone bled amazingly little and Van Rieten dressed the wound as if it had been a bruise or scrape.

Stone had stopped talking the instant the excrescent head was severed. Van Rieten did all that could be done for Stone and then fairly grabbed the light from me. Snatching up a gun he scanned the ground by the cot and brought the butt down once and twice, viciously.

We went back to our hut, but I doubt if I slept.

VI

Next day, near noon, in broad daylight, we heard the two voices from Stone's hut. We found Etcham dropped asleep by his charge. The swelling on the left had broken, and just such another head was there miauling and spluttering. Etcham woke up and the three of us stood there and glared. Stone interjected hoarse vocables into the tinkling gurgle of the portent's utterance.

Van Rieten stepped forward, took up Stone's razor and knelt down by the cot. The atomy of a head squealed a wheezy snarl at him.

Then suddenly Stone spoke English.

"Who are you with my razor?"

Van Rieten started back and stood up.

Stone's eyes were clear now and bright, they roved about the hut.

"The end," he said; "I recognize the end. I seem to see Etcham, as if in life. But Singleton! Ah, Singleton! Ghosts of my boyhood come to watch me pass! And you, strange specter with the black beard, and my razor! Aroint ye all!"

"I'm no ghost, Stone," I managed to say. "I'm alive. So are Etcham and Van Rieten. We are here to help you."

"Van Rieten!" he exclaimed. "My work passes on to a better man. Luck go with you, Van Rieten."

Van Rieten went nearer to him.

"Just hold still a moment, old man," he said soothingly. "It will be only one twinge."

"I've held still for many such twinges," Stone answered quite distinctly. "Let me be. Let me die my own way. The hydra was nothing to this. You can cut off ten, a hundred, a thousand heads, but the curse you can not cut off, or take off. What's soaked into the bone won't come out of the flesh, any more than what's bred there. Don't hack me any more. Promise!"

His voice had all the old commanding tone of his boyhood and it swayed Van Rieten as it always had swayed everybody.

"I promise," said Van Rieten.

Almost as he said the word Stone's eyes filmed again.

Then we three sat about Stone and watched that hideous, gibbering prodigy grow up out of Stone's flesh, till two horrid, spindling little black arms disengaged themselves. The infinitesimal nails were perfect to the barely perceptible moon at the quick, the pink spot on the palm was horridly natural. These arms gesticulated and the right plucked toward Stone's blond beard.

"I can't stand this," Van Rieten exclaimed and took up the razor again.

Instantly Stone's eyes opened, hard and glittering.

"Van Rieten break his word?" he enunciated slowly. "Never!"

"But we must help you," Van Rieten gasped.

"I am past all help and all hurting," said Stone. "This is my hour. This curse is not put on me; it grew out of me, like this horror here. Even now I go."

His eyes closed and we stood helpless, the adherent figure spouting shrill sentences.

In a moment Stone spoke again.

"You speak all tongues?" he asked thickly.

And the emergent minikin replied in sudden English:

"Yea, verily, all that you speak," putting out its microscopic tongue, writhing its lips and wagging its head from side to side. We could see the thready ribs on its exiguous flanks heave as if the thing breathed.

"Has she forgiven me?" Stone asked in a muffled strangle.

"Not while the moss hangs from the cypresses," the head squeaked. "Not while the stars shine on Lake Pontchartrain will she forgive."

And then Stone, all with one motion, wrenched himself over on his side. The next instant he was dead.

When Singleton's voice ceased the room was hushed for a space. We could hear each other breathing. Twombly, the tactless, broke the silence.

"I presume," he said, "you cut off the little minikin and brought it home in alcohol."

Singleton turned on him a stern countenance.

"We buried Stone," he said, "unmutilated as he died."

"But," said the unconscionable Twombly, "the whole thing is incredible."

Singleton stiffened.

"I did not expect you to believe it," he said; "I began by saying that although I heard and saw it, when I look back on it I cannot credit it myself."

1907

OLIVIA HOWARD DUNBAR

(1873–1953)

The Shell of Sense

It was intolerably unchanged, the dim, dark-toned room. In an agony of recognition my glance ran from one to another of the comfortable, familiar things that my earthly life had been passed among. Incredibly distant from it all as I essentially was, I noted sharply that the very gaps that I myself had left in my bookshelves still stood unfilled; that the delicate fingers of the ferns that I had tended were still stretched futilely toward the light; that the soft agreeable chuckle of my own little clock, like some elderly woman with whom conversation has become automatic, was undiminished.

Unchanged—or so it seemed at first. But there were certain trivial differences that shortly smote me. The windows were closed too tightly; for I had always kept the house very cool, although I had known that Theresa preferred warm rooms. And my work-basket was in disorder: it was preposterous that so small a thing should hurt me so. Then, for this was my first experience of the shadow-folded transition, the odd alternation of my emotions bewildered me. For at one moment the place seemed so humanly familiar, so distinctly my own proper envelope, that for love of it I could have laid my cheek against the wall; while in the next I was miserably conscious of strange new shrillnesses. How could they be endured—and had I ever endured them?—those harsh influences that I now perceived at the window; light and color so blinding that they obscured the form of the wind, tumult so discordant that one could scarcely hear the roses open in the garden below?

But Theresa did not seem to mind any of these things. Disorder, it is true, the dear child had never minded. She was sitting all this time at my desk—at *my* desk,—occupied, I could only too easily surmise how. In the light of my own habits of precision it was plain that that sombre correspondence should have been attended to before; but I believe that I did not really reproach Theresa, for I knew that her notes, when she did write them, were perhaps less perfunctory than mine. She finished the last one as I watched her, and added it to the heap of black-bordered envelopes that lay on the desk. Poor girl! I saw now that they had cost her tears. Yet, living beside her day after day, year after year, I had never discovered what deep tenderness my sister possessed. Toward each other it had been our habit to display only a temperate affection, and I remember having always thought it distinctly fortunate for Theresa, since she was denied my happiness, that she could live so easily and pleasantly without emotions of the devastating sort. . . . And now, for the first time, I was really to behold her. . . . Could it be Theresa, after all, this tangle of subdued turbulences? Let no one suppose that it is an easy thing to bear, the relentlessly lucid understanding that I then first exercised; or that, in its first enfranchisement, the timid vision does not yearn for its old screens and mists.

Suddenly, as Theresa sat there, her head, filled with its tender thoughts of me, held in her gentle hands, I felt Allan's step on the carpeted stair outside. Theresa felt it, too,—but how? for it was not audible. She gave a start, swept the black envelopes out of sight, and pretended to be writing in a little book. Then I forgot to watch her any longer in my absorption in Allan's coming. It was he, of course, that I was awaiting. It was for him that I had made this first lonely, frightened effort to return, to recover. . . . It was not that I had supposed he would allow himself to recognize my presence, for I had long been sufficiently familiar with his hard and fast denials of the invisible. He was so reasonable always, so sane—so blindfolded. But I had hoped that because of his very rejection of the ether that now contained me I could perhaps all the more safely, the more secretly, watch him, linger near him. He was near now, very near,—but why did Theresa, sitting there in the room that had never belonged to her, appropriate for herself his coming? It was so manifestly I who had drawn him, I whom he had come to seek.

The door was ajar. He knocked softly at it. "Are you there, Theresa?" he called. He expected to find her, then, there in my room? I shrank back, fearing, almost, to stay.

"I shall have finished in a moment," Theresa told him, and he sat down to wait for her.

No spirit still unreleased can understand the pang that I felt with Allan sitting almost within my touch. Almost irresistibly the wish beset me to let him for an instant feel my nearness. Then I checked myself, remembering—oh, absurd, piteous human fears!—that my too unguarded closeness might alarm him. It was not so remote a time that I myself had known them, those blind, uncouth timidities. I came, therefore, somewhat nearer— but I did not touch him. I merely leaned toward him and with incredible softness whispered his name. That much I could not have forborne; the spell of life was still too strong in me.

But it gave him no comfort, no delight. "Theresa!" he called, in a voice dreadful with alarm—and in that instant the last veil fell, and desperately, scarce believingly, I beheld how it stood between them, those two.

She turned to him that gentle look of hers.

"Forgive me," came from him hoarsely. "But I had suddenly the most—unaccountable sensation. Can there be too many windows open? There is such a—chill—about."

"There are no windows open," Theresa assured him. "I took care to shut out the chill. You are not well, Allan!"

"Perhaps not." He embraced the suggestion. "And yet I feel no illness apart from this abominable sensation that persists— persists. . . . Theresa, you must tell me: do I fancy it, or do you, too, feel—something—strange here?"

"Oh, there is something very strange here," she half sobbed. "There always will be."

"Good heavens, child, I didn't mean that!" He rose and stood looking about him. "I know, of course, that you have your beliefs, and I respect them, but you know equally well that I have nothing of the sort! So—don't let us conjure up anything inexplicable."

I stayed impalpably, imponderably near him. Wretched and bereft though I was, I could not have left him while he stood denying me.

"What I mean," he went on, in his low, distinct voice, "is a special, an almost ominous sense of cold. Upon my soul, Theresa,"—he paused—"if I *were* superstitious, if I *were* a woman, I should probably imagine it to seem—a presence!"

He spoke the last word very faintly, but Theresa shrank from it nevertheless.

"*Don't* say that, Allan!" she cried out. "Don't think it, I beg of you! I've tried so hard myself not to think it—and you must help me. You know it is only perturbed, uneasy spirits that wander. With her it is quite different. She has always been so happy—she must still be."

I listened, stunned, to Theresa's sweet dogmatism. From what blind distances came her confident misapprehensions, how dense, both for her and for Allan, was the separating vapor!

Allan frowned. "Don't take me literally, Theresa," he explained; and I, who a moment before had almost touched him, now held myself aloof and heard him with a strange untried pity, new born in me. "I'm not speaking of what you call—spirits. It's something much more terrible." He allowed his head to sink heavily on his chest. "If I did not positively know that I had never done her any harm, I should suppose myself to be suffering from guilt, from remorse. . . . Theresa, you know better than I, perhaps. Was she content, always? Did she believe in me?"

"Believe in you?—when she knew you to be so good!—when you adored her!"

"She thought that? She said it? Then what in Heaven's name ails me?—unless it is all as you believe, Theresa, and she knows now what she didn't know then, poor dear, and minds—"

"Minds what? What do you mean, Allan?"

I, who with my perhaps illegitimate advantage saw so clear, knew that he had not meant to tell her: I did him that justice, even in my first jealousy. If I had not tortured him so by clinging near him, he would not have told her. But the moment came, and overflowed, and he did tell her—passionate, tumultuous story that it was. During all our life together, Allan's and mine, he had spared me, had kept me wrapped in the white cloak of an unblemished loyalty. But it would have been kinder, I now bitterly thought, if, like many husbands, he had years ago found for the story he now poured forth some clandestine listener; I should not have known. But he was faithful and good, and so he waited till I, mute and chained, was there to hear him. So well did I know him, as I thought, so thoroughly had he once been mine, that I saw it in his eyes, heard it in his voice, before the words came. And yet, when it came, it lashed me with the whips of an unbearable humiliation. For I, his wife, had not known how greatly he could love.

And that Theresa, soft little traitor, should, in her still way, have cared too! Where was the iron in her, I moaned within my stricken spirit, where the steadfastness? From the moment he bade her, she turned her soft little petals up to him—and my last delusion was spent. It was intolerable; and none the less so that in another moment she had, prompted by some belated thought of me, renounced him. Allan was hers, yet she put him from her; and it was my part to watch them both.

Then in the anguish of it all I remembered, awkward, untutored spirit that I was, that I now had the Great Recourse. Whatever human things were unbearable, I had no need to bear. I ceased, therefore, to make the effort that kept me with them. The pitiless poignancy was dulled, the sounds and the light ceased, the lovers faded from me, and again I was mercifully drawn into the dim, infinite spaces.

There followed a period whose length I cannot measure and during which I was able to make no progress in the difficult, dizzying experience of release. "Earth-bound" my jealousy relentlessly kept me. Though my two dear ones had forsworn each other, I could not trust them, for theirs seemed to me an affectation of a more than mortal magnanimity. Without a ghostly sentinel to prick them with sharp fears and recollections, who could believe that they would keep to it? Of the efficacy of my own vigilance, so long as I might choose to exercise it, I could have no doubt, for I had by this time come to have a dreadful exultation in the new power that lived in me. Repeated delicate experiment had taught me how a touch or a breath, a wish or a whisper, could control Allan's acts, could keep him from Theresa. I could manifest myself as palely, as transiently, as a thought. I could produce the merest necessary flicker, like the shadow of a just-opened leaf, on his trembling, tortured consciousness. And these unrealized perceptions of me he interpreted, as I had known that he would, as his soul's inevitable penance. He had come to believe that he had done evil in silently loving Theresa all these years, and it was my vengeance to allow him to believe this, to prod him ever to believe it afresh.

I am conscious that this frame of mind was not continuous in me. For I remember, too, that when Allan and Theresa were safely apart and sufficiently miserable I loved them as dearly as I ever had, more dearly perhaps. For it was impossible that I should not perceive, in my new emancipation, that they were, each of them, something more and greater than the two beings I had once ignorantly pictured them. For years they had practised a selflessness of which I could once scarcely have conceived, and which even now I could only admire without entering into its mystery. While I had lived solely for myself, these two divine creatures had lived exquisitely for me. They had granted me everything, themselves nothing. For my undeserving sake their lives had been a constant torment of renunciation—a torment they had not sought to alleviate by the exchange of a single glance of understanding. There were even marvellous moments when, from the depths of my newly informed heart, I pitied them:—poor creatures, who, withheld from the infinite solaces that I had come to know, were still utterly within that

Shell of sense
So frail, so piteously contrived for pain.

Within it, yes; yet exercising qualities that so sublimely transcended it. Yet the shy, hesitating compassion that thus had birth in me was far from being able to defeat the earlier, earthlier emotion. The two, I recognized, were in a sort of conflict; and I, regarding it, assumed that the conflict would never end; that for years, as Allan and Theresa reckoned time, I should be obliged to withhold myself from the great spaces and linger suffering, grudging, shamed, where they lingered.

It can never have been explained, I suppose, what, to devitalized perception such as mine, the contact of mortal beings with each other appears to be. Once to have exercised this sense-freed perception is to realize that the gift of prophecy, although the subject of such frequent marvel, is no longer mysterious. The merest glance of our sensitive and uncloyed vision can detect the strength of the relation between two beings, and therefore instantly calculate its duration. If you see a heavy weight suspended from a slender string, you can know, without any wizardry, that in a few moments the string will snap; well, such, if you admit the analogy, is prophecy, is foreknowledge. And it was thus that I saw it with Theresa and Allan. For it was perfectly visible to me that they would very little longer have the strength to preserve, near each other, the denuded impersonal relation that they, and that I, behind them, insisted on; and that they would have to separate. It was my sister, perhaps the more sensitive, who first realized this. It had now become possible for me to observe them almost constantly, the effort necessary to visit them had so greatly diminished; so that I watched her, poor, anguished girl, prepare to leave him. I saw each reluctant movement that she made. I saw her eyes, worn from self-searching; I heard her step grown timid from inexplicable fears; I entered her very heart and heard its pitiful, wild beating. And still I did not interfere.

For at this time I had a wonderful, almost demoniacal sense of disposing of matters to suit my own selfish will. At any moment I could have checked their miseries, could have restored happiness and peace. Yet it gave me, and I could weep to admit it, a monstrous joy to know that Theresa thought she was leaving Allan of her own free intention, when it was I who was contriving, arranging, insisting. . . . And yet she wretchedly felt my presence near her; I am certain of that.

A few days before the time of her intended departure my sister told Allan that she must speak with him after dinner. Our beautiful old house branched out from a circular hall with great arched doors at either end; and it was through the rear doorway that always in summer, after dinner, we passed out into the garden adjoining. As usual, therefore, when the hour came, Theresa led the way. That dreadful daytime brilliance that in my present state I found so hard to endure was now becoming softer. A delicate, capricious twilight breeze danced inconsequently through languidly whispering leaves. Lovely pale flowers blossomed like little moons in the dusk, and over them the breath of mignonette hung heavily. It was a perfect place—and it had so long been ours, Allan's and mine. It made me restless and a little wicked that those two should be there together now.

For a little they walked about together, speaking of common, daily things. Then suddenly Theresa burst out:

"I am going away, Allan. I have stayed to do everything that needed to be done. Now your mother will be here to care for you, and it is time for me to go."

He stared at her and stood still. Theresa had been there so long, she so definitely, to his mind, belonged there. And she was, as I also had jealously known, so lovely there, the small, dark, dainty creature, in the old hall, on the wide staircases, in the garden. . . . Life there without Theresa, even the intentionally remote, the perpetually renounced Theresa—he had not dreamed of it, he could not, so suddenly, conceive of it.

"Sit here," he said, and drew her down beside him on a bench, "and tell me what it means, why you are going. Is it because of something that I have been—have done?"

She hesitated. I wondered if she would dare tell him. She looked out and away from him, and he waited long for her to speak.

The pale stars were sliding into their places. The whispering of the leaves was almost hushed. All about them it was still and shadowy and sweet. It was that wonderful moment when, for lack of a visible horizon, the not yet darkened world seems infinitely greater—a moment when anything can happen, anything be believed in. To me, watching, listening, hovering, there came a dreadful purpose and a dreadful courage. Suppose, for one moment, Theresa should not only feel, but *see* me—would she dare to tell him then?

There came a brief space of terrible effort, all my fluttering, uncertain forces strained to the utmost. The instant of my struggle was endlessly long and the transition seemed to take place outside me—as one sitting in a train, motionless, sees the leagues of earth float by. And then, in a bright, terrible flash I knew I had achieved it—I had *attained visibility*. Shuddering, insubstantial, but luminously apparent, I stood there before them. And for the instant that I maintained the visible state I looked straight into Theresa's soul.

She gave a cry. And then, thing of silly, cruel impulses that I was, I saw what I had done. The very thing that I wished to avert I had precipitated. For Allan, in his sudden terror and pity, had bent and caught her in his arms. For the first time they were together; and it was I who had brought them.

Then, to his whispered urging to tell the reason of her cry, Theresa said:

"Frances was here. You did not see her, standing there, under the lilacs, with no smile on her face?"

"My dear, my dear!" was all that Allan said. I had so long now lived invisibly with them, he knew that she was right.

"I suppose you know what it means?" she asked him, calmly.

"Dear Theresa," Allan said, slowly, "if you and I should go away somewhere, could we not evade all this ghostliness? And will you come with me?"

"Distance would not banish her," my sister confidently asserted. And then she said, softly: "Have you thought what a lonely, awesome thing it must be to be so newly dead? Pity her, Allan. We who are warm and alive should pity her. She loves you still,—that is the meaning of it all, you know—and she wants us to understand that for that reason we must keep apart. Oh, it was so plain in her white face as she stood there. And you did not see her?"

"It was your face that I saw," Allan solemnly told her—oh, how different he had grown from the Allan that I had known!— "and yours is the only face that I shall ever see." And again he drew her to him.

She sprang from him. "You are defying her, Allan!" she cried. "And you must not. It is her right to keep us apart, if she wishes. It must be as she insists. I shall go, as I told you. And, Allan, I beg of you, leave me the courage to do as she demands!"

They stood facing each other in the deep dusk, and the wounds that I had dealt them gaped red and accusing. "We must pity her," Theresa had said. And as I remembered that extraordinary speech, and saw the agony in her face, and the greater agony in Allan's, there came the great irreparable cleavage between mortality and me. In a swift, merciful flame the last of my mortal emotions—gross and tenacious they must have been—was consumed. My cold grasp of Allan loosened and a new unearthly love of him bloomed in my heart.

I was now, however, in a difficulty with which my experience in the newer state was scarcely sufficient to deal. How could I make it plain to Allan and Theresa that I wished to bring them together, to heal the wounds that I had made?

Pityingly, remorsefully, I lingered near them all that night and the next day. And by that time I had brought myself to the point of a great determination. In the little time that was left, before Theresa should be gone and Allan bereft and desolate, I saw the one way that lay open to me to convince them of my acquiescence in their destiny.

In the deepest darkness and silence of the next night I made a greater effort than it will ever be necessary for me to make again. When they think of me, Allan and Theresa, I pray now that they will recall what I did that night, and that my thousand frustrations and selfishnesses may shrivel and be blown from their indulgent memories.

Yet the following morning, as she had planned, Theresa appeared at breakfast dressed for her journey. Above in her room there were the sounds of departure. They spoke little during the brief meal, but when it was ended Allan said:

"Theresa, there is half an hour before you go. Will you come up-stairs with me? I had a dream that I must tell you of."

"Allan!" She looked at him, frightened, but went with him. "It was of Frances you dreamed," she said, quietly, as they entered the library together.

"Did I say it was a dream? But I was awake—thoroughly awake. I had not been sleeping well, and I heard, twice, the striking of the clock. And as I lay there, looking out at the stars, and thinking—thinking of you, Theresa,—she came to me, stood there before me, in my room. It was no sheeted spectre, you understand; it was Frances, literally she. In some inexplicable fashion I seemed to be aware that she wanted to make me know something, and I waited, watching her face. After a few moments it came. She did not speak, precisely. That is, I am sure I heard no sound. Yet the words that came from her were definite enough. She said: 'Don't let Theresa leave you. Take her and keep her.' Then she went away. Was that a dream?"

"I had not meant to tell you," Theresa eagerly answered, "but now I must. It is too wonderful. What time did your clock strike, Allan?"

"One, the last time."

"Yes; it was then that I awoke. And she had been with me. I had not seen her, but her arm had been about me and her kiss was on my cheek. Oh, I knew; it was unmistakable. And the sound of her voice was with me."

"Then she bade you, too—"

"Yes, to stay with you. I am glad we told each other." She smiled tearfully and began to fasten her wrap.

"But you are not going—*now*!" Allan cried. "You know that you cannot, now that she has asked you to stay."

"Then you believe, as I do, that it was she?" Theresa demanded.

"I can never understand, but I know," he answered her. "And now you will not go?"

I am freed. There will be no further semblance of me in my old home, no sound of my voice, no dimmest echo of my earthly self. They have no further need of me, the two that I have brought together. Theirs is the fullest joy that the dwellers in the shell of sense can know. Mine is the transcendent joy of the unseen spaces.

1908

HENRY JAMES

(1843–1916)

The Jolly Corner

"Every one asks me what I 'think' of everything," said Spencer Brydon; "and I make answer as I can—begging or dodging the question, putting them off with any nonsense. It wouldn't matter to any of them really," he went on, "for, even were it possible to meet in that stand-and-deliver way so silly a demand on so big a subject, my 'thoughts' would still be almost altogether about something that concerns only myself." He was talking to Miss Staverton, with whom for a couple of months now he had availed himself of every possible occasion to talk; this disposition and this resource, this comfort and support, as the situation in fact presented itself, having promptly enough taken the first place in the considerable array of rather unattenuated surprises attending his so strangely belated return to America. Everything was somehow a surprise; and that might be natural when one had so long and so consistently neglected everything, taken pains to give surprises so much margin for play. He had given them more than thirty years—thirty-three, to be exact; and they now seemed to him to have organised their performance quite on the scale of that licence. He had been twenty-three on leaving New York—he was fifty-six to-day: unless indeed he were to reckon as he had sometimes, since his repatriation, found himself feeling; in which case he would have lived longer than is often allotted to man. It would have taken a century, he repeatedly said to himself, and said also to Alice Staverton, it would have taken a longer absence and a more averted mind than those even of which he had been guilty, to pile up the differences, the newnesses, the queernesses, above all the bignesses, for the better or the worse, that at present assaulted his vision wherever he looked.

The great fact all the while however had been the incalculability; since he *had* supposed himself, from decade to decade, to be allowing, and in the most liberal and intelligent manner, for brilliancy of change. He actually saw that he had allowed for nothing; he missed what he would have been sure of finding, he found what he would never have imagined. Proportions and values were upside-down; the ugly things he had expected, the ugly things of his far-away youth, when he had too promptly waked up to a sense of the ugly—these uncanny phenomena placed him rather, as it happened, under the charm; whereas the "swagger" things, the modern, the monstrous, the famous things, those he had more particularly, like thousands of ingenuous enquirers every year, come over to see, were exactly his sources of dismay. They were as so many set traps for displeasure, above all for reaction, of which his restless tread was constantly pressing the spring. It was interesting, doubtless, the whole show, but it would have been too disconcerting hadn't a certain finer truth saved the situation. He had distinctly not, in this steadier light, come over *all* for the monstrosities; he had come, not only in the last analysis but quite on the face of the act, under an impulse with which they had nothing to do. He had come—putting the thing pompously— to look at his "property," which he had thus for a third of a century not been within four thousand miles of; or, expressing it less sordidly, he had yielded to the humour of seeing again his house on the jolly corner, as he usually, and quite fondly, described it—the one in which he had first seen the light, in which various members of his family had lived and had died, in which the holidays of his overschooled boyhood had been passed and the few social flowers of his chilled adolescence gathered, and which, alienated then for so long a period, had, through the successive deaths of his two brothers and the termination of old arrangements, come wholly into his hands. He was the owner of another, not quite so "good"—the jolly corner having been, from far back, superlatively extended and consecrated; and the value of the pair represented his main capital, with an income consisting, in these later years, of their respective rents which (thanks precisely to their original excellent type) had never been depressingly low. He could live in "Europe," as he had been in the habit of living, on the product of these flourishing New York leases, and all the better since, that of the second structure, the mere number in its long row, having within a twelvemonth fallen in, renovation at a high advance had proved beautifully possible.

These were items of property indeed, but he had found himself since his arrival distinguishing more than ever between them. The house within the street, two bristling blocks westward, was already in course of reconstruction as a tall mass of flats; he had acceded, some time before, to overtures for this conversion—in which, now that it was going forward, it had been not the least of his astonishments to find himself able, on the spot, and though without a previous ounce of such experience, to participate with a certain intelligence, almost with a certain authority. He had lived his life with his back so turned to such concerns and his face addressed to those of so different an order that he scarce knew what to make of this lively stir, in a compartment of his mind never yet penetrated, of a capacity for business and a sense for construction. These virtues, so common all round him now, had been dormant in his own organism—where it might be said of them perhaps that they had slept the sleep of the just. At present, in the splendid autumn weather—the autumn at least was a pure boon in the terrible place—he loafed about his "work" undeterred, secretly agitated; not in the least "minding" that the whole proposition, as they said, was vulgar and sordid, and ready to climb ladders, to walk the plank, to handle materials and look wise about them, to ask questions, in fine, and challenge explanations and really "go into" figures.

It amused, it verily quite charmed him; and, by the same stroke, it amused, and even more, Alice Staverton, though perhaps charming her perceptibly less. She wasn't however going to be better-off for it, as *he* was—and so astonishingly much: nothing was now likely, he knew, ever to make her better-off than she found herself, in the afternoon of life, as the delicately frugal possessor and tenant of the small house in Irving Place to which she had subtly managed to cling through her almost unbroken New York career. If he knew the way to it now better than to any other address among the dreadful multiplied numberings which seemed to him to reduce the whole place to some vast ledger-page, overgrown, fantastic, of ruled and criss-crossed lines and figures—if he had formed, for his consolation, that habit, it was really not a little because of the charm of his having encountered and recognised, in the vast wilderness of the wholesale, breaking through the mere gross generalisation of wealth and force and success, a small still scene where items and shades, all delicate things, kept the sharpness of the notes of a high voice perfectly trained, and where economy hung about like the scent of a garden. His old friend lived with one maid and herself dusted her relics and trimmed her lamps and polished her silver; she stood off, in the awful modern crush, when she could, but she sallied forth and did battle when the challenge was really to "spirit," the spirit she after all confessed to, proudly and a little shyly, as to that of the better time, that of *their* common, their quite far-away and antediluvian social period and order. She made use of the street-cars when need be, the terrible things that people scrambled for as the panic-stricken at sea scramble for the boats; she affronted, inscrutably, under stress, all the public concussions and ordeals; and yet, with that slim mystifying grace of her appearance, which defied you to say if she were a fair young woman who looked older through trouble, or a fine smooth older one who looked young through successful indifference; with her precious reference, above all, to memories and histories into which he could enter, she was as exquisite for him as some pale pressed flower (a rarity to begin with), and, failing other sweetnesses, she was a sufficient reward of his effort. They had communities of knowledge, "their" knowledge (this discriminating possessive was always on her lips) of presences of the other age, presences all overlaid, in his case, by the experience of a man and the freedom of a wanderer, overlaid by pleasure, by infidelity, by passages of life that were strange and dim to her, just by "Europe" in short, but still unobscured, still exposed and cherished, under that pious visitation of the spirit from which she had never been diverted.

She had come with him one day to see how his "apartment-house" was rising; he had helped her over gaps and explained to her plans, and while they were there had happened to have, before her, a brief but lively discussion with the man in charge, the representative of the building-firm that had undertaken his work. He had found himself quite "standing-up" to this personage over a failure on the latter's part to observe some detail of one of their noted conditions, and had so lucidly argued his case that, besides ever so prettily flushing, at the time, for sympathy in his triumph, she had afterwards said to him (though to a slightly greater effect of irony) that he had clearly for too many years neglected a real gift. If he had but stayed at home he would have anticipated the inventor of the sky-scraper. If he had but stayed at home he would have discovered his genius in time really to start some new variety of awful architectural hare and run it till it burrowed in a goldmine. He was to remember these words, while the weeks elapsed, for the small silver ring they had sounded over the queerest and deepest of his own lately most disguised and most muffled vibrations.

It had begun to be present to him after the first fortnight, it had broken out with the oddest abruptness, this particular wanton wonderment: it met him there—and this was the image under which he himself judged the matter, or at least, not a little, thrilled and flushed with it—very much as he might have been met by some strange figure, some unexpected occupant, at a turn of one of the dim passages of an empty house. The quaint analogy quite hauntingly remained with him, when he didn't indeed rather improve it by a still intenser form: that of his opening a door behind which he would have made sure of finding nothing, a door into a room shuttered and void, and yet so coming, with a great suppressed start, on some quite erect confronting presence, something planted in the middle of the place and facing him through the dusk. After that visit to the house in construction he walked with his companion to see the other and always so much the better one, which in the eastward direction formed one of the corners, the "jolly" one precisely, of the street now so generally dishonoured and disfigured in its westward reaches, and of the comparatively conservative Avenue. The Avenue still had pretensions, as Miss Staverton said, to decency; the old people had mostly gone, the old names were unknown, and here and there an old association seemed to stray, all vaguely, like some very aged person, out too late, whom you might meet and feel the impulse to watch or follow, in kindness, for safe restoration to shelter.

They went in together, our friends; he admitted himself with his key, as he kept no one there, he explained, preferring, for his reasons, to leave the place empty, under a simple arrangement with a good woman living in the neighbourhood and who came for a daily hour to open windows and dust and sweep. Spencer Brydon had his reasons and was growingly aware of them; they seemed to him better each time he was there, though he didn't name them all to his companion, any more than he told her as yet how often, how quite absurdly often, he himself came. He only let her see for the present, while they walked through the great blank rooms, that absolute vacancy reigned and that, from top to bottom, there was nothing but Mrs. Muldoon's broomstick, in a corner, to tempt the burglar. Mrs. Muldoon was then on the premises, and she loquaciously attended the visitors, preceding them from room to room and pushing back shutters and throwing up sashes—all to show them, as she remarked, how little there was to see. There was little indeed to see in the great gaunt shell where the main dispositions and the general apportionment of space, the style of an age of ampler allowances, had nevertheless for its master their honest pleading message, affecting him as some good old servant's, some lifelong retainer's appeal for a character, or even for a retiring-pension; yet it was also a remark of Mrs. Muldoon's that, glad as she was to oblige him by her noonday round, there was a request she greatly hoped he would never make of her. If he should wish her for any reason to come in after dark she would just tell him, if he "plased," that he must ask it of somebody else.

The fact that there was nothing to see didn't militate for the worthy woman against what one *might* see, and she put it frankly to Miss Staverton that no lady could be expected to like, could she? "craping up to thim top storeys in the ayvil hours." The gas and the electric light were off the house, and she fairly evoked a gruesome vision of her march through the great grey rooms—so many of them as there were too!—with her glimmering taper. Miss Staverton met her honest glare with a smile and the profession that she herself certainly would recoil from such an adventure. Spencer Brydon meanwhile held his peace —for the moment; the question of the "evil" hours in his old home had already become too grave for him. He had begun some time since to "crape," and he knew just why a packet of candles addressed to that pursuit had been stowed by his own hand, three weeks before, at the back of a drawer of the fine old sideboard that occupied, as a "fixture," the deep recess in the dining-room. Just now he laughed at his companions—quickly however changing the subject; for the reason that, in the first place, his laugh struck him even at that moment as starting the odd echo, the conscious human resonance (he scarce knew how to qualify it) that sounds made while he was there alone sent back to his ear or his fancy; and that, in the second, he imagined Alice Staverton for the instant on the point of asking him, with a divination, if he ever so prowled. There were divinations he was unprepared for, and he had at all events averted enquiry by the time Mrs. Muldoon had left them, passing on to other parts.

There was happily enough to say, on so consecrated a spot, that could be said freely and fairly; so that a whole train of declarations was precipitated by his friend's having herself broken out, after a yearning look round: "But I hope you don't mean they want you to pull *this* to pieces!" His answer came, promptly, with his re-awakened wrath: it was of course exactly what they wanted, and what they were "at" him for, daily, with the iteration of people who couldn't for their life understand a man's liability to decent feelings. He had found the place, just as it stood and beyond what he could express, an interest and a joy. There were values other than the beastly rent-values, and in short, in short—! But it was thus Miss Staverton took him up. "In short you're to make so good a thing of your sky-scraper that, living in luxury on *those* ill-gotten gains, you can afford for a while to be sentimental here!" Her smile had for him, with the words, the particular mild irony with which he found half her talk suffused; an irony without bitterness and that came, exactly, from her having so much imagination—not, like the cheap sarcasms with which one heard most people, about the world of "society," bid for the reputation of cleverness, from nobody's really having any. It was agreeable to him at this very moment to be sure that when he had answered, after a brief demur, "Well yes: so, precisely, you may put it!" her imagination would still do him justice. He explained that even if never a dollar were to come to him from the other house he would nevertheless cherish this one; and he dwelt, further, while they lingered and wandered, on the fact of the stupefaction he was already exciting, the positive mystification he felt himself create.

He spoke of the value of all he read into it, into the mere sight of the walls, mere shapes of the rooms, mere sound of the floors, mere feel, in his hand, of the old silver-plated knobs of the several mahogany doors, which suggested the pressure of the palms of the dead; the seventy years of the past in fine that these things represented, the annals of nearly three generations, counting his grandfather's, the one that had ended there, and the impalpable ashes of his long-extinct youth, afloat in the very air like microscopic motes. She listened to everything; she was a woman who answered intimately but who utterly didn't chatter. She scattered abroad therefore no cloud of words; she could assent, she could agree, above all she could encourage, without doing that. Only at the last she went a little further than he had done himself. "And then how do you know? You may still, after all, want to live here." It rather indeed pulled him up, for it wasn't what he had been thinking, at least in her sense of the words. "You mean I may decide to stay on for the sake of it?"

"Well, *with* such a home—!" But, quite beautifully, she had too much tact to dot so monstrous an *i*, and it was precisely an illustration of the way she didn't rattle. How could any one—of any wit—insist on any one else's "wanting" to live in New York?

"Oh," he said, "I *might* have lived here (since I had my opportunity early in life); I might have put in here all these years. Then everything would have been different enough—and, I dare say, 'funny' enough. But that's another matter. And then the beauty of it—I mean of my perversity, of my refusal to agree to a 'deal'—is just in the total absence of a reason. Don't you see that if I had a reason about the matter at all it would *have* to be the other way, and would then be inevitably a reason of dollars? There are no reasons here *but* of dollars. Let us therefore have none whatever—not the ghost of one."

They were back in the hall then for departure, but from where they stood the vista was large, through an open door, into the great square main saloon, with its almost antique felicity of brave spaces between windows. Her eyes came back from that reach and met his own a moment. "Are you very sure the 'ghost' of one doesn't, much rather, serve—?"

He had a positive sense of turning pale. But it was as near as they were then to come. For he made answer, he believed, between a glare and a grin: "Oh ghosts—of course the place must swarm with them! I should be ashamed of it if it didn't. Poor Mrs. Muldoon's right, and it's why I haven't asked her to do more than look in."

Miss Staverton's gaze again lost itself, and things she didn't utter, it was clear, came and went in her mind. She might even for the minute, off there in the fine room, have imagined some element dimly gathering. Simplified like the death-mask of a handsome face, it perhaps produced for her just then an effect akin to the stir of an expression in the "set" commemorative plaster. Yet whatever her impression may have been she produced instead a vague platitude. "Well, if it were only furnished and lived in—!"

She appeared to imply that in case of its being still furnished he might have been a little less opposed to the idea of a return. But she passed straight into the vestibule, as if to leave her words behind her, and the next moment he had opened the house-door and was standing with her on the steps. He closed the door and, while he re-pocketed his key, looking up and down, they took in the comparatively harsh actuality of the Avenue, which reminded him of the assault of the outer light of the Desert on the traveller emerging from an Egyptian tomb. But he risked before they stepped into the street his gathered answer to her speech. "For me it *is* lived in. For me it *is* furnished." At which it was easy for her to sigh "Ah yes—!" all vaguely and discreetly; since his parents and his favourite sister, to say nothing of other kin, in numbers, had run their course and met their end there. That represented, within the walls, ineffaceable life.

It was a few days after this that, during an hour passed with her again, he had expressed his impatience of the too flattering curiosity—among the people he met—about his appreciation of New York. He had arrived at none at all that was socially producible, and as for that matter of his "thinking" (thinking the better or the worse of anything there) he was wholly taken up with one subject of thought. It was mere vain egoism, and it was moreover, if she liked, a morbid obsession. He found all things come back to the question of what he personally might have been, how he might have led his life and "turned out," if he had not so, at the outset, given it up. And confessing for the first time to the intensity within him of this absurd speculation —which but proved also, no doubt, the habit of too selfishly thinking—he affirmed the impotence there of any other source of interest, any other native appeal. "What would it have made of me, what would it have made of me? I keep for ever wondering, all idiotically; as if I could possibly know! I see what it has made of dozens of others, those I meet, and it positively aches within me, to the point of exasperation, that it would have made something of me as well. Only I can't make out *what*, and the worry of it, the small rage of curiosity never to be satisfied, brings back what I remember to have felt, once or twice, after judging best, for reasons, to burn some important letter unopened. I've been sorry, I've hated it—I've never known what was in the letter. You may of course say it's a trifle—!"

"I don't say it's a trifle," Miss Staverton gravely interrupted.

She was seated by her fire, and before her, on his feet and restless, he turned to and fro between this intensity of his idea and a fitful and unseeing inspection, through his single eyeglass, of the dear little old objects on her chimney-piece. Her interruption made him for an instant look at her harder. "I shouldn't care if you did!" he laughed, however; "and it's only a figure, at any rate, for the way I now feel. *Not* to have followed my perverse young course—and almost in the teeth of my father's curse, as I may say; not to have kept it up, so, 'over there,' from that day to this, without a doubt or a pang; not, above all, to have liked it, to have loved it, so much, loved it, no doubt, with such an abysmal conceit of my own preference: some variation from *that*, I say, must have produced some different effect for my life and for my 'form.' I should have stuck here—if it had been possible; and I was too young, at twenty-three, to judge, *pour deux sous*, whether it *were* possible. If I had waited I might have seen it was, and then I might have been, by staying here, something nearer to one of these types who have been hammered so hard and made so keen by their conditions. It isn't that I admire them so much—the question of any charm in them, or of any charm, beyond that of the rank money-passion, exerted by their conditions *for* them, has nothing to do with the matter: it's only a question of what fantastic, yet perfectly possible, development of my own nature I mayn't have missed. It comes over me that I had then a strange *alter ego* deep down somewhere within me, as the full-blown flower is in the small tight bud, and that I just took the course, I just transferred him to the climate, that blighted him for once and for ever."

"And you wonder about the flower," Miss Staverton said. "So do I, if you want to know; and so I've been wondering these several weeks. I believe in the flower," she continued, "I feel it would have been quite splendid, quite huge and monstrous."

"Monstrous above all!" her visitor echoed; "and I imagine, by the same stroke, quite hideous and offensive."

"You don't believe that," she returned; "if you did you wouldn't wonder. You'd know, and that would be enough for you. What you feel—and what I feel *for* you—is that you'd have had power."

"You'd have liked me that way?" he asked.

She barely hung fire. "How should I not have liked you?"

"I see. You'd have liked me, have preferred me, a billionaire!"

"How should I not have liked you?" she simply again asked.

He stood before her still—her question kept him motionless. He took it in, so much there was of it; and indeed his not otherwise meeting it testified to that. "I know at least what I am," he simply went on; "the other side of the medal's clear enough. I've not been edifying—I believe I'm thought in a hundred quarters to have been barely decent. I've followed strange paths and worshipped strange gods; it must have come to you again and again—in fact you've admitted to me as much —that I was leading, at any time these thirty years, a selfish frivolous scandalous life. And you see what it has made of me."

She just waited, smiling at him. "You see what it has made of *me*."

"Oh you're a person whom nothing can have altered. You were born to be what you are, anywhere, anyway: you've the perfection nothing else could have blighted. And don't you see how, without my exile, I shouldn't have been waiting till now—?" But he pulled up for the strange pang.

"The great thing to see," she presently said, "seems to me to be that it has spoiled nothing. It hasn't spoiled your being here at last. It hasn't spoiled this. It hasn't spoiled your speaking—" She also however faltered.

He wondered at everything her controlled emotion might mean. "Do you believe then—too dreadfully!—that I *am* as good as I might ever have been?"

"Oh no! Far from it!" With which she got up from her chair and was nearer to him. "But I don't care," she smiled.

"You mean I'm good enough?"

She considered a little. "Will you believe it if I say so? I mean will you let that settle your question for you?" And then as if making out in his face that he drew back from this, that he had some idea which, however absurd, he couldn't yet bargain away: "Oh you don't care either—but very differently: you don't care for anything but yourself."

Spencer Brydon recognised it—it was in fact what he had absolutely professed. Yet he importantly qualified. "*He* isn't myself. He's the just so totally other person. But I do want to see him," he added. "And I can. And I shall."

Their eyes met for a minute while he guessed from something in hers that she divined his strange sense. But neither of them otherwise expressed it, and her apparent understanding, with no protesting shock, no easy derision, touched him more deeply than anything yet, constituting for his stifled perversity, on the spot, an element that was like breatheable air. What she said however was unexpected. "Well, *I've* seen him."

"You—?"

"I've seen him in a dream."

"Oh a 'dream'—!" It let him down.

"But twice over," she continued. "I saw him as I see you now."

"You've dreamed the same dream-—?"

"Twice over," she repeated. "The very same."

This did somehow a little speak to him, as it also gratified him. "You dream about me at that rate?"

"Ah about *him*!" she smiled.

His eyes again sounded her. "Then you know all about him." And as she said nothing more: "What's the wretch like?"

She hesitated, and it was as if he were pressing her so hard that, resisting for reasons of her own, she had to turn away. "I'll tell you some other time!"

II

It was after this that there was most of a virtue for him, most of a cultivated charm, most of a preposterous secret thrill, in the particular form of surrender to his obsession and of address to what he more and more believed to be his privilege. It was what in these weeks he was living for—since he really felt life to begin but after Mrs. Muldoon had retired from the scene and, visiting the ample house from attic to cellar, making sure he was alone, he knew himself in safe possession and, as he tacitly expressed it, let himself go. He sometimes came twice in the twenty-four hours; the moments he liked best were those of gathering dusk, of the short autumn twilight; this was the time of which, again and again, he found himself hoping most. Then he could, as seemed to him, most intimately wander and wait, linger and listen, feel his fine attention, never in his life before so fine, on the pulse of the great vague place: he pre-ferred the lampless hour and only wished he might have pro-longed each day the deep crepuscular spell. Later—rarely much before midnight, but then for a considerable vigil—he watched with his glimmering light; moving slowly, holding it high, playing it far, rejoicing above all, as much as he might, in open vistas, reaches of communication between rooms and by pas-sages; the long straight chance or show, as he would have called it, for the revelation he pretended to invite. It was a practice he found he could perfectly "work" without exciting remark; no one was in the least the wiser for it; even Alice Staverton, who was moreover a well of discretion, didn't quite fully imagine.

He let himself in and let himself out with the assurance of calm proprietorship; and accident so far favoured him that, if a fat Avenue "officer" had happened on occasion to see him en-tering at eleven-thirty, he had never yet, to the best of his be-lief, been noticed as emerging at two. He walked there on the crisp November nights, arrived regularly at the evening's end; it was as easy to do this after dining out as to take his way to a club or to his hotel. When he left his club, if he hadn't been dining out, it was ostensibly to go to his hotel; and when he left his hotel, if he had spent a part of the evening there, it was ostensibly to go to his club. Everything was easy in fine; every-thing conspired and promoted: there was truly even in the strain of his experience something that glossed over, something that salved and simplified, all the rest of consciousness. He circulated, talked, renewed, loosely and pleasantly, old relations—met indeed, so far as he could, new expectations and seemed to make out on the whole that in spite of the career, of such different contacts, which he had spoken of to Miss Staverton as ministering so little, for those who might have watched it, to edification, he was positively rather liked than not. He was a dim secondary social success—and all with people who had truly not an idea of him. It was all mere surface sound, this murmur of their welcome, this popping of their corks—just as his gestures of response were the extravagant shadows, emphatic in proportion as they meant little, of some game of *ombres chinoises*. He projected himself all day, in thought, straight over the bristling line of hard unconscious heads and into the other, the real, the waiting life; the life that, as soon as he had heard behind him the click of his great house-door, began for him, on the jolly corner, as beguilingly as the slow opening bars of some rich music follows the tap of the conductor's wand.

He always caught the first effect of the steel point of his stick on the old marble of the hall pavement, large black-and-white squares that he remembered as the admiration of his childhood and that had then made in him, as he now saw, for the growth of an early conception of style. This effect was the dim reverberating tinkle as of some far-off bell hung who should say where?—in the depths of the house, of the past, of that mystical other world that might have flourished for him had he not, for weal or woe, abandoned it. On this impression he did ever the same thing; he put his stick noiselessly away in a corner—feeling the place once more in the likeness of some great glass bowl, all precious concave crystal, set delicately humming by the play of a moist finger round its edge. The concave crystal held, as it were, this mystical other world, and the indescribably fine murmur of its rim was the sigh there, the scarce audible pathetic wail to his strained ear, of all the old baffled forsworn possibilities. What he did therefore by this appeal of his hushed presence was to wake them into such measure of ghostly life as they might still enjoy. They were shy, all but unappeasably shy, but they weren't really sinister; at least they weren't as he had hitherto felt them—before they had taken the Form he so yearned to make them take, the Form he at moments saw himself in the light of fairly hunting on tiptoe, the points of his evening-shoes, from room to room and from storey to storey.

That was the essence of his vision—which was all rank folly, if one would, while he was out of the house and otherwise occupied, but which took on the last verisimilitude as soon as he was placed and posted. He knew what he meant and what he wanted; it was as clear as the figure on a cheque presented in demand for cash. His *alter ego* "walked"—that was the note of his image of him, while his image of his motive for his own odd pastime was the desire to waylay him and meet him. He roamed, slowly, warily, but all restlessly, he himself did—Mrs. Muldoon had been right, absolutely, with her figure of their "craping"; and the presence he watched for would roam restlessly too. But it would be as cautious and as shifty; the conviction of its probable, in fact its already quite sensible, quite audible evasion of pursuit grew for him from night to night, laying on him finally a rigour to which nothing in his life had been comparable. It had been the theory of many superficially-judging persons, he knew, that he was wasting that life in a surrender to sensations, but he had tasted of no pleasure so fine as his actual tension, had been introduced to no sport that demanded at once the patience and the nerve of this stalking of a creature more subtle, yet at bay perhaps more formidable, than any beast of the forest. The terms, the comparisons, the very practices of the chase positively came again into play; there were even moments when passages of his occasional experience as a sportsman, stirred memories, from his younger time, of moor and mountain and desert, revived for him—and to the increase of his keenness—by the tremendous force of analogy. He found himself at moments—once he had placed his single light on some mantel-shelf or in some recess—stepping back into shelter or shade, effacing himself behind a door or in an embrasure, as he had sought of old the vantage of rock and tree; he found himself holding his breath and living in the joy of the instant, the supreme suspense created by big game alone.

He wasn't afraid (though putting himself the question as he believed gentlemen on Bengal tiger-shoots or in close quarters

with the great bear of the Rockies had been known to confess
to having put it); and this indeed—since here at least he might
be frank!—because of the impression, so intimate and so
strange, that he himself produced as yet a dread, produced certainly a strain, beyond the liveliest he was likely to feel. They
fell for him into categories, they fairly became familiar, the signs,
for his own perception, of the alarm his presence and his vigilance created; though leaving him always to remark, porten-
tously, on his probably having formed a relation, his probably
enjoying a consciousness, unique in the experience of man.
People enough, first and last, had been in terror of apparitions,
but who had ever before so turned the tables and become himself, in the apparitional world, an incalculable terror? He might
have found this sublime had he quite dared to think of it; but
he didn't too much insist, truly, on that side of his privilege.
With habit and repetition he gained to an extraordinary degree
the power to penetrate the dusk of distances and the darkness
of corners, to resolve back into their innocence the treacheries
of uncertain light, the evil-looking forms taken in the gloom
by mere shadows, by accidents of the air, by shifting effects of
perspective; putting down his dim luminary he could still wander on without it, pass into other rooms and, only knowing it
was there behind him in case of need, see his way about, visually project for his purpose a comparative clearness. It made
him feel, this acquired faculty, like some monstrous stealthy
cat; he wondered if he would have glared at these moments
with large shining yellow eyes, and what it mightn't verily be,
for the poor hard-pressed *alter ego*, to be confronted with such
a type.

He liked however the open shutters; he opened everywhere
those Mrs. Muldoon had closed, closing them as carefully afterwards, so that she shouldn't notice: he liked—oh this he did like,
and above all in the upper rooms!—the sense of the hard silver
of the autumn stars through the window-panes, and scarcely
less the flare of the street-lamps below, the white electric lustre
which it would have taken curtains to keep out. This was
human actual social; this was of the world he had lived in, and
he was more at his ease certainly for the countenance, coldly
general and impersonal, that all the while and in spite of his
detachment it seemed to give him. He had support of course

mostly in the rooms at the wide front and the prolonged side; it failed him considerably in the central shades and the parts at the back. But if he sometimes, on his rounds, was glad of his optical reach, so none the less often the rear of the house affected him as the very jungle of his prey. The place was there more subdivided; a large "extension" in particular, where small rooms for servants had been multiplied, abounded in nooks and corners, in closets and passages, in the ramifications especially of an ample back staircase over which he leaned, many a time, to look far down—not deterred from his gravity even while aware that he might, for a spectator, have figured some solemn simpleton playing at hide-and-seek. Outside in fact he might himself make that ironic *rapprochement*; but within the walls, and in spite of the clear windows, his consistency was proof against the cynical light of New York.

It had belonged to that idea of the exasperated consciousness of his victim to become a real test for him; since he had quite put it to himself from the first that, oh distinctly! he could "cultivate" his whole perception. He had felt it as above all open to cultivation—which indeed was but another name for his manner of spending his time. He was bringing it on, bringing it to perfection, by practice; in consequence of which it had grown so fine that he was now aware of impressions, attestations of his general postulate, that couldn't have broken upon him at once. This was the case more specifically with a phenomenon at last quite frequent for him in the upper rooms, the recognition—absolutely unmistakeable, and by a turn dating from a particular hour, his resumption of his campaign after a diplomatic drop, a calculated absence of three nights—of his being definitely followed, tracked at a distance carefully taken and to the express end that he should the less confidently, less arrogantly, appear to himself merely to pursue. It worried, it finally quite broke him up, for it proved, of all the conceivable impressions, the one least suited to his book. He was kept in sight while remaining himself—as regards the essence of his position—sightless, and his only recourse then was in abrupt turns, rapid recoveries of ground. He wheeled about, retracing his steps, as if he might so catch in his face at least the stirred air of some other quick revolution. It was indeed true that his fully dislocalised thought of these manœuvres recalled to him

Pantaloon, at the Christmas farce, buffeted and tricked from behind by ubiquitous Harlequin; but it left intact the influence of the conditions themselves each time he was re-exposed to them, so that in fact this association, had he suffered it to become constant, would on a certain side have but ministered to his intenser gravity. He had made, as I have said, to create on the premises the baseless sense of a reprieve, his three absences; and the result of the third was to confirm the after-effect of the second.

On his return, that night—the night succeeding his last intermission—he stood in the hall and looked up the staircase with a certainty more intimate than any he had yet known. "He's *there*, at the top, and waiting—not, as in general, falling back for disappearance. He's holding his ground, and it's the first time—which is a proof, isn't it? that something has happened for him." So Brydon argued with his hand on the banister and his foot on the lowest stair; in which position he felt as never before the air chilled by his logic. He himself turned cold in it, for he seemed of a sudden to know what now was involved. "Harder pressed?—yes, he takes it in, with its thus making clear to him that I've come, as they say, 'to stay.' He finally doesn't like and can't bear it, in the sense, I mean, that his wrath, his menaced interest, now balances with his dread. I've hunted him till he has 'turned': that, up there, is what has happened—he's the fanged or the antlered animal brought at last to bay." There came to him, as I say—but determined by an influence beyond my notation!—the acuteness of this certainty; under which however the next moment he had broken into a sweat that he would as little have consented to attribute to fear as he would have dared immediately to act upon it for enterprise. It marked none the less a prodigious thrill, a thrill that represented sudden dismay, no doubt, but also represented, and with the selfsame throb, the strangest, the most joyous, possibly the next minute almost the proudest, duplication of consciousness.

"He has been dodging, retreating, hiding, but now, worked up to anger, he'll fight!"—this intense impression made a single mouthful, as it were, of terror and applause. But what was wondrous was that the applause, for the felt fact, was so eager, since, if it was his other self he was running to earth, this ineffable identity was thus in the last resort not unworthy of him. It bristled there—somewhere near at hand, however unseen still—as the hunted thing, even as the trodden worm of the adage *must* at last bristle; and Brydon at this instant tasted probably of a sensation more complex than had ever before found itself consistent with sanity. It was as if it would have shamed him that a character so associated with his own should triumphantly succeed in just skulking, should to the end not risk the open; so that the drop of this danger was, on the spot, a great lift of the whole situation. Yet with another rare shift of the same subtlety he was already trying to measure by how much more he himself might now be in peril of fear; so rejoicing that he could, in another form, actively inspire that fear, and simultaneously quaking for the form in which he might passively know it.

The apprehension of knowing it must after a little have grown in him, and the strangest moment of his adventure perhaps, the most memorable or really most interesting, afterwards, of his crisis, was the lapse of certain instants of concentrated conscious *combat*, the sense of a need to hold on to something, even after the manner of a man slipping and slipping on some awful incline; the vivid impulse, above all, to move, to act, to charge, somehow and upon something—to show himself, in a word, that he wasn't afraid. The state of "holding-on" was thus the state to which he was momentarily reduced; if there had been anything, in the great vacancy, to seize, he would presently have been aware of having clutched it as he might under a shock at home have clutched the nearest chairback. He had been surprised at any rate—of this he *was* aware—into something unprecedented since his original appropriation of the place; he had closed his eyes, held them tight, for a long minute, as with that instinct of dismay and that terror of vision. When he opened them the room, the other contiguous rooms, extraordinarily, seemed lighter—so light, almost, that at first he took the change for day. He stood firm, however that might be, just where he had paused; his resistance had helped him—it was as if there were something he had tided over. He knew after a little what this was—it had been in the imminent danger of flight. He had stiffened his will against going; without this he would have made for the stairs, and it

seemed to him that, still with his eyes closed, he would have
descended them, would have known how, straight and swiftly,
to the bottom.

Well, as he had held out, here he was—still at the top, among
the more intricate upper rooms and with the gauntlet of the
others, of all the rest of the house, still to run when it should
be his time to go. He would go at his time—only at his time:
didn't he go every night very much at the same hour? He took
out his watch—there was light for that: it was scarcely a quarter
past one, and he had never withdrawn so soon. He reached his
lodgings for the most part at two—with his walk of a quarter
of an hour. He would wait for the last quarter—he wouldn't
stir till then; and he kept his watch there with his eyes on it, reflecting while he held it that this deliberate wait, a wait with an
effort, which he recognised, would serve perfectly for the at-
testation he desired to make. It would prove his courage—
unless indeed the latter might most be proved by his budging
at last from his place. What he mainly felt now was that, since
he hadn't originally scuttled, he had his dignities—which had
never in his life seemed so many—all to preserve and to carry
aloft. This was before him in truth as a physical image, an image almost worthy of an age of greater romance. That remark
indeed glimmered for him only to glow the next instant with a
finer light; since what age of romance, after all, could have
matched either the state of his mind or, "objectively," as they
said, the wonder of his situation? The only difference would
have been that, brandishing his dignities over his head as in a
parchment scroll, he might then—that is in the heroic time—
have proceeded downstairs with a drawn sword in his other
grasp.

At present, really, the light he had set down on the mantel of
the next room would have to figure his sword; which utensil,
in the course of a minute, he had taken the requisite number
of steps to possess himself of. The door between the rooms was
open, and from the second another door opened to a third.
These rooms, as he remembered, gave all three upon a common corridor as well, but there was a fourth, beyond them,
without issue save through the preceding. To have moved, to
have heard his step again, was appreciably a help; though even
in recognising this he lingered once more a little by the chim-

ney-piece on which his light had rested. When he next moved, just hesitating where to turn, he found himself considering a circumstance that, after his first and comparatively vague apprehension of it, produced in him the start that often attends some pang of recollection, the violent shock of having ceased happily to forget. He had come into sight of the door in which the brief chain of communication ended and which he now surveyed from the nearer threshold, the one not directly facing it. Placed at some distance to the left of this point, it would have admitted him to the last room of the four, the room without other approach or egress, had it not, to his intimate conviction, been closed *since* his former visitation, the matter probably of a quarter of an hour before. He stared with all his eyes at the wonder of the fact, arrested again where he stood and again holding his breath while he sounded its sense. Surely it had been *subsequently* closed—that is it had been on his previous passage indubitably open!

He took it full in the face that something had happened between—that he couldn't not have noticed before (by which he meant on his original tour of all the rooms that evening) that such a barrier had exceptionally presented itself. He had indeed since that moment undergone an agitation so extraordinary that it might have muddled for him any earlier view; and he tried to convince himself that he might perhaps then have gone into the room and, inadvertently, automatically, on coming out, have drawn the door after him. The difficulty was that this exactly was what he never did; it was against his whole policy, as he might have said, the essence of which was to keep vistas clear. He had them from the first, as he was well aware, quite on the brain: the strange apparition, at the far end of one of them, of his baffled "prey" (which had become by so sharp an irony so little the term now to apply!) was the form of success his imagination had most cherished, projecting into it always a refinement of beauty. He had known fifty times the start of perception that had afterwards dropped; had fifty times gasped to himself "There!" under some fond brief hallucination. The house, as the case stood, admirably lent itself; he might wonder at the taste, the native architecture of the particular time, which could rejoice so in the multiplication of doors— the opposite extreme to the modern, the actual almost complete proscription of them; but it had fairly contributed to provoke this obsession of the presence encountered telescopically, as he might say, focussed and studied in diminishing perspective and as by a rest for the elbow.

It was with these considerations that his present attention was charged—they perfectly availed to make what he saw portentous. He *couldn't*, by any lapse, have blocked that aperture; and if he hadn't, if it was unthinkable, why what else was clear but that there had been another agent? Another agent?—he had been catching, as he felt, a moment back, the very breath of him; but when had he been so close as in this simple, this logical, this completely personal act? It was so logical, that is, that one might have *taken* it for personal; yet for what did Brydon take it, he asked himself, while, softly panting, he felt his eyes almost leave their sockets. Ah this time at last they *were*, the two, the opposed projections of him, in presence; and this time, as much as one would, the question of danger loomed. With it rose, as not before, the question of courage—for what he knew the blank face of the door to say to him was "Show us how much you have!" It stared, it glared back at him with that challenge; it put to him the two alternatives: should he just push it open or not? Oh to have this consciousness was to *think*— and to think, Brydon knew, as he stood there, was, with the lapsing moments, not to have acted! Not to have acted—that was the misery and the pang—was even still not to act; was in fact *all* to feel the thing in another, in a new and terrible way. How long did he pause and how long did he debate? There was presently nothing to measure it; for his vibration had already changed—as just by the effect of its intensity. Shut up there, at bay, defiant, and with the prodigy of the thing palpably proveably *done*, thus giving notice like some stark signboard—under that accession of accent the situation itself had turned; and Brydon at last remarkably made up his mind on what it had turned to.

It had turned altogether to a different admonition; to a supreme hint, for him, of the value of Discretion! This slowly dawned, no doubt—for it could take its time; so perfectly, on his threshold, had he been stayed, so little as yet had he either advanced or retreated. It was the strangest of all things that now when, by his taking ten steps and applying his hand to a latch, or even his shoulder and his knee, if necessary, to a panel, all the hunger of his prime need might have been met, his high curiosity crowned, his unrest assuaged—it was amazing, but it was also exquisite and rare, that insistence should have, at a touch, quite dropped from him. Discretion—he jumped at that; and yet not, verily, at such a pitch, because it saved his nerves or his skin, but because, much more valuably, it saved the situation. When I say he "jumped" at it I feel the consonance of this term with the fact that—at the end indeed of I know not how long—he did move again, he crossed straight to the door. He wouldn't touch it—it seemed now that he might *if* he would: he would only just wait there a little, to show, to prove, that he wouldn't. He had thus another station, close to the thin partition by which revelation was denied him; but with his eyes bent and his hands held off in a mere intensity of stillness. He listened as if there had been something to hear, but this attitude, while it lasted, was his own communication. "If you won't then—good: I spare you and I give up. You affect me as by the appeal positively for pity: you convince me that for reasons rigid and sublime—what do I know?—we both of us should have suffered. I respect them then, and, though moved and privileged as, I believe, it has never been given to man, I retire, I renounce—never, on my honour, to try again. So rest for ever—and let *me!*"

That, for Brydon was the deep sense of this last demonstration—solemn, measured, directed, as he felt it to be. He brought it to a close, he turned away; and now verily he knew how deeply he had been stirred. He retraced his steps, taking up his candle, burnt, he observed, well-nigh to the socket, and marking again, lighten it as he would, the distinctness of his footfall; after which, in a moment, he knew himself at the other side of the house. He did here what he had not yet done at these hours—he opened half a casement, one of those in the front, and let in the air of the night; a thing he would have taken at any time previous for a sharp rupture of his spell. His spell was broken now, and it didn't matter—broken by his concession and his surrender, which made it idle henceforth that he should ever come back. The empty street—its other life so marked even by the great lamplit vacancy—was within call, within touch; he stayed there as to be in it again, high above

it though he was still perched; he watched as for some comforting common fact, some vulgar human note, the passage of
a scavenger or a thief, some night-bird however base. He would
have blessed that sign of life; he would have welcomed positively the slow approach of his friend the policeman, whom he
had hitherto only sought to avoid, and was not sure that if the
patrol had come into sight he mightn't have felt the impulse to
get into relation with it, to hail it, on some pretext, from his
fourth floor.

The pretext that wouldn't have been too silly or too com-
promising, the explanation that would have saved his dignity
and kept his name, in such a case, out of the papers, was not definite to him: he was so occupied with the thought of recording
his Discretion—as an effect of the vow he had just uttered to
his intimate adversary—that the importance of this loomed large
and something had overtaken all ironically his sense of proportion. If there had been a ladder applied to the front of the house,
even one of the vertiginous perpendiculars employed by
painters and roofers and sometimes left standing overnight, he
would have managed somehow, astride of the window-sill, to
compass by outstretched leg and arm that mode of descent. If
there had been some such uncanny thing as he had found in
his room at hotels, a workable fire-escape in the form of
notched cable or a canvas shoot, he would have availed himself
of it as a proof—well, of his present delicacy. He nursed that
sentiment, as the question stood, a little in vain, and even—at
the end of he scarce knew, once more, how long—found it, as
by the action on his mind of the failure of response of the
outer world, sinking back to vague anguish. It seemed to him
he had waited an age for some stir of the great grim hush; the
life of the town was itself under a spell—so unnaturally, up and
down the whole prospect of known and rather ugly objects,
the blankness and the silence lasted. Had they ever, he asked
himself, the hard-faced houses, which had begun to look livid
in the dim dawn, had they ever spoken so little to any need of
his spirit? Great builded voids, great crowded stillnesses put on,
often, in the heart of cities, for the small hours, a sort of sinister mask, and it was of this large collective negation that Brydon presently became conscious—all the more that the break

of day was, almost incredibly, now at hand, proving to him what a night he had made of it.

He looked again at his watch, saw what had become of his time-values (he had taken hours for minutes—not, as in other tense situations, minutes for hours) and the strange air of the streets was but the weak, the sullen flush of a dawn in which everything was still locked up. His choked appeal from his own open window had been the sole note of life, and he could but break off at last as for a worse despair. Yet while so deeply demoralised he was capable again of an impulse denoting—at least by his present measure—extraordinary resolution; of retracing his steps to the spot where he had turned cold with the extinction of his last pulse of doubt as to there being in the place another presence than his own. This required an effort strong enough to sicken him; but he had his reason, which overmastered for the moment everything else. There was the whole of the rest of the house to traverse, and how should he screw himself to that if the door he had seen closed were at present open? He could hold to the idea that the closing had practically been for him an act of mercy, a chance offered him to descend, depart, get off the ground and never again profane it. This conception held together, it worked; but what it meant for him depended now clearly on the amount of forbearance his recent action, or rather his recent inaction, had engendered. The image of the "presence," whatever it was, waiting there for him to go—this image had not yet been so concrete for his nerves as when he stopped short of the point at which certainty would have come to him. For, with all his resolution, or more exactly with all his dread, he did stop short—he hung back from really seeing. The risk was too great and his fear too definite: it took at this moment an awful specific form.

He knew—yes, as he had never known anything—that, *should* he see the door open, it would all too abjectly be the end of him. It would mean that the agent of his shame—for his shame was the deep abjection—was once more at large and in general possession; and what glared him thus in the face was the act that this would determine for him. It would send him straight about to the window he had left open, and by that window, be long ladder and dangling rope as absent as they would, he saw himself uncontrollably insanely fatally take his way to the street. The hideous chance of this he at least could avert; but he could only avert it by recoiling in time from assurance. He had the whole house to deal with, this fact was still there; only he now knew that uncertainty alone could start him. He stole back from where he had checked himself—merely to do so was suddenly like safety—and, making blindly for the greater staircase, left gaping rooms and sounding passages behind. Here was the top of the stairs, with a fine large dim descent and three spacious landings to mark off. His instinct was all for mildness, but his feet were harsh on the floors, and, strangely, when he had in a couple of minutes become aware of this, it counted somehow for help. He couldn't have spoken, the tone of his voice would have scared him, and the common conceit or resource of "whistling in the dark" (whether literally or figuratively) have appeared basely vulgar; yet he liked none the less to hear himself go, and when he had reached his first landing —taking it all with no rush, but quite steadily—that stage of success drew from him a gasp of relief.

The house, withal, seemed immense, the scale of space again inordinate; the open rooms, to no one of which his eyes deflected, gloomed in their shuttered state like mouths of caverns; only the high skylight that formed the crown of the deep well created for him a medium in which he could advance, but which might have been, for queerness of colour, some watery under-world. He tried to think of something noble, as that his property was really grand, a splendid possession; but this nobleness took the form too of the clear delight with which he was finally to sacrifice it. They might come in now, the builders, the destroyers—they might come as soon as they would. At the end of two flights he had dropped to another zone, and from the middle of the third, with only one more left, he recognised the influence of the lower windows, of half-drawn blinds, of the occasional gleam of streetlamps, of the glazed spaces of the vestibule. This was the bottom of the sea, which showed an illumination of its own and which he even saw paved—when at a given moment he drew up to sink a long look over the banisters—with the marble squares of his childhood. By that time indubitably he felt, as he might have said in a commoner cause, better; it had allowed him to stop and draw breath, and the ease increased with the sight of the old black-and-white slabs. But what he most felt was that now surely, with the element of impunity pulling him as by hard firm hands, the case was settled for what he might have seen above had he dared that last look. The closed door, blessedly remote now, was still closed—and he had only in short to reach that of the house.

He came down further, he crossed the passage forming the access to the last flight; and if here again he stopped an instant it was almost for the sharpness of the thrill of assured escape. It made him shut his eyes—which opened again to the straight slope of the remainder of the stairs. Here was impunity still, but impunity almost excessive; inasmuch as the sidelights and the high fan-tracery of the entrance were glimmering straight into the hall; an appearance produced, he the next instant saw, by the fact that the vestibule gaped wide, that the hinged halves of the inner door had been thrown far back. Out of that again the *question* sprang at him, making his eyes, as he felt, half-start from his head, as they had done, at the top of the house, before the sign of the other door. If he had left that one open, hadn't he left this one closed, and wasn't he now in *most* immediate presence of some inconceivable occult activity? It was as sharp, the question, as a knife in his side, but the answer hung fire still and seemed to lose itself in the vague darkness to which the thin admitted dawn, glimmering archwise over the whole outer door, made a semicircular margin, a cold silvery nimbus that seemed to play a little as he looked—to shift and expand and contract.

It was as if there had been something within it, protected by indistinctness and corresponding in extent with the opaque surface behind, the painted panels of the last barrier to his escape, of which the key was in his pocket. The indistinctness mocked him even while he stared, affected him as somehow shrouding or challenging certitude, so that after faltering an instant on his step he let himself go with the sense that here *was* at last something to meet, to touch, to take, to know—something all unnatural and dreadful, but to advance upon which was the condition for him either of liberation or of supreme defeat. The penumbra, dense and dark, was the virtual screen of a figure which stood in it as still as some image erect in a niche or as some black-vizored sentinel guarding a treasure. Brydon was to know afterwards, was to recall and make out, the particular thing he had believed during the rest of his descent. He saw, in its great grey glimmering margin, the central vagueness diminish, and he felt it to be taking the very form toward which, for so many days, the passion of his curiosity had yearned. It gloomed, it loomed, it was something, it was somebody, the prodigy of a personal presence.

Rigid and conscious, spectral yet human, a man of his own substance and stature waited there to measure himself with his power to dismay. This only could it be—this only till he recognised, with his advance, that what made the face dim was the pair of raised hands that covered it and in which, so far from being offered in defiance, it was buried as for dark deprecation. So Brydon, before him, took him in; with every fact of him now, in the higher light, hard and acute—his planted stillness, his vivid truth, his grizzled bent head and white masking hands, his queer actuality of evening-dress, of dangling double eye-glass, of gleaming silk lappet and white linen, of pearl button and gold watch-guard and polished shoe. No portrait by a great modern master could have presented him with more intensity, thrust him out of his frame with more art, as if there had been "treatment," of the consummate sort, in his every shade and salience. The revulsion, for our friend, had become, before he knew it, immense—this drop, in the act of apprehension, to the sense of his adversary's inscrutable manœuvre. That meaning at least, while he gaped, it offered him; for he could but gape at his other self in this other anguish, gape as a proof that *he*, standing there for the achieved, the enjoyed, the triumphant life, couldn't be faced in his triumph. Wasn't the proof in the splendid covering hands, strong and completely spread?—so spread and so intentional that, in spite of a special verity that surpassed every other, the fact that one of these hands had lost two fingers, which were reduced to stumps, as if accidentally shot away, the face was effectually guarded and saved.

"Saved," though, *would* it be?—Brydon breathed his wonder till the very impunity of his attitude and the very insistence of his eyes produced, as he felt, a sudden stir which showed the next instant as a deeper portent, while the head raised itself, the betrayal of a braver purpose. The hands, as he looked, began to move, to open; then, as if deciding in a flash, dropped from the face and left it uncovered and presented. Horror, with the sight, had leaped into Brydon's throat, gasping there in a sound he couldn't utter; for the bared identity was too hideous as *his*, and his glare was the passion of his protest. The face, *that* face, Spencer Brydon's?—he searched it still, but looking away from it in dismay and denial, falling straight from his height of sublimity. It was unknown, inconceivable, awful, disconnected from any possibility—! He had been "sold," he inwardly moaned, stalking such game as this: the presence before him was a presence, the horror within him a horror, but the waste of his nights had been only grotesque and the success of his adventure an irony. Such an identity fitted his at *no* point, made its alternative monstrous. A thousand times yes, as it came upon him nearer now—the face was the face of a stranger. It came upon him nearer now, quite as one of those expanding fantastic images projected by the magic lantern of childhood; for the stranger, whoever he might be, evil, odious, blatant, vulgar, had advanced as for aggression, and he knew himself give ground. Then harder pressed still, sick with the force of his shock, and falling back as under the hot breath and the roused passion of a life larger than his own, a rage of personality before which his own collapsed, he felt the whole vision turn to darkness and his very feet give way. His head went round; he was going; he had gone.

III

What had next brought him back, clearly—though after how long?—was Mrs. Muldoon's voice, coming to him from quite near, from so near that he seemed presently to see her as kneeling on the ground before him while he lay looking up at her; himself not wholly on the ground, but half-raised and upheld—conscious, yes, of tenderness of support and, more particularly, of a head pillowed in extraordinary softness and fainly refreshing fragrance. He considered, he wondered, his wit but half at his service; then another face intervened, bending more directly over him, and he finally knew that Alice Staverton had made her lap an ample and perfect cushion to him, and that she had to this end seated herself on the lowest degree of the staircase, the rest of his long person remaining stretched on his old black-and-white slabs. They were cold, these marble squares of his youth; but *he* somehow was not, in this rich return of consciousness—the most wonderful hour, little by little, that he had ever known, leaving him, as it did, so gratefully, so abysmally passive, and yet as with a treasure of intelligence waiting all round him for quiet appropriation; dissolved, he might call it, in the air of the place and producing the golden glow of a late autumn afternoon. He had come back, yes—come back from further away than any man but himself had ever travelled; but it was strange how with this sense what he had come back *to* seemed really the great thing, and as if his prodigious journey had been all for the sake of it. Slowly but surely his consciousness grew, his vision of his state thus completing itself: he had been miraculously *carried* back—lifted and carefully borne as from where he had been picked up, the uttermost end of an interminable grey passage. Even with this he was suffered to rest, and what had now brought him to knowledge was the break in the long mild motion.

It had brought him to knowledge, to knowledge—yes, this was the beauty of his state; which came to resemble more and more that of a man who has gone to sleep on some news of a great inheritance, and then, after dreaming it away, after profaning it with matters strange to it, has waked up again to serenity of certitude and has only to lie and watch it grow. This was the drift of his patience—that he had only to let it shine on him. He must moreover, with intermissions, still have been lifted and borne; since why and how else should he have known himself, later on, with the afternoon glow intenser, no longer at the foot of his stairs—situated as these now seemed at that dark other end of his tunnel—but on a deep window-bench of his high saloon, over which had been spread, couch-fashion, a mantle of soft stuff lined with grey fur that was familiar to his eyes and that one of his hands kept fondly feeling as for its pledge of truth. Mrs. Muldoon's face had gone, but the other, the second he had recognised, hung over him in a way that showed how he was still propped and pillowed. He took it all in, and the more he took it the more it seemed to suffice: he was as much at peace as if he had had food and drink. It was the two women who had found him, on Mrs. Muldoon's having plied, at her usual hour, her latch-key—and on her having above all arrived while Miss Staverton still lingered near the house. She had been turning away, all anxiety, from worrying the vain bell-handle—her calculation having been of the hour of the good woman's visit; but the latter, blessedly, had come up while she was still there, and they had entered together. He had then lain, beyond the vestibule, very much as he was lying now—quite, that is, as he appeared to have fallen, but all so wondrously without bruise or gash; only in a depth of stupor. What he most took in, however, at present, with the steadier clearance, was that Alice Staverton had for a long unspeakable moment not doubted he was dead.

"It must have been that I *was*." He made it out as she held him. "Yes—I can only have died. You brought me literally to life. Only," he wondered, his eyes rising to her, "only, in the name of all the benedictions, how?"

It took her but an instant to bend her face and kiss him, and something in the manner of it, and in the way her hands clasped and locked his head while he felt the cool charity and virtue of her lips, something in all this beatitude somehow answered everything. "And now I keep you," she said.

"Oh keep me, keep me!" he pleaded while her face still hung over him: in response to which it dropped again and stayed close, clingingly close. It was the seal of their situation—of which he tasted the impress for a long blissful moment in silence. But he came back. "Yet how did you know—?"

"I was uneasy. You were to have come, you remember—and you had sent no word."

"Yes, I remember—I was to have gone to you at one today." It caught on to their "old" life and relation—which were so near and so far. "I was still out there in my strange darkness—where was it, what was it? I must have stayed there so long." He could but wonder at the depth and the duration of his swoon.

"Since last night?" she asked with a shade of fear for her possible indiscretion.

"Since this morning—it must have been: the cold dim dawn of to-day. Where have I been," he vaguely wailed, "where have

I been?" He felt her hold him close, and it was as if this helped him now to make in all security his mild moan. "What a long dark day!"

All in her tenderness she had waited a moment. "In the cold dim dawn?" she quavered.

But he had already gone on piecing together the parts of the whole prodigy. "As I didn't turn up you came straight—?"

She barely cast about. "I went first to your hotel—where they told me of your absence. You had dined out last evening and hadn't been back since. But they appeared to know you had been at your club."

"So you had the idea of *this*—?"

"Of what?" she asked in a moment.

"Well—of what has happened."

"I believed at least you'd have been here. I've known, all along," she said, "that you've been coming."

"'Known' it—?"

"Well, I've believed it. I said nothing to you after that talk we had a month ago—but I felt sure. I knew you *would*," she declared.

"That I'd persist, you mean?"

"That you'd see him."

"Ah but I didn't!" cried Brydon with his long wail. "There's somebody—an awful beast; whom I brought, too horribly, to bay. But it's not me."

At this she bent over him again, and her eyes were in his eyes. "No—it's not you." And it was as if, while her face hovered, he might have made out in it, hadn't it been so near, some particular meaning blurred by a smile. "No, thank heaven," she repeated—"it's not you! Of course it wasn't to have been."

"Ah but it *was*," he gently insisted. And he stared before him now as he had been staring for so many weeks. "I was to have known myself."

"You couldn't!" she returned consolingly. And then reverting, and as if to account further for what she had herself done, "But it wasn't only *that*, that you hadn't been at home," she went on. "I waited till the hour at which we had found Mrs. Muldoon that day of my going with you; and she arrived, as I've told you, while, failing to bring any one to the door, I lingered in my despair on the steps. After a little, if she hadn't come, by such a mercy, I should have found means to hunt her up. But it wasn't," said Alice Staverton, as if once more with her fine intention—"it wasn't only that."

His eyes, as he lay, turned back to her. "What more then?"

She met it, the wonder she had stirred. "In the cold dim dawn, you say? Well, in the cold dim dawn of this morning I too saw you."

"Saw *me*—?"

"Saw *him*," said Alice Staverton. "It must have been at the same moment."

He lay an instant taking it in—as if he wished to be quite reasonable. "At the same moment?"

"Yes—in my dream again, the same one I've named to you. He came back to me. Then I knew it for a sign. He had come to you."

At this Brydon raised himself; he had to see her better. She helped him when she understood his movement, and he sat up, steadying himself beside her there on the window-bench and with his right hand grasping her left. "*He* didn't come to me."

"You came to yourself," she beautifully smiled.

"Ah I've come to myself now—thanks to you, dearest. But this brute, with his awful face—this brute's a black stranger. He's none of *me*, even as I *might* have been," Brydon sturdily declared.

But she kept the clearness that was like the breath of infallibility. "Isn't the whole point that you'd have been different?"

He almost scowled for it. "As different as *that*—?"

Her look again was more beautiful to him than the things of this world. "Haven't you exactly wanted to know *how* different? So this morning," she said, "you appeared to me."

"Like *him*?"

"A black stranger!"

"Then how did you know it was I?"

"Because, as I told you weeks ago, my mind, my imagination, had worked so over what you might, what you mightn't have been—to show you, you see, how I've thought of you. In the midst of that you came to me—that my wonder might be answered. So I knew," she went on; "and believed that, since the question held you too so fast, as you told me that day, you too would see for yourself. And when this morning I again saw

I knew it would be because you had—and also then, from the first moment, because you somehow wanted me. *He* seemed to tell me of that. So why," she strangely smiled, "shouldn't I like him?"

It brought Spencer Brydon to his feet. "You 'like' that horror—?"

"I *could* have liked him. And to me," she said, "he was no horror. I had accepted him."

" 'Accepted'—?" Brydon oddly sounded.

"Before, for the interest of his difference—yes. And as *I* didn't disown him, as *I* knew him—which you at last, confronted with him in his difference, so cruelly didn't, my dear—well, he must have been, you see, less dreadful to me. And it may have pleased him that I pitied him."

She was beside him on her feet, but still holding his hand—still with her arm supporting him. But though it all brought for him thus a dim light, "You 'pitied' him?" he grudgingly, resentfully asked.

"He has been unhappy, he has been ravaged," she said.

"And haven't I been unhappy? Am not I—you've only to look at me!—ravaged?"

"Ah I don't say I like him *better*," she granted after a thought. "But he's grim, he's worn—and things have happened to him. He doesn't make shift, for sight, with your charming monocle."

"No"—it struck Brydon: "I couldn't have sported mine 'downtown.' They'd have guyed me there."

"His great convex pince-nez—I saw it, I recognised the kind —is for his poor ruined sight. And his poor right hand—!"

"Ah!" Brydon winced—whether for his proved identity or for his lost fingers. Then, "He has a million a year," he lucidly added. "But he hasn't you."

"And he isn't—no, he isn't—*you!*" she murmured as he drew her to his breast.

1908

ALICE BROWN

(1857–1948)

Golden Baby

WE were in the *Sycorax* smoking-room, within an hour of turning the lights out for the night. The air was gray with smoke, and everybody, even the men that made it, looked dulled by it. The scion of one of our oldest families, who had seized the occasion of an ocean voyage for extravagant over-indulgence, sat at a little table, monotonously repeating, "She was the fairest of all the country round," in a tone of eccentric rhetorical emphasis. Nobody took any notice of him, because we had ceased doing that when he introduced us, one by one, to the aura of his ancestor who had "preceded Sir Philip Sidney at the battle of Zutphen." What he meant by that initiatory phrase we never knew. We were merely convinced, one after another, by the sound of it, that we weren't strong enough to hear it again. The man who was travelling round the globe on his own private fortune to discover a parasite for hostile bugs was absorbedly making diagrams of larvæ and what he called winged coleoptera for a buyer of seersucker, who was not listening to him, and the big fellow with the grizzled beard and the William Morris look of the eyes was sunk in some private reverie of his own. Suddenly the clerical young fellow opposite him asked him a question, whereupon he leaned back in his chair, gripped the beer glass before him as if he might sling it, and began, in a voice like a bell:

"Logic is a fool. The mystery your calling is founded on is no more a mystery than a million others. You simply fail to get the connections. I could tell you a dozen tales more unaccountable than that, because they're just ripped out of the air and made manifest. It's as if you should go out there on deck and see a film of some kind of impalpable parchment hanging from the topmast. You'd send up a man, he'd bring it down to you, and you'd find on it characters you could seem to read; but the story they made would say nothing whatever to you. I mean, it couldn't be hitched on to the general course of things. Now I'll give you a case in point."

He had given us no cases in point throughout the voyage. He had simply rowed about labor and capital, and said one was as bad as the other, capital being only labor reversed, and we thought we had discovered his pet nursling of a fad and just what road it was leading him. Now two or three other men looked up, and then moved a little nearer. They scented story as you do when you buy the new magazine and are lotting on having it to go to bed on. The scion of the noble family leaned back in his chair, regarded us haughtily, and said, "What's all this?" in a loud tone nobody noticed except discouragingly because he was making more noise. We left him to the solace of it, and drew up in a circle about the William Morris man. He had put the tip of his blunt finger—the kind of digit artisans work wonders with—delicately into a little pond of beer on the table and drawn out a line from it like a peninsula. Then he dabbled his finger again and put it down in another place, to make an island, and another. A merchant of many sorts of goods, who sailed all seas, burst out there, with a sudden recognition:

"Why, you're making islands!"

A white-faced young man of no breadth and inconsiderable stature, who, we understood, had some reputation as a poet of the minor variety, bent over the table and put on his large horn-bowed spectacles to look. He, too, spoke with an irrational quickness, as if everything the William Morris man did suddenly bore a meaning. It seemed as if the man had turned on his battery and we had become aware of his voltage.

"Do you suppose that's how God did it?" asked the little poet. "Before He 'came to the making of man'?"

But the William Morris man never answered him. He did look up at the merchant.

"Yes," he said, "it's the West Indies." Then he hunched his big frame back in his chair and began speaking, rather slowly and in a quiet voice, as if what he had to tell bore for him a significance of a particular and really a solemn nature.

"It was a week before Christmas when we sailed. Some company—it was a bum company and went to pieces afterward when its unseaworthy boats had all gone cranky, one way or another, and the public had turned back to the old standbys that rule the wave and sap the pocket—this company —I forget the name—had bought an old boat for a song and a promise, knocked out bulkheads, furbished up some dog-holes for new staterooms, put in red velvet and gilding, called her the *Siren*, and advertised a grand excursion to the West Indies. Somehow the idea took. It had been a nasty winter, there was easy money, and without much delay the *Siren's* list was full. I was among the first to take passage. I was done up that winter with statistics and the deviltry of the rich and, besides, I'd always wanted a sniff of sugar, rum and spices on their own ground. When I went on board there was a great copper sunset; it looked as if it belonged to the land exclusively and we might never have a whack at such another when we'd left New York behind us. I turned to look at it, as I'd been turning all the way along, and I stood there till the splendors and banners of it blinded me. So when I went aboard things were dark before me momentarily, in queer shapes, the outlines of warehouses and such, and I didn't feel that I'd really seen anything, until, on the deck at the end of the gangplank, I came face to face with a coolie woman, the thinnest of her sort, with bare feet and legs, bare arms, the slightest possible garment, and a weight of silver bangles on her wrists and collars round her neck. She stood there holding a child, a baby with a queer expression of maturity, and her eyes as she looked at me were black and solemn. They seemed to talk in a language of their own, to sing things maybe, chant 'em—talking wasn't good enough—and they made me shiver. The child sat there supported on the crook of her arm and looked at me as seriously as she did, but with a kind of well-wishing, too, as if he said:

"'Old man, you're tired, aren't you? Everybody's tired. Glad you're shut of little old New York for a spell. Wish all of 'em could do the same.'

"What came into my mind—I don't see why—was that he was a kind of golden baby. Maybe it was because he had bright hair—an image to be worshipped—and my mind said inside, as plain as your lips might speak it, 'Golden Baby!' I felt I liked him, too, better than any piece of littleness I'd ever seen. And then, in the same minute—for it all passed as quickly as you might set your foot on deck and lift the other foot to keep it company—the coolie woman and the golden baby were gone, and there was a spot of blackness where he'd been.

"A sailor was passing me with an end of a rope.

" 'Where's the woman?' I asked, before I could stop myself.

"He gave me a glance, and said, 'Sir?' without stopping, because he was evidently on business of the ship.

" 'The woman and the child,' I called after him.

"I felt I'd got to know. But he shook his head and went along, and I felt disappointed, as if I'd lost something. But there was one queer thing. A darkness in the outline of the child stood before my eyes until I'd got into my stateroom and after. I couldn't rub it away.

"Well, gentlemen, that voyage was a corker for sheer madness of the human creature let loose. We hadn't been a day out before I knew what we'd got aboard—mothers that regarded the boat as a summer hotel and had fitted out their daughters with every rag known to milliners, to sell 'em in the market of some rich man's desire. That was the first—exhibit A. Then there were copper kings whose copper queens hadn't any chance to show off their diamonds and pearls and loot of the earth and sea in the regulation manner, and brought it all on board to flout the moon and stars, I guess, and the Creator of the moon and stars, and the other folks He'd made that had more or hadn't so many, each in a different way. It was all money and class hatred and scorn and contumely."

Here the scion of a noble stock broke in, his dreary drone addressed to none of us in particular:

"Sir Philip Sidney, let me inform you. Sir Philip Sidney! Battle of Zutphen!"

"That's it," said the William Morris man, quietly. "That just it. There were a few of 'em on board just like him. They'd had ancestors at Zutphen, and they wouldn't speak to the Semitic walking diamond-shops, nor me because I said I'd been in a foundry, nor the captain even, because he wasn't a *von*. Intercourse was restricted because they could only speak to one another, and they'd trodden that ground so long that they had only common recollections to go on, and I felt they were the best bored set on the boat. But in spite of all the hatreds and mildew of exclusiveness, the same old farce obtained that they were all enjoying themselves immensely. The decks were canvassed in nearly every night and the stars shut out, so that those apes of various degrees could put on their gimcracks borrowed from the earth and sea, and dance and strut under the light of electric bulbs with backgrounds of flags and paper garlands. Great Israel! I wonder the Lord of all don't turn His face away from the whole bloomin' show sometimes and say, 'I'm sick of vaudeville.'

"Well, as days went on, I can't tell you how or why, I began to be conscious of hate, hate everywhere. Whether it was the heat and madness of the tropics that got into our blood and set it seething, I don't know, or whether it was the revenge of big nature rising up against fool civilization—we were separated into as many little cliques and parties as the factions in a South-American state. I was out of the whole thing, not because I was better, but because I was worse. They hated one another, and I hated them all with a glorious impartiality. We'd gone due south, struck Jamaica, steamed on to the Isthmus, and then skirted the coast to Trinidad and dipped down beyond the mouth of the Orinoco, with the Southern Cross dominant now and the Dipper selling short. And suddenly one night about eleven, when the band was whanging away at a popular waltz and girls were swishing their muslins and laces round the deck in time, the boat stopped. You know there's always an underconsciousness of danger at sea, in the thickest-hided. No man forgets he's over an unplumbed abyss, except maybe he's in his cups and taking the return trip to Zutphen. So when the motion—there wasn't much of it on that sea— when it fell into a calm, the dancing grigs stopped, I suppose as the dancers did in 'Belgium's capital' when George Osborne got his summons to go and be killed, and wondered what the god of the machinery was going to do to them. We stopped, and we stayed so. I was on the hurricane-deck, and I came down with that same premonition of panic in me—I'm an old sailor, but I did feel actual panic—and the first man I met, making his thirty-six-inch strides along the deck, was the second officer. He was a good fellow; I hadn't hated him. We'd chummed together quite a lot on the voyage. I've grinned since to think how I greeted him inanely.

" 'We've stopped,' said I.

" 'Yes,' said he, two paces away from me.

"'What for?' I called, knowing I shouldn't be told.

"'Don't know, sir,' he returned. I knew he was entrenched in official reserve and not the accessible fellow I'd smoked my pipe with.

"Well, gentlemen, we had stopped, and there we hung all that night, and the next morning we were there still, a little motion under us, the very least, like the sound, so far as motion might be, of tiny ripples lapping on the beach. Everybody came haggard to breakfast. Nobody had slept, except some of the rummies who were in that condition of tissue where you might call 'em permanently asleep. The crew, such of them as I saw at intervals, seemed also to be in a state of tension. Then the questions began, fired by the broadside and popping like guerrilla warfare, always to the same tune: What was the matter? The answer reassured us briefly. It was no longer, 'We don't know.' 'Some trouble with the engine,' we were assured. 'The engineer's at it now.' So we went on eating, and fault-finding when our toast varied in brownness, and hating one another; but the day, the sulky, burning tropical day, went by, and the tropical night with its quick onrush of stars, and still we hadn't moved. That next morning I met the wireless man at the rail, where he's gone to lean both arms and, it seemed, throw some problem of his own at the bright horizon-line. He was a little, round, oily, dark fellow with curly hair, and in spite of his fatness his face looked funnily tragic with anxiety, as if he were going to cry. At once I felt he was pretty well shaken, and he'd tell me what's the matter.

"'Have you tried wireless?' I asked, in the fatuous way we have of baiting with a commonplace when we mean to fish up something that might dart and elude us unless it thought it was snapping at the same old fly. He shook his head as if he shook me off. I'd thought he knew nothing but wireless, but it was evident he sized me up for the ass I was.

"'Tried it?' he said. 'What else?'

"'Well, don't you get anything?'

"He shook his head again.

"'Why don't you keep on trying? There must be stations down here—there must be ships—'

"'They don't answer,' he said. It was almost as if with

another word he might break down actually. 'I've changed my tune, and changed it—changed it. I can't get them.'

"He turned abruptly as if he were really concealing tears now, and ran up the ladder to his post. Then I went away to think. I was afraid, sheer afraid, and wondered at myself. You see, I've no more pluck than any man of my inches, but I'd been about a good bit. I'd seen adventure and heard other fellows talk it over, and I knew you're pretty sure to get out of everything with a whole skin till that last particular time when you don't—so what's the use of grizzling? But this time there was panic in my left waistcoat pocket, neatly sewed in to stay, and I knew it and hated it for being there. There was foul weather all over the ship. Nobody sang, nobody strummed the light guitar as one girl had been doing till we wished she was at home in the kitchen with a consignment of pots and pans to wash. New York hated Jerusalem more frankly than ever, and Jerusalem wagged its fat chin and openly put up its beak at New York. Hate! Talk about the wars of nations! If that ship couldn't have made use of a whole Hague conference all to herself, it wasn't because she wasn't sick for it and only needed diagnosis to have it prescribed. Toward night I climbed up to the door of the little wireless cage, and stopped there, hat in hand, if you'll believe me. I don't know what kind of besetment made me feel as if every Jack on board that ship was in as tight a place as he could breathe in, and that every lubber that spoke to them had got to walk Spanish. He looked up at me. His tired little eyes were set in a bed of wrinkles. It hadn't been long, this universal panic of the ship, but it had had time to eat into him and change him, from a fat little manipulator who'd learned to do a certain thing, to a crying, hungering soul in trouble, beseeching—maybe with no voice, only with those eyes and that quiver of a mouth—beseeching the Lord of things big and little to lift him out of the pit he's stumbled into. I don't know whether the wireless chap ever heard of the Psalmist, but if he had, I bet he was tuning his own little pipe to him that minute.

"'Go down,' said he, looking at me as if I were in pinafores.

"That was all. But I felt I must speak. I had an ass's desire to bray and a meddler's insane push to help on somehow.

I'd got to help the ship on. We all felt so. One man in the smoking-room—we kept it all of a cloud now, we smoked so hard and universally—he told me he felt as if he must get out and push, even if he drowned in doing it. He gave a queer little catch in his throat when he said it. If it had been a woman that gave that sound, you'd have said it was a sob. 'That's it,' two or three other men had said, and looked the same way, and it was ten to one that, give them a lead, they'd have sobbed, too. It was then I had lighted out. I was afraid we should all be in hysterics together like a girls' boarding-school. But the wireless man:

"'I beg pardon,' I said to him.

"'Go down,' said he.

"'I beg your pardon,' I said again, 'but mightn't there be—isn't there—some sort of magnetic field, and mightn't we be inside it?'

"He laughed a little—a shrill hoot all scorn and tiredness.

"'Magnetic grandmother!' said he. 'Go down.'

"Then I went.

"Well, whatever it was that stopped stayed stopped. Life hung fire. Electricity hadn't played us false. There were plenty of lights, as faithful as the night. It wasn't true that according to the old tune—it ran in my head all the time then—'water wouldn't quench fire, fire wouldn't burn axe,' and the rest of it. Fire was faithful and cooked us three—no, by George! six times a day the most elaborate and embroidered and sinful meals for richness the tropics ever saw. But we simply didn't move, and now the mischief was so patent, the whole thing grew so upsetting and queer, that the usual disciplinary silence cracked and broke. The captain made no secret of it. The mate made none, nor the chief engineer. He, I found out, was spending his time digging into his engine, prying into her heart to find out whether she'd got some deadly secret he hadn't shared. At last he was crying over her, the chief electrician told me afterward. But they made no secret, any of them. There was nothing the matter anywhere. The engine simply would not go. And we saw no ship and we saw no land, and wireless wouldn't talk. The only creatures on the ship that showed any animation because they hadn't time to break, were the stewards and I suppose the *chef*, though I never saw him, and the band. For according to the notion that you can ensure a man against panic by making a noise or stuffing him, they kept the band playing the last comic-opera airs, and the stewards brought on more food, food, food, and offered it up to the god that's in every man's belly. I'll say right here that I never knew stewards so overworked as those poor devils had been from the start, and by now they were so pasty-pale it made you ashamed of yourself, if you were an able-bodied man, to ring a bell and see 'em totter out and start into that perfunctory sprightliness—you know it. See it here on this very ship; but these boys look better, a heap better. The stewards on the *Siren* made you want to say, 'For God's sake, give me the key of the pantry and I'll get it myself.'

"Well, one night, as if a great bubble burst in the air, something happened. Don't you know how it feels when your head's sort of muffled and woozy, and suddenly something clicks in your ear, and everything clears and lightens, and you find yourself out in the open? This was exactly that way. We were all on deck, packed into our rows of steamer chairs—I believe we were afraid of going below, and besides it was hot—and the band was dashing along from:

> " 'Oh, I am the King of Gold,
>   And I made it all myself;
>   My heart and brain I sold
>   In accumulating pelf,'

to the Sylvia ballet music, when a man down the line of chairs somewhere—I never knew who he was—burst out into a kind of screech: 'Stop that band! For God's sake, stop that band!'

"We didn't have to. The band stopped. I believe it knew, instruments and all, that we had had every hair's weight we could endure, and that it had blared out all the breath it could spare, and had got either to scream or die dead from tiredness and fear. And then I turned my head a little—I don't know why: I felt as if I had been called—and in a veil of darkness by the rail pretty well aft I saw them, the coolie woman and the baby. 'Golden Baby!' I caught myself saying, under my breath, 'Golden Baby!'

"And at once my fear passed away from me as the shadow passes when the cloud moves on. Something snapped—that same lightening like a bubble's breaking—and something came up in me that was like summer mornings and being young. I felt it going all over the ship, as if there'd been long breaths—what the stories call breaths of relief—and I knew I was in the midst of a flood of the same kind of sudden happiness. I had time to ask myself why, why, and to wonder a little, because the ship hadn't started and we were in exactly as bad case as before. But that I couldn't stop to think of, for my eyes were on the Golden Baby, and I seemed to be wanting to learn everything I could about him by heart, for fear I should never see him again. You know some minutes warn you they're going to be mighty short and you'd better take a snapshot of 'em while you can. The coolie woman stood there exactly as she'd stood on deck the first minute I saw her. She had on the same scanty, dignified garment down to her bare knees and thin legs, and the silver round her neck and on her arms shone out there in the dark. It seemed to shine like moonlight. The electric lights didn't touch her or the child. They were there in a darkness of their own, and it seemed as if they made their own light. The child sat on her arm and looked toward us and smiled. His hair was bright. His face was bright. Afterward I had a kind of feeling that he stretched out his arms toward us, but that I couldn't swear to. His smile was queer, too. Or, no, it wasn't queer. It was pretty much what you'd see in any baby, only more so. It wasn't—well, it wasn't benignant, you know; spiritual, you might call it, same as it is in pictures of—" He hesitated here, being, we thought, diffident about matters of accepted religion.

"Madonnas," said the little poet, raptly. He had hung on every word.

"Exactly, Madonnas. No, it was the way you'd like to have your own baby look, if he'd come in from play with his hands full of flowers. But the coolie woman smiled. She held out her arms toward us, and him in them. And all along the line I knew women were holding out their arms toward the child; and the men—well, I guess they did what I did. I brought my feet down to the deck and sat up straight and bent forward. That's all the way I know how to express it. I wanted to get there, somewhere near the baby, and same time I knew I mustn't go any nearer, not a step. And the only relief I had was muttering, just as you'd breathe hard, 'Golden Baby!' Then the woman spoke. It was a kind of voice—well, I don't know exactly, a cool voice, smooth, kind of like a silver horn. Something shaking in it, too, something that trembled and yet had a power of its own, a vibration—I've never been able to describe it to myself, all the times I've tried, and I'm not having any better luck now. But there wasn't any mistake about what she said. 'You're keeping him back, and he's got to be there. Oh, don't! You mustn't keep him back.'"

"What language did she speak in?" asked the man that sought the parasites. He'd been listening very seriously, not in any spirit of unbelief, I could see, but with the gravity due a marvel.

The William Morris man nodded at him.

"I knew that would come," he said. "It came that very night, before we turned in. 'What language did she speak?' says the wireless man to me, and I carried the question on to the first mate. 'God, man, I don't know,' says he. 'She spoke, that's all I can say.'

"And a Frenchman that was going to write up Martinique as he saw it from the deck swore she spoke in French, and the German that played the trombone said it was the best Hanoverian German. I knew well enough it wasn't either, but I didn't know what it was, and I didn't care. I only know she spoke and we understood. I didn't have much eyesight to spare from looking at the baby; but somehow I did realize that everything round me was different, and different all over the ship. Mrs.—I forget her condemned and sacred name—she was one of your Boston Apocalypse people, the kind that got transfigured on some mount or other and haven't spoken to anybody since—why, up to now she hadn't accepted anybody's being on that boat but herself and her two long-footed daughters and their following. And now she sat there with her hand on a bedizened Jewess's fat knee, and her daughters had hold of a school-teacher from the West—not with a ten-foot pole and a hook on the end of it, mind you, but as if they were constrained to hug somebody and it didn't matter whom. It was the same all over the ship. Something had lubricated us.

Something had washed us clean. I understood, and at the same minute I knew they all understood, too. Hate had passed away, and in its place was the other word that's just as big. 'Golden Baby!' I says to myself. I saw he had done it, though I didn't know how. That didn't concern us somehow.

"The coolie woman seemed to come forward. I say seemed, though she didn't move a step, but we all knew she was nearer, every one of us, and that it wasn't important except as she brought the child. Anyhow, he seemed nearer, and if every-body felt as I did it was as if the child was warm and bright right in the midst of us. She spoke again.

" 'That's it,' she said. 'That's good. When you feel like this it doesn't keep him back. Don't keep him back. He's needed so.'

"And then something happened. It was so gradual and so natural that at first we didn't realize what it was, only that every-thing in general was all right, and the sun would rise to-morrow on the good old practical world with no fear in it, and God was up there in His heavens wishing us well and not playing tricks on us. The ship was moving, that's what it was. There was the beat of the engine and the little heaving motion of a ship that begins to feel herself, though on smooth water. Then some-body began to cry and somebody else laughed, and we hugged each other, I guess, nobody particularly anxious to know whether he was hugging out of his class or not, and somehow or other the coolie woman and the Golden Baby were gone. But that night it seemed no more incredible to have them go than it did to have them come. And the engine was beating and the wireless man suddenly appeared among us, his flabby round face all puffed out again with satisfaction in his box of tricks, and he says:

" 'There's a revolution in Haiti!'

"And we laughed louder and more foolishly, not because there was a revolution, but because it was such a joyful thing to have wireless say anything at all.

" 'Let's have something to eat,' says somebody then, because we'd got used to eating as a kind of expression of emotion of any sort; but somebody else roared out: 'Let the stewards rest, can't you? Poor devils!'

" 'Poor devils!' said somebody else, and then I understood,

and I guess everybody else did, that we not only impossibly loved one another, but we loved the pasty stewards, too.

"And we bunked down quietly that night, and there was no eating or drinking, only a kind of prayerful yearning over the engine that kept beating on, and thoughts we didn't dare to put into words about the Baby. And next day the engines were still going, and there was a breeze, and in some queer way we were a quiet, happy crew of people. And everybody spoke to everybody else."

"Where were the woman and the baby?" asked the parasite man. He was frowning a good deal and beating a forefinger silently on the table.

"I don't know."

"Don't know? Didn't you ask for them?"

"No."

"Didn't anybody?"

"No."

"Why didn't you ask?"

The William Morris man paused a long time here, and seemed to study the question in many aspects. Then he answered slowly:

"We knew we were not to ask. We knew they'd come for a special purpose. What it was didn't concern us, and we felt— we felt a loyalty to the child, a loyalty bigger than anything I'd ever felt before. I guess it was so with all of 'em."

"Did you ever see them again?"

"Oh, yes. We sailed north, touching at an island now and then, contented as you please, but solemn, changed in a way. I was changed. I guess they all were. I haven't been the same man since. It was the pasty stewards on that trip that set me thinking labor and capital wasn't an institution to be sworn over. There was something to be done about it. Well, we kept our course north, and then we slid along the coast of Haiti, and the wireless man picked up more about the revolution. Hot as pepper it was, black as ink. And then one night off that coast—I never knew whether there was a harbor or not—the engines slowed down and we stopped. But queer as it was to stop again we didn't feel a breath of our old panic, only a solemn expectation. And we heard a stroke of oars, and before

I knew what was doing there was the coolie woman, Golden Baby in her arms, going over the side. They seemed to make their own light—the child did. His hair was bright almost like flame. His face—I never saw—"

Here he stopped a moment, as if the memory were too blinding to be borne.

"I heard a woman say—it wasn't as if she was afraid, but only awed and wondering—'Don't let them go there into that island in the dark. Don't let them go!' And somebody else said:

"'Hush!'

"I jumped to the rail and looked over, and I got a glimpse— I swear I did—of a boat full of blacks and the stern seat vacant for a passenger. And the boat moved away, and there was a light in it there hadn't been before. It was bright, like the baby's hair. We put on steam again, and that was all."

Nobody spoke for a while, and the steward, perking out the curtains at the port-holes, to give himself pretence for lingering while our talk shut down, ventured to look at us imploringly, like a tired clock striking the hour. The parasite man began to feel his way cautiously through a sentence, evidently not knowing where he was to come out.

"It's your theory, is it, that—that the spirit of those on board ship delayed—well, it's absurd to say it—stopped the machinery?"

The William Morris man nodded.

"When you put in that way," he owned, "of course there's nothing for it but to laugh. But there were evil passions aboard that ship, envy, pride, covetousness, lust, hate—chiefly hate. Now if you should ask me if hate could stop an engine, I should say, 'No, it can't,' and so would you. Still, the hate was there and the engine stopped."

"Ah!" This was a breath in unison from us all, not a breath of understanding, but of concurrence. The scion of a noble stock, who'd been cooling off a little, got on his wobbly pins and stretched himself cautiously, with regard to equipoise.

"Look here, old chap," said he, "I've heard that story before."

The William Morris man was too much absorbed in the after-tang of his renewed memory of it to notice who spoke, or he wouldn't have answered. Nobody answered the Sidney man.

"Not likely," said he. He spoke briefly, absently. "None of us who were there were likely to tell it. I never told it before in my life."

"But I've heard it," said the little poet.

"Have you?'" asked the William Morris man. He looked up at him and spoke as if in that quarter something might be doing. "Have you?"

"Yes," said the little poet. His eyes shone. His hair seemed to bristle and come alive with some new excitement under his poll. "Oh yes, I've heard it."

"When d' you hear it?"

"Long ago—oh, long ago!"

"Who told you?"

"A man named Coleridge. He called it 'The Ancient Mariner'."

1910

EDITH WHARTON

(1862–1937)

Afterward

"Oh, there *is* one, of course, but you'll never know it."

The assertion, laughingly flung out six months earlier in a bright June garden, came back to Mary Boyne with a new perception of its significance as she stood, in the December dusk, waiting for the lamps to be brought into the library.

The words had been spoken by their friend Alida Stair, as they sat at tea on her lawn at Pangbourne, in reference to the very house of which the library in question was the central, the pivotal "feature." Mary Boyne and her husband, in quest of a country place in one of the southern or southwestern counties, had, on their arrival in England, carried their problem straight to Alida Stair, who had successfully solved it in her own case; but it was not until they had rejected, almost capriciously, several practical and judicious suggestions that she threw out: "Well, there's Lyng, in Dorsetshire. It belongs to Hugo's cousins, and you can get it for a song."

The reason she gave for its being obtainable on these terms —its remoteness from a station, its lack of electric light, hot-water pipes, and other vulgar necessities—were exactly those pleading in its favour with two romantic Americans perversely in search of the economic drawbacks which were associated, in their tradition, with unusual architectural felicities.

"I should never believe I was living in an old house unless I was thoroughly uncomfortable," Ned Boyne, the more extravagant of the two, had jocosely insisted; "the least hint of 'convenience' would make me think it had been bought out of an exhibition, with the pieces numbered, and set up again." And they had proceeded to enumerate, with humorous precision, their various doubts and demands, refusing to believe that the house their cousin recommended was *really* Tudor till they learned it had no heating system, or that the village church was literally in the grounds till she assured them of the deplorable uncertainty of the water-supply.

"It's too uncomfortable to be true!" Edward Boyne had continued to exult as the avowal of each disadvantage was successively wrung from her; but he had cut short his rhapsody to ask, with a relapse to distrust: "And the ghost? You've been concealing from us the fact that there is no ghost!"

Mary, at the moment, had laughed with him, yet almost with her laugh, being possessed of several sets of independent perceptions, had been struck by a note of flatness in Alida's answering hilarity.

"Oh, Dorsetshire's full of ghosts, you know."

"Yes, yes; but that won't do. I don't want to have to drive ten miles to see somebody else's ghost. I want one of my own on the premises. *Is* there a ghost at Lyng?"

His rejoinder had made Alida laugh again, and it was then that she had flung back tantalisingly: "Oh, there *is* one, of course, but you'll never know it."

"Never know it?" Boyne pulled her up. "But what in the world constitutes a ghost except the fact of its being known for one?"

"I can't say. But that's the story."

"That there's a ghost, but that nobody knows it's a ghost?"

"Well—not till afterward, at any rate."

"Till afterward?"

"Not till long long afterward."

"But if it's once been identified as an unearthly visitant, why hasn't its *signalement* been handed down in the family? How has it managed to preserve its incognito?"

Alida could only shake her head. "Don't ask me. But it has."

"And then suddenly—" Mary spoke up as if from cavernous depths of divination— "suddenly, long afterward, one says to one's self *'That was it?'*"

She was startled at the sepulchral sound with which her question fell on the banter of the other two, and she saw the shadow of the same surprise flit across Alida's pupils. "I suppose so. One just has to wait."

"Oh, hang waiting!" Ned broke in. "Life's too short for a ghost who can only be enjoyed in retrospect. Can't we do better than that, Mary?"

But it turned out that in the event they were not destined to, for within three months of their conversation with Mrs. Stair they were settled at Lyng, and the life they had yearned for, to the point of planning it in advance in all its daily details, had actually begun for them.

It was to sit, in the thick December dusk, by just such a wide-hooded fireplace, under just such black oak rafters, with the sense that beyond the mullioned panes the downs were darkened to a deeper solitude: it was for the ultimate indulgence of such sensations that Mary Boyne, abruptly exiled from New York by her husband's business, had endured for nearly fourteen years the soul-deadening ugliness of a Middle Western town, and that Boyne had ground on doggedly at his engineering till, with a suddenness that still made her blink, the prodigious windfall of the Blue Star Mine had put them at a stroke in possession of life and the leisure to taste it. They had never for a moment meant their new state to be one of idleness; but they meant to give themselves only to harmonious activities. She had her vision of painting and gardening (against a background of grey walls), he dreamed of the production of his long-planned book on the "Economic Basis of Culture"; and with such absorbing work ahead no existence could be too sequestered: they could not get far enough from the world, or plunge deep enough into the past.

Dorsetshire had attracted them from the first by an air of remoteness out of all proportion to its geographical position. But to the Boynes it was one of the ever-recurring wonders of the whole incredibly compressed island—a nest of counties, as they put it—that for the production of its effects so little of a given quality went so far: that so few miles made a distance, and so short a distance a difference.

"It's that," Ned had once enthusiastically explained, "that gives such depth to their effects, such relief to their contrasts. They've been able to lay the butter so thick on every delicious mouthful."

The butter had certainly been laid on thick at Lyng: the old house hidden under a shoulder of the downs had almost all the finer marks of commerce with a protracted past. The mere fact that it was neither large nor exceptional made it, to the Boynes, abound the more completely in its special charm—the charm of having been for centuries a deep dim reservoir of life. The life had probably not been of the most vivid order: for long periods, no doubt, it had fallen as noiselessly into the past as the quiet drizzle of autumn fell, hour after hour, into the fish-pond between the yews; but these backwaters of existence sometimes breed, in their sluggish depths, strange acuities of emotion, and Mary Boyne had felt from the first the mysterious stir of intenser memories.

The feeling had never been stronger than on this particular afternoon when, waiting in the library for the lamps to come, she rose from her seat and stood among the shadows of the hearth. Her husband had gone off, after luncheon, for one of his long tramps on the downs. She had noticed of late that he preferred to go alone; and, in the tried security of their personal relations, had been driven to conclude that his book was bothering him, and that he needed the afternoons to turn over in solitude the problems left from the morning's work. Certainly the book was not going as smoothly as she had thought it would, and there were lines of perplexity between his eyes such as had never been there in his engineering days. He had often, then, looked fagged to the verge of illness, but the native demon of "worry" had never branded his brow. Yet the few pages he had so far read to her—the introduction, and a summary of the opening chapter—showed a firm hold on his subject, and an increasing confidence in his powers.

The fact threw her into deeper perplexity, since, now that he had done with "business" and its disturbing contingencies, the one other possible source of anxiety was eliminated. Unless it were his health, then? But physically he had gained since they had come to Dorsetshire, grown robuster, ruddier and fresher-eyed. It was only within the last week that she had felt in him the undefinable change which made her restless in his absence, and as tongue-tied in his presence as though it were *she* who had a secret to keep from him!

The thought that there *was* a secret somewhere between them struck her with a sudden rap of wonder, and she looked about her down the long room.

"Can it be the house?" she mused.

The room itself might have been full of secrets. They seemed to be piling themselves up, as evening fell, like the layers and layers of velvet shadow dropping from the low ceiling, the rows of books, the smoke-blurred sculpture of the hearth.

"Why, of course—the house is haunted!" she reflected.

The ghost—Alida's imperceptible ghost—after figuring largely in the banter of their first month or two at Lyng, had been gradually left aside as too ineffectual for imaginative use. Mary had, indeed, as became the tenant of a haunted house, made the customary inquiries among her rural neighbours, but, beyond a vague "They dü say so, Ma'am," the villagers had nothing to impart. The elusive spectre had apparently never had sufficient identity for a legend to crystallise about it, and after a time the Boynes had set the matter down to their profit-and-loss account, agreeing that Lyng was one of the few houses good enough in itself to dispense with supernatural enhancements.

"And I suppose, poor ineffectual demon, that's why it beats its beautiful wings in vain in the void," Mary had laughingly concluded.

"Or, rather," Ned answered in the same strain, "why, amid so much that's ghostly, it can never affirm its separate existence as *the* ghost." And thereupon their invisible housemate had finally dropped out of their references, which were numerous enough to make them soon unaware of the loss.

Now, as she stood on the hearth, the subject of their earlier curiosity revived in her with a new sense of its meaning—a sense gradually acquired through daily contact with the scene of the lurking mystery. It was the house itself, of course, that possessed the ghost-seeing faculty, that communed visually but secretly with its own past; if one could only get into close enough communion with the house, one might surprise its secret, and acquire the ghost-sight on one's own account. Perhaps, in his long hours in this very room, where she never trespassed till the afternoon, her husband *had* acquired it already, and was silently carrying about the weight of whatever it had revealed to him. Mary was too well versed in the code of the spectral world not to know that one could not talk about the ghosts one saw: to do so was almost as great a breach of taste as to name a lady in a club. But this explanation did not really satisfy her. "What, after all, except for the fun of the shudder," she reflected, "would he really care for any of their old ghosts?"

And thence she was thrown back once more on the fundamental dilemma: the fact that one's greater or less susceptibility to spectral influences had no particular bearing on the case, since, when one *did* see a ghost at Lyng, one did not know it.

"Not till long afterward," Alida Stair had said. Well, supposing Ned *had* seen one when they first came, and had known only within the last week what had happened to him? More and more under the spell of the hour, she threw back her thoughts to the early days of their tenancy, but at first only to recall a lively confusion of unpacking, settling, arranging of books, and calling to each other from remote corners of the house as, treasure after treasure, it revealed itself to them. It was in this particular connection that she presently recalled a certain soft afternoon of the previous October, when, passing from the first rapturous flurry of exploration to a detailed inspection of the old house, she had pressed (like a novel heroine) a panel that opened on a flight of corkscrew stairs leading to a flat ledge of the roof—the roof which, from below, seemed to slope away on all sides too abruptly for any but practised feet to scale.

The view from this hidden coign was enchanting, and she had flown down to snatch Ned from his papers and give him the freedom of her discovery. She remembered still how, standing at her side, he had passed his arm about her while their gaze flew to the long tossed horizon-line of the downs, and then dropped contentedly back to trace the arabesque of yew hedges about the fish-pond, and the shadow of the cedar on the lawn.

"And now the other way," he had said, turning her about within his arm; and closely pressed to him, she had absorbed, like some long satisfying draught, the picture of the grey-walled court, the squat lions on the gates, and the lime-avenue reaching up to the highroad under the downs.

It was just then, while they gazed and held each other, that she had felt his arm relax, and heard a sharp "Hullo!" that made her turn to glance at him.

Distinctly, yes, she now recalled that she had seen, as she glanced, a shadow of anxiety, of perplexity, rather, fall across his face; and, following his eyes, had beheld the figure of a man —a man in loose greyish clothes, as it appeared to her—who was sauntering down the lime-avenue to the court with the doubtful gait of a stranger who seeks his way. Her short-sighted eyes had given her but a blurred impression of slightness and greyishness, with something foreign, or at least unlocal, in the cut of the figure or its dress; but her husband had apparently seen more—seen enough to make him push past her with a hasty "Wait!" and dash down the stairs without pausing to give her a hand.

A slight tendency to dizziness obliged her, after a provisional clutch at the chimney against which they had been leaning, to follow him first more cautiously; and when she had reached the landing she paused again, for a less definite reason, leaning over the banister to strain her eyes through the silence of the brown sun-flecked depths. She lingered there till, somewhere in those depths, she heard the closing of a door; then, mechanically impelled, she went down the shallow flights of steps till she reached the lower hall.

The front door stood open on the sunlight of the court, and hall and court were empty. The library door was open, too, and after listening in vain for any sound of voices within, she crossed the threshold, and found her husband alone, vaguely fingering the papers on his desk.

He looked up, as if surprised at her entrance, but the shadow of anxiety had passed from his face, leaving it even, as she fancied, a little brighter and clearer than usual.

"What was it? Who was it?" she asked.

"Who?" he repeated, with the surprise still all on his side.

"The man we saw coming toward the house."

He seemed to reflect. "The man? Why, I thought I saw Peters; I dashed after him to say a word about the stable drains, but he had disappeared before I could get down."

"Disappeared? But he seemed to be walking so slowly when we saw him."

Boyne shrugged his shoulders. "So I thought; but he must have got up steam in the interval. What do you say to our trying a scramble up Meldon Steep before sunset?"

That was all. At the time the occurrence had been less than nothing, had, indeed, been immediately obliterated by the magic of their first vision from Meldon Steep, a height which they had dreamed of climbing ever since they had first seen its bare spine rising above the roof of Lyng. Doubtless it was the mere fact of the other incident's having occurred on the very day of their ascent to Meldon that had kept it stored away in the fold of memory from which it now emerged; for in itself it had no mark of the portentous. At the moment there could have been nothing more natural than that Ned should dash himself from the roof in the pursuit of dilatory tradesmen. It was the period when they were always on the watch for one or the other of the specialists employed about the place; always lying in wait for them, and rushing out at them with questions, reproaches or reminders. And certainly in the distance the grey figure had looked like Peters.

Yet now, as she reviewed the scene, she felt her husband's explanation of it to have been invalidated by the look of anxiety on his face. Why had the familiar appearance of Peters made him anxious? Why, above all, if it was of such prime necessity to confer with him on the subject of the stable drains, had the failure to find him produced such a look of relief? Mary could not say that any one of these questions had occurred to her at the time, yet, from the promptness with which they now marshalled themselves at her summons, she had a sense that they must all along have been there, waiting their hour.

II

Weary with her thoughts, she moved to the window. The library was now quite dark, and she was surprised to see how much faint light the outer world still held.

As she peered out into it across the court, a figure shaped itself far down the perspective of bare limes: it looked a mere blot of deeper grey in the greyness, and for an instant, as it moved toward her, her heart thumped to the thought "It's the ghost!"

She had time, in that long instant, to feel suddenly that the man of whom, two months earlier, she had had a distant vision from the roof, was now, at his predestined hour, about to reveal himself as *not* having been Peters; and her spirit sank under the impending fear of the disclosure. But almost with the next tick of the clock the figure, gaining substance and character, showed itself even to her weak sight as her husband's;

and she turned to meet him, as he entered, with the confession of her folly.

"It's really too absurd," she laughed out, "but I never *can* remember!"

"Remember what?" Boyne questioned as they drew together.

"That when one sees the Lyng ghost one never knows it."

Her hand was on his sleeve, and he kept it there, but with no response in his gesture or in the lines of his preoccupied face.

"Did you think you'd seen it?" he asked, after an appreciable interval.

"Why, I actually took *you* for it, my dear, in my mad determination to spot it!"

"Me—just now?" His arm dropped away, and he turned from her with a faint echo of her laugh. "Really, dearest, you'd better give it up, if that's the best you can do."

"Oh, yes, I give it up. Have *you*?" she asked, turning round on him abruptly.

The parlour-maid had entered with letters and a lamp, and the light struck up into Boyne's face as he bent above the tray she presented.

"Have *you*?" Mary perversely insisted, when the servant had disappeared on her errand of illumination.

"Have I what?" he rejoined absently, the light bringing out the sharp stamp of worry between his brows as he turned over the letters.

"Given up trying to see the ghost." Her heart beat a little at the experiment she was making.

Her husband, laying his letters aside, moved away into the shadow of the hearth.

"I never tried," he said, tearing open the wrapper of a newspaper.

"Well, of course," Mary persisted, "the exasperating thing is that there's no use trying, since one can't be sure till so long afterward."

He was unfolding the paper as if he had hardly heard her; but after a pause, during which the sheets rustled spasmodically between his hands, he looked up to ask, "Have you any idea *how long*?"

Mary had sunk into a low chair beside the fireplace. From

her seat she glanced over, startled, at her husband's profile, which was projected against the circle of lamplight.

"No; none. Have *you*?" she retorted, repeating her former phrase with an added stress of intention.

Boyne crumpled the paper into a bunch, and then, inconsequently, turned back with it toward the lamp.

"Lord, no! I only meant," he explained, with a faint tinge of impatience, "is there any legend, any tradition, as to that?"

"Not that I know of," she answered; but the impulse to add "What makes you ask?" was checked by the reappearance of the parlour-maid, with tea and a second lamp.

With the dispersal of shadows, and the repetition of the daily domestic office, Mary Boyne felt herself less oppressed by that sense of something mutely imminent which had darkened her afternoon. For a few moments she gave herself to the details of her task, and when she looked up from it she was struck to the point of bewilderment by the change in her husband's face. He had seated himself near the farther lamp, and was absorbed in the perusal of his letters; but was it something he had found in them, or merely the shifting of her own point of view, that had restored his features to their normal aspect? The longer she looked the more definitely the change affirmed itself. The lines of tension had vanished, and such traces of fatigue as lingered were of the kind easily attributable to steady mental effort. He glanced up, as if drawn by her gaze, and met her eyes with a smile.

"I'm dying for my tea, you know; and here's a letter for you," he said.

She took the letter he held out in exchange for the cup she proffered him, and, returning to her seat, broke the seal with the languid gesture of the reader whose interests are all enclosed in the circle of one cherished presence.

Her next conscious motion was that of starting to her feet, the letter falling to them as she rose, while she held out to her husband a newspaper clipping.

"Ned! What's this? What does it mean?"

He had risen at the same instant, almost as if hearing her cry before she uttered it; and for a perceptible space of time he and she studied each other, like adversaries watching for an advantage, across the space between her chair and his desk.

"What's what? You fairly made me jump!" Boyne said at length, moving toward her with a sudden half-exasperated laugh. The shadow of apprehension was on his face again, not now a look of fixed foreboding, but a shifting vigilance of lips and eyes that gave her the sense of his feeling himself invisibly surrounded.

Her hand shook so that she could hardly give him the clipping.

"This article—from the *Waukesha Sentinel*—that a man named Elwell has brought suit against you—that there was something wrong about the Blue Star Mine. I can't understand more than half."

They continued to face each other as she spoke, and to her astonishment she saw that her words had the almost immediate effect of dissipating the strained watchfulness of his look.

"Oh, *that!*" He glanced down the printed slip, and then folded it with the gesture of one who handles something harmless and familiar. "What's the matter with you this afternoon, Mary? I thought you'd got bad news."

She stood before him with her undefinable terror subsiding slowly under the reassurance of his tone.

"You knew about this, then—it's all right?"

"Certainly I knew about it; and it's all right."

"But what *is* it? I don't understand. What does this man accuse you of?"

"Pretty nearly every crime in the calendar." Boyne had tossed the clipping down, and thrown himself into an armchair near the fire. "Do you want to hear the story? It's not particularly interesting—just a squabble over interests in the Blue Star."

"But who is this Elwell? I don't know the name."

"Oh, he's a fellow I put into it—gave him a hand up. I told you all about him at the time."

"I daresay. I must have forgotten." Vainly she strained back among her memories. "But if you helped him, why does he make this return?"

"Probably some shyster lawyer got hold of him and talked him over. It's all rather technical and complicated. I thought that kind of thing bored you."

His wife felt a sting of compunction. Theoretically, she deprecated the American wife's detachment from her husband's professional interests, but in practice she had always found it difficult to fix her attention on Boyne's report of the transactions in which his varied interests involved him. Besides, she had felt during their years of exile, that, in a community where the amenities of living could be obtained only at the cost of efforts as arduous as her husband's professional labours, such brief leisure as he and she could command should be used as an escape from immediate preoccupations, a flight to the life they always dreamed of living. Once or twice, now that this new life had actually drawn its magic circle about them, she had asked herself if she had done right; but hitherto such conjectures had been no more than the retrospective excursions of an active fancy. Now, for the first time, it startled her a little to find how little she knew of the material foundation on which her happiness was built.

She glanced at her husband, and was again reassured by the composure of his face; yet she felt the need of more definite grounds for her reassurance.

"But doesn't this suit worry you? Why have you never spoken to me about it?"

He answered both questions at once. "I didn't speak of it at first because it *did* worry me—annoyed me, rather. But it's all ancient history now. Your correspondent must have got hold of a back number of the *Sentinel*."

She felt a quick thrill of relief. "You mean it's over? He's lost his case?"

There was a just perceptible delay in Boyne's reply. "The suit's been withdrawn—that's all."

But she persisted, as if to exonerate herself from the inward charge of being too easily put off. "Withdrawn it because he saw he had no chance?"

"Oh, he had no chance," Boyne answered.

She was still struggling with a dimly felt perplexity at the back of her thoughts.

"How long ago was it withdrawn?"

He paused, as if with a slight return of his former uncertainty. "I've just had the news now; but I've been expecting it."

"Just now—in one of your letters?"

"Yes; in one of my letters."

She made no answer, and was aware only, after a short interval of waiting, that he had risen, and, strolling across the room, had placed himself on the sofa at her side. She felt him, as he did so, pass an arm about her, she felt his hand seek hers and clasp it, and turning slowly, drawn by the warmth of his cheek, she met his smiling eyes.

"It's all right—it's all right?" she questioned, through the flood of her dissolving doubts; and "I give you my word it was never righter!" he laughed back at her, holding her close.

III

One of the strangest things she was afterward to recall out of all the next day's strangeness was the sudden and complete recovery of her sense of security.

It was in the air when she woke in her low-ceiled, dusky room; it went with her down-stairs to the breakfast-table, flashed out at her from the fire, and reduplicated itself from the flanks of the urn and the sturdy flutings of the Georgian teapot. It was as if, in some roundabout way, all her diffused fears of the previous day, with their moment of sharp concentration about the newspaper article—as if this dim questioning of the future, and startled return upon the past, had between them liquidated the arrears of some haunting moral obligation. If she had indeed been careless of her husband's affairs, it was, her new state seemed to prove, because her faith in him instinctively justified such carelessness; and his right to her faith had now affirmed itself in the very face of menace and suspicion. She had never seen him more untroubled, more naturally and unconsciously himself, than after the cross-examination to which she had subjected him: it was almost as if he had been aware of her doubts, and had wanted the air cleared as much as she did.

It was as clear, thank Heaven! as the bright outer light that surprised her almost with a touch of summer when she issued from the house for her daily round of the gardens. She had left Boyne at his desk, indulging herself, as she passed the library door, by a last peep at his quiet face, where he bent, pipe in mouth, above his papers; and now she had her own morning's task to perform. The task involved, on such charmed winter days, almost as much happy loitering about the different quarters of her demesne as if spring were already at work there. There were such endless possibilities still before her, such opportunities to bring out the latent graces of the old place, without a single irreverent touch of alteration, that the winter was all too short to plan what spring and autumn executed. And her recovered sense of safety gave, on this particular morning, a peculiar zest to her progress through the sweet still place. She went first to the kitchen-garden, where the espaliered pear-trees drew complicated patterns on the walls, and pigeons were fluttering and preening about the silvery-slated roof of their cot. There was something wrong about the piping of the hot-house, and she was expecting an authority from Dorchester, who was to drive out between trains and make a diagnosis of the boiler. But when she dipped into the damp heat of the green-houses, among the spiced scents and waxy pinks and reds of old-fashioned exotics—even the flora of Lyng was in the note! —she learned that the great man had not arrived, and, the day being too rare to waste in an artificial atmosphere, she came out again and paced along the springy turf of the bowling-green to the gardens behind the house. At their farther end rose a grass terrace, looking across the fish-pond and yew hedges to the long house-front with its twisted chimney-stacks and blue roof angles all drenched in the pale gold moisture of the air.

Seen thus, across the level tracery of the gardens, it sent her, from open windows and hospitably smoking chimneys, the look of some warm human presence, of a mind slowly ripened on a sunny wall of experience. She had never before had such a sense of her intimacy with it, such a conviction that its secrets were all beneficent, kept, as they said to children, "for one's good," such a trust in its power to gather up her life and Ned's into the harmonious pattern of the long long story it sat there weaving in the sun.

She heard steps behind her, and turned, expecting to see the gardener accompanied by the engineer from Dorchester. But only one figure was in sight, that of a youngish slightly built man, who, for reasons she could not on the spot have given, did not remotely resemble her notion of an authority on hot-house boilers. The new-comer, on seeing her, lifted his hat, and paused with the air of a gentleman—perhaps a traveller—who wishes to make it known that his intrusion is involuntary. Lyng occasionally attracted the more cultivated traveller, and Mary half-expected to see the stranger dissemble a camera, or justify his presence by producing it. But he made no gesture of any sort, and after a moment she asked, in a tone responding to the courteous hesitation of his attitude: "Is there any one you wish to see?"

"I came to see Mr. Boyne," he answered. His intonation, rather than his accent, was faintly American, and Mary, at the note, looked at him more closely. The brim of his soft felt hat cast a shade on his face, which, thus obscured, wore to her short-sighted gaze a look of seriousness, as of a person arriving "on business," and civilly but firmly aware of his rights.

Past experience had made her equally sensible to such claims; but she was jealous of her husband's morning hours, and doubtful of his having given any one the right to intrude on them.

"Have you an appointment with my husband?" she asked.

The visitor hesitated, as if unprepared for the question.

"I think he expects me," he replied.

It was Mary's turn to hesitate. "You see this is his time for work: he never sees any one in the morning."

He looked at her a moment without answering; then, as if accepting her decision, he began to move away. As he turned, Mary saw him pause and glance up at the peaceful house-front. Something in his air suggested weariness and disappointment, the dejection of the traveller who has come from far off and whose hours are limited by the time-table. It occurred to her that if this were the case her refusal might have made his errand vain, and a sense of compunction caused her to hasten after him.

"May I ask if you have come a long way?"

He gave her the same grave look. "Yes—I have come a long way."

"Then, if you'll go to the house, no doubt my husband will see you now. You'll find him in the library."

She did not know why she had added the last phrase, except from a vague impulse to atone for her previous inhospitality. The visitor seemed about to express his thanks, but her attention was distracted by the approach of the gardener with a companion who bore all the marks of being the expert from Dorchester.

"This way," she said, waving the stranger to the house; and

an instant later she had forgotten him in the absorption of her meeting with the boiler-maker.

The encounter led to such far-reaching results that the engineer ended by finding it expedient to ignore his train, and Mary was beguiled into spending the remainder of the morning in absorbed confabulation among the flower-pots. When the colloquy ended, she was surprised to find that it was nearly luncheon-time, and she half expected, as she hurried back to the house, to see her husband coming out to meet her. But she found no one in the court but an under-gardener raking the gravel, and the hall, when she entered it, was so silent that she guessed Boyne to be still at work.

Not wishing to disturb him, she turned into the drawing-room, and there, at her writing-table, lost herself in renewed calculations of the outlay to which the morning's conference had pledged her. The fact that she could permit herself such follies had not yet lost its novelty; and somehow, in contrast to the vague fears of the previous days, it now seemed an element of her recovered security, of the sense that, as Ned had said, things in general had never been "righter."

She was still luxuriating in a lavish play of figures when the parlour-maid, from the threshold, roused her with an enquiry as to the expediency of serving luncheon. It was one of their jokes that Trimmle announced luncheon as if she were divulging a state secret and Mary, intent upon her papers, merely murmured an absent-minded assent.

She felt Trimmle wavering doubtfully on the threshold, as if in rebuke of such unconsidered assent; then her retreating steps sounded down the passage, and Mary, pushing away her papers, crossed the hall and went to the library door. It was still closed, and she wavered in her turn, disliking to disturb her husband, yet anxious that he should not exceed his usual measure of work. As she stood there, balancing her impulses, Trimmle returned with the announcement of luncheon, and Mary, thus impelled, opened the library door.

Boyne was not at his desk, and she peered about her, expecting to discover him before the book-shelves, somewhere down the length of the room; but her call brought no response, and gradually it became clear to her that he was not there.

She turned back to the parlour-maid.

"Mr. Boyne must be up-stairs. Please tell him that luncheon is ready."

Trimmle appeared to hesitate between the obvious duty of obedience and an equally obvious conviction of the foolishness of the injunction laid on her. The struggle resulted in her saying: "If you please, Madam, Mr. Boyne's not up-stairs."

"Not in his room? Are you sure?"

"I'm sure, Madam."

Mary consulted the clock. "Where is he, then?"

"He's gone out," Trimmle announced, with the superior air of one who has respectfully waited for the question that a well-ordered mind would have put first.

Mary's conjecture had been right, then. Boyne must have gone to the gardens to meet her, and since she had missed him, it was clear that he had taken the shorter way by the south door, instead of going round to the court. She crossed the hall to the French window opening directly on the yew garden, but the parlour-maid, after another moment of inner conflict, decided to bring out: "Please, Madam, Mr. Boyne didn't go that way."

Mary turned back. "Where *did* he go? And when?"

"He went out of the front door, up the drive, Madam." It was a matter of principle with Trimmle never to answer more than one question at a time.

"Up the drive? At this hour?" Mary went to the door herself, and glanced across the court through the tunnel of bare limes. But its perspective was as empty as when she had scanned it on entering.

"Did Mr. Boyne leave no message?"

Trimmle seemed to surrender herself to a last struggle with the forces of chaos.

"No, Madam. He just went out with the gentleman."

"The gentleman? What gentleman?" Mary wheeled about, as if to front this new factor.

"The gentleman who called, Madam," said Trimmle resignedly.

"When did a gentleman call? Do explain yourself, Trimmle!"

Only the fact that Mary was very hungry, and that she wanted to consult her husband about the greenhouses, would have caused her to lay so unusual an injunction on her attendant; and even now she was detached enough to note in Trimmle's eye the dawning defiance of the respectful subordinate who has been pressed too hard.

"I couldn't exactly say the hour, Madam, because I didn't let the gentleman in," she replied, with an air of discreetly ignoring the irregularity of her mistress's course.

"You didn't let him in?"

"No, Madam. When the bell rang I was dressing, and Agnes——"

"Go and ask Agnes, then," said Mary.

Trimmle still wore her look of patient magnanimity. "Agnes would not know, Madam, for she had unfortunately burnt her hand in trimming the wick of the new lamp from town" —Trimmle, as Mary was aware, had always been opposed to the new lamp— "and so Mrs. Dockett sent the kitchen-maid instead."

Mary looked again at the clock. "It's after two! Go and ask the kitchen-maid if Mr. Boyne left any word."

She went into luncheon without waiting, and Trimmle presently brought her there the kitchen-maid's statement that the gentleman had called about eleven o'clock, and that Mr. Boyne had gone out with him without leaving any message. The kitchen-maid did not even know the caller's name, for he had written it on a slip of paper, which he had folded and handed to her, with the injunction to deliver it at once to Mr. Boyne.

Mary finished her luncheon, still wondering, and when it was over, and Trimmle had brought the coffee to the drawing-room, her wonder had deepened to a first faint tinge of disquietude. It was unlike Boyne to absent himself without explanation at so unwonted an hour, and the difficulty of identifying the visitor whose summons he had apparently obeyed made his disappearance the more unaccountable. Mary Boyne's experience as the wife of a busy engineer, subject to sudden calls and compelled to keep irregular hours, had trained her to the philosophic acceptance of surprises; but since Boyne's withdrawal from business he had adopted a Benedictine regularity of life. As if to make up for the dispersed and agitated years, with their "stand-up" lunches, and dinners rattled down to the joltings of the dining-cars, he cultivated the last refinements of punctuality and monotony, discouraging his wife's fancy for the unexpected, and declaring that to a delicate taste there were infinite gradations of pleasure in the recurrences of habit.

Still, since no life can completely defend itself from the unforeseen, it was evident that all Boyne's precautions would sooner or later prove unavailable, and Mary concluded that he had cut short a tiresome visit by walking with his caller to the station, or at least accompanying him for part of the way.

This conclusion relieved her from farther preoccupation, and she went out herself to take up her conference with the gardener. Thence she walked to the village post-office, a mile or so away; and when she turned toward home the early twilight was setting in.

She had taken a foot-path across the downs, and as Boyne, meanwhile, had probably returned from the station by the highroad, there was little likelihood of their meeting. She felt sure, however, of his having reached the house before her; so sure that, when she entered it herself, without even pausing to inquire of Trimmle, she made directly for the library. But the library was still empty, and with an unwonted exactness of visual memory she observed that the papers on her husband's desk lay precisely as they had lain when she had gone in to call him to luncheon.

Then of a sudden she was seized by a vague dread of the unknown. She had closed the door behind her on entering, and as she stood alone in the long silent room, her dread seemed to take shape and sound, to be there breathing and lurking among the shadows. Her short-sighted eyes strained through them, half-discerning an actual presence, something aloof, that watched and knew; and in the recoil from that intangible presence she threw herself on the bell-rope and gave it a sharp pull.

The sharp summons brought Trimmle in precipitately with a lamp, and Mary breathed again at this sobering reappearance of the usual.

"You may bring tea if Mr. Boyne is in," she said, to justify her ring.

"Very well, Madam. But Mr. Boyne is not in," said Trimmle, putting down the lamp.

"Not in? You mean he's come back and gone out again?"

"No, Madam. He's never been back."

The dread stirred again, and Mary knew that now it had her fast.

"Not since he went out with—the gentleman?"

"Not since he went out with the gentleman."

"But who *was* the gentleman?" Mary insisted, with the shrill note of some one trying to be heard through a confusion of noises.

"That I couldn't say, Madam." Trimmle, standing there by the lamp, seemed suddenly to grow less round and rosy, as though eclipsed by the same creeping shade of apprehension.

"But the kitchen-maid knows—wasn't it the kitchen-maid who let him in?"

"She doesn't know either, Madam, for he wrote his name on a folded paper."

Mary, through her agitation, was aware that they were both designating the unknown visitor by a vague pronoun, instead of the conventional formula which, till then, had kept their allusions within the bounds of conformity. And at the same moment her mind caught at the suggestion of the folded paper.

"But he must have a name! Where's the paper?"

She moved to the desk, and began to turn over the documents that littered it. The first that caught her eye was an unfinished letter in her husband's hand, with his pen lying across it, as though dropped there at a sudden summons.

"My dear Parvis"—who was Parvis?— "I have just received your letter announcing Elwell's death, and while I suppose there is now no farther risk of trouble, it might be safer——"

She tossed the sheet aside, and continued her search; but no folded paper was discoverable among the letters and pages of manuscript which had been swept together in a heap, as if by a hurried or a startled gesture.

"But the kitchen-maid *saw* him. Send her here," she commanded, wondering at her dulness in not thinking sooner of so simple a solution.

Trimmle vanished in a flash, as if thankful to be out of the room, and when she reappeared, conducting the agitated underling, Mary had regained her self-possession, and had her questions ready.

The gentleman was a stranger, yes—that she understood.

But what had he said? And, above all, what had he looked like? The first question was easily enough answered, for the disconcerting reason that he had said so little—had merely asked for Mr. Boyne, and, scribbling something on a bit of paper, had requested that it should at once be carried in to him.

"Then you don't know what he wrote? You're not sure it *was* his name?"

The kitchen-maid was not sure, but supposed it was, since he had written it in answer to her inquiry as to whom she should announce.

"And when you carried the paper in to Mr. Boyne, what did he say?"

The kitchen-maid did not think that Mr. Boyne had said anything, but she could not be sure, for just as she had handed him the paper and he was opening it, she had become aware that the visitor had followed her into the library, and she had slipped out, leaving the two gentlemen together.

"But then, if you left them in the library, how do you know that they went out of the house?"

This question plunged the witness into a momentary inarticulateness, from which she was rescued by Trimmle, who, by means of ingenious circumlocutions, elicited the statement that before she could cross the hall to the back passage she had heard the two gentlemen behind her, and had seen them go out of the front door together.

"Then, if you saw the strange gentleman twice, you must be able to tell me what he looked like."

But with this final challenge to her powers of expression it became clear that the limit of the kitchen-maid's endurance had been reached. The obligation of going to the front door to "show in" a visitor was in itself so subversive of the fundamental order of things that it had thrown her faculties into hopeless disarray, and she could only stammer out, after various panting efforts: "His hat, mum, was different-like, as you might say——"

"Different? How different?" Mary flashed out, her own mind, in the same instant, leaping back to an image left on it that morning, and then lost under layers of subsequent impressions.

"His hat had a wide brim, you mean? and his face was pale—a youngish face?" Mary pressed her, with a white-lipped inten-

sity of interrogation. But if the kitchen-maid found any adequate answer to this challenge, it was swept away for her listener down the rushing current of her own convictions. The
stranger—the stranger in the garden! Why had Mary not
thought of him before? She needed no one now to tell her that
it was he who had called for her husband and gone away with
him. But who was he, and why had Boyne obeyed him?

IV

It leaped out at her suddenly, like a grin out of the dark, that
they had often called England so little—"such a confoundedly
hard place to get lost in."

A confoundedly hard place to get lost in! That had been her
husband's phrase. And now, with the whole machinery of official investigation sweeping its flash-lights from shore to shore,
and across the dividing straits; now, with Boyne's name blazing
from the walls of every town and village, his portrait (how that
wrung her!) hawked up and down the country like the image
of a hunted criminal; now the little compact populous island,
so policed, surveyed and administered, revealed itself as a
Sphinx-like guardian of abysmal mysteries, staring back into his
wife's anguished eyes as if with the wicked joy of knowing
something they would never know!

In the fortnight since Boyne's disappearance there had been
no word of him, no trace of his movements. Even the usual
misleading reports that raise expectancy in tortured bosoms
had been few and fleeting. No one but the kitchen-maid had
seen Boyne leave the house, and no one else had seen "the
gentleman" who accompanied him. All enquiries in the neighbourhood failed to elicit the memory of a stranger's presence
that day in the neighbourhood of Lyng. And no one had met
Edward Boyne, either alone or in company, in any of the neighbouring villages, or on the road across the downs, or at either
of the local railway-stations. The sunny English noon had swallowed him as completely as if he had gone out into Cimmerian
night.

Mary, while every official means of investigation was working
at its highest pressure, had ransacked her husband's papers for
any trace of antecedent complications, of entanglements or

obligations unknown to her, that might throw a ray into the darkness. But if any such had existed in the background of Boyne's life, they had vanished like the slip of paper on which the visitor had written his name. There remained no possible thread of guidance except—if it were indeed an exception—the letter which Boyne had apparently been in the act of writing when he received his mysterious summons. That letter, read and reread by his wife, and submitted by her to the police, yielded little enough to feed conjecture.

"I have just heard of Elwell's death, and while I suppose there is now no farther risk of trouble, it might be safer——" That was all. The "risk of trouble" was easily explained by the newspaper clipping which had apprised Mary of the suit brought against her husband by one of his associates in the Blue Star enterprise. The only new information conveyed by the letter was the fact of its showing Boyne, when he wrote it, to be still apprehensive of the results of the suit, though he had told his wife that it had been withdrawn, and though the letter itself proved that the plaintiff was dead. It took several days of cabling to fix the identity of the "Parvis" to whom the fragment was addressed, but even after these enquiries had shown him to be a Waukesha lawyer, no new facts concerning the Elwell suit were elicited. He appeared to have had no direct concern in it, but to have been conversant with the facts merely as an acquaintance, and possible intermediary; and he declared himself unable to guess with what object Boyne intended to seek his assistance.

This negative information, sole fruit of the first fortnight's search, was not increased by a jot during the slow weeks that followed. Mary knew that the investigations were still being carried on, but she had a vague sense of their gradually slackening, as the actual march of time seemed to slacken. It was as though the days, flying horror-struck from the shrouded image of the one inscrutable day, gained assurance as the distance lengthened, till at last they fell back into their normal gait. And so with the human imaginations at work on the dark event. No doubt it occupied them still, but week by week and hour by hour it grew less absorbing, took up less space, was slowly but inevitably crowded out of the foreground of consciousness by the new problems perpetually bubbling up from the cloudy caldron of human experience.

Even Mary Boyne's consciousness gradually felt the same lowering of velocity. It still swayed with the incessant oscillations of conjecture; but they were slower, more rhythmical in their beat. There were even moments of weariness when, like the victim of some poison which leaves the brain clear, but holds the body motionless, she saw herself domesticated with the Horror, accepting its perpetual presence as one of the fixed conditions of life.

These moments lengthened into hours and days, till she passed into a phase of stolid acquiescence. She watched the routine of daily life with the incurious eye of a savage on whom the meaningless processes of civilisation make but the faintest impression. She had come to regard herself as part of the routine, a spoke of the wheel, revolving with its motion; she felt almost like the furniture of the room in which she sat, an insensate object to be dusted and pushed about with the chairs and tables. And this deepening apathy held her fast at Lyng, in spite of the entreaties of friends and the usual medical recommendation of "change." Her friends supposed that her refusal to move was inspired by the belief that her husband would one day return to the spot from which he had vanished, and a beautiful legend grew up about this imaginary state of waiting. But in reality she had no such belief: the depths of anguish enclosing her were no longer lighted by flashes of hope. She was sure that Boyne would never come back, that he had gone out of her sight as completely as if Death itself had waited that day on the threshold. She had even renounced, one by one, the various theories as to his disappearance which had been advanced by the press, the police, and her own agonised imagination. In sheer lassitude her mind turned from these alternatives of horror, and sank back into the blank fact that he was gone.

No, she would never know what had become of him—no one would ever know. But the house *knew*; the library in which she spent her long lonely evenings knew. For it was here that the last scene had been enacted, here that the stranger had come, and spoken the word which had caused Boyne to rise and follow him. The floor she trod had felt his tread; the books on the shelves had seen his face; and there were moments when the intense consciousness of the old dusky walls seemed about to break out into some audible revelation of their secret. But the revelation never came, and she knew it would never come. Lyng was not one of the garrulous old houses that betray the secrets entrusted to them. Its very legend proved that it had always been the mute accomplice, the incorruptible custodian, of the mysteries it had surprised. And Mary Boyne, sitting face to face with its silence, felt the futility of seeking to break it by any human means.

V

"I don't say it *wasn't* straight, and yet I don't say it *was* straight. It was business."

Mary, at the words, lifted her head with a start, and looked intently at the speaker.

When, half an hour before, a card with "Mr. Parvis" on it had been brought up to her, she had been immediately aware that the name had been a part of her consciousness ever since she had read it at the head of Boyne's unfinished letter. In the library she had found awaiting her a small sallow man with a bald head and gold eye-glasses, and it sent a tremor through her to know that this was the person to whom her husband's last known thought had been directed.

Parvis, civilly, but without vain preamble—in the manner of a man who has his watch in his hand—had set forth the object of his visit. He had "run over" to England on business, and finding himself in the neighbourhood of Dorchester, had not wished to leave it without paying his respects to Mrs. Boyne; and without asking her, if the occasion offered, what she meant to do about Bob Elwell's family.

The words touched the spring of some obscure dread in Mary's bosom. Did her visitor, after all, know what Boyne had meant by his unfinished phrase? She asked for an elucidation of his question, and noticed at once that he seemed surprised at her continued ignorance of the subject. Was it possible that she really knew as little as she said?

"I know nothing—you must tell me," she faltered out; and her visitor thereupon proceeded to unfold his story. It threw, even to her confused perceptions, and imperfectly initiated vision, a lurid glare on the whole hazy episode of the Blue Star Mine. Her husband had made his money in that brilliant speculation at the cost of "getting ahead" of some one less alert to seize the chance; and the victim of his ingenuity was young Robert Elwell, who had "put him on" to the Blue Star scheme.

Parvis, at Mary's first cry, had thrown her a sobering glance through his impartial glasses.

"Bob Elwell wasn't smart enough, that's all; if he had been, he might have turned round and served Boyne the same way. It's the kind of thing that happens every day in business. I guess it's what the scientists call the survival of the fittest—see?" said Mr. Parvis, evidently pleased with the aptness of his analogy.

Mary felt a physical shrinking from the next question she tried to frame: it was as though the words on her lips had a taste that nauseated her.

"But then—you accuse my husband of doing something dishonourable?"

Mr. Parvis surveyed the question dispassionately. "Oh, no, I don't. I don't even say it wasn't straight." He glanced up and down the long lines of books, as if one of them might have supplied him with the definition he sought. "I don't say it *wasn't* straight, and yet I don't say it *was* straight. It was business." After all, no definition in his category could be more comprehensive than that.

Mary sat staring at him with a look of terror. He seemed to her like the indifferent emissary of some evil power.

"But Mr. Elwell's lawyers apparently did not take your view, since I suppose the suit was withdrawn by their advice."

"Oh, yes; they knew he hadn't a leg to stand on, technically. It was when they advised him to withdraw the suit that he got desperate. You see, he'd borrowed most of the money he lost in the Blue Star, and he was up a tree. That's why he shot himself when they told him he had no show."

The horror was sweeping over Mary in great deafening waves.

"He shot himself? He killed himself because of *that*?"

"Well, he didn't kill himself, exactly. He dragged on two months before he died." Parvis emitted the statement as unemotionally as a gramophone grinding out its "record."

"You mean that he tried to kill himself, and failed? And tried again?"

"Oh, he didn't have to *try* again," said Parvis grimly.

They sat opposite each other in silence, he swinging his eye-glasses thoughtfully about his finger, she, motionless, her arms stretched along her knees in an attitude of rigid tension.

"But if you knew all this," she began at length, hardly able to force her voice above a whisper, "how is it that when I wrote you at the time of my husband's disappearance you said you didn't understand his letter?"

Parvis received this without perceptible embarrassment: "Why, I didn't understand it—strictly speaking. And it wasn't the time to talk about it, if I had. The Elwell business was settled when the suit was withdrawn. Nothing I could have told you would have helped you to find your husband."

Mary continued to scrutinise him. "Then why are you telling me now?"

Still Parvis did not hesitate. "Well, to begin with, I supposed you knew more than you appear to—I mean about the circumstances of Elwell's death. And then people are talking of it now; the whole matter's been raked up again. And I thought if you didn't know you ought to."

She remained silent, and he continued: "You see, it's only come out lately what a bad state Elwell's affairs were in. His wife's a proud woman, and she fought on as long as she could, going out to work, and taking sewing at home when she got too sick—something with the heart, I believe. But she had his mother to look after, and the children, and she broke down under it, and finally had to ask for help. That called attention to the case, and the papers took it up, and a subscription was started. Everybody out there liked Bob Elwell, and most of the prominent names in the place are down on the list, and people began to wonder why——"

Parvis broke off to fumble in an inner pocket. "Here," he continued, "here's an account of the whole thing from the *Sentinel*—a little sensational, of course. But I guess you'd better look it over."

He held out a newspaper to Mary, who unfolded it slowly, remembering, as she did so, the evening when, in that same room, the perusal of a clipping from the *Sentinel* had first shaken the depths of her security.

As she opened the paper, her eyes, shrinking from the glaring headlines, "Widow of Boyne's Victim Forced to Appeal for Aid," ran down the column of text to two portraits inserted in it. The first was her husband's, taken from a photograph made the year they had come to England. It was the picture of him that she liked best, the one that stood on the writing-table upstairs in her bedroom. As the eyes in the photograph met hers, she felt it would be impossible to read what was said of him, and closed her lids with the sharpness of the pain.

"I thought if you felt disposed to put your name down——" she heard Parvis continue.

She opened her eyes with an effort, and they fell on the other portrait. It was that of a youngish man, slightly built, with features somewhat blurred by the shadow of a projecting hat-brim. Where had she seen that outline before? She stared at it confusedly, her heart hammering in her ears. Then she gave a cry.

"This is the man—the man who came for my husband!"

She heard Parvis start to his feet, and was dimly aware that she had slipped backward into the corner of the sofa, and that he was bending above her in alarm. She straightened herself, and reached out for the paper, which she had dropped.

"It's the man! I should know him anywhere!" she persisted in a voice that sounded to her own ears like a scream.

Parvis's answer seemed to come to her from far off, down endless fog-muffled windings.

"Mrs. Boyne, you're not very well. Shall I call somebody? Shall I get a glass of water?"

"No, no, no!" She threw herself toward him, her hand frantically clutching the newspaper. "I tell you, it's the man! I *know* him! He spoke to me in the garden!"

Parvis took the journal from her, directing his glasses to the portrait. "It can't be, Mrs. Boyne. It's Robert Elwell."

"Robert Elwell?" Her white stare seemed to travel into space. "Then it was Robert Elwell who came for him."

"Came for Boyne? The day he went away from here?" Parvis's voice dropped as hers rose. He bent over, laying a fraternal hand on her, as if to coax her gently back into her seat. "Why, Elwell was dead! Don't you remember?"

Mary sat with her eyes fixed on the picture, unconscious of what he was saying.

"Don't you remember Boyne's unfinished letter to me—the one you found on his desk that day? It was written just after he'd heard of Elwell's death." She noticed an odd shake in Parvis's unemotional voice. "Surely you remember!" he urged her.

Yes, she remembered: that was the profoundest horror of it. Elwell had died the day before her husband's disappearance; and this was Elwell's portrait; and it was the portrait of the man who had spoken to her in the garden. She lifted her head and looked slowly about the library. The library could have borne witness that it was also the portrait of the man who had come in that day to call Boyne from his unfinished letter. Through the misty surgings of her brain she heard the faint boom of half-forgotten words—words spoken by Alida Stair on the lawn at Pangbourne before Boyne and his wife had ever seen the house at Lyng, or had imagined that they might one day live there.

"This was the man who spoke to me," she repeated.

She looked again at Parvis. He was trying to conceal his disturbance under what he probably imagined to be an expression of indulgent commiseration; but the edges of his lips were blue. "He thinks me mad; but I'm not mad," she reflected; and suddenly there flashed upon her a way of justifying her strange affirmation.

She sat quiet, controlling the quiver of her lips, and waiting till she could trust her voice; then she said, looking straight at Parvis: "Will you answer me one question, please? When was it that Robert Elwell tried to kill himself?"

"When—when?" Parvis stammered.

"Yes; the date. Please try to remember."

She saw that he was growing still more afraid of her. "I have a reason," she insisted.

"Yes, yes. Only I can't remember. About two months before, I should say."

"I want the date," she repeated.

Parvis picked up the newspaper. "We might see here," he said, still humouring her. He ran his eyes down the page. "Here it is. Last October—the——"

She caught the words from him. "The 20th, wasn't it?" With a sharp look at her, he verified. "Yes, the 20th. Then you *did* know?"

"I know now." Her gaze continued to travel past him. "Sunday, the 20th—that was the day he came first."

Parvis's voice was almost inaudible. "Came *here* first?"

"Yes."

"You saw him twice, then?"

"Yes, twice." She just breathed it at him. "He came first on the 20th of October. I remember the date because it was the day we went up Meldon Steep for the first time." She felt a faint gasp of inward laughter at the thought that but for that she might have forgotten.

Parvis continued to scrutinise her, as if trying to intercept her gaze.

"We saw him from the roof," she went on. "He came down the lime-avenue toward the house. He was dressed just as he is in that picture. My husband saw him first. He was frightened, and ran down ahead of me; but there was no one there. He had vanished."

"Elwell had vanished?" Parvis faltered.

"Yes." Their two whispers seemed to grope for each other. "I couldn't think what had happened. I see now. He *tried* to come then; but he wasn't dead enough—he couldn't reach us. He had to wait for two months to die; and then he came back again—and Ned went with him."

She nodded at Parvis with the look of triumph of a child who has worked out a difficult puzzle. But suddenly she lifted her hands with a desperate gesture, pressing them to her temples.

"Oh, my God! I sent him to Ned—I told him where to go! I sent him to this room!" she screamed.

She felt the walls of books rush toward her, like inward falling ruins; and she heard Parvis, a long way off, through the ruins, crying to her, and struggling to get at her. But she was numb to his touch, she did not know what he was saying. Through the tumult she heard but one clear note, the voice of Alida Stair, speaking on the lawn at Pangbourne.

"You won't know till afterward," it said. "You won't know till long, long afterward."

1910

WILLA CATHER

(1873–1947)

Consequences

HENRY EASTMAN, a lawyer, aged forty, was standing beside the
Flatiron building in a driving November rain-storm, signaling
frantically for a taxi. It was six-thirty, and everything on wheels
was engaged. The streets were in confusion about him, the sky
was in turmoil above him, and the Flatiron building, which
seemed about to blow down, threw water like a mill-shoot.
Suddenly, out of the brutal struggle of men and cars and ma-
chines and people tilting at each other with umbrellas, a quiet,
well-mannered limousine paused before him, at the curb, and
an agreeable, ruddy countenance confronted him through the
open window of the car.

"Don't you want me to pick you up, Mr. Eastman? I'm running directly home now."

Eastman recognized Kier Cavenaugh, a young man of pleasure, who lived in the house on Central Park South, where he
himself had an apartment.

"Don't I?" he exclaimed, bolting into the car. "I'll risk getting your cushions wet without compunction. I came up in a
taxi, but I didn't hold it. Bad economy. I thought I saw your
car down on Fourteenth Street about half an hour ago."

The owner of the car smiled. He had a pleasant, round face
and round eyes, and a fringe of smooth, yellow hair showed
under the rim of his soft felt hat. "With a lot of little broilers
fluttering into it? You did. I know some girls who work in the
cheap shops down there. I happened to be down-town and I
stopped and took a load of them home. I do sometimes. Saves
their poor little clothes, you know. Their shoes are never any
good."

Eastman looked at his rescuer. "Aren't they notoriously afraid
of cars and smooth young men?" he inquired.

Cavenaugh shook his head. "They know which cars are safe
and which are chancy. They put each other wise. You have to

take a bunch at a time, of course. The Italian girls can never come along; their men shoot. The girls understand, all right; but their fathers don't. One gets to see queer places, sometimes, taking them home."

Eastman laughed drily. "Every time I touch the circle of your acquaintance, Cavenaugh, it's a little wider. You must know New York pretty well by this time."

"Yes, but I'm on my good behavior below Twenty-third Street," the young man replied with simplicity. "My little friends down there would give me a good character. They're wise little girls. They have grand ways with each other, a romantic code of loyalty. You can find a good many of the lost virtues among them."

The car was standing still in a traffic block at Fortieth Street, when Cavenaugh suddenly drew his face away from the window and touched Eastman's arm. "Look, please. You see that hansom with the bony gray horse—driver has a broken hat and red flannel around his throat. Can you see who is inside?"

Eastman peered out. The hansom was just cutting across the line, and the driver was making a great fuss about it, bobbing his head and waving his whip. He jerked his dripping old horse into Fortieth Street and clattered off past the Public Library grounds toward Sixth Avenue. "No, I couldn't see the passenger. Someone you know?"

"Could you see whether there was a passenger?" Cavenaugh asked.

"Why, yes. A man, I think. I saw his elbow on the apron. No driver ever behaves like that unless he has a passenger."

"Yes, I may have been mistaken," Cavenaugh murmured absent-mindedly. Ten minutes or so later, after Cavenaugh's car had turned off Fifth Avenue into Fifty-eighth Street, Eastman exclaimed, "There's your same cabby, and his cart's empty. He's headed for a drink now, I suppose." The driver in the broken hat and the red flannel neck cloth was still brandishing the whip over his old gray. He was coming from the west now, and turned down Sixth Avenue, under the elevated.

Cavenaugh's car stopped at the bachelor apartment house between Sixth and Seventh Avenues where he and Eastman lived, and they went up in the elevator together. They were still talking when the lift stopped at Cavenaugh's floor, and

Eastman stepped out with him and walked down the hall, finishing his sentence while Cavenaugh found his latch-key. When he opened the door, a wave of fresh cigarette smoke greeted them. Cavenaugh stopped short and stared into his hallway. "Now how in the devil—!" he exclaimed angrily.

"Someone waiting for you? Oh, no, thanks. I wasn't coming in. I have to work to-night. Thank you, but I couldn't." Eastman nodded and went up the two flights to his own rooms.

Though Eastman did not customarily keep a servant he had this winter a man who had been lent to him by a friend who was abroad. Rollins met him at the door and took his coat and hat.

"Put out my dinner clothes, Rollins, and then get out of here until ten o'clock. I've promised to go to a supper tonight. I shan't be dining. I've had a late tea and I'm going to work until ten. You put out some kumiss and biscuit for me."

Rollins took himself off, and Eastman settled down at the big table in his sitting-room. He had to read a lot of letters submitted as evidence in a breach of contract case, and before he got very far he found that long paragraphs in some of the letters were written in German. He had a German dictionary at his office, but none here. Rollins had gone, and anyhow, the bookstores would be closed. He remembered having seen a row of dictionaries on the lower shelf of one of Cavenaugh's bookcases. Cavenaugh had a lot of books, though he never read anything but new stuff. Eastman prudently turned down his student's lamp very low—the thing had an evil habit of smoking—and went down two flights to Cavenaugh's door.

The young man himself answered Eastman's ring. He was freshly dressed for the evening, except for a brown smoking jacket, and his yellow hair had been brushed until it shone. He hesitated as he confronted his caller, still holding the door knob, and his round eyes and smooth forehead made their best imitation of a frown. When Eastman began to apologize, Cavenaugh's manner suddenly changed. He caught his arm and jerked him into the narrow hall. "Come in, come in. Right along!" he said excitedly. "Right along," he repeated as he pushed Eastman before him into his sitting-room. "Well I'll—" he stopped short at the door and looked about his own room with an air of complete mystification. The back window was wide open and a strong wind was blowing in. Cavenaugh walked over to the window and stuck out his head, looking up and down the fire escape. When he pulled his head in, he drew down the sash.

"I had a visitor I wanted you to see," he explained with a nervous smile. "At least I thought I had. He must have gone out that way," nodding toward the window.

"Call him back. I only came to borrow a German dictionary, if you have one. Can't stay. Call him back."

Cavenaugh shook his head despondently. "No use. He's beat it. Nowhere in sight."

"He must be active. Has he left something?" Eastman pointed to a very dirty white glove that lay on the floor under the window.

"Yes, that's his." Cavenaugh reached for his tongs, picked up the glove, and tossed it into the grate, where it quickly shriveled on the coals. Eastman felt that he had happened in upon something disagreeable, possibly something shady, and he wanted to get away at once. Cavenaugh stood staring at the fire and seemed stupid and dazed; so he repeated his request rather sternly, "I think I've seen a German dictionary down there among your books. May I have it?"

Cavenaugh blinked at him. "A German dictionary? Oh, possibly! Those were my father's. I scarcely know what there is." He put down the tongs and began to wipe his hands nervously with his handkerchief.

Eastman went over to the bookcase behind the Chesterfield, opened the door, swooped upon the book he wanted and stuck it under his arm. He felt perfectly certain now that something shady had been going on in Cavenaugh's rooms, and he saw no reason why he should come in for any hangover. "Thanks. I'll send it back to-morrow," he said curtly as he made for the door.

Cavenaugh followed him. "Wait a moment. I wanted you to see him. You did see his glove," glancing at the grate.

Eastman laughed disagreeably. "I saw a glove. That's not evidence. Do your friends often use that means of exit? Somewhat inconvenient."

Cavenaugh gave him a startled glance. "Wouldn't you think so? For an old man, a very rickety old party? The ladders are steep, you know, and rusty." He approached the window again and put it up softly. In a moment he drew his head back with a jerk. He caught Eastman's arm and shoved him toward the window. "Hurry, please. Look! Down there." He pointed to the little patch of paved court four flights down.

The square of pavement was so small and the walls about it were so high, that it was a good deal like looking down a well. Four tall buildings backed upon the same court and made a kind of shaft, with flagstones at the bottom, and at the top a square of dark blue with some stars in it. At the bottom of the shaft Eastman saw a black figure, a man in a caped coat and a tall hat stealing cautiously around, not across the square of pavement, keeping close to the dark wall and avoiding the streak of light that fell on the flagstones from a window in the opposite house. Seen from that height he was of course fore-shortened and probably looked more shambling and decrepit than he was. He picked his way along with exaggerated care and looked like a silly old cat crossing a wet street. When he reached the gate that led into an alley way between two buildings, he felt about for the latch, opened the door a mere crack, and then shot out under the feeble lamp that burned in the brick arch over the gateway. The door closed after him.

"He'll get run in," Eastman remarked curtly, turning away from the window. "That door shouldn't be left unlocked. Any crook could come in. I'll speak to the janitor about it, if you don't mind," he added sarcastically.

"Wish you would." Cavenaugh stood brushing down the front of his jacket, first with his right hand and then with his left. "You saw him, didn't you?"

"Enough of him. Seems eccentric. I have to see a lot of buggy people. They don't take me in any more. But I'm keeping you and I'm in a hurry myself. Good night."

Cavenaugh put out his hand detainingly and started to say something; but Eastman rudely turned his back and went down the hall and out of the door. He had never felt anything shady about Cavenaugh before, and he was sorry he had gone down for the dictionary. In five minutes he was deep in his papers; but in the half hour when he was loafing before he dressed to go out, the young man's curious behavior came into his mind again.

Eastman had merely a neighborly acquaintance with Cavenaugh. He had been to a supper at the young man's rooms once, but he didn't particularly like Cavenaugh's friends; so the next time he was asked, he had another engagement. He liked Cavenaugh himself, if for nothing else than because he was so cheerful and trim and ruddy. A good complexion is always at a premium in New York, especially when it shines reassuringly on a man who does everything in the world to lose it. It encourages fellow mortals as to the inherent vigor of the human organism and the amount of bad treatment it will stand for. "Footprints that perhaps another," etc.

Cavenaugh, he knew, had plenty of money. He was the son of a Pennsylvania preacher, who died soon after he discovered that his ancestral acres were full of petroleum, and Kier had come to New York to burn some of the oil. He was thirty-two and was still at it; spent his life, literally, among the breakers. His motor hit the Park every morning as if it were the first time ever. He took people out to supper every night. He went from restaurant to restaurant, sometimes to half-a-dozen in an evening. The head waiters were his hosts and their cordiality made him happy. They made a life-line for him up Broadway and down Fifth Avenue. Cavenaugh was still fresh and smooth, round and plump, with a lustre to his hair and white teeth and a clear look in his round eyes. He seemed absolutely unwearied and unimpaired; never bored and never carried away.

Eastman always smiled when he met Cavenaugh in the entrance hall, serenely going forth to or returning from gladiatorial combats with joy, or when he saw him rolling smoothly up to the door in his car in the morning after a restful night in one of the remarkable new roadhouses he was always finding. Eastman had seen a good many young men disappear on Cavenaugh's route, and he admired this young man's endurance.

To-night, for the first time, he had got a whiff of something unwholesome about the fellow—bad nerves, bad company, something on hand that he was ashamed of, a visitor old and vicious, who must have had a key to Cavenaugh's apartment, for he was evidently there when Cavenaugh returned at seven o'clock. Probably it was the same man Cavenaugh had seen in the hansom. He must have been able to let himself in, for Cavenaugh kept no man but his chauffeur; or perhaps the janitor had been instructed to let him in. In either case, and whoever he was, it was clear enough that Cavenaugh was ashamed of him and was mixing up in questionable business of some kind.

Eastman sent Cavenaugh's book back by Rollins, and for the next few weeks he had no word with him beyond a casual greeting when they happened to meet in the hall or the elevator. One Sunday morning Cavenaugh telephoned up to him to ask if he could motor out to a roadhouse in Connecticut that afternoon and have supper; but when Eastman found there were to be other guests he declined.

On New Year's eve Eastman dined at the University Club at six o'clock and hurried home before the usual manifestations of insanity had begun in the streets. When Rollins brought his smoking coat, he asked him whether he wouldn't like to get off early.

"Yes, sir. But won't you be dressing, Mr. Eastman?" he inquired.

"Not to-night." Eastman handed him a bill. "Bring some change in the morning. There'll be fees."

Rollins lost no time in putting everything to rights for the night, and Eastman couldn't help wishing that he were in such a hurry to be off somewhere himself. When he heard the hall door close softly, he wondered if there were any place, after all, that he wanted to go. From his window he looked down at the long lines of motors and taxis waiting for a signal to cross Broadway. He thought of some of their probable destinations and decided that none of those places pulled him very hard. The night was warm and wet, the air was drizzly. Vapor hung in clouds about the *Times* Building, half hid the top of it, and made a luminous haze along Broadway. While he was looking down at the army of wet, black carriage-tops and their reflected headlights and tail-lights, Eastman heard a ring at his door. He deliberated. If it were a caller, the hall porter would have telephoned up. It must be the janitor. When he opened the door, there stood a rosy young man in a tuxedo, without a coat or hat.

"Pardon. Should I have telephoned? I half thought you wouldn't be in."

Eastman laughed. "Come in, Cavenaugh. You weren't sure whether you wanted company or not, eh, and you were trying to let chance decide it? That was exactly my state of mind. Let's accept the verdict." When they emerged from the narrow hall into his sitting-room, he pointed out a seat by the fire to his guest. He brought a tray of decanters and soda bottles and placed it on his writing table.

Cavenaugh hesitated, standing by the fire. "Sure you weren't starting for somewhere?"

"Do I look it? No, I was just making up my mind to stick it out alone when you rang. Have one?" He picked up a tall tumbler.

"Yes, thank you. I always do."

Eastman chuckled. "Lucky boy! So will I. I had a very early dinner. New York is the most arid place on holidays," he continued as he rattled the ice in the glasses. "When one gets too old to hit the rapids down there, and tired of gobbling food to heathenish dance music, there is absolutely no place where you can get a chop and some milk toast in peace, unless you have strong ties of blood brotherhood on upper Fifth Avenue. But you, why aren't you starting for somewhere?"

The young man sipped his soda and shook his head as he replied:

"Oh, I couldn't get a chop, either. I know only flashy people, of course." He looked up at his host with such a grave and candid expression that Eastman decided there couldn't be anything very crooked about the fellow. His smooth cheeks were positively cherubic.

"Well, what's the matter with them? Aren't they flashing to-night?"

"Only the very new ones seem to flash on New Year's eve. The older ones fade away. Maybe they are hunting a chop, too."

"Well"—Eastman sat down—"holidays do dash one. I was just about to write a letter to a pair of maiden aunts in my old home town, up-state; old coasting hill, snow-covered pines, lights in the church windows. That's what you've saved me from."

Cavenaugh shook himself. "Oh, I'm sure that wouldn't have been good for you. Pardon me," he rose and took a photograph from the bookcase, a handsome man in shooting clothes. "Dudley, isn't it? Did you know him well?"

"Yes. An old friend. Terrible thing, wasn't it? I haven't got over the jolt yet."

"His suicide? Yes, terrible! Did you know his wife?"

"Slightly. Well enough to admire her very much. She must be terribly broken up. I wonder Dudley didn't think of that."

Cavenaugh replaced the photograph carefully, lit a cigarette, and standing before the fire began to smoke. "Would you mind telling me about him? I never met him, but of course I'd read a lot about him, and I can't help feeling interested. It was a queer thing."

Eastman took out his cigar case and leaned back in his deep chair. "In the days when I knew him best he hadn't any story, like the happy nations. Everything was properly arranged for him before he was born. He came into the world happy, healthy, clever, straight, with the right sort of connections and the right kind of fortune, neither too large nor too small. He helped to make the world an agreeable place to live in until he was twenty-six. Then he married as he should have married. His wife was a Californian, educated abroad. Beautiful. You have seen her picture?"

Cavenaugh nodded. "Oh, many of them."

"She was interesting, too. Though she was distinctly a person of the world, she had retained something, just enough of the large Western manner. She had the habit of authority, of calling out a special train if she needed it, of using all our ingenious mechanical contrivances lightly and easily, without over-rating them. She and Dudley knew how to live better than most people. Their house was the most charming one I have ever known in New York. You felt freedom there, and a zest of life, and safety—absolute sanctuary—from everything sordid or petty. A whole society like that would justify the creation of man and would make our planet shine with a soft, peculiar radiance among the constellations. You think I'm putting it on thick?"

The young man sighed gently. "Oh, no! One has always felt there must be people like that. I've never known any."

"They had two children, beautiful ones. After they had been married for eight years, Rosina met this Spaniard. He must have amounted to something. She wasn't a flighty woman. She came home and told Dudley how matters stood. He persuaded her to stay at home for six months and try to pull up. They were both fair-minded people, and I'm as sure as if I were the Almighty, that she did try. But at the end of the time, Rosina went quietly off to Spain, and Dudley went to hunt in the Canadian Rockies. I met his party out there. I didn't know his wife had left him and talked about her a good deal. I noticed that he never drank anything, and his light used to shine through the log chinks of his room until all hours, even after a hard day's hunting. When I got back to New York, rumors were creeping about. Dudley did not come back. He bought a ranch in Wyoming, built a big log house and kept splendid dogs and horses. One of his sisters went out to keep house for him, and the children were there when they were not in school. He had a great many visitors, and everyone who came back talked about how well Dudley kept things going.

"He put in two years out there. Then, last month, he had to come back on business. A trust fund had to be settled up, and he was administrator. I saw him at the club; same light, quick step, same gracious handshake. He was getting gray, and there was something softer in his manner; but he had a fine red tan on his face and said he found it delightful to be here in the season when everything is going hard. The Madison Avenue house had been closed since Rosina left it. He went there to get some things his sister wanted. That, of course, was the mistake. He went alone, in the afternoon, and didn't go out for dinner—found some sherry and tins of biscuit in the sideboard. He shot himself sometime that night. There were pistols in his smoking-room. They found burnt out candles beside him in the morning. The gas and electricity were shut off. I suppose there, in his own house, among his own things, it was too much for him. He left no letters."

Cavenaugh blinked and brushed the lapel of his coat. "I suppose," he said slowly, "that every suicide is logical and reasonable, if one knew all the facts."

Eastman roused himself. "No, I don't think so. I've known too many fellows who went off like that—more than I deserve, I think—and some of them were absolutely inexplicable. I can understand Dudley; but I can't see why healthy bachelors, with money enough, like ourselves, need such a device. It reminds me of what Dr. Johnson said, that the most discouraging thing about life is the number of fads and hobbies and fake religions it takes to put people through a few years of it."

"Dr. Johnson? The specialist? Oh, the old fellow!" said Cavenaugh imperturbably. "Yes, that's interesting. Still, I fancy if one knew the facts— Did you know about Wyatt?"

"I don't think so."

"You wouldn't, probably. He was just a fellow about town who spent money. He wasn't one of the *forestieri*, though. Had connections here and owned a fine old place over on Staten Island. He went in for botany, and had been all over, hunting things; rusts, I believe. He had a yacht and used to take a gay crowd down about the South Seas, botanizing. He really did botanize, I believe. I never knew such a spender—only not flashy. He helped a lot of fellows and he was awfully good to girls, the kind who come down here to get a little fun, who don't like to work and still aren't really tough, the kind you see talking hard for their dinner. Nobody knows what becomes of them, or what they get out of it, and there are hundreds of new ones every year. He helped dozens of 'em; it was he who got me curious about the little shop girls. Well, one afternoon when his tea was brought, he took prussic acid instead. He didn't leave any letters, either; people of any taste don't. They wouldn't leave any material reminder if they could help it. His lawyers found that he had just $314.72 above his debts when he died. He had planned to spend all his money, and then take his tea; he had worked it out carefully."

Eastman reached for his pipe and pushed his chair away from the fire. "That looks like a considered case, but I don't think philosophical suicides like that are common. I think they usually come from stress of feeling and are really, as the newspapers call them, desperate acts; done without a motive. You remember when Anna Karenina was under the wheels, she kept saying, 'Why am I here?'"

Cavenaugh rubbed his upper lip with his pink finger and made an effort to wrinkle his brows. "May I, please?" reaching for the whiskey. "But have you," he asked, blinking as the soda flew at him, "have you ever known, yourself, cases that were really inexplicable?"

"A few too many. I was in Washington just before Captain Jack Purden was married and I saw a good deal of him. Popular army man, fine record in the Philippines, married a charming girl with lots of money; mutual devotion. It was the gayest wedding of the winter, and they started for Japan. They stopped in San Francisco for a week and missed their boat because, as the bride wrote back to Washington, they were too happy to move. They took the next boat, were both good sailors, had exceptional weather. After they had been out for two weeks, Jack got up from his deck chair one afternoon, yawned, put down his book, and stood before his wife. 'Stop reading for a moment and look at me.' She laughed and asked him why. 'Because you happen to be good to look at.' He nodded to her, went back to the stern and was never seen again. Must have gone down to the lower deck and slipped overboard, behind the machinery. It was the luncheon hour, not many people about; steamer cutting through a soft green sea. That's one of the most baffling cases I know. His friends raked up his past, and it was as trim as a cottage garden. If he'd so much as dropped an ink spot on his fatigue uniform, they'd have found it. He wasn't emotional or moody; wasn't, indeed, very inter-esting; simply a good soldier, fond of all the pompous little formalities that make up a military man's life. What do you make of that, my boy?"

Cavenaugh stroked his chin. "It's very puzzling, I admit. Still, if one knew everything——"

"But we do know everything. His friends wanted to find something to help them out, to help the girl out, to help the case of the human creature."

"Oh, I don't mean things that people could unearth," said Cavenaugh uneasily. "But possibly there were things that couldn't be found out."

Eastman shrugged his shoulders. "It's my experience that when there are 'things' as you call them, they're very apt to be found. There is no such thing as a secret. To make any move at all one has to employ human agencies, employ at least one human agent. Even when the pirates killed the men who buried their gold for them, the bones told the story."

Cavenaugh rubbed his hands together and smiled his sunny smile.

"I like that idea. It's reassuring. If we can have no secrets, it means that we can't, after all, go so far afield as we might," he hesitated, "yes, as we might."

Eastman looked at him sourly. "Cavenaugh, when you've

practised law in New York for twelve years, you find that people can't go far in any direction, except—" He thrust his forefinger sharply at the floor. "Even in that direction, few people can do anything out of the ordinary. Our range is limited. Skip a few baths, and we become personally objectionable. The slightest carelessness can rot a man's integrity or give him ptomaine poisoning. We keep up only by incessant cleansing operations, of mind and body. What we call character, is held together by all sorts of tacks and strings and glue."

Cavenaugh looked startled. "Come now, it's not so bad as that, is it? I've always thought that a serious man, like you, must know a lot of Launcelots." When Eastman only laughed, the younger man squirmed about in his chair. He spoke again hastily, as if he were embarrassed. "Your military friend may have had personal experiences, however, that his friends couldn't possibly get a line on. He may accidentally have come to a place where he saw himself in too unpleasant a light. I believe people can be chilled by a draft from outside, somewhere."

"Outside?" Eastman echoed. "Ah, you mean the far out-side! Ghosts, delusions, eh?"

Cavenaugh winced. "That's putting it strong. Why not say tips from the outside? Delusions belong to a diseased mind, don't they? There are some of us who have no minds to speak of, who yet have had experiences. I've had a little something in that line myself and I don't look it, do I?"

Eastman looked at the bland countenance turned toward him. "Not exactly. What's your delusion?"

"It's not a delusion. It's a haunt."

The lawyer chuckled. "Soul of a lost Casino girl?"

"No; an old gentleman. A most unattractive old gentleman, who follows me about."

"Does he want money?"

Cavenaugh sat up straight. "No. I wish to God he wanted anything—but the pleasure of my society! I'd let him clean me out to be rid of him. He's a real article. You saw him yourself that night when you came to my rooms to borrow a dictio-nary, and he went down the fire-escape. You saw him down in the court."

"Well, I saw somebody down in the court, but I'm too cautious to take it for granted that I saw what you saw. Why, any-how, should I see your haunt? If it was your friend I saw, he impressed me disagreeably. How did you pick him up?"

Cavenaugh looked gloomy. "That was queer, too. Charley Burke and I had motored out to Long Beach, about a year ago, sometime in October, I think. We had supper and stayed until late. When we were coming home, my car broke down. We had a lot of girls along who had to get back for morning rehearsals and things; so I sent them all into town in Charley's car, and he was to send a man back to tow me home. I was driving myself, and didn't want to leave my machine. We had not taken a direct road back; so I was stuck in a lonesome, woody place, no houses about. I got chilly and made a fire, and was putting in the time comfortably enough, when this old party steps up. He was in shabby evening clothes and a top hat, and had on his usual white gloves. How he got there, at three o'clock in the morning, miles from any town or railway, I'll leave it to you to figure out. *He* surely had no car. When I saw him coming up to the fire, I disliked him. He had a silly, apolo-getic walk. His teeth were chattering, and I asked him to sit down. He got down like a clothes-horse folding up. I offered him a cigarette, and when he took off his gloves I couldn't help noticing how knotted and spotty his hands were. He was asthmatic, and took his breath with a wheeze. 'Haven't you got anything—refreshing in there?' he asked, nodding at the car. When I told him I hadn't, he sighed. 'Ah, you young fel-lows are greedy. You drink it all up. You drink it all up, all up—up!' he kept chewing it over."

Cavenaugh paused and looked embarrassed again. "The thing that was most unpleasant is difficult to explain. The old man sat there by the fire and leered at me with a silly sort of admiration that was—well, more than humiliating. 'Gay boy, gay dog!' he would mutter, and when he grinned he showed his teeth, worn and yellow—shells. I remembered that it was better to talk casually to insane people; so I remarked carelessly that I had been out with a party and got stuck.

"'Oh yes, I remember,' he said, 'Flora and Lottie and May-belle and Marcelline, and poor Kate.'

"He had named them correctly; so I began to think I had been hitting the bright waters too hard.

"Things I drank never had seemed to make me woody; but you can never tell when trouble is going to hit you. I pulled my hat down and tried to look as uncommunicative as possible; but he kept croaking on from time to time, like this: 'Poor Kate! Splendid arms, but dope got her. She took up with Eastern religions after she had her hair dyed. Got to going to a Swami's joint, and smoking opium. Temple of the Lotus, it was called, and the police raided it.'

"This was nonsense, of course; the young woman was in the pink of condition. I let him rave, but I decided that if something didn't come out for me pretty soon, I'd foot it across Long Island. There wasn't room enough for the two of us. I got up and took another try at my car. He hopped right after me.

" 'Good car,' he wheezed, 'better than the little Ford.'

"I'd had a Ford before, but so has everybody; that was a safe guess.

" 'Still,' he went on, 'that run in from Huntington Bay in the rain wasn't bad. Arrested for speeding, he-he.'

"It was true I had made such a run, under rather unusual circumstances, and had been arrested. When at last I heard my life-boat snorting up the road, my visitor got up, sighed, and stepped back into the shadow of the trees. I didn't wait to see what became of him, you may believe. That was visitation number one. What do you think of it?"

Cavenaugh looked at his host defiantly. Eastman smiled.

"I think you'd better change your mode of life, Cavenaugh. Had many returns?" he inquired.

"Too many, by far." The young man took a turn about the room and came back to the fire. Standing by the mantel he lit another cigarette before going on with his story:

"The second visitation happened in the street, early in the evening, about eight o'clock. I was held up in a traffic block before the Plaza. My chauffeur was driving. Old Nibbs steps up out of the crowd, opens the door of my car, gets in and sits down beside me. He had on wilted evening clothes, same as before, and there was some sort of heavy scent about him. Such an unpleasant old party! A thorough-going rotter; you knew it at once. This time he wasn't talkative, as he had been when I first saw him. He leaned back in the car as if he owned

it, crossed his hands on his stick and looked out at the crowd
—sort of hungrily.

"I own I really felt a loathing compassion for him. We got
down the avenue slowly. I kept looking out at the mounted
police. But what could I do? Have him pulled? I was afraid to.
I was awfully afraid of getting him into the papers.

" 'I'm going to the New Astor,' I said at last. 'Can I take you
anywhere?'

" 'No, thank you,' says he. 'I get out when you do. I'm due
on West 44th. I'm dining to-night with Marcelline—all that is
left of her!'

"He put his hand to his hat brim with a grewsome salute.
Such a scandalous, foolish old face as he had! When we pulled
up at the Astor, I stuck my hand in my pocket and asked him if
he'd like a little loan.

" 'No, thank you, but'—he leaned over and whispered, ugh!
—'but save a little, save a little. Forty years from now—a little—
comes in handy. Save a little.'

"His eyes fairly glittered as he made his remark. I jumped
out. I'd have jumped into the North River. When he tripped
off, I asked my chauffeur if he'd noticed the man who got into
the car with me. He said he knew someone was with me, but
he hadn't noticed just when he got in. Want to hear any more?"

Cavenaugh dropped into his chair again. His plump cheeks
were a trifle more flushed than usual, but he was perfectly
calm. Eastman felt that the young man believed what he was
telling him.

"Of course I do. It's very interesting. I don't see quite
where you are coming out though."

Cavenaugh sniffed. "No more do I. I really feel that I've
been put upon. I haven't deserved it any more than any other
fellow of my kind. Doesn't it impress you disagreeably?"

"Well, rather so. Has anyone else seen your friend?"

"You saw him."

"We won't count that. As I said, there's no certainty that you
and I saw the same person in the court that night. Has anyone
else had a look in?"

"People sense him rather than see him. He usually crops
up when I'm alone or in a crowd on the street. He never

approaches me when I'm with people I know, though I've seen him hanging about the doors of theatres when I come out with a party; loafing around the stage exit, under a wall; or across the street, in a doorway. To be frank, I'm not anxious to introduce him. The third time, it was I who came upon him. In November my driver, Harry, had a sudden attack of appendicitis. I took him to the Presbyterian Hospital in the car, early in the evening. When I came home, I found the old villain in my rooms. I offered him a drink, and he sat down. It was the first time I had seen him in a steady light, with his hat off.

"His face is lined like a railway map, and as to color—Lord, what a liver! His scalp grows tight to his skull, and his hair is dyed until it's perfectly dead, like a piece of black cloth."

Cavenaugh ran his fingers through his own neatly trimmed thatch, and seemed to forget where he was for a moment.

"I had a twin brother, Brian, who died when we were sixteen. I have a photograph of him on my wall, an enlargement from a kodak of him, doing a high jump, rather good thing, full of action. It seemed to annoy the old gentleman. He kept looking at it and lifting his eyebrows, and finally he got up, tiptoed across the room, and turned the picture to the wall.

"'Poor Brian! Fine fellow, but died young,' says he.

"Next morning, there was the picture, still reversed."

"Did he stay long?" Eastman asked interestedly.

"Half an hour, by the clock."

"Did he talk?"

"Well, he rambled."

"What about?"

Cavenaugh rubbed his pale eyebrows before answering.

"About things that an old man ought to want to forget. His conversation is highly objectionable. Of course he knows me like a book; everything I've ever done or thought. But when he recalls them, he throws a bad light on them, somehow. Things that weren't much off color, look rotten. He doesn't leave one a shred of self-respect, he really doesn't. That's the amount of it." The young man whipped out his handkerchief and wiped his face.

"You mean he really talks about things that none of your friends know?"

"Oh, dear, yes! Recalls things that happened in school. Anything disagreeable. Funny thing, he always turns Brian's picture to the wall."

"Does he come often?"

"Yes, oftener, now. Of course I don't know how he gets in down-stairs. The hall boys never see him. But he has a key to my door. I don't know how he got it, but I can hear him turn it in the lock."

"Why don't you keep your driver with you, or telephone for me to come down?"

"He'd only grin and go down the fire escape as he did before. He's often done it when Harry's come in suddenly. Everybody has to be alone sometimes, you know. Besides, I don't want anybody to see him. He has me there."

"But why not? Why do you feel responsible for him?"

Cavenaugh smiled wearily. "That's rather the point, isn't it? Why do I? But I absolutely do. That identifies him, more than his knowing all about my life and my affairs."

Eastman looked at Cavenaugh thoughtfully. "Well, I should advise you to go in for something altogether different and new, and go in for it hard; business, engineering, metallurgy, something this old fellow wouldn't be interested in. See if you can make him remember logarithms."

Cavenaugh sighed. "No, he has me there, too. People never really change; they go on being themselves. But I would never make much trouble. Why can't they let me alone, damn it! I'd never hurt anybody, except, perhaps——"

"Except your old gentleman, eh?" Eastman laughed. "Seriously, Cavenaugh, if you want to shake him, I think a year on a ranch would do it. He would never be coaxed far from his favorite haunts. He would dread Montana."

Cavenaugh pursed up his lips. "So do I!"

"Oh, you think you do. Try it, and you'll find out. A gun and a horse beats all this sort of thing. Besides losing your haunt, you'd be putting ten years in the bank for yourself. I know a good ranch where they take people, if you want to try it."

"Thank you. I'll consider. Do you think I'm batty?"

"No, but I think you've been doing one sort of thing too long. You need big horizons. Get out of this."

Cavenaugh smiled meekly. He rose lazily and yawned behind his hand. "It's late, and I've taken your whole evening." He strolled over to the window and looked out. "Queer place, New York; rough on the little fellows. Don't you feel sorry for them, the girls especially? I do. What a fight they put up for a little fun! Why, even that old goat is sorry for them, the only decent thing he kept."

Eastman followed him to the door and stood in the hall, while Cavenaugh waited for the elevator. When the car came up Cavenaugh extended his pink, warm hand. "Good night."

The cage sank and his rosy countenance disappeared, his round-eyed smile being the last thing to go.

Weeks passed before Eastman saw Cavenaugh again. One morning, just as he was starting for Washington to argue a case before the Supreme Court, Cavenaugh telephoned him at his office to ask him about the Montana ranch he had recommended; said he meant to take his advice and go out there for the spring and summer.

When Eastman got back from Washington, he saw dusty trunks, just up from the trunk room, before Cavenaugh's door. Next morning, when he stopped to see what the young man was about, he found Cavenaugh in his shirt sleeves, packing.

"I'm really going; off to-morrow night. You didn't think it of me, did you?" he asked gaily.

"Oh, I've always had hopes of you!" Eastman declared. "But you are in a hurry, it seems to me."

"Yes, I am in a hurry." Cavenaugh shot a pair of leggings into one of the open trunks. "I telegraphed your ranch people, used your name, and they said it would be all right. By the way, some of my crowd are giving a little dinner for me at Rector's to-night. Couldn't you be persuaded, as it's a farewell occasion?" Cavenaugh looked at him hopefully.

Eastman laughed and shook his head. "Sorry, Cavenaugh, but that's too gay a world for me. I've got too much work lined up before me. I wish I had time to stop and look at your guns, though. You seem to know something about guns. You've more than you'll need, but nobody can have too many good ones." He put down one of the revolvers regretfully. "I'll drop in to see you in the morning, if you're up."

"I shall be up, all right. I've warned my crowd that I'll cut away before midnight."

"You won't, though," Eastman called back over his shoulder as he hurried down-stairs.

The next morning, while Eastman was dressing, Rollins came in greatly excited.

"I'm a little late, sir. I was stopped by Harry, Mr. Cavenaugh's driver. Mr. Cavenaugh shot himself last night, sir."

Eastman dropped his vest and sat down on his shoe-box. "You're drunk, Rollins," he shouted. "He's going away to-day!"

"Yes, sir. Harry found him this morning. Ah, he's quite dead, sir. Harry's telephoned for the coroner. Harry don't know what to do with the ticket."

Eastman pulled on his coat and ran down the stairway. Cavenaugh's trunks were strapped and piled before the door. Harry was walking up and down the hall with a long green railroad ticket in his hand and a look of complete stupidity on his face.

"What shall I do about this ticket, Mr. Eastman?" he whispered. "And what about his trunks? He had me tell the transfer people to come early. They may be here any minute. Yes, sir. I brought him home in the car last night, before twelve, as cheerful as could be."

"Be quiet, Harry. Where is he?"

"In his bed, sir."

Eastman went into Cavenaugh's sleeping-room. When he came back to the sitting-room, he looked over the writing table; railway folders, time-tables, receipted bills, nothing else. He looked up for the photograph of Cavenaugh's twin brother. There it was, turned to the wall. Eastman took it down and looked at it; a boy in track clothes, half lying in the air, going over the string shoulders first, above the heads of a crowd of lads who were running and cheering. The face was somewhat blurred by the motion and the bright sunlight. Eastman put the picture back, as he found it. Had Cavenaugh entertained his visitor last night, and had the old man been more convincing than usual? "Well, at any rate, he's seen to it that the old man can't establish identity. What a soft lot they are, fellows like poor Cavenaugh!" Eastman thought of his office as a delightful place.

1915

ELLEN GLASGOW
(1873–1945)

The Shadowy Third

WHEN the call came I remember that I turned from the telephone in a romantic flutter. Though I had spoken only once to the great surgeon, Roland Maradick, I felt on that December afternoon that to speak to him only once—to watch him in the operating-room for a single hour—was an adventure which drained the colour and the excitement from the rest of life. After all these years of work on typhoid and pneumonia cases, I can still feel the delicious tremor of my young pulses; I can still see the winter sunshine slanting through the hospital windows over the white uniforms of the nurses.

"He didn't mention me by name. Can there be a mistake?" I stood, incredulous yet ecstatic, before the superintendent of the hospital.

"No, there isn't a mistake. I was talking to him before you came down." Miss Hemphill's strong face softened while she looked at me. She was a big, resolute woman, a distant Canadian relative of my mother's, and the kind of nurse I had discovered in the month since I had come up from Richmond, that Northern hospital boards, if not Northern patients, appear instinctively to select. From the first, in spite of her hardness, she had taken a liking—I hesitate to use the word "fancy" for a preference so impersonal—to her Virginia cousin. After all, it isn't every Southern nurse, just out of training, who can boast a kinswoman in the superintendent of a New York hospital.

"And he made you understand positively that he meant me?" The thing was so wonderful that I simply couldn't believe it.

"He asked particularly for the nurse who was with Miss Hudson last week when he operated. I think he didn't even remember that you had a name. When I asked if he meant Miss Randolph, he repeated that he wanted the nurse who had been with Miss Hudson. She was small, he said, and cheerful-looking. This, of course, might apply to one or two of the others, but none of these was with Miss Hudson."

"Then I suppose it is really true?" My pulses were tingling. "And I am to be there at six o'clock?"

"Not a minute later. The day nurse goes off duty at that hour, and Mrs. Maradick is never left by herself for an instant."

"It is her mind, isn't it? And that makes it all the stranger that he should select me, for I have had so few mental cases."

"So few cases of any kind," Miss Hemphill was smiling, and when she smiled I wondered if the other nurses would know her. "By the time you have gone through the treadmill in New York, Margaret, you will have lost a good many things besides your inexperience. I wonder how long you will keep your sympathy and your imagination? After all, wouldn't you have made a better novelist than a nurse?"

"I can't help putting myself into my cases. I suppose one ought not to?"

"It isn't a question of what one ought to do, but of what one must. When you are drained of every bit of sympathy and enthusiasm, and have got nothing in return for it, not even thanks, you will understand why I try to keep you from wasting yourself."

"But surely in a case like this—for Doctor Maradick?"

"Oh, well, of course—for Doctor Maradick." She must have seen that I implored her confidence, for, after a minute, she let fall carelessly a gleam of light on the situation: "It is a very sad case when you think what a charming man and a great surgeon Doctor Maradick is."

Above the starched collar of my uniform I felt the blood leap in bounds to my cheeks. "I have spoken to him only once," I murmured, "but he is charming, and so kind and handsome, isn't he?"

"His patients adore him."

"Oh, yes, I've seen that. Everyone hangs on his visits." Like the patients and the other nurses, I also had come by delightful, if imperceptible, degrees to hang on the daily visits of Doctor Maradick. He was, I suppose, born to be a hero to women. From my first day in his hospital, from the moment when I watched, through closed shutters, while he stepped out of his

car, I have never doubted that he was assigned to the great
part in the play. If I had been ignorant of his spell—of the
charm he exercised over his hospital—I should have felt it in
the waiting hush, like a drawn breath, which followed his ring
at the door and preceded his imperious footstep on the stairs.
My first impression of him, even after the terrible events of the
next year, records a memory that is both careless and splendid.
At that moment, when, gazing through the chinks in the shutters, I watched him, in his coat of dark fur, cross the pavement
over the pale streaks of sunshine, I knew beyond any doubt—I
knew with a sort of infallible prescience—that my fate was irre-
trievably bound up with his in the future. I knew this, I repeat,
though Miss Hemphill would still insist that my foreknowledge was merely a sentimental gleaning from indiscriminate
novels. But it wasn't only first love, impressionable as my kinswoman believed me to be. It wasn't only the way he looked.
Even more than his appearance—more than the shining dark
of his eyes, the silvery brown of his hair, the dusky glow in his
face—even more than his charm and his magnificence, I think,
the beauty and sympathy in his voice won my heart. It was a
voice, I heard someone say afterwards, that ought always to
speak poetry.

So you will see why—if you do not understand at the beginning, I can never hope to make you believe impossible things!
—so you will see why I accepted the call when it came as an
imperative summons. I couldn't have stayed away after he sent
for me. However much I may have tried not to go, I know that
in the end I must have gone. In those days, while I was still
hoping to write novels, I used to talk a great deal about "destiny" (I have learned since then how silly all such talk is), and I
suppose it was my "destiny" to be caught in the web of Roland
Maradick's personality. But I am not the first nurse to grow
love-sick about a doctor who never gave her a thought.

"I am glad you got the call, Margaret. It may mean a great
deal to you. Only try not to be too emotional." I remember
that Miss Hemphill was holding a bit of rose-geranium in
her hand while she spoke—one of the patients had given it to
her from a pot she kept in her room, and the scent of the flower
is still in my nostrils—or my memory. Since then—oh, long since
then—I have wondered if she also had been caught in the web.

"I wish I knew more about the case." I was pressing for light. "Have you ever seen Mrs. Maradick?"

"Oh, dear, yes. They have been married only a little over a year, and in the beginning she used to come sometimes to the hospital and wait outside while the doctor made his visits. She was a very sweet-looking woman then—not exactly pretty, but fair and slight, with the loveliest smile, I think, I have ever seen. In those first months she was so much in love that we used to laugh about it among ourselves. To see her face light up when the doctor came out of the hospital and crossed the pavement to his car, was as good as a play. We never tired of watching her—I wasn't superintendent then, so I had more time to look out of the window while I was on day duty. Once or twice she brought her little girl in to see one of the patients. The child was so much like her that you would have known them anywhere for mother and daughter."

I had heard that Mrs. Maradick was a widow, with one child, when she first met the doctor, and I asked now, still seeking an illumination I had not found, "There was a great deal of money, wasn't there?"

"A great fortune. If she hadn't been so attractive, people would have said, I suppose, that Doctor Maradick married her for her money. Only," she appeared to make an effort of memory, "I believe I've heard somehow that it was all left in trust away from Mrs. Maradick if she married again. I can't, to save my life, remember just how it was; but it was a queer will, I know, and Mrs. Maradick wasn't to come into the money unless the child didn't live to grow up. The pity of it——"

A young nurse came into the office to ask for something—the keys, I think, of the operating-room, and Miss Hemphill broke off inconclusively as she hurried out of the door. I was sorry that she left off just when she did. Poor Mrs. Maradick! Perhaps I was too emotional, but even before I saw her I had begun to feel her pathos and her strangeness.

My preparations took only a few minutes. In those days I always kept a suitcase packed and ready for sudden calls; and it was not yet six o'clock when I turned from Tenth Street into Fifth Avenue, and stopped for a minute, before ascending the steps, to look at the house in which Doctor Maradick lived. A fine rain was falling, and I remember thinking, as I turned the corner, how depressing the weather must be for Mrs. Maradick. It was an old house, with damp-looking walls (though that may have been because of the rain) and a spindle-shaped iron railing which ran up the stone steps to the black door, where I noticed a dim flicker through the old-fashioned fanlight. Afterwards I discovered that Mrs. Maradick had been born in the house—her maiden name was Calloran—and that she had never wanted to live anywhere else. She was a woman —this I found out when I knew her better—of strong attachments to both persons and places; and though Doctor Maradick had tried to persuade her to move uptown after her marriage, she had clung, against his wishes, to the old house in lower Fifth Avenue. I dare say she was obstinate about it in spite of her gentleness and her passion for the doctor. Those sweet, soft women, especially when they have always been rich, are sometimes amazingly obstinate. I have nursed so many of them since—women with strong affections and weak intellects —that I have come to recognize the type as soon as I set eyes upon it.

My ring at the bell was answered after a little delay, and when I entered the house I saw that the hall was quite dark except for the waning glow from an open fire which burned in the library. When I gave my name, and added that I was the night nurse, the servant appeared to think my humble presence unworthy of illumination. He was an old negro butler, inherited perhaps from Mrs. Maradick's mother, who, I learned afterwards, was from South Carolina; and while he passed me on his way up the staircase, I heard him vaguely muttering that he "wa'n't gwinter tu'n on dem lights twel de chile had done playin'."

To the right of the hall, the soft glow drew me into the library, and crossing the threshold timidly, I stooped to dry my wet coat by the fire. As I bent there, meaning to start up at the first sound of a footstep, I thought how cosy the room was after the damp walls outside to which some bared creepers were clinging; and I was watching the strange shapes and patterns the firelight made on the old Persian rug, when the lamps of a slowly turning motor flashed on me through the white shades at the window. Still dazzled by the glare, I looked round in the dimness and saw a child's ball of red and blue rubber roll towards me out of the gloom of the adjoining room. A moment later, while I made a vain attempt to capture the toy as it spun past me, a little girl darted airily, with peculiar lightness and grace, through the doorway, and stopped quickly, as if in surprise at the sight of a stranger. She was a small child—so small and slight that her footsteps made no sound on the polished floor of the threshold; and I remember thinking while I looked at her that she had the gravest and sweetest face I had ever seen. She couldn't—I decided this afterwards—have been more than six or seven years old, yet she stood there with a curious prim dignity, like the dignity of an elderly person, and gazed up at me with enigmatical eyes. She was dressed in Scotch plaid, with a bit of red ribbon in her hair, which was cut in a fringe over her forehead and hung very straight to her shoulders. Charming as she was, from her uncurled brown hair to the white socks and black slippers on her little feet, I recall most vividly the singular look in her eyes, which appeared in the shifting light to be of an indeterminate colour. For the odd thing about this look was that it was not the look of childhood at all. It was the look of profound experience, of bitter knowledge.

"Have you come for your ball?" I asked; but while the friendly question was still on my lips, I heard the servant returning. In my confusion I made a second ineffectual grasp at the play-thing, which had rolled away from me into the dusk of the drawing-room. Then, as I raised my head, I saw that the child also had slipped from the room; and without looking after her I followed the old negro into the pleasant study above, where the great surgeon awaited me.

Ten years ago, before hard nursing had taken so much out of me, I blushed very easily, and I was aware at the moment when I crossed Doctor Maradick's study that my cheeks were the colour of peonies. Of course, I was a fool—no one knows this better than I do—but I had never been alone, even for an instant, with him before, and the man was more than a hero to me, he was—there isn't any reason now why I should blush over the confession—almost a god. At that age I was mad about the wonders of surgery, and Roland Maradick in the operating-room was magician enough to have turned an older and more sensible head than mine. Added to his great reputation and his marvelous skill, he was, I am sure of this, the most splendid-looking man, even at forty-five, that one could imagine. Had he been ungracious—had he been positively rude to me, I should still have adored him; but when he held out his hand, and greeted me in the charming way he had with women, I felt that I would have died for him. It is no wonder that a saying went about the hospital that every woman he operated on fell in love with him. As for the nurses—well, there wasn't a single one of them who had escaped his spell—not even Miss Hemphill, who could have been scarcely a day under fifty.

"I am glad you could come, Miss Randolph. You were with Miss Hudson last week when I operated?"

I bowed. To save my life I couldn't have spoken without blushing the redder.

"I noticed your bright face at the time. Brightness, I think, is what Mrs. Maradick needs. She finds her day nurse depressing." His eyes rested so kindly upon me that I have suspected since that he was not entirely unaware of my worship. It was a small thing, heaven knows, to flatter his vanity—a nurse just out of a training-school—but to some men no tribute is too insignificant to give pleasure.

"You will do your best, I am sure." He hesitated an instant —just long enough for me to perceive the anxiety beneath the genial smile on his face—and then added gravely, "We wish to avoid, if possible, having to send her away."

I could only murmur in response, and after a few carefully chosen words about his wife's illness, he rang the bell and directed the maid to take me upstairs to my room. Not until I was ascending the stairs to the third storey did it occur to me that he had really told me nothing. I was as perplexed about the nature of Mrs. Maradick's malady as I had been when I entered the house.

I found my room pleasant enough. It had been arranged— at Doctor Maradick's request, I think—that I was to sleep in the house, and after my austere little bed at the hospital, I was agreeably surprised by the cheerful look of the apartment into which the maid led me. The walls were papered in roses, and there were curtains of flowered chintz at the window, which looked down on a small formal garden at the rear of the house. This the maid told me, for it was too dark for me to distinguish more than a marble fountain and a fir-tree, which looked old, though I afterwards learned that it was replanted almost every season.

In ten minutes I had slipped into my uniform and was ready to go to my patient; but for some reason—to this day I have never found out what it was that turned her against me at the start—Mrs. Maradick refused to receive me. While I stood outside her door I heard the day nurse trying to persuade her to let me come in. It wasn't any use, however, and in the end I was obliged to go back to my room and wait until the poor lady got over her whim and consented to see me. That was long after dinner—it must have been nearer eleven than ten o'clock —and Miss Peterson was quite worn out by the time she came for me.

"I'm afraid you'll have a bad night," she said as we went downstairs together. That was her way, I soon saw, to expect the worst of everything and everybody.

"Does she often keep you up like this?"

"Oh, no, she is usually very considerate. I never knew a sweeter character. But she still has this hallucination——"

Here again, as in the scene with Doctor Maradick, I felt that the explanation had only deepened the mystery. Mrs. Maradick's hallucination, whatever form it assumed, was evidently a subject for evasion and subterfuge in the household. It was on the tip of my tongue to ask, "What is her hallucination?"—but before I could get the words past my lips we had reached Mrs. Maradick's door, and Miss Peterson motioned me to be silent. As the door opened a little way to admit me, I saw that Mrs. Maradick was already in bed, and that the lights were out except for a night-lamp burning on a candle-stand beside a book and a carafe of water.

"I won't go in with you," said Miss Peterson in a whisper; and I was on the point of stepping over the threshold when I saw the little girl, in the dress of Scotch plaid, slip by me from the dusk of the room into the electric light of the hall. She held a doll in her arms, and as she went by she dropped a doll's work-basket in the doorway. Miss Peterson must have picked up the toy, for when I turned in a minute to look for it I found that it was gone. I remember thinking that it was late for a child to be up—she looked delicate, too—but, after all, it was no business of mine, and four years in a hospital had taught me never to meddle in things that do not concern me. There is nothing a nurse learns quicker than not to try to put the world to rights in a day.

When I crossed the floor to the chair by Mrs. Maradick's bed, she turned over on her side and looked at me with the sweetest and saddest smile.

"You are the night nurse," she said in a gentle voice; and from the moment she spoke I knew that there was nothing hysterical or violent about her mania—or hallucination, as they called it. "They told me your name, but I have forgotten it."

"Randolph—Margaret Randolph." I liked her from the start, and I think she must have seen it.

"You look very young, Miss Randolph."

"I am twenty-two, but I suppose I don't look quite my age. People usually think I am younger."

For a minute she was silent, and while I settled myself in the chair by the bed, I thought how strikingly she resembled the little girl I had seen first in the afternoon, and then leaving her room a few moments before. They had the same small, heart-shaped faces, coloured ever so faintly; the same straight, soft hair, between brown and flaxen; and the same large, grave eyes, set very far apart under arched eyebrows. What surprised me most, however, was that they both looked at me with that enigmatical and vaguely wondering expression—only in Mrs. Maradick's face the vagueness seemed to change now and then to a definite fear—a flash, I had almost said, of startled horror.

I sat quite still in my chair, and until the time came for Mrs. Maradick to take her medicine not a word passed between us. Then, when I bent over her with the glass in my hand, she raised her head from the pillow and said in a whisper of suppressed intensity:

"You look kind. I wonder if you could have seen my little girl?"

As I slipped my arm under the pillow I tried to smile cheerfully down on her. "Yes, I've seen her twice. I'd know her anywhere by her likeness to you."

A glow shone in her eyes, and I thought how pretty she must have been before illness took the life and animation out of her features. "Then I know you're good." Her voice was so strained and low that I could barely hear it. "If you weren't good you couldn't have seen her."

I thought this queer enough, but all I answered was, "She looked delicate to be sitting up so late."

A quiver passed over her thin features, and for a minute I thought she was going to burst into tears. As she had taken the medicine, I put the glass back on the candle-stand, and bending over the bed, smoothed the straight brown hair, which was as fine and soft as spun silk, back from her forehead. There was something about her—I don't know what it was—that made you love her as soon as she looked at you.

"She always had that light and airy way, though she was never sick a day in her life," she answered calmly after a pause. Then, groping for my hand, she whispered passionately, "You must not tell him—you must not tell any one that you have seen her!"

"I must not tell any one?" Again I had the impression that had come to me first in Doctor Maradick's study, and afterwards with Miss Peterson on the staircase, that I was seeking a gleam of light in the midst of obscurity.

"Are you sure there isn't any one listening—that there isn't any one at the door?" she asked, pushing aside my arm and raising herself on the pillows.

"Quite, quite sure. They have put out the lights in the hall."

"And you will not tell him? Promise me that you will not tell him." The startled horror flashed from the vague wonder of her expression. "He doesn't like her to come back, because he killed her."

"Because he killed her!" Then it was that light burst on me in a blaze. So this was Mrs. Maradick's hallucination! She believed that her child was dead—the little girl I had seen with my own eyes leaving her room; and she believed that her husband—the great surgeon we worshipped in the hospital—had murdered her. No wonder they veiled the dreadful obsession in mystery! No wonder that even Miss Peterson had not dared to drag the horrid thing out into the light! It was the kind of hallucination one simply couldn't stand having to face.

"There is no use telling people things that nobody believes," she resumed slowly, still holding my hand in a grasp that would have hurt me if her fingers had not been so fragile. "Nobody believes that he killed her. Nobody believes that she comes back every day to the house. Nobody believes—and yet you saw her——"

"Yes, I saw her—but why should your husband have killed her?" I spoke soothingly, as one would speak to a person who was quite mad. Yet she was not mad, I could have sworn this while I looked at her.

For a moment she moaned inarticulately, as if the horror of her thoughts were too great to pass into speech. Then she flung out her thin, bare arm with a wild gesture.

"Because he never loved me!" she said. "He never loved me!"

"But he married you," I urged gently while I stroked her hair. "If he hadn't loved you, why should he have married you?"

"He wanted the money—my little girl's money. It all goes to him when I die."

"But he is rich himself. He must make a fortune from his profession."

"It isn't enough. He wanted millions." She had grown stern and tragic. "No, he never loved me. He loved someone else from the beginning—before I knew him."

It was quite useless, I saw, to reason with her. If she wasn't mad, she was in a state of terror and despondency so black that it had almost crossed the border-line into madness. I thought once that I would go upstairs and bring the child down from her nursery; but, after a moment's hesitation, I realized that Miss Peterson and Doctor Maradick must have long ago tried all these measures. Clearly, there was nothing to do except soothe and quiet her as much as I could; and this I did until she dropped into a light sleep which lasted well into the morning.

By seven o'clock I was worn out—not from work but from the strain on my sympathy—and I was glad, indeed, when one of the maids came in to bring me an early cup of coffee. Mrs. Maradick was still sleeping—it was a mixture of bromide and chloral I had given her—and she did not wake until Miss Peterson came on duty an hour or two later. Then, when I went downstairs, I found the dining-room deserted except for the old housekeeper, who was looking over the silver. Doctor

Maradick, she explained to me presently, had his breakfast served in the morning-room on the other side of the house.

"And the little girl? Does she take her meals in the nursery?"

She threw me a startled glance. Was it, I questioned afterwards, one of distrust or apprehension?

"There isn't any little girl. Haven't you heard?"

"Heard? No. Why, I saw her only yesterday."

The look she gave me—I was sure of it now—was full of alarm.

"The little girl—she was the sweetest child I ever saw—died just two months ago of pneumonia."

"But she couldn't have died." I was a fool to let this out, but the shock had completely unnerved me. "I tell you I saw her yesterday."

The alarm in her face deepened. "That is Mrs. Maradick's trouble. She believes that she still sees her."

"But don't you see her?" I drove the question home bluntly.

"No." She set her lips tightly. "I never see anything."

So I had been wrong, after all, and the explanation, when it came, only accentuated the terror. The child was dead—she had died of pneumonia two months ago—and yet I had seen her, with my own eyes, playing ball in the library; I had seen her slipping out of her mother's room, with her doll in her arms.

"Is there another child in the house? Could there be a child belonging to one of the servants?" A gleam had shot through the fog in which I was groping.

"No, there isn't any other. The doctors tried bringing one once, but it threw the poor lady into such a state she almost died of it. Besides, there wouldn't be any other child as quiet and sweet-looking as Dorothea. To see her skipping along in her dress of Scotch plaid used to make me think of a fairy, though they say that fairies wear nothing but white or green."

"Has any one else seen her—the child, I mean—any of the servants?"

"Only old Gabriel, the coloured butler, who came with Mrs. Maradick's mother from South Carolina. I've heard that negroes often have a kind of second sight—though I don't know that that is just what you would call it. But they seem to believe in the supernatural by instinct, and Gabriel is so old and doty—he does no work except answer the door-bell and clean the silver—that nobody pays much attention to anything that he sees——"

"Is the child's nursery kept as it used to be?"

"Oh, no. The doctor had all the toys sent to the children's hospital. That was a great grief to Mrs. Maradick; but Doctor Brandon thought, and all the nurses agreed with him, that it was best for her not to be allowed to keep the room as it was when Dorothea was living."

"Dorothea? Was that the child's name?"

"Yes, it means the gift of God, doesn't it? She was named after the mother of Mrs. Maradick's first husband, Mr. Ballard. He was the grave, quiet kind—not the least like the doctor."

I wondered if the other dreadful obsession of Mrs. Maradick's had drifted down through the nurses or the servants to the housekeeper; but she said nothing about it, and since she was, I suspected, a garrulous person, I thought it wiser to assume that the gossip had not reached her.

A little later, when breakfast was over and I had not yet gone upstairs to my room, I had my first interview with Doctor Brandon, the famous alienist who was in charge of the case. I had never seen him before, but from the first moment that I looked at him I took his measure almost by intuition. He was, I suppose, honest enough—I have always granted him that, bitterly as I have felt towards him. It wasn't his fault that he lacked red blood in his brain, or that he had formed the habit, from long association with abnormal phenomena, of regarding all life as a disease. He was the sort of physician—every nurse will understand what I mean—who deals instinctively with groups instead of with individuals. He was long and solemn and very round in the face; and I hadn't talked to him ten minutes before I knew he had been educated in Germany, and that he had learned over there to treat every emotion as a pathological manifestation. I used to wonder what he got out of life —what any one got out of life who had analyzed away everything except the bare structure.

When I reached my room at last, I was so tired that I could barely remember either the questions Doctor Brandon had asked or the directions he had given me. I fell asleep, I know, almost as soon as my head touched the pillow; and the maid who came to inquire if I wanted luncheon decided to let me finish my nap. In the afternoon, when she returned with a cup of tea, she found me still heavy and drowsy. Though I was used to night nursing, I felt as if I had danced from sunset to daybreak. It was fortunate, I reflected, while I drank my tea, that every case didn't wear on one's sympathies as acutely as Mrs. Maradick's hallucination had worn on mine.

Through the day I did not see Doctor Maradick; but at seven o'clock when I came up from my early dinner on my way to take the place of Miss Peterson, who had kept on duty an hour later than usual, he met me in the hall and asked me to come into his study. I thought him handsomer than ever in his evening clothes, with a white flower in his buttonhole. He was going to some public dinner, the housekeeper told me, but, then, he was always going somewhere. I believe he didn't dine at home a single evening that winter.

"Did Mrs. Maradick have a good night?" He had closed the door after us, and turning now with the question, he smiled kindly, as if he wished to put me at ease in the beginning.

"She slept very well after she took the medicine. I gave her that at eleven o'clock."

For a minute he regarded me silently, and I was aware that his personality—his charm—was focussed upon me. It was almost as if I stood in the centre of converging rays of light, so vivid was my impression of him.

"Did she allude in any way to her—to her hallucination?" he asked.

How the warning reached me—what invisible waves of sense-perception transmitted the message—I have never known; but while I stood there, facing the splendour of the doctor's presence, every intuition cautioned me that the time had come when I must take sides in the household. While I stayed there I must stand either with Mrs. Maradick or against her.

"She talked quite rationally," I replied after a moment.

"What did she say?"

"She told me how she was feeling, that she missed her child, and that she walked a little every day about her room."

His face changed—how I could not at first determine.

"Have you seen Doctor Brandon?"

"He came this morning to give me his directions."

"He thought her less well to-day. He has advised me to send her to Rosedale."

I have never, even in secret, tried to account for Doctor Maradick. He may have been sincere. I tell only what I know —not what I believe or imagine—and the human is sometimes as inscrutable, as inexplicable, as the supernatural.

While he watched me I was conscious of an inner struggle, as if opposing angels warred somewhere in the depths of my being. When at last I made my decision, I was acting less from reason, I knew, than in obedience to the pressure of some secret current of thought. Heaven knows, even then, the man held me captive while I defied him.

"Doctor Maradick," I lifted my eyes for the first time frankly to his, "I believe that your wife is as sane as I am—or as you are."

He started. "Then she did not talk freely to you?"

"She may be mistaken, unstrung, piteously distressed in mind"—I brought this out with emphasis—"but she is not—I am willing to stake my future on it—a fit subject for an asylum. It would be foolish—it would be cruel to send her to Rosedale."

"Cruel, you say?" A troubled look crossed his face, and his voice grew very gentle. "You do not imagine that I could be cruel to her?"

"No, I do not think that." My voice also had softened.

"We will let things go on as they are. Perhaps Doctor Brandon may have some other suggestion to make." He drew out his watch and compared it with the clock—nervously, I observed, as if his action were a screen for his discomfiture or perplexity. "I must be going now. We will speak of this again in the morning."

But in the morning we did not speak of it, and during the month that I nursed Mrs. Maradick I was not called again into her husband's study. When I met him in the hall or on the staircase, which was seldom, he was as charming as ever; yet, in spite of his courtesy, I had a persistent feeling that he had taken my measure on that evening, and that he had no further use for me.

As the days went by Mrs. Maradick seemed to grow stronger.

Never, after our first night together, had she mentioned the child to me; never had she alluded by so much as a word to her dreadful charge against her husband. She was like any woman recovering from a great sorrow, except that she was sweeter and gentler. It is no wonder that everyone who came near her loved her; for there was a mysterious loveliness about her like the mystery of light, not of darkness. She was, I have always thought, as much of an angel as it is possible for a woman to be on this earth. And yet, angelic as she was, there were times when it seemed to me that she both hated and feared her husband. Though he never entered her room while I was there, and I never heard his name on her lips until an hour before the end, still I could tell by the look of terror in her face whenever his step passed down the hall that her very soul shivered at his approach.

During the whole month I did not see the child again, though one night, when I came suddenly into Mrs. Maradick's room, I found a little garden, such as children make out of pebbles and bits of box, on the window-sill. I did not mention it to Mrs. Maradick, and a little later, as the maid lowered the shades, I noticed that the garden had vanished. Since then I have often wondered if the child were invisible only to the rest of us, and if her mother still saw her. But there was no way of finding out except by questioning, and Mrs. Maradick was so well and patient that I hadn't the heart to question. Things couldn't have been better with her than they were, and I was beginning to tell myself that she might soon go out for an airing, when the end came so suddenly.

It was a mild January day—the kind of day that brings the foretaste of spring in the middle of winter, and when I came downstairs in the afternoon, I stopped a minute by the window at the end of the hall to look down on the box maze in the garden. There was an old fountain, bearing two laughing boys in marble, in the centre of the gravelled walk, and the water, which had been turned on that morning for Mrs. Maradick's pleasure, sparkled now like silver as the sunlight splashed over it. I had never before felt the air quite so soft and springlike in January; and I thought, as I gazed down on the garden, that it would be a good idea for Mrs. Maradick to go out and bask for an hour or so in the sunshine. It seemed strange to me that she was never allowed to get any fresh air except the air that came through her windows.

When I went into her room, however, I found that she had no wish to go out. She was sitting, wrapped in shawls, by the open window, which looked down on the fountain; and as I entered she glanced up from a little book she was reading. A pot of daffodils stood on the window-sill—she was very fond of flowers and we tried always to keep some growing in her room.

"Do you know what I am reading, Miss Randolph?" she asked in her soft voice; and she read aloud a verse while I went over to the candle-stand to measure out a dose of medicine.

" 'If thou hast two loaves of bread, sell one and buy daffodils, for bread nourisheth the body, but daffodils delight the soul.' That is very beautiful, don't you think so?"

I said "Yes," that it was beautiful; and then I asked her if she wouldn't go downstairs and walk about in the garden.

"He wouldn't like it," she answered; and it was the first time she had mentioned her husband to me since the night I came to her. "He doesn't want me to go out."

I tried to laugh her out of the idea; but it was no use, and after a few minutes I gave up and began talking of other things. Even then it did not occur to me that her fear of Doctor Maradick was anything but a fancy. I could see, of course, that she wasn't out of her head; but sane persons, I knew, sometimes have unaccountable prejudices, and I accepted her dislike as a mere whim or aversion. I did not understand then and—I may as well confess this before the end comes—I do not understand any better to-day. I am writing down the things I actually saw, and I repeat that I have never had the slightest twist in the direction of the miraculous.

The afternoon slipped away while we talked—she talked brightly when any subject came up that interested her—and it was the last hour of day—that grave, still hour when the movement of life seems to droop and falter for a few precious minutes—that brought us the thing I had dreaded silently since my first night in the house. I remember that I had risen to close the window, and was leaning out for a breath of the mild air, when there was the sound of steps, consciously softened, in the hall outside, and Doctor Brandon's usual knock fell on my ears. Then, before I could cross the room, the door opened, and the doctor entered with Miss Peterson. The day nurse, I knew, was a stupid woman; but she had never appeared to me so stupid, so armoured and encased in her professional manner, as she did at that moment.

"I am glad to see that you are taking the air." As Doctor Brandon came over to the window, I wondered maliciously what devil of contradictions had made him a distinguished specialist in nervous diseases.

"Who was the other doctor you brought this morning?" asked Mrs. Maradick gravely; and that was all I ever heard about the visit of the second alienist.

"Someone who is anxious to cure you." He dropped into a chair beside her and patted her hand with his long, pale fingers. "We are so anxious to cure you that we want to send you away to the country for a fortnight or so. Miss Peterson has come to help you to get ready, and I've kept my car waiting for you. There couldn't be a nicer day for a trip, could there?"

The moment had come at last. I knew at once what he meant, and so did Mrs. Maradick. A wave of colour flowed and ebbed in her thin cheeks, and I felt her body quiver when I moved from the window and put my arms on her shoulders. I was aware again, as I had been aware that evening in Doctor Maradick's study, of a current of thought that beat from the air around into my brain. Though it cost me my career as a nurse and my reputation for sanity, I knew that I must obey that invisible warning.

"You are going to take me to an asylum," said Mrs. Maradick.

He made some foolish denial or evasion; but before he had finished I turned from Mrs. Maradick and faced him impulsively. In a nurse this was flagrant rebellion, and I realized that the act wrecked my professional future. Yet I did not care—I did not hesitate. Something stronger than I was driving me on.

"Doctor Brandon," I said, "I beg you—I implore you to wait until to-morrow. There are things I must tell you."

A queer look came into his face, and I understood, even in

my excitement, that he was mentally deciding in which group he should place me—to which class of morbid manifestations I must belong.

"Very well, very well, we will hear everything," he replied soothingly; but I saw him glance at Miss Peterson, and she went over to the wardrobe for Mrs. Maradick's fur coat and hat.

Suddenly, without warning, Mrs. Maradick threw the shawls away from her, and stood up. "If you send me away," she said, "I shall never come back. I shall never live to come back."

The grey of twilight was just beginning, and while she stood there, in the dusk of the room, her face shone out as pale and flower-like as the daffodils on the window-sill. "I cannot go away!" she cried in a sharper voice. "I cannot go away from my child!"

I saw her face clearly; I heard her voice; and then—the horror of the scene sweeps back over me!—I saw the door open slowly and the little girl run across the room to her mother. I saw the child lift her little arms, and I saw the mother stoop and gather her to her bosom. So closely locked were they in that passionate embrace that their forms seemed to mingle in the gloom that enveloped them.

"After this can you doubt?" I threw out the words almost savagely—and then, when I turned from the mother and child to Doctor Brandon and Miss Peterson, I knew breathlessly— oh, there was a shock in the discovery!—that they were blind to the child. Their blank faces revealed the consternation of ignorance, not of conviction. They had seen nothing except the vacant arms of the mother and the swift, erratic gesture with which she stooped to embrace some invisible presence. Only my vision—and I have asked myself since if the power of sympathy enabled me to penetrate the web of material fact and see the spiritual form of the child—only my vision was not blinded by the clay through which I looked.

"After this can you doubt?" Doctor Brandon had flung my words back to me. Was it his fault, poor man, if life had granted him only the eyes of flesh? Was it his fault if he could see only half of the thing there before him?

But they couldn't see, and since they couldn't see I realized that it was useless to tell them. Within an hour they took Mrs.

Maradick to the asylum; and she went quietly, though when the time came for parting from me she showed some faint trace of feeling. I remember that at the last, while we stood on the pavement, she lifted her black veil, which she wore for the child, and said: "Stay with her, Miss Randolph, as long as you can. I shall never come back."

Then she got into the car and was driven off, while I stood looking after her with a sob in my throat. Dreadful as I felt it to be, I didn't, of course, realize the full horror of it, or I couldn't have stood there quietly on the pavement. I didn't realize it, indeed, until several months afterwards when word came that she had died in the asylum. I never knew what her illness was, though I vaguely recall that something was said about "heart failure"—a loose enough term. My own belief is that she died simply of the terror of life.

To my surprise Doctor Maradick asked me to stay on as his office nurse after his wife went to Rosedale; and when the news of her death came there was no suggestion of my leaving. I don't know to this day why he wanted me in the house. Perhaps he thought I should have less opportunity to gossip if I stayed under his roof; perhaps he still wished to test the power of his charm over me. His vanity was incredible in so great a man. I have seen him flush with pleasure when people turned to look at him in the street, and I know that he was not above playing on the sentimental weakness of his patients. But he was magnificent, heaven knows! Few men, I imagine, have been the objects of so many foolish infatuations.

The next summer Doctor Maradick went abroad for two months, and while he was away I took my vacation in Virginia. When we came back the work was heavier than ever—his reputation by this time was tremendous—and my days were so crowded with appointments, and hurried flittings to emergency cases, that I had scarcely a minute left in which to remember poor Mrs. Maradick. Since the afternoon when she went to the asylum the child had not been in the house; and at last I was beginning to persuade myself that the little figure had been an optical illusion—the effect of shifting lights in the gloom of the old rooms—not the apparition I had once believed it to be. It does not take long for a phantom to fade from the memory—especially when one leads the active and methodical life I was forced into that winter. Perhaps—who knows?—(I remember telling myself) the doctors may have been right, after all, and the poor lady may have actually been out of her mind. With this view of the past, my judgment of Doctor Maradick insensibly altered. It ended, I think, in my acquitting him altogether. And then, just as he stood clear and splendid in my verdict of him, the reversal came so precipitately that I grow breathless now whenever I try to live it over again. The violence of the next turn in affairs left me, I often fancy, with a perpetual dizziness of the imagination.

It was in May that we heard of Mrs. Maradick's death, and exactly a year later, on a mild and fragrant afternoon, when the daffodils were blooming in patches around the old fountain in the garden, the housekeeper came into the office, where I lingered over some accounts, to bring me news of the doctor's approaching marriage.

"It is no more than we might have expected," she concluded rationally. "The house must be lonely for him—he is such a sociable man. But I can't help feeling," she brought out slowly after a pause in which I felt a shiver pass over me, "I can't help feeling that it is hard for that other woman to have all the money poor Mrs. Maradick's first husband left her."

"There is a great deal of money, then?" I asked curiously.

"A great deal." She waved her hand, as if words were futile to express the sum. "Millions and millions!"

"They will give up this house, of course?"

"That's done already, my dear. There won't be a brick left of it by this time next year. It's to be pulled down and an apartment-house built on the ground."

Again the shiver passed over me. I couldn't bear to think of Mrs. Maradick's old home falling to pieces.

"You didn't tell me the name of the bride," I said. "Is she someone he met while he was in Europe?"

"Dear me, no! She is the very lady he was engaged to before he married Mrs. Maradick, only she threw him over, so people said, because he wasn't rich enough. Then she married some lord or prince from over the water; but there was a divorce, and now she has turned again to her old lover. He is rich enough now, I guess, even for her!"

It was all perfectly true, I suppose; it sounded as plausible as a story out of a newspaper; and yet while she told me I felt, or dreamed that I felt, a sinister, an impalpable hush in the air. I was nervous, no doubt; I was shaken by the suddenness with which the housekeeper had sprung her news on me; but as I sat there I had quite vividly an impression that the old house was listening—that there was a real, if invisible, presence somewhere in the room or the garden. Yet, when an instant afterwards I glanced through the long window which opened down to the brick terrace, I saw only the faint sunshine over the deserted garden, with its maze of box, its marble fountain, and its patches of daffodils.

The housekeeper had gone—one of the servants, I think, came for her—and I was sitting at my desk when the words of Mrs. Maradick on that last evening floated into my mind. The daffodils brought her back to me; for I thought, as I watched them growing, so still and golden in the sunshine, how she would have enjoyed them. Almost unconsciously I repeated the verse she had read to me:

"If thou hast two loaves of bread, sell one and buy daffodils" —and it was at this very instant, while the words were still on my lips, that I turned my eyes to the box maze, and saw the child skipping rope along the gravelled path to the fountain. Quite distinctly, as clear as day, I saw her come, with what children call the dancing step, between the low box borders to the place where the daffodils bloomed by the fountain. From her straight brown hair to her frock of Scotch plaid and her little feet, which twinkled in white socks and black slippers over the turning rope, she was as real to me as the ground on which she trod or the laughing marble boys under the splashing water. Starting up from my chair, I made a single step to the terrace. If I could only reach her—only speak to her—I felt that I might at last solve the mystery. But with the first flutter of my dress on the terrace, the airy little form melted into the quiet dusk of the maze. Not a breath stirred the daffodils, not a shadow passed over the sparkling flow of the water; yet, weak and shaken in every nerve, I sat down on the brick step of the terrace and burst into tears. I must have known that something terrible would happen before they pulled down Mrs. Maradick's home.

The doctor dined out that night. He was with the lady he

was going to marry, the housekeeper told me; and it must have been almost midnight when I heard him come in and go upstairs to his room. I was downstairs because I had been unable to sleep, and the book I wanted to finish I had left that afternoon in the office. The book—I can't remember what it was—had seemed to me very exciting when I began it in the morning; but after the visit of the child I found the romantic novel as dull as a treatise on nursing. It was impossible for me to follow the lines, and I was on the point of giving up and going to bed, when Doctor Maradick opened the front door with his latch-key and went up the staircase. "There can't be a bit of truth in it," I thought over and over again as I listened to his even step ascending the stairs. "There can't be a bit of truth in it." And yet, though I assured myself that "there couldn't be a bit of truth in it," I shrank, with a creepy sensation, from going through the house to my room in the third storey. I was tired out after a hard day, and my nerves must have reacted morbidly to the silence and the darkness. For the first time in my life I knew what it was to be afraid of the unknown, of the unseen; and while I bent over my book, in the glare of the electric light, I became conscious presently that I was straining my senses for some sound in the spacious emptiness of the rooms overhead. The noise of a passing motor-car in the street jerked me back from the intense hush of expectancy; and I can recall the wave of relief that swept over me as I turned to my book again and tried to fix my distracted mind on its pages.

I was still sitting there when the telephone on my desk rang, with what seemed to my overwrought nerves a startling abruptness, and the voice of the superintendent told me hurriedly that Doctor Maradick was needed at the hospital. I had become so accustomed to these emergency calls in the night that I felt reassured when I had rung up the doctor in his room and had heard the hearty sound of his response. He had not yet undressed, he said, and would come down immediately while I ordered back his car, which must just have reached the garage.

"I'll be with you in five minutes!" he called as cheerfully as if I had summoned him to his wedding.

I heard him cross the floor of his room; and before he could reach the head of the staircase, I opened the door and went out into the hall in order that I might turn on the light and have his hat and coat waiting. The electric button was at the end of the hall, and as I moved towards it, guided by the glimmer that fell from the landing above, I lifted my eyes to the staircase, which climbed dimly, with its slender mahogany balustrade, as far as the third storey. Then it was, at the very moment when the doctor, humming gaily, began his quick descent of the steps, that I distinctly saw—I will swear to this on my deathbed—a child's skipping-rope lying loosely coiled, as if it had dropped from a careless little hand, in the bend of the staircase. With a spring I had reached the electric button, flooding the hall with light; but as I did so, while my arm was still outstretched behind me, I heard the humming voice change to a cry of surprise or terror, and the figure on the staircase tripped heavily and stumbled with groping hands into emptiness. The scream of warning died in my throat while I watched him pitch forward down the long flight of stairs to the floor at my feet. Even before I bent over him, before I wiped the blood from his brow and felt for his silent heart, I knew that he was dead.

Something—it may have been, as the world believes, a misstep in the dimness, or it may have been, as I am ready to bear witness, an invisible judgment—something had killed him at the very moment when he most wanted to live.

1916

JULIAN HAWTHORNE

(1846–1934)

Absolute Evil

I

I WAS half-way between twenty and thirty when I joined the Pleasances' house-boat party on their adventure to Thirteen-Mile Beach. Nobody—no society women, at any rate—had been there before, and we called ourselves pioneers.

What made it our objective was the tale of its being haunted. Haunted houses were a fashionable subject of polite investigation at that period; and to test out a haunted island was an enterprise even more engaging.

Our route lay along that chain of sounds or inland seas which extend from Chesapeake to below Hatteras. The island was one of those long, narrow sand-bars that form outlying buttresses against Atlantic storms. That, apart from legend, was all that any of us knew about it at starting. And even legend did not inform us by whom it was haunted, or why.

Two years after our expedition I was led by circumstances, chiefly subjective, to repeat the trip; this time alone. It is of this last occasion that I am to tell you; but first I must say a little more about our pioneering.

II

The house-boat belonged to the Pleasances, very nice, middle-aged Philadelphia people, of Quaker stock, but reconciled to the world, while still retaining between each other their thee-and-thy locution. They were rich, of course, and childless; but they brought along their ward, Ann Marlowe, a pretty girl of demure bearing, but with fire in her eye.

To amuse her came Jack Peters, a gilded youth of that epoch, with many suits of wonderful clothes, including two yachting-suits, in anticipation of maritime vicissitudes.

Of somewhat older years than Jack was Topham Brent, an old friend of my own, already a distinguished surgeon. Topham ought not to have come, for I had refused his offer of marriage not long before; but he was of the persistent sort, and, I admit, the finest sort of fellow.

Then there was the Rev. Nathaniel Tyler, a young New England divine, high-bred and learned, with a fine pulpit reputation, but suffering from nervous breakdown, owing to too assiduous study, no doubt. This did not prevent him from being very seriously interested in me, and we spent much of our time in intimate conversations about original sin and esoteric philosophy, with sentiment never far off; while Topham rambled about the craft, smoking cigars and trying to look indifferent.

Finally, there was myself, Martha Klemm, a handsome spinster, of the Beacon Street, Boston, brand. After this rather long interval I am a spinster still.

The house-boat was sixty or seventy feet long and more than half as wide, luxuriously decorated and furnished, with a chef and two other servants, and an inexhaustible supply of good things to eat and drink. Philadelphia Quakers know how to live.

III

I was interested in original sin, and had dabbled in esoteric philosophy; my remote ancestors had been Salem witches. So, on these grounds at least, I was ready to meet Nat Tyler half-way.

He was magnetic, fine-looking, and anything but a fool. He was tall, spare, dark-browed, with deep-set, gray eyes rather near together. His long hands were very sensitive and expressive. His lips were thin, but sharply curved, implying eloquence and secret voluptuousness. There was a conspicuous black mole on his left cheek, close to the furrow that went from the arched nostril to the corner of the mouth. His voice was a deep barytone, agreeably modulated, with reserves of power. I had heard him preach, and he could send forth notes like an organ.

Every once in a while something peeped forth from the shadows of those eyes of his that made me jump—interiorly, of course; I was woman of the world enough to betray nothing. It was as if somebody I knew very well had suddenly peeped out at me from a window in a strange place, where that face was the last I should have expected to see.

It seemed to have nothing to do with the personality of Nat Tyler himself; he was a clergyman, and this was suggestive of anything but divinity. It conveyed a profound, fascinating wickedness. It was as old as the pyramids, yet riotous with vitality. Perhaps I ought not to speak in this way of a thing which belonged to imagination; this reverend young gentleman's life had always been open as daylight, and more than blameless— apostolic. His family was as old-established as my own, and I had known of him long, though our first personal meeting was recent.

Nothing diabolic, therefore, could justly be inferred from what I have mentioned. Call it just a grotesque notion of mine. I'm sure nobody but I had noticed it, not even Topham Brent, who might have been not unwilling to detect anything objectionable in my reverend crony.

Topham was not so wise then as he is now, and may not have known that women are often attracted by what ought to repel them—some women! I confess I was on the lookout for that satanic drama in Tyler's eyes, and enjoyed the little fillip it gave me. By no word or gesture did Tyler himself betray consciousness of his peculiarity.

We discovered that we both had queer books—antique lore about witchcraft and the like. This gave us common ground, and, what was more to the point, uncommon, too.

Imagine us side by side in our reclining chairs on a moonlight evening, with the calm, watery expanse far and near, and a dark line of low shore on the horizon. Yonder the red, reflected light of a fisherman's dory; around one corner of the deck-house the giggle and babble of Jack Peters entertaining Ann, and her brief rejoinders; round the other occasional smoke-drifts from the excellent cigar Topham was smoking; inside the house was the placid silence of the benign old Pleasances reading magazines to themselves.

Tyler, in his agreeable murmur, is speculating in my ear on the origin of evil.

"Thomas Aquinas says that angels, white and black, can

change men into beasts permanently; enchanters could do it, too, but not for long. Seventeenth century witchcraft affirmed that certain natural objects and rites could produce strange effects without aid of God or devil. But the operator must renounce God and Christ, be re-baptised, trample on the cross, and be marked in a certain way—a symbolic transaction. The person could then do only evil—good was forbidden to him, or her!"

"Do you believe people can be changed into beasts?" I inquired, as if we were talking of the weather to-morrow.

"Spiritually, I know they can be, and we often notice the resemblance of some one to an animal. Well, if, as the poet Spencer says, 'Soul is form and doth the body make,' why mightn't the body of a man with the soul of a hog assume, under favorable conditions, hoggish lineaments?"

"I wonder. But what are the favorable conditions?"

"His own persistent will, or dominating suggestion from another."

Here there was the creaking of a chair and Jack came grinning round the corner.

"Say, parson, here's Ann says there are ghosts, and I'll leave it to you; are there?"

Ann, with her inscrutable smile, appeared in the background.

"Ghosts, yes; but can we see them?" returned Tyler. "Ask Dr. Brent?"

"How about it, doc?" Jack called out.

"We're on our way to Thirteen-Mile Beach to find out," answered Topham's voice, with a whiff of cigar-smoke.

"I'll bet a dozen pairs of gloves to a cigarette we don't see one."

Mr. Pleasance put his head out of the window.

"Quarter of twelve, folks; wife and I are going to bed."

"Run along, Mr. Peters," said Ann.

The currents were mixed, and we all stood up. Tyler and I, however, found ourselves leaning over the taffrail at the front of our old vehicle, as it slowly pushed its way through the liquid wilderness. The moonlight fell upon his aquiline features, as he faced toward me, and I involuntarily watched for Satan.

"I wish we could have met sooner," he remarked. "I have

longed for stimulus and companionship in my researches; such things are perilous when one goes alone. The absolute evil!— is there such a thing? Until we know, how can we understand and combat it?"

"The difficulty seems to be," I said, "that those who know it don't care to combat it. We'll assume, for the sake of argument, that witches really existed, as well as ghosts. But, for my part, I don't feel sure that we ought to combat it—that is, if we felt any assurance of extirpating it. Evil is as necessary an ingredient of life as red pepper is of an epicure's menu—it stimulates one to enjoy the banquet of life."

Out peeped Beelzebub for a moment. "You are incomparable!" murmured the parson.

"It's a fine night for a broomstick ride," I said; "but we'd better go in."

" 'The bridal of the earth and sky!' " he quoted, from Herbert, I think, looking round admiringly on the tranquil prospect. When he turned back the devil had vanished, and we went inside like two Christians.

IV

No place to compare with a house-boat for being bored, or for a flirtation, has been invented; and when the youth of one flirtation is complicated by the animated corpse of a former one, the resources of the situation might keep anyone awake. But I shall not adduce further illustrations; and I am free to confess that although I afforded my reverend friend adequate opportunities, he did not come to a technical issue. Something kept him back at the critical juncture; whether it was Satan, or whether Satan lacked power to bring on the avowal, I won't decide.

Or maybe that the fatuity of poor Jack being slowly eviscerated by that demure little devil of an Ann Marlowe deterred me from putting forth all my spells; or, possibly, it may have been a stroke of altruistic conscience about Topham Brent, who vainly and intemperately sought an anodyne in tobacco.

Howbeit, neither Ann nor I was engaged when we arrived at Thirteen-Mile Beach and set forth in quest of the ghost.

All we found there was endless prolongation of sand, with a

low backbone of tussocks tufted with beach-grass, and a few groups of storm-stunted cedars. Nothing seemed farther from any taint of the supernatural as we four young people tramped hither and yon, and the Pleasance pair sat in their beach-chairs and contemplated the incoming or withdrawing tides.

The place was not wholly destitute of incarnate human beings, however. I must give a word to the Duckworths.

What a spot for a man to bring his bride to! Old Tom Duckworth had been a sailor originally, and after giving up the Seven Seas had become a sort of beach-comber. He had put together a hut on the highest part of the beach, at its hither end; had fished the Sound and the ocean, and had salvaged flotsam and jetsam from wrecks, of which there was always a tolerable supply after a gale. He had a little garden, and kept goats, pigs, and poultry. And there he dwelt in a solitude more unmitigated than Alexander Selkirk's.

One or twice a year, though, he rowed across the ten miles of Sound, and made his way to a neighboring town for provisions.

And it chanced, on an excursion of this kind, that he encountered an elderly female.

Jane—I never learned her maiden name—had been a schoolteacher in the vicinity for half a lifetime, but had been recently retired by the school board in favor of some younger and postdiluvian rival. She was thrown upon her own resources, which was exactly nothing, for either from inability or from moral principle she had contracted no debts.

Tom proposed marriage, she accepted him; and here they were, and for the past ten years had been, contented with their environment and each other.

Tom had added to his mansion (made of old ships' timbers) two more rooms, and a fence circumventing the building, five feet high, and sunk at least as far into the sand, as a protection against storm-tides. The enclosure was about forty feet square; the pigs had their sty, and the goats and the hens wandered at will.

I once spent a summer at Étretat, on the Normandy coast, where the old sailors' huts are made of overturned boats with windows cut in the sides, a flue sticking up at one end, and a hole at the other by way of a door. They have been painted by a thousand artists, but were less picturesque than Tom Duck-worth's contrivance. Within, the rooms were kept rigorously neat by Jane, and she did much useful domestic knitting in addition to her other household duties.

They were a healthy, wholesome old couple, and may have been more than a hundred and twenty years old, combined. They had no children, and both seemed to be sorry for it.

After a first shyness they allowed us to become well acquainted with them. You might think there wasn't much of them or theirs for us to get acquainted with; but the natures of solitary people are apt to have more unmapped country in them than worldly folk imagine. They see and think and do things peculiar to themselves, and one may turn up buried treasure in them at any moment.

Our house-boat was moored off their garden for three days while we explored the island. Sea, sand, and sky—that was all, a portentous, desolate monotony. But I began to feel the spell of it, and so, I think, did Tyler.

On our last day he and I, both good walkers, tramped to the other end of the island and back, a long twenty-five miles. We had gone pretty deep into each other's minds before we returned; but, as I said, nothing ever took place. Our only substantial discovery was another hut, or shack, perched on a hummock in a kind of marsh near the southern extremity of the beach. It was uninhabited.

Tyler observed: "What a chance for a hermit!"

The Duckworths told us on our return that legend said it had been occupied many years before by a fugitive negro murderer, and was supposed to be haunted. So here was what we had come for, after all!

But the dear old Pleasances wanted to be heading for Philadelphia, and it was agreed that Jack had won his cigarettes by default. A twenty-five-mile journey and a night in the shack was voted to be too high a price to pay to decide the problem of the supernatural. We left the ghost on the fence.

At Beaufort, on our way back, we met our forwarded mail, and Tyler, after reading his, said he would have to leave us there and get home by rail.

"I hope, Martha," he said, as he held my hand at parting—

we had got as far as first names—"that we may soon meet again, and arrive at more definite conclusions."

"As to the origin of evil?" I inquired with simplicity.

I felt his eyes for a moment, but I happened to be facing the sun, and could not be sure whether or not that interesting hobby of his made its appearance.

"So far as I am concerned," he replied after a little, "intimacy with you could be only a source of good."

It was a clever turn, and now I saw that his glance was as innocent as a child's. Topham, with his broad shoulders and square face, was puffing his cigar near by, leaning back against the rail and looking quite happy. He was to stick to the ship until the last. Jack, who was dejected, suddenly resolved to accompany Tyler, and his two big trunks and four suit-cases went over the side, Ann Marlowe looking serenely on. She afterwards married Philip Bramwell, a banker of fifty.

Between Topham and me during the rest of the voyage, nothing important transpired. In Boston I learned that the Rev. Nathaniel Tyler had resigned his pastorate, and would spend some years in Europe, especially Palestine.

I had meditations over that news, but could make nothing of it. I dreamed of him several times, vividly, a most unusual thing for me. In these dreams we were always traveling somewhere at great speed, I reluctantly, he with eagerness. We never arrived.

I will end this prologue, as I might term it, here. After two years I went back to Thirteen-Mile Beach, alone, and making no one privy to my destination.

V

Not only did I tell no one, not even Topham, where I was going, but I could not myself reasonably account for my escapade. If you are indulging the notion that some hypnotic influence was involved, dismiss it immediately.

I have said that I am a descendant of witches. My exterior motive was an intense craving for solitude. Many good-looking and affluent young women in society might feel the same, after too much social dissipation. I thought of that endless, desolate beach with a longing which at last became irresistible.

It did not occur to me that absence of human companionship does not assure solitude. It may, on the contrary, plunge one into an environment compared with which New York or London would appear deserts. For we take memory and imagination with us. The seabirds that scream overhead or waddle along the margins of the surf; the grotesque forms of twisted cedars; the rustle of sea-grass in the wind; the interminable percussion of the breakers; the dead infinity of the sand itself—there can be no solitude, in the sense of freedom from disturbances of thought, in the presence of such things. They draw us back into the maelstrom.

I meant to spend a month on Thirteen-Mile Beach, and sent a message to the Duckworths asking shelter with them, and naming the date of my arrival. Should they refuse it—which I was confident they would not—I was prepared to camp out on the sands; the weather was warm and I was hardy.

I remitted money to cover extra expenses for board and lodging. I took with me a trunk full of necessities, my bicycle (a chainless one), and a revolver; not for self-defense, but I am a good shot, and might amuse myself by practising at the gulls.

After leaving the train I had to drive forty miles in an open wagon over the preposterous roads; and then, not finding Duckworth as I had expected, was obliged to hunt up a local clam-digger and get him to row me across. He explained Duckworth's failure to appear; the poor fellow had been drowned in a great storm that winter. But Jane, he said, was still there, and he believed there was "a little gal" with her.

It was near sunset when the dory stuck its nose in the mud at the end of the Duckworths' thin-legged little pier. Jane was waiting there; she had seen our approach from afar. She greeted me with a sober countenance and words, but the grip of her lean old hand was expressive of a dreary kind of satisfaction. I asked if the young woman could help us up with the trunk. She stared; young woman?

Just then the gate of the fence was pushed open, and a child of four came trudging down the path. I understood.

My clam-digger got his bony back under the trunk and

plodded up with it. Jane had made ready my room for me; she gave the clam-digger a slice of pork and some baked beans as refreshment after his trip. I glanced at myself in the crooked bit of looking-glass and shook down my hair and combed it out, and changed my traveling-dress for a jersey and a pair of loose knee-breeches, which was to be my costume in this re-tirement, and then came into the combination kitchen and sitting-room to drink a dish of tea, as Jane called it.

The little gal stood between my knees all the while and stared up in my face. She had taken to me at first sight, and was interested in my black stream of hair. When I asked her name she puffed out her mouth and said something like "Puhd!" Jane explained:

"I named her Perdita; she was lost, you see, and my Tom, he was lost getting her ashore."

The child was sturdy, and had thick, yellow hair, cut square off at the back, like a fourteenth century page's.

My room being on the side of the sea, I had already seen through the window the ribs of the wrecked vessel—a schooner —sticking up outside the breakers and deeply embedded in the sand. Jane told me the story, not consecutively, but a little now and then, day after day. The gale—"Tom called it a hurri-cane, and I reckon he knew"—had blown two days, and the evening of the third was approaching when the vessel was sighted, driving straight on the beach, only the stumps of the masts left, and nobody, as it turned out, on board.

When she struck, the wind stopped, as if it had done its job and quit. The surf was too high to go out to her, however; the clouds broke away overhead, and the full moon shone down, it being then midnight.

As the two old people stood watching, Jane had fancied she heard a sound of crying from the wreck—the crying of a child. Tom had finally agreed he heard something, too, in the inter-vals of the breakers. He got out his old binoculars, but could make out nothing on the deck; but the name of the vessel, painted in white letters on her bows, was discernible—"Jane—New Orleans."

"Tom looks at me," said the old woman, "and says he: 'Jane —and a child crying! Looks like the Lord sent us a baby, after all!' And when that idee struck him, Miss Klemm, there was nothing could hold him. 'Tide's goin' out,' says he, 'and sea calmin' down; I got to get that kid!'"

The stout old mariner brought out the life-belt and line, hitched one end of the line to the post and went in. Jane stood by the post and watched. Tom passed the breakers safely and struck out for the ship. He would disappear in the trough of the seas and then reappear when she thought him lost.

But as he approached the side of the vessel, which lay broad-side-on, a big comber lapped over her from seaward and came on, bearing something with it from the deck. It was an impromptu raft, made of heavy timbers, and the child had been made fast to it. A corner of the structure, carried on the crest of the wave, was dashed against Tom Duckworth's head. Jane ran down into the froth of the breakers and received the raft, with the little child upon it, still living, and her husband's dead body.

I suppose such things are not uncommon on this treacherous coast. But what a simple, appalling drama! There was nothing dramatic in Jane's temperament, and no gift of expression but might have been beggared in portraying such a catastrophe. She told me the thing without emphasis or gesture—doing her knitting or stirring the contents of the saucepan on the kitchen stove. There had been no one present to sympathize with her agony—only the thunder of the waves upon the sand, the screaming sea-gulls, the moon staring down from the cloud-rifts.

She drew the body up beyond the reach of the waves, and took the child into the cabin, fed it, and warmed it. The next day men came over from the mainland.

"It wasn't any use hating the child; it wasn't to blame, so I got fond of it," she remarked. The Lord had sent it to her, a substitute for what He had taken away! That was her interpretation. Perdita was not a marvel of beauty, but she was an active, smiling, affectionate little thing, and kept Jane busy looking after her.

"She keeps the loneliness off," Jane observed.

VI

I took up my regimen of life immediately. The sand was hard and elastic, just the consistency for bicycle-riding. It was September, and warm for the season. I had the freedom of the island—nobody ever visited it. I would ride out before breakfast eight or ten miles down the beach, and then take a surf bath, unimpeded by a bathing-dress. Coming out I would get on my wheel again and enjoy a wild witch-ride to and fro till my skin was dry and glowing.

What a tonic for body and mind! No born savage could have had a tithe my delight in it. The sun, the sea, the sand, the gulls were my sole playmates. I would throw a long wreath of kelp over my shoulder and speed till it flew out behind me, mingling with the fluttering flag of my hair. Nature seems to welcome defiance of conventions, and to say, with a smile, 'So, the truant has come back again!'"

How men and women interfere with and imprison one another!

After breakfast and washing up the things, in which I collaborated with Jane, though she didn't wish it, I would go out and sprawl in the sun and play with Perdita and feed the pigs and chickens and have fun with the goat. An hour or two of this and then, with a little bundle of lunch at my belt, I would jump on the wheel again and be off till late afternoon. Dismounting, I would make ready for another bath of sun and air, if not of sea, and seldom resumed my riding-dress till it was time to go home.

It was not many days before I might have been taken for a wild Indian: I was golden brown from head to feet.

Why not live this way always? The thought of going back to Boston was intolerable! Nature and I were one thing.

One evening, after Perdita had been got to her crib and was asleep, and Jane and I were sitting beside the driftwood fire, and all was still except the deep, soft rhythm of the surf, a strange, remote sound came vibrating to my ears. Jane gave a slight movement, but did not look up from her knitting. The sound came again.

"Are there dogs on the island?" I asked.

"Best not notice it, Miss Klemm," said Jane; she seemed embarrassed. "Gulls, maybe."

This evasion roused my curiosity. No sea-bird could emit a call like that. It had reminded me of the coyotes, as I had heard them on the western deserts at night; but, of course, it

couldn't be that! It must be a dog, running wild. But how had
a dog got over here? Some man must have brought it; but the
idea of a man coming to the island was disquieting. It would
be an invasion of my liberties!

The sound came once more—now further off.

"Just not mind it—that's my plan," repeated Jane. "My
mother, she was born in Ireland, and used to tell us about the
banshee. I reckon this is something in that way. Nothing there
—only the sound. I heard it first after Tom died!"

"Never before that?"

"No, miss; and if you're agreeable I'd sooner not talk of it.
Things like that comes oftener if you worry about 'em."

"I thought you had more sense, Jane!" I said. "I know all
about banshees; but we're not children—we're two women
out here alone. A wild dog like that might kill one of your pigs
or chickens. Besides, where there's a dog a man is apt to be not
far off. The creature ought to be hunted down and killed, and
I'll do it to-morrow!" I added, remembering my revolver at
the bottom of my trunk. "Its howling is disagreeable, and its
being here interferes with my privacy."

Jane heaved a sigh, and went on with her knitting in silence;
and there was no further disturbance that night. Next morning
there was a northerly wind, with gusts of rain, and I omitted
my early ride. But going out, during an intermission of the
showers, I met Perdita at the seaward gate of the palisade, crying
lustily.

In explanation she pointed over to Tom Duckworth's grave,
which had been made about thirty yards south of the enclosure; it was surrounded with a little picket, and Jane had
planted flowers on it.

But mischief had been at work there the night before. The
flowers had been violently dug up and scattered about, and a
hole of some depth hollowed out, as if to get at what lay beneath. There were no marks of spade or pickax, but there were
other traces that left no doubt as to the perpetrator—it was the
howling beast of the foregoing evening. Perdita, going out to
pluck a flower and finding the destruction, had been smitten
with indignation and grief.

I would have kept knowledge of it from Jane, but the child's lamentations had drawn her out of the kitchen—she came, wiping her hands on her apron, and beheld the desecration. She stood rigid a minute, her meager old face twisted with horror; then her lips trembled, and she said, "I didn't know I'd an enemy in the world!"

"Enemy? It's that damned hound!" I answered in wrath. "Clear your imagination of enemies and banshees, woman. The plundering beast has lived too long."

But Jane's reticence being thus broken she became almost voluble, and her supernatural fears came out. The howling, she told me, had begun soon after Tom's death—it was an evil spirit! The physical attack upon the grave seemed to confirm her in that conviction. Once, she declared, when she had gone out at night to bring in a skirt that had been blown over the fence, and the thing had made a swoop at her through the air! No, not a gull, nor a hawk—no mortal creature went on such wings!

She didn't know whether the things were the souls of the folks that had been swept off the ship before she struck, and had been carried away in the sea and never had burial; or whether the persecution was aimed at poor Tom for something he might have done when he was a sailor before the mast; or whether it was something about Perdita, who had appeared miraculously, as one might say; or whether, finally, she herself were the person concerned.

In short, to my surprise, the old schoolmistress confessed herself a prey to the rankest superstition, and reason and ridicule were alike wasted on her. The only thing to do was to kill the dog and show her its remains.

The rain-clouds drifted away during the night, and the sun rose clear for a day of perfect beauty and radiance. I awoke betimes and hastened to get abroad, not delaying to delve into my trunk for the revolver; neither concrete dogs nor ghosts were likely to be out so early. I swept down the beach as swiftly as I could drive; reached the point where I was accustomed to take my dip, threw off my clothes and ran in, eager to feel the thrill of the breakers on my body.

I came out breathing hard and tingling with joy of life. I had been carried down some distance by the set of the current; and

as I debouched beyond the reach of the sliding surf I saw
something which startled me not a little—a man's bare footprint in the sand!

VII

Without staying to examine it, I scuttled to my jersey and
breeches and huddled them on in a jiffy. Then my panic
changed to anger: I regretted not having brought my revolver,
and went back to investigate.

There were several of them; they emerged from below the
surf line and proceeded diagonally inland till they were lost in
the loose, grass-grown sand. The tide was ebbing; they might
be two or three hours old. They were long and narrow.

Where was the man?

From the little elevation, where I now stood, the surface of
the island was visible for miles in all directions; but no living
creature was in sight. My eyes are good, and I could have seen
any moving object in that clear atmosphere, with the sun
standing an hour high above the sea at a great distance. Of
course the fellow might be hiding behind one of the little
clumps of cedars that dotted the expanse.

A man and a dog on my island! Howlings by night and footprints in the morning! There were no dog footprints, to be
sure, but it was inevitable to associate the evidences to ear and
eye. They must have a habitation—where was it?

I recalled, for the first time, the little abandoned shack at the
further end of the island, said to have been the refuge of the
negro murderer of old times. I had never yet ridden more than
ten or twelve miles from the Duckworth cabin. Had the shack
a new tenant? If so, he could hardly be a desirable neighbor.
Thirteen miles was, indeed, a considerable distance to go and
return, for a man, if not for a dog. But, if the man were a "wild
man," distance might be no hindrance to him. There had been
no indications, however, that he had accompanied his dog on
the nocturnal excursions.

I was now much nearer his abode than the Duckworths.

I took another look at the footprints and noticed their great
distance apart—more than five feet. Thirty inches is a good
average stride for a man, walking on sand. The sixty-inch in-

tervals showed that he must have been running. Perhaps there was nothing singular in that; but it gave me an unpleasant sensation—a naked man running insanely along the beach! But I laughed at myself—I was giving imagination too much rein. The tracks could not be traced more than thirty or forty yards, and a barefoot man is not necessarily bare all over. Possibly he had been merely taking a bath, like myself, and had run out of the water, as I had, under a natural stimulus.

After all, too, he had as much ostensible right to be on the island as I had.

Nevertheless—and I am sensitive to such impressions—there was an evil "vibration," as the saying is, from the footprints. And, at any rate, their presence destroyed my freedom. I determined to get my gun and explore. Meanwhile I would say nothing to Jane. She had enough to tax her nerves as it was!

As I rode home my fancy pictured a big, shambling negro, with an ugly dog, roaming about the place; an outlaw, doubtless, subsisting on clams—what else was there for him to eat? He must be ripe for robbery and violence. And to oppose him, two lone women and a child, forty miles from help! I was glad of my revolver.

On my arrival at the cabin I took a look at the place as a post of defense. The palisade completely surrounded it, and was five feet in height; made of massive pieces of ship-timber, planted deep and firm in the sand. This strength had been designed to resist the onset of the waves in case they should come up so far; but, of course, an athletic man could easily vault over it—unless he were shot down in the act!

The cabin itself was also very strongly constructed, as strong as an ordinary blockhouse. I was confident I could defend it against any single assailant, especially were he unarmed, as the negro would most likely be. A surprise assault was the thing to be guarded against. A small dog of our own would have been useful—to give the alarm at night. Perhaps we could procure one.

After breakfast I spent an hour cleaning my revolver and trying my skill at a target. Jane shook her head, probably thinking that bullets were vain against demonic powers. But Perdita was hugely delighted with the shining little instrument, and wanted it for a plaything; women of all ages will play with death! When

I fired it the explosion didn't frighten her; her little heart had never learned to tremble, but she couldn't grasp the connection between the sharp, sudden noise, and the hole in the plank thirty yards distant. I took a shot at a gull on the wing, and by chance cut a piece of a feather from its tail; Perdita shouted with astonishment and delight; it was wondrous magic to her.

About ten o'clock I mounted my wheel again and set off down the beach—the gun in my belt. In the broad sunshine, beside the sparkling sea, I felt secure and adventurous; after all, there was good New England fighting blood in my veins!

It was my purpose to ride to the end of the beach and take a look at the negro's shack. My apprehensions might prove groundless. The owner of the footprints might be a harmless hunter in quest of ducks, or even a wandering tourist on a vacation hike. Old Jane's supernatural gossip had perhaps caused me to take too romantic a view of the situation. I would solve the problem forthwith.

The tide, since my early excursion, had passed its low mark, and was now making again. But when I got to the place where I had bathed the footprints were still uncovered. They were three inches longer than my own beside them. The fellow must be immense!

I rode on slowly, pondering, but, under the genial moisture of exercise on my body, neither uneasy nor as much irritated as before. The Atlantic coast of the United States was long enough to accommodate two persons without crowding. Very likely this was the first, and would be the last time the invader would leave his trail on this part of it!

But a mile or so beyond I halted sharply. The trail again— and something more!

I dismounted. The footsteps, still indicating a running gait, came down toward the sea again; but after going parallel with the surf-line for a little began circling around, as if the crazy negro—such I now imagined him—were in a fit. Some of the prints were deep driven. At first I thought there were two sets of prints. But, no! All were made by the same pair of feet. The circuits they traced were narrow and irregular; the marks often crossed one another—a sort of insane dance.

But there was something else, and it turned me cold when I realized what it meant.

The footprints didn't go on beyond the general circle in any direction! Where, then, was the man—unless a balloon had swooped down and borne him away?

That was one bad thing; the other was quite as bad.

The human footprints were intermingled with others, not human—the marks of the four paws of an enormous dog! But this beast had not entered the circle from any point outside of it—at least, if he had, the man must have carried him in his arms. But this was unthinkable; and if the man had carried him in the beast had left the circle on its own foot, continuing at full speed down the beach, leaving behind it—what? Nothing at all!

I was armed, and am far from being a timorous person. But this weird thing crawled into my nerves with a sensation, compared with which the threat of impending death would have seemed trivial.

A man had entered that circle and had vanished there. A beast had run out of that circle without having entered it.

As I rode slowly homeward, beside the sparkling sea, under the cloudless sky, that was all I could make of it; and I didn't like it.

VIII

But the creeping paralysis of helpless dismay—helpless against I knew not what—presently changed into a passion of black anger. I would have it out with this thing and be done with it—one way or another. To flinch from it would be to lose nerve and self-respect forever.

At the cabin I was monosyllabic with Jane, and in no mood to respond to Perdita's invitations to play with her, or give her the shining toy to play with. I wanted to take counsel with myself—by myself. I would have dismissed even Topham Brent, though I was used to think of him as a counselor. I would rather have discussed the matter with that very different person, the Rev. Nathaniel Tyler, with whom, as I have said, I had ground in common.

Upon second thought, however, I dismissed him, too; he would be too refined and fastidious to take hold of this brutal event efficiently. I must deal with it alone!

But thinking about it only made it worse. I must act. I must hunt the enigma down, solve it, and destroy it, or be destroyed by it. Still I stayed in my room, unable to decide how to go about the adventure. I sat listening to the surf and to the gulls and to the occasional voices of the child and Jane; once or twice the rap of soft little knuckles came on my door, but I kept silence.

When, later, Jane summoned me to dinner, I declined to come out. I wasn't hungry, I told her; had a headache.

Through my uneasy preoccupation I was sensible by familiar sounds that Perdita was being put to bed. I had usually helped at this ceremony, and the child asked after me. "I want Aunt Martha"—such was my title in her list of friends. Jane and I were the only persons represented there. I had an impulse to go to her, but resisted it. After she had gone to sleep the silence in the cabin was complete; there was only the heavy chanting of the surf coming through my open window.

A couple of hours passed and it was now dark—the moon had not yet risen. Jane's voice at my door; she hoped I was feeling better, she had put a dish of victuals on the stove for me, in case I got an appetite; she was going to bed.

"Good night, Jane; I'll be all right tomorrow!" I said.

Should I too turn in? What was the use of sitting up?

But I was in no condition to sleep, and it was better to be awake standing than lying down. I leaned out of the window and breathed in the soft air from the sea; there was a light breeze from the south. I could see the long, level line of the horizon, and part of the black ribs of the wrecked schooner, thrusting up against the sky.

All at once, between the ribs, appeared a pyramid of bright red light—the gibbous moon rising in the east. A moment after I thought I heard, very far away, a long ululation, which crisped my nerves.

The dog was abroad!

Since childhood I have always been affected by the changes of the moon, sometimes very much so. As the light of the satellite fell on my face my mind cleared, and I knew what was to be done. I had partly undressed; I pulled on my sweater again and buckled on the revolver. I had left my bicycle under the lean-to outside; to avoid disturbing Jane I slipped out of the window. One of the hens uttered an interrogative croak as I passed the coop.

I got my wheel, opened the gate of the palisade, closed it behind me, and ran the wheel down to the firm sand of the beach, where I mounted; it was just past eleven o'clock. I set off in the old direction, glad to be in action and strung up to meet anything.

The horizon line had been clear a few minutes before; but now I observed a low, gray fog moving in toward the coast, with the mysteriously slow yet swift movement characteristic of sea fogs. It had seemed distant, yet now it had reached out a long, silent arm, and had touched the beach ahead. The moon hung a little way above it. The fog clung close to the surface of the scene—seemed hardly more than a man's height in thickness.

In another minute it had swathed me in its gray impalpability; and at the same time I heard again the howl of the dog, much more distinct than at first. My pedals revolved more swiftly, and the revolver thumped against my hip; I hoped the negro was with his dog. My only fear was lest they should pass me in the obscurity of the flowing mist.

The line of the beach was not straight; there were wide, shallow bays and projections, and the mist confused me, so that occasionally I found myself running close to the surf, or away from it. But the sea was a safeguard against losing my direction entirely, and I kept on at a fast pace. But was that which I sought coming toward me, or fleeing before me? If the latter, my best speed would be needed to catch up with it. I bent over the handlebars; speed in either case!

Three short barks, followed by a long howl, sounded not fifty yards away. In the few seconds that followed I halted, leaped off the wheel, snatched the revolver from my belt, and held it ready in my right hand, standing behind the wheel. I could not risk a shot while mounted; but afoot I was confident of my aim, and could use the saddle as a rest.

Then, at last, the beast disclosed itself. It was alone. Itself gray, it seemed formed out of the fog. The cantering movement was what I first discerned; but when within a dozen yards it stopped, plunging its forepaws in the sand, its head extended forward.

Shreds of mist drifted past it, and perhaps exaggerated its apparent size, but it seemed much bigger than I had anticipated. And the long, dripping jaws, the short, thick ears, the build of the chest and shoulders, and the shaggy tail flung out behind, showed me at a glance that this was no dog of any breed; it was a wolf!

Unaccountable though its presence in this region might be, there could be no doubt of that. I had to deal with a savage wild beast—a giant of its kind.

For an instant a perplexing thought of its association with a human being, even a crazy negro, flashed across my brain; but the present emergency was enough, and I gripped myself to meet it.

"*The absolute evil—is there such a thing?*" This saying of Tyler's recurred to my mind as I faced the creature, challenging the glare of its close-set eyes down the barrel of my weapon. The aspect of the monster answered the question. Hell could engender nothing more diabolical than this!

My hand did not tremble as I sighted to a point between the glaring eyes and touched the trigger. The detonation sounded flat in the boundless gray expanse that surrounded us.

The beast gave a lurch of the head, uttered a harsh bark, swung round in its tracks, and was out of sight in a moment. I had missed it clean!

I sent a second bullet after it at hazard. Another long howl was the answer, and already it seemed to be a mile away.

The fog thickened and now obscured the moon. I had sprung to my saddle, but almost immediately gave up the pursuit. There wasn't a chance in a million that I would set eyes upon the creature again that night.

I turned and rode back, feeling upon the whole glad of the encounter. I had met the thing and knew what it was; and though I had incredibly missed killing it, I had put it to flight, and perhaps driven it off the island entirely.

But there was a feeling in me that I should meet it again. I didn't believe that an incident so out of the ordinary would have no sequel.

IX

Time passed on, however, and there was no more baying at the moon or alarms in our household, nor did I find any more tracks on the beach. The weather was the most exhilarating I had ever known, and Diana, the goddess—to whom fanciful admirers had often compared me—couldn't have felt more of the elixir of immortality in her than I did.

The moon, after her brief retirement, appeared once more, a lovely crescent, in the west, and, gradually attaining her full splendor, shone at last transcendent in the pallid sky. I was in the pink of condition, as the young fellows in training for a race say. I had ceased thinking of the wolf, and had never told Jane of my meeting with it. Either she had forgotten her misgivings, or some odd reluctance prevented her mentioning them. Perdita and I had become sworn play-fellows—her innocence and confidence had made me love her.

"Absolute evil" seemed a grotesque hallucination. Absolute good was more real and near.

One thing only marred my tranquillity—though the wolf never occurred to my mind in waking hours, I dreamed of it several times at night. I was alone in some desolate place, deeply preoccupied, and suddenly felt that I had lost my way. Looking up, I saw the wolf before me. Nothing but its head was clearly visible, however. And in this head the terrible, glaring, close-set eyes drew mine irresistibly till, after a moment, the eyes alone seemed there. Behind them spread a region of darkness, out of which the beast had emerged, and into which it seemed striving to entice me, as a snake fascinates a bird.

I struggled against the hideous lure, but felt I was yielding —at which juncture I awoke.

This dream, almost the same in details, visited me three or four times. In sleep only the nature of the sleeper is active; what belongs to acquired character no longer exists. And the nature possesses impulse, but not will. My resistance could never have been overcome in my waking state.

There was one other feature of this experience to which I will merely allude; I didn't understand it at the time. It was the most revolting of all. The eyes of the beast reminded me of eyes that I had seen before. Not the eyes themselves, either, but the look that came from them. I could not trace this impression back to its source, though that seemed only just beyond my reach. It disturbed me.

But by the time the moon had filled her circle, this obsession, too, left me, and there was no cloud on my sky except regret at my approaching departure from the beach. When I spoke of it to Jane, her face fell.

"I'd be thankful if you'd stay longer, miss," she said. "And the child—what'll *she* do?" She pressed her lips together, as if trying to keep something back; but it came. She bent forward and whispered, "I'm afeared of the dog!"

I laughed with ruddy-cheeked assurance.

"I think the dog, as you call it, won't trouble you again." Then I told her my story. "I fancy I must have wounded it," I said; "it's either dead or gone for good. I've been down and back scores of times since, and seen no trace of it. Put it out of your mind."

I did not tell her of that insoluble enigma of the mingled tracks of the beast and the man. In truth, I preferred to keep away from it. There must have been some error in my observation; impossibilities don't happen.

Jane said no more, and after sitting in a brown study for a while, got up and went about her domestic affairs. Perdita, from outside, called me to come and have some fun with the goat. But the goat was perverse that day, and I, being in my bathing-dress—it was the forenoon—proposed to take the child in with me for a bath.

The sea was as smooth as a pond and the sun warm. Perdita was fearless, and could swim well. The tide was low, and we managed to get out to the wreck, where we amused ourselves with the sea anemones and shells sticking to the old timbers.

Children, brought up naturally and in freedom, not only have imagination, but live in a world of imagination more real to them than our reality. Perdita, perched on one of the cross-pieces, with her small feet dabbling in the water, and a ribbon of green seaweed twisted round her head for a crown, said: "This ship mine. By 'n' by, when I'm big, I make it all new and sail to Boston!"

"This is a much nicer place than Boston," said I.

"No!" She insisted. "Sail to Boston and get away from naughty dog."

I hadn't supposed that she knew anything about the dog. "There is no dog," I said, "and dogs don't hurt little children."

But she looked at me, rounding her blue eyes and holding up her arms to express something vast and intimidating, and repeated, "Bi-ig dog! Make noise—so!"—she threw back her head and gave an absurd imitation of a howl—"and bite poor Pudh."

Then her mood changed, and she burst into uproarious laughter. I caught her up in my arms and kissed her.

The weather changed that afternoon, with the abruptness peculiar to this coast; a wind began blowing from the south, the temperature rose and became sticky and uncomfortable, and the sea "got up," as Jane expressed it.

States of the atmosphere pass into us as water through the meshes of a sieve, and storms occur in us before they break upon the world without, creating restless sensations. The cabin became oppressive, and we opened the doors and windows to let the air through. Perdita was so uneasy, after being put into her crib, that we drew the crib to the seaward door to give her the benefit of the draft.

Jane went to bed about nine o'clock as usual; but I remained sitting in the doorway, beside Perdita, who now seemed to sleep quietly. The moon, now riding high, broke through the hurrying clouds once in a while, and sent broad rays across the rough backs of the seas. The wind was not violent, except in gusts; but the heat of it was extraordinary—it seemed to come out of an oven.

I stood up at last out of patience, and going to my room, took off my skirt and waist and put on my pajamas, in which I returned to the doorway. It was some relief; but now, as I looked over to the breaking surf, an impulse came upon me to go down and take one dip in the cool waves and out again.

I didn't pause to debate the matter, but with a glance at the child, peaceful on her little pillow, I crossed the yard quickly and out at the gate of the palisade, which I left open behind me. I would let the sea just wet me as I was, and return; by the time the wind had dried my pajamas I should be cool enough to sleep.

As I stood upon the margin, the on-driving waves loomed gigantic, and the force of them appeared so great that I wouldn't venture far in: I stepped into the sliding tongues of water, and threw myself down at full length where the depth was not above my knees. Even there the drag of the withdrawing wave was very strong. But the coolness was delicious, and I may have lain wallowing there as much as five minutes. The thunder and rush of sound filled my ears. What an incomparable creature is the sea!

I got to my feet, thoroughly revived, and turned toward the cabin.

As I did so a shrill scream, which was more like a squeal, pierced my brain like a needle. It defined itself against the surf-roar like a slender stab of light against the dark. Almost simultaneously, out through the gate of the palisade, which my neglect had left open, plunged the gray shape of the wolf, bearing in its jaws a bundle of whiteness, partly trailing on the ground. He headed down the beach in a long, swinging canter, his pace hardly impeded by the weight he carried.

My knees weakened for an instant as if from a violent blow in the breast. An instant more I wavered, prompted to pursue on foot. That folly forced back, I leaped toward the cabin for my wheel and revolver.

I rushed against something in the doorway—Jane, distracted, frantically moaning—and we stumbled together over the over-turned crib. In another breath I was in my room, had snatched the revolver from the dressing-table, was out again, and on my wheel. After a fierce interval of plowing through heavy sand, I felt the firm beach under my tires, and was off.

Beneath this frenzy of physical effort, some region far within me seemed to remain cold and unflurried, calculating chances, foreseeing obstacles, measuring advantages.

Be the strength of the beast what it might—and it appeared supernatural—I knew that I should overtake it. There was supernatural vigor in my limbs, too, and my heart was firm as granite and hot as fire. I would not miss my aim this time, but I clearly perceived the danger of sending a bullet through Perdita as well as through the beast.

There was another possibility—the child might be already

dead. I must accept these risks; get her, alive or dead, and deal out vengeance.

The wind, meanwhile, had backed to the north and blew much harder, but being more behind me than in front, aided rather than hindered my speed. There was great darkness, so that I could see nothing except the relative blanching of the breakers as they foamed up to me on my left hand. The temperature fell headlong, and I felt the sting of hail on the thin wet silk of my pajamas. But I was warm, and my body exulted, in spite of the wrath in my soul.

I was steering with my left hand only on the handlebars, my right being occupied with the revolver, but my arm felt as strong as a steel bar. No sound reached me from ahead; the beast could not bark, and Perdita had not screamed after the first. How far had I ridden?—miles probably; but distance seemed nothing, and I felt that nature, to which I so loved to give myself, was on my side. Absolute evil could not prevail.

The crisis came unawares, yet found me ready.

There—almost under my wheel! The beast, with its burden, was revealed suddenly in the darkness, huddled back upon its haunches, snarling, dripping froth, at bay. Before it lay the child on the wet sand, her arms tossed up beyond her head, her cheek resting on a roll of brown seaweed, as if asleep, swathed in her torn white wrappings. Gale, sea, and sky drove upon us.

The beast seemed to tower up, huge, hideous and fatal; it hurtled at me, snarling, and I fired.

I think I laughed aloud as I saw the bullet strike its left shoulder. The coarse, gray hair was dabbled with spurting blood. I leaped from my wheel, which fell to the left, and stepped forward to complete my work.

But the beast had vanished. The gale shrieked; in the blackness the gray form of a wave surged almost to my feet—gray and writhing like the beast itself. But the wind swept the spume away, and there was nothing visible but the white, precious bundle that was Perdita. From somewhere far off, against the gale, came faintly back the long-drawn howl. It sounded to my fancy like the despairing call of a damned soul.

I lifted the child from the sand, and holding her on my left arm, regained my seat and began to fight my way back to the cabin.

X

Perdita was alive. Hardly a scratch marred her little body; there were only a few bruises on her head and shoulder, which, combined with the shock of fear, had made her unconscious. She had stirred and whimpered before we reached home, and Jane and I ministered to her, and before morning she slept in comfort. Marvelous beings are little children!

These things went by like the figures of a magic lantern to which one pays but dim attention. I was reliving that wild hour, and answered Jane at random. I was content; the beast had not died on the spot, but I knew it must die. The corpse could be found later.

I felt no curiosity about it. I had done my part—saved Perdita, and freed Jane from the forebodings that had haunted her. The rest would take care of itself. Nature, through my agency, had been relieved of an ulcer that had been festering in her breast, and her wholesome law had been reestablished. I felt like a soldier returned from an honorable campaign, conscious of duty done, and indifferent to what fame rumored of the battle. Enough for him that the enemy was defeated; for me that the beast was no more.

I don't deny that this has a mystical sound. Probably our lives are full of symbols which only an unacknowledged sense perceives. Spiritual events assume a material guise, in accordance with some creative principle, but do not insist on recognition. The soul is wounded, or is healed, as the case may be, and the effect, echoed upon the mortal plane, exercises in silence its benign office as penalty or reward.

The storm continued for three days; it has happened twice or thrice to me that memorable events in my life have been ushered in or accompanied by great storms. When the turmoil and darkness passed away, a new, crisp brightness began, as of approaching winter. The black bones of the wreck upon the beach had been broken up by the waves, and lay scattered for miles along the shore. Jane congratulated herself on the supply of firewood, but Perdita was displeased; how was she to get to Boston?

That problem has since been solved in a less magical manner than her fancy had provided. I kept alive the link between myself and these two. Jane died after a few years; Perdita, after adventures not to be told here, is a fortunate and happy woman.

But why do I dilly-dally and gossip and procrastinate? I must tell the end of this story, great as is my unwillingness to do it. It is inhuman and incredible, but the truth has no concern with such adjectives. And you may give it lodging according to the character of your philosophy; you have your choice and opportunity.

But perhaps you know the end already. I thought, afterward, that I had known it. No secrets are better hidden than are those that we hide from ourselves.

I got back to Boston about the middle of November of that year, and was enjoying, I must admit, the various luxuries abounding in that most respectable old house of mine, which I had so well dispensed with, and with such a glow of fresh life, in the primitive cabin on Thirteen-Mile Beach. My friends in society had also returned from their holidays, and we were practising upon one another our old, urbane amenities.

One of the first to call on me was, of course, Topham Brent. I flirted artistically with him, as it is my fate to do with some men. He told me I looked tremendously fit, and wanted to know what adventures I had had. I answered "None," and inquired whether he had heard anything of the Rev. Nathaniel Tyler. "That man interested me," I remarked.

"Not really?—never should have imagined it!" was his ironic rejoinder. "Why, seems to me I heard somewhere that he was back from the Orient, or some such place. They said he was in bad health, too—worse than when we had the benefit of his company on the Pleasances' house-boat two years ago. But he hasn't called me in, so I'm unable to present any pathological details."

"I must drop him a line; I'd like to see him," said I.

But the next day I received a note from him. He wrote:

I've dwelt in the desert since we met, and while there sustained an injury which confines me to my house. I can never expect to appear in a pulpit again. It would afford me great pleasure if you would come to see me. I have never forgotten our talks on the house-boat, and I have reached some conclusions on the subjects we discussed which I would like to submit to you.

I was promised an invitation to a lunch next day, Tuesday, and to a reception the same evening. On Wednesday I had tickets for an afternoon concert, and a dinner later. On Thursday I was particularly desired to attend the meeting of the Homogeneity Club, and on Friday— No matter what; I made up my mind to give my Friday to the afflicted clergyman.

I found him in his study, which apparently adjoined his bed-room; a soothing brown effect of furniture and decoration, steel engravings of sacred subjects on the walls, shelves of books, old quartos, volumes of recent philosophical and scientific essays; on the table a portfolio of designs of "The Dance of Death," and several French and Russian novels; on the mantel-piece a bronze replica of the Venus Kallipygos, of Naples.

These things reported themselves to the corners of my eyes, the direct look of which, of course, was fixed upon Tyler. He reclined in an invalid's chair, fronting an open coal grate fire; his attitude reminded me of how he and I used to recline side by side in our deck chairs on the house-boat.

Otherwise he was strangely altered. His hair was gray and thin, and hung down to his neck. A thin gray beard was on his cheeks and chin and upper lip. His former spareness had become mere boniness; the sutures of his head, his cheek-bones, the angles of the jaw might have been a skull's, and his body, as indicated beneath the wrappings over him, was but a skeleton.

His eyes, sunken deep under the tufted eyebrows, appeared almost black in the subdued light of the room; they seemed to draw inward toward the narrow dividing ridge of his high nose, giving his gaze an intense concentration. His long hands rested on the arms of his chair; they were like talons, with prominent knuckles, and narrow, polished nails of a purplish hue. But his mouth had still its sharp, voluptuous curves, and smiled as he greeted me, though the eyes had no part in the smile. There was a sort of bunch over his left shoulder which the drapery didn't wholly conceal.

I said to myself, "The man will be dead in a few days." I felt this, quite as much as I inferred it from his aspect.

But the tones of his voice were firm and cheerful, with even a half-laughing accent of raillery in them.

"If you were a disciple of mine, Miss Klemm, summoned here for ghostly counsel, you'd need no better symbol of *memento mori* than myself, I fancy. But it is I who am under obligation to you—for this and other favors. I won't keep you long. I'm mortified at not being able to get up and fetch you a chair; will you pardon me, and be seated?"

As I sat down beside him he made a movement of the head, upon which the young woman in the attire of a professional nurse, who had been standing near his chair, silently withdrew into the bedroom and softly closed the door.

"As you've surmised," he then said, "I shall shortly lay aside this muddy vesture of decay; but I thought, in deference to your feelings and many social engagements that it would be more considerate to arrange our interview before than after that event; it was bound to take place one way or the other. You—er—enjoyed yourself last summer?"

"I'm feeling the better for it," I replied.

"You have the goddesslike quality of sweeping obstacles from your path, and punishing interlopers," he rejoined; and as he spoke that satanic presence sparkled in the depths of his eyes. "When Diana, your prototype, was surprised at her bath by Actæon, she didn't suffer him to live to boast of his enjoyment of her perfections. But I dare say he was as willing as I am to pay that price for the privilege."

"I hear you've been abroad," said I, not ready to understand him.

"Oh, that is for the vulgar ear. You and I are augurs, and have no subterfuges. Perhaps, in good old Cotton Mather's day, we may have bestridden a broomstick together. I've always had a notion that our acquaintance is of long standing."

I kept silence, instinctively shutting my mind.

"Abroad, yes: far abroad!—and in the desert, to which the Sahara or the plain of Nineveh would be populous." He pointed to his own breast with a light laugh. "There, like our friend Walt Whitman, I invited my soul, and we had it out *à outrance*—thanks to my friend, Miss Martha Klemm."

"What do you expect me to say, Mr Tyler?"

"My dear young lady, you are voluble! From the moment of

your entrance—if not before—you and I have been conversing like babbling brooks, though even had my clinical attendant not so discreetly retired, she couldn't have heard a syllable of it. The footprints perplexed you, possibly; but that first moonlight tryst, which ended so explosively—surely you've had no doubts since then?"

The sensation was as if he were throwing invisible nets around me. I stood up, with angry eyes. "Shall I call the nurse?"

"Ah, have a little patience! Give a poor moribund wretch the consolation of shriving himself. Don't let me perish quite alone in the world—alone—with the beast!"

At that word, and at that thought, I sat down again. I put out all my self-command to keep from trembling. He nodded thankfully, but for some moments, contending against the exhaustion which his assumption of mockery had, as I now perceived, cost him, he could not speak. When he did, it was in another vein.

"It needed a man like me—if I am a man—to conceive it and to do it. Learning, culture, the religious training and atmosphere, personal sanctity, esthetic sensitiveness, a heredity without blemish—I abounded in all that. I was vowed to God. To descend deep, you must first go high—touch the halo before polluting it. I can say that I went deep, at least. None has been lower. Yes, I went into the desert—but not to pray. It was a wonderful journey! Not for the elixir of life, not for gold, not for holiness. And, oh, if I could have gone with your hand in mine! It might have been, Martha, that if we'd gone on the quest together, we might not only have found what we sought, but have returned alive!"

"Am I a part of your confession, Mr Tyler?" I said with a coldness which was partly designed to chill him back to earth from this feverish flight.

"Ah, well, I ask your pardon!" he returned, his smile ghastly. "I shouldn't have ventured on the liberty if I hadn't thought my condition might excuse it. Really, though, as a rank outsider, which I certainly am now, I may say that you are the only woman with whom I ever desired an intimate connection. Possibly I led you to suspect as much on the boat; and I will add that I was withheld from proposing (as they say) by the very strength of the sentiment; that is, the risk of the enterprise I had undertaken. Had you happened to accept me, you see, and braved the desert with me, we might, so far from getting back alive, have shared in the disaster—made it even worse, if possible!"

"Put what you have to say in plain words," I said, not trusting myself to a longer speech.

"Thank you! Yes, it's the pulpiteer's vice—phrases, circumlocutions! Thank you! The quest of the absolute evil—that's a phrase, too." He set his teeth, and partly rose on his right elbow. "I went to find the devil, and I found him! He's all they say of him and more. I looked down—down; I thought away everything human, sacred, innocent, pure; I desecrated and profaned the Holy of Holies, burned every bridge, worshiped the black he-goat with the flame between his horns—ha, ha, ha! —and at last the beast was there! Squatting there in the little shack in the marsh, I felt the transformation—oh, the agony and triumph of it! The big, grizzled, shaggy body—the crooked thighs and sharp, pointed hocks behind—the clawed forepaws, the long, slavering grin, thick ears, and those eyes— those eyes! You recognized them, my dear Miss Klemm—yes, you did! And the odor—pah!"

"Stop!" I whispered. But he had gone too far.

"Then out I galloped into the moonlight, and howled— how I howled! You heard me; not quite the popular preacher's voice, but you recognized it! Fancy the Rev. Nathaniel Tyler cantering down the aisle of his church, and addressing his congregation with a howl—'Ha, ha, hoo!'"

I leaned forward and put my hand resolutely on his, bending my will to check his hysteria. He panted, gurgled in his throat, and presently expressed his gratitude in a look once more human. I didn't like to think what might have come to pass in another moment! Indeed, the next thing he said, speaking now very faintly, with closed eyes, "There was no telling when— where—!" confirmed my misgiving.

The flicker of life almost failed in him, but he feebly resisted my attempt to remove my hand. "You know," he said, with trembling eyelids, "persons fed on poisons are poisoned by the antidote. Your touch would have saved me at first—now it brings a delicious death! It finishes what your bullet began. I'm glad to die a—man!" The words were low, but distinct.

At last he lifted himself and gathered energy. "The—child—lived?"

"She was not hurt."

He relaxed, a convulsion that I couldn't interpret passed over his face. But I knew this was the end, and called sharply to the nurse. His grip on my hand had not loosened.

The nurse bent over him, and turned back the wrap on his left shoulder, and then loosened the bandage beneath. A puncture, not large, but with inflamed edges, was revealed; my bullet must have passed just above the heart.

"An odd case," said the woman. "He'd been away on a trip for several weeks, and came back wounded; wouldn't have a doctor, and acted strange about it. When he got weak, they had a surgeon in to examine him. Not a mortal wound at all, but his neglect of it, or something, gave it a bad turn; likely his vitality was low, too."

After death his lips gradually drew back in a sort of grimace, disclosing both the upper and lower teeth, which were remarkably perfect and white. Efforts to correct the contraction of the facial muscles were futile. It gave the narrow, lean face a sort of wolfish look.

Sometimes, even after so many years, I feel the grip of his fingers on my arm.

1918

FRANCIS STEVENS

(1883–1948)

Unseen—Unfeared

I HAD been dining with my ever-interesting friend, Mark Jenkins, at a little Italian restaurant near South Street. It was a chance meeting. Jenkins is too busy, usually, to make dinner engagements. Over our highly seasoned food and sour, thin, red wine, he spoke of little odd incidents and adventures of his profession. Nothing very vital or important, of course. Jenkins is not the sort of detective who first detects and then pours the egotistical and revealing details of achievement in the ears of every acquaintance, however appreciative.

But when I spoke of something I had seen in the morning papers, he laughed. "Poor old 'Doc' Holt! Fascinating old codger, to any one who really knows him. I've had his friendship for years—since I was first on the city force and saved a young assistant of his from jail on a false charge. And they had to drag him into the poisoning of this young sport, Ralph Peeler!"

"Why are you so sure he couldn't have been implicated?" I asked.

But Jenkins only shook his head, with a quiet smile. "I have reasons for believing otherwise," was all I could get out of him on that score. "But," he added, "the only reason he was suspected at all is the superstitious dread of these ignorant people around him. Can't see why he lives in such a place. I know for a fact he doesn't have to. Doc's got money of his own. He's an amateur chemist and dabbler in different sorts of research work, and I suspect he's been guilty of 'showing off.' Result, they all swear he has the evil eye and holds forbidden communion with invisible powers. Smoke?"

Jenkins offered me one of his invariably good cigars, which I accepted, saying thoughtfully: "A man has no right to trifle with the superstitions of ignorant people. Sooner or later, it spells trouble."

"Did in his case. They swore up and down that he sold love charms openly and poisons secretly, and that, together with his living so near to—somebody else—got him temporarily suspected. But my tongue's running away with me, as usual!"

"As usual," I retorted impatiently, "you open up with all the frankness of a Chinese diplomat."

He beamed upon me engagingly and rose from the table, with a glance at his watch. "Sorry to leave you, Blaisdell, but I have to meet Jimmy Brennan in ten minutes."

He so clearly did not invite my further company that I remained seated for a little while after his departure; then took my own way homeward. Those streets always held for me a certain fascination, particularly at night. They are so unlike the rest of the city, so foreign in appearance, with their little shabby stores, always open until late evening, their unbelievably cheap goods, displayed as much outside the shops as in them, hung on the fronts and laid out on tables by the curb and in the street itself. To-night, however, neither people nor stores in any sense appealed to me. The mixture of Italians, Jews and a few negroes, mostly bareheaded, unkempt and generally unhygienic in appearance, struck me as merely revolting. They were all humans, and I, too, was human. Some way I did not like the idea.

Puzzled a trifle, for I am more inclined to sympathize with poverty than accuse it, I watched the faces that I passed. Never before had I observed how stupid, how bestial, how brutal were the countenances of the dwellers in this region. I actually shuddered when an old-clothes man, a gray-bearded Hebrew, brushed me as he toiled past with his barrow.

There was a sense of evil in the air, a warning of things which it is wise for a clean man to shun and keep clear of. The impression became so strong that before I had walked two squares I began to feel physically ill. Then it occurred to me that the one glass of cheap Chianti I had drunk might have something to do with the feeling. Who knew how that stuff had been manufactured, or whether the juice of the grape entered at all into its ill-flavored composition? Yet I doubted if that were the real cause of my discomfort.

By nature I am rather a sensitive, impressionable sort of

chap. In some way to-night this neighborhood, with its sordid sights and smells, had struck me wrong.

My sense of impending evil was merging into actual fear. This would never do. There is only one way to deal with an imaginative temperament like mine—conquer its vagaries. If I left South Street with this nameless dread upon me, I could never pass down it again without a recurrence of the feeling. I should simply have to stay here until I got the better of it— that was all.

I paused on a corner before a shabby but brightly lighted little drug store. Its gleaming windows and the luminous green of its conventional glass show jars made the brightest spot on the block. I realized that I was tired, but hardly wanted to go in there and rest. I knew what the company would be like at its shabby, sticky soda fountain. As I stood there, my eyes fell on a long white canvas sign across from me, and its black-and-red lettering caught my attention.

SEE THE GREAT UNSEEN!
Come in! This Means You!
Free to All!

A museum of fakes, I thought, but also reflected that if it were a show of some kind I could sit down for a while, rest, and fight off this increasing obsession of nonexistent evil. That side of the street was almost deserted, and the place itself might well be nearly empty.

II.

I walked over, but with every step my sense of dread increased. Dread of I knew not what. Bodiless, inexplicable horror had me as in a net, whose strands, being intangible, without reason for existence, I could by no means throw off. It was not the people now. None of them were about me. There, in the open, lighted street, with no sight nor sound of terror to assail me, I was the shivering victim of such fear as I had never known was possible. Yet still I would not yield.

Setting my teeth, and fighting with myself as with some pet animal gone mad, I forced my steps to slowness and walked along the sidewalk, seeking entrance. Just here there were no shops, but several doors reached in each case by means of a few iron-railed stone steps. I chose the one in the middle beneath the sign. In that neighborhood there are museums, shops and other commercial enterprises conducted in many shabby old residences, such as were these. Behind the glazing of the door I had chosen I could see a dim, pinkish light, but on either side the windows were quite dark.

Trying the door, I found it unlocked. As I opened it a party of Italians passed on the pavement below and I looked back at them over my shoulder. They were gayly dressed, men, women and children, laughing and chattering to one another; probably on their way to some wedding or other festivity.

In passing, one of the men glanced up at me and involuntarily I shuddered back against the door. He was a young man, handsome after the swarthy manner of his race, but never in my life had I seen a face so expressive of pure, malicious cruelty, naked and unashamed. Our eyes met and his seemed to light up with a vile gleaming, as if all the wickedness of his nature had come to a focus in the look of concentrated hate he gave me.

They went by, but for some distance I could see him watching me, chin on shoulder, till he and his party were swallowed up in the crowd of marketers farther down the street.

Sick and trembling from that encounter, merely of eyes though it had been, I threw aside my partly smoked cigar and entered. Within there was a small vestibule, whose ancient tesselated floor was grimy with the passing of many feet. I could feel the grit of dirt under my shoes, and it rasped on my rawly quivering nerves. The inner door stood partly open, and going on I found myself in a bare, dirty hallway, and was greeted by the sour, musty, poverty-stricken smell common to dwellings of the very ill-to-do. Beyond there was a stairway, carpeted with ragged grass matting. A gas jet, turned low inside a very dusty pink globe, was the light I had seen from without.

Listening, the house seemed entirely silent. Surely, this was no place of public amusement of any kind whatever. More likely it was a rooming house, and I had, after all, mistaken the entrance.

To my intense relief, since coming inside, the worst agony of my unreasonable terror had passed away. If I could only get in some place where I could sit down and be quiet, probably I should be rid of it for good. Determining to try another entrance, I was about to leave the bare hallway when one of several doors along the side of it suddenly opened and a man stepped out into the hall.

"Well?" he said, looking at me keenly, but with not the least show of surprise at my presence.

"I beg your pardon," I replied. "The door was unlocked and I came in here, thinking it was the entrance to the exhibit —what do they call it?—the 'Great Unseen.' The one that is mentioned on that long white sign. Can you tell me which door is the right one?"

"I can."

With that brief answer he stopped and stared at me again. He was a tall, lean man, somewhat stooped, but possessing considerable dignity of bearing. For that neighborhood, he appeared uncommonly well dressed, and his long, smooth-shaven face was noticeable because, while his complexion was dark and his eyes coal-black, above them the heavy brows and his hair were almost silvery-white. His age might have been anything over the threescore mark.

I grew tired of being stared at. "If you can and—won't, then never mind," I observed a trifle irritably, and turned to go. But his sharp exclamation halted me.

"No!" he said. "No—no! Forgive me for pausing—it was not hesitation, I assure you. To think that one—one, even, has come! All day they pass my sign up there—pass and fear to enter. But you are different. *You* are not of these timorous, ignorant foreign peasants. You ask me to tell you the right door? Here it is! Here!"

And he struck the panel of the door, which he had closed behind him, so that the sharp yet hollow sound of it echoed up through the silent house.

Now it may be thought that after all my senseless terror in the open street, so strange a welcome from so odd a showman would have brought the feeling back, full force. But there is an emotion stronger, to a certain point, than fear. This queer old fellow aroused my curiosity. What kind of museum could it be that he accused the passing public of fearing to enter? Nothing really terrible, surely, or it would have been closed by the

police. And normally I am not an unduly timorous person.
"So, it's in there, is it?" I asked, coming toward him. "And I'm
to be sole audience? Come, that will be an interesting experience." I was half laughing now.

"The most interesting in the world," said the old man, with
a solemnity which rebuked my lightness.

With that he opened the door, passed inward and closed it
again—in my very face. I stood staring at it blankly. The panels, I remember, had been originally painted white, but now
the paint was flaked and blistered, gray with dirt and dirty finger marks. Suddenly it occurred to me that I had no wish to
enter there. Whatever was behind it could be scarcely worth
seeing, or he would not choose such a place for its exhibition.
With the old man's vanishing my curiosity had cooled, but just
as I again turned to leave, the door opened and this singular
showman stuck his white-eyebrowed face through the aperture. He was frowning impatiently. "Come in—come in!" he
snapped, and promptly withdrawing his head, once more closed
the door.

"He has something in there he doesn't want should get out,"
was the very natural conclusion which I drew. "Well, since it
can hardly be anything dangerous, and he's so anxious I should
see it—here goes!"

With that I turned the soiled white porcelain handle, and
entered.

The room I came into was neither very large nor very
brightly lighted. In no way did it resemble a museum or lecture room. On the contrary, it seemed to have been fitted up
as a quite well-appointed laboratory. The floor was linoleum-
covered, there were glass cases along the walls whose shelves
were filled with bottles, specimen jars, graduates, and the like.
A large table in one corner bore what looked like some odd
sort of camera, and a larger one in the middle of the room was
fitted with a long rack filled with bottles and test tubes, and was
besides littered with papers, glass slides, and various paraphernalia which my ignorance failed to identify. There were several
cases of books, a few plain wooden chairs, and in the corner a
large iron sink with running water.

My host of the white hair and black eyes was awaiting me,
standing near the larger table. He indicated one of the wooden

chairs with a thin forefinger that shook a little, either from age or eagerness. "Sit down—sit down! Have no fear but that you will be interested, my friend. Have no fear at all—of anything!"

As he said it he fixed his dark eyes upon me and stared harder than ever. But the effect of his words was the opposite of their meaning. I did sit down, because my knees gave under me, but if in the outer hall I had lost my terror, it now returned twofold upon me. Out there the light had been faint, dingily roseate, indefinite. By it I had not perceived how this old man's face was a mask of living malice—of cruelty, hate and a certain masterful contempt. Now I knew the meaning of my fear, whose warning I would not heed. Now I knew that I had walked into the very trap from which my abnormal sensitiveness had striven in vain to save me.

III.

Again I struggled within me, bit at my lip till I tasted blood, and presently the blind paroxysm passed. It must have been longer in going than I thought, and the old man must have all that time been speaking, for when I could once more control my attention, hear and see him, he had taken up a position near the sink, about ten feet away, and was addressing me with a sort of "platform" manner, as if I had been the large audience whose absence he had deplored.

"And so," he was saying, "I was forced to make these plates very carefully, to truly represent the characteristic hues of each separate organism. Now, in color work of every kind the film is necessarily extremely sensitive. Doubtless you are familiar in a general way with the exquisite transparencies produced by color photography of the single-plate type."

He paused, and, trying to act like a normal human being, I observed: "I saw some nice landscapes done in that way—last week at an illustrated lecture in Franklin Hall."

He scowled, and made an impatient gesture at me with his hand. "I can proceed better without interruptions," he said. "My pause was purely oratorical."

I meekly subsided, and he went on in his original loud, clear voice. He would have made an excellent lecturer before a much larger audience—if only his voice could have lost that eerie, ringing note. Thinking of that I must have missed some more, and when I caught it again he was saying:

"As I have indicated, the original plate is the final picture. Now, many of these organisms are extremely hard to photograph, and microphotography in color is particularly difficult. In consequence, to spoil a plate tries the patience of the photographer. They are so sensitive that the ordinary darkroom ruby lamp would instantly ruin them, and they must therefore be developed either in darkness or by a special light produced by interposing thin sheets of tissue of a particular shade of green and of yellow between lamp and plate, and even that will often cause ruinous fog. Now I, finding it hard to handle them so, made numerous experiments with a view to discovering some glass or fabric of a color which should add to the safety of the green, without robbing it of all efficiency. All proved equally useless, but intermittently I persevered—until last week."

His voice dropped to an almost confidential tone, and he leaned slightly toward me. I was cold from my neck to my feet, though my head was burning, but I tried to force an appreciative smile.

"Last week," he continued impressively, "I had a prescription filled at the corner drug store. The bottle was sent home to me wrapped in a piece of what I at first took to be whitish, slightly opalescent paper. Later I decided that it was some kind of membrane. When I questioned the druggist, seeking its source, he said it was a sheet of 'paper' that was around a bundle of herbs from South America. That he had no more, and doubted if I could trace it. He had wrapped my bottle so, because he was in haste and the sheet was handy.

"I can hardly tell you what first inspired me to try that membrane in my photographic work. It was merely dull white with a faint hint of opalescence, except when held against the light. Then it became quite translucent and quite brightly prismatic. For some reason it occurred to me that this refractive effect might help in breaking up the actinic rays—the rays which affect the sensitive emulsion. So that night I inserted it behind the sheets of green and yellow tissue, next the lamp, prepared my trays and chemicals, laid my plate holders to hand, turned off the white light and—turned on the green!"

There was nothing in his words to inspire fear. It was a

wearisomely detailed account of his struggles with photography. Yet, as he again paused impressively, I wished that he might never speak again. I was desperately, contemptibly in dread of the thing he might say next.

Suddenly he drew himself erect, the stoop went out of his shoulders, he threw back his head and laughed. It was a hollow sound, as if he laughed into a trumpet. "I won't tell you what I saw! Why should I? Your own eyes shall bear witness. But this much I'll say, so that you may better understand—later. When our poor, faultily sensitive vision can perceive a thing, we say that it is visible. When the nerves of touch can feel it, we say that it is tangible. Yet I tell you there are beings intangible to our physical sense, yet whose presence is felt by the spirit, and invisible to our eyes merely because those organs are not attuned to the light as reflected from their bodies. But light passed through the screen which we are about to use has a wave length novel to the scientific world, and by it you shall see with the eyes of the flesh that which has been invisible since life began. Have no fear!"

He stopped to laugh again, and his mirth was yellow-toothed—menacing.

"*Have no fear!*" he reiterated, and with that stretched his hand toward the wall, there came a click and we were in black, impenetrable darkness. I wanted to spring up, to seek the door by which I had entered and rush out of it, but the paralysis of unreasoning terror held me fast.

I could hear him moving about in the darkness, and a moment later a faint green glimmer sprang up in the room. Its source was over the large sink, where I suppose he developed his precious "color plates."

Every instant, as my eyes became accustomed to the dimness, I could see more clearly. Green light is peculiar. It may be far fainter than red, and at the same time far more illuminating. The old man was standing beneath it, and his face by that ghastly radiance had the exact look of a dead man's. Beside this, however, I could observe nothing appalling.

"That," continued the man, "is the simple developing light of which I have spoken—now watch, for what you are about to behold no mortal man but myself has ever seen before."

For a moment he fussed with the green lamp over the sink.

It was so constructed that all the direct rays struck downward. He opened a flap at the side, for a moment there was a streak of comforting white luminance from within, then he inserted something, slid it slowly in—and closed the flap.

The thing he put in—that South American "membrane" it must have been—instead of decreasing the light increased it—amazingly. The hue was changed from green to greenish-gray, and the whole room sprang into view, a livid, ghastly chamber, filled with—overcrawled by—what?

My eyes fixed themselves, fascinated, on something that moved by the old man's feet. It writhed there on the floor like a huge, repulsive starfish, an immense, armed, legged thing, that twisted convulsively. It was smooth, as if made of rubber, was whitish-green in color; and presently raised its great round blob of a body on tottering tentacles, crept toward my host and writhed upward—yes, climbed up his legs, his body. And he stood there, erect, arms folded, and stared sternly down at the thing which climbed.

But the room—the whole room was alive with other creatures than that. Everywhere I looked they were—centipedish things, with yard-long bodies, detestable, furry spiders that lurked in shadows, and sausage-shaped translucent horrors that moved—and floated through the air. They dived here and there between me and the light, and I could see its brighter greenness through their greenish bodies.

Worse, though, far worse than these were the *things with human faces*. Mask-like, monstrous, huge gaping mouths and slitlike eyes—I find I cannot write of them. There was that about them which makes their memory even now intolerable.

The old man was speaking again, and every word echoed in my brain like the ringing of a gong. "Fear nothing! Among such as these do you move every hour of the day and the night. Only you and I have seen, for God is merciful and has spared our race from sight. But I am not merciful! I loathe the race which gave these creatures birth—the race which might be so surrounded by invisible, unguessed but blessed beings—and chooses these for its companions! All the world shall see and know. One by one shall they come here, learn the truth, and perish. For who can survive the ultimate of terror? Then I, too, shall find peace, and leave the earth to its heritage of man-created horrors. Do you know what these are—whence they come?"

His voice boomed now like a cathedral bell. I could not answer him, but he waited for no reply. "Out of the ether—out of the omnipresent ether from whose intangible substance the mind of God made the planets, all living things, and man— man has made these! By his evil thoughts, by his selfish panics, by his lusts and his interminable, never-ending hate he has made them, and they are everywhere! Fear nothing—they cannot harm your body—but let your spirit beware! Fear nothing— but see where there comes to you, its creator, the shape and the body of your FEAR!"

And as he said it I perceived a great Thing coming toward me—a Thing—but consciousness could endure no more. The ringing, threatening voice merged in a roar within my ears, there came a merciful dimming of the terrible, lurid vision, and blank nothingness succeeded upon horror too great for bearing.

IV.

There was a dull, heavy pain above my eyes. I knew that they were closed, that I was dreaming, and that the rack full of colored bottles which I seemed to see so clearly was no more than a part of the dream. There was some vague but imperative reason why I should rouse myself. I wanted to awaken, and thought that by staring very hard indeed I could dissolve this foolish vision of blue and yellow-brown bottles. But instead of dissolving they grew clearer, more solid and substantial of appearance, until suddenly the rest of my senses rushed to the support of sight, and I became aware that my eyes were open, the bottles were quite real, and that I was sitting in a chair, fallen sideways so that my cheek rested most uncomfortably on the table which held the rack.

I straightened up slowly and with difficulty, groping in my dulled brain for some clew to my presence in this unfamiliar place, this laboratory that was lighted only by the rays of an arc light in the street outside its three large windows. Here I sat, alone, and if the aching of cramped limbs meant anything, here I had sat for more than a little time.

Then, with the painful shock which accompanies awakening to the knowledge of some great catastrophe, came memory. It was this very room, shown by the street lamp's rays to be empty of life, which I had seen thronged with creatures too loathsome for description. I staggered to my feet, staring fearfully about. There were the glass-doored cases, the bookshelves, the two tables with their burdens, and the long iron sink above which, now only a dark blotch of shadow, hung the lamp from which had emanated that livid, terrifically revealing illumination. Then the experience had been no dream, but a frightful reality. I was alone here now. With callous indifference my strange host had allowed me to remain for hours unconscious, with not the least effort to aid or revive me. Perhaps, hating me so, he had hoped that I would die there.

At first I made no effort to leave the place. Its appearance filled me with reminiscent loathing. I longed to go, but as yet felt too weak and ill for the effort. Both mentally and physically my condition was deplorable, and for the first time I realized that a shock to the mind may react upon the body as vilely as any debauch of self-indulgence.

Quivering in every nerve and muscle, dizzy with headache and nausea, I dropped back into the chair, hoping that before the old man returned I might recover sufficient self-control to escape him. I knew that he hated me, and why. As I waited, sick, miserable, I understood the man. Shuddering, I recalled the loathsome horrors he had shown me. If the mere desires and emotions of mankind were daily carnified in such forms as those, no wonder that he viewed his fellow beings with detestation and longed only to destroy them.

I thought, too, of the cruel, sensuous faces I had seen in the streets outside—seen for the first time, as if a veil had been withdrawn from eyes hitherto blinded by self-delusion. Fatuously trustful as a month-old puppy, I had lived in a grim, evil world, where goodness is a word and crude selfishness the only actuality. Drearily my thoughts drifted back through my own life, its futile purposes, mistakes and activities. All of evil that I knew returned to overwhelm me. Our gropings toward divinity were a sham, a writhing sunward of slime-covered beasts who claimed sunlight as their heritage, but in their hearts preferred the foul and easy depths.

Even now, though I could neither see nor feel them, this room, the entire world, was acrawl with the beings created by our real natures. I recalled the cringing, contemptible fear to which my spirit had so readily yielded, and the faceless Thing to which the emotion had given birth.

Then abruptly, shockingly, I remembered that every moment I was adding to the horde. Since my mind could conceive only repulsive incubi, and since while I lived I must think, feel, and so continue to shape them, was there no way to check so abominable a succession? My eyes fell on the long shelves with their many-colored bottles. In the chemistry of photography there are deadly poisons—I knew that. Now was the time to end it—now! Let him return and find his desire accomplished. One good thing I could do, if one only. I could abolish my monster-creating self.

V.

My friend Mark Jenkins is an intelligent and usually a very careful man. When he took from "Smiler" Callahan a cigar which had every appearance of being excellent, innocent Havana, the act denoted both intelligence and caution. By very clever work he had traced the poisoning of young Ralph Peeler to Mr. Callahan's door, and he believed this particular cigar to be the mate of one smoked by Peeler just previous to his demise. And if, upon arresting Callahan, he had not confiscated this bit of evidence, it would have doubtless been destroyed by its regrettably unconscientious owner.

But when Jenkins shortly afterward gave me that cigar, as one of his own, he committed one of those almost inconceivable blunders which, I think, are occasionally forced upon clever men to keep them from overweening vanity. Discovering his slight mistake, my detective friend spent the night searching for his unintended victim, myself, and that his search was successful was due to Pietro Marini, a young Italian of Jenkins' acquaintance, whom he met about the hour of two a.m. returning from a dance.

Now, Marini had seen me standing on the steps of the house where Doctor Frederick Holt had his laboratory and living rooms, and he had stared at me, not with any ill intent, but because he thought I was the sickest-looking, most ghastly specimen of humanity that he had ever beheld. And, sharing the superstition of his South Street neighbors, he wondered if the worthy doctor had poisoned me as well as Peeler. This suspicion he imparted to Jenkins, who, however, had the best of reasons for believing otherwise. Moreover, as he informed Marini, Holt was dead, having drowned himself late the previous afternoon. An hour or so after our talk in the restaurant news of his suicide reached Jenkins.

It seemed wise to search any place where a very sick-looking young man had been seen to enter, so Jenkins came straight to the laboratory. Across the fronts of those houses was the long sign with its mysterious inscription, "See the Great Unseen," not at all mysterious to the detective. He knew that next door to Doctor Holt's the second floor had been thrown together into a lecture room, where at certain hours a young man employed by settlement workers displayed upon a screen stereopticon views of various deadly bacilli, the germs of diseases appropriate to dirt and indifference. He knew, too, that Doctor Holt himself had helped the educational effort along by providing some really wonderful lantern slides, done by microcolor photography.

On the pavement outside, Jenkins found the two-thirds remnant of a cigar, which he gathered in and came up the steps, a very miserable and self-reproachful detective. Neither outer nor inner door was locked, and in the laboratory he found me, alive, but on the verge of death by another means than he had feared.

In the extreme physical depression following my awakening from drugged sleep, and knowing nothing of its cause, I believed my adventure fact in its entirety. My mentality was at too low an ebb to resist its dreadful suggestion. I was searching among Holt's various bottles when Jenkins burst in. At first I was merely annoyed at the interruption of my purpose, but before the anticlimax of his explanation the mists of obsession drifted away and left me still sick in body, but in spirit happy as any man may well be who has suffered a delusion that the world is wholly bad—and learned that its badness springs from his own poisoned brain.

The malice which I had observed in every face, including

young Marini's, existed only in my drug-affected vision. Last week's "popular-science" lecture had been recalled to my subconscious mind—the mind that rules dreams and delirium— by the photographic apparatus in Holt's workroom. "See the Great Unseen" assisted materially, and even the corner drug store before which I had paused, with its green-lit show vases, had doubtless played a part. But presently, following something Jenkins told me, I was driven to one protest. "If Holt was not here," I demanded, "if Holt is dead, as you say, how do you account for the fact that I, who have never seen the man, was able to give you an accurate description which you admit to be that of Doctor Frederick Holt?"

He pointed across the room. "See that?" It was a life-size bust portrait, in crayons, the picture of a white-haired man with bushy eyebrows and the most piercing black eyes I had ever seen—until the previous evening. It hung facing the door and near the windows, and the features stood out with a strangely lifelike appearance in the white rays of the arc lamp just outside. "Upon entering," continued Jenkins, "the first thing you saw was that portrait, and from it your delirium built a living, speaking man. So, there are your white-haired showman, your unnatural fear, your color photography and your pretty green golliwogs all nicely explained for you, Blaisdell, and thank God you're alive to hear the explanation. If you had smoked the whole of that cigar—well, never mind. You didn't. And now, my very dear friend, I think it's high time that you interviewed a real, flesh-and-blood doctor. I'll phone for a taxi."

"Don't," I said. "A walk in the fresh air will do me more good than fifty doctors."

"Fresh air! There's no fresh air on South Street in July," complained Jenkins, but reluctantly yielded.

I had a reason for my preference. I wished to see people, to meet face to face even such stray prowlers as might be about at this hour, nearer sunrise than midnight, and rejoice in the goodness and kindliness of the human countenance—particularly as found in the lower classes.

But even as we were leaving there occurred to me a curious inconsistency.

"Jenkins," I said, "you claim that the reason Holt, when I first met him in the hall, appeared to twice close the door in

my face, was because the door never opened until I myself un-
latched it."

"Yes," confirmed Jenkins, but he frowned, foreseeing my
next question.

"Then why, if it was from that picture that I built so solid, so
convincing a vision of the man, did I see Holt in the hall
before the door was open?"

"You confuse your memories," retorted Jenkins rather
shortly.

"Do I? Holt was dead at that hour, but—*I tell you I saw
Holt outside the door!* And what was his reason for committing
suicide?"

Before my friend could reply I was across the room, fumbling in the dusk there at the electric lamp above the sink. I
got the tin flap open and pulled out the sliding screen, which
consisted of two sheets of glass with fabric between, dark on
one side, yellow on the other. With it came the very thing I
dreaded—a sheet of whitish, parchmentlike, slightly opalescent stuff.

Jenkins was beside me as I held it at arm's length toward the
windows. Through it the light of the arc lamp fell—divided
into the most astonishingly brilliant rainbow hues. And instead
of diminishing the light, it was perceptibly increased in the
oddest way. Almost one thought that the sheet itself was luminous, and yet when held in shadow it gave off no light at all.

"Shall we—put it in the lamp again—and try it?" asked
Jenkins slowly, and in his voice there was no hint of mockery.

I looked him straight in the eyes. "No," I said, "we won't. I
was drugged. Perhaps in that condition I received a merciless
revelation of the discovery that caused Holt's suicide, but I
don't believe it. Ghost or no ghost, I refuse to ever again
believe in the depravity of the human race. If the air and the
earth are teeming with invisible horrors, they are *not* of our
making, and—the study of demonology is better let alone.
Shall we burn this thing, or tear it up?"

"We have no right to do either," returned Jenkins thoughtfully, "but you know, Blaisdell, there's a little too darn much
realism about some parts of your 'dream.' I haven't been
smoking any doped cigars, but when you held that up to the

light, I'll swear I saw—well, never mind. Burn it—send it back to the place it came from."

"South America?" said I.

"A hotter place than that. Burn it."

So he struck a match and we did. It was gone in one great white flash.

A large place was given by morning papers to the suicide of Doctor Frederick Holt, caused, it was surmised, by mental derangement brought about by his unjust implication in the Peeler murder. It seemed an inadequate reason, since he had never been arrested, but no other was ever discovered.

Of course, our action in destroying that "membrane" was illegal and rather precipitate, but, though he won't talk about it, I know that Jenkins agrees with me—doubt is sometimes better than certainty, and there are marvels better left unproved. Those, for instance, which concern the Powers of Evil.

1919

F. SCOTT FITZGERALD
(1896–1940)

The Curious Case of Benjamin Button

I

As long ago as 1860 it was the proper thing to be born at home. At present, so I am told, the high gods of medicine have decreed that the first cries of the young shall be uttered upon the anesthetic air of a hospital, preferably a fashionable one. So young Mr. and Mrs. Roger Button were fifty years ahead of style when they decided, one day in the summer of 1860, that their first baby should be born in a hospital. Whether this anachronism had any bearing upon the astonishing history I am about to set down will never be known.

I shall tell you what occurred, and let you judge for yourself.

The Roger Buttons held an enviable position, both social and financial, in ante-bellum Baltimore. They were related to the This Family and the That Family, which, as every Southerner knew, entitled them to membership in that enormous peerage which largely populated the Confederacy. This was their first experience with the charming old custom of having babies— Mr. Button was naturally nervous. He hoped it would be a boy so that he could be sent to Yale College in Connecticut, at which institution Mr. Button himself had been known for four years by the somewhat obvious nickname of "Cuff."

On the September morning consecrated to the enormous event he arose nervously at six o'clock, dressed himself, adjusted an impeccable stock, and hurried forth through the streets of Baltimore to the hospital, to determine whether the darkness of the night had borne in new life upon its bosom.

When he was approximately a hundred yards from the Maryland Private Hospital for Ladies and Gentlemen he saw Doctor Keene, the family physician, descending the front steps, rubbing his hands together with a washing movement—as all

doctors are required to do by the unwritten ethics of their profession.

Mr. Roger Button, the president of Roger Button & Co.,
Wholesale Hardware, began to run toward Doctor Keene with
much less dignity than was expected from a Southern gentleman of that picturesque period. "Doctor Keene!" he called.
"Oh, Doctor Keene!"

The doctor heard him, faced around, and stood waiting, a
curious expression settling on his harsh, medicinal face as Mr.
Button drew near.

"What happened?" demanded Mr. Button, as he came up in
a gasping rush. "What was it? How is she? A boy? Who is it?
What——"

"Talk sense!" said Doctor Keene sharply. He appeared
somewhat irritated.

"Is the child born?" begged Mr. Button.

Doctor Keene frowned. "Why, yes, I suppose so—after a
fashion." Again he threw a curious glance at Mr. Button.

"Is my wife all right?"

"Yes."

"Is it a boy or a girl?"

"Here now!" cried Doctor Keene in a perfect passion of irri-
tation, "I'll ask you to go and see for yourself. Outrageous!"
He snapped the last word out in almost one syllable, then he
turned away muttering: "Do you imagine a case like this will
help my professional reputation? One more would ruin me—
ruin anybody."

"What's the matter?" demanded Mr. Button, appalled.
"Triplets?"

"No, not triplets!" answered the doctor cuttingly. "What's
more, you can go and see for yourself. And get another doctor.
I brought you into the world, young man, and I've been physician to your family for forty years, but I'm through with you! I
don't want to see you or any of your relatives ever again!
Good-by!"

Then he turned sharply, and without another word climbed
into his phaeton, which was waiting at the curbstone, and drove
severely away.

Mr. Button stood there upon the sidewalk, stupefied and

trembling from head to foot. What horrible mishap had oc-curred? He had suddenly lost all desire to go into the Maryland Private Hospital for Ladies and Gentlemen—it was with the greatest difficulty that, a moment later, he forced himself to mount the steps and enter the front door.

A nurse was sitting behind a desk in the opaque gloom of the hall. Swallowing his shame, Mr. Button approached her.

"Good-morning," she remarked, looking up at him pleasantly.

"Good-morning. I—I am Mr. Button."

At this a look of utter terror spread itself over the girl's face. She rose to her feet and seemed about to fly from the hall, re-straining herself only with the most apparent difficulty.

"I want to see my child," said Mr. Button.

The nurse gave a little scream. "Oh—of course!" she cried hysterically. "Up-stairs. Right up-stairs. Go—*up!*"

She pointed the direction, and Mr. Button, bathed in a cool perspiration, turned falteringly, and began to mount to the second floor. In the upper hall he addressed another nurse who approached him, basin in hand. "I'm Mr. Button," he man-aged to articulate. "I want to see my——"

Clank! The basin clattered to the floor and rolled in the di-rection of the stairs. Clank! Clank! It began a methodical de-scent as if sharing in the general terror which this gentleman provoked.

"I want to see my child!" Mr. Button almost shrieked. He was on the verge of collapse.

Clank! The basin had reached the first floor. The nurse re-gained control of herself, and threw Mr. Button a look of hearty contempt.

"All *right*, Mr. Button," she agreed in a hushed voice. "Very *well!* But if you *knew* what state it's put us all in this morning! It's perfectly outrageous! The hospital will never have the ghost of a reputation after——"

"Hurry!" he cried hoarsely. "I can't stand this!"

"Come this way, then, Mr. Button."

He dragged himself after her. At the end of a long hall they reached a room from which proceeded a variety of howls—indeed, a room which, in later parlance, would have been known as the "crying-room." They entered. Ranged around the walls were half a dozen white-enameled rolling cribs, each with a tag tied at the head.

"Well," gasped Mr. Button, "which is mine?"

"There!" said the nurse.

Mr. Button's eyes followed her pointing finger, and this is what he saw. Wrapped in a voluminous white blanket, and partially crammed into one of the cribs, there sat an old man apparently about seventy years of age. His sparse hair was almost white, and from his chin dripped a long smoke-colored beard, which waved absurdly back and forth, fanned by the breeze coming in at the window. He looked up at Mr. Button with dim, faded eyes in which lurked a puzzled question.

"Am I mad?" thundered Mr. Button, his terror resolving into rage. "Is this some ghastly hospital joke?"

"It doesn't seem like a joke to us," replied the nurse severely. "And I don't know whether you're mad or not—but that is most certainly your child."

The cool perspiration redoubled on Mr. Button's forehead. He closed his eyes, and then, opening them, looked again. There was no mistake—he was gazing at a man of threescore and ten—a *baby* of threescore and ten, a baby whose feet hung over the sides of the crib in which it was reposing.

The old man looked placidly from one to the other for a moment, and then suddenly spoke in a cracked and ancient voice. "Are you my father?" he demanded.

Mr. Button and the nurse started violently.

"Because if you are," went on the old man querulously, "I wish you'd get me out of this place—or, at least, get them to put a comfortable rocker in here."

"Where in God's name did you come from? Who are you?" burst out Mr. Button frantically.

"I can't tell you *exactly* who I am," replied the querulous whine, "because I've only been born a few hours—but my last name is certainly Button."

"You lie! You're an impostor!"

The old man turned wearily to the nurse. "Nice way to welcome a new-born child," he complained in a weak voice. "Tell him he's wrong, why don't you?"

"You're wrong, Mr. Button," said the nurse severely. "This is your child, and you'll have to make the best of it. We're going

to ask you to take him home with you as soon as possible—
some time to-day."

"Home?" repeated Mr. Button incredulously.

"Yes, we can't have him here. We really can't, you know?"

"I'm right glad of it," whined the old man. "This is a fine
place to keep a youngster of quiet tastes. With all this yelling and
howling, I haven't been able to get a wink of sleep. I asked for
something to eat"—here his voice rose to a shrill note of
protest—"and they brought me a bottle of milk!"

Mr. Button sank down upon a chair near his son and concealed his face in his hands. "My heavens!" he murmured, in
an ecstasy of horror. "What will people say? What must I do?"

"You'll have to take him home," insisted the nurse—
"immediately!"

A grotesque picture formed itself with dreadful clarity before
the eyes of the tortured man—a picture of himself walking
through the crowded streets of the city with this appalling apparition stalking by his side. "I can't. I can't," he moaned.

People would stop to speak to him, and what was he going
to say? He would have to introduce this—this septuagenarian:
"This is my son, born early this morning." And then the old
man would gather his blanket around him and they would
plod on, past the bustling stores, the slave market—for a dark
instant Mr. Button wished passionately that his son was black
—past the luxurious houses of the residential district, past the
home for the aged. . . .

"Come! Pull yourself together," commanded the nurse.

"See here," the old man announced suddenly, "if you think
I'm going to walk home in this blanket, you're entirely
mistaken."

"Babies always have blankets."

With a malicious crackle the old man held up a small white
swaddling garment. "Look!" he quavered. "*This* is what they
had ready for me."

"Babies always wear those," said the nurse primly.

"Well," said the old man, "this baby's not going to wear
anything in about two minutes. This blanket itches. They
might at least have given me a sheet."

"Keep it on! Keep it on!" said Mr. Button hurriedly. He
turned to the nurse. "What'll I do?"

"Go down town and buy your son some clothes."

Mr. Button's son's voice followed him down into the hall: "And a cane, father. I want to have a cane."

Mr. Button banged the outer door savagely. . . .

II

"Good-morning," Mr. Button said, nervously, to the clerk in the Chesapeake Dry Goods Company. "I want to buy some clothes for my child."

"How old is your child, sir?"

"About six hours," answered Mr. Button, without due consideration.

"Babies' supply department in the rear."

"Why, I don't think—I'm not sure that's what I want. It's—he's an unusually large-size child. Exceptionally—ah—large."

"They have the largest child's sizes."

"Where is the boys' department?" inquired Mr. Button, shifting his ground desperately. He felt that the clerk must surely scent his shameful secret.

"Right here."

"Well—" He hesitated. The notion of dressing his son in men's clothes was repugnant to him. If, say, he could only find a *very* large boy's suit, he might cut off that long and awful beard, dye the white hair brown, and thus manage to conceal the worst, and to retain something of his own self-respect—not to mention his position in Baltimore society.

But a frantic inspection of the boys' department revealed no suits to fit the new-born Button. He blamed the store, of course—in such cases it is the thing to blame the store.

"How old did you say that boy of yours was?" demanded the clerk curiously.

"He's—sixteen."

"Oh, I beg your pardon. I thought you said six *hours.* You'll find the youths' department in the next aisle."

Mr. Button turned miserably away. Then he stopped, brightened, and pointed his finger toward a dressed dummy in the window display. "There!" he exclaimed. "I'll take that suit, out there on the dummy."

The clerk stared. "Why," he protested, "that's not a child's suit. At least it *is*, but it's for fancy dress. You could wear it yourself!"

"Wrap it up," insisted his customer nervously. "That's what I want."

The astonished clerk obeyed.

Back at the hospital Mr. Button entered the nursery and almost threw the package at his son. "Here's your clothes," he snapped out.

The old man untied the package and viewed the contents with a quizzical eye.

"They look sort of funny to me," he complained. "I don't want to be made a monkey of——"

"You've made a monkey of me!" retorted Mr. Button fiercely. "Never you mind how funny you look. Put them on—or I'll—or I'll *spank* you." He swallowed uneasily at the penultimate word, feeling nevertheless that it was the proper thing to say.

"All right, father"—this with a grotesque simulation of filial respect—"you've lived longer; you know best. Just as you say."

As before, the sound of the word "father" caused Mr. Button to start violently.

"And hurry."

"I'm hurrying, father."

When his son was dressed Mr. Button regarded him with depression. The costume consisted of dotted socks, pink pants, and a belted blouse with a wide white collar. Over the latter waved the long whitish beard, drooping almost to the waist. The effect was not good.

"Wait!"

Mr. Button seized a hospital shears and with three quick snaps amputated a large section of the beard. But even with this improvement the ensemble fell far short of perfection. The remaining brush of scraggly hair, the watery eyes, the ancient teeth, seemed oddly out of tone with the gayety of the costume. Mr. Button, however, was obdurate—he held out his hand. "Come along!" he said sternly.

His son took the hand trustingly. "What are you going to call me, dad?" he quavered as they walked from the nursery—"just 'baby' for a while? till you think of a better name?"

Mr. Button grunted. "I don't know," he answered harshly. "I think we'll call you Methuselah."

III

Even after the new addition to the Button family had had his hair cut short and then dyed to a sparse unnatural black, had had his face shaved so close that it glistened, and had been attired in small-boy clothes made to order by a flabbergasted tailor, it was impossible for Mr. Button to ignore the fact that his son was a poor excuse for a first family baby. Despite his aged stoop, Benjamin Button—for it was by this name they called him instead of by the appropriate but invidious Methuselah—was five feet eight inches tall. His clothes did not conceal this, nor did the clipping and dyeing of his eyebrows disguise the fact that the eyes underneath were faded and watery and tired. In fact, the baby-nurse who had been engaged in advance left the house after one look, in a state of considerable indignation.

But Mr. Button persisted in his unwavering purpose. Benjamin was a baby, and a baby he should remain. At first he declared that if Benjamin didn't like warm milk he could go without food altogether, but he was finally prevailed upon to allow his son bread and butter, and even oatmeal by way of a compromise. One day he brought home a rattle and, giving it to Benjamin, insisted in no uncertain terms that he should "play with it," whereupon the old man took it with a weary expression and could be heard jingling it obediently at intervals throughout the day.

There can be no doubt, though, that the rattle bored him, and that he found other and more soothing amusements when he was left alone. For instance, Mr. Button discovered one day that during the preceding week he had smoked more cigars than ever before—a phenomenon which was explained a few days later when, entering the nursery unexpectedly, he found the room full of faint blue haze and Benjamin, with a guilty expression on his face, trying to conceal the butt of a dark Havana. This, of course, called for a severe spanking, but Mr. Button found that he could not bring himself to administer it. He merely warned his son that he would "stunt his growth."

Nevertheless he persisted in his attitude. He brought home lead soldiers, he brought toy trains, he brought large pleasant animals made of cotton, and, to perfect the illusion which he was creating—for himself at least—he passionately demanded of the clerk in the toy-store whether "the paint would come off the pink duck if the baby put it in his mouth." But, despite all his father's efforts, Benjamin refused to be interested. He would steal down the back stairs and return to the nursery with a volume of the "Encyclopædia Britannica," over which he would pore through an afternoon, while his cotton cows and his Noah's ark were left neglected on the floor. Against such a stubbornness Mr. Button's efforts were of little avail.

The sensation created in Baltimore was, at first, prodigious. What the mishap would have cost the Buttons and their kins-folk socially cannot be determined, for the outbreak of the Civil War drew the city's attention to other things. A few people who were unfailingly polite racked their brains for compliments to give to the parents—and finally hit upon the ingenious device of declaring that the baby resembled his grandfather, a fact which, due to the standard state of decay common to all men of seventy, could not be denied. Mr. and Mrs. Roger Button were not pleased, and Benjamin's grandfather was furiously insulted.

Benjamin, once he left the hospital, took life as he found it. Several small boys were brought to see him, and he spent a stiff-jointed afternoon trying to work up an interest in tops and marbles—he even managed, quite accidentally, to break a kitchen window with a stone from a sling shot, a feat which se-cretly delighted his father.

Thereafter Benjamin contrived to break something every day, but he did these things only because they were expected of him, and because he was by nature obliging.

When his grandfather's initial antagonism wore off, Ben-jamin and that gentleman took enormous pleasure in one an-other's company. They would sit for hours, these two so far apart in age and experience, and, like old cronies, discuss with tire-less monotony the slow events of the day. Benjamin felt more at ease in his grandfather's presence than in his parents'—they seemed always somewhat in awe of him and, despite the dicta-torial authority they exercised over him, frequently addressed him as "Mr."

He was as puzzled as any one else at the apparently advanced age of his mind and body at birth. He read up on it in the medical journal, but found that no such case had been previously recorded. At his father's urging he made an honest attempt to play with other boys, and frequently he joined in the milder games—football shook him up too much, and he feared that in case of a fracture his ancient bones would refuse to knit.

When he was five he was sent to kindergarten, where he was initiated into the art of pasting green paper on orange paper, of weaving colored maps and manufacturing eternal cardboard necklaces. He was inclined to drowse off to sleep in the middle of these tasks, a habit which both irritated and frightened his young teacher. To his relief she complained to his parents, and he was removed from the school. The Roger Buttons told their friends that they felt he was too young.

By the time he was twelve years old his parents had grown used to him. Indeed, so strong is the force of custom that they no longer felt that he was different from any other child—except when some curious anomaly reminded them of the fact. But one day a few weeks after his twelfth birthday, while looking in the mirror, Benjamin made, or thought he made, an astonishing discovery. Did his eyes deceive him, or had his hair turned in the dozen years of his life from white to iron-gray under its concealing dye? Was the network of wrinkles on his face becoming less pronounced? Was his skin healthier and firmer, with even a touch of ruddy winter color? He could not tell. He knew that he no longer stooped and that his physical condition had improved since the early days of his life.

"Can it be——?" he thought to himself, or, rather, scarcely dared to think.

He went to his father. "I am grown," he announced determinedly. "I want to put on long trousers."

His father hesitated. "Well," he said finally, "I don't know. Fourteen is the age for putting on long trousers—and you are only twelve."

"But you'll have to admit," protested Benjamin, "that I'm big for my age."

His father looked at him with illusory speculation. "Oh, I'm not so sure of that," he said. "I was as big as you when I was twelve."

This was not true—it was all part of Roger Button's silent agreement with himself to believe in his son's normality.

Finally a compromise was reached. Benjamin was to continue to dye his hair. He was to make a better attempt to play with boys of his own age. He was not to wear his spectacles or carry a cane in the street. In return for these concessions he was allowed his first suit of long trousers. . . .

IV

Of the life of Benjamin Button between his twelfth and twenty-first year I intend to say little. Suffice to record that they were years of normal ungrowth. When Benjamin was eighteen he was erect as a man of fifty; he had more hair and it was of a dark gray; his step was firm, his voice had lost its cracked quaver and descended to a healthy baritone. So his father sent him up to Connecticut to take examinations for entrance to Yale College. Benjamin passed his examination and became a member of the freshman class.

On the third day following his matriculation he received a notification from Mr. Hart, the college registrar, to call at his office and arrange his schedule. Benjamin, glancing in the mirror, decided that his hair needed a new application of its brown dye, but an anxious inspection of his bureau drawer disclosed that the dye bottle was not there. Then he remembered—he had emptied it the day before and thrown it away.

He was in a dilemma. He was due at the registrar's in five minutes. There seemed to be no help for it—he must go as he was. He did.

"Good-morning," said the registrar politely. "You've come to inquire about your son."

"Why, as a matter of fact, my name's Button—" began Benjamin, but Mr. Hart cut him off.

"I'm very glad to meet you, Mr. Button. I'm expecting your son here any minute."

"That's me!" burst out Benjamin. "I'm a freshman."

"What!"

"I'm a freshman."

"Surely you're joking."

"Not at all."

The registrar frowned and glanced at a card before him. "Why, I have Mr. Benjamin Button's age down here as eighteen."

"That's my age," asserted Benjamin, flushing slightly.

The registrar eyed him wearily. "Now surely, Mr. Button, you don't expect me to believe that."

Benjamin smiled wearily. "I am eighteen," he repeated.

The registrar pointed sternly to the door. "Get out," he said. "Get out of college and get out of town. You are a dangerous lunatic."

"I am eighteen."

Mr. Hart opened the door. "The idea!" he shouted. "A man of your age trying to enter here as a freshman. Eighteen years old, are you? Well, I'll give you eighteen minutes to get out of town."

Benjamin Button walked with dignity from the room, and half a dozen undergraduates, who were waiting in the hall, followed him curiously with their eyes. When he had gone a little way he turned around, faced the infuriated registrar, who was still standing in the doorway, and repeated in a firm voice: "I am eighteen years old."

To a chorus of titters which went up from the group of undergraduates, Benjamin walked away.

But he was not fated to escape so easily. On his melancholy walk to the railroad station he found that he was being followed by a group, then by a swarm, and finally by a dense mass of undergraduates. The word had gone around that a lunatic had passed the entrance examinations for Yale and attempted to palm himself off as a youth of eighteen. A fever of excitement permeated the college. Men ran hatless out of classes, the football team abandoned its practice and joined the mob, professors' wives with bonnets awry and bustles out of position, ran shouting after the procession, from which proceeded a continual succession of remarks aimed at the tender sensibilities of Benjamin Button.

"He must be the Wandering Jew!"

"He ought to go to prep school at his age!"

"Look at the infant prodigy!"

"He thought this was the old men's home."

"Go up to Harvard!"

Benjamin increased his gait, and soon he was running. He

would show them! He *would* go to Harvard, and then they would regret these ill-considered taunts!

Safely on board the train for Baltimore, he put his head from the window. "You'll regret this!" he shouted.

"Ha-ha!" the undergraduates laughed. "Ha-ha-ha!" It was the biggest mistake that Yale College had ever made. . . .

v

In 1880 Benjamin Button was twenty years old, and he signalized his birthday by going to work for his father in Roger Button & Co., Wholesale Hardware. It was in that same year that he began "going out socially"—that is, his father insisted on taking him to several fashionable dances. Roger Button was now fifty, and he and his son were more and more companionable—in fact, since Benjamin had ceased to dye his hair (which was still grayish) they appeared about the same age, and could have passed for brothers.

One night in August they got into the phaeton attired in their full-dress suits and drove out to a dance at the Shevlins' country house, situated just outside of Baltimore. It was a gorgeous evening. A full moon drenched the road to the lustreless color of platinum, and late-blooming harvest flowers breathed into the motionless air aromas that were like low, half-heard laughter. The open country, carpeted for rods around with bright wheat, was translucent as in the day. It was almost impossible not to be affected by the sheer beauty of the sky—almost.

"There's a great future in the dry-goods business," Roger Button was saying. He was not a spiritual man—his esthetic sense was rudimentary.

"Old fellows like me can't learn new tricks," he observed profoundly. "It's you youngsters with energy and vitality that have the great future before you."

Far up the road the lights of the Shevlins' country house drifted into view, and presently there was a sighing sound that crept persistently toward them—it might have been the fine plaint of violins or the rustle of the silver wheat under the moon.

They pulled up behind a handsome brougham whose passengers were disembarking at the door. A lady got out, then an elderly gentleman, then another young lady, beautiful as sin.

Benjamin started; an almost chemical change seemed to dissolve and recompose the very elements of his body. A rigor passed over him, blood rose into his cheeks, his forehead, and there was a steady thumping in his ears. It was first love.

The girl was slender and frail, with hair that was ashen under the moon and honey-colored under the sputtering gas-lamps of the porch. Over her shoulders was thrown a Spanish mantilla of softest yellow, butterflied in black; her feet were glittering buttons at the hem of her bustled dress.

Roger Button leaned over to his son. "That," he said, "is young Hildegarde Moncrief, the daughter of General Moncrief."

Benjamin nodded coldly. "Pretty little thing," he said indifferently. But when the negro boy had led the buggy away, he added: "Dad, you might introduce me to her."

They approached a group of which Miss Moncrief was the centre. Reared in the old tradition, she courtesied low before Benjamin. Yes, he might have a dance. He thanked her and walked away—staggered away.

The interval until the time for his turn should arrive dragged itself out interminably. He stood close to the wall, silent, inscrutable, watching with murderous eyes the young bloods of Baltimore as they eddied around Hildegarde Moncrief, passionate admiration in their faces. How obnoxious they seemed to Benjamin; how intolerably rosy! Their curling brown whiskers aroused in him a feeling equivalent to indigestion.

But when his own time came, and he drifted with her out upon the changing floor to the music of the latest waltz from Paris, his jealousies and anxieties melted from him like a mantle of snow. Blind with enchantment, he felt that life was just beginning.

"You and your brother got here just as we did, didn't you?" asked Hildegarde, looking up at him with eyes that were like bright blue enamel.

Benjamin hesitated. If she took him for his father's brother, would it be best to enlighten her? He remembered his experience at Yale, so he decided against it. It would be rude to contradict a lady; it would be criminal to mar this exquisite occasion with the grotesque story of his origin. Later, perhaps. So he nodded, smiled, listened, was happy.

"I like men of your age," Hildegarde told him. "Young boys are so idiotic. They tell me how much champagne they drink at college, and how much money they lose playing cards. Men of your age know how to appreciate women."

Benjamin felt himself on the verge of a proposal—with an effort he choked back the impulse.

"You're just the romantic age," she continued—"fifty. Twenty-five is too worldly-wise; thirty is apt to be pale from overwork; forty is the age of long stories that take a whole cigar to tell; sixty is—oh, sixty is too near seventy; but fifty is the mellow age. I love fifty."

Fifty seemed to Benjamin a glorious age. He longed passionately to be fifty.

"I've always said," went on Hildegarde, "that I'd rather marry a man of fifty and be taken care of than marry a man of thirty and take care of *him*."

For Benjamin the rest of the evening was bathed in a honey-colored mist. Hildegarde gave him two more dances, and they discovered that they were marvellously in accord on all the questions of the day. She was to go driving with him on the following Sunday, and then they would discuss all these questions further.

Going home in the phaeton just before the crack of dawn, when the first bees were humming and the fading moon glimmered in the cool dew, Benjamin knew vaguely that his father was discussing wholesale hardware.

". . . . And what do you think should merit our biggest attention after hammers and nails?" the elder Button was saying.

"Love," replied Benjamin absent-mindedly.

"Lugs?" exclaimed Roger Button. "Why, I've just covered the question of lugs."

Benjamin regarded him with dazed eyes just as the eastern sky was suddenly cracked with light, and an oriole yawned piercingly in the quickening trees. . . .

VI

When, six months later, the engagement of Miss Hildegarde Moncrief to Mr. Benjamin Button was made known (I say "made known," for General Moncrief declared he would rather fall upon his sword than announce it), the excitement in Balti-more society reached a feverish pitch. The almost forgotten story of Benjamin's birth was remembered and sent out upon the winds of scandal in picaresque and incredible forms. It was said that Benjamin was really the father of Roger Button, that he was his brother who had been in prison for forty years, that he was John Wilkes Booth in disguise—and, finally, that he had two small conical horns sprouting from his head.

The Sunday supplements of the New York papers played up the case with fascinating sketches which showed the head of Benjamin Button attached to a fish, to a snake, and, finally, to a body of solid brass. He became known, journalistically, as the Mystery Man of Maryland. But the true story, as is usually the case, had a very small circulation.

However, every one agreed with General Moncrief that it was "criminal" for a lovely girl who could have married any beau in Baltimore to throw herself into the arms of a man who was assuredly fifty. In vain Mr. Roger Button published his son's birth certificate in large type in the Baltimore *Blaze*. No one believed it. You had only to look at Benjamin and see.

On the part of the two people most concerned there was no wavering. So many of the stories about her fiancé were false that Hildegarde refused stubbornly to believe even the true one. In vain General Moncrief pointed out to her the high mortality among men of fifty—or, at least, among men who looked fifty; in vain he told her of the instability of the whole-sale hardware business. Hildegarde had chosen to marry for mellowness —and marry she did. . . .

VII

In one particular, at least, the friends of Hildegarde Moncrief were mistaken. The wholesale hardware business prospered amazingly. In the fifteen years between Benjamin Button's marriage in 1880 and his father's retirement in 1895, the family fortune was doubled—and this was due largely to the younger member of the firm.

Needless to say, Baltimore eventually received the couple to its bosom. Even old General Moncrief became reconciled to his son-in-law when Benjamin gave him the money to bring out his "History of the Civil War" in twenty volumes, which had been refused by nine prominent publishers.

In Benjamin himself fifteen years had wrought many changes. It seemed to him that the blood flowed with new vigor through his veins. It began to be a pleasure to rise in the morning, to walk with an active step along the busy, sunny street, to work untiringly with his shipments of hammers and his cargoes of nails. It was in 1890 that he executed his famous business coup: he brought up the suggestion that *all nails used in nailing up the boxes in which nails are shipped are the property of the shippee*, a proposal which became a statute, was approved by Chief Justice Fossile, and saved Roger Button and Company, Wholesale Hardware, more than *six hundred nails every year*.

In addition, Benjamin discovered that he was becoming more and more attracted by the gay side of life. It was typical of his growing enthusiasm for pleasure that he was the first man in the city of Baltimore to own and run an automobile. Meeting him on the street, his contemporaries would stare enviously at the picture he made of health and vitality.

"He seems to grow younger every year," they would remark. And if old Roger Button, now sixty-five years old, had failed at first to give a proper welcome to his son he atoned at last by bestowing on him what amounted to adulation.

And here we come to an unpleasant subject which it will be well to pass over as quickly as possible. There was only one thing that worried Benjamin Button: his wife had ceased to attract him.

At that time Hildegarde was a woman of thirty-five, with a son, Roscoe, fourteen years old. In the early days of their marriage Benjamin had worshipped her. But, as the years passed, her honey-colored hair became an unexciting brown, the blue enamel of her eyes assumed the aspect of cheap crockery—moreover, and most of all, she had become too settled in her ways, too placid, too content, too anemic in her excitements, and too sober in her taste. As a bride it had been she who had "dragged" Benjamin to dances and dinners—now conditions were reversed. She went out socially with him, but without enthusiasm, devoured already by that eternal inertia which comes to live with each of us one day and stays with us to the end.

Benjamin's discontent waxed stronger. At the outbreak of

the Spanish-American War in 1898 his home had for him so little charm that he decided to join the army. With his business influence he obtained a commission as captain, and proved so adaptable to the work that he was made a major, and finally a lieutenant-colonel just in time to participate in the celebrated charge up San Juan Hill. He was slightly wounded, and received a medal.

Benjamin had become so attached to the activity and excitement of army life that he regretted to give it up, but his business required attention, so he resigned his commission and came home. He was met at the station by a brass band and escorted to his house.

VIII

Hildegarde, waving a large silk flag, greeted him on the porch, and even as he kissed her he felt with a sinking of the heart that these three years had taken their toll. She was a woman of forty now, with a faint skirmish line of gray hairs in her head. The sight depressed him.

Up in his room he saw his reflection in the familiar mirror—he went closer and examined his own face with anxiety, comparing it after a moment with a photograph of himself in uniform taken just before the war.

"Good Lord!" he said aloud. The process was continuing. There was no doubt of it—he looked now like a man of thirty. Instead of being delighted, he was uneasy—he was growing younger. He had hitherto hoped that once he reached a bodily age equivalent to his age in years, the grotesque phenomenon which had marked his birth would cease to function. He shuddered. His destiny seemed to him awful, incredible.

When he came down-stairs Hildegarde was waiting for him. She appeared annoyed, and he wondered if she had at last discovered that there was something amiss. It was with an effort to relieve the tension between them that he broached the matter at dinner in what he considered a delicate way.

"Well," he remarked lightly, "everybody says I look younger than ever."

Hildegarde regarded him with scorn. She sniffed. "Do you think it's anything to boast about?"

"I'm not boasting," he asserted uncomfortably.

She sniffed again. "The idea," she said, and after a moment: "I should think you'd have enough pride to stop it."

"How can I?" he demanded.

"I'm not going to argue with you," she retorted. "But there's a right way of doing things and a wrong way. If you've made up your mind to be different from everybody else, I don't suppose I can stop you, but I really don't think it's very considerate."

"But, Hildegarde, I can't help it."

"You can too. You're simply stubborn. You think you don't want to be like any one else. You always have been that way, and you always will be. But just think how it would be if every one else looked at things as you do—what would the world be like?"

As this was an inane and unanswerable argument Benjamin made no reply, and from that time on a chasm began to widen between them. He wondered what possible fascination she had ever exercised over him.

To add to the breach, he found, as the new century gathered headway, that his thirst for gayety grew stronger. Never a party of any kind in the city of Baltimore but he was there, dancing with the prettiest of the young married women, chatting with the most popular of the débutantes, and finding their company charming, while his wife, a dowager of evil omen, sat among the chaperons, now in haughty disapproval, and now following him with solemn, puzzled, and reproachful eyes.

"Look!" people would remark. "What a pity! A young fellow that age tied to a woman of forty-five. He must be twenty years younger than his wife." They had forgotten—as people inevitably forget—that back in 1880 their mammas and papas had also remarked about this same ill-matched pair.

Benjamin's growing unhappiness at home was compensated for by his many new interests. He took up golf and made a great success of it. He went in for dancing: in 1906 he was an expert at "The Boston," and in 1908 he was considered proficient at the "Maxixe," while in 1909 his "Castle Walk" was the envy of every young man in town.

His social activities, of course, interfered to some extent with his business, but then he had worked hard at wholesale hardware for twenty-five years and felt that he could soon hand it on to his son, Roscoe, who had recently graduated from Harvard.

He and his son were, in fact, often mistaken for each other. This pleased Benjamin—he soon forgot the insidious fear which had come over him on his return from the Spanish-American War, and grew to take a naïve pleasure in his appearance. There was only one fly in the delicious ointment—he hated to appear in public with his wife. Hildegarde was almost fifty, and the sight of her made him feel absurd. . . .

IX

One September day in 1910—a few years after Roger Button & Co., Wholesale Hardware, had been handed over to young Roscoe Button—a man, apparently about twenty years old, entered himself as a freshman at Harvard University in Cambridge. He did not make the mistake of announcing that he would never see fifty again nor did he mention the fact that his son had been graduated from the same institution ten years before.

He was admitted, and almost immediately attained a prominent position in the class, partly because he seemed a little older than the other freshmen, whose average age was about eighteen.

But his success was largely due to the fact that in the football game with Yale he played so brilliantly, with so much dash and with such a cold, remorseless anger that he scored seven touchdowns and fourteen field goals for Harvard, and caused one entire eleven of Yale men to be carried singly from the field, unconscious. He was the most celebrated man in college.

Strange to say, in his third or junior year he was scarcely able to "make" the team. The coaches said that he had lost weight, and it seemed to the more observant among them that he was not quite as tall as before. He made no touchdowns—indeed, he was retained on the team chiefly in hope that his enormous reputation would bring terror and disorganization to the Yale team.

In his senior year he did not make the team at all. He had grown so slight and frail that one day he was taken by some sophomores for a freshman, an incident which humiliated him terribly. He became known as something of a prodigy—a senior who was surely no more than sixteen—and he was often shocked at the worldliness of some of his classmates. His studies seemed harder to him—he felt that they were too advanced. He had heard his classmates speak of St. Midas', the famous preparatory school, at which so many of them had prepared for college, and he determined after his graduation to enter himself at St. Midas', where the sheltered life among boys his own size would be more congenial to him.

Upon his graduation in 1914 he went home to Baltimore with his Harvard diploma in his pocket. Hildegarde was now residing in Italy, so Benjamin went to live with his son, Roscoe. But though he was welcomed in a general way, there was obviously no heartiness in Roscoe's feeling toward him—there was even perceptible a tendency on his son's part to think that Benjamin, as he moped about the house in adolescent mooniness, was somewhat in the way. Roscoe was married now and prominent in Baltimore life, and he wanted no scandal to creep out in connection with his family.

Benjamin, no longer persona grata with the débutantes and younger college set, found himself left much alone, except for the companionship of three or four fifteen-year-old boys in the neighborhood. His idea of going to St. Midas' school recurred to him.

"Say," he said to Roscoe one day, "I've told you over and over that I want to go to prep school."

"Well, go, then," replied Roscoe shortly. The matter was distasteful to him, and he wished to avoid a discussion.

"I can't go alone," said Benjamin helplessly. "You'll have to enter me and take me up there."

"I haven't got time," declared Roscoe abruptly. His eyes narrowed and he looked uneasily at his father. "As a matter of fact," he added, "you'd better not go on with this business much longer. You better pull up short. You better—you better"—he paused and his face crimsoned as he sought for words—"you better turn right around and start back the other way. This has gone too far to be a joke. It isn't funny any longer. You—you behave yourself!"

Benjamin looked at him, on the verge of tears.

"And another thing," continued Roscoe, "when visitors are

in the house I want you to call me 'Uncle'—not 'Roscoe,' but 'Uncle,' do you understand? It looks absurd for a boy of fifteen to call me by my first name. Perhaps you'd better call me 'Uncle' *all* the time, so you'll get used to it."

With a harsh look at his father, Roscoe turned away. . . .

X

At the termination of this interview, Benjamin wandered dismally up-stairs and stared at himself in the mirror. He had not shaved for three months, but he could find nothing on his face but a faint white down with which it seemed unnecessary to meddle. When he had first come home from Harvard, Roscoe had approached him with the proposition that he should wear eye-glasses and imitation whiskers glued to his cheeks, and it had seemed for a moment that the farce of his early years was to be repeated. But whiskers had itched and made him ashamed. He wept and Roscoe had reluctantly relented.

Benjamin opened a book of boys' stories, "The Boy Scouts in Bimini Bay," and began to read. But he found himself thinking persistently about the war. America had joined the Allied cause during the preceding month, and Benjamin wanted to enlist, but, alas, sixteen was the minimum age, and he did not look that old. His true age which was fifty-seven, would have disqualified him, anyway.

There was a knock at his door, and the butler appeared with a letter bearing a large official legend in the corner and addressed to Mr. Benjamin Button. Benjamin tore it open eagerly, and read the enclosure with delight. It informed him that many reserve officers who had served in the Spanish-American War were being called back into service with a higher rank, and it enclosed his commission as brigadier-general in the United States army with orders to report immediately.

Benjamin jumped to his feet fairly quivering with enthusiasm. This was what he had wanted. He seized his cap and ten minutes later he had entered a large tailoring establishment on Charles Street, and asked in his uncertain treble to be measured for a uniform.

"Want to play soldier, sonny?" demanded a clerk, casually.

Benjamin flushed. "Say! Never mind what I want!" he

retorted angrily. "My name's Button and I live on Mt. Vernon Place, so you know I'm good for it."

"Well," admitted the clerk, hesitantly, "if you're not, I guess your daddy is, all right."

Benjamin was measured, and a week later his uniform was completed. He had difficulty in obtaining the proper general's insignia because the dealer kept insisting to Benjamin that a nice Y.W.C.A. badge would look just as well and be much more fun to play with.

Saying nothing to Roscoe, he left the house one night and proceeded by train to Camp Mosby, in South Carolina, where he was to command an infantry brigade. On a sultry April day he approached the entrance to the camp, paid off the taxicab which had brought him from the station, and turned to the sentry on guard.

"Get some one to handle my luggage!" he said briskly.

The sentry eyed him reproachfully. "Say," he remarked, "where you goin' with the general's duds, sonny?"

Benjamin, veteran of the Spanish-American War, whirled upon him with fire in his eye, but with, alas, a changing treble voice.

"Come to attention!" he tried to thunder; he paused for breath—then suddenly he saw the sentry snap his heels together and bring his rifle to the present. Benjamin concealed a smile of gratification, but when he glanced around his smile faded. It was not he who had inspired obedience, but an imposing artillery colonel who was approaching on horseback.

"Colonel!" called Benjamin shrilly.

The colonel came up, drew rein, and looked coolly down at him with a twinkle in his eyes. "Whose little boy are you?" he demanded kindly.

"I'll soon darn well show you whose little boy I am!" retorted Benjamin in a ferocious voice. "Get down off that horse!"

The colonel roared with laughter.

"You want him, eh, general?"

"Here!" cried Benjamin desperately. "Read this." And he thrust his commission toward the colonel.

The colonel read it, his eyes popping from their sockets.

"Where'd you get this?" he demanded, slipping the document into his own pocket.

"I got it from the Government, as you'll soon find out!"

"You come along with me," said the colonel with a peculiar look. "We'll go up to headquarters and talk this over. Come along."

The colonel turned and began walking his horse in the direction of headquarters. There was nothing for Benjamin to do but follow with as much dignity as possible—meanwhile promising himself a stern revenge.

But this revenge did not materialize. Two days later, however, his son Roscoe materialized from Baltimore, hot and cross from a hasty trip, and escorted the weeping general, *sans* uniform, back to his home.

XI

In 1920 Roscoe Button's first child was born. During the attendant festivities, however, no one thought it "the thing" to mention that the little grubby boy, apparently about ten years of age who played around the house with lead soldiers and a miniature circus, was the new baby's own grandfather.

No one disliked the little boy whose fresh, cheerful face was crossed with just a hint of sadness, but to Roscoe Button his presence was a source of torment. In the idiom of his generation Roscoe did not consider the matter "efficient." It seemed to him that his father, in refusing to look sixty, had not behaved like a "red-blooded he-man"—this was Roscoe's favorite expression—but in a curious and perverse manner. Indeed, to think about the matter for as much as a half an hour drove him to the edge of insanity. Roscoe believed that "live wires" should keep young, but carrying it out on such a scale was—was—was inefficient. And there Roscoe rested.

Five years later Roscoe's little boy had grown old enough to play childish games with little Benjamin under the supervision of the same nurse. Roscoe took them both to kindergarten on the same day and Benjamin found that playing with little strips of colored paper, making mats and chains and curious and beautiful designs, was the most fascinating game in the world. Once he was bad and had to stand in the corner—then he cried —but for the most part there were gay hours in the cheerful room, with the sunlight coming in the windows and Miss

Bailey's kind hand resting for a moment now and then in his tousled hair.

Roscoe's son moved up into the first grade after a year, but Benjamin stayed on in the kindergarten. He was very happy. Sometimes when other tots talked about what they would do when they grew up a shadow would cross his little face as if in a dim, childish way he realized that those were things in which he was never to share.

The days flowed on in monotonous content. He went back a third year to the kindergarten, but he was too little now to understand what the bright shining strips of paper were for. He cried because the other boys were bigger than he and he was afraid of them. The teacher talked to him, but though he tried to understand he could not understand at all.

He was taken from the kindergarten. His nurse, Nana, in her starched gingham dress, became the centre of his tiny world. On bright days they walked in the park; Nana would point at a great gray monster and say "elephant," and Benjamin would say it after her, and when he was being undressed for bed that night he would say it over and over aloud to her: "Elyphant, elyphant, elyphant." Sometimes Nana let him jump on the bed, which was fun, because if you sat down exactly right it would bounce you up on your feet again, and if you said "Ah" for a long time while you jumped you got a very pleasing broken vocal effect.

He loved to take a big cane from the hatrack and go around hitting chairs and tables with it and saying: "Fight, fight, fight." When there were people there the old ladies would cluck at him, which interested him, and the young ladies would try to kiss him, which he submitted to with mild boredom. And when the long day was done at five o'clock he would go upstairs with Nana and be fed oatmeal and nice soft mushy foods with a spoon.

There were no troublesome memories in his childish sleep; no token came to him of his brave days at college, of the glittering years when he flustered the hearts of many girls. There were only the white, safe walls of his crib and Nana and a man who came to see him sometimes, and a great big orange ball that Nana pointed at just before his twilight bed hour and called "sun." When the sun went his eyes were sleepy—there were no dreams, no dreams to haunt him.

The past—the wild charge at the head of his men up San Juan Hill; the first years of his marriage when he worked late into the summer dusk down in the busy city for young Hildegarde whom he loved; the days before that when he sat smoking far into the night in the gloomy old Button house on Monroe Street with his grandfather—all these had faded like unsubstantial dreams from his mind as though they had never been.

He did not remember. He did not remember clearly whether the milk was warm or cool at his last feeding or how the days passed—there was only his crib and Nana's familiar presence. And then he remembered nothing. When he was hungry he cried—that was all. Through the noons and nights he breathed and over him there were soft mumblings and murmurings that he scarcely heard, and faintly differentiated smells, and light and darkness.

Then it was all dark, and his white crib and the dim faces that moved above him, and the warm sweet aroma of the milk, faded out altogether from his mind.

1922

SEABURY QUINN

(1889–1969)

The Curse of Everard Maundy

"*Mort d'un chat!* I do not like this!" Jules de Grandin slammed the evening paper down upon the table and glared ferociously at me through the library lamplight.

"What's up now?" I asked, wondering vaguely what the cause of his latest grievance was. "Some reporter say something personal about you?"

"*Parbleu, non*, he would better not!" the little Frenchman replied, his round blue eyes flashing ominously. "Me, I would pull his nose and tweak his ears. But it is not of the reporter's insolence I speak, my friend; I do not like these suicides; there are too many of them."

"Of course there are," I conceded soothingly, "one suicide is that much too many; people have no right to——"

"Ah bah!" he cut in. "You do misapprehend me, *mon vieux*. Excuse me one moment, if you please." He rose hurriedly from his chair and left the room. A moment later I heard him rummaging about in the cellar.

In a few minutes he returned, the week's supply of discarded newspapers salvaged from the dust bin in his arms.

"Now, attend me," he ordered as he spread the sheets out before him and began scanning the columns hastily. "Here is an item from Monday's *Journal*:

Two Motorists Die While Driving Cars

The impulse to end their lives apparently attacked two automobile drivers on the Albemarle turnpike near Lonesome Swamp, two miles out of Harrisonville, last night. Carl Planz, thirty-one years old, of Martins Falls, took his own life by shooting himself in the head with a shotgun while seated in his automobile, which he had parked at the roadside where the pike passes nearest the swamp. His remains were identified by two letters, one addressed to his wife, the other to his father, Joseph Planz, with whom he was associated in the real estate

536

business at Martins Falls. A check for three hundred dollars and several other papers found in his pockets completed identification. The letters, which merely declared his intention to kill himself, failed to establish any motive for the act.

Almost at the same time, and within a hundred yards of the spot where Planz's body was found by State Trooper Henry Anderson this morning, the body of Henry William Nixon, of New Rochelle, N.Y., was discovered partly sitting, partly lying on the rear seat of his automobile, an empty bottle of windshield cleaner lying on the floor beside him. It is thought this liquid, which contained a small amount of cyanide of potassium, was used to inflict death. Police Surgeon Stevens, who examined both bodies, declared that the men had been dead approximately the same length of time when brought to the station house.

"What think you of that, my friend, *hein*?" de Grandin demanded, looking up from the paper with one of his direct, challenging stares.

"Why—er——" I began, but he interrupted.

"Hear this," he commanded, taking up a second paper, "this is from the *News* of Tuesday:

Mother and Daughters Die in Death Pact

Police and heartbroken relatives are today trying to trace a motive for the triple suicide of Mrs. Ruby Westerfelt and her daughters, Joan and Elizabeth, who perished by leaping from the eighth floor of the Hotel Dolores, Newark, late yesterday afternoon. The women registered at the hotel under assumed names, went immediately to the room assigned them, and ten minutes later Miss Gladys Walsh, who occupied a room on the fourth floor, was startled to see a dark form hurtle past her window. A moment later a second body flashed past on its downward flight, and as Miss Walsh, horrified, rushed toward the window, a loud crash sounded outside. Looking out, Miss Walsh saw the body of a third woman partly impaled on the spikes of a balcony rail.

Miss Walsh sought to aid the woman. As she leaned from her window and reached out with a trembling arm she was greeted by a scream: "Don't try! I won't be saved; I must go with Mother and Sister!" A moment later the woman had managed to free herself from the restraining iron spikes and fell to the cement areaway four floors below.

"And here is still another account, this one from tonight's paper," he continued, unfolding the sheet which had caused his original protest:

High School Co-ed Takes Life in Attic

The family and friends of Edna May McCarty, fifteen-year-old co-ed of Harrisonville High School, are at a loss to assign a cause for her suicide early this morning. The girl had no love affairs, as far as is known, and had not failed in her examinations. On the contrary, she had passed the school's latest test with flying colors. Her mother told investigating police officials that overstudy might have temporarily unbalanced the child's mind. Miss McCarty's body was found suspended from the rafters of her father's attic by her mother this morning when the young woman did not respond to a call for breakfast and could not be found in her room on the second floor of the house. A clothesline, used to hang clothes which were dried inside the house in rainy weather, was used to form the fatal noose.

"Now then, my friend," de Grandin reseated himself and lighted a vile-smelling French cigarette, puffing furiously, till the smoke surrounded his sleek, blond head like a mephitic nimbus, "what have you to say to those reports? Am I not right? Are there not too many—*mordieu*, entirely too many!—suicides in our city?"

"All of them weren't committed here," I objected practically, "and besides, there couldn't very well be any connection between them. Mrs. Westerfelt and her daughters carried out a suicide pact, it appears, but they certainly could have had no understanding with the two men and the young girl——"

"Perhaps, maybe, possibly," he agreed, nodding his head so vigorously that a little column of ash detached itself from his cigarette and dropped unnoticed on the bosom of his stiffly starched evening shirt. "You may be right, Friend Trowbridge, but then, as is so often the case, you may be entirely wrong. One thing I know: I, Jules de Grandin, shall investigate these cases myself personally. *Cordieu*, they do interest me! I shall ascertain what is the what here."

"Go ahead," I encouraged. "The investigation will keep you out of mischief," and I returned to the second chapter of Haggard's *The Wanderer's Necklace*, a book which I have read at least half a dozen times, yet find as fascinating at each rereading as when I first perused its pages.

The matter of the six suicides still bothered him next morning. "Trowbridge, my friend," he asked abruptly as he disposed of his second helping of coffee and passed his cup for replenishment, "why is it that people destroy themselves?"

"Oh," I answered evasively, "different reasons, I suppose. Some are crossed in love, some meet financial reverses and some do it while temporarily deranged."

"Yes," he agreed thoughtfully, "yet every self-murderer has a real or fancied reason for quitting the world, and there is apparently no reason why any of these six poor ones who hurled themselves into outer darkness during the past week should have done so. All, apparently, were well provided for, none of them, as far as is known, had any reason to regret the past or fear the future; yet"—he shrugged his narrow shoulders significantly—"*voilà*, they are gone!

"Another thing: At the *Faculté de Médicine Légal* and the *Sûreté* in Paris we keep most careful statistics, not only on the number, but on the manner of suicides. I do not think your Frenchman differs radically from your American when it comes to taking his life, so the figures for one nation may well be a signpost for the other. These self-inflicted deaths, they are not right. They do not follow the rules. Men prefer to hang, slash or shoot themselves; women favor drowning, poison or gas; yet here we have one of the men taking poison, one of the women hanging herself, and three of them jumping to death. *Nom d'un canard*, I am not satisfied with it!"

"H'm, neither are the unfortunate parties who killed themselves, if the theologians are to be believed," I returned.

"You speak right," he returned, then muttered dreamily to himself: "Destruction—destruction of body and imperilment of soul—*mordieu*, it is strange, it is not righteous!" He disposed of his coffee at a gulp and leaped from his chair. "I go!" he declared dramatically, turning toward the door.

"Where?"

"Where? Where should I go, if not to secure the history of these so puzzling cases? I shall not rest nor sleep nor eat until I have the string of the mystery's skein in my hands." He paused at the door, a quick, elfin smile playing across his usually stern features. "And should I return before my work is complete," he suggested, "I pray you, have the excellent Nora prepare another of her so magnificent apple pies for dinner."

Forty seconds later the front door clicked shut, and from

the dining room's oriel window I saw his neat little figure, trimly encased in blue chinchilla and gray worsted, pass quickly down the sidewalk, his ebony cane hammering a rapid tattoo on the stones as it kept time to the thoughts racing through his active brain.

"I am desolated that my capacity is exhausted," he announced that evening as he finished his third portion of deep-dish apple pie smothered in pungent rum sauce and regarded his empty plate sadly. "*Eh bien*, perhaps it is as well. Did I eat more I might not be able to think clearly, and clear thought is what I shall need this night, my friend. Come; we must be going."

"Going where?" I demanded.

"To hear the reverend and estimable Monsieur Maundy deliver his sermon."

"Who? Everard Maundy?"

"But of course, who else?"

"But—but," I stammered, looking at him incredulously, "why should we go to the tabernacle to hear this man? I can't say I'm particularly impressed with his system, and—aren't you a Catholic, de Grandin?"

"Who can say?" he replied as he lighted a cigarette and stared thoughtfully at his coffee cup. "My father was a Huguenot of the Huguenots; a several times great-grandsire of his cut his way to freedom through the Paris streets on the fateful night of August 24, 1572. My mother was convent-bred, and as pious as anyone with a sense of humor and the gift of thinking for herself could well be. One of my uncles—he for whom I am named—was like a blood brother to Darwin the magnificent, and Huxley the scarcely less magnificent, also. Me, I am"—he elevated his eyebrows and shoulders at once and pursed his lips comically—"what should a man with such a heritage be, my friend? But come, we delay, we tarry, we lose time. Let us hasten. I have a fancy to hear what this Monsieur Maundy has to say, and to observe him. See, I have here tickets for the fourth row of the hall."

Very much puzzled, but never doubting that something more than the idle wish to hear a sensational evangelist urged the little Frenchman toward the tabernacle, I rose and accompanied him.

"*Parbleu*, what a day!" he sighed as I turned my car toward the downtown section. "From coroner's office to undertakers' I have run; and from undertakers' to hospitals. I have interviewed everyone who could shed the smallest light on these strange deaths, yet I seem no further advanced than when I began. What I have found out serves only to whet my curiosity; what I have not discovered——" He spread his hands in a world-embracing gesture and lapsed into silence.

The Jachin Tabernacle, where the Rev. Everard Maundy was holding his series of non-sectarian revival meetings, was crowded to overflowing when we arrived, but our tickets passed us through the jostling crowd of half-skeptical, half-believing people who thronged the lobby, and we were soon ensconced in seats where every word the preacher uttered could be heard with ease.

Before the introductory hymn had been finished, de Grandin mumbled a wholly unintelligible excuse in my ear and disappeared up the aisle, and I settled myself in my seat to enjoy the service as best I might.

The Rev. Mr. Maundy was a tall, hatchet-faced man in early middle life, a little inclined to rant and make use of worked-over platitudes, but obviously sincere in the message he had for his congregation. From the half-cynical attitude of a regularly-enrolled church member who looks on revivals with a certain disdain, I found myself taking keener and keener interest in the story of regeneration the preacher had to tell, my attention compelled not so much by his words as by the earnestness of his manner and the wonderful stage presence the man possessed. When the ushers had taken up the collection and the final hymn was sung, I was surprized to find we had been two hours in the tabernacle. If anyone had asked me, I should have said half an hour would have been nearer the time consumed by the service.

"Eh, my friend, did you find it interesting?" de Grandin asked as he joined me in the lobby and linked his arm in mine.

"Yes, very," I admitted, then, somewhat sulkily: "I thought you wanted to hear him, too—it was your idea that we came here—what made you run away?"

"I am sorry," he replied with a chuckle which belied his words, "but it was *necessaire* that I fry other fish while you listened to the reverend gentleman's discourse. Will you drive me home?"

The March wind cut shrewdly through my overcoat after the super-heated atmosphere of the tabernacle, and I felt myself shivering involuntarily more than once as we drove through the quiet streets. Strangely, too, I felt rather sleepy and ill at ease. By the time we reached the wide, tree-bordered avenue before my house I was conscious of a distinctly unpleasant sensation, a constantly-growing feeling of malaise, a sort of baseless, irritating uneasiness. Thoughts of years long forgotten seemed summoned to my memory without rime or reason. An incident of an unfair advantage I had taken of a younger boy while at public school, recollections of petty, useless lies and bits of naughtiness committed when I could not have been more than three came flooding back on my consciousness, finally an episode of my early youth which I had forgotten some forty years.

My father had brought a little stray kitten into the house, and I, with the tiny lad's unconscious cruelty, had fallen to teasing the wretched bundle of bedraggled fur, finally tossing it nearly to the ceiling to test the tale I had so often heard that a cat always lands on its feet. My experiment was the exception which demonstrated the rule, it seemed, for the poor, half-starved feline hit the hardwood floor squarely on its back, struggled feebly a moment, then yielded up its entire nine-fold expectancy of life.

Long after the smart of the whipping I received in consequence had been forgotten, the memory of that unintentional murder had plagued my boyish conscience, and many were the times I had awakened at dead of night, weeping bitter repentance out upon my pillow.

Now, some forty years later, the thought of that kitten's death came back as clearly as the night the unkempt little thing thrashed out its life upon our kitchen floor. Strive as I would, I could not drive the memory from me, and it seemed as though the unwitting crime of my childhood was assuming an enormity out of all proportion to its true importance.

I shook my head and passed my hand across my brow, as a sleeper suddenly wakened does to drive away the lingering memory of an unpleasant dream, but the kitten's ghost, like Banquo's, would not down.

"What is it, Friend Trowbridge?" de Grandin asked as he eyed me shrewdly.

"Oh, nothing," I replied as I parked the car before our door and leaped to the curb, "I was just thinking."

"Ah?" he responded on a rising accent. "And of what do you think, my friend? Something unpleasant?"

"Oh, no; nothing important enough to dignify by that term," I answered shortly, and led the way to the house, keeping well ahead of him, lest he push his inquiries farther.

In this, however, I did him wrong. Tactful women and Jules de Grandin have the talent of feeling without being told when conversation is unwelcome, and besides wishing me a pleasant good-night, he spoke not a word until we had gone upstairs to bed. As I was opening my door, he called down the hall, "Should you want me, remember, you have but to call."

"Humph!" I muttered ungraciously as I shut the door. "Want him? What the devil should I want him for?" And so I pulled off my clothes and climbed into bed, the thought of the murdered kitten still with me and annoying me more by its persistence than by the faint sting of remorse it evoked.

How long I had slept I do not know, but I do know I was wide-awake in a single second, sitting up in bed and staring through the darkened chamber with eyes which strove desperately to pierce the gloom.

Somewhere—whether far or near I could not tell—a cat had raised its voice in a long-drawn, wailing cry, kept silence a moment, then given tongue again with increased volume.

There are few sounds more eery to hear in the dead of night than the cry of a prowling feline, and this one was of a particularly sad, almost reproachful tone.

"Confound the beast!" I exclaimed angrily, and lay back on my pillow, striving vainly to recapture my broken sleep.

Again the wail sounded, indefinite as to location, but louder, more prolonged, even, it seemed, fiercer in its timbre than when I first heard it in my sleep.

I glanced toward the window with the vague thought of

hurling a book or boot or other handy missile at the disturber, then held my breath in sudden affright. Staring through the aperture between the scrim curtains was the biggest, most ferocious-looking tom-cat I had ever seen. Its eyes, seemingly as large as butter dishes, glared at me with the green phosphorescence of its tribe, and with an added demoniacal glow the like of which I had never seen. Its red mouth, opened to full compass in a venomous, soundless "spit," seemed almost as large as that of a lion, and the wicked, pointed ears above its rounded face were laid back against its head, as though it were crouching for combat.

"Get out! Scat!" I called feebly, but making no move toward the thing.

"S-s-s-sssh!" a hiss of incomparable fury answered me, and the creature put one heavy, padded paw tentatively over the window-sill, still regarding me with its unchanging, hateful stare.

"Get!" I repeated, and stopped abruptly. Before my eyes the great beast was *growing*, increasing in size till its chest and shoulders completely blocked the window. Should it attack me I would be as helpless in its claws as a Hindoo under the paws of a Bengal tiger.

Slowly, stealthily, its cushioned feet making no sound as it set them down daintily, the monstrous creature advanced into the room, crouched on its haunches and regarded me steadily, wickedly, malevolently.

I rose a little higher on my elbow. The great brute twitched the tip of its sable tail warningly, half lifted one of its forepaws from the floor, and set it down again, never shifting its sulfurous eyes from my face.

Inch by inch I moved my farther foot from the bed, felt the floor beneath it, and pivoted slowly in a sitting position until my other foot was free of the bedclothes. Apparently the cat did not notice my strategy, for it made no menacing move till I flexed my muscles for a leap, suddenly flung myself from the bedstead, and leaped toward the door.

With a snarl, white teeth flashing, green eyes glaring, ears laid back, the beast moved between me and the exit, and began slowly advancing on me, hate and menace in every line of its giant body.

I gave ground before it, retreating step by step and striving desperately to hold its eyes with mine, as I had heard hunters sometimes do when suddenly confronted by wild animals.

Back, back I crept, the ogreish visitant keeping pace with my retreat, never suffering me to increase the distance between us.

I felt the cold draft of the window on my back; the pressure of the sill against me; behind me, from the waist up, was the open night, before me the slowly advancing monster.

It was a thirty-foot drop to a cemented roadway, but death on the pavement was preferable to the slashing claws and grinding teeth of the terrible thing creeping toward me.

I threw one leg over the sill, watching constantly, lest the cat-thing leap on me before I could cheat it by dashing myself to the ground——

"Trowbridge, *mon Dieu*, Trowbridge, my friend! What is it you would do?" The frenzied hail of Jules de Grandin cut through the dark, and a flood of light from the hallway swept into the room as he flung the door violently open and raced across the room, seizing my arm in both hands and dragging me from the window.

"Look out, de Grandin!" I screamed. "The cat! It'll get you!"

"Cat?" he echoed, looking about him uncomprehendingly. "Do you say 'cat,' my friend? A cat will get *me*? *Mort d'un chou*, the cat which can make a mouse of Jules de Grandin is not yet whelped! Where is it, this cat of yours?"

"There! Th——" I began, then stopped, rubbing my eyes. The room was empty. Save for de Grandin and me there was nothing animate in the place.

"But it *was* here," I insisted. "I tell you, I saw it; a great, black cat, as big as a lion. It came in the window and crouched right over there, and was driving me to jump to the ground when you came——"

"*Nom d'un porc!* Do you say so?" he exclaimed, seizing my arm again and shaking me. "Tell me of this cat, my friend. I would learn more of this puss-puss who comes into Friend Trowbridge's house, grows great as a lion and drives him to his death on the stones below. Ha, I think maybe the trail of these mysterious deaths is not altogether lost! Tell me more, *mon ami*; I would know all—all!"

"Of course, it was just a bad dream," I concluded as I finished the recital of my midnight visitation, "but it seemed terribly real to me while it lasted."

"I doubt it not," he agreed with a quick, nervous nod. "And on our way from the tabernacle tonight, my friend, I noticed you were much *distrait*. Were you, perhaps, feeling ill at the time?"

"Not at all," I replied. "The truth is, I was remembering something which occurred when I was a lad four or five years old; something which had to do with a kitten I killed," and I told him the whole wretched business.

"U'm?" he commented when I had done. "You are a good man, Trowbridge, my friend. In all your life, since you attained to years of discretion, I do not believe you have done a wicked or ignoble act."

"Oh, I wouldn't say that," I returned, "we all——"

"*Parbleu*, I have said it. That kitten incident, now, is probably the single tiny skeleton in the entire closet of your existence, yet sustained thought upon it will magnify it even as the cat of your dream grew from cat's to lion's size. *Pardieu*, my friend, I am not so sure you did dream of that abomination in the shape of a cat which visited you. Suppose——" he broke off, staring intently before him, twisting first one, then the other end of his trimly waxed mustache.

"Suppose what?" I prompted.

"*Non*, we will suppose nothing to-night," he replied. "You will please go to sleep once more, my friend, and I shall remain in the room to frighten away any more dream-demons which may come to plague you. Come, let us sleep. Here I do remain." He leaped into the wide bed beside me and pulled the down comforter snuggly up about his pointed chin.

". . . . and I'd like very much to have you come right over to see her, if you will," Mrs. Weaver finished. "I can't imagine whatever made her attempt such a thing—she's never shown any signs of it before."

I hung up the telephone receiver and turned to de Grandin. "Here's another suicide, or almost-suicide, for you," I told him half teasingly. "The daughter of one of my patients attempted her life by hanging in the bathroom this morning."

"*Par la tête bleu*, do you tell me so?" he exclaimed eagerly. "I go with you, *cher ami*. I see this young woman; I examine her. Perhaps I shall find some key to the riddle there. *Parbleu*, me, I itch, I burn, I am all on fire with this mystery! Certainly, there must be an answer to it; but it remains hidden like a peasant's pig when the tax collector arrives."

"Well, young lady, what's this I hear about you?" I demanded severely as we entered Grace Weaver's bedroom a few minutes later. "What on earth have you to die for?"

"I—I don't know what made me want to do it, Doctor," the girl replied with a wan smile. "I hadn't thought of it before —ever. But I just got to—oh, you know, sort of brooding over things last night, and when I went into the bathroom this morning, something—something inside my head, like those ringing noises you hear when you have a head-cold, you know —seemed to be whispering, 'Go on, kill yourself, you've nothing to live for. Go on, do it!' So I just stood on the scales and took the cord from my bathrobe and tied it over the transom, then knotted the other end about my neck. Then I kicked the scales away and"—she gave another faint smile—"I'm glad I hadn't locked the door before I did it," she admitted.

De Grandin had been staring unwinkingly at her with his curiously level glance throughout her recital. As she concluded he bent forward and asked: "This voice which you heard bidding you commit an unpardonable sin, *Mademoiselle*, did you, perhaps, recognize it?"

The girl shuddered. "No!" she replied, but a sudden paling of her face about the lips gave the lie to her word.

"*Pardonnez-moi, Mademoiselle*," the Frenchman returned. "I think you do not tell the truth. Now, whose voice was it, if you please?"

A sullen, stubborn look spread over the girl's features, to be replaced a moment later by the muscular spasm which preludes weeping. "It—it sounded like Fanny's," she cried, and turning her face to the pillow, fell to sobbing bitterly.

"And Fanny, who is she?" de Grandin began, but Mrs. Weaver motioned him to silence with an imploring gesture.

I prescribed a mild bromide and left the patient, wondering what mad impulse could have led a girl in the first flush of young womanhood, happily situated in the home of parents who idolized her, engaged to a fine young man, and without bodily or spiritual ill of any sort, to attempt her life. Outside, de Grandin seized the mother's arm and whispered fiercely: "Who is this Fanny, Madame Weaver? Believe me, I ask not from idle curiosity, but because I seek vital information!"

"Fanny Briggs was Grace's chum two years ago," Mrs. Weaver answered. "My husband and I never quite approved of her, for she was several years older than Grace, and had such pronounced modern ideas that we didn't think her a suitable companion for our daughter, but you know how girls are with their 'crushes'. The more we objected to her going with Fanny, the more she used to seek her company, and we were both at our wits' ends when the Briggs girl was drowned while swimming at Asbury Park. I hate to say it, but it was almost a positive relief to us when the news came. Grace was almost broken-hearted about it at first, but she met Charley this summer, and I haven't heard her mention Fanny's name since her engagement until just now."

"Ah?" de Grandin tweaked the tip of his mustache meditatively. "And perhaps Mademoiselle Grace was somewhere to be reminded of Mademoiselle Fanny last night?"

"No," Mrs. Weaver replied, "she went with a crowd of young folks to hear Maundy preach. There was a big party of them at the tabernacle—I'm afraid they went more to make fun than in a religious frame of mind, but he made quite an impression on Grace, she told us."

"*Feu de Dieu!*" de Grandin exploded, twisting his mustache furiously. "Do you tell me so, *Madame?* This is of the interest. *Madame*, I salute you," he bowed formally to Mrs. Weaver, then seized me by the arm and fairly dragged me away.

"Trowbridge, my friend," he informed me as we descended the steps of the Weaver portico, "this business, it has *l'odeur du poisson*—how is it you say?—the fishy smell."

"What do you mean?" I asked.

"*Parbleu*, what should I mean except that we go to interview this Monsieur Everard Maundy immediately, right away, at once? *Mordieu*, I damn think I have the tail of this mystery in my hand, and may the blight of prohibition fall upon France if I do not twist it!"

*

The Rev. Everard Maundy's rooms in the Tremont Hotel were not hard to locate, for a constant stream of visitors went to and from them.

"Have you an appointment with Mr. Maundy?" the secretary asked as we were ushered into the ante-room.

"Not we," de Grandin denied, "but if you will be so kind as to tell him that Dr. Jules de Grandin, of the Paris *Sûreté*, desires to speak with him for five small minutes, I shall be in your debt."

The young man looked doubtful, but de Grandin's steady, catlike stare never wavered, and he finally rose and took our message to his employer.

In a few minutes he returned and admitted us to the big room where the evangelist received his callers behind a wide, flat-topped desk.

"Ah, Mr. de Grandin," the exhorter began with a professionally bland smile as we entered, "you are from France, are you not, sir? What can I do to help you toward the light?"

"*Cordieu, Monsieur*," de Grandin barked, for once forgetting his courtesy and ignoring the preacher's outstretched hand, "you can do much. You can explain these so unexplainable suicides which have taken place during the past week—the time you have preached here. That is the light we do desire to see."

Maundy's face went masklike and expressionless. "Suicides? Suicides?" he echoed. "What should I know of——"

The Frenchman shrugged his narrow shoulders impatiently. "We do fence with words, *Monsieur*," he interrupted testily. "Behold the facts: Messieurs Planz and Nixon, young men with no reason for such desperate deeds, did kill themselves by violence; Madame Westerfelt and her two daughters, who were happy in their home, as everyone thought, did hurl themselves from an hotel window; a little schoolgirl hanged herself; last night my good friend Trowbridge, who never understandingly harmed man or beast, and whose life is dedicated to the healing of the sick, did almost take his life; and this very morning a young girl, wealthy, beloved, with every reason to be happy, did almost succeed in dispatching herself.

"Now, *Monsieur le prédicateur*, the only thing this miscellaneous assortment of persons had in common is the fact that *each of them did hear you preach the night before, or the same night, he attempted self-destruction*. That is the light we seek. Explain us the mystery, if you please."

Maundy's lean, rugged face had undergone a strange transformation while the little Frenchman spoke. Gone was his smug, professional smirk, gone the forced and meaningless expression of benignity, and in their place a look of such anguish and horror as might rest on the face of one who hears his sentence of damnation read.

"Don't—don't!" he besought, covering his writhing face with his hands and bowing his head upon his desk while his shoulders shook with deep, soul-racking sobs. "Oh, miserable me! My sin has found me out!"

For a moment he wrestled in spiritual anguish, then raised his stricken countenance and regarded us with tear-dimmed eyes. "I am the greatest sinner in the world," he announced sorrowfully. "There is no hope for me on earth or yet in heaven!"

De Grandin tweaked the ends of his mustache alternately as he gazed curiously at the man before us. "*Monsieur*," he replied at length, "I think you do exaggerate. There are surely greater sinners than you. But if you would shrive you of the sin which gnaws your heart, I pray you shed what light you can upon these deaths, for there may be more to follow, and who knows that I shall not be able to stop them if you will but tell me all?"

"*Mea culpa!*" Maundy exclaimed, and struck his chest with his clenched fists like a Hebrew prophet of old. "In my younger days, gentlemen, before I dedicated myself to the salvaging of souls, I was a scoffer. What I could not feel or weigh or measure, I disbelieved. I mocked at all religion and sneered at all the things which others held sacred.

"One night I went to a Spiritualistic séance, intent on scoffing, and forced my young wife to accompany me. The medium was an old colored woman, wrinkled, half-blind and unbelievably ignorant, but she had something—some secret power—which was denied the rest of us. Even I, atheist and derider of the truth that I was, could see that.

"As the old woman called on the spirits of the departed, I laughed out loud, and told her it was all a fake. The negress came out of her trance and turned her deep-set, burning old eyes on me. 'White man,' she said, 'yuh is gwine ter feel mighty sorry fo' dem words. Ah tells yuh de speerits can heah whut yuh says, an' dey will take deir revenge on yuh an' yours—yas, an' on dem as follers yuh—till yuh wishes yo' tongue had been cut out befo' yuh said dem words dis yere night.'

"I tried to laugh at her—to curse her for a sniveling old faker—but there was something so terrible in her wrinkled old face that the words froze on my lips, and I hurried away.

"The next night my wife—my young, lovely bride—drowned herself in the river, and I have been a marked man ever since. Wherever I go it is the same. God has seen fit to open my eyes to the light of Truth and give me words to place His message before His people, and many who come to sneer at me go away believers; but wherever throngs gather to hear me bear my testimony there are always these tragedies. Tell me, gentlemen" —he threw out his hands in a gesture of surrender—"must I forever cease to preach the message of the Lord to His people? I have told myself that these self-murders would have occurred whether I came to town or not, but—is this a judgment which pursues me forever?"

Jules de Grandin regarded him thoughtfully. "*Monsieur*," he murmured, "I fear you make the mistakes we are all too prone to make. You do saddle *le bon Dieu* with all the sins with which the face of man is blackened. What if this were no judgment of heaven, but a curse of a very different sort, *hein?*"

"You mean the devil might be striving to overthrow the effects of my work?" the other asked, a light of hope breaking over his haggard face.

"U'm, perhaps; let us take that for our working hypothesis," de Grandin replied. "At present we may not say whether it be devil or devilkin which dogs your footsteps; but at the least we are greatly indebted to you for what you have told. Go, my friend; continue to preach the Truth as you conceive the Truth to be, and may the God of all peoples uphold your hands. Me, I have other work to do, but it may be scarcely less important." He bowed formally and, turning on his heel, strode quickly from the room.

"That's the most fantastic story I ever heard!" I declared as we entered the hotel elevator. "The idea! As if an ignorant old negress could put a curse on——"

"*Zut!*" de Grandin shut me off. "You are a most excellent physician in the State of New Jersey, Friend Trowbridge, but have you ever been in Martinique, or Haiti, or in the jungles of the Congo Belgique?"

"Of course not," I admitted, "but——"

"I have. I have seen things so strange among the *Voudois* people that you would wish to have me committed to a mad-house did I but relate them to you. However, as that Monsieur Kipling says, 'that is another story.' At the present we are pledged to the solving of another mystery. Let us go to your house. I would think, I would consider all this business-of-the-monkey. *Pardieu*, it has as many angles as a diamond cut in Amsterdam!"

"Tell me, Friend Trowbridge," he demanded as we concluded our evening meal, "have you perhaps among your patients some young man who has met with a great sorrow recently; some-one who has sustained a loss of wife or child or parents?"

I looked at him in amazement, but the serious expression on his little heart-shaped face told me he was in earnest, not making some ill-timed jest at my expense.

"Why, yes," I responded. "There is young Alvin Spence. His wife died in childbirth last June, and the poor chap has been half beside himself ever since. Thank God I was out of town at the time and didn't have the responsibility of the case."

"Thank God, indeed," de Grandin nodded gravely. "It is not easy for us, though we do ply our trade among the dying, to tell those who remain behind of their bereavement. But this Monsieur Spence; will you call on him this evening? Will you give him a ticket to the lecture of Monsieur Maundy?"

"No!" I blazed, half rising from my chair. "I've known that boy since he was a little toddler—knew his dead wife from child-hood, too; and if you're figuring on making him the subject of some experiment——"

"Softly, my friend," he besought. "There is a terrible Thing loose among us. Remember the noble martyrs of science, those so magnificent men who risked their lives that yellow fever and malaria should be no more. Was not their work a holy one? Cer-tainly. I do but wish that this young man may attend the lecture tonight, and on my honor, I shall guard him until all danger of attempted self-murder is passed. You will do what I say?"

He was so earnest in his plea that, though I felt like an accessory before the fact in a murder, I agreed.

Meantime, his little blue eyes snapping and sparkling with the zest of the chase, de Grandin had busied himself with the telephone directory, looking up a number of addresses, culling through them, discarding some, adding others, until he had obtained a list of some five or six. "Now, *mon vieux*," he begged as I made ready to visit Alvin Spence on my treacherous errand, "I would that you convey me to the rectory of St. Benedict's Church. The priest in charge there is Irish, and the Irish have the gift of seeing things which you colder-blooded Saxons may not. I must have a confab with this good Father O'Brien before I can permit that you interview the young Monsieur Spence. *Mordieu*, me, I am a scientist; no murderer!"

I drove him past the rectory and parked my motor at the curb, waiting impatiently while he thundered at the door with the handle of his ebony walking stick. His knock was answered by a little old man in clerical garb and a face as round and ruddy as a winter apple.

De Grandin spoke hurriedly to him in a low voice, waving his hands, shaking his head, shrugging his shoulders, as was his wont when the earnestness of his argument bore him before it. The priest's round face showed first incredulity, then mild skepticism, finally absorbed interest. In a moment the pair of them had vanished inside the house, leaving me to cool my heels in the bitter March air.

"You were long enough," I grumbled as he emerged from the rectory.

"*Pardieu*, yes, just long enough," he agreed. "I did accomplish my purpose, and no visit is either too long or too short when you can say that. Now to the house of the good Monsieur Spence, if you will. *Mordieu*, but we shall see what we shall see this night!"

Six hours later de Grandin and I crouched shivering at the roadside where the winding, serpentine Albemarle Pike dips into the hollow beside the Lonesome Swamp. The wind which had been trenchant as a shrew's tongue earlier in the evening had died away, and a hard, dull bitterness of cold hung over the hills and hollows of the rolling country-side. From the wide salt marshes where the bay's tide crept up to mingle with the swamp's brackish waters twice a day there came great sheets of brumous, impenetrable vapor which shrouded the landscape and distorted commonplace objects into hideous, gigantic monstrosities.

"*Mort d'un petit bonhomme*, my friend," de Grandin commented between chattering teeth, "I do not like this place; it has an evil air. There are spots where the very earth does breathe of unholy deeds, and by the sacred name of a rooster, this is one such. Look you at this accursed fog. Is it not as if the specters of those drowned at sea were marching up the shore this night?"

"Umph!" I replied, sinking my neck lower in the collar of my ulster and silently cursing myself for a fool.

A moment's silence, then: "You are sure Monsieur Spence must come this way? There is no other road by which he can reach his home?"

"Of course not," I answered shortly. "He lives out in the new Weiss development with his mother and sister—you were there this evening—and this is the only direct motor route to the subdivision from the city."

"Ah, that is well," he replied, hitching the collar of his great-coat higher about his ears. "You will recognize his car—surely?"

"I'll try to," I promised, "but you can't be sure of anything on a night like this. I'd not guarantee to pick out my own—there's somebody pulling up beside the road now," I interrupted myself as a roadster came to an abrupt halt and stood panting, its headlights forming vague, luminous spots in the haze.

"*Mais oui*," he agreed, "and no one stops at this spot for any good until *It* has been conquered. Come, let us investigate." He started forward, body bent, head advanced, like a motion picture conception of an Indian on the warpath.

Half a hundred stealthy steps brought us abreast of the parked car. Its occupant was sitting back on the driving seat, his hands resting listlessly on the steering wheel, his eyes up-turned, as though he saw a vision in the trailing wisps of fog before him. I needed no second chance to recognize Alvin Spence, though the rapt look upon his white, set face trans-figured it almost beyond recognition. He was like a poet be-holding the beatific vision of his mistress or a medieval eremite gazing through the opened portals of Paradise.

"A-a-ah!" de Grandin's whisper cut like a wire-edged knife through the silence of the fog-bound air, "do you behold it, Friend Trowbridge?"

"Wha——" I whispered back, but broke the syllable half uttered. Thin, tenuous, scarcely to be distinguished from the lazily drifting festoons of the fog itself, there was a *something* in midair before the car where Alvin Spence sat with his yearning soul looking from his eyes. I seemed to see clear through the thing, yet its outlines were plainly perceptible, and as I looked and looked again, I recognized the unmistakable features of Dorothy Spence, the young man's dead wife. Her body—if the tenuous, ethereal mass of static vapor could be called such—was bare of clothing, and seemed endued with a voluptuous grace and allure the living woman had never possessed, but her face was that of the young woman who had lain in Rosedale Cemetery for three-quarters of a year. If ever living man be-held the simulacrum of the dead, we three gazed on the wraith of Dorothy Spence that moment.

"Dorothy—my beloved, my dear, my dear!" the man half whispered, half sobbed, stretching forth his hands to the spirit-woman, then falling back on the seat as the vision seemed to elude his grasp when a sudden puff of breeze stirred the fog.

We could not catch the answer he received, close as we stood, but we could see the pale, curving lips frame the single word, "Come!" and saw the transparent arms stretched out to beckon him forward.

The man half rose from his seat, then sank back, set his face in sudden resolution and plunged his hand into the pocket of his overcoat.

Beside me de Grandin had been fumbling with something in his inside pocket. As Alvin Spence drew forth his hand and the dull gleam of a polished revolver shone in the light from his dashboard lamp, the Frenchman leaped forward like a panther. "Stop him, Friend Trowbridge!" he called shrilly, and to the hovering vision:

"Avaunt, accursed one! Begone, thou exile from heaven! Away, snake-spawn!"

As he shouted he drew a tiny pellet from his inner pocket and hurled it point-blank through the vaporous body of the specter.

Even as I seized Spence's hand and fought with him for possession of the pistol, I saw the transformation from the tail of my eye. As de Grandin's missile tore through its unsubstantial substance, the vision-woman seemed to shrink in upon herself, to become suddenly more compact, thinner, scrawny. Her rounded bosom flattened to mere folds of leatherlike skin stretched drum-tight above staring ribs, her slender graceful hands were horrid, claw-tipped talons, and the yearning, enticing face of Dorothy Spence became a mask of hideous, implacable hate, great-eyed, thin-lipped, beak-nosed—such a face as the demons of hell might show after a million million years of burning in the infernal fires. A screech like the keening of all the owls in the world together split the fog-wrapped stillness of the night, and the monstrous thing before us seemed suddenly to shrivel, shrink to a mere spot of baleful, phosphorescent fire, and disappear like a snuffed-out candle's flame.

Spence saw it, too. The pistol dropped from his nerveless fingers to the car's floor with a soft thud, and his arm went limp in my grasp as he fell forward in a dead faint.

"*Parbleu*," de Grandin swore softly as he climbed into the unconscious lad's car. "Let us drive forward, friend Trowbridge. We will take him home and administer a soporific. He must sleep, this poor one, or the memory of what we have shown him will rob him of his reason."

So we carried Alvin Spence to his home, administered a hypnotic and left him in the care of his wondering mother with instructions to repeat the dose if he should wake.

It was a mile or more to the nearest bus station, and we set out at a brisk walk, our heels hitting sharply against the frosty concrete of the road.

"What in the world was it, de Grandin?" I asked as we

marched in step down the darkened highway. "It was the most horrible——"

"*Parbleu*," he interrupted, "someone comes this way in a monstrous hurry!"

His remark was no exaggeration. Driven as though pursued by all the furies from pandemonium, came a light motor car with plain black sides and a curving top. "Look out!" the driver warned as he recognized me and came to a bumping halt. "Look out, Dr. Trowbridge, it's walking! It got out and walked!"

De Grandin regarded him with an expression of comic bewilderment. "Now what is it that walks, *mon brave?*" he demanded. "*Mordieu*, you chatter like a monkey with a handful of hot chestnuts! What is it that walks, and why must we look out for it, *hein?*"

"Sile Gregory," the young man answered. "He died this mornin', an' Mr. Johnson took him to th' parlors to fix 'im up, an' sent me an' Joe Williams out with him this evenin'. I was just drivin' up to th' house, an' Joe hopped out to give me a lift with th' casket, an' old Silas *got up an' walked away!* An' Mr. Johnson embalmed 'im this mornin', I tell you!"

"*Nom d'un chou-fleur!*" de Grandin shot back. "And where did this so remarkable demonstration take place, *mon vieux?* Also, what of the excellent Williams, your partner?"

"I don't know, an' I don't care," the other replied. "When a dead corpse I saw embalmed this mornin' gets outa its casket an' walks, I ain't gonna wait for nobody. Jump up here, if you want to go with me; I ain't gonna stay here no longer!"

"*Bien*," de Grandin acquiesced. "Go your way, my excellent one. Should we encounter your truant corpse, we will direct him to his waiting *bière.*"

The young man waited no second invitation, but started his car down the road at a speed which would bring him into certain trouble if observed by a state trooper.

"Now, what the devil do you make of that?" I asked. "I know Johnson, the funeral director, well, and I always thought he had a pretty level-headed crowd of boys about his place, but if that lad hasn't been drinking some powerful liquor, I'll be——"

"Not necessarily, my friend," de Grandin interrupted. "I

think it not at all impossible that he tells but the sober truth. It may well be that the dead do walk this road tonight."

I shivered with something other than the night's chill as he made the matter-of-fact assertion, but forbore pressing him for an explanation. There are times when ignorance is a happier portion than knowledge.

We had marched perhaps another quarter-mile in silence when de Grandin suddenly plucked my sleeve. "Have you noticed nothing, my friend?" he asked.

"What d'ye mean?" I demanded sharply, for my nerves were worn tender by the night's events.

"I am not certain, but it seems to me we are followed."

"Followed? Nonsense! *Who* would be following us?" I returned, unconsciously stressing the personal pronoun, for I had almost said, "What would follow us," and the implication raised by the impersonal form sent tiny shivers racing along my back and neck.

De Grandin cast me a quick, appraising glance, and I saw the ends of his spiked mustache lift suddenly as his lips framed a sardonic smile, but instead of answering he swung round on his heel and faced the shadows behind us.

"*Holà, Monsieur le Cadavre!*" he called sharply. "Here we are, and—*sang du diable!*—here we shall stand."

I looked at him in open-mouthed amazement, but his gaze was turned stedfastly on something half seen in the mist which lay along the road.

Next instant my heart seemed pounding through my ribs and my breath came hot and choking in my throat, for a tall, gangling man suddenly emerged from the fog and made for us at a shambling gait.

He was clothed in a long, old-fashioned double-breasted frock coat and stiffly starched shirt topped by a standing collar and white, ministerial tie. His hair was neatly, though somewhat unnaturally, arranged in a central part above a face the color and smoothness of wax, and little flecks of talcum powder still clung here and there to his eyebrows. No mistaking it! Johnson, artist that he was, had arrayed the dead farmer in the manner of all his kind for their last public appearance before relatives and friends. One look told me the horrible, incredible truth. It was the body of old Silas Gregory which stumbled toward us through the fog. Dressed, greased and powdered for its last, long rest, the thing came toward us with faltering, uncertain strides, and I noticed, with the sudden ability for minute inventory fear sometimes lends our senses, that his old, sunburned skin showed more than one brand where the formaldehyde embalming fluid had burned it.

In one long, thin hand the horrible thing grasped the helve of a farmyard ax, the other hand lay stiffly folded across the midriff as the embalmer had placed it when his professional ministrations were finished that morning.

"My God!" I cried, shrinking back toward the roadside. But de Grandin ran forward to meet the charging horror with a cry which was almost like a welcome.

"Stand clear, Friend Trowbridge," he warned, "we will fight this to a finish, I and It!" His little, round eyes were flashing with the zest of combat, his mouth was set in a straight, uncompromising line beneath the sharply waxed ends of his diminutive mustache, and his shoulders hunched forward like those of a practised wrestler before he comes to grips with his opponent.

With a quick, whipping motion, he ripped the razor-sharp blade of his sword-cane from its ebony sheath and swung the flashing steel in a whirring circle about his head, then sank to a defensive posture, one foot advanced, one retracted, the leg bent at the knee, the triple-edged sword dancing before him like the darting tongue of an angry serpent.

The dead thing never faltered in its stride. Three feet or so from Jules de Grandin it swung the heavy, rust-encrusted ax above its shoulder and brought it downward, its dull, lackluster eyes staring straight before it with an impassivity more terrible than any glare of hate.

"Sa ha!" de Grandin's blade flickered forward like a streak of storm lightning, and fleshed itself to the hilt in the corpse's shoulder.

He might as well have struck his steel into a bag of meal.

The ax descended with a crushing, devastating blow.

De Grandin leaped nimbly aside, disengaging his blade and swinging it again before him, but an expression of surprise—almost of consternation—was on his face.

I felt my mouth go dry with excitement, and a queer, weak

feeling hit me at the pit of the stomach. The Frenchman had driven his sword home with the skill of a practised fencer and the precision of a skilled anatomist. His blade had pierced the dead man's body at the junction of the short head of the biceps and the great pectoral muscle, at the coracoid process, inflicting a wound which should have paralyzed the arm—yet the terrible ax rose for a second blow as though de Grandin's steel had struck wide of the mark.

"Ah?" de Grandin nodded understandingly as he leaped backward, avoiding the ax-blade by the breadth of a hair. "*Bien. À la fin!*"

His defensive tactics changed instantly. Flickeringly his sword lashed forward, then came down and back with a sharp, whipping motion. The keen edge of the angular blade bit deeply into the corpse's wrist, laying bare the bone. Still the ax rose and fell and rose again.

Slash after slash de Grandin gave, his slicing cuts falling with almost mathematical precision in the same spot, shearing deeper and deeper into his dreadful opponent's wrist. At last, with a short, clucking exclamation, he drew his blade sharply back for the last time, severing the ax-hand from the arm.

The dead thing collapsed like a deflated balloon at his feet as hand and ax fell together to the cement roadway.

Quick as a mink, de Grandin thrust his left hand within his coat, drew forth a pellet similar to that with which he had transformed the counterfeit of Dorothy Spence, and hurled it straight into the upturned, ghastly-calm face of the mutilated body before him.

The dead lips did not part, for the embalmer's sutures had closed them forever that morning, but the body writhed upward from the road, and a groan which was a muted scream came from its flat chest. It twisted back and forth a moment, like a mortally stricken serpent in its death agony, then lay still.

Seizing the corpse by its grave-clothes, de Grandin dragged it through the line of roadside hazel bushes to the rim of the swamp, and busied himself cutting long, straight withes from the brushwood, then disappeared again behind the tangled branches. At last:

"It is finished," he remarked, stepping back to the road. "Let us go."

"Wha—what did you do?" I faltered.

"I did the needful, my friend. *Morbleu*, we had an evil, a very evil thing imprisoned in that dead man, and I took such precautions as were necessary to fix it in its prison. A stake through the heart, a severed head, and the whole firmly thrust into the ooze of the swamp—*voilà*. It will be long before other innocent ones are induced to destroy themselves by *that*."

"But——" I began.

"*Non, non*," he replied, half laughing. "*En avant, mon ami!* I would that we return home as quickly as possible. Much work creates much appetite, and I make small doubt that I shall consume the remainder of that so delicious apple pie which I could not eat at dinner."

Jules de Grandin regarded the empty plate before him with a look of comic tragedy. "May endless benisons rest upon your amiable cook, Friend Trowbridge," he pronounced, "but may the curse of heaven forever pursue the villain who manufactures the wofully inadequate pans in which she bakes her pies."

"Hang the pies, and the plate-makers, too!" I burst out. "You promised to explain all this hocus-pocus, and I've been patient long enough. Stop sitting there like a glutton, wailing for more pie, and tell me about it."

"Oh, the mystery?" he replied, stifling a yawn and lighting a cigarette. "That is simple, my friend, but these so delicious pies—however, I do digress:

"When first I saw the accounts of so many strange suicides within one little week I was interested, but not greatly puzzled. People have slain themselves since the beginning of time, and yet"—he shrugged his shoulders deprecatingly—"what is it that makes the hound scent his quarry, the war-horse sniff the battle afar off? Who can tell?

"I said to me: 'There is undoubtlessly more to these deaths than the newspapers have said. I shall investigate.'

"From the coroner's to the undertakers', and from the undertakers' to the physicians', yes, *parbleu!* and to the family residences, as well, I did go, gleaning here a bit and there a bit of information which seemed to mean nothing, but which might mean much did I but have other information to add to it.

"One thing I ascertained early: In each instance the suicides had been to hear this reverend Maundy the night before or the same night they did away with themselves. This was perhaps insignificant; perhaps it meant much. I determined to hear this Monsieur Maundy with my own two ears; but I would not hear him too close by.

"Forgive me, my friend, for I did make of you the guinea-pig for my laboratory experiment. You I left in a forward seat while the reverend gentleman preached, me, I stayed in the rear of the hall and used my eyes as well as my ears.

"What happened that night? Why, my good, kind Friend Trowbridge, who in all his life had done no greater wrong than thoughtlessly to kill a little, so harmless kitten, did almost *seemingly* commit suicide. But I was not asleep by the switch, my friend. Not Jules de Grandin! All the way home I saw you were *distrait*, and I did fear something would happen, and I did therefore watch beside your door with my eye and ear alternately glued to the keyhole. *Parbleu*, I entered the chamber not one little second too soon, either!

"'This is truly strange,' I tell me. 'My friend hears this preacher and nearly destroys himself. Six others have heard him, and have quite killed themselves. If Friend Trowbridge were haunted by the ghost of a dead kitten, why should not those others, who also undoubtlessly possessed distressing memories, have been hounded to their graves by them?'

"'There is no reason why they should not,' I tell me.

"Next morning comes the summons to attend the young Mademoiselle Weaver. She, too, have heard the preacher; she, too, have attempted her life. And what does she tell us? That she fancied the voice of her dead friend urged her to kill herself.

"'Ah, ha!' I say to me. 'This whatever-it-is which causes so much suicide may appeal by fear, or perhaps by love, or by whatever will most strongly affect the person who dies by his own hand. We must see this Monsieur Maundy. It is perhaps possible he can tell us much.'

"As yet I can see no light—I am still in darkness—but far ahead I already see the gleam of a promise of information. When we see Monsieur Everard Maundy and he tells us of his experience at that séance so many years ago—*parbleu*, I see it all, or almost all.

"Now, what was it acted as agent for that aged sorceress' curse?"

He elevated one shoulder and looked questioningly at me.

"How should I know?" I answered.

"Correct," he nodded, "how, indeed? Beyond doubt it were a spirit of some sort; what sort we do not know. Perhaps it were the spirit of some unfortunate who had destroyed himself and was earthbound as a consequence. There are such. And, as misery loves company in the proverb, so do these wretched ones seek to lure others to join them in their unhappy state. Or, maybe, it were an Elemental."

"A *what?*" I demanded.

"An Elemental—a Neutrarian."

"What the deuce is that?"

For answer he left the table and entered the library, returning with a small red-leather bound volume in his hand. "You have read the works of Monsieur Rossetti?" he asked.

"Yes."

"You recall his poem, *Eden Bowers*, perhaps?"

"H'm; yes, I've read it, but I never could make anything of it."

"Quite likely," he agreed, "its meaning is most obscure, but I shall enlighten you. *Attendez-moi!*"

Thumbing through the thin pages he began reading at random:

> It was Lilith, the wife of Adam,
> Not a drop of her blood was human,
> But she was made like a soft, sweet woman . . . .

> Lilith stood on the skirts of Eden,
> She was the first that thence was driven,
> With her was hell and with Eve was heaven . . . .

> What bright babes had Lilith and Adam,
> Shapes that coiled in the woods and waters,
> Glittering sons and radiant daughters . . . .

"You see, my friend?"

"No, I'm hanged if I do."

"Very well, then, according to the rabbinical lore, before Eve was created, Adam, our first father, had a demon wife named

Lilith. And by her he had many children, not human, nor yet wholly demon.

"For her sins Lilith was expelled from Eden's bowers, and Adam was given Eve to wife. With Lilith was driven out all her progeny by Adam, and Lilith and her half-man, half-demon brood declared war on Adam and Eve and their descendants for ever. These descendants of Lilith and Adam have ever since roamed the earth and air, incorporeal, having no bodies like men, yet having always a hatred for flesh and blood. Because they were the first, or elder race, they are sometimes called Elementals in the ancient lore; sometimes they are called Neutrarians, because they are neither wholly men nor wholly devils. Me, I do not take sides in the controversy; I care not what they are called, but I know what I have seen. I think it is highly possible those ancient Hebrews, misinterpreting the manifestations they observed, accounted for them by their so fantastic legends. We are told these Neutrarians or Elementals are immaterial beings. Absurd? Not necessarily. What is matter—material? Electricity, perhaps—a great system of law and order throughout the universe and all the millions of worlds extending throughout infinity.

"Very good, so far; but when we have said matter is electricity, what have we to say if asked, 'What is electricity?' Me, I think it a modification of the ether.

"'Very good,' you say; 'but what is ether?'

"*Parbleu*, I do not know. The matter—or material—of the universe is little, if anything, more than electrons flowing about in all directions. Now here, now there, the electrons coalesce and form what we call solids—rocks and trees and men and woman. But may they not coalesce at a different rate of speed, or vibration, to form beings which are real, with emotions and loves and hates similar to ours, yet for the most part invisible to us, as is the air? Why not? No man can truthfully say, 'I have seen the air,' yet no one is so great a fool as to doubt its existence for that reason."

"Yes, but we can see the effects of air," I objected. "Air in motion, for instance, becomes wind, and——"

"*Mort d'un crapaud!*" he burst out. "And have we not observed the effects of these Elementals—these Neutrarians, or whatsoever their name may be? How of the six suicides; how of that which tempted the young Mademoiselle Weaver and the young Monsieur Spence to self-murder? How of the cat which entered your room? Did we see no effects there, *hein?*"

"But the thing we saw with young Spence, and the cat, were visible," I objected.

"But of course. When you fancied you saw the cat, you were influenced from within, even as Mademoiselle Weaver was when she heard the voice of her dead friend. What we saw with the young Spence was the shadow of his desire—the intensified love and longing for his dead wife, plus the evil entity which urged him to unpardonable sin."

"Oh, all right," I conceded. "Go on with your theory."

He stared thoughtfully at the glowing tip of his cigarette a moment, then: "It has been observed, my friend, that he who goes to a Spiritualistic séance may come away with some evil spirit attached to him—whether it be a spirit which once inhabited human form or an Elemental, it is no matter; the evil ones swarm about the lowered lights of the Spiritualistic meeting as flies congregate at the honey-pot in summer. It appears such an one fastened to Everard Maundy. His wife was its first victim, afterward those who heard him preach were attacked.

"Consider the scene at the tabernacle when Monsieur Maundy preaches: Emotion, emotion—all is emotion; reason is lulled to sleep by the power of his words; and the minds of his hearers are not on their guard against the entrance of evil spirits; they are too intent on what he is saying. Their consciousness is absent. *Pouf!* The evil one fastens firmly on some unwary person, explores his innermost mind, finds out his weakest point of defense. With you it was the kitten; with young Mademoiselle Weaver, her dead friend; with Monsieur Spence, his lost wife. Even love can be turned to evil purposes by such an one.

"These things I did consider most carefully, and then I did enlist the services of young Monsieur Spence. You saw what you saw on the lonely road this night. Appearing to him in the form of his dead beloved, this wicked one had all but persuaded him to destroy himself when we intervened.

"*Très bien.* We triumphed then; the night before I had prevented your death. The evil one was angry at me; also it was frightened. If I continued, I would rob it of much prey, so it sought to do me harm. Me, I am ever on guard, for knowledge is power. It could not lead me to my death, and, being spirit, it could not directly attack me. It had recourse to its last resort. While the young undertaker's assistant was about to deliver the body of the old Monsieur Gregory, the spirit seized the corpse and animated it, then pursued me.

"Ha, almost, I thought, it had done for me at one time, for I forgot it was no living thing I fought, and attacked it as if it could be killed. But when I found my sword could not kill that which was already dead, I did cut off its so abominable hand. I am very clever, my friend. The evil spirit reaped small profits from fighting with me."

He made the boastful admission in all seriousness, entirely unaware of its sound, for to him it was but a straightforward statement of undisputed fact. I grinned in spite of myself, then curiosity got the better of amusement. "What were those little pellets you threw at the spirit when it was luring young Spence to commit suicide, and later at the corpse of Silas Gregory?" I asked.

"Ah"—his elfish smile flickered across his lips, then disappeared so quickly as it came—"it is better you do not ask me that, *mon cher*. Let it suffice when I tell you I convinced the good *Père* O'Brien that he should let me have what no layman is supposed to touch, that I might use the ammunition of heaven against the forces of hell."

"But how do we know this Elemental, or whatever it is, won't come back again?" I persisted.

"Little fear," he encouraged. "The resort to the dead man's body was its last desperate chance. Having elected to fight me physically, it must stand or fall by the result of the fight. Once inside the body, it could not quickly extricate itself. Half an hour, at least, must elapse before it could withdraw, and before that time had passed I had fixed it there for all time. The stake through the heart and the severed head makes that body as harmless as any other, and the wicked spirit which animated it must remain with the flesh it sought to pervert to its own evil ends henceforth and forever."

"But——"

"*Ah bah!*" He dropped his cigarette end into his empty coffee cup and yawned frankly. "We do talk too much, my friend. This night's work has made me heavy with sleep. Let us take a tiny sip of cognac, that the pie may not give us unhappy dreams, and then to bed. Tomorrow is another day, and who knows what new task lies before us?"

1927

STEPHEN VINCENT BENÉT

(1889–1943)

The King of the Cats

"But, my *dear*," said Mrs. Culverin, with a tiny gasp, "you can't actually mean—a *tail*!"

Mrs. Dingle nodded impressively. "Exactly. I've seen him. Twice. Paris, of course, and then, a command appearance at Rome—we were in the Royal box. He conducted—my dear, you've never heard such effects from an orchestra—and, my dear," she hesitated slightly, "he conducted *with it*."

"How perfectly, fascinatingly too horrid for words!" said Mrs. Culverin in a dazed but greedy voice. "We *must* have him to dinner as soon as he comes over—he is coming over, isn't he?"

"The twelfth," said Mrs. Dingle with a gleam in her eyes. "The New Symphony people have asked him to be guest-conductor for three special concerts—I do hope you can dine with *us* some night while he's here—he'll be very busy, of course —but he's promised to give us what time he can spare——"

"Oh, thank you, dear," said Mrs. Culverin, abstractedly, her last raid upon Mrs. Dingle's pet British novelist still fresh in her mind. "You're always so delightfully hospitable—but you mustn't wear yourself out—the rest of us must do *our* part—I know Henry and myself would be only too glad to——"

"That's very sweet of you, darling." Mrs. Dingle also remembered the larceny of the British novelist. "But we're just going to give Monsieur Tibault—sweet name, isn't it! They say he's descended from the Tybalt in 'Romeo and Juliet' and that's why he doesn't like Shakespeare—we're just going to give Monsieur Tibault the simplest sort of time—a little reception after his first concert, perhaps. He hates," she looked around the table, "large, mixed parties. And then, of course, his—er— little idiosyncrasy——" she coughed delicately. "It makes him feel a trifle shy with strangers."

"But I don't understand yet, Aunt Emily," said Tommy

Brooks, Mrs. Dingle's nephew. "Do you really mean this Tibault bozo has a tail? Like a monkey and everything?"

"Tommy dear," said Mrs. Culverin, crushingly, "in the first place Monsieur Tibault is not a bozo—he is a very distinguished musician—the finest conductor in Europe. And in the second place——"

"He has," Mrs. Dingle was firm. "He has a tail. He conducts with it."

"Oh, but honestly!" said Tommy, his ears pinkening. "I mean —of course, if you say so, Aunt Emily, I'm sure he has—but still, it sounds pretty steep, if you know what I mean! How about it, Professor Tatto?"

Professor Tatto cleared his throat. "Tck," he said, putting his fingertips together cautiously, "I shall be very anxious to see this Monsieur Tibault. For myself, I have never observed a genuine specimen of *homo caudatus*, so I should be inclined to doubt, and yet . . . In the Middle Ages, for instance, the belief in men—er—tailed or with caudal appendages of some sort, was both widespread and, as far as we can gather, well-founded. As late as the Eighteenth Century, a Dutch sea-captain with some character for veracity recounts the discovery of a pair of such creatures in the island of Formosa. They were in a low state of civilization, I believe, but the appendages in question were quite distinct. And in 1860, Dr. Grimbrook, the English surgeon, claims to have treated no less than three African natives with short but evident tails—though his testimony rests upon his unsupported word. After all, the thing is not impossible, though doubtless unusual. Web feet—rudimentary gills —these occur with some frequency. The appendix we have with us always. The chain of our descent from the ape-like form is by no means complete. For that matter," he beamed around the table, "what can we call the last few vertebrae of the normal spine but the beginnings of a concealed and rudimentary tail? Oh, yes—yes—it's possible—quite—that in an extraordinary case—a reversion to type—a survival—though, of course——"

"I told you so," said Mrs. Dingle triumphantly. "*Isn't* it fascinating? Isn't it, Princess?"

The Princess Vivrakanarda's eyes, blue as a field of larkspur, fathomless as the centre of heaven, rested lightly for a moment on Mrs. Dingle's excited countenance.

"Ve-ry fascinating," she said, in a voice like stroked, golden velvet. "I should like—I should like ve-ry much to meet this Monsieur Tibault."

"Well, *I* hope he breaks his neck!" said Tommy Brooks, under his breath—but nobody ever paid much attention to Tommy.

Nevertheless as the time for Mr. Tibault's arrival in these States drew nearer and nearer, people in general began to wonder whether the Princess had spoken quite truthfully—for there was no doubt of the fact that, up till then, she had been the unique sensation of the season—and you know what social lions and lionesses are.

It was, if you remember, a Siamese season, and genuine Siamese were at quite as much of a premium as Russian accents had been in the quaint old days when the Chauve-Souris was a novelty. The Siamese Art Theatre, imported at terrific expense, was playing to packed houses. "Gushuptzgu," an epic novel of Siamese farm life, in nineteen closely-printed volumes, had just been awarded the Nobel prize. Prominent pet-and-newt dealers reported no cessation in the appalling demand for Siamese cats. And upon the crest of this wave of interest in things Siamese, the Princess Vivrakanarda poised with the elegant nonchalance of a Hawaiian water-baby upon its surfboard. She was indispensable. She was incomparable. She was everywhere.

Youthful, enormously wealthy, allied on one hand to the Royal Family of Siam and on the other to the Cabots (and yet with the first eighteen of her twenty-one years shrouded from speculation in a golden zone of mystery), the mingling of races in her had produced an exotic beauty as distinguished as it was strange. She moved with a feline, effortless grace, and her skin was as if it had been gently powdered with tiny grains of the purest gold—yet the blueness of her eyes, set just a trifle slantingly, was as pure and startling as the sea on the rocks of Maine. Her brown hair fell to her knees—she had been offered extraordinary sums by the Master Barbers' Protective Association to have it shingled. Straight as a waterfall tumbling over brown rocks, it had a vague perfume of sandalwood and suave spices and held tints of rust and the sun. She did not talk very much—but then she did not have to—her voice had an odd, small, melodious huskiness that haunted the mind. She lived alone and was reputed to be very lazy—at least it was known that she slept during most of the day—but at night she bloomed like a moon-flower and a depth came into her eyes.

It was no wonder that Tommy Brooks fell in love with her. The wonder was that she let him. There was nothing exotic or distinguished about Tommy—he was just one of those pleasant, normal young men who seem created to carry on the bond business by reading the newspapers in the University Club during most of the day, and can always be relied upon at night to fill an unexpected hole in a dinner-party. It is true that the Princess could hardly be said to do more than tolerate any of her suitors—no one had ever seen those aloofly arrogant eyes enliven at the entrance of any male. But she seemed to be able to tolerate Tommy a little more than the rest—and that young man's infatuated day-dreams were beginning to be beset by smart solitaires and imaginary apartments on Park Avenue, when the famous M. Tibault conducted his first concert at Carnegie Hall.

Tommy Brooks sat beside the Princess. The eyes he turned upon her were eyes of longing and love, but her face was as impassive as a mask, and the only remark she made during the preliminary bustlings was that there seemed to be a number of people in the audience. But Tommy was relieved, if anything, to find her even a little more aloof than usual, for, ever since Mrs. Culverin's dinner-party, a vague disquiet as to the possible impression which this Tibault creature might make upon her had been growing in his mind. It shows his devotion that he was present at all. To a man whose simple Princetonian nature found in "Just a Little Love, a Little Kiss," the quintessence of musical art, the average symphony was a positive torture, and he looked forward to the evening's programme itself with a grim, brave smile.

"Ssh!" said Mrs. Dingle, breathlessly. "He's coming!" It seemed to the startled Tommy as if he were suddenly back in the trenches under a heavy barrage, as M. Tibault made his entrance to a perfect bombardment of applause.

Then the enthusiastic noise was sliced off in the middle and a gasp took its place—a vast, windy sigh, as if every person in that multitude had suddenly said, "Ah." For the papers had not lied about him. The tail was there.

They called him theatric—but how well he understood the uses of theatricalism! Dressed in unrelieved black from head to foot (the black dress-shirt had been a special token of Mussolini's esteem), he did not walk on, he strolled, leisurely, easily, aloofly, the famous tail curled nonchalantly about one wrist—a suave, black panther lounging through a summer garden with that little mysterious weave of the head that panthers have when they pad behind bars—the glittering darkness of his eyes unmoved by any surprise or elation. He nodded, twice, in regal acknowledgment, as the clapping reached an apogee of frenzy. To Tommy there was something dreadfully reminiscent of the Princess in the way he nodded. Then he turned to his orchestra.

A second and louder gasp went up from the audience at this point, for, as he turned, the tip of that incredible tail twined with dainty carelessness into some hidden pocket and produced a black baton. But Tommy did not even notice. He was looking at the Princess instead.

She had not even bothered to clap, at first, but now— He had never seen her moved like this, never. She was not applauding, her hands were clenched in her lap, but her whole body was rigid, rigid as a steel bar, and the blue flowers of her eyes were bent upon the figure of M. Tibault in a terrible concentration. The pose of her entire figure was so still and intense that for an instant Tommy had the lunatic idea that any moment she might leap from her seat beside him as lightly as a moth, and land, with no sound, at M. Tibault's side to—yes—to rub her proud head against his coat in worship. Even Mrs. Dingle would notice in a moment.

"Princess——" he said, in a horrified whisper, "Princess——"

Slowly the tenseness of her body relaxed, her eyes veiled again, she grew calm.

"Yes, Tommy?" she said, in her usual voice, but there was still something about her . . .

"Nothing, only—oh, hang—he's starting!" said Tommy, as M. Tibault, his hands loosely clasped before him, turned and *faced* the audience. His eyes dropped, his tail switched once impressively, then gave three little preliminary taps with his baton on the floor.

Seldom has Gluck's overture to "Iphigenie in Aulis" received such an ovation. But it was not until the Eighth Symphony that the hysteria of the audience reached its climax. Never before had the New Symphony played so superbly—and certainly never before had it been led with such genius. Three prominent conductors in the audience were sobbing with the despairing admiration of envious children toward the close, and one at least was heard to offer wildly ten thousand dollars to a well-known facial surgeon there present for a shred of evidence that tails of some variety could by any stretch of science be grafted upon a normally decaudate form. There was no doubt about it—no mortal hand and arm, be they ever so dexterous, could combine the delicate elan and powerful grace displayed in every gesture of M. Tibault's tail.

A sable staff, it dominated the brasses like a flicker of black lightning; an ebon, elusive whip, it drew the last exquisite breath of melody from the woodwinds and ruled the stormy strings like a magician's rod. M. Tibault bowed and bowed again—roar after roar of frenzied admiration shook the hall to its foundations—and when he finally staggered, exhausted, from the platform, the president of the Wednesday Sonata Club was only restrained by force from flinging her ninety-thousand-dollar string of pearls after him in an excess of aesthetic appreciation. New York had come and seen—and New York was conquered. Mrs. Dingle was immediately besieged by reporters, and Tommy Brooks looked forward to the "little party" at which he was to meet the new hero of the hour with feelings only a little less lugubrious than those that would have come to him just before taking his seat in the electric chair.

The meeting between his Princess and M. Tibault was worse and better than he expected. Better because, after all, they did not say much to each other—and worse because it seemed to him, somehow, that some curious kinship of mind between them made words unnecessary. They were certainly the most distinguished-looking couple in the room, as he bent over her hand. "So darlingly foreign, both of them, and yet so different," babbled Mrs. Dingle—but Tommy couldn't agree.

They were different, yes—the dark, lithe stranger with the bizarre appendage tucked carelessly in his pocket, and the blue-eyed, brown-haired girl. But that difference only accentuated what they had in common—something in the way they moved, in the suavity of their gestures, in the set of their eyes. Something deeper, even, than race. He tried to puzzle it out— then, looking around at the others, he had a flash of revelation. It was as if that couple were foreign, indeed—not only to New York but to all common humanity. As if they were polite guests from a different star.

Tommy did not have a very happy evening, on the whole. But his mind worked slowly, and it was not until much later that the mad suspicion came upon him in full force.

Perhaps he is not to be blamed for his lack of immediate comprehension. The next few weeks were weeks of bewildered misery for him. It was not that the Princess's attitude toward him had changed—she was just as tolerant of him as before, but M. Tibault was always there. He had a faculty of appearing as out of thin air—he walked, for all his height, as lightly as a butterfly—and Tommy grew to hate that faintest shuffle on the carpet that announced his presence.

And then, hang it all, the man was so smooth, so infernally, unrufflably smooth! He was never out of temper, never embarrassed. He treated Tommy with the extreme of urbanity, and yet his eyes mocked, deep-down, and Tommy could do nothing. And, gradually, the Princess became more and more drawn to this stranger, in a soundless communion that found little need for speech—and that, too, Tommy saw and hated, and that, too, he could not mend.

He began to be haunted not only by M. Tibault in the flesh, but by M. Tibault in the spirit. He slept badly, and when he slept, he dreamed—of M. Tibault, a man no longer, but a shadow, a spectre, the limber ghost of an animal whose words came purringly between sharp little pointed teeth. There was certainly something odd about the whole shape of the fellow —his fluid ease, the mould of his head, even the cut of his fingernails—but just what it was escaped Tommy's intensest cogitation. And when he did put his finger on it at length, at first he refused to believe.

A pair of petty incidents decided him, finally, against all reason. He had gone to Mrs. Dingle's, one winter afternoon, hoping to find the Princess. She was out with his aunt, but was expected back for tea, and he wandered idly into the library to wait. He was just about to switch on the lights, for the library was always dark even in summer, when he heard a sound of light breathing that seemed to come from the leather couch in the corner. He approached it cautiously and dimly made out the form of M. Tibault, curled up on the couch, peacefully asleep.

The sight annoyed Tommy so that he swore under his breath and was back near the door on his way out, when the feeling we all know and hate, the feeling that eyes we cannot see are watching us, arrested him. He turned back—M. Tibault had not moved a muscle of his body to all appearance—but his eyes were open now. And those eyes were black and human no longer. They were green—Tommy could have sworn it—and he could have sworn that they had no bottom and gleamed like little emeralds in the dark. It only lasted a moment, for Tommy pressed the light-button automatically—and there was M. Tibault, his normal self, yawning a little but urbanely apologetic, but it gave Tommy time to think. Nor did what happened a trifle later increase his peace of mind.

They had lit a fire and were talking in front of it—by now Tommy hated M. Tibault so thoroughly that he felt that odd yearning for his company that often occurs in such cases. M. Tibault was telling some anecdote and Tommy was hating him worse than ever for basking with such obvious enjoyment in the heat of the flames and the ripple of his own voice.

Then they heard the street-door open, and M. Tibault jumped up—and jumping, caught one sock on a sharp corner of the brass fire-rail and tore it open in a jagged flap. Tommy looked down mechanically at the tear—a second's glance, but enough—for M. Tibault, for the first time in Tommy's experience, lost his temper completely. He swore violently in some spitting, foreign tongue—his face distorted suddenly—he clapped his hand over his sock. Then, glaring furiously at Tommy, he fairly sprang from the room, and Tommy could hear him scaling the stairs in long, agile bounds.

Tommy sank into a chair, careless for once of the fact that he heard the Princess's light laugh in the hall. He didn't want to see the Princess. He didn't want to see anybody. There had been something revealed when M. Tibault had torn that hole in his sock—and it was not the skin of a man. Tommy had caught a glimpse of—black plush. Black velvet. And then had come M. Tibault's sudden explosion of fury. Good *Lord*—did the man wear black velvet stockings under his ordinary socks? Or could he—could he—but here Tommy held his fevered head in his hands.

He went to Professor Tatto that evening with a series of hypothetical questions, but as he did not dare confide his real suspicions to the Professor, the hypothetical answers he received served only to confuse him the more. Then he thought of Billy Strange. Billy was a good sort, and his mind had a turn for the bizarre. Billy might be able to help.

He couldn't get hold of Billy for three days and lived through the interval in a fever of impatience. But finally they had dinner together at Billy's apartment, where his queer books were, and Tommy was able to blurt out the whole disordered jumble of his suspicions.

Billy listened without interrupting until Tommy was quite through. Then he pulled at his pipe. "But, my dear *man*——" he said, protestingly.

"Oh, I know—I know——" said Tommy, and waved his hands, "I know I'm crazy—you needn't tell me that—but I tell you, the man's a cat all the same—no, I don't see how he could be, but he is—why, hang it, in the first place, everybody knows he's got a tail!"

"Even so," said Billy, puffing. "Oh, my dear Tommy, I don't doubt you saw, or think you saw, everything you say. But, even so——" He shook his head.

"But what about those other birds, werwolves and things?" said Tommy.

Billy looked dubious. "We-ll," he admitted, "you've got me there, of course. At least—a tailed man *is* possible. And the yarns about werwolves go back far enough, so that—well, I wouldn't say there aren't or haven't been werwolves—but then I'm willing to believe more things than most people. But a wer-cat—or a man that's a cat and a cat that's a man—honestly, Tommy——"

"If I don't get some real advice I'll go clean off my hinge. For Heaven's sake, tell me something to *do!*"

"Lemme think," said Billy. "First, you're pizen-sure this man is——"

"A cat. Yeah," and Tommy nodded violently.

"Check. And second—if it doesn't hurt your feelings, Tommy—you're afraid this girl you're in love with has—er—at least a streak of—felinity—in her—and so she's drawn to him?"

"Oh, Lord, Billy, if I only knew!"

"Well—er—suppose she really is, too, you know—would you still be keen on her?"

"I'd marry her if she turned into a dragon every Wednesday!" said Tommy, fervently.

Billy smiled. "H'm," he said, "then the obvious thing to do is to get rid of this M. Tibault. Lemme think."

He thought about two pipes full, while Tommy sat on pins and needles. Then, finally, he burst out laughing.

"What's so darn funny?" said Tommy, aggrievedly.

"Nothing, Tommy, only I've just thought of a stunt—something so blooming crazy—but if he is—h'm—what you think he is—it *might* work——" And, going to the bookcase, he took down a book.

"If you think you're going to quiet my nerves by reading me a bedtime story——"

"Shut up, Tommy, and listen to this—if you really want to get rid of your feline friend."

"What is it?"

"Book of Agnes Repplier's. About cats. Listen.

"'There is also a Scandinavian version of the ever famous story which Sir Walter Scott told to Washington Irving, which Monk Lewis told to Shelley and which, in one form or another, we find embodied in the folklore of every land'—now, Tommy, pay attention—'the story of the traveller who saw within a ruined abbey, a procession of cats, lowering into a grave a little coffin with a crown upon it. Filled with horror, he hastened from the spot; but when he had reached his destination, he could not forbear relating to a friend the wonder he had seen. Scarcely had the tale been told when his friend's cat, who lay curled up tranquilly by the fire, sprang to its feet, cried out, "Then I am the King of the Cats!" and disappeared in a flash up the chimney.'

"Well?" said Billy, shutting the book.

"By gum!" said Tommy, staring. "By gum! Do you think there's a chance?"

"*I* think we're both in the booby-hatch. But if you want to try it——"

"Try it! I'll spring it on him the next time I see him. But—listen—I can't make it a ruined abbey——"

"Oh, use your imagination! Make it Central Park—anywhere. Tell it as if it happened to you—seeing the funeral procession and all that. You can lead into it somehow—let's see—some general line—oh, yes—'Strange, isn't it, how fact so often copies fiction. Why, only yesterday——' See?"

"Strange, isn't it, how fact so often copies fiction," repeated Tommy dutifully. "Why, only yesterday——"

"I happened to be strolling through Central Park when I saw something very odd."

"I happened to be strolling through—here, gimme that book!" said Tommy, "I want to learn the rest of it by heart!"

Mrs. Dingle's farewell dinner to the famous Monsieur Tibault, on the occasion of his departure for his Western tour, was looked forward to with the greatest expectations. Not only would everybody be there, including the Princess Vivrakanarda, but Mrs. Dingle, a hinter if there ever was one, had let it be known that at this dinner an announcement of very unusual interest to Society might be made. So everyone, for once, was almost on time, except for Tommy. He was at least fifteen minutes early, for he wanted to have speech with his aunt alone. Unfortunately, however, he had hardly taken off his overcoat when she was whispering some news in his ear so rapidly that he found it difficult to understand a word of it.

"And you mustn't breathe it to a soul!" she ended, beaming. "That is, not before the announcement—I think we'll have *that* with the salad—people never pay very much attention to salad——"

"Breathe what, Aunt Emily?" said Tommy, confused.

"The Princess, darling—the dear Princess and Monsieur Tibault—they just got engaged this afternoon, dear things! Isn't it *fascinating*?"

"Yeah," said Tommy, and started to walk blindly through the nearest door. His aunt restrained him.

"Not there, dear—not in the library. You can congratulate them later. They're just having a sweet little moment alone there now——" And she turned away to harry the butler, leaving Tommy stunned.

But his chin came up after a moment. He wasn't beaten yet.

"Strange, isn't it, how often fact copies fiction?" he repeated to himself in dull mnemonics, and, as he did so, he shook his fist at the library door.

Mrs. Dingle was wrong, as usual. The Princess and M. Tibault were not in the library—they were in the conservatory, as Tommy discovered when he wandered aimlessly past the glass doors.

He didn't mean to look, and after a second he turned away. But that second was enough.

Tibault was seated in a chair and she was crouched on a stool at his side, while his hand, softly, smoothly, stroked her brown hair. Black cat and Siamese kitten. Her face was hidden from Tommy, but he could see Tibault's face. And he could hear.

They were not talking, but there was a sound between them. A warm and contented sound like the murmur of giant bees in a hollow tree—a golden, musical rumble, deep-throated, that came from Tibault's lips and was answered by hers—a golden purr.

Tommy found himself back in the drawing-room, shaking hands with Mrs. Culverin, who said, frankly, that she had seldom seen him look so pale.

The first two courses of the dinner passed Tommy like dreams, but Mrs. Dingle's cellar was notable, and by the middle of the meat course, he began to come to himself. He had only one resolve now.

For the next few moments he tried desperately to break into the conversation, but Mrs. Dingle was talking, and even Gabriel will have a time interrupting Mrs. Dingle. At last, though, she paused for breath and Tommy saw his chance.

"Speaking of that," said Tommy, piercingly, without knowing in the least what he was referring to, "Speaking of that——"

"As I was saying," said Professor Tatto. But Tommy would not yield. The plates were being taken away. It was time for salad.

"Speaking of that," he said again, so loudly and strangely that Mrs. Culverin jumped and an awkward hush fell over the table. "Strange, isn't it, how often fact copies fiction?" There, he was started. His voice rose even higher. "Why, only to-day I was strolling through——" and, word for word, he repeated his lesson. He could see Tibault's eyes glowing at him, as he described the funeral. He could see the Princess, tense.

He could not have said what he had expected might happen when he came to the end; but it was not bored silence, everywhere, to be followed by Mrs. Dingle's acrid, "Well, Tommy, is that *quite* all?"

He slumped back in his chair, sick at heart. He was a fool and his last resource had failed. Dimly he heard his aunt's voice, saying, "Well, then——" and realized that she was about to make the fatal announcement.

But just then Monsieur Tibault spoke.

"One moment, Mrs. Dingle," he said, with extreme politeness, and she was silent. He turned to Tommy.

"You are—positive, I suppose, of what you saw this afternoon, Brooks?" he said, in tones of light mockery.

"Absolutely," said Tommy sullenly. "Do you think I'd——"

"Oh, no, no, no," Monsieur Tibault waved the implication aside, "but—such an interesting story—one likes to be sure of the details—and, of course, you *are* sure—*quite* sure—that the kind of crown you describe was on the coffin?"

"Of course," said Tommy, wondering, "but——"

"Then I'm the King of the Cats!" cried Monsieur Tibault in a voice of thunder, and, even as he cried it, the house-lights blinked—there was the soft thud of an explosion that seemed muffled in cotton-wool from the minstrel gallery—and the scene was lit for a second by an obliterating and painful burst of light that vanished in an instant and was succeeded by heavy, blinding clouds of white, pungent smoke.

"Oh, those *horrid* photographers," came Mrs. Dingle's voice in a melodious wail. "I *told* them not to take the flashlight picture till dinner was over, and now they've taken it *just* as I was nibbling lettuce!"

Someone tittered a little nervously. Someone coughed. Then, gradually the veils of smoke dislimned and the green-and-black spots in front of Tommy's eyes died away.

They were blinking at each other like people who have just come out of a cave into brilliant sun. Even yet their eyes stung with the fierceness of that abrupt illumination and Tommy found it hard to make out the faces across the table from him.

Mrs. Dingle took command of the half-blinded company with her accustomed poise. She rose, glass in hand. "And now, dear friends," she said in a clear voice, "I'm sure all of us are very happy to——" Then she stopped, open-mouthed, an expression of incredulous horror on her features. The lifted glass began to spill its contents on the tablecloth in a little stream of amber. As she spoke, she had turned directly to Monsieur Tibault's place at the table—and Monsieur Tibault was no longer there.

Some say there was a bursting flash of fire that disappeared up the chimney—some say it was a giant cat that leaped through the window at a bound, without breaking the glass. Professor Tatto puts it down to a mysterious chemical disturbance operating only over M. Tibault's chair. The butler, who is pious, believes the devil in person flew away with him, and Mrs. Dingle hesitates between witchcraft and a malicious ectoplasm dematerializing on the wrong cosmic plane. But be that as it may, one thing is certain—in the instant of fictive darkness which followed the glare of the flashlight, Monsieur Tibault, the great conductor, disappeared forever from mortal sight, tail and all.

Mrs. Culverin swears he was an international burglar and that she was just about to unmask him, when he slipped away under cover of the flashlight smoke, but no one else who sat at that historic dinner-table believes her. No, there are no sound explanations, but Tommy thinks he knows, and he will never be able to pass a cat again without wondering.

Mrs. Tommy is quite of her husband's mind regarding cats—she was Gretchen Woolwine, of Chicago—for Tommy told her his whole story, and while she doesn't believe a great deal of it, there is no doubt in her heart that one person concerned in the affair was a *perfect* cat. Doubtless it would have been more romantic to relate how Tommy's daring finally won him his Princess—but, unfortunately, it would not be veracious. For the Princess Vivrakanarda, also, is with us no longer. Her nerves, shattered by the spectacular denouement of Mrs. Dingle's dinner, required a sea-voyage, and from that voyage she has never returned to America.

Of course, there are the usual stories—one hears of her, a nun in a Siamese convent, or a masked dancer at Le Jardin de ma Soeur—one hears that she has been murdered in Patagonia or married in Trebizond—but, as far as can be ascertained, not one of these gaudy fables has the slightest basis of fact. I believe that Tommy, in his heart of hearts, is quite convinced that the sea-voyage was only a pretext, and that by some unheard-of means, she has managed to rejoin the formidable Monsieur Tibault, wherever in the world of the visible or the invisible he may be—in fact, that in some ruined city or subterranean palace they reign together now, King and Queen of all the mysterious Kingdom of Cats. But that, of course, is quite impossible.

1929

DAVID H. KELLER

(1880–1966)

The Jelly-Fish

"All space is relative. There is no such thing as size. The telescope and the microscope have produced a deadly leveling of great and small, far and near. The only little thing is sin, the only great thing is fear!"

For the hundredth time Professor Queirling repeated his statement, and for the hundredth time we listened in silence, afraid to enter into a controversy with him. It was not the fact that he knew more than we did that kept us quiet, but the haunting fear that filled us when we listened to him or watched him at work.

Working at an unsolved problem, he seemed a soul detached, a spirit separated from its earthly home, a being living only in the realm of thought. His body sat motionless, his eyes catatonic, unwinking stared until his mind, satisfied, deigned to return to bone-bound cell. Then in magnificent condescension he would talk freely in limpid phrases of the things he had considered and the conclusions he had deduced. We, chosen scientists, university graduates, hailed him as our master and hated him for admitting his mastery.

We hoped some evil might befall him, and yet we admitted that the success of the expedition depended upon his continued leadership. It was vitally necessary for our future: we were struggling young men with all life ahead of us, and if we failed in our first effort there would be no other opportunities for fame granted us.

In a specially constructed yacht, a veritable floating laboratory, we were south of Borneo, making a detailed study of microscopic sea life. In deep-sea nets we gathered the tiny organisms and then, with microscope, photography, and the cinema we observed them for the future instruction of the human race. There were hundreds of species, thousands of varieties, each to be identified, classified, described, studied, and photographed. We gathered in the morning, studied until midnight and slept restlessly until morning. The only thing in which we were agreed was ambition, our sole united emotion was hatred of the professor.

He knew how we felt and enjoyed taunting us: "I am your leader because I willed it so," he would say, speaking in a low restrained voice. "With me the will to attain is synonymous with accomplishment. I believe in myself and through this irreducible faith I succeed. There is nothing a strong man cannot do if he wills to do it and believes in his strength. Our ideas of space, size, and time are but the fanciful dreams of children. I am fifty-nine inches tall and fully clothed, weigh one hundred and ten pounds. If I desired I could make myself a colossus and swallow the earth as a child swallows a pill. If I willed it I could fly through space like a comet or hang suspended in the ether like the morning star. My will is greater than any other physical force, because I believe in it: I have confidence in my ability to do whatever I wish. So far I have conducted myself like an average man because I desire to so behave and not because of any limitations: Man has a soul and that ethereal force is greater than any law of nature that man ever thought of or any God ever created. He is purely and totally supreme—if he so desires."

It was after such a defiant declaration to us that our chemist, Bullard, gathered courage to challenge his power. He stated his opinion sharply and to the point, "I do not believe you."

"What is that to me?" answered the professor.

"Simply this: You make a statement that you have certain powers. I say that it is not true: Of what good to boast if you know we think you a liar? Can you do these things? If you can, do them for us, and I for one, will hail you as greater than God. Fail to do them and I will brand you a boasting poseur."

The professor looked steadily at the chemist. We waited breathlessly for the blow to fall, but he only laughed.

"You want a sign? A proof? I have thought of just such a thing and I would have proposed it myself had one of you not asked for it. The thing must be visible to all of you, something that I can demonstrate, a thing unheard of, an act all men consider impossible and yet I will do it. Listen to me.

"You have all seen the jellyfish called the Bishop's Miter.

When it is magnified three hundred times under the microscope it looks like a small balloon with a large opening at one end. It propels itself through the water by the flagellate movement of its cilia. The walls are translucent and transparent. At the top there are two specialized groups of nerve cells which we believe may serve as eyes. The opening at the bottom serves as a mouth. Smaller cells enter there and are absorbed. I describe it to refresh your memory, though you have all seen it. I will secure one in a hanging drop under the microscope and then we will attach the camera and cinema to it. We will project the picture on our screen. You will see the Miter move and live; you will observe the cilia move.

"While we have the actual specimen under observation I will look at it through the microscope. Then I will demonstrate to you that I am not the idle boaster you think me. I will force myself to pass through the glass eye-piece down into the brass tube. As I go, I will make myself grow smaller. Finally I will pass through the objective and jump into the hanging drop. I will swim in that drop—swim up to the jellyfish and touch it, make actual observations concerning its structure and functions. While I am in the drop of water you will be able to observe my every motion on the screen: Then I will disappear, pass through the microscope upwards and finally resume my original size and position in the room. I presume that if I do this you will be satisfied."

We were too astonished to reply. It was evident that the man had suddenly become insane. He smiled superciliously, as though we were children.

He waited for an answer, but we had none and then he began to prepare the apparatus for the experiment. Finally all was to his satisfaction. After examining several drops of water from our specimen-jar he was able to imprison a Bishop's Miter in the hanging drop under the microscope. He switched on the electricity and we saw the jellyfish move upon the screen.

The professor carefully adjusted the apparatus until the organism appeared with more than usual distinctness. We saw the little animal he had so carefully described to us. We even saw the little projections which we believed were its rudimentary visual organs.

Then Professor Queirling told the cinema operator what he

wanted done. He was to take a picture starting from the time the professor disappeared down the brass tube of the microscope and continue until he reappeared. No matter what happened, he was to go on taking pictures.

"It is all well enough," said our master, "for you children to see what is happening and to talk about it later on, but who would believe you? We know that the camera cannot lie. That is why it is important to take a consecutive picture of what occurs. Otherwise you might think that I have been able to hypnotize you. Now I will look down this tube. At the bottom of the hanging drop I see a transparent balloon. It is a pretty sight. Now watch me carefully as I will myself to shrink. I will go on talking as long as I can and you must listen carefully because the smaller I am the less audible will be my voice.

"Now I am twelve inches high. I am standing near the microscope. I grow still smaller and now I am only one inch tall and am standing on the eye-piece. No doubt you can barely hear me. Now I am smaller yet and am ready to will myself through the glass of the eye-piece."

The room became silent. Shivering, we looked at the microscope. The professor was gone. The chemist staggered over to the instrument, looked into it, and silently reeled back to his seat.

On the screen before us, the living inhabitants of the drop of water lived and moved and had their being. Largest of all was the transparent jellyfish, which was moving restlessly as though seeking a way of escape. The only sound in the room was the hum of the cinema and the stertorous breathing of the chemist.

Then on the screen came a new figure we were able to identify as the professor, swimming among the infusoria. Gaining his balance, at last he stood upright and waved his hand at us. It was easy to see his smile, that condescending smug smile that had so often driven us frantic. There was no doubt from his expression that he was highly pleased with his performance. None of us dared look at his fellow; not one of the audience thought for a second of taking his eyes off the silver screen. We were stunned, stupefied, and filled with a wild terror all the more horrible because of the silence.

The professor started to swim again and now approached

the jellyfish. He tapped the crystal walls. Then as though seized with a sudden impulse, he went to the bottom, jumped up through the mouth, and entered the translucent ball of protoplasm. He peered at us through the transparent walls. His arms made a series of peculiar movements and once again he smiled at us.

"My God!" exclaimed the artist. "He is wigwagging to us in army code. He says, 'I have done it, and now I will return to your world.' "

As though to keep his promise he started for the mouth of the jellyfish, and then—*the mouth closed.*

The professor circled the glasslike ball seeking a way of exit. Once he waved at us in a peculiar manner and then suddenly he sought the wall and with arms and feet tried to break through. On his face was now the look of ghastly despair. The things on top of the jellyfish began to glow—no doubt now that they were eyes, and bright ones.

Before our eyes the professor slowly disappeared into a globule of milky protoplasm. The jellyfish not only had made him a prisoner, but had actually dissolved and digested him. With a shriek the artist went over to the wall and turned on the electric lights. Trembling, the chemist looked down the tube of the microscope and told us that there was nothing in the hanging drop save the jellyfish.

The next day, after a conference, in which each of us said only part of what he thought, we decided to destroy the roll of film—and sent word to the university that the professor had disappeared from the ship and our only explanation was that he had been drowned.

1929

CONRAD AIKEN

(1889–1973)

Mr. Arcularis

MR. ARCULARIS stood at the window of his room in the hospital and looked down at the street. There had been a light shower, which had patterned the sidewalks with large drops, but now again the sun was out, blue sky was showing here and there between the swift white clouds, a cold wind was blowing the poplar trees. An itinerant band had stopped before the building and was playing, with violin, harp, and flute, the finale of "Cavalleria Rusticana." Leaning against the window-sill—for he felt extraordinarily weak after his operation—Mr. Arcularis suddenly, listening to the wretched music, felt like crying. He rested the palm of one hand against a cold window-pane and stared down at the old man who was blowing the flute, and blinked his eyes. It seemed absurd that he should be so weak, so emotional, so like a child—and especially now that everything was over at last. In spite of all their predictions, in spite, too, of his own dreadful certainty that he was going to die, here he was, as fit as a fiddle—but what a fiddle it was, so out of tune!—with a long life before him. And to begin with, a voyage to England ordered by the doctor. What could be more delightful? Why should he feel sad about it and want to cry like a baby? In a few minutes Harry would arrive with his car to take him to the wharf; in an hour he would be on the sea, in two hours he would see the sunset behind him, where Boston had been, and his new life would be opening before him. It was many years since he had been abroad. June, the best of the year to come—England, France, the Rhine—how ridiculous that he should already be homesick!

There was a light footstep outside the door, a knock, the door opened, and Harry came in.

"Well, old man, I've come to get you. The old bus actually got here. Are you ready? Here, let me take your arm. You're tottering like an octogenarian!"

Mr. Arcularis submitted gratefully, laughing, and they made the journey slowly along the bleak corridor and down the stairs to the entrance hall. Miss Hoyle, his nurse, was there, and the Matron, and the charming little assistant with freckles who had helped to prepare him for the operation. Miss Hoyle put out her hand.

"Good-by, Mr. Arcularis," she said, "and *bon voyage*."

"Good-by, Miss Hoyle, and thank you for everything. You were very kind to me. And I fear I was a nuisance."

The girl with the freckles, too, gave him her hand, smiling. She was very pretty, and it would have been easy to fall in love with her. She reminded him of some one. Who was it? He tried in vain to remember while he said good-by to her and turned to the Matron.

"And not too many latitudes with the young ladies, Mr. Arcularis!" she was saying.

Mr. Arcularis was pleased, flattered, by all this attention to a middle-aged invalid, and felt a joke taking shape in his mind, and no sooner in his mind than on his tongue.

"Oh, no latitudes," he said, laughing. "I'll leave the latitudes to the ship!"

"Oh, come now," said the Matron, "we don't seem to have hurt him much, do we?"

"I think we'll have to operate on him again and *really* cure him," said Miss Hoyle.

He was going down the front steps, between the potted palmettos, and they all laughed and waved. The wind was cold, very cold for June, and he was glad he had put on his coat. He shivered.

"Damned cold for June!" he said. "Why should it be so cold?"

"East wind," Harry said, arranging the rug over his knees. "Sorry it's an open car, but I believe in fresh air and all that sort of thing. I'll drive slowly. We've got plenty of time."

They coasted gently down the long hill toward Beacon Street, but the road was badly surfaced, and despite Harry's care Mr. Arcularis felt his pain again. He found that he could alleviate it a little by leaning to the right, against the arm-rest, and not breathing too deeply. But how glorious to be out again! How strange and vivid the world looked! The trees had innumerable green fresh leaves—they were all blowing and shifting and turning and flashing in the wind; drops of rain-water fell downward sparkling; the robins were singing their absurd, delicious little four-noted songs; even the street cars looked unusually bright and beautiful, just as they used to look when he was a child and had wanted above all things to be a motorman. He found himself smiling foolishly at everything, foolishly and weakly, and wanted to say something about it to Harry. It was no use, though—he had no strength, and the mere finding of words would almost more than he could manage. And even if he should succeed in saying it, he would then most likely burst into tears. He shook his head slowly from side to side.

"Ain't it grand?" he said.

"I'll bet it looks good," said Harry.

"Words fail me."

"You wait till you get out to sea. You'll have a swell time."

"Oh, swell! . . . I hope not. I hope it'll be calm."

"Tut tut."

When they passed the Harvard Club Mr. Arcularis made a slow and somewhat painful effort to turn in his seat and look at it. It might be the last chance to see it for a long time. Why this sentimental longing to stare at it, though? There it was, with the great flag blowing in the wind, the Harvard seal now concealed by the swift folds and now revealed, and there were the windows in the library, where he had spent so many de-lightful hours reading—Plato, and Kipling, and the Lord knows what—and the balconies from which for so many years he had watched the Marathon. Old Talbot might be in there now, sleeping with a book on his knee, hoping forlornly to be inter-rupted by any one, for anything.

"Good-by to the old club," he said.

"The bar will miss you," said Harry, smiling with friendly irony and looking straight ahead.

"But let there be no moaning," said Mr. Arcularis.

"What's *that* a quotation from?"

"'The Odyssey.'"

In spite of the cold, he was glad of the wind on his face, for it helped to dissipate the feeling of vagueness and dizziness that came over him in a sickening wave from time to time. All of a sudden everything would begin to swim and dissolve, the houses would lean their heads together, he had to close his eyes, and there would be a curious and dreadful humming noise, which at regular intervals rose to a crescendo and then drawlingly subsided again. It was disconcerting. Perhaps he still had a trace of fever. When he got on the ship he would have a glass of whisky. . . . From one of these spells he opened his eyes and found that they were on the ferry, crossing to East Boston. It must have been the ferry's engines that he had heard. From another spell he woke to find himself on the wharf, the car at a standstill beside a pile of yellow packing-cases.

"We're here because we're here because we're here," said Harry.

"Because we're here," added Mr. Arcularis.

He dozed in the car while Harry—and what a good friend Harry was!—attended to all the details. He went and came with tickets and passports and baggage checks and porters. And at last he unwrapped Mr. Arcularis from the rugs and led him up the steep gangplank to the deck, and thence by devious windings to a small cold stateroom with a solitary porthole like the eye of a cyclops.

"Here you are," he said, "and now I've got to go. Did you hear the whistle?"

"No."

"Well, you're half asleep. It's sounded the all-ashore. Good-by, old fellow, and take care of yourself. Bring me back a spray of edelweiss. And send me a picture post-card from the Absolute."

"Will you have it finite or infinite?"

"Oh, infinite. But with your signature on it. Now you'd better turn in for a while and have a nap. Cheerio!"

Mr. Arcularis took his hand and pressed it hard, and once more felt like crying. Absurd! Had he become a child again?

"Good-by," he said.

He sat down in the little wicker chair, with his overcoat still on, closed his eyes, and listened to the humming of the air in the ventilator. Hurried footsteps ran up and down the corridor. The chair was not too comfortable, and his pain began to bother him again, so he moved, with his coat still on, to the narrow berth and fell asleep. When he woke up, it was dark, and the porthole had been partly opened. He groped for the switch and turned on the light. Then he rang for the steward.

"It's cold in here," he said. "Would you mind closing the port?"

The girl who sat opposite him at dinner was charming. Who was it she reminded him of? Why, of course, the girl at the hospital, the girl with the freckles. Her hair was beautiful, not quite red, not quite gold, nor had it been bobbed; arranged with a sort of graceful untidiness, it made him think of a Melozzo da Forli angel. Her face was freckled, she had a mouth which was both humorous and voluptuous. And she seemed to be alone.

He frowned at the bill of fare and ordered the thick soup.

"No hors d'œuvres?" asked the steward.

"I think not," said Mr. Arcularis. "They might kill me."

The steward permitted himself to be amused and deposited the menu card on the table against the water-bottle. His eyebrows were lifted. As he moved away, the girl followed him with her eyes and smiled.

"I'm afraid you shocked him," she said.

"Impossible," said Mr. Arcularis. "These stewards, they're dead souls. How could they be stewards otherwise? And they think they've seen and known everything. They suffer terribly from the *déjà vu*. Personally, I don't blame them."

"It must be a dreadful sort of life."

"It's because they're dead that they accept it."

"Do you think so?"

"I'm sure of it. I'm enough of a dead soul myself to know the signs!"

"Well, I don't know what you mean by that!"

"But nothing mysterious! I'm just out of hospital, after an operation. I was given up for dead. For six months I had given *myself* up for dead. If you've ever been seriously ill you know the feeling. You have a posthumous feeling—a mild, cynical tolerance for everything and every one. What is there you haven't seen or done or understood? Nothing."

Mr. Arcularis waved his hands and smiled.

"I wish I could understand you," said the girl, "but I've never been ill in my life."

"Never?"

"Never."

"Good God!"

The torrent of the unexpressed and inexpressible paralyzed him and rendered him speechless. He stared at the girl, wondering who she was and then, realizing that he had perhaps stared too fixedly, averted his gaze, gave a little laugh, rolled a pill of bread between his fingers. After a second or two he allowed himself to look at her again and found her smiling.

"Never pay any attention to invalids," he said, "or they'll drag you to the hospital."

She examined him critically, with her head tilted a little to one side, but with friendliness.

"You don't *look* like an invalid," she said.

Mr. Arcularis thought her charming. His pain ceased to bother him, the disagreeable humming disappeared, or rather, it was dissociated from himself and became merely, as it should be, the sound of the ship's engines, and he began to think the voyage was going to be really delightful. The parson on his right passed him the salt.

"I fear you will need this in your soup," he said.

"Thank you. Is it as bad as that?"

The steward, overhearing, was immediately apologetic and solicitous. He explained that on the first day everything was at sixes and sevens. The girl looked up at him and asked him a question.

"Do you think we'll have a good voyage?" she said.

He was passing the hot rolls to the parson, removing the napkins from them with a deprecatory finger.

"Well, madam, I don't like to be a Jeremiah, but——"

"Oh, come," said the parson, "I hope we have no Jeremiahs."

"What do you mean?" said the girl.

Mr. Arcularis ate his soup with gusto—it was nice and hot.

"Well, maybe I shouldn't say it, but there's a corpse on board, going to Ireland; and I never yet knew a voyage with a corpse on board that we didn't have bad weather."

"Why, steward, you're just superstitious! What nonsense!"

"That's a very ancient superstition," said Mr. Arcularis. "I've heard it many times. Maybe it's true. Maybe we'll be wrecked. And what does it matter, after all?" He was very bland.

"Then let's be wrecked," said the parson coldly.

Nevertheless, Mr. Arcularis felt a shudder go through him

on hearing the steward's remark. A corpse in the hold—a coffin? Perhaps it was true. Perhaps some disaster would befall them. There might be fogs. There might be icebergs. He thought of all the wrecks of which he had read. There was the *Titanic*, which he had read about in the warm newspaper room at the Harvard Club—it had seemed dreadfully real, even there. That band, playing "Nearer My God to Thee" on the after-deck while the ship sank! It was one of the darkest of his memories. And the *Empress of Ireland*—all those poor people trapped in the smoking-room, with only one door between them and life, and that door locked for the night by the deck-steward, and the deck-steward nowhere to be found! He shivered, feeling a draft, and turned to the parson.

"How do these strange delusions arise?" he said.

The parson looked at him searchingly, appraisingly—from chin to forehead, from forehead to chin—and Mr. Arcularis, feeling uncomfortable, straightened his tie.

"From nothing but fear," said the parson. "Nothing on earth but fear."

"How strange!" said the girl.

Mr. Arcularis again looked at her—she had lowered her face—and again tried to think of whom she reminded him. It wasn't only the little freckle-faced girl at the hospital—both of them had reminded him of some one else. Some one far back in his life: remote, beautiful, lovely. But he couldn't think. The meal came to an end, they all rose, the ship's orchestra played a feeble fox-trot, and Mr. Arcularis, once more alone, went to the bar to have his whisky. The room was stuffy, and the ship's engines were both audible and palpable. The humming and throbbing oppressed him, the rhythm seemed to be the rhythm of his own pain, and after a short time he found his way, with slow steps, holding on to the walls in his moments of weakness and dizziness, to his forlorn and white little room. The port had been—thank God!—closed for the night: it was cold enough anyway. The white and blue ribbons fluttered from the ventilator, the bottle and glasses clicked and clucked as the ship swayed gently to the long, slow motion of the sea. It was all very peculiar—it was all like something he had experienced somewhere before. What was it? Where was it? . . . He untied his tie, looking at his face in the glass, and wondered, and from time to time put his hand to his side to hold in the pain. It wasn't at Portsmouth, in his childhood, nor at Salem, nor in the rose-garden at his Aunt Julia's, nor in the schoolroom at Cambridge. It was something very queer, very intimate, very precious. The jackstones, the Sunday-school cards which he had loved when he was a child . . . He fell asleep.

The sense of time was already hopelessly confused. One hour was like another, the sea looked always the same, morning was indistinguishable from afternoon—and was it Tuesday or Wednesday? Mr. Arcularis was sitting in the smoking-room, in his favorite corner, watching the parson teach Miss Dean to play chess. On the deck outside he could see the people passing and repassing in their restless round of the ship. The red jacket went by, then the black hat with the white feather, then the purple scarf, the brown tweed coat, the Bulgarian mustache, the monocle, the Scotch cap with fluttering ribbons, and in no time at all the red jacket again, dipping past the windows with its own peculiar rhythm, followed once more by the black hat and the purple scarf. How odd to reflect on the fixed little orbits of these things—as definite and profound, perhaps, as the orbits of the stars, and as important to God or the Absolute. There was a kind of tyranny in this fixedness, too—to think of it too much made one uncomfortable. He closed his eyes for a moment, to avoid seeing for the fortieth time the Bulgarian mustache and the pursuing monocle. The parson was explaining the movements of knights. Two forward and one to the side. Eight possible moves, always to the opposite color from that on which the piece stands. Two forward and one to the side: Miss Dean repeated the words several times with reflective emphasis. Here, too, was the terrifying fixed curve of the infinite, the creeping curve of logic which at last must become the final signpost at the edge of nothing. After that— the deluge. The great white light of annihilation. The bright flash of death. . . . Was it merely the sea which made these abstractions so insistent, so intrusive? The mere notion of *orbit* had somehow become extraordinarily naked; and to rid himself of the discomfort and also to forget a little the pain which bothered his side whenever he sat down, he walked slowly and carefully into the writing-room, and examined a pile of super-annuated magazines and catalogues of travel. The bright colors amused him, the photographs of remote islands and moun-tains, savages in sampans or sarongs or both—it was all very far off and delightful, like something in a dream or a fever. But he found that he was too tired to read and was incapable of con-centration. Dreams! Yes, that reminded him. That rather alarming business—sleep-walking!

Later in the evening—at what hour he didn't know—he was telling Miss Dean about it, as he had intended to do. They were sitting in deck-chairs on the sheltered side. The sea was black, and there was a cold wind. He wished they had chosen to sit in the lounge.

Miss Dean was extremely pretty—no, beautiful. She looked at him, too, in a very strange and lovely way, with something of inquiry, something of sympathy, something of affection. It seemed as if, between the question and the answer, they had sat thus for a very long time, exchanging an unspoken secret, simply looking at each other quietly and kindly. Had an hour or two passed? And was it at all necessary to speak?

"No," she said, "I never have."

She breathed into the low words a note of interrogation and gave him a slow smile.

"That's the funny part of it. I never had either until last night. Never in my life. I hardly ever even dream. And it really rather frightens me."

"Tell me about it, Mr. Arcularis."

"I dreamed at first that I was walking, alone, in a wide plain covered with snow. It was growing dark, I was very cold, my feet were frozen and numb, and I was lost. I came then to a signpost—at first it seemed to me there was nothing on it. Nothing but ice. Just before it grew finally dark, however, I made out on it the one word 'Polaris.'"

"The Pole Star."

"Yes—and you see, I didn't myself know that. I looked it up only this morning. I suppose I must have seen it somewhere? And of course it rhymes with my name."

"Why, so it does!"

"Anyway, it gave me—in the dream—an awful feeling of despair, and the dream changed. This time, I dreamed I was standing *outside* my state-room in the little dark corridor, or *cul-de-sac*, and trying to find the door-handle to let myself in. I was in my pajamas, and again I was very cold. And at this point I woke up. . . . The extraordinary thing is that's exactly where I was!"

"Good heavens. How strange!"

"Yes. And now the question is, *where had I been?* I was frightened, when I came to—not unnaturally. For among other things I *did* have, quite definitely, the feeling that I *had been* somewhere. Somewhere where it was very cold. It doesn't sound very proper. Suppose I had been seen!"

"That might have been awkward," said Miss Dean.

"Awkward! It might indeed. It's very singular. I've never done such a thing before. It's this sort of thing that reminds one—rather wholesomely, perhaps, don't you think?"—and Mr. Arcularis gave a nervous little laugh—"how extraordinarily little we know about the workings of our own minds or souls. After all, what *do* we know?"

"Nothing—nothing—nothing—nothing," said Miss Dean slowly.

"*Absolutely* nothing."

Their voices had dropped, and again they were silent; and again they looked at each other gently and sympathetically, as if for the exchange of something unspoken and perhaps unspeakable. Time ceased. The orbit—so it seemed to Mr. Arcularis—once more became pure, became absolute. And once more he found himself wondering who it was that Miss Dean—Clarice Dean—reminded him of. Long ago and far away. Like those pictures of the islands and mountains. The little freckle-faced girl at the hospital was merely, as it were, the stepping-stone, the signpost, or, as in algebra, the "equals" sign. But what was it they both "equalled"? The jackstones came again into his mind and his Aunt Julia's rose-garden—at sunset; but this was ridiculous. It couldn't be simply that they reminded him of his childhood! And yet why not?

They went into the lounge. The ship's orchestra, in the oval-shaped balcony among faded palms, was playing the finale of "Cavalleria Rusticana," playing it badly.

"Good God!" said Mr. Arcularis, "can't I ever escape from that damned sentimental tune? It's the last thing I heard in America, and the last thing I *want* to hear."

"But don't you like it?"

"As music? No! It moves me too much, but in the wrong way."

"What, exactly, do you mean?"

"Exactly? Nothing. When I heard it at the hospital—when was it?—it made me feel like crying. Three old Italians tootling it in the rain. I suppose, like most people, I'm afraid of my feelings."

"Are they so dangerous?"

"Now then, young woman! Are you pulling my leg?"

The stewards had rolled away the carpets, and the passengers were beginning to dance. Miss Dean accepted the invitation of a young officer, and Mr. Arcularis watched them with envy. Odd, that last exchange of remarks—very odd; in fact, everything was odd. Was it possible that they were falling in love? Was that what it was all about—all these concealed references and recollections? He had read of such things. But at his age! And with a girl of twenty-two! It was ridiculous.

After an amused look at his old friend Polaris from the open door on the sheltered side, he went to bed.

The rhythm of the ship's engines was positively a persecution. It gave one no rest, it followed one like the Hound of Heaven, it drove one out into space and across the Milky Way and then back home by way of Betelgeuse. It was cold there, too. Mr. Arcularis, making the round trip by way of Betelgeuse and Polaris, sparkled with frost. He felt like a Christmas tree. Icicles on his fingers and icicles on his toes. He tinkled and spangled in the void, hallooed to the waste echoes, rounded the buoy on the verge of the Unknown, and tacked glitteringly homeward. The wind whistled. He was barefooted. Snowflakes and tinsel blew past him. Next time, by George, he would go farther still—for altogether it was rather a lark. Forward into the untrodden! as somebody said. Some intrepid explorer of his own backyard, probably, some middle-aged professor with an umbrella: those were the fellows for courage! But give us time, thought Mr. Arcularis, give us time, and we will bring back with us the night-rime of the Absolute. Or was it Abso-

lete? If only there weren't this perpetual throbbing, this iteration of sound, like a pain, these circles and repetitions of
light—the feeling as of everything coiling inward to a centre of
misery . . .

Suddenly it was dark, and he was lost. He was groping, he
touched the cold, white, slippery woodwork with his fingernails, looking for an electric switch. The throbbing, of course,
was the throbbing of the ship. But he was almost home—almost
home. Another corner to round, a door to be opened, and there
he would be. Safe and sound. Safe in his father's home.

It was at this point that he woke up: in the corridor that led
to the dining saloon. Such pure terror, such horror, seized him
as he had never known. His heart felt as if it would stop beating.
His back was toward the dining saloon; apparently he had just
come from it. He was in his pajamas. The corridor was dim, all
but two lights having been turned out for the night, and—
thank God!—deserted. Not a soul, not a sound. He was perhaps fifty yards from his room. With luck he could get to it
unseen. Holding tremulously to the rail that ran along the
wall, a brown, greasy rail, he began to creep his way forward.
He felt very weak, very dizzy, and his thoughts refused to concentrate. Vaguely he remembered Miss Dean—Clarice—and
the freckled girl, as if they were one and the same person. But
he wasn't in the hospital, he was on the ship. Of course. How
absurd. The Great Circle. Here we are, old fellow . . . steady
round the corner . . . hold hard to your umbrella . . .

In his room, with the door safely shut behind him, Mr. Arcularis broke into a cold sweat. He had no sooner got into his
bunk, shivering, than he heard the night watchman pass.

"But where—" he thought, closing his eyes in agony—
"have I been? . . ."

A dreadful idea had occurred to him.

"It's nothing serious—how could it be anything serious? Of
course it's nothing serious," said Mr. Arcularis.

"No, it's nothing serious," said the ship's doctor urbanely.

"I knew you'd think so. But just the same——"

"Such a condition is the result of worry," said the doctor.
"Are you worried—do you mind telling me—about something?
Just try to think."

"Worried?"

Mr. Arcularis knitted his brows. *Was* there something? Some little mosquito of a cloud disappearing into the southwest, the northeast? Some little gnat-song of despair? But no, that was all over. All over.

"Nothing," he said, "nothing whatever."

"It's very strange," said the doctor.

"Strange! I should say so. I've come to sea for a rest, not for a nightmare! What about a bromide?"

"Well, I can give you a bromide, Mr. Arcularis——"

"Then, please, if you don't mind, give me a bromide."

He carried the little phial hopefully to his stateroom, and took a dose at once. He could see the sun through his porthole. It looked northern and pale and small, like a little peppermint, which was only natural enough, for the latitude was changing with every hour. But why was it that doctors were all alike? and all, for that matter, like his father, or that other fellow at the hospital? Smythe, his name was. Doctor Smythe. A nice, dry little fellow, and they said he was a writer. Wrote poetry, or something like that. Poor fellow—disappointed. Like everybody else. Crouched in there, in his cabin, night after night, writing blank verse or something—all about the stars and flowers and love and death; ice and the sea and the infinite; time and tide—well, every man to his own taste.

"But it's nothing serious," said Mr. Arcularis, later, to the parson. "How could it be?"

"Why, of course not, my dear fellow," said the parson, patting his back. "How could it be?"

"I know it isn't and yet I worry about it."

"It would be ridiculous to think it serious," said the parson.

Mr. Arcularis shivered: it was colder than ever. It was said that they were near icebergs. For a few hours in the morning there had been a fog, and the siren had blown—devastatingly—at three-minute intervals. Icebergs caused fog—he knew that.

"These things always come," said the parson, "from a sense of guilt. You feel guilty about something. I won't be so rude as to inquire what it is. But if you could rid yourself of the sense of guilt——"

And later still, when the sky was pink:

"But is it anything to worry about?" said Miss Dean. "Really?"

"No, I suppose not."

"Then don't worry. We aren't children any longer!"

"Aren't we? I wonder!"

They leaned, shoulders touching, on the deck-rail, and looked at the sea, which was multitudinously incarnadined. Mr. Arcularis scanned the horizon in vain for an iceberg.

"Anyway," he said, "the colder we are the less we feel!"

"I hope that's no reflection on *you*," said Miss Dean.

"Here . . . feel my hand," said Mr. Arcularis.

"Heaven knows it's cold!"

"It's been to Polaris and back! No wonder."

"Poor thing, poor thing!"

"Warm it."

"May I?"

"You can."

"I'll try."

Laughing, she took his hand between both of hers, one palm under and one palm over, and began rubbing it briskly. The decks were deserted, no one was near them, every one was dressing for dinner. The sea grew darker, the wind blew colder.

"I wish I could remember who you are," he said.

"And you—who are you?"

"Myself."

"Then perhaps *I* am yourself."

"Don't be metaphysical!"

"But I *am* metaphysical!"

She laughed, withdrew, pulled the light coat about her shoulders.

The bugle blew the summons for dinner—"The Roast Beef of Old England"—and they walked together along the darkening deck toward the door, from which a shaft of soft light fell across the deck-rail. As they stepped over the brass door-sill Mr. Arcularis felt the throb of the engines again; he put his hand quickly to his side.

"*Auf wiedersehen*," he said. "*To-morrow and to-morrow and to-morrow.*"

Mr. Arcularis was finding it impossible, absolutely impossible, to keep warm. A cold fog surrounded the ship, had done so, it seemed, for days. The sun had all but disappeared, the transition from day to night was almost unnoticeable. The ship, too, seemed scarcely to be moving—it was as if anchored among walls of ice and rime. Monstrous, that merely because it was June, and supposed, therefore, to be warm, the ship's authorities should consider it unnecessary to turn on the heat! By day, he wore his heavy coat and sat shivering in the corner of the smoking-room. His teeth chattered, his hands were blue. By night, he heaped blankets on his bed, closed the porthole's black eye against the sea, and drew the yellow curtains across it, but in vain. Somehow, despite everything, the fog crept in, and the icy fingers touched his throat. The steward, questioned about it, merely said, "Icebergs." Of course—any fool knew that. But how long, in God's name, was it going to last? They surely ought to be past the Grand Banks by this time! And surely it wasn't necessary to sail to England by way of Greenland and Iceland!

Miss Dean—Clarice—was sympathetic.

"It's simply because," she said, "your vitality has been lowered by your illness. You can't expect to be your normal self so soon after an operation! When *was* your operation, by the way?"

Mr. Arcularis considered. Strange—he couldn't be quite sure. It was all a little vague—his sense of time had disappeared.

"Heavens knows!" he said. "Centuries ago. When I was a tadpole and you were a fish. I should think it must have been at about the time of the Battle of Teutoburg Forest. Or perhaps when I was a Neanderthal man with a club!"

"Are you sure it wasn't farther back still?"

What did she mean by that?

"Not at all. Obviously, we've been on this damned ship for ages—for eras—for æons. And even on this ship, you must remember, I've had plenty of time, in my nocturnal wanderings, to go several times to Orion and back. I'm thinking, by the way, of going farther still. There's a nice little star off to the left, as you round Betelgeuse, which looks as if it might be right at the edge. The last outpost of the finite. I think I'll have a look at it and bring you back a frozen rime-feather."

"It would melt when you got it back."

"Oh, no, it wouldn't—not on *this* ship!"

Clarice laughed.

"I wish I could go with you," she said.

"If only you would! If only——"

He broke off his sentence and looked hard at her—how lovely she was, and how desirable! No such woman had ever before come into his life; there had been no one with whom he had at once felt so profound a sympathy and understanding. It was a miracle, simply—a miracle. No need to put his arm around her or to kiss her—delightful as such small vulgarities would be. He had only to look at her, and to feel, gazing into those extraordinary eyes, that she knew him, had always known him. It was as if, indeed, she might be his own soul.

But as he looked thus at her, reflecting, he noticed that she was frowning.

"What is it?" he said.

She shook her head, slowly.

"I don't know."

"Tell me."

"Nothing. It just occurred to me that perhaps you weren't looking quite so well."

Mr. Arcularis was startled. He straightened himself up.

"What nonsense! Of course this pain bothers me—and I feel astonishingly weak——"

"It's more than that—much more than that. Something is worrying you horribly." She paused, and then with an air of challenging him, added, "Tell me, did you——"

Her eyes were suddenly asking him blazingly the question he had been afraid of. He flinched, caught his breath, looked away. But it was no use, as he knew: he would have to tell her. He had known all along that he would have to tell her.

"Clarice," he said—and his voice broke in spite of his effort to control it—"It's killing me, it's ghastly! Yes, I did."

His eyes filled with tears, he saw that her own had done so also. She put her hand on his arm.

"I knew," she said. "I knew. But tell me."

"It's happened twice again—*twice*—and each time I was farther away. The same dream of going round a star, the same terrible coldness and helplessness. That awful whistling curve . . ." He shuddered.

"And when you woke up——" she spoke quietly— "where were you when you woke up? Don't be afraid!"

"The first time I was at the farther end of the dining saloon. I had my hand on the door that leads into the pantry."

"I see. Yes. And the next time?"

Mr. Arcularis wanted to close his eyes in terror—he felt as if he were going mad. His lips moved before he could speak, and when at last he did speak it was in a voice so low as to be almost a whisper.

"I was at the bottom of the stairway that leads down from the pantry to the hold, past the refrigerating-plant. It was dark, and I was crawling on my hands and knees . . . *Crawling on my hands and knees! . . .*"

"Oh!" she said, and again, "Oh!"

He began to tremble violently; he felt the hand on his arm trembling also. And then he watched a look of unmistakable horror come slowly into Clarice's eyes, and a look of understanding, as if she saw . . . She tightened her hold on his arm.

"Do you think . . ." she whispered.

They stared at each other.

"I know," he said. "And so do you . . . Twice more—three times—and I'll be looking down into an empty . . ."

It was then that they first embraced—then, at the edge of the infinite, at the last signpost of the finite. They clung together desperately, forlornly, weeping as they kissed each other, staring hard one moment and closing their eyes the next. Passionately, passionately, she kissed him, as if she were indeed trying to give him her warmth, her life.

"But what nonsense!" she cried, leaning back, and holding his face between her hands, her hands which were wet with his tears. "What nonsense! It can't be!"

"It is," said Mr. Arcularis slowly.

"But how do you know? . . . How do you know where the——"

For the first time Mr. Arcularis smiled.

"Don't be afraid, darling—you mean the coffin?"

"How could you know where it is?"

"I don't need to," said Mr. Arcularis . . . "I'm already almost there."

Before they separated for the night, in the smoking-room, they had several whisky cocktails.

"We must make it gay!" Mr. Arcularis said. "Above all, we must make it gay. Perhaps even now it will turn out to be nothing but a nightmare from which both of us will wake! And even at the worst, at my present rate of travel, I ought to need two more nights! It's a long way, still, to that little star."

The parson passed them at the door.

"What! turning in so soon?" he said. "I was hoping for a game of chess."

"Yes, both turning in. But to-morrow?"

"To-morrow, then, Miss Dean! And good night!"

"Good night."

They walked once round the deck, then leaned on the railing and stared into the fog. It was thicker and whiter than ever. The ship was moving barely perceptibly, the rhythm of the engines was slower, more subdued and remote, and at regular intervals, mournfully, came the long reverberating cry of the foghorn. The sea was calm, and lapped only very tenderly against the side of the ship, the sound coming up to them clearly, however, because of the profound stillness.

" 'On such a night as this—' " quoted Mr. Arcularis grimly.

" 'On such a night as this——' "

Their voices hung suspended in the night, time ceased for them, for an eternal instant they were happy. When at last they parted it was by tacit agreement on a note of the ridiculous.

"Be a good boy and take your bromide!" she said.

"Yes, mother, I'll take my medicine!"

In his stateroom, he mixed himself a strong potion of bromide, a very strong one, and got into bed. He would have no trouble in falling asleep: he felt more tired, more supremely exhausted, than he had ever been in his life; nor had bed ever seemed so delicious. And that long, magnificent, delirious swoop of dizziness . . . the Great Circle . . . the swift pathway to Arcturus . . .

It was all as before, but infinitely more rapid. Never had Mr. Arcularis achieved such phenomenal, such supernatural, speed. In no time at all he was beyond the moon, shot past the North Star as if it were standing still (which perhaps it was?), swooped in a long, bright curve round the Pleiades, shouted his frosty greetings to Betelgeuse, and was off to the little blue star which pointed the way to the Unknown. Forward into the untrodden! Courage, old man, and hold on to your umbrella! Have you got your garters on? Mind your hat! In no time at all we'll be back to Clarice with the frozen rime-feather, the rime-feather, the snowflake of the Absolute, the Obsolete. If only we don't wake . . . if only we needn't wake . . . if only we don't wake in that—in that—time and space . . . somewhere or nowhere . . . cold and dark . . . "Cavalleria Rusticana" sobbing among the palms; if a lonely . . . if only . . . the coffers of the poor—not coffers, not coffers, not coffers, Oh, God, not coffers, but light, delight, supreme white and brightness, whirling lightness above all—and freezing—freezing— freezing . . .

At this point in the void the surgeon's last effort to save Mr. Arcularis's life had failed. He stood back from the operating table and made a tired gesture with a rubber-gloved hand.

"It's all over," he said. "As I expected."

He looked at Miss Hoyle, whose gaze was downward, at the basin she held. There was a moment's stillness, a pause, a brief flight of unexchanged comment, and then the ordered life of the hospital was resumed.

1931

ROBERT E. HOWARD

(1906–1936)

The Black Stone

*"They say foul beings of Old Times still lurk
In dark forgotten corners of the world,
And Gates still gape to loose, on certain nights,
Shapes pent in Hell."*
                                        —JUSTIN GEOFFREY

I READ of it first in the strange book of Von Junzt, the German eccentric who lived so curiously and died in such grisly and mysterious fashion. It was my fortune to have access to his *Nameless Cults* in the original edition, the so-called Black Book, published in Düsseldorf in 1839, shortly before a hounding doom overtook the author. Collectors of rare literature are familiar with *Nameless Cults* mainly through the cheap and faulty translation which was pirated in London by Bridewall in 1845, and the carefully expurgated edition put out by the Golden Goblin Press of New York in 1909. But the volume I stumbled upon was one of the unexpurgated German copies, with heavy leather covers and rusty iron hasps. I doubt if there are more than half a dozen such volumes in the entire world today, for the quantity issued was not great, and when the manner of the author's demise was bruited about, many possessors of the book burned their volumes in panic.

Von Junzt spent his entire life (1795–1840) delving into forbidden subjects; he traveled in all parts of the world, gained entrance into innumerable secret societies, and read countless little-known and esoteric books and manuscripts in the original; and in the chapters of the Black Book, which range from startling clarity of exposition to murky ambiguity, there are statements and hints to freeze the blood of a thinking man. Reading what Von Junzt *dared* put in print arouses uneasy speculations as to what it was that he dared *not* tell. What dark matters, for instance, were contained in those closely written pages that formed the unpublished manuscript on which he

worked unceasingly for months before his death, and which
lay torn and scattered all over the floor of the locked and
bolted chamber in which Von Junzt was found dead with the
marks of taloned fingers on his throat? It will never be known,
for the author's closest friend, the Frenchman Alexis Ladeau,
after having spent a whole night piecing the fragments together and reading what was written, burnt them to ashes and
cut his own throat with a razor.

But the contents of the published matter are shuddersome
enough, even if one accepts the general view that they but represent the ravings of a madman. There among many strange
things I found mention of the Black Stone, that curious, sinister monolith that broods among the mountains of Hungary,
and about which so many dark legends cluster. Von Junzt did
not devote much space to it—the bulk of his grim work concerns cults and objects of dark worship which he maintained
existed in his day, and it would seem that the Black Stone rep-
resents some order or being lost and forgotten centuries ago.
But he spoke of it as one of the *keys*—a phrase used many times
by him, in various relations, and constituting one of the ob-
scurities of his work. And he hinted briefly at curious sights
to be seen about the monolith on midsummer's night. He
mentioned Otto Dostmann's theory that this monolith was a
remnant of the Hunnish invasion and had been erected to
commemorate a victory of Attila over the Goths. Von Junzt
contradicted this assertion without giving any refutory facts,
merely remarking that to attribute the origin of the Black
Stone to the Huns was as logical as assuming that William the
Conqueror reared Stonehenge.

This implication of enormous antiquity piqued my interest
immensely and after some difficulty I succeeded in locating a
rat-eaten and moldering copy of Dostmann's *Remnants of Lost
Empires* (Berlin, 1809, "Der Drachenhaus" Press). I was disappointed to find that Dostmann referred to the Black Stone even
more briefly than had Von Junzt, dimmissing it with a few
lines as an artifact comparatively modern in contrast with the
Greco-Roman ruins of Asia Minor which were his pet theme.
He admitted his inability to make out the defaced characters on
the monolith but pronounced them unmistakably Mongoloid.
However, little as I learned from Dostmann, he did mention the

name of the village adjacent to the Black Stone—Stregoicavar
—an ominous name, meaning something like Witch-Town.

A close scrutiny of guide-books and travel articles gave me no
further information—Stregoicavar, not on any map that I could
find, lay in a wild, little-frequented region, out of the path of
casual tourists. But I did find subject for thought in Dornly's
Magyar Folklore. In his chapter on *Dream Myths* he mentions
the Black Stone and tells of some curious superstitions regarding
it—especially the belief that if any one sleeps in the vicinity of
the monolith, that person will be haunted by monstrous nightmares for ever after; and he cited tales of the peasants regarding
too-curious people who ventured to visit the Stone on Midsummer Night and who died raving mad because of *something*
they saw there.

That was all I could gleam from Dornly, but my interest was
even more intensely roused as I sensed a distinctly sinister aura
about the Stone. The suggestion of dark antiquity, the recurrent hint of unnatural events on Midsummer Night, touched
some slumbering instinct in my being, as one senses, rather
than hears, the flowing of some dark subterraneous river in the
night.

And I suddenly saw a connection between this Stone and a
certain weird and fantastic poem written by the mad poet
Justin Geoffrey: *The People of the Monolith*. Inquiries led to the
information that Geoffrey had indeed written that poem while
traveling in Hungary, and I could not doubt that the Black
Stone was the very monolith to which he referred in his strange
verse. Reading his stanzas again, I felt once more the strange
dim stirrings of subconscious promptings that I had noticed
when first reading of the Stone.

I had been casting about for a place to spend a short vacation
and I made up my mind. I went to Stregoicavar. A train of obsolete style carried me from Temesvar to within striking distance, at least, of my objective, and a three days' ride in a
jouncing coach brought me to the little village which lay in a
fertile valley high up in the fir-clad mountains. The journey itself was uneventful, but during the first day we passed the old
battlefield of Schomvaal where the brave Polish-Hungarian
knight, Count Boris Vladinoff, made his gallant and futile

stand against the victorious hosts of Suleiman the Magnificent, when the Grand Turk swept over eastern Europe in 1526.

The driver of the coach pointed out to me a great heap of crumbling stones on a hill near by, under which, he said, the bones of the brave Count lay. I remembered a passage from Larson's *Turkish Wars*: "After the skirmish" (in which the Count with his small army had beaten back the Turkish advance-guard) "the Count was standing beneath the half-ruined walls of the old castle on the hill, giving orders as to the disposition of his forces, when an aide brought to him a small lacquered case which had been taken from the body of the famous Turk-ish scribe and historian, Selim Bahadur, who had fallen in the fight. The Count took therefrom a roll of parchment and began to read, but he had not read far before he turned very pale and without saying a word, replaced the parchment in the case and thrust the case into his cloak. At that very instant a hidden Turkish battery suddenly opened fire, and the balls striking the old castle, the Hungarians were horrified to see the walls crash down in ruin, completely covering the brave Count. Without a leader the gallant little army was cut to pieces, and in the war-swept years which followed, the bones of the nobleman were never recovered. Today the natives point out a huge and moldering pile of ruins near Schomvaal beneath which, they say, still rests all that the centuries have left of Count Boris Vladinoff."

I found the village of Stregoicavar a dreamy, drowsy little village that apparently belied its sinister cognomen—a forgot-ten black-eddy that Progress had passed by. The quaint houses and the quainter dress and manners of the people were those of an earlier century. They were friendly, mildly curious but not inquisitive, though visitors from the outside world were ex-tremely rare.

"Ten years ago another American came here and stayed a few days in the village," said the owner of the tavern where I had put up, "a young fellow and queer-acting—mumbled to himself— a poet, I think."

I knew he must mean Justin Geoffrey.

"Yes, he was a poet," I answered, "and he wrote a poem about a bit of scenery near this very village."

"Indeed?" mine host's interest was aroused. "Then, since all great poets are strange in their speech and actions, he must have achieved great fame, for his actions and conversations were the strangest of any man I ever knew."

"As is usual with artists," I answered, "most of his recognition has come since his death."

"He is dead, then?"

"He died screaming in a madhouse five years ago."

"Too bad, too bad," sighed mine host sympathetically. "Poor lad—he looked too long at the Black Stone."

My heart gave a leap, but I masked my keen interest and said casually: "I have heard something of this Black Stone; somewhere near this village, is it not?"

"Nearer than Christian folk wish," he responded. "Look!" He drew me to a latticed window and pointed up at the fir-clad slopes of the brooding blue mountains. "There beyond where you see the bare face of that jutting cliff stands that accursed Stone. Would that it were ground to powder and the powder flung into the Danube to be carried to the deepest ocean! Once men tried to destroy the thing, but each man who laid hammer or maul against it came to an evil end. So now the people shun it."

"What is there so evil about it?" I asked curiously.

"It is a demon-haunted thing," he answered uneasily and with the suggestion of a shudder. "In my childhood I knew a young man who came up from below and laughed at our traditions—in his foolhardiness he went to the Stone one Midsummer Night and at dawn stumbled into the village again, stricken dumb and mad. Something had shattered his brain and sealed his lips, for until the day of his death, which came soon after, he spoke only to utter terrible blasphemies or to slaver gibberish.

"My own nephew when very small was lost in the mountains and slept in the woods near the Stone, and now in his manhood he is tortured by foul dreams, so that at times he makes the night hideous with his screams and wakes with cold sweat upon him.

"But let us talk of something else, *Herr*; it is not good to dwell upon such things."

I remarked on the evident age of the tavern and he answered with pride: "The foundations are more than four hundred years old; the original house was the only one in the village which was not burned to the ground when Suleiman's devils swept through the mountains. Here, in the house that then stood on these same foundations, it is said, the scribe Selim Bahadur had his headquarters while ravaging the country hereabouts."

I learned then that the present inhabitants of Stregoicavar are not descendants of the people who dwelt there before the Turkish raid of 1526. The victorious Moslems left no living human in the village or the vicinity thereabouts when they passed over. Men, women and children they wiped out in one red holocaust of murder, leaving a vast stretch of country silent and utterly deserted. The present people of Stregoicavar are descended from hardy settlers from the lower valleys who came into the upper levels and rebuilt the ruined village after the Turk was thrust back.

Mine host did not speak of the extermination of the original inhabitants with any great resentment and I learned that his ancestors in the lower levels had looked on the mountaineers with even more hatred and aversion than they regarded the Turks. He was rather vague regarding the causes of this feud, but said that the original inhabitants of Stregoicavar had been in the habit of making stealthy raids on the lowlands and stealing girls and children. Moreover, he said that they were not exactly of the same blood as his own people; the sturdy, original Magyar-Slavic stock had mixed and intermarried with a degraded aboriginal race until the breeds had blended, producing an unsavory amalgamation. Who these aborigines were, he had not the slightest idea, but maintained that they were "pagans" and had dwelt in the mountains since time immemorial, before the coming of the conquering peoples.

I attached little importance to this tale; seeing in it merely a parallel to the amalgamation of Celtic tribes with Mediterranean aborigines in the Galloway hills, with the resultant mixed race which, as Picts, has such an extensive part in Scotch legendry. Time has a curiously foreshortening effect on folklore, and just as tales of the Picts became intertwined with legends of an older Mongoloid race, so that eventually the Picts were ascribed the repulsive appearance of the squat primitives, whose individuality merged, in the telling, into Pictish tales, and was forgotten; so, I felt, the supposed inhuman attributes of the first villagers of Stregoicavar could be traced to older, outworn myths with invading Huns and Mongols.

The morning after my arrival I received directions from my host, who gave them worriedly, and set out to find the Black Stone. A few hours' tramp up the fir-covered slopes brought me to the face of the rugged, solid stone cliff which jutted boldly from the mountainside. A narrow trail wound up it, and mounting this, I looked out over the peaceful valley of Stregoicavar, which seemed to drowse, guarded on either hand by the great blue mountains. No huts or any sign of human tenancy showed between the cliff whereon I stood and the village. I saw numbers of scattering farms in the valley but all lay on the other side of Stregoicavar, which itself seemed to shrink from the brooding slopes which masked the Black Stone.

The summit of the cliffs proved to be a sort of thickly wooded plateau. I made my way through the dense growth for a short distance and came into a wide glade; and in the center of the glade reared a gaunt figure of black stone.

It was octagonal in shape, some sixteen feet in height and about a foot and a half thick. It had once evidently been highly polished, but now the surface was thickly dinted as if savage efforts had been made to demolish it; but the hammers had done little more than to flake off small bits of stone and mutilate the characters which once had evidently marched in a spiraling line round and round the shaft to the top. Up to ten feet from the base these characters were almost completely blotted out, so that it was very difficult to trace their direction. Higher up they were plainer, and I managed to squirm part of the way up the shaft and scan them at close range. All were more or less defaced, but I was positive that they symbolized no language now remembered on the face of the earth. I am fairly familiar with all hieroglyphics known to researchers and philologists and I can say with certainty that those characters were like nothing of which I have ever read or heard. The nearest approach to them that I ever saw were some crude scratches on a gigantic and strangely symmetrical rock in a lost valley of Yucatan. I remember that when I pointed out these marks to the archeologist who was my companion, he maintained that they either represented natural weathering or the idle scratching of some Indian. To my theory that the rock was really the base of a long-vanished column, he merely laughed, calling my attention to the dimensions of it, which suggested, if it were built with any natural rules of architectural symmetry, a column a thousand feet high. But I was not convinced.

I will not say that the characters on the Black Stone were similar to those on that colossal rock in Yucatan; but one suggested the other. As to the substance of the monolith, again I was baffled. The stone of which it was composed was a dully gleaming black, whose surface, where it was not dinted and roughened, created a curious illusion of semi-transparency.

I spent most of the morning there and came away baffled. No connection of the Stone with any other artifact in the world suggested itself to me. It was as if the monolith had been reared by alien hands, in an age distant and apart from human ken.

I returned to the village with my interest in no way abated. Now that I had seen the curious thing, my desire was still more keenly whetted to investigate the matter further and seek to learn by what strange hands and for what strange purpose the Black Stone had been reared in the long ago.

I sought out the tavern-keeper's nephew and questioned him in regard to his dreams, but he was vague, though willing to oblige. He did not mind discussing them, but was unable to describe them with any clarity. Though he dreamed the same dreams repeatedly, and though they were hideously vivid at the time, they left no distinct impression on his waking mind. He remembered them only as chaotic nightmares through which huge whirling fires shot lurid tongues of flame and a black drum bellowed incessantly. One thing only he clearly remembered—in one dream he had seen the Black Stone, not on a mountain slope but set like a spire on a colossal black castle.

As for the rest of the villagers I found them not inclined to talk about the Stone, with the exception of the schoolmaster, a man of surprising education, who spent much more of his time out in the world than any of the rest.

He was much interested in what I told him of Von Junzt's remarks about the Stone, and warmly agreed with the German author in the alleged age of the monolith. He believed that a coven had once existed in the vicinity and that possibly all of the original villagers had been members of that fertility cult which once threatened to undermine European civilization and gave rise to the tales of witchcraft. He cited the very name of the village to prove his point; it had not been originally named Stregoicavar, he said; according to legends the builders had called it Xuthltan, which was the aboriginal name of the site on which the village had been built many centuries ago.

This fact routed again an indescribable feeling of uneasiness. The barbarous name did not suggest connection with any Scythic, Slavic or Mongolian race to which an aboriginal people of these mountains would, under natural circumstances, have belonged.

That the Magyars and Slavs of the lower valleys believed the original inhabitants of the village to be members of the witch-craft cult was evident, the schoolmaster said, by the name they gave it, which name continued to be used even after the older settlers had been massacred by the Turks, and the village re-built by a cleaner and more wholesome breed.

He did not believe that the members of the cult erected the monolith but he did believe that they used it as a center of their activities, and repeating vague legends which had been handed down since before the Turkish invasion, he advanced the the-ory that the degenerate villagers had used it as a sort of altar on which they offered human sacrifices, using as victims the girls and babies stolen from his own ancestors in the lower valleys.

He discounted the myths of weird events on Midsummer Night, as well as a curious legend of a strange deity which the witch-people of Xuthltan were said to have invoked with chants and wild rituals of flagellation and slaughter.

He had never visited the Stone on Midsummer Night, he said, but he would not fear to do so; whatever *had* existed or taken place there in the past, had been long engulfed in the mists of time and oblivion. The Black Stone had lost its meaning save as a link to a dead and dusty past.

It was while returning from a visit with this schoolmaster one night about a week after my arrival at Stregoicavar that a sud-den recollection struck me—it was Midsummer Night! The very time that the legends linked with grisly implications to the Black Stone. I turned away from the tavern and strode swiftly through the village. Stregoicavar lay silent; the villagers retired early. I saw no one as I passed rapidly out of the village and up into the firs which masked the mountain slopes with whispering darkness. A broad silver moon hung above the valley, flooding the crags and slopes in a weird light and etching the shadows blackly. No wind blew through the firs, but a mysterious, intangible rustling and whispering was abroad. Surely on such nights in past centuries, my whimsical imagination told me, naked witches astride magic broomsticks had flown across this valley, pursued by jeering demoniac familiars.

I came to the cliffs and was somewhat disquieted to note that the illusive moonlight lent them a subtle appearance I had not noticed before—in the weird light they appeared less like natural cliffs and more like the ruins of cyclopean and Titan-reared battlements jutting from the mountain-slope.

Shaking off this hallucination with difficulty I came upon the plateau and hesitated a moment before I plunged into the brooding darkness of the woods. A sort of breathless tenseness hung over the shadows, like an unseen monster holding its breath lest it scare away its prey.

I shook off the sensation—a natural one, considering the eeriness of the place and its evil reputation—and made my way through the wood, experiencing a most unpleasant sensation that I was being followed, and halting once, sure that something clammy and unstable had brushed against my face in the darkness.

I came out into the glade and saw the tall monolith rearing its gaunt height above the sward. At the edge of the woods on the side toward the cliffs was a stone which formed a sort of natural seat. I sat down, reflecting that it was probably while there that the mad poet, Justin Geoffrey, had written his fantastic *People of the Monolith*. Mine host thought that it was the Stone which had caused Geoffrey's insanity, but the seeds of madness had been sown in the poet's brain long before he ever came to Stregoicavar.

A glance at my watch showed that the hour of midnight was close at hand. I leaned back, waiting whatever ghostly demonstration might appear. A thin night wind started up among the branches of the firs, with an uncanny suggestion of faint, unseen pipes whispering an eery and evil tune. The monotony of the sound and my steady gazing at the monolith produced a sort of self-hypnosis upon me; I grew drowsy. I fought this feeling, but sleep stole on me in spite of myself; the monolith seemed to sway and dance, strangely distorted to my gaze, and then I slept.

I opened my eyes and sought to rise, but lay still, as if an icy hand gripped me helpless. Cold terror stole over me. The glade was no longer deserted. It was thronged by a silent crowd of strange people, and my distended eyes took in strange barbaric details of costume which my reason told me were archaic and forgotten even in this backward land. Surely, I thought, these are villagers who have come here to hold some fantastic conclave—but another glance told me that these people were not of the folk of Stregoicavar. They were a shorter, more squat race, whose brows were lower, whose faces were broader and duller. Some had Slavic or Magyar features, but those features were degraded as from a mixture of some baser, alien strain I could not classify. Many wore the hides of wild beasts, and their whole appearance, both men and women, was one of sensual brutishness. They terrified and repelled me, but they gave me no heed. They formed in a vast half-circle in front of the monolith and began a sort of chant, flinging their arms in unison and weaving their bodies rythmically from the waist upward. All eyes were fixed on the top of the Stone which they seemed to be invoking. But the strangest of all was the dimness of their voices; not fifty yards from me hundreds of men and women were unmistakably lifting their voices in a wild chant, yet those voices came to me as a faint indistinguishable murmur as if from across vast leagues of Space —or *time*.

Before the monolith stood a sort of brazier from which a vile, nauseous yellow smoke billowed upward, curling curiously in an undulating spiral around the black shaft, like a vast unstable serpent.

On one side of this brazier lay two figures—a young girl, stark naked and bound hand and foot, and an infant, apparently only a few months old. On the other side of the brazier squatted a hideous old hag with a queer sort of black drum on her lap; this drum she beat with slow, light blows of her open palms, but I could not hear the sound.

The rhythm of the swaying bodies grew faster and into the space between the people and the monolith sprang a naked young woman, her eyes blazing, her long black hair flying loose. Spinning dizzily on her toes, she whirled across the open space and fell prostrate before the Stone, where she lay motionless. The next instant a fantastic figure followed her—a man from whose waist hung a goatskin, and whose features were entirely hidden by a sort of mask made from a huge wolf's head, so that he looked like a monstrous, nightmare being, horribly compounded of elements both human and bestial. In his hand he held a bunch of long fir switches bound together at the larger ends, and the moonlight glinted on a chain of heavy gold looped about his neck. A smaller chain depending from it suggested a pendant of some sort, but this was missing.

The people tossed their arms violently and seemed to redouble their shouts as this grotesque creature loped across the open space with many a fantastic leap and caper. Coming to the woman who lay before the monolith, he began to lash her with the switches he bore, and she leaped up and spun into the wild mazes of the most incredible dance I have ever seen. And her tormentor danced with her, keeping the wild rhythm, matching her every whirl and bond, while incessantly raining cruel blows on her naked body. And at every blow he shouted a single word, over and over, and all the people shouted it back. I could see the working of their lips, and now the faint far-off murmur of their voices merged and blended into one distant shout, repeated over and over with slobbering ecstasy. But what that one word was, I could not make out.

In dizzy whirls spun the wild dancers, while the lookers-on, standing still in their tracks, followed the rhythm of their dance with swaying bodies and weaving arms. Madness grew in the eyes of the capering votaress and was reflected in the eyes of the watchers. Wilder and more extravagant grew the whirling frenzy of that mad dance—it became a bestial and obscene thing, while the old hag howled and battered the drum like a crazy woman, and the switches cracked out a devil's tune.

Blood trickled down the dancer's limbs but she seemed not to feel the lashing save as a stimulus for further enormities of outrageous motion; bounding into the midst of the yellow smoke which now spread out tenuous tentacles to embrace both flying figures, she seemed to merge with that foul fog and veil herself with it. Then emerging into plain view, closely followed by the beast-thing that flogged her, she shot into an indescribable, explosive burst of dynamic mad motion, and on the very crest of that mad wave, she dropped suddenly to the sward, quivering and panting as if completely overcome by her frenzied exertions. The lashing continued with unabated violence and intensity and she began to wriggle toward the monolith on her belly. The priest—or such I will call him—followed, lashing her unprotected body with all the power of his arm as she writhed along, leaving a heavy track of blood on the trampled earth. She reached the monolith, and gasping and panting, flung both arms about it and covered the cold stone with fierce hot kisses, as in frenzied and unholy adoration.

The fantastic priest bounded high in the air, flinging away the red-dabbled switches, and the worshippers, howling and foaming at the mouths, turned on each other with tooth and nail, rending one another's garments and flesh in a blind passion of bestiality. The priest swept up the infant with a long arm, and shouting again that Name, whirled the wailing babe high in the air and dashed its brains out against the monolith, leaving a ghastly stain on the black surface. Cold with horror I saw him rip the tiny body open with his bare brutish fingers and fling handfuls of blood on the shaft, then toss the red and torn shape into the brazier, extinguishing flame and smoke in a crimson rain, while the maddened brutes behind him howled over and over that Name. Then suddenly they all fell prostrate, writhing like snakes, while the priest flung wide his gory hands as in triumph. I opened my mouth to scream my horror and loathing, but only a dry rattle sounded; a huge monstrous toad-like *thing* squatted on the top of the monolith!

I saw its bloated, repulsive and unstable outline against the moonlight, and set in what would have been the face of a natural creature, its huge, blinking eyes which reflected all the lust, abysmal greed, obscene cruelty and monstrous evil that has stalked the sons of men since their ancestors mowed blind and hairless in the tree-tops. In those grisly eyes were mirrored all the unholy things and vile secrets that sleep in the cities under the sea, and that skulk from the light of day in the blackness of primordial caverns. And so that ghastly thing that the unhallowed ritual of cruelty and sadism and blood had evoked from the silence of the hills, leered and blinked down on its bestial worshippers, who groveled in abhorrent abasement before it.

Now the beast-masked priest lifted the bound and weakly writhing girl in his brutish hands and held her up toward that horror on the monolith. And as that monstrosity sucked in its breath, lustfully and slobberingly, something snapped in my brain and I fell into a merciful faint.

I opened my eyes on a still white dawn. All events of the night rushed back on me and I sprang up, then stared about me in amazement. The monolith brooded gaunt and silent above the sward which waved, green and untrampled, in the morning breeze. A few quick strides took me across the glade; here had the dancers leaped and bounded until the ground should have been trampled bare, and here had the votaress wriggled her painful way to the Stone, streaming blood on the earth. But no drop of crimson showed on the uncrushed sward. I looked, shudderingly, at the side of the monolith against which the bestial priest had brained the stolen baby—but no dark stain nor grisly clot showed there.

A dream! It had been a wild nightmare—or else—I shrugged my shoulders. What vivid clarity for a dream!

I returned quietly to the village and entered the inn without being seen. And there I sat meditating over the strange events of the night. More and more was I prone to discard the dream-theory. That what I had seen was illusion and without material substance, was evident. But I believed that I had looked on the mirrored shadow of a deed perpetrated in ghastly actuality in bygone days. But how was I to know? What proof to show that my vision had been a gathering of foul specters rather than a mere nightmare originating in my own brain?

As if for answer a name flashed into my mind—Selim Bahadur! According to legend this man, who had been a solider as well as a scribe, had commanded that part of Suleiman's army which had devastated Stregoicavar; it seemed logical enough; and if so, he had gone straight from the blotted-out country-side to the bloody field of Schomvaal, and his doom. I sprang up with a sudden shout—that manuscript which was taken from the Turk's body, and which Count Boris shuddered over—might it not contain some narration of what the conquering Turks found in Stregoicavar? What else could have shaken the iron nerves of the Polish adventurer? And since the bones of the Count had never been recovered, what more certain than that the lacquered case, with its mysterious contents, still lay hidden beneath the ruins that covered Boris Vladinoff? I began packing my bag with fierce haste.

Three days later found me ensconced in a little village a few miles from the old battlefield, and when the moon rose I was working with savage intensity on the great pile of crumbling stone that crowned the hill. It was back-breaking toil—looking back now I can not see how I accomplished it, though I labored without a pause from moonrise to dawn. Just as the sun was coming up I tore aside the last tangle of stones and looked on all that was mortal of Count Boris Vladinoff—only a few pitiful fragments of crumbling bone—and among them, crushed out of all original shape, lay a case whose lacquered surface had kept it from complete decay through the centuries.

I seized it with frenzied eagerness, and piling back some of the stones on the bones I hurried away; for I did not care to be discovered by the suspicious peasants in an act of apparent desecration.

Back in my tavern chamber I opened the case and found the parchment comparatively intact; and there was something else in the case—a small squat object wrapped in silk. I was wild to plumb the secrets of those yellowed pages, but weariness forbade me. Since leaving Stregoicavar I had hardly slept at all, and the terrific exertions of the previous night combined to overcome me. In spite of myself I was forced to stretch myself on my bed, nor did I awake until sundown.

I snatched a hasty supper, and then in the light of a flickering candle, I set myself to read the neat Turkish characters that covered the parchment. It was difficult work, for I am not deeply versed in the language and the archaic style of the narrative baffled me. But as I toiled through it a word or a phrase here and there leaped at me and a dimly growing horror shook me in its grip. I bent my energies fiercely to the task, and as the tale grew clearer and took more tangible form my blood chilled in my veins, my hair stood up and my tongue clove to my mouth. All external things partook of the grisly madness of that infernal manuscript until the night sounds of insects and creatures in the woods took the form of ghastly murmurings and stealthy treadings of ghoulish horrors and the sighing of the night wind changed to tittering obscene gloating of evil over the souls of men.

At last when gray dawn was stealing through the latticed window, I laid down the manuscript and took up and unwrapped the thing in the bit of silk. Staring at it with haggard eyes I knew the truth of the matter was clinched, even had it been possible to doubt the veractiy of that terrible manuscript.

And I replaced both obscene things in the case, nor did I rest or sleep or eat until that case containing them had been weighted with stones and flung into the deepest current of the Danube which, God grant, carried them back into the Hell from which they came.

It was no dream I dreamed on Midsummer Midnight in the hills above Stregoicavar. Well for Justin Geoffrey that he tarried there only in the sunlight and went his way, for had he gazed upon that ghastly conclave, his mad brain would have snapped before it did. How my own reason held, I do not know.

No—it was no dream—I gazed upon a foul rout of votaries long dead, come up from Hell to worship as of old; ghosts that bowed before a ghost. For Hell has long claimed their hideous god. Long, long he dwelt among the hills, a brain-shattering vestige of an outworn age, but no longer his obscene talons clutch for the souls of living men, and his kingdom is a dead kingdom, peopled only by the ghosts of those who served him in his lifetime and theirs.

By what foul alchemy or godless sorcery the Gates of Hell are opened on that one eery night I do not know, but mine own eyes have seen. And I know I looked on no living thing that night, for the manuscript written in the careful hand of Selim Bahadur narrated at length what he and his raiders found in the valley of Stregoicavar; and I read, set down in detail, the blasphemous obscenities that torture wrung from the lips of screaming worshippers; and I read, too, of the lost, grim black cavern high in the hills where the horrified Turks hemmed a monstrous, bloated, wallowing toad-like being and slew it with flame and ancient steel blessed in old times by Muhammad, and with incantations that were old when Arabia was young. And even staunch old Selim's hand shook as he recorded the cataclysmic, earth-shaking death-howls of the monstrosity, which died not alone; for a half-score of his slayers perished with him, in ways that Selim would not or could not describe.

And the squat idol carved of gold and wrapped in silk was an image of *himself*, and Selim tore it from the golden chain that looped the neck of the slain high priest of the mask.

Well that the Turks swept that foul valley with torch and cleanly steel! Such sights as those brooding mountains have looked on belong to the darkness and abysses of lost eons. No—it is not fear of the toad-thing that makes me shudder in the night. He is made fast in Hell with his nauseous horde, freed only for an hour on the most weird night of the year, as I have seen. And of his worshippers, none remains.

But it is the realization that such things once crouched beast-like above the souls of men which brings cold sweat to my brow; and I fear to peer again into the leaves of Von Junzt's abomination. For now I understand his repeated phrase of *keys!*—aye! Keys to Outer Doors—links with an abhorrent past and—who knows?—of abhorrent spheres of the *present*. And I understand why the cliffs look like battlements in the moonlight and why the tavern-keeper's nightmare-haunted nephew saw in his dream, the Black Stone like a spire on a cyclopean black castle. If men ever excavate among those mountains they may find incredible things below those masking slopes. For the cave wherein the Turks trapped the—*thing*—was not truly a cavern, and I shudder to contemplate the gigantic gulf of eons which must stretch between this age and the time when the earth shook herself and reared up, like a wave, those blue mountains that, rising, enveloped unthinkable things. May no man ever seek to uproot that ghastly spire men call the Black Stone!

A Key! Aye, it is a Key, symbol of a forgotten horror. That horror has faded into the limbo from which it crawled, loathsomely, in the black dawn of the earth. But what of the other fiendish possibilities hinted at by Von Junzt—what of the monstrous hand which strangled out his life? Since reading what Selim Bahadur wrote, I can no longer doubt anything in the Black Book. Man was not always master of the earth—*and is he now?*

And the thought recurs to me—if such a monstrous entity as the Master of the Monolith somehow survived its own unspeakably distant epoch so long—*what nameless shapes may even now lurk in the dark places of the world?*

1931

HENRY S. WHITEHEAD

(1882–1932)

Passing of a God

"You say that when Carswell came into your hospital over in Port au Prince his fingers looked as though they had been wound with string," said I, encouragingly.

"It is a very ugly story, that, Canevin," replied Doctor Pelletier, still reluctant, it appeared.

"You promised to tell me," I threw in.

"I know it, Canevin," admitted Doctor Pelletier of The U.S. Navy Medical Corps, now stationed here in the Virgin Islands. "But," he proceeded, "you couldn't use this story, anyhow. There are editorial *tabus*, aren't there? The thing is too—what shall I say?—too outrageous, too incredible."

"Yes," I admitted in turn, "there are *tabus*, plenty of them. Still, after hearing about those fingers, as though wound with string—why not give me the story, Pelletier; leave it to me whether or not I 'use' it. It's the story I want, mostly. I'm burning up for it!"

"I suppose it's your lookout," said my guest. "If you find it too gruesome for you, tell me and I'll quit."

I plucked up hope once more. I had been trying for this story, after getting little scraps of it which allured and intrigued me, for weeks.

"Start in," I ventured, soothingly, pushing the silver swizzel-jug after the humidor of cigarettes from which Pelletier was even now making a selection. Pelletier helped himself to the swizzel frowningly. Evidently he was torn between the desire to pour out the story of Arthur Carswell and some complication of feelings against doing so. I sat back in my wicker lounge-chair and waited.

Pelletier moved his large bulk about in his chair. Plainly now he was cogitating how to open the tale. He began, meditatively:

"I don't know as I ever heard public discussion of the ma-

625

lignant bodily growths except among medical people. Science knows little about them. The fact of such diseases, though, is well known to everybody, through campaigns of prevention, the life insurance companies, appeals for funds——

"Well, Carswell's case, primarily, is one of those cases."

He paused and gazed into the glowing end of his cigarette.

"'Primarily?'" I threw in encouragingly.

"Yes. Speaking as a surgeon, that's where this thing begins, I suppose."

I kept still, waiting.

"Have you read Seabrook's book, *The Magic Island*, Canevin?" asked Pelletier suddenly.

"Yes," I answered. "What about it?"

"Then I suppose that from your own experience knocking around the West Indies and your study of it all, a good bit of that stuff of Seabrook's is familiar to you, isn't it?—the *vodu*, and the hill customs, and all the rest of it, especially over in Haiti—you could check up on a writer like Seabrook, couldn't you, more or less?"

"Yes," said I, "practically all of it was an old story to me—a very fine piece of work, however, the thing clicks all the way through—an honest and thorough piece of investigation."

"Anything in it new to you?"

"Yes——Seabrook's statement that there was an exchange of personalities between the sacrificial goat—at the 'baptism'—and the young Black girl, the chapter he calls: *Girl-Cry—Goat-Cry*. That, at least, was a new one on me, I admit."

"You will recall, if you read it carefully, that he attributed that phenomenon to his own personal 'slant' on the thing. Isn't that the case, Canevin?"

"Yes," I agreed, "I think that is the way he put it."

"Then," resumed Doctor Pelletier, "I take it that all that material of his—I notice that there have been a lot of story-writers using his terms lately!—is sufficiently familiar to you so that you have some clear idea of the Haitian-African demi-gods, like Ogoun Badagris, Damballa, and the others, taking up their residence for a short time in some devotee?"

"The idea is very well understood," said I. "Mr. Seabrook mentions it among a number of other local phenomena. It was an old negro who came up to him while he was eating,

thrust his soiled hands into the dishes of food, surprized him
considerably—then was surrounded by worshippers who took
him to the nearest *houmfort* or *vodu*-house, let him sit on the
altar, brought him food, hung all their jewelry on him, worshipped him for the time being; then, characteristically, quite
utterly ignored the original old fellow after the 'possession' on
the part of the 'deity' ceased and reduced him to an unimpor-
tant old pantaloon as he was before."

"That summarizes it exactly," agreed Doctor Pelletier. "That,
Canevin, that kind of thing, I mean, is the real starting-place
of this dreadful matter of Arthur Carswell."

"You mean——?" I barged out at Pelletier, vastly intrigued.
I had had no idea that there was *vodu* mixed in with the case.

"I mean that Arthur Carswell's first intimation that there
was anything pressingly wrong with him was just such a 'possession' as the one you have recounted."

"But—but," I protested, "I had supposed—I had every reason to believe, that it was a surgical matter! Why, you just objected to telling about it on the ground that——"

"Precisely," said Doctor Pelletier, calmly. "It was such a surgical case, but, as I say, it *began* in much the same way as the
'occupation' of that old negro's body by Ogoun Badagris or
whichever one of their devilish deities that happened to be,
just as, you say, is well known to fellows like yourself who go in
for such things, and just as Seabrook recorded it."

"Well," said I, "you go ahead in your own way, Pelletier. I'll
do my best to listen. Do you mind an occasional question?"

"Not in the least," said Doctor Pelletier considerately,
shifted himself to a still more pronouncedly recumbent position in my Chinese rattan lounge-chair, lit a fresh cigarette,
and proceeded:

"Carswell had worked up a considerable intimacy with the
snake-worship of interior Haiti, all the sort of thing familiar to
you; the sort of thing set out, probably for the first time in English at least, in Seabrook's book; all the gatherings, and the
'baptism,' and the sacrifices of the fowls and the bull, and the
goats; the orgies of the worshippers, the boom and thrill of
the *rata* drums—all that strange, incomprehensible, rather silly-
surfaced, deadly-underneathed worship of 'the Snake' which

the Dahomeyans brought with them to old Hispaniola, now
Haiti and the Dominican Republic.

"He had been there, as you may have heard, for a number of
years; went there in the first place because everybody thought
he was a kind of failure at home; made a good living, too, in a
way nobody but an original-minded fellow like him would have
thought of—shot ducks on the Léogane marshes, dried them,
and exported them to New York and San Francisco to the
United States' two largest Chinatowns!

"For a 'failure,' too, Carswell was a particularly smart-
looking chap, smart, I mean, in the English sense of that word.
He was one of those fellows who was always shaved, clean,
freshly groomed, even under the rather adverse conditions of
his living, there in Léogane by the salt marshes; and of his trade,
which was to kill and dry ducks. A fellow can get pretty careless and let himself go at that sort of thing, away from 'home';
away, too, from such niceties as there are in a place like Port au
Prince.

"He looked, in fact, like a fellow just off somebody's yacht
the first time I saw him, there in the hospital in Port au Prince,
and that, too, was right after a rather singular experience which
would have unnerved or unsettled pretty nearly anybody.

"But not so old Carswell. No, indeed. I speak of him as 'Old
Carswell,' Canevin. That, though, is a kind of affectionate term.
He was somewhere about forty-five then; it was two years ago,
you see, and, in addition to his being very spick and span, well
groomed, you know, he looked surprizingly young, somehow.
One of those faces which showed experience, but, along with
the experience, a philosophy. The lines in his face were *good*
lines, if you get what I mean—lines of humor and courage; no
dissipation, no let-down kind of lines, nothing of slackness
such as you would see in the face of even a comparatively
young beach-comber. No, as he strode into my office, almost
jauntily, there in the hospital, there was nothing, nothing
whatever, about him, to suggest anything else but a prosperous fellow American, a professional chap, for choice, who
might, as I say, have just come ashore from somebody's yacht.

"And yet—good God, Canevin, the story that came
out——!"

Naval surgeon though he was, with service in Haiti, at sea,

in Nicaragua, and the China Station to his credit, Doctor Pelletier rose at this point, and, almost agitatedly, walked up and down my gallery. Then he sat down and lit a fresh cigarette.

"There is," he said, reflectively, and as though weighing his words carefully, "there is, Canevin, among various others, a somewhat 'wild' theory that somebody put forward several years ago, about the origin of malignant tumors. It never gained very much approval among the medical profession, but it has, at least, the merit of originality, and—it was new. Because of those facts, it had a certain amount of currency, and there are those, in and out of medicine, who still believe in it. It is that there are certain *nuclei*, certain masses, so to speak, of the bodily material which have persisted—not generally, you understand, but in certain cases—among certain persons, the kind who are 'susceptible' to this horrible disease, which, in the pre-natal state, did not develop fully or normally—little places in the bodily structure, that is—if I make myself clear?—which remain undeveloped.

"Something, according to this hypothesis, something like a sudden jar, or a bruise, a kick, a blow with the fist, the result of a fall, or whatnot, causes traumatism—physical injury, that is, you know—to one of the focus-places, and the undeveloped little mass of material *starts in to grow*, and so displaces the normal tissue which surrounds it.

"One objection to the theory is that there are at least two varieties, well-known and recognized scientifically; the carcinoma, which is itelf subdivided into two kinds, the hard and the soft carcinomæ, and the sarcoma, which is a soft thing, like what is popularly understood by a 'tumor.' Of course they are all 'tumors,' particular kinds of tumors, malignant tumors. What lends a certain credibility to the theory I have just mentioned is the malignancy, the growing element. For, whatever the underlying reason, they grow, Canevin, as is well recognized, and this explanation I have been talking about gives a reason for the growth. The 'malignancy' is, really, that one of the things seems to have, as it were, its own life. All this, probably, you know?"

I nodded. I did not wish to interrupt. I could see that this side-issue on a scientific by-path must have something to do with the story of Carswell.

"Now," resumed Pelletier, "notice this fact, Canevin. Let me put it in the form of a question, like this: To what kind, or type, of *vodu* worshipper, does the 'possession' by one of their deities occur—from your own knowledge of such things, what would you say?"

"To the incomplete; the abnormal, to an *old* man, or woman," said I, slowly, reflecting, "or—to a child, or, perhaps, to an idiot. Idiots, ancient crones, backward children, 'town-fools' and the like, all over Europe, are supposed to be in some mysterious way *en rapport* with deity—or with Satan! It is an established peasant belief. Even among the Mahometans, the moron or idiot is 'the afflicted of God.' There is no other better established belief along such lines of thought."

"Precisely!" exclaimed Pelletier, "and, Canevin, go back once more to Seabrook's instance that we spoke about. What type of person was 'possessed'?"

"An old doddering man," said I, "one well gone in his dotage apparently."

"Right once more! Note now, two things. First, I will admit to you, Canevin, that that theory I have just been expounding never made much of a hit with me. It might be true, but—very few first-rate men in our profession thought much of it, and I followed that negative lead and didn't think much of it, or, in-deed, much about it. I put it down to the vaporings of the theorist who first thought it out and published it, and let it go at that. Now, Canevin, *I am convinced that it is true!* The second thing, then: When Carswell came into my office in the hospital over there in Port au Prince, the first thing I noticed about him—I had never seen him before, you see—was a peculiar, almost an indescribable, discrepancy. It was between his general appearance of weather-worn cleanliness, general fitness, his 'smart' appearance in his clothes—all that, which fitted together about the clean-cut, open character of the fellow; and what I can only describe as a pursiness. He seemed in good condition, I mean to say, and yet—there was something, somehow, *flabby* some-where in his makeup. I couldn't put my finger on it, but—it was there, a suggestion of something that detracted from the impression he gave as being an upstanding fellow, a good-fellow-to-have-beside-you-in-a-pinch—that kind of person.

*

"The second thing I noticed, it was just after he had taken a chair beside my desk, was his fingers, and thumbs. They were swollen, Canevin, looked sore, as though they had been wound with string. That was the first thing I thought of, being wound with string. He saw me looking at them, held them out to me abruptly, laid them side by side, his hands I mean, on my desk, and smiled at me.

"'I see you have noticed them, Doctor,' he remarked, almost jovially. 'That makes it a little easier for me to tell you what I'm here for. It's—well, you might put it down as a "symptom".'

"I looked at his fingers and thumbs; every one of them was affected in the same way; and ended up with putting a magnifying glass over them.

"They were all bruised and reddened, and here and there on several of them, the skin was abraded, broken, *circularly*—it was a most curious-looking set of digits. My new patient was addressing me again:

"'I'm not here to ask you riddles, Doctor,' he said, gravely, this time, 'but—would you care to make a guess at what did that to those fingers and thumbs of mine?'

"'Well,' I came back at him, 'without knowing what's happened, it *looks* as if you'd been trying to wear about a hundred rings, all at one time, and most of them didn't fit!'

"Carswell nodded his head at me. 'Score one for the medico,' said he, and laughed. 'Even numerically you're almost on the dot, sir. The precise number was one hundred and six!'

"I confess, I stared at him then. But he wasn't fooling. It was a cold, sober, serious fact that he was stating; only, he saw that it had a humorous side, and that intrigued him, as anything humorous always did, I found out after I got to know Carswell a lot better than I did then."

"You said you wouldn't mind a few questions, Pelletier," I interjected.

"Fire away," said Pelletier. "Do you see any light, so far?"

"I was naturally figuring along with you, as you told about it all," said I. "Do I infer correctly that Carswell, having lived there—how long, four or five years or so?——"

"Seven, to be exact," put in Pelletier.

"——that Carswell, being pretty familiar with the native

doings, had mixed into things, got the confidence of his Black neighbors in and around Léogane, become somewhat 'adept', had the run of the *houmforts*, so to speak—'*votre bougie, M'sieu*' —the fortune-telling at the festivals, and so forth, and—had been 'visited' by one of the Black deities? That, apparently, if I'm any judge of tendencies, is what your account seems to be leading up to. Those bruised fingers—the one hundred and six rings—good heavens, man, is it really possible?"

"Carswell told me all about that end of it, a little later—yes, that was, precisely, what happened, but—that, surprizing, incredible as it seems, is only the small end of it all. You just wait——"

"Go ahead," said I, "I am all ears, I assure you!"

"Well, Carswell took his hands off the desk after I had looked at them through my magnifying glass, and then waved one of them at me in a kind of deprecating gesture.

"'I'll go into all that, if you're interested to hear about it, Doctor,' he assured me, 'but that isn't what I'm here about.' His face grew suddenly very grave. 'Have you plenty of time?' he asked. 'I don't want to let my case interfere with anything.'

"'Fire ahead,' says I, and he leaned forward in his chair.

"'Doctor,' says he, 'I don't know whether or not you ever heard of me before. My name's Carswell, and I live over Léogane way. I'm an American, like yourself, as you can probably see, and, even after seven years of it, out there, duck-hunting, mostly, with virtually no White-man's doings for a pretty long time, I haven't "gone native" or anything of the sort. I wouldn't want you to think I'm one of those wasters.' He looked up at me inquiringly for my estimate of him. He had been by himself a good deal; perhaps too much. I nodded at him. He looked me in the eye, squarely, and nodded back. 'I guess we understand each other,' he said. Then he went on.

"'Seven years ago, it was, I came down here. I've lived over there ever since. What few people know about me regard me as a kind of failure, I daresay. But—Doctor, there was a reason for that, a pretty definite reason. I won't go into it beyond your end of it—the medical end, I mean. I came down because of this.'

"He stood up then, and I saw what made that 'discrepancy' I spoke about, that 'flabbiness' which went so ill with the general cut of the man. He turned up the lower ends of his white drill jacket and put his hand a little to the left of the middle of his stomach. 'Just notice this,' he said, and stepped toward me.

"There, just over the left center of that area and extending up toward the spleen, on the left side, you know, there was a protuberance. Seen closely it was apparent that here was some sort of internal growth. It was that which had made him look flabby, stomachish.

" 'This was diagnosed for me in New York,' Carswell explained, 'a little more than seven years ago. They told me it was inoperable then. After seven years, probably, I daresay it's worse, if anything. To put the thing in a nutshell, Doctor, I had to "let go" then. I got out of a promising business, broke off my engagement, came here. I won't expatiate on it all, but —it was pretty tough, Doctor, pretty tough. I've lasted all right, so far. It hasn't troubled me—until just lately. That's why I drove in this afternoon, to see you, to see if anything could be done.'

" 'Has it been kicking up lately?' I asked him.

" 'Yes,' said Carswell, simply. 'They said it would kill me, probably within a year or so, as it grew. It hasn't grown— much. I've lasted a little more than seven years, so far.'

" 'Come in to the operating-room,' I invited him, 'and take your clothes off, and let's get a good look at it.'

" 'Anything you say,' returned Carswell, and followed me back into the operating-room then and there.

"I had a good look at Carswell, first, superficially. That preliminary examination revealed a growth quite typical, the self-contained, not the 'fibrous' type, in the location I've already described, and about the size of an average man's head. It lay imbedded, fairly deep. It was what we call 'encapsulated.' That, of course, is what had kept Carswell alive.

"Then we put the X-rays on it, fore-and-aft, and sidewise. One of those things doesn't always respond very well to skia-graphic examination, to the X-ray, that is, but this one showed clearly enough. Inside it appeared a kind of dark, triangular mass, with the small end at the top. When Doctor Smithson and I had looked him over thoroughly, I asked Carswell whether or not he wanted to stay with us, to come into the hospital as a patient, for treatment.

" 'I'm quite in your hands, Doctor,' he told me. 'I'll stay, or do whatever you want me to. But, first,' and for the first time he looked a trifle embarrassed, 'I think I'd better tell you the story that goes with my coming here! However, speaking plainly, do you think I have a chance?'

" 'Well,' said I, 'speaking plainly, yes, there is a chance, maybe a "fifty-fifty" chance, maybe a little less. On the one hand, this thing has been let alone for seven years since original diagnosis. It's probably less operable than it was when you were in New York. On the other hand, we know a lot more, not about these things, Mr. Carswell, but about surgical technique, than they did seven years ago. On the whole, I'd advise you to stay and get ready for an operation, and, say about "forty-sixty" you'll go back to Léogane, or back to New York if you feel like it, several pounds lighter in weight and a new man. If it takes you, on the table, well, you've had a lot more time out there gunning for ducks in Léogane than those New York fellows allowed you.'

" 'I'm with you,' said Carswell, and we assigned him a room, took his 'history', and began, to get him ready for his operation.

"We did the operation two days later, at ten-thirty in the morning, and in the meantime Carswell told me his 'story' about it.

"It seems that he had made quite a place for himself, there in Léogane, among the negroes and the ducks. In seven years a man like Carswell, with his mental and dispositional equipment, can go quite a long way, anywhere. He had managed to make quite a good thing out of his duck-drying industry, employed five or six 'hands' in his little wooden 'factory,' rebuilt a rather good house he had secured there for a song right after he had arrived, collected local antiques to add to the equipment he had brought along with him, made himself a real home of a peculiar, bachelor kind, and, above all, got in solid with the Black People all around him. Almost incidentally I gathered from him—he had no gift of narrative, and I had to question him a great deal—he had got onto, and into, the know in the *vodu* thing. There wasn't, as far as I could get it, any aspect of it all that he hadn't been in on, except, that is, '*la chevre sans cornes*'—the goat without horns, you know—the human sacrifice on great occasions. In fact, he strenuously denied that the *voduists* resorted to that; said it was a *canard* against them; that they never, really, did such things, never had, unless back in prehistoric times, in Guinea—Africa.

"But, there wasn't anything about it all that he hadn't at his very finger-ends, and at first-hand, too. The man was a walking encyclopedia of the native beliefs, customs, and practises. He knew, too, every turn and twist of their speech. He hadn't, as he had said at first, 'gone native' in the slightest degree, and yet, without lowering his White Man's dignity by a trifle, he had got it all.

"That brings us to the specific happening, the 'story' which, he had said, went along with his reason for coming in to the hospital in Port au Prince, to us.

"It appears that his sarcoma had never, practically, troubled. Beyond noting a very gradual increase in its size from year to year, he said, he 'wouldn't know he had one.' In other words, characteristically, it never gave him any pain or direct annoyance beyond the sense of the wretched thing being there, and increasing on him, and always drawing him closer to that end of life which the New York doctors had warned him about.

"Then, it had happened only three days before he came to the hospital, he had gone suddenly unconscious one afternoon, as he was walking down his shell path to his gateway. The last thing he remembered then was being 'about four steps from the gate.' When he woke up, it was dark. He was seated in a big chair on his own front gallery, and the first thing he noticed was that his fingers and thumbs were sore and ached very painfully. The next thing was that there were flares burning all along the edge of the gallery, and down in the front yard, and along the road outside the paling fence that divided his property from the road, and in the light of these flares, there swarmed literally hundreds of negroes, gathered about him and mostly on their knees; lined along the gallery and on the grounds below it; prostrating themselves, chanting, putting earth and sand on their heads; and, when he leaned back in his chair, something hurt the back of his neck, and he found that he was being nearly choked with the necklaces, strings of beads, gold and silver coin-strings, and other kinds, that had been draped over his head. His fingers, and the thumbs as well, were covered with gold and silver rings, many of them jammed on so as to stop the circulation.

"From his knowledge of their beliefs, he recognized what had happened to him. He had, he figured, probably fainted, although such a thing was not at all common with him, going down the pathway to the yard gate, and the Blacks had supposed him to be 'possessed' as he had several times seen Black people, children, old men and women, morons, chiefly, similarly 'possessed.' He knew that, now that he was recovered from whatever had happened to him, the 'worship' ought to cease and if he simply sat quiet and took what was coming to him, they would, as soon as they realized he was 'himself' once more, leave him alone and he would get some relief from this uncomfortable set of surroundings; get rid of the necklaces and the rings; get a little privacy.

"But—the queer part of it all was that they didn't quit. No, the mob around the house and on the gallery increased rather than diminished, and at last he was put to it, from sheer discomfort—he said he came to the point where he felt he couldn't stand it all another instant—to speak up and ask the people to leave him in peace.

"They left him, he says, at that, right off the bat, immediately, without a protesting voice, but—and here was what started him on his major puzzlement—they didn't take off the necklaces and rings. No—they left the whole set of that metallic drapery which they had hung and thrust upon him right there, and, after he had been left alone, as he had requested, and had gone into his house, and lifted off the necklaces and worked the rings loose, the *next* thing that happened was that old Pa'p Josef, the local *papaloi*, together with three or four other neighboring *papalois*, witch-doctors from nearby villages, and followed by a very old man who was known to Carswell as the *hougan*, or head witch-doctor of the whole countryside thereabouts, came in to him in a kind of procession, and knelt down all around him on the floor of his living-room, and laid down gourds of cream and bottles of red rum and cooked chickens, and even a big china bowl of Tannia soup—a dish he abominated, said it always tasted like soapy water to him!— and then backed out leaving him to these comestibles.

"He said that this sort of attention persisted in his case, right

through the three days that he remained in his house in Léogane, before he started out for the hospital; would, apparently,
be still going on if he hadn't come in to Port au Prince to us.

"But—his coming in was not, in the least, because of this. It
had puzzled him a great deal, for there was nothing like it in
his experience, nor, so far as he could gather from their attitude, in the experience of the people about him, of the *papalois*, or even of the *hougan* himself. They acted, in other words,
precisely as though the 'deity' supposed to have taken up his
abode within him had remained there, although there seemed
no precedent for such an occurrence, and, so far as he knew, he
felt precisely just as he had felt right along, that is, fully awake,
and, certainly, not in anything like an abnormal condition,
and, very positively, not in anything like a fainting-fit!

"That is to say—he felt precisely the same as usual except
that—he attributed it to the probability that he must have
fallen on the ground that time when he lost consciousness
going down the pathway to the gate (he had been told that
passers-by had picked him up and carried him to the gallery
where he had awakened, later, these Good Samaritans meanwhile recognizing that one of the 'deities' had indwelt him)—
he felt the same except for recurrent, almost unbearable pains
in the vicinity of his lower abdominal region.

"There was nothing surprizing to him in this accession of
the new painfulness. He had been warned that that would be the
beginning of the end. It was in the rather faint hope that something might be done that he had come in to the hospital. It
speaks volumes for the man's fortitude, for his strength of
character, that he came in so cheerfully; acquiesced in what we
suggested to him to do; remained with us, facing those comparatively slim chances with complete cheerfulness.

"For—we did not deceive Carswell—the chances were somewhat slim. 'Sixty-forty' I had said, but as I afterward made
clear to him, the favorable chances, as gleaned from the mortality tables, were a good deal less than that.

"He went to the table in a state of mind quite unchanged
from his accustomed cheerfulness. He shook hands good-bye
with Doctor Smithson and me, 'in case,' and also with Doctor
Jackson, who acted as anesthetist.

*

"Carswell took an enormous amount of ether to get him off. His consciousness persisted longer, perhaps, than that of any surgical patient I can remember. At last, however, Doctor Jackson intimated to me that I might begin, and, Doctor Smithson standing by with the retracting forceps, I made the first incision. It was my intention, after careful study of the X-ray plates, to open it up from in front, in an up-and-down direction, establish drainage directly, and, leaving the wound in the sound tissue in front of it open, to attempt to get it healed up after removing its contents. Such is the technique of the major portion of successful operations.

"It was a comparatively simple matter to expose the outer wall. This accomplished, and after a few words of consultation with my colleague, I very carefully opened it. We recalled that the X-ray had shown, as I mentioned, a triangular-shaped mass within. This apparent content we attributed to some obscure chemical coloration of the contents. I made my incisions with the greatest care and delicacy, of course. The critical part of the operation lay right at this point, and the greatest exactitude was indicated, of course.

"At last the outer coats of it were cut through, and retracted, and with renewed caution I made the incision through the inmost wall of tissue. To my surprize, and to Doctor Smithson's, the inside was comparatively dry. The gauze which the nurse attending had caused to follow the path of the knife, was hardly moistened. I ran my knife down below the original scope of that last incision, then upward from its upper extremity, greatly lengthening the incision as a whole, if you are following me.

"Then, reaching my gloved hand within this long up-and-down aperture, I felt about and at once discovered that I could get my fingers in around the inner containing wall quite easily. I reached and worked my fingers in farther and farther, finally getting both hands inside and at last feeling my fingers touch inside the posterior or rear wall. Rapidly, now, I ran the edges of my hands around inside, and, quite easily, lifted out the 'inside.' This, a mass weighing several pounds, of more or less solid material, was laid aside on the small table beside the operating-table, and, again pausing to consult with Doctor Smithson—the operation was going, you see, a lot better than either of us had dared to anticipate—and being encouraged by him to proceed to a radical step which we had not hoped to be able to take, I began the dissection from the surrounding, normal tissue, of the now collapsed walls. This, a long, difficult, and harassing job, was accomplished at the end of, perhaps, ten or twelve minutes of gruelling work, and the bag-like thing, now completely severed from the tissues in which it had been for so long imbedded, was placed also on the side table.

"Doctor Jackson reporting favorably on our patient's condition under the anesthetic, I now proceeded to dress the large aperture, and to close the body-wound. This was accomplished in a routine manner, and then, together, we bandaged Carswell, and he was taken back to his room to await awakening from the ether.

"Carswell disposed of, Doctor Jackson and Doctor Smithson left the operating-room and the nurse started in cleaning up after the operation; dropping the instruments into the boiler, and so on—a routine set of duties. As for me, I picked up the shell in a pair of forceps, turned it about under the strong electric operating-light, and laid it down again. It presented nothing of interest for a possible laboratory examination.

"Then I picked up the more or less solid contents which I had laid, very hastily, and without looking at it—you see, my actual removal of it had been done inside, in the dark for the most part and by the sense of feeling, with my hands, you will remember—I picked it up; I still had my operating-gloves on to prevent infection when looking over these specimens, and, still, not looking at it particularly, carried it out into the laboratory.

"Canevin"—Doctor Pelletier looked at me somberly through the very gradually fading light of late afternoon, the period just before the abrupt falling of our tropic dusk— "Canevin," he repeated, "honestly, I don't know how to tell you! Listen now, old man, do something for me, will you?"

"Why, yes—of course," said I, considerably mystified. "What is it you want me to do, Pelletier?"

"My car is out in front of the house. Come on home with me, up to my house, will you? Let's say I want to give you a cocktail! Anyhow, maybe you'll understand better when you are there, *I want to tell you the rest up at my house, not here.* Will you please come, Canevin?"

I looked at him closely. This seemed to me a very strange, an abrupt, request. Still, there was nothing whatever unreasonable about such a sudden whim on Pelletier's part.

"Why, yes, certainly I'll go with you, Pelletier, if you want me to."

"Come on, then," said Pelletier, and we started for his car.

The doctor drove himself, and after we had taken the first turn in the rather complicated route from my house to his, on the extreme airy top of Denmark Hill, he said, in a quiet voice:

"Put together, now, Canevin, certain points, if you please, in this story. Note, kindly, how the Black people over in Léogane acted, according to Carswell's story. Note, too, that theory I was telling you about; do you recollect it clearly?"

"Yes," said I, still more mystified.

"Just keep those two points in mind, then," added Doctor Pelletier, and devoted himself to navigating sharp turns and plodding up two steep roadways for the rest of the drive to his house.

We went in and found his houseboy laying the table for his dinner. Doctor Pelletier is unmarried, keeps a hospitable bachelor establishment. He ordered cocktails, and the houseboy departed on this errand. Then he led me into a kind of office, littered with medical and surgical paraphernalia. He lifted some papers off a chair, motioned me into it, and took another near by. "Listen, now!" he said, and held up a finger at me.

"I took that thing, as I mentioned, into the laboratory," said he. "I carried it in my hand, with my gloves still on, as aforesaid. I laid it down on a table and turned on a powerful light over it. It was only then that I took a good look at it. It weighed several pounds at least, was about the bulk and heft of a full-grown coconut, and about the same color as a hulled coconut, that is, a kind of medium brown. As I looked at it, I saw that it was, as the X-ray had indicated, vaguely triangular in shape. It lay over on one of its sides under that powerful light, and—Canevin, so help me God"—Doctor Pelletier leaned toward me, his face working, a great seriousness in his eyes—"it moved, Canevin," he murmured; "and, as I looked— the thing *breathed*! I was just plain dumfounded. A biological specimen like that—does not move, Canevin! I shook all over, suddenly. I felt my hair prickle on the roots of my scalp. I felt chills go down my spine. Then I remembered that here I was, after an operation, in my own biological laboratory. I came close to the thing and propped it up, on what might be called its logical base, if you see what I mean, so that it stood as nearly upright as its triangular conformation permitted.

"And then I saw that it had faint yellowish markings over the brown, and that what you might call its skin was moving, and—as I stared at the thing, Canevin—two things like little arms began to move, and the top of it gave a kind of convulsive shudder, and it opened straight at me, Canevin, a pair of eyes and looked me in the face.

"Those eyes—my God, Canevin, those eyes! They were eyes of something more than human, Canevin, something incredibly evil, something vastly old, sophisticated, cold, immune from anything except pure evil, the eyes of something that had been worshipped, Canevin, from ages and ages out of a past that went back before all known human calculation, eyes that showed all the deliberate, lurking wickedness that has ever been in the world. The eyes closed, Canevin, and the thing sank over onto its side, and heaved and shuddered convulsively.

"*It was sick, Canevin*; and now, emboldened, holding myself together, repeating over and over to myself that I had a case of the quavers, of post-operative 'nerves,' I forced myself to look closer, and as I did so I got from it a faint whiff of ether. Two tiny, ape-like nostrils, over a clamped-shut slit of a mouth, were exhaling and inhaling; drawing in the good, pure air, exhaling ether fumes. It popped into my head that Carswell had consumed a terrific amount of ether before he went under; we had commented on that, Doctor Jackson particularly. I put two and two together, Canevin, remembered we were in Haiti, where things are not like New York, or Boston, or Baltimore! Those negroes had believed that the 'deity' had not come out of Carswell, do you see? *That* was the thing that held the edge of my mind. The thing stirred uneasily, put out one of its 'arms,' groped about, stiffened.

"I reached for a near-by specimen-jar, Canevin, reasoning, almost blindly, that if this thing were susceptible to ether, it would be susceptible to—well, my gloves were still on my hands, and—now shuddering so that I could hardly move at all, I had to force every motion—I reached out and took hold of the thing—it felt like moist leather—and dropped it into the jar. Then I carried the carboy of preserving alcohol over to the table and poured it in till the ghastly thing was entirely covered, the alcohol near the top of the jar. It writhed once, then rolled over on its 'back,' and lay still, the mouth now open. Do you believe me, Canevin?"

"I have always said that I would believe anything, on proper evidence," said I, slowly, "and I would be the last to question a statement of yours, Pelletier. However, although I have, as you say, looked into some of these things perhaps more than most, it seems, well——"

Doctor Pelletier said nothing. Then he slowly got up out of his chair. He stepped over to a wall-cupboard and returned, a wide-mouthed specimen-jar in his hand. He laid the jar down before me, in silence.

I looked into it, through the slightly discolored alcohol with which the jar, tightly sealed with rubber-tape and sealing-wax, was filled nearly to the brim. There, on the jar's bottom, lay such a thing as Pelletier had described (a thing which, if it had been "seated," upright, would somewhat have resembled that representation of the happy little godling 'Billiken' which was popular twenty years ago as a desk ornament), a thing suggesting the sinister, the unearthly, even in this dessicated form. I looked long at the thing.

"Excuse me for even seeming to hesitate, Pelletier," said I, reflectively.

"I can't say that I blame you," returned the genial doctor. "It is, by the way, the first and only time I have ever tried to tell the story to anybody."

"And Carswell?" I asked. "I've been intrigued with that good fellow and his difficulties. How did he come out of it all?"

"He made a magnificent recovery from the operation," said Pelletier, "and afterward, when he went back to Léogane, he told me that the negroes, while glad to see him quite as usual, had quite lost interest in him as the throne of a 'divinity'."

"H'm," I remarked, "it would seem, that, to bear out——"

"Yes," said Pelletier, "I have always regarded that fact as absolutely conclusive. Indeed, how otherwise could one possibly account for—*this?*" He indicated the contents of the laboratory jar.

I nodded my head, in agreement with him. "I can only say that—if you won't feel insulted, Pelletier—that you are singularly open-minded, for a man of science! What, by the way, became of Carswell?"

The houseboy came in with a tray, and Pelletier and I drank to each other's good health.

"He came in to Port au Prince," replied Pelletier after he had done the honors. "He did not want to go back to the States, he said. The lady to whom he had been engaged had died a couple of years before; he felt that he would be out of touch with American business. The fact is—he had stayed out here too long, too continuously. But, he remains an 'authority' on Haitian native affairs, and is consulted by the High Commissioner. He knows, literally, more about Haiti than the Haitians themselves. I wish you might meet him; you'd have a lot in common."

"I'll hope to do that," said I, and rose to leave. The houseboy appeared at the door, smiling in my direction.

"The table is set for two, sar," said he.

Doctor Pelletier led the way into the dining-room, taking it for granted that I would remain and dine with him. We are informal in St. Thomas, about such matters. I telephoned home and sat down with him.

Pelletier suddenly laughed—he was half-way through his soup at the moment. I looked up inquiringly. He put down his soup spoon and looked across the table at me.

"It's a bit odd," he remarked, "when you stop to think of it! There's one thing Carswell doesn't know about Haiti and what happens there!"

"What's that?" I inquired.

"That—thing—in there," said Pelletier, indicating the office with his thumb in the way artists and surgeons do. "I thought he'd had troubles enough without *that* on his mind, too."

I nodded in agreement and resumed my soup. Pelletier has a cook in a thousand. . . .

1931

AUGUST DERLETH

(1909–1971)

The Panelled Room

WHEN Father Brauman could not change Mrs. Grant's mind,
Miss Barbara Allen, seeing him come dolefully down the steps
from the porch flung proudly across the face of the house Mrs.
Grant had taken, thought she would try. People said that if
Miss Barbara Allen could do nothing there was no use trying
longer. But it was necessary to do everything possible to convince Mrs. Grant that the house on Main Street was not a
healthy place to live in, because of the things that were whispered and sometimes openly said about it—since the murder
some years back. So, after announcing her intention to the
town through her friends, Miss Barbara Allen paid a visit to
Mrs. Grant a week after that lady had moved into the house on
Main Street with her sister and her sister's little daughter.

Her reception was not too cordial, and when she mentioned
the house and spoke about what people said of it, Mrs. Grant
put up her lorgnette and told the old lady that as she was a
Freethinker she didn't believe in such things.

"I'm a Freethinker, too, Mrs. Grant," said Miss Barbara,
"but I lived in this house once."

Mrs. Grant smiled politely and patiently and said, "Nothing
seems to have happened to you," her inference clear and her
manner no less so.

Miss Barbara blinked a little and said, "My sister died here,"
announcing it rather, as if this fact alone were incontestable
proof of the strange rumors current about the house in which
they sat.

Mrs. Grant thought, How provincial! and raised her eyebrows a little. "Surely you don't think this house had anything
to do with that?" she asked, her voice more kind now.

The old lady was firm. "I know it did. If it wouldn't be for
wanting to tell you, that being my duty, as I said to Elvira—
that's my other sister—I'd never've set foot in this house

again. My sister was found dead in the panelled room, the parlor—at least, it was our parlor."

"Heart attack, I suppose?"

Miss Barbara shook her head. "There was never anything the matter with Abby. She was just found dead. Old Doctor Brown, he said it was shock—a scare, most likely. That was after poor Abby began to see things in that room."

"What things?"

The old lady picked at her shawl and looked at Mrs. Grant over her spectacles, as if trying to discover from Mrs. Grant's features how much she had already been told. "Fifty years ago, come next month, Peter Mason killed his wife in that room and then he killed himself. They found them both the next day, she choked to death, and he hanging there. Sometimes you can see him hanging there yet—and she a-lying on the floor pale and white."

"Why, Miss Allen, that's a childish invention!"

Miss Barbara smiled faintly. "Almost my very words, when Abby and I took this house. But I've seen Peter Mason hanging, myself—and I've seen his wife there, too." There was an intensity in her voice, but no flicker of emotion disturbed her face.

Mrs. Grant leaned forward a little, saying, "Yes?", still polite, still patient, urging her visitor to continue, though she did not wish to hear more.

"He was hanging from the cross-beam over the bookcase—just like they found him when I was a little girl. You don't know what it is to walk into that room and see him there all unexpected—you don't know, yet. And to see her like that again—all crumpled up on the floor, her face twisted! I wouldn't want to be in your place for anything. I'd move out right away, this very minute!"

Mrs. Grant sighed, having heard the admonition many times since she had come to the town and taken the house. Miss Barbara Allen began to feel uncomfortable and rose presently to go, feeling that she had done what she could.

"Will you promise me something, Mrs. Grant?" she asked.

Mrs. Grant hesitated. "That can be almost anything," she said, feeling her position becoming intolerable and wanting this woman to go away.

Miss Barbara said, "It's nothing unreasonable. Promise me

that when you see the panels moving in the parlor, you'll leave this house right away. There's a horror hanging over this house —and it may be too late to get away when you see the panels move."

Curiosity prompted Mrs. Grant to ask, "What do you mean, Miss Allen?"

"If you're staying, you'll see soon enough. But I hope you'll change your mind before then." Then she was gone, the door closing heavily behind her.

Mrs. Grant watched the old woman go down the outer steps, thinking, What a queer person! Then she turned away and went into the living room, where she sat down, aware of the critical eye her sister turned on her.

"The usual thing, Irma," said Mrs. Grant. "We are to move right away."

The child in one corner of the room took up the words. "I like moving, Mamma. When are we going to move?" She allowed her block building to tumble to the floor and jumped to her feet, clapping her hands.

"Do be quiet, Ellen," said her mother, fixing the child with her eyes while Mrs. Grant nodded stern but not unkind approval. "We aren't going to move, dear." Then she turned again to her older sister.

"But there's something new, this time," Mrs. Grant went on. "The panels in the parlor are said to move—that serpent design, I suppose Miss Allen meant."

Irma smiled. "An illusion, Lydia. Everyone knows that if you look at a design like that long enough, your eyes will seem to see movement."

Mrs. Grant nodded, clasping her fingers and looking down at them in a moment of silent speculation. Presently she spoke again. "True, Irma. Still, there was something about Miss Allen I didn't understand."

"What?"

"Why, I don't know. A peculiar earnestness—that's the best I can do by way of describing her attitude. She sat there telling me her story so simply, expecting me to believe every word of it. It was uncanny, Irma. I mean, she didn't look like the kind of woman who's very easily taken in by such things."

"I do believe the old lady's story has affected you," said

Irma, not without impatience. "But I shan't let you fall under her spell. I declare, Lydia, you're white as a sheet, just thinking about it."

Mrs. Grant felt considerably better on coming down to breakfast next morning, for indeed Miss Allen's simple earnestness had insidiously destroyed her confident superiority the evening before. The prattle of Irma's child this unusually bright morning took her mind away from Peter Mason and his unfortunate wife, and the unbelievable stories of weird hauntings that had been current since then.

In the afternoon Mrs. Grant let it be known that she would not welcome any more people, however well-intentioned, who came to warn her about the house. When she dropped this hint to her callers, she sensed immediately an air of restraint. Later, when she walked down Main Street at dusk, she felt a frightening air of waiting in the half-hidden faces peering out at her from behind the curtained windows of houses she passed.

In the evening she was afraid. With some reluctance, she said to her sister, "Really, the house *is* beginning to oppress me," and when Irma said, "Nonsense, Lydia!" she was afraid to say more. She sat in comparative silence for the rest of the evening, an obvious air of unnatural restraint cloaking her. For this she could not entirely account, Miss Allen's story being already too far in the past to explain it.

Mrs. Grant's strange oppression grew.

It crept upon her from all sides, day by day, and she felt it suddenly even when doing the most ordinary things—when dusting the room, or rearranging the furniture, things she trusted no maid with doing. She could not understand this oppression's growing in, building itself stronger about and within her, but when fear found her she knew.

Ten days after Miss Barbara Allen's call, Mrs. Grant walked into the panelled room one evening and saw a man hanging in the shadows where the bookcase was—and a crumpled shape oddly darkening the floor nearby. She fell back against the wall, but the thing was gone. She thought, It's nothing. There is nothing there at all. But it was two hours before she had convinced herself that she had seen nothing. When she came out of the parlor, Irma noticed her paleness.

"Well, I declare, Lydia, there's something the matter with you!" she exclaimed.

Mrs. Grant looked at her sister and knew she could not tell her, knew she could not face Irma's scornful skepticism. "I've got a terrible headache," she said.

Irma was surprised. "A headache—that's strange. You've never had one before, Lydia." She looked queerly at Mrs. Grant for a moment before she said, "You'll find aspirin tablets in my purse. You'd better take one. But I can't understand your having a headache like this."

Mrs. Grant did not reply. Irma did not notice that Mrs. Grant went directly upstairs, avoiding the purse on the side table. In the night, Mrs. Grant's sleep was haunted by dreams of the panelled room and what she had seen there, and in her dreams there was no illusion.

After Mrs. Grant had seen the man hanging and the form huddled on the floor beneath four times, she steeled herself to speak to her sister, thinking that this was the only way, for it must come some time. "I've seen him," she said abruptly one day while the two of them sat at the table.

Irma put down her cup of coffee and looked at her sister with a frown on her forehead. "You've seen him," she said. "What do you mean? Who is it you've seen?"

"Why, Peter Mason—the man who killed his wife. And I've seen her, too." Mrs. Grant made a vague and uncertain gesture in the direction of the panelled room.

A sudden comprehension came to Irma, and a strange gleam began to grow in her eyes. Mrs. Grant did not understand, but Irma was thinking, *If anything happens to her, I'll get everything!* The thought had come to her with startling suddenness, but she made no attempt to beat it down. It would mean freedom for her and Ellen. No more bending to Lydia's wish. With an effort she controlled her voice, for her abrupt excitement was beating in her. "You imagined it," she said calmly, but her fingers trembled as she took up a tea-cake.

"I think we *had* better give up this house," said Mrs. Grant.

Irma smiled in a superior fashion calculated to disarm her sister. "Nonsense, Lydia. I refuse to consider giving up this fine old house because of a few stories—like as not unfounded, my dear."

"*But Irma, I have seen him!*" Her voice was strong with the intensity of conviction that had grown in her during the past few days.

Irma stirred her coffee and said, "That is a peculiar arrangement of the shadows from the street-lamp, Lydia. I myself have got that impression several times—of someone hanging there. I had hoped you wouldn't see it because I knew you half-believed those stories."

Mrs. Grant said "Oh," weakly, and Irma thought, *If anything should happen to her: if anything . . .*

Abruptly Irma pressed the temporary advantage she had gained. "I'll go into the parlor with you, Lydia. Then we'll see." She got up immediately and took her sister's arm.

If Irma noticed the shadow, she gave no sign, even when Mrs. Grant clutched her arm in fright. "There's nothing there, Lydia," she said, patting her sister's hand.

"Oh, you can't see him," breathed Mrs. Grant. "And now he's gone . . . he's gone."

Irma said, "You're tired, Lydia, dear."

Mrs. Grant stared at her sister in the semi-dusk and said, "I want to go away." Her voice was thick and rough. Her hands were shuddering.

"You must face what's worrying you, Lydia; that's the only way."

Mrs. Grant nodded and said, "Yes. I will." She did not notice the strange fixity of Irma's eyes.

Miss Barbara Allen called the next day. She sat in the living room, fixing Mrs. Grant with her eyes. She looked tired, yet there was a curious alertness about her. The two of them— Irma had not come into the room—talked of everything but the house. Mrs. Grant did not want to give the old lady a chance to say anything; so she spoke a great deal and repeated many things she had said once already. And then, in spite of her talking, there came a lull in the conversation, and Miss Barbara said what she had come to say.

"Why are you staying here, Mrs. Grant?"

Mrs. Grant asked, "What do you mean?" She had meant her voice to be polite and calm; it was unsteady, alarmed.

"I know you've seen him," said the old lady, dropping her voice. "And I had hoped you would leave when you saw—

before the panels start moving. It's unbearable, it's awful, when they start. It works on your mind, Mrs. Grant."

"How did you know I'd seen him, Miss Allen?"

The old lady said, "It's in your eyes, Mrs. Grant. I know what it is to see him, because I've seen him, too—and her. And I remember Abby's eyes: waiting, always waiting, frightened."

Mrs. Grant made a nervous gesture with her hands as if seeking to brush the suggestion away like a tangible thing. "I've seen them both," she said, her words coming rapidly, "but it can't be real, because Irma can't see them."

Miss Barbara was obviously startled, for she jerked her head up and looked at her hostess as if she believed that Mrs. Grant was deliberately misleading her. Her eyes narrowed, her thin lips folded together, and abruptly she said, "Your sister lies!" her voice sharp and accusing.

Mrs. Grant was confused. "There's no reason why she should lie to me, Miss Allen."

"If your sister says she can't see them, it's because she wants you to stay here for a very strong reason. Does she go often into the panelled room?" Mrs. Grant's sudden start, her widened eyes, answered the old lady; she went on. "Are you sure there's no reason for her wanting you to stay, Mrs. Grant? Perhaps it would be better for her—if something happened to you? I understand she's entirely dependent on you, and as she's very young yet, I don't suppose she'd like that. Seems to me it's your sister who's keeping you here, Mrs. Grant."

Mrs. Grant's confusion became even more evident. "I don't know," she said. "I really don't. Irma doesn't go into the parlor at all. And she wouldn't want anything to happen to me. I know she wouldn't. No, no, it's unthinkable, Miss Allen. I feel bound to resent such a suggestion."

But the old lady paid no attention. "I think you'd better leave the house right away, Mrs. Grant. Tomorrow is a day no one should be in this house, an anniversary. It was seventeen years ago tomorrow . . ."

At this moment Irma swept into the room, eyeing the old lady in cold hostility. Miss Allen nodded politely, but she rose to go immediately. When she left the house, the old lady's eyes were pleading with Mrs. Grant to follow.

That afternoon Mrs. Grant called on Miss Barbara Allen. She had dropped all pretense and began to talk frankly about the house, admitting her inability to understand Irma's liking for it, and her being unable to see the man hanging—and what lay behind. Miss Barbara let her talk awhile before she advanced the plan which she had been formulating. She outlined it patiently, urging it upon Mrs. Grant as a means with which to test her sister—and to punish her if anything should happen. After a while the two women went downtown to the local lawyer, and Mrs. Grant made her will. In the evening Miss Barbara, having seen Mrs. Grant leave the house, made a short call on Irma.

"I don't know what you're up to," she said in her mild voice. "But I think you should know that Mrs. Grant has just made her will."

For a moment Irma was surprised. Then she drew herself together and said, "Really, Miss Allen, I don't understand." Her voice was edged and hostile.

"I think you do," the old lady went on, standing firmly before the younger woman. "I think you know as well as I do that Mrs. Grant should leave this house before anything happens—and I'm afraid something will happen."

"That's nonsense, Miss Allen, and you know it," Irma flung back. But her voice was not as firm as she would have liked it because she was thinking, *Then something will happen, something will happen* . . .

The old lady disregarded this. "Mrs. Grant has put in her will that if anything happens to her here, if she's not gone tomorrow because you've kept her back, then you'll get all she has—*providing you spend the rest of your life in this house!*"

Miss Barbara Allen went out of the house, and Irma stood in the dusk of the dimly lit room with her hands pressed to her breast. It was some moments before the full import of what the old lady had said broke in upon her, and then she thrust it blindly away, refusing to see it. It isn't true, she told herself. But she looked at her little girl in growing fear. Something will happen tomorrow, she thought. Something must happen—afterwards, we can go, Ellen and I.

Mrs. Grant got up early the next morning. She was definitely nervous and made little effort to hide it. At the breakfast table she said, "I must go away today. I can't stand this house any longer."

Irma steeled herself for combat. "Are you going to let children's tales and shadows affect you that way?" she demanded. Her voice was purposely very cold, and Mrs. Grant wavered in her resolve. Perhaps after all she *had* allowed herself to fall too easily a prey to unfounded fancies to which her imaginative mind had lent support by conjuring up before her suggestive hallucinations. And yet . . . Irma went on, "If you want, I shall send for a doctor. I can't help feeling that something's the matter with you. You've been acting so strangely of late, Lydia."

In the end, Mrs. Grant surrendered her resolve, so that when evening came, she was still in the house. Irma sat in the living room with her, waiting, wondering whether her sister would go into the parlor. In her own mind was forming a question of her right. But she crushed her conscience and said quickly, "Will you get my gold thimble from the parlor, Lydia?" Her voice was casual, and her question suggested that she had already been in the parlor during the day.

Mrs. Grant looked at her sister, sitting calmly near her with folds of embroidery over her knees. She conquered the abrupt apprehension that had risen in her with patient effort, and presently she said, "Yes, I'll go," her voice as casual as Irma's.

She took a lamp and lit it, and went slowly toward the closed double doors leading into the panelled room. She opened them and went into the room. A moment of breathless silence descended, hanging in the house. And then Irma heard a short, shrill scream of terror. She sat there half-paralyzed, thinking of Miss Barbara's accusing eyes. Then she sprang up with a cry and ran toward the panelled room, Ellen following.

Mrs. Grant was standing in the middle of the room, pointing at the walls. Little choking sounds came from her throat, and her hands went up to tear at her high collar. Then, before Irma could reach her, she fell in a heap on the floor. Irma came to her knees and caught up her sister's head.

"Lydia!—Lydia!" she moaned.

Even while she knelt there, she felt a horror such as she had never known, and she knew what it was that had stopped the beating of her sister's heart. She felt the brooding fear that came throbbing toward her from the walls, and she knew that unless she escaped, she too would be smothered and choked, this fear pressing in upon her with its icy hands until her life was gone. Her sister's collar came open, and Irma saw on her throat a faint line, red and bruised, as if the collar had strangled her. Irma's hands began to tremble, and her lips fell open and shut. She thought with sudden horror of Lydia's will and as she strove to push away the thought, she heard Ellen's voice coming it seemed from very far away.

"Mamma, will they do it again?"

The child was standing near her, pointing at the panels of the walls. Irma put one hand up to her throat, and her voice, as she answered the child, was little more than a whisper. "What?" she asked harshly. God, there's nothing, she thought. There's nothing.

The child continued to point at the panels, and she said, "I saw them move. I saw them."

There's nothing.—There's nothing there at all. Irma began to sway, and then suddenly she reached out and began to strike the child unmercifully, striking blindly, until at last the child's crying brought her to her senses. She crouched there on her knees looking with unseeing eyes at the crying child and screamed to her. "*You didn't see anything! You didn't see anything! You didn't—You didn't . . . !*"

1933

H. P. LOVECRAFT

(1890-1937)

The Thing on the Doorstep

It is true that I have sent six bullets through the head of my best friend, and yet I hope to shew by this statement that I am not his murderer. At first I shall be called a madman—madder than the man I shot in his cell at the Arkham Sanitarium. Later some of my readers will weigh each statement, correlate it with the known facts, and ask themselves how I could have believed otherwise than as I did after facing the evidence of that horror—that thing on the doorstep.

Until then I also saw nothing but madness in the wild tales I have acted on. Even now I ask myself whether I was misled— or whether I am not mad after all. I do not know—but others have strange things to tell of Edward and Asenath Derby, and even the stolid police are at their wits' end to account for that last terrible visit. They have tried weakly to concoct a theory of a ghastly jest or warning by discharged servants, yet they know in their hearts that the truth is something infinitely more terrible and incredible.

So I say that I have not murdered Edward Derby. Rather have I avenged him, and in so doing purged the earth of a horror whose survival might have loosed untold terrors on all mankind. There are black zones of shadow close to our daily paths, and now and then some evil soul breaks a passage through. When that happens, the man who knows must strike before reckoning the consequences.

I have known Edward Pickman Derby all his life. Eight years my junior, he was so precocious that we had much in common from the time he was eight and I sixteen. He was the most phenomenal child scholar I have ever known, and at seven was writing verse of a sombre, fantastic, almost morbid cast which astonished the tutors surrounding him. Perhaps his private education and coddled seclusion had something to do with his premature flowering. An only child, he had organic weaknesses which startled his doting parents and caused them to keep him closely chained to their side. He was never allowed out without his nurse, and seldom had a chance to play unconstrainedly with other children. All this doubtless fostered a strange, secretive inner life in the boy, with imagination as his one avenue of freedom.

At any rate, his juvenile learning was prodigious and bizarre; and his facile writings such as to captivate me despite my greater age. About that time I had leanings toward art of a somewhat grotesque cast, and I found in this younger child a rare kindred spirit. What lay behind our joint love of shadows and marvels was, no doubt, the ancient, mouldering, and subtly fearsome town in which we lived—witch-cursed, legend-haunted Arkham, whose huddled, sagging gambrel roofs and crumbling Georgian balustrades brood out the centuries beside the darkly muttering Miskatonic.

As time went by I turned to architecture and gave up my design of illustrating a book of Edward's daemoniac poems, yet our comradeship suffered no lessening. Young Derby's odd genius developed remarkably, and in his eighteenth year his collected nightmare-lyrics made a real sensation when issued under the title *Azathoth and Other Horrors*. He was a close correspondent of the notorious Baudelairean poet Justin Geoffrey, who wrote *The People of the Monolith* and died screaming in a madhouse in 1926 after a visit to a sinister, ill-regarded village in Hungary.

In self-reliance and practical affairs, however, Derby was greatly retarded because of his coddled existence. His health had improved, but his habits of childish dependence were fostered by overcareful parents; so that he never travelled alone, made independent decisions, or assumed responsibilities. It was early seen that he would not be equal to a struggle in the business or professional arena, but the family fortune was so ample that this formed no tragedy. As he grew to years of manhood he retained a deceptive aspect of boyishness. Blond and blue-eyed, he had the fresh complexion of a child; and his attempts to raise a moustache were discernible only with difficulty. His voice was soft and light, and his pampered, unexercised life gave him a juvenile chubbiness rather than the paunchiness of premature middle age. He was of good height, and his handsome face would have made him a notable gallant had not his shyness held him to seclusion and bookishness.

Derby's parents took him abroad every summer, and he was quick to seize on the surface aspects of European thought and expression. His Poe-like talents turned more and more toward the decadent, and other artistic sensitivenesses and yearnings were half-aroused in him. We had great discussions in those days. I had been through Harvard, had studied in a Boston architect's office, had married, and had finally returned to Arkham to practice my profession—settling in the family homestead in Saltonstall St. since my father had moved to Florida for his health. Edward used to call almost every evening, till I came to regard him as one of the household. He had a characteristic way of ringing the doorbell or sounding the knocker that grew to be a veritable code signal, so that after dinner I always listened for the familiar three brisk strokes followed by two more after a pause. Less frequently I would visit at his house and note with envy the obscure volumes in his constantly growing library.

Derby went through Miskatonic University in Arkham, since his parents would not let him board away from them. He entered at sixteen and completed his course in three years, majoring in English and French literature and receiving high marks in everything but mathematics and the sciences. He mingled very little with the other students, though looking enviously at the "daring" or "Bohemian" set—whose superficially "smart" language and meaninglessly ironic pose he aped, and whose dubious conduct he wished he dared adopt.

What he did do was to become an almost fanatical devotee of subterranean magical lore, for which Miskatonic's library was and is famous. Always a dweller on the surface of phantasy and strangeness, he now delved deep into the actual runes and riddles left by a fabulous past for the guidance or puzzlement of posterity. He read things like the frightful *Book of Eibon*, the *Unaussprechlichen Kulten* of von Junzt, and the forbidden *Necronomicon* of the mad Arab Abdul Alhazred, though he did not tell his parents he had seen them. Edward was twenty when my son and only child was born, and seemed pleased when I named the newcomer Edward Derby Upton, after him.

By the time he was twenty-five Edward Derby was a prodi-

giously learned man and a fairly well-known poet and fantai-
siste, though his lack of contacts and responsibilities had slowed
down his literary growth by making his products derivative
and overbookish. I was perhaps his closest friend—finding him
an inexhaustible mine of vital theoretical topics, while he relied
on me for advice in whatever matters he did not wish to refer
to his parents. He remained single—more through shyness,
inertia, and parental protectiveness than through inclination—
and moved in society only to the slightest and most perfunctory extent. When the war came both health and ingrained
timidity kept him at home. I went to Plattsburg for a commission, but never got overseas.

So the years wore on. Edward's mother died when he was
thirty-four, and for months he was incapacitated by some odd
psychological malady. His father took him to Europe, however, and he managed to pull out of his trouble without visible
effects. Afterward he seemed to feel a sort of grotesque exhilaration, as if of partial escape from some unseen bondage. He
began to mingle in the more "advanced" college set despite his
middle age, and was present at some extremely wild doings—
on one occasion paying heavy blackmail (which he borrowed
of me) to keep his presence at a certain affair from his father's
notice. Some of the whispered rumours about the wild Miskatonic set were extremely singular. There was even talk of black
magic and of happenings utterly beyond credibility.

II.

Edward was thirty-eight when he met Asenath Waite. She
was, I judge, about twenty-three at the time; and was taking a
special course in mediaeval metaphysics at Miskatonic. The
daughter of a friend of mine had met her before—in the Hall
School at Kingsport—and had been inclined to shun her
because of her odd reputation. She was dark, smallish, and
very good-looking except for overprotuberant eyes; but something in her expression alienated extremely sensitive people. It
was, however, largely her origin and conversation which caused
average folk to avoid her. She was one of the Innsmouth
Waites, and dark legends have clustered for generations about
crumbling, half-deserted Innsmouth and its people. There are

tales of horrible bargains about the year 1850, and of a strange element "not quite human" in the ancient families of the run-down fishing port—tales such as only old-time Yankees can devise and repeat with proper awesomeness.

Asenath's case was aggravated by the fact that she was Ephraim Waite's daughter—the child of his old age by an unknown wife who always went veiled. Ephraim lived in a half-decayed mansion in Washington Street, Innsmouth, and those who had seen the place (Arkham folk avoid going to Innsmouth whenever they can) declared that the attic windows were always boarded, and that strange sounds sometimes floated from within as evening drew on. The old man was known to have been a prodigious magical student in his day, and legend averred that he could raise or quell storms at sea according to his whim. I had seen him once or twice in my youth as he came to Arkham to consult forbidden tomes at the college library, and had hated his wolfish, saturnine face with its tangle of iron-grey beard. He had died insane—under rather queer circumstances—just before his daughter (by his will made a nominal ward of the principal) entered the Hall School, but she had been his morbidly avid pupil and looked fiendishly like him at times.

The friend whose daughter had gone to school with Asenath Waite repeated many curious things when the news of Edward's acquaintance with her began to spread about. Asenath, it seemed, had posed as a kind of magician at school; and had really seemed able to accomplish some highly baffling marvels. She professed to be able to raise thunderstorms, though her seeming success was generally laid to some uncanny knack at prediction. All animals markedly disliked her, and she could make any dog howl by certain motions of her right hand. There were times when she displayed snatches of knowledge and language very singular—and very shocking—for a young girl; when she would frighten her schoolmates with leers and winks of an inexplicable kind, and would seem to extract an obscene and zestful irony from her present situation.

Most unusual, though, were the well-attested cases of her influence over other persons. She was, beyond question, a genuine hypnotist. By gazing perculiarly at a fellow-student she would often give the latter a distinct feeling of *exchanged personality*—as if the subject were placed momentarily in the magician's body and able to stare half across the room at her real body, whose eyes blazed and protruded with an alien expression. Asenath often made wild claims about the nature of consciousness and about its independence of the physical frame —or at least from the life-processes of the physical frame. Her crowning rage, however, was that she was not a man; since she believed a male brain had certain unique and far-reaching cosmic powers. Given a man's brain, she declared, she could not only equal but surpass her father in mastery of unknown forces.

Edward met Asenath at a gathering of "intelligentsia" held in one of the students' rooms, and could talk of nothing else when he came to see me the next day. He had found her full of the interests and erudition which engrossed him most, and was in addition wildly taken with her appearance. I had never seen the young woman, and recalled casual references only faintly, but I knew who she was. It seemed rather regrettable that Derby should become so upheaved about her; but I said nothing to discourage him, since infatuation thrives on opposition. He was not, he said, mentioning her to his father.

In the next few weeks I heard of very little but Asenath from young Derby. Others now remarked Edward's autumnal gallantry, though they agreed that he did not look even nearly his actual age, or seem at all inappropriate as an escort for his bizarre divinity. He was only a trifle paunchy despite his indolence and self-indulgence, and his face was absolutely without lines. Asenath, on the other hand, had the premature crow's feet which come from the exercise of an intense will.

About this time Edward brought the girl to call on me, and I at once saw that his interest was by no means one-sided. She eyed him continually with an almost predatory air, and I perceived that their intimacy was beyond untangling. Soon afterward I had a visit from old Mr. Derby, whom I had always admired and respected. He had heard the tales of his son's new friendship, and had wormed the whole truth out of "the boy". Edward meant to marry Asenath, and had even been looking at houses in the suburbs. Knowing my usually great influence with his son, the father wondered if I could help to break the ill-advised affair off; but I regretfully expressed my doubts. This time it was not a question of Edward's weak will but of the woman's strong will. The perennial child had transferred his dependence from the parental image to a new and stronger image, and nothing could be done about it.

The wedding was performed a month later—by a justice of the peace, according to the bride's request. Mr. Derby, at my advice, offered no opposition; and he, my wife, my son, and I attended the brief ceremony—the other guests being wild young people from the college. Asenath had bought the old Crowninshield place in the country at the end of High Street, and they proposed to settle there after a short trip to Innsmouth, whence three servants and some books and household goods were to be brought. It was probably not so much consideration for Edward and his father as a personal wish to be near the college, its library, and its crowd of "sophisticates", that made Asenath settle in Arkham instead of returning permanently home.

When Edward called on me after the honeymoon I thought he looked slightly changed. Asenath had made him get rid of the undeveloped moustache, but there was more than that. He looked soberer and more thoughtful, his habitual pout of childish rebelliousness being exchanged for a look almost of genuine sadness. I was puzzled to decide whether I liked or disliked the change. Certainly, he seemed for the moment more normally adult than ever before. Perhaps the marriage was a good thing—might not the *change* of dependence form a start toward actual *neutralisation*, leading ultimately to responsible independence? He came alone, for Asenath was very busy. She had brought a vast store of books and apparatus from Innsmouth (Derby shuddered as he spoke the name), and was finishing the restoration of the Crowninshield house and grounds.

Her home in—that town—was a rather disquieting place, but certain objects in it had taught him some surprising things. He was progressing fast in esoteric lore now that he had Asenath's guidance. Some of the experiments she proposed were very daring and radical—he did not feel at liberty to describe them—but he had confidence in her powers and intentions. The three servants were very queer—an incredibly aged couple who had been with old Ephraim and referred occasionally to him and to Asenath's dead mother in a cryptic way, and a swarthy young wench who had marked anomalies of feature and seemed to exude a perpetual odour of fish.

III.

For the next two years I saw less and less of Derby. A fortnight would sometimes slip by without the familiar three-and-two strokes at the front door; and when he did call—or when, as happened with increasing infrequency, I called on him—he was very little disposed to converse on vital topics. He had become secretive about those occult studies which he used to describe and discuss so minutely, and preferred not to talk of his wife. She had aged tremendously since her marriage, till now —oddly enough—she seemed the elder of the two. Her face held the most concentratedly determined expression I had ever seen, and her whole aspect seemed to gain a vague, unplaceable repulsiveness. My wife and son noticed it as much as I, and we all ceased gradually to call on her—for which, Edward admitted in one of his boyishly tactless moments, she was unmitigatedly grateful. Occasionally the Derbys would go on long trips—ostensibly to Europe, though Edward sometimes hinted at obscurer destinations.

It was after the first year that people began talking about the change in Edward Derby. It was very casual talk, for the change was purely psychological; but it brought up some interesting points. Now and then, it seemed, Edward was observed to wear an expression and to do things wholly incompatible with his usual flabby nature. For example—although in the old days he could not drive a car, he was now seen occasionally to dash into or out of the old Crowninshield driveway with Asenath's powerful Packard, handling it like a master, and meeting traffic entanglements with a skill and determination utterly alien to his accustomed nature. In such cases he seemed always to be just back from some trip or just starting on one—what sort of trip, no one could guess, although he mostly favoured the old Innsmouth road.

Oddly, the metamorphosis did not seem altogether pleasing. People said he looked too much like his wife, or like old Ephraim Waite himself, in these moments—or perhaps these moments seemed unnatural because they were so rare. Sometimes, hours after starting out in this way, he would return listlessly sprawled on the rear seat of his car while an obviously hired chauffeur or mechanic drove. Also, his preponderant aspect on the streets during his decreasing round of social contacts (including, I may say, his calls on me) was the old-time indecisive one—its irresponsible childishness even more marked than in the past. While Asenath's face aged, Edward's—aside from those exceptional occasions—actually relaxed into a kind of exaggerated immaturity, save when a trace of the new sadness or understanding would flash across it. It was really very puzzling. Meanwhile the Derbys almost dropped out of the gay college circle—not through their own disgust, we heard, but because something about their present studies shocked even the most callous of the other decadents.

It was in the third year of the marriage that Edward began to hint openly to me of a certain fear and dissatisfaction. He would let fall remarks about things 'going too far', and would talk darkly about the need of 'saving his identity'. At first I ignored such references, but in time I began to question him guardedly, remembering what my friend's daughter had said about Asenath's hypnotic influence over the other girls at school—the cases where students had thought they were in her body looking across the room at themselves. This questioning seemed to make him at once alarmed and grateful, and once he mumbled something about having a serious talk with me later.

About this time old Mr. Derby died, for which I was afterward very thankful. Edward was badly upset, though by no means disorganised. He had seen astonishingly little of his parent since his marriage, for Asenath had concentrated in herself all his vital sense of family linkage. Some called him callous in his loss—especially since those jaunty and confident moods in the car began to increase. He now wished to move back into the old Derby mansion, but Asenath insisted on staying in the Crowninshield house, to which she had become well adjusted.

Not long afterward my wife heard a curious thing from a friend—one of the few who had not dropped the Derbys. She had been out to the end of High St. to call on the couple, and had seen a car shoot briskly out of the drive with Edward's oddly confident and almost sneering face above the wheel. Ringing the bell, she had been told by the repulsive wench that Asenath was also out; but had chanced to look up at the house in leaving. There, at one of Edward's library windows, she had glimpsed a hastily withdrawn face—a face whose expression of pain, defeat, and wistful hopelessness was poignant beyond description. It was—incredibly enough in view of its usual domineering cast—Asenath's; yet the caller had vowed that in that instant the sad, muddled eyes of poor Edward were gazing out from it.

Edward's calls now grew a trifle more frequent, and his hints occasionally became concrete. What he said was not to be believed, even in centuried and legend-haunted Arkham; but he threw out his dark lore with a sincerity and convincingness which made one fear for his sanity. He talked about terrible meetings in lonely places, of Cyclopean ruins in the heart of the Maine woods beneath which vast staircases lead down to abysses of nighted secrets, of complex angles that lead through invisible walls to other regions of space and time, and of hideous exchanges of personality that permitted explorations in remote and forbidden places, on other worlds, and in different space-time continua.

He would now and then back up certain crazy hints by exhibiting objects which utterly nonplussed me—elusively coloured and bafflingly textured objects like nothing ever heard of on earth, whose insane curves and surfaces answered no conceivable purpose and followed no conceivable geometry. These things, he said, came 'from outside'; and his wife knew how to get them. Sometimes—but always in frightened and ambiguous whispers—he would suggest things about old Ephraim Waite, whom he had seen occasionally at the college library in the old days. These adumbrations were never specific, but seemed to revolve around some especially horrible doubt as to whether the old wizard were really dead—in a spiritual as well as corporeal sense.

At times Derby would halt abruptly in his revelations, and I wondered whether Asenath could possibly have divined his speech at a distance and cut him off through some unknown sort of telepathic mesmerism—some power of the kind she had displayed at school. Certainly, she suspected that he told me things, for as the weeks passed she tried to stop his visits with words and glances of a most inexplicable potency. Only with difficulty could he get to see me, for although he would pretend to be going somewhere else, some invisible force would generally clog his motions or make him forget his destination for the time being. His visits usually came when Asenath was away—'away in her own body', as he once oddly put it. She always found out later—the servants watched his goings and comings—but evidently she thought it inexpedient to do anything drastic.

IV.

Derby had been married more than three years on that August day when I got the telegram from Maine. I had not seen him for two months, but had heard he was away "on business". Asenath was supposed to be with him, though watchful gossips declared there was someone upstairs in the house behind the doubly curtained windows. They had watched the purchases made by the servants. And now the town marshal of Chesuncook had wired of the draggled madman who stumbled out of the woods with delirious ravings and screamed to me for protection. It was Edward—and he had been just able to recall his own name and my name and address.

Chesuncook is close to the wildest, deepest, and least explored forest belt in Maine, and it took a whole day of feverish jolting through fantastic and forbidding scenery to get there in a car. I found Derby in a cell at the town farm, vacillating between frenzy and apathy. He knew me at once, and began pouring out a meaningless, half-incoherent torrent of words in my direction.

"Dan—for God's sake! The pit of the shoggoths! Down the six thousand steps . . . the abomination of abominations . . . I never would let her take me, and then I found myself there. . . . Iä! Shub-Niggurath! . . . The shape rose up from the altar, and there were 500 that howled. . . . The Hooded Thing bleated 'Kamog! Kamog!'—that was old Ephraim's secret name in the coven. . . . I was there, where she promised she wouldn't take me. . . . A minute before I was locked in the library, and then I was there where she had gone with my body—in the place of utter blasphemy, the unholy pit where the black realm begins and the watcher guards the gate. . . .

I saw a shoggoth—it changed shape. . . . I can't stand it. . . . I won't stand it. . . . I'll kill her if she ever sends me there again. . . . I'll kill that entity . . . her, him, it . . . I'll kill it! I'll kill it with my own hands!"

It took me an hour to quiet him, but he subsided at last. The next day I got him decent clothes in the village, and set out with him for Arkham. His fury of hysteria was spent, and he was inclined to be silent; though he began muttering darkly to himself when the car passed through Augusta—as if the sight of a city aroused unpleasant memories. It was clear that he did not wish to go home; and considering the fantastic delusions he seemed to have about his wife—delusions undoubtedly springing from some actual hypnotic ordeal to which he had been subjected—I thought it would be better if he did not. I would, I resolved, put him up myself for a time; no matter what unpleasantness it would make with Asenath. Later I would help him get a divorce, for most assuredly there were mental factors which made this marriage suicidal for him. When we struck open country again Derby's muttering faded away, and I let him nod and drowse on the seat beside me as I drove.

During our sunset dash through Portland the muttering commenced again, more distinctly than before, and as I listened I caught a stream of utterly insane drivel about Asenath. The extent to which she had preyed on Edward's nerves was plain, for he had woven a whole set of hallucinations around her. His present predicament, he mumbled furtively, was only one of a long series. She was getting hold of him, and he knew that some day she would never let go. Even now she probably let him go only when she had to, because she couldn't hold on long at a time. She constantly took his body and went to nameless places for nameless rites, leaving him in her body and locking him upstairs—but sometimes she couldn't hold on, and he would find himself suddenly in his own body again in some far-off, horrible, and perhaps unknown place. Sometimes she'd get hold of him again and sometimes she couldn't. Often he was left stranded somewhere as I had found him . . . time and again he had to find his way home from frightful distances, getting somebody to drive the car after he found it.

The worst thing was that she was holding on to him longer

and longer at a time. She wanted to be a man—to be fully human—that was why she got hold of him. She had sensed the mixture of fine-wrought brain and weak will in him. Some day she would crowd him out and disappear with his body—disappear to become a great magician like her father and leave him marooned in that female shell that wasn't even quite human. Yes, he knew about the Innsmouth blood now. There had been traffick with things from the sea—it was horrible. . . . And old Ephraim—he had known the secret, and when he grew old did a hideous thing to keep alive . . . he wanted to live forever . . . Asenath would succeed—one successful demonstration had taken place already.

As Derby muttered on I turned to look at him closely, verifying the impression of change which an earlier scrutiny had given me. Paradoxically, he seemed in better shape than usual —harder, more normally developed, and without the trace of sickly flabbiness caused by his indolent habits. It was as if he had been really active and properly exercised for the first time in his coddled life, and I judged that Asenath's force must have pushed him into unwonted channels of motion and alertness. But just now his mind was in a pitiable state; for he was mumbling wild extravagances about his wife, about black magic, about old Ephraim, and about some revelation which would convince even me. He repeated names which I recognised from bygone browsings in forbidden volumes, and at times made me shudder with a certain thread of mythological consistency—of convincing coherence—which ran through his maundering. Again and again he would pause, as if to gather courage for some final and terrible disclosure.

"Dan, Dan, don't you remember him—the wild eyes and the unkempt beard that never turned white? He glared at me once, and I never forgot it. Now *she* glares that way. *And I know why!* He found it in the *Necronomicon*—the formula. I don't dare tell you the page yet, but when I do you can read and understand. Then you will know what has engulfed me. On, on, on, on—body to body to body—he means never to die. The life-glow—he knows how to break the link . . . it can flicker on a while even when the body is dead. I'll give you hints, and maybe you'll guess. Listen, Dan—do you know why my wife always takes such pains with that silly backhand writing? Have you ever seen a manuscript of old Ephraim's? Do you want to know why I shivered when I saw some hasty notes Asenath had jotted down?

"Asenath . . . *is there such a person?* Why did they half think there was poison in old Ephraim's stomach? Why do the Gilmans whisper about the way he shrieked—like a frightened child—when he went mad and Asenath locked him up in the padded attic room where—the other—had been? *Was it old Ephraim's soul that was locked in? Who locked in whom?* Why had he been looking for months for someone with a fine mind and a weak will? Why did he curse that his daughter wasn't a son? Tell me, Daniel Upton—*what devilish exchange was perpetuated in the house of horror where that blasphemous monster had his trusting, weak-willed, half-human child at his mercy?* Didn't he make it permanent—as she'll do in the end with me? Tell me why that thing that calls itself Asenath writes differently when off guard, *so that you can't tell its script from . . .*"

Then the thing happened. Derby's voice was rising to a thin treble scream as he raved, when suddenly it was shut off with an almost mechanical click. I thought of those other occasions at my home when his confidences had abruptly ceased—when I had half fancied that some obscure telepathic wave of Asenath's mental force was intervening to keep him silent. This, though, was something altogether different—and, I felt, infinitely more horrible. The face beside me was twisted almost unrecognisably for a moment, while through the whole body there passed a shivering motion—as if all the bones, organs, muscles, nerves, and glands were readjusting themselves to a radically different posture, set of stresses, and general personality.

Just where the supreme horror lay, I could not for my life tell; yet there swept over me such a swamping wave of sickness and repulsion—such a freezing, petrifying sense of utter alienage and abnormality—that my grasp of the wheel grew feeble and uncertain. The figure beside me seemed less like a lifelong friend than like some monstrous intrusion from outer space—some damnable, utterly accursed focus of unknown and malign cosmic forces.

I had faltered only a moment, but before another moment was over my companion had seized the wheel and forced me to change places with him. The dusk was now very thick, and the lights of Portland far behind, so I could not see much of his face. The blaze of his eyes, though, was phenomenal; and I knew that he must now be in that queerly energised state—so unlike his usual self—which so many people had noticed. It seemed odd and incredible that listless Edward Derby—he who could never assert himself, and who had never learned to drive—should be ordering me about and taking the wheel of my own car, yet that was precisely what had happened. He did not speak for some time, and in my inexplicable horror I was glad he did not.

In the lights of Biddeford and Saco I saw his firmly set mouth, and shivered at the blaze of his eyes. The people were right—he did look damnably like his wife and like old Ephraim when in these moods. I did not wonder that the moods were disliked—there was something unnatural and diabolic in them, and I felt the sinister element all the more because of the wild ravings I had been hearing. This man, for all my lifelong knowledge of Edward Pickman Derby, was a stranger—an intrusion of some sort from the black abyss.

He did not speak until we were on a dark stretch of road, and when he did his voice seemed utterly unfamiliar. It was deeper, firmer, and more decisive than I had ever known it to be; while its accent and pronunciation were altogether changed —though vaguely, remotely, and rather disturbingly recalling something I could not quite place. There was, I thought, a trace of very profound and very genuine irony in the timbre— not the flashy, meaninglessly jaunty pseudo-irony of the callow "sophisticate", which Derby had habitually affected, but something grim, basic, pervasive, and potentially evil. I marvelled at the self-possession so soon following the spell of panic-struck muttering.

"I hope you'll forget my attack back there, Upton," he was saying. "You know what my nerves are, and I guess you can excuse such things. I'm enormously grateful, of course, for this lift home.

"And you must forget, too, any crazy things I may have been saying about my wife—and about things in general. That's what comes from overstudy in a field like mine. My philosophy is full of bizarre concepts, and when the mind gets worn out it cooks up all sorts of imaginary concrete applications. I shall take a rest from now on—you probably won't see me for some time, and you needn't blame Asenath for it.

"This trip was a bit queer, but it's really very simple. There are certain Indian relics in the north woods—standing stones, and all that—which mean a good deal in folklore, and Asenath and I are following that stuff up. It was a hard search, so I seem to have gone off my head. I must send somebody for the car when I get home. A month's relaxation will put me back on my feet."

I do not recall just what my own part of the conversation was, for the baffling alienage of my seatmate filled my consciousness. With every moment my feeling of elusive cosmic horror increased, till at length I was in a virtual delirium of longing for the end of the drive. Derby did not offer to relinquish the wheel, and I was glad of the speed with which Portsmouth and Newburyport flashed by.

At the junction where the main highway runs inland and avoids Innsmouth I was half afraid my driver would take the bleak shore road that goes through that damnable place. He did not, however, but darted rapidly past Rowley and Ipswich toward our destination. We reached Arkham before midnight, and found the lights still on at the old Crowninshield house. Derby left the car with a hasty repetition of his thanks, and I drove home alone with a curious feeling of relief. It had been a terrible drive—all the more terrible because I could not quite tell why—and I did not regret Derby's forecast of a long absence from my company.

V.

The next two months were full of rumours. People spoke of seeing Derby more and more in his new energised state, and Asenath was scarcely ever in to her few callers. I had only one visit from Edward, when he called briefly in Asenath's car— duly reclaimed from wherever he had left it in Maine—to get some books he had lent me. He was in his new state, and paused only long enough for some evasively polite remarks. It was plain that he had nothing to discuss with me when in this condition—and I noticed that he did not even trouble to give the old three-and-two signal when ringing the doorbell. As on that evening in the car, I felt a faint, infinitely deep horror which I could not explain; so that his swift departure was a prodigious relief.

In mid-September Derby was away for a week, and some of the decadent college set talked knowingly of the matter—hinting at a meeting with a notorious cult-leader, lately expelled from England, who had established headquarters in New York. For my part I could not get that strange ride from Maine out of my head. The transformation I had witnessed had affected me profoundly, and I caught myself again and again trying to account for the thing—and for the extreme horror it had inspired in me.

But the oddest rumours were those about the sobbing in the old Crowninshield house. The voice seemed to be a woman's, and some of the younger people thought it sounded like Asenath's. It was heard only at rare intervals, and would sometimes be choked off as if by force. There was talk of an investigation, but this was dispelled one day when Asenath appeared in the streets and chatted in a sprightly way with a large number of acquaintances—apologising for her recent absences and speaking incidentally about the nervous breakdown and hysteria of a guest from Boston. The guest was never seen, but Asenath's appearance left nothing to be said. And then someone complicated matters by whispering that the sobs had once or twice been in a man's voice.

One evening in mid-October I heard the familiar three-and-two ring at the front door. Answering it myself, I found Edward on the steps, and saw in a moment that his personality was the old one which I had not encountered since the day of his ravings on that terrible ride from Chesuncook. His face was twitching with a mixture of odd emotions in which fear and triumph seemed to share dominion, and he looked furtively over his shoulder as I closed the door behind him.

Following me clumsily to the study, he asked for some whiskey to steady his nerves. I forbore to question him, but waited till he felt like beginning whatever he wanted to say. At length he ventured some information in a choking voice.

"Asenath has gone, Dan. We had a long talk last night while the servants were out, and I made her promise to stop preying on me. Of course I had certain—certain occult defences I never told you about. She had to give in, but got frightfully angry. Just packed up and started for New York—walked right out to catch the 8:20 in to Boston. I suppose people will talk, but I can't help that. You needn't mention that there was any trouble—just say she's gone on a long research trip.

"She's probably going to stay with one of her horrible groups of devotees. I hope she'll go west and get a divorce—anyhow, I've made her promise to keep away and let me alone. It was horrible, Dan—she was stealing my body—crowding me out—making a prisoner of me. I laid low and pretended to let her do it, but I had to be on the watch. I could plan if I was careful, for she can't read my mind literally, or in detail. All she could read of my planning was a sort of general mood of rebellion—and she always thought I was helpless. Never thought I could get the best of her . . . but I had a spell or two that worked."

Derby looked over his shoulder and took some more whiskey.

"I paid off those damned servants this morning when they got back. They were ugly about it, and asked questions, but they went. They're her kind—Innsmouth people—and were hand and glove with her. I hope they'll let me alone—I didn't like the way they laughed when they walked away. I must get as many of Dad's old servants again as I can. I'll move back home now.

"I suppose you think I'm crazy, Dan—but Arkham history ought to hint at things that back up what I've told you—and what I'm going to tell you. You've seen one of the changes, too—in your car after I told you about Asenath that day coming home from Maine. That was when she got me—drove me out of my body. The last thing of the ride I remember was when I was all worked up trying to tell you *what that she-devil is.* Then she got me, and in a flash I was back at the house—in the library where those damned servants had me locked up—and in that cursed fiend's body . . . that isn't even human. . . . You know, it was she you must have ridden home with . . . that preying wolf in my body. . . . You ought to have known the difference!"

I shuddered as Derby paused. Surely, I *had* known the

difference—yet could I accept an explanation as insane as this? But my distracted caller was growing even wilder.

"I had to save myself—I had to, Dan! She'd have got me for good at Hallowmass—they hold a Sabbat up there beyond Chesuncook, and the sacrifice would have clinched things. She'd have got me for good . . . she'd have been I, and I'd have been she . . . forever . . . too late. . . . My body'd have been hers for good. . . . She'd have been a man, and fully human, just as she wanted to be. . . . I suppose she'd have put me out of the way—killed her own ex-body with me in it, damn her, *just as she did before*—just as she, he, or it did before. . . ."

Edward's face was now atrociously distorted, and he bent it uncomfortably close to mine as his voice fell to a whisper.

"You must know what I hinted in the car—*that she isn't Asenath at all, but really old Ephraim himself.* I suspected it a year and a half ago, but I know it now. Her handwriting shews it when she's off guard—sometimes she jots down a note in writing that's just like her father's manuscripts, stroke for stroke —and sometimes she says things that nobody but an old man like Ephraim could say. He changed forms with her when he felt death coming—she was the only one he could find with the right kind of brain and a weak enough will—he got her body permanently, just as she almost got mine, and then poisoned the old body he'd put her into. Haven't you seen old Ephraim's soul glaring out of that she-devil's eyes dozens of times . . . and out of mine when she had control of my body?"

The whisperer was panting, and paused for breath. I said nothing, and when he resumed his voice was nearer normal. This, I reflected, was a case for the asylum, but I would not be the one to send him there. Perhaps time and freedom from Asenath would do its work. I could see that he would never wish to dabble in morbid occultism again.

"I'll tell you more later—I must have a long rest now. I'll tell you something of the forbidden horrors she led me into— something of the age-old horrors that even now are festering in out-of-the-way corners with a few monstrous priests to keep them alive. Some people know things about the universe that nobody ought to know, and can do things that nobody ought to be able to do. I've been in it up to my neck, but that's the end. Today I'd burn that damned *Necronomicon* and all the rest if I were librarian at Miskatonic.

"But she can't get me now. I must get out of that accursed house as soon as I can, and settle down at home. You'll help me, I know, if I need help. Those devilish servants, you know . . . and if people should get too inquisitive about Asenath. You see, I can't give them her address. . . . Then there are certain groups of searchers—certain cults, you know—that might misunderstand our breaking up . . . some of them have damnably curious ideas and methods. I know you'll stand by me if anything happens—even if I have to tell you a lot that will shock you. . . ."

I had Edward stay and sleep in one of the guest-chambers that night, and in the morning he seemed calmer. We discussed certain possible arrangements for his moving back into the Derby mansion, and I hoped he would lose no time in making the change. He did not call the next evening, but I saw him frequently during the ensuing weeks. We talked as little as possible about strange and unpleasant things, but discussed the renovation of the old Derby house, and the travels which Edward promised to take with my son and me the following summer.

Of Asenath we said almost nothing, for I saw that the subject was a peculiarly disturbing one. Gossip, of course, was rife; but that was no novelty in connexion with the strange ménage at the old Crowninshield house. One thing I did not like was what Derby's banker let fall in an overexpansive mood at the Miskatonic Club—about the cheques Edward was sending regularly to a Moses and Abigail Sargent and a Eunice Babson in Innsmouth. That looked as if those evil-faced servants were extorting some kind of tribute from him—yet he had not mentioned the matter to me.

I wished that the summer—and my son's Harvard vacation —would come, so that we could get Edward to Europe. He was not, I soon saw, mending as rapidly as I had hoped he would; for there was something a bit hysterical in his occasional exhilaration, while the moods of fright and depression were altogether too frequent. The old Derby house was ready by December, yet Edward constantly put off moving. Though he hated and seemed to fear the Crowninshield place, he was at the same time queerly enslaved by it. He could not seem to begin dismantling things, and invented every kind of excuse to postpone action. When I pointed this out to him he appeared unaccountably frightened. His father's old butler—who was there with other reacquired family servants—told me one day that Edward's occasional prowlings about the house, and especially down cellar, looked odd and unwholesome to him. I wondered if Asenath had been writing disturbing letters, but the butler said there was no mail which could have come from her.

VI.

It was about Christmas that Derby broke down one evening while calling on me. I was steering the conversation toward next summer's travels when he suddenly shrieked and leaped up from his chair with a look of shocking, uncontrollable fright—a cosmic panic and loathing such as only the nether gulfs of nightmare could bring to any sane mind.

"My brain! My brain! God, Dan—it's tugging—from beyond—knocking—clawing—that she-devil—even now—Ephraim—Kamog! Kamog!—The pit of the shoggoths—Iä! Shub-Niggurath! The Goat with a Thousand Young! . . .

"The flame—the flame . . . beyond body, beyond life . . . in the earth . . . oh, God! . . ."

I pulled him back to his chair and poured some wine down his throat as his frenzy sank to a dull apathy. He did not resist, but kept his lips moving as if talking to himself. Presently I realised that he was trying to talk to me, and bent my ear to his mouth to catch the feeble words.

". . . again, again . . . she's trying . . . I might have known . . . nothing can stop that force; not distance, nor magic, nor death . . . it comes and comes, mostly in the night . . . I can't leave . . . it's horrible . . . oh, God, Dan, *if you only knew as I do just how horrible it is.* . . ."

When he had slumped down into a stupor I propped him with pillows and let normal sleep overtake him. I did not call a doctor, for I knew what would be said of his sanity, and wished to give nature a chance if I possibly could. He waked at midnight, and I put him to bed upstairs, but he was gone by morning. He had let himself quietly out of the house—and his butler, when called on the wire, said he was at home pacing restlessly about the library.

Edward went to pieces rapidly after that. He did not call again, but I went daily to see him. He would always be sitting in his library, staring at nothing and having an air of abnormal *listening*. Sometimes he talked rationally, but always on trivial topics. Any mention of his trouble, of future plans, or of Asenath would send him into a frenzy. His butler said he had frightful seizures at night, during which he might eventually do himself harm.

I had a long talk with his doctor, banker, and lawyer, and finally took the physician with two specialist colleagues to visit him. The spasms that resulted from the first questions were violent and pitiable—and that evening a closed car took his poor struggling body to the Arkham Sanitarium. I was made his guardian and called on him twice weekly—almost weeping to hear his wild shrieks, awesome whispers, and dreadful, droning repetitions of such phrases as "I had to do it—I had to do it . . . it'll get me . . . it'll get me . . . down there . . . down there in the dark. . . . Mother, mother! Dan! Save me. . . . save me . . ."

How much hope of recovery there was, no one could say; but I tried my best to be optimistic. Edward must have a home if he emerged, so I transferred his servants to the Derby mansion, which would surely be his sane choice. What to do about the Crowninshield place with its complex arrangements and collections of utterly inexplicable objects I could not decide, so left it momentarily untouched—telling the Derby household to go over and dust the chief rooms once a week, and ordering the furnace man to have a fire on those days.

The final nightmare came before Candlemas—heralded, in cruel irony, by a false gleam of hope. One morning late in January the sanitarium telephoned to report that Edward's reason had suddenly come back. His continuous memory, they said, was badly impaired; but sanity itself was certain. Of course he must remain some time for observation, but there could be little doubt of the outcome. All going well, he would surely be free in a week.

I hastened over in a flood of delight, but stood bewildered

when a nurse took me to Edward's room. The patient rose to greet me, extending his hand with a polite smile; but I saw in an instant that he bore the strangely energised personality which had seemed so foreign to his own nature—the competent personality I had found so vaguely horrible, and which Edward himself had once vowed was the intruding soul of his wife. There was the same blazing vision—so like Asenath's and old Ephraim's—and the same firm mouth; and when he spoke I could sense the same grim, pervasive irony in his voice—the deep irony so redolent of potential evil. This was the person who had driven my car through the night five months before—the person I had not seen since that brief call when he had forgotten the old-time doorbell signal and stirred such nebulous fears in me—and now he filled me with the same dim feeling of blasphemous alienage and ineffable cosmic hideousness.

He spoke affably of arrangements for release—and there was nothing for me to do but assent, despite some remarkable gaps in his recent memories. Yet I felt that something was terribly, inexplicably wrong and abnormal. There were horrors in this thing that I could not reach. This was a sane person—but was it indeed the Edward Derby I had known? If not, who or what was it—*and where was Edward?* Ought it to be free or confined . . . or ought it to be extirpated from the face of the earth? There was a hint of the abysmally sardonic in everything the creature said—the Asenath-like eyes lent a special and baffling mockery to certain words about the 'early liberty earned by an *especially close confinement*'. I must have behaved very awkwardly, and was glad to beat a retreat.

All that day and the next I racked my brain over the problem. What had happened? What sort of mind looked out through those alien eyes in Edward's face? I could think of nothing but this dimly terrible enigma, and gave up all efforts to perform my usual work. The second morning the hospital called up to say that the recovered patient was unchanged, and by evening I was close to a nervous collapse—a state I admit, though others will vow it coloured my subsequent vision. I have nothing to say on this point except that no madness of mine could account for *all* the evidence.

VII.

It was in the night—after that second evening—that stark, utter horror burst over me and weighted my spirit with a black, clutching panic from which it can never shake free. It began with a telephone call just before midnight. I was the only one up, and sleepily took down the receiver in the library. No one seemed to be on the wire, and I was about to hang up and go to bed when my ear caught a very faint suspicion of sound at the other end. Was someone trying under great difficulties to talk? As I listened I thought I heard a sort of half-liquid bubbling noise—"*glub . . . glub . . . glub*"—which had an odd suggestion of inarticulate, unintelligible word and syllable divisions. I called, "Who is it?" But the only answer was "*glub-glub . . . glub-glub.*" I could only assume that the noise was mechanical; but fancying that it might be a case of a broken instrument able to receive but not to send, I added, "I can't hear you. Better hang up and try Information." Immediately I heard the receiver go on the hook at the other end.

This, I say, was just before midnight. When that call was traced afterward it was found to come from the old Crownin-shield house, though it was fully half a week from the housemaid's day to be there. I shall only hint what was found at that house—the upheaval in a remote cellar storeroom, the tracks, the dirt, the hastily rifled wardrobe, the baffling marks on the telephone, the clumsily used stationery, and the detestable stench lingering over everything. The police, poor fools, have their smug little theories, and are still searching for those sinister discharged servants—who have dropped out of sight amidst the present furore. They speak of a ghoulish revenge for things that were done, and say I was included because I was Edward's best friend and adviser.

Idiots!—do they fancy those brutish clowns could have forged that handwriting? Do they fancy they could have brought what later came? Are they blind to the changes in that body that was Edward's? As for me, *I now believe all that Edward Derby ever told me.* There are horrors beyond life's edge that we do not suspect, and once in a while man's evil prying calls them just within our range. Ephraim—Asenath—that devil called them in, and they engulfed Edward as they are engulfing me.

Can I be sure that I am safe? Those powers survive the life of the physical form. The next day—in the afternoon, when I pulled out of my prostration and was able to walk and talk coherently—I went to the madhouse and shot him dead for Edward's and the world's sake, but can I be sure till he is cremated? They are keeping the body for some silly autopsies by different doctors—but I say he must be cremated. *He must be cremated—he who was not Edward Derby when I shot him.* I shall go mad if he is not, for I may be the next. But my will is not weak—and I shall not let it be undermined by the terrors I know are seething around it. One life—Ephraim, Asenath, and Edward—who now? I *will not* be driven out of my body . . . I *will not* change souls with that bullet-ridden lich in the madhouse!

But let me try to tell coherently of that final horror. I will not speak of what the police persistently ignored—the tales of that dwarfed, grotesque, malodorous thing met by at least three wayfarers in High St. just before two o'clock, and the nature of the single footprints in certain places. I will say only that just about two the doorbell and knocker waked me—doorbell and knocker both, plied alternately and uncertainly in a kind of weak desperation, *and each trying to keep to Edward's old signal of three-and-two strokes.*

Roused from sound sleep, my mind leaped into a turmoil. Derby at the door—and remembering the old code! That new personality had not remembered it . . . was Edward suddenly back in his rightful state? Why was he here in such evident stress and haste? Had he been released ahead of time, or had he escaped? Perhaps, I thought as I flung on a robe and bounded downstairs, his return to his own self had brought raving and violence, revoking his discharge and driving him to a desperate dash for freedom. Whatever had happened, he was good old Edward again, and I would help him!

When I opened the door into the elm-arched blackness a gust of insufferably foetid wind almost flung me prostrate. I choked in nausea, and for a second scarcely saw the dwarfed, humped figure on the steps. The summons had been Edward's, but who was this foul, stunted parody? Where had Edward had time to go? His ring had sounded only a second before the door opened.

The caller had on one of Edward's overcoats—its bottom almost touching the ground, and its sleeves rolled back yet still covering the hands. On the head was a slouch hat pulled low, while a black silk muffler concealed the face. As I stepped unsteadily forward, the figure made a semi-liquid sound like that I had heard over the telephone—"*glub . . . glub . . .*"—and thrust at me a large, closely written paper impaled on the end of a long pencil. Still reeling from the morbid and unaccountable foetor, I seized this paper and tried to read it in the light from the doorway.

Beyond question, it was in Edward's script. But why had he written when he was close enough to ring—and why was the script so awkward, coarse, and shaky? I could make out nothing in the dim half light, so edged back into the hall, the dwarf figure clumping mechanically after but pausing on the inner door's threshold. The odour of this singular messenger was really appalling, and I hoped (not in vain, thank God!) that my wife would not wake and confront it.

Then, as I read the paper, I felt my knees give under me and my vision go black. I was lying on the floor when I came to, that accursed sheet still clutched in my fear-rigid hand. This is what it said.

"Dan—go to the sanitarium and kill it. Exterminate it. It isn't Edward Derby any more. She got me—it's Asenath—*and she has been dead three months and a half.* I lied when I said she had gone away. I killed her. I had to. It was sudden, but we were alone and I was in my right body. I saw a candlestick and smashed her head in. She would have got me for good at Hallowmass.

"I buried her in the farther cellar storeroom under some old boxes and cleaned up all the traces. The servants suspected next morning, but they have such secrets that they dare not tell the police. I sent them off, but God knows what they—and others of the cult—will do.

"I thought for a while I was all right, and then I felt the tugging at my brain. I knew what it was—I ought to have remembered. A soul like hers—or Ephraim's—is half detached, and keeps right on after death as long as the body lasts. She was getting me—making me change bodies with her—*seizing my body and putting me in that corpse of hers buried in the cellar.*

"I knew what was coming—that's why I snapped and had to go to the asylum. Then it came—I found myself choked in the dark—in Asenath's rotting carcass down there in the cellar under the boxes where I put it. And I knew she must be in my body at the sanitarium—*permanently*, for it was after Hallowmass, and the sacrifice would work even without her being there—sane, and ready for release as a menace to the world. I was desperate, *and in spite of everything I clawed my way out.*

"I'm too far gone to talk—I couldn't manage to telephone—but I can still write. I'll get fixed up somehow and bring you this last word and warning. *Kill that fiend* if you value the peace and comfort of the world. *See that it is cremated.* If you don't, it will live on and on, body to body forever, and I can't tell you what it will do. Keep clear of black magic, Dan, it's the devil's business. Goodbye—you've been a great friend. Tell the police whatever they'll believe—and I'm damnably sorry to drag all this on you. I'll be at peace before long—this thing won't hold together much more. Hope you can read this. *And kill that thing—kill it.*

Yours—Ed."

It was only afterward that I read the last half of this paper, for I had fainted at the end of the third paragraph. I fainted again when I saw and smelled what cluttered up the threshold where the warm air had struck it. The messenger would not move or have consciousness any more.

The butler, tougher-fibred than I, did not faint at what met him in the hall in the morning. Instead, he telephoned the police. When they came I had been taken upstairs to bed, but the—other mass—lay where it had collapsed in the night. The men put handkerchiefs to their noses.

What they finally found inside Edward's oddly assorted clothes was mostly liquescent horror. There were bones, too—and a crushed-in skull. Some dental work positively identified the skull as Asenath's.

1933

CLARK ASHTON SMITH

(1893–1961)

Genius Loci

"It is a very strange place," said Amberville, "but I scarcely know how to convey the impression it made upon me. It will all sound so simple and ordinary. There is nothing but a sedgy meadow, surrounded on three sides by slopes of yellow pine. A dreary little stream flows in from the open end, to lose itself in a *cul-de-sac* of cat-tails and boggy ground. The stream, running slowly and more slowly, forms a stagnant pool of some extent, from which several sickly-looking alders seem to fling themselves backward, as if unwilling to approach it. A dead willow leans above the pool, tangling its wan, skeleton-like reflection with the green scum that mottles the water. There are no blackbirds, no kildees, no dragon-flies even, such as one usually finds in a place of that sort. It is all silent and desolate. The spot is evil—it is unholy in a way that I simply can't describe. I was compelled to make a drawing of it, almost against my will, since anything so outré is hardly in my line. In fact, I made two drawings. I'll show them to you, if you like."

Since I had a high opinion of Amberville's artistic abilities, and had long considered him one of the foremost landscape painters of his generation, I was naturally eager to see the drawings. He, however, did not even pause to await my avowal of interest, but began at once to open his portfolio. His facial expression, the very movements of his hands, were somehow eloquent of a strange mixture of compulsion and repugnance as he brought out and displayed the two watercolor sketches he had mentioned.

I could not recognize the scene depicted from either of them. Plainly it was one that I had missed in my desultory rambling about the foot-hill environs of the tiny hamlet of Bowman, where, two years before, I had purchased an uncultivated ranch and had retired for the privacy so essential to prolonged literary effort. Francis Amberville, in the one

fortnight of his visit, through his flair for the pictorial poten-
tialities of landscape, had doubtless grown more familiar with
the neighborhood than I. It had been his habit to roam about
in the forenoon, armed with sketching-materials; and in this
way he had already found the theme of more than one lovely
painting. The arrangement was mutually convenient, since I,
in his absence, was wont to apply myself assiduously to an antique Remington typewriter.

I examined the drawings attentively. Both, though of hurried execution, were highly meritorious, and showed the characteristic grace and vigor of Amberville's style. And yet, even
at first glance, I found a quality that was more alien to the
spirit of his work. The elements of the scene were those he had
described. In one picture, the pool was half hidden by a fringe
of mace-reeds, and the dead willow was leaning across it at a
prone, despondent angle, as if mysteriously arrested in its fall
toward the stagnant waters. Beyond, the alders seemed to
strain away from the pool, exposing their knotted roots as if in
eternal effort. In the other drawing, the pool formed the main
portion of the foreground, with the skeleton tree looming
drearily at one side. At the water's farther end, the cat-tails
seemed to wave and whisper among themselves in a dying
wind; and the steeply barring slope of pine at the meadow's
terminus was indicated as a wall of gloomy green that closed in
the picture, leaving only a pale margin of autumnal sky at the
top.

All this, as the painter had said, was ordinary enough. But I
was impressed immediately by a profound horror that lurked
in these simple elements and was expressed by them as if by the
balefully contorted features of some demoniac face. In both
drawings, this sinister character was equally evident, as if the
same face had been shown in profile and front view. I could
not trace the separate details that composed the impressions;
but ever, as I looked, the abomination of a strange evil, a spirit
of despair, malignity, desolation, leered from the drawing
more openly and hatefully. The spot seemed to wear a macabre
and Satanic grimace. One felt that it might speak aloud, might
utter the imprecations of some gigantic devil, or the raucous
derision of a thousand birds of ill omen. The evil conveyed was
something wholly outside of humanity—more ancient than

man. Somehow—fantastic as this will seem—the meadow had
the air of a vampire, grown old and hideous with unutterable
infamies. Subtly, indefinably, it thirsted for other things than
the sluggish trickle of water by which it was fed.

"Where is the place?" I asked, after a minute or two of silent
inspection. It was incredible that anything of the sort could
really exist—and equally incredible that a nature so robust as
Amberville should have been sensitive to its quality.

"It's in the bottom of that abandoned ranch, a mile or less
down the little road toward Bear River," he replied. "You must
know it. There's a small orchard about the house, on the
upper hillside; but the lower portion, ending in that meadow,
is all wild land."

I began to visualize the vicinity in question. "Guess it must
be the old Chapman place," I decided. "No other ranch along
that road would answer your specifications."

"Well, whoever it belongs to, that meadow is the most horrible spot I have ever encountered. I've known other landscapes
that had something wrong with them, but never anything like
this."

"Maybe it's haunted," I said, half in jest. "From your description, it must be the very meadow where old Chapman was
found dead one morning by his youngest daughter. It happened a few months after I moved here. He was supposed to
have died of heart failure. His body was quite cold, and he had
probably been lying there all night, since the family had missed
him at suppertime. I don't remember him very clearly, but I
remember that he had a reputation for eccentricity. For some
time before his death, people thought he was going mad. I
forget the details. Anyway, his wife and children left, not long
after he died, and no one has occupied the house or cultivated
the orchard since. It was a commonplace rural tragedy."

"I'm not much of a believer in spooks," observed Amberville, who seemed to have taken my suggestion of haunting
in a literal sense. "Whatever the influence is, it's hardly of
human origin. Come to think of it, though, I received a very
silly impression once or twice—the idea that some one was
watching me while I did those drawings. Queer—I had almost
forgotten that, till you brought up the possibility of haunting.
I seemed to see him out of the tail of my eye, just beyond the

radius that I was putting into the picture: a dilapidated old scoundrel with dirty gray whiskers and an evil scowl. It's odd, too, that I should have gotten such a definite conception of him, without ever seeing him squarely. I thought it was a tramp who had strayed into the meadow bottom. But when I turned to give him a level glance, he simply wasn't there. It was as if he melted into the miry ground, the cat-tails, the sedges."

"That isn't a bad description of Chapman," I said. "I remember his whiskers—they were almost white, except for the tobacco juice. A battered antique, if there ever was one—and very unamiable, too. He had a poisonous glare toward the end, which no doubt helped along the legend of his insanity. Some of the tales about him come back to me now. People said that he neglected the care of his orchard more and more. Visitors used to find him in that lower meadow, standing idly about and staring vacantly at the trees and water. Probably that was one reason they thought he was losing his mind. But I'm sure I never heard that there was anything unusual or queer about the meadow, either at the time of Chapman's death, or since. It's a lonely spot, and I don't imagine that any one ever goes there now."

"I stumbled on it quite by accident," said Amberville. "The place isn't visible from the road, on account of the thick pines. . . . But there's another odd thing: I went out this morning with a very strong and clear intuition that I might find something of uncommon interest. I made a bee-line for that meadow, so to speak; and I'll have to admit that the intuition justified itself. The place repels me—but it fascinates me, too. I've simply got to solve the mystery, if it has a solution," he added, with a slightly defensive air. "I'm going back early tomorrow, with my oils, to start a real painting of it."

I was surprised, knowing that predilection of Amberville for scenic brilliance and gayety which had caused him to be likened to Sorolla. "The painting will be a novelty for you," I commented. "I'll have to come and take a look at the place myself, before long. It should really be more in my line than yours. There ought to be a weird story in it somewhere, if it lives up to your drawings and description."

Several days passed. I was deeply preoccupied, at the time,

with the toilsome and intricate problems offered by the concluding chapters of a new novel; and I put off my proposed visit to the meadow discovered by Amberville. My friend, on his part, was evidently engrossed by his new theme. He sallied forth each morning with his easel and oil-colors, and returned later each day, forgetful of the luncheon-hour that had formerly brought him back from such expeditions. On the third day, he did not reappear till sunset. Contrary to his custom, he did not show me what he had done, and his answers to my queries regarding the progress of the picture were somewhat vague and evasive. For some reason, he was unwilling to talk about it. Also, he was apparently loth to discuss the meadow itself, and in answer to direct questions, merely reiterated in an absent and perfunctory manner the account he had given me following his discovery of the place. In some mysterious way that I could not define, his attitude seemed to have changed.

There were other changes, too. He seemed to have lost his usual blitheness. Often I caught him frowning intently, and surprised the lurking of some equivocal shadow in his frank eyes. There was a moodiness, a morbidity, which, as far as our five years' friendship enabled me to observe, was a new aspect of his temperament. Perhaps, if I had not been so preoccupied with my own difficulties, I might have wondered more as to the causation of his gloom, which I attributed readily enough at first to some technical dilemma that was baffling him. He was less and less the Amberville that I knew; and on the fourth day, when he came back at twilight, I perceived an actual surliness that was quite foreign to his nature.

"What's wrong?" I ventured to inquire. "Have you struck a snag? Or is old Chapman's meadow getting on your nerves with its ghostly influences?"

He seemed, for once, to make an effort to throw off his gloom, his taciturnity and ill humor.

"It's the infernal mystery of the thing," he declared. "I've simply got to solve it, in one way or another. The place has an entity of its own—an indwelling personality. It's there, like the soul in a human body, but I can't pin it down or touch it. You know that I'm not superstitious—but, on the other hand, I'm not a bigoted materialist, either; and I've run across some odd phenomena in my time. That meadow, perhaps, is inhabited by

what the ancients called a *Genius Loci*. More than once, before
this, I have suspected that such things might exist—might re-
side, inherent, in some particular spot. But this is the first time
that I've had reason to suspect anything of an actively malignant or inimical nature. The other influences, whose presence
I have felt, were benign in some large, vague, impersonal way
—or were else wholly indifferent to human welfare—perhaps
oblivious of human existence. This thing, however, is hatefully
aware and watchful: I feel that the meadow itself—or the force
embodied in the meadow—is scrutinizing me all the time. The
place has the air of a thirsty vampire, waiting to drink me in
somehow, if it can. It is a *cul-de-sac* of everything evil, in which
an unwary soul might well be caught and absorbed. But I tell
you, Murray, I can't keep away from it."

"It looks as if the place *were* getting you," I said, thoroughly
astonished by his extraordinary declaration, and by the air of
fearful and morbid conviction with which he uttered it.

Apparently he had not heard me, for he made no reply to
my observation. "There's another angle," he went on, with a
feverish tensity in his voice. "You remember my impression of
an old man lurking in the background and watching me, on
my first visit. Well, I have seen him again, many times, out of
the corner of my eye; and during the last two days, he has appeared more directly, though in a queer, partial way. Sometimes, when I am studying the dead willow very intently, I see
his scowling filthy-bearded face as a part of the bole. Then,
again, it will float among the leafless twigs, as if it had been
caught there. Sometimes a knotty hand, a tattered coat-sleeve,
will emerge through the mantling algae in the pool, as if a
drowned body were rising to the surface. Then, a moment
later—or simultaneously—there will be something of him
among the alders or the cat-tails. These apparitions are always
brief, and when I try to scutinize them closely, they melt like
films of vapor into the surrounding scene. But the old
scoundrel, whoever or whatever he may be, is a sort of fixture.
He is no less vile than everything else about the place, though
I feel that he isn't the main element of the vileness."

"Good Lord!" I exclaimed. "You certainly have been seeing
things. If you don't mind, I'll come down and join you for

a while, tomorrow afternoon. The mystery begins to invei-
gle me."

"Of course I don't mind. Come ahead." His manner, all at
once, for no tangible reason, had resumed the unnatural taciturnity of the past four days. He gave me a furtive look that
was sullen and almost unfriendly. It was as if an obscure barrier, temporarily laid aside, had again risen between us. The
shadows of his strange mood returned upon him visibly; and
my efforts to continue the conversation were rewarded only by
half-surly, half-absent monosyllables. Feeling an aroused concern, rather than any offense, I began to note, for the first
time, the unwonted pallor of his face, and the bright, febrile
luster of his eyes. He looked vaguely unwell, I thought, as if
something of his exuberant vitality had gone out of him, and
had left in its place an alien energy of doubtful and less healthy
nature. Tacitly, I gave up any attempt to bring him back from
the secretive twilight into which he had withdrawn. For the
rest of the evening, I pretended to read a novel, while Amberville maintained his singular abstraction. Somewhat inconclusively, I puzzled over the matter till bedtime. I made up my
mind, however, that I would visit Chapman's meadow. I did
not believe in the supernatural, but it seemed apparent that the
place was exerting a deleterious influence upon Amberville.

The next morning, when I arose, my Chinese servant informed me that the painter had already breakfasted and had
gone out with his easel and colors. This further proof of his
obsession troubled me; but I applied myself rigorously to a
forenoon of writing.

Immediately after luncheon, I drove down the highway, followed the narrow dirt road that branched off toward Bear
River, and left my car on the pine-thick hill above the old
Chapman place. Though I had never visited the meadow, I
had a pretty clear idea of its location. Disregarding the grassy,
half-obliterated road into the upper portion of the property,
I struck down through the woods into the little blind valley,
seeing more than once, on the opposite slope, the dying orchard of pear and apple trees, and the tumbledown shanty that
had belonged to the Chapmans.

It was a warm October day; and the serene solitude of the

forest, the autumnal softness of light and air, made the idea of anything malign or sinister seem impossible. When I came to the meadow bottom, I was ready to laugh at Amberville's notions; and the place itself, at first sight, merely impressed me as being rather dreary and dismal. The features of the scene were those that he had described so clearly, but I could not find the open evil that had leered from the pool, the willow, the alders and the cat-tails in his drawings.

Amberville, with his back toward me, was seated on a folding stool before his easel, which he had placed among the plots of dark green wire-grass in the open ground above the pool. He did not seem to be working, however, but was staring intently at the scene beyond him, while a loaded brush drooped idly in his fingers. The sedges deadened my footfalls; and he did not hear me as I drew near.

With much curiosity, I peered over his shoulder at the large canvas on which he had been engaged. As far as I could tell, the picture had already been carried to a consummate degree of technical perfection. It was an almost photographic rendering of the scummy water, the whitish skeleton of the leaning willow, the unhealthy, half-disrooted alders, and the cluster of nodding mace-reeds. But in it I found the macabre and demoniac spirit of the sketches: the meadow seemed to wait and watch like an evilly distorted face. It was a deadfall of malignity and despair, lying apart from the autumn world around it; a plague-spot of nature, for ever accursed and alone.

Again I looked at the landscape itself—and saw that the spot was indeed as Amberville had depicted it. It wore the grimace of a mad vampire, hateful and alert! At the same time, I became disagreeably conscious of the unnatural silence. There were no birds, no insects, as the painter had said; and it seemed that only spent and dying winds could ever enter that depressed valley-bottom. The thin stream that lost itself in the boggy ground was like a soul that went down to perdition. It was part of the mystery, too; for I could not remember any stream on the lower side of the barring hill that would indicate a subterranean outlet.

Amberville's intentness, and the very posture of his head and shoulders, were like those of a man who has been mesmerized. I was about to make my presence known to him; but at that instant there came to me the apperception that we were not alone in the meadow. Just beyond the focus of my vision, a figure seemed to stand in a furtive attitude, as if watching us both. I whirled about—and there was no one. Then I heard a startled cry from Amberville, and turned to find him staring at me. His features wore a wild look of terror and surprise, which had not wholly erased a hypnotic absorption.

"My God!" he said. "I thought you were the old man!"

I can not be sure whether anything more was said by either of us. I have, however, the impression of a blank silence. After his single exclamation of surprise, Amberville seemed to retreat into an impenetrable abstraction, as if he were no longer conscious of my presence; as if, having identified me, he had forgotten me at once. On my part, I felt a weird and overpowering constraint. That infamous, eery scene depressed me beyond measure. It seemed that the boggy bottom was trying to drag me down in some intangible way. The boughs of the sick alders beckoned. The pool, over which the bony willow presided like an arboreal death, was wooing me foully with its stagnant waters.

Moreover, apart from the ominous atmosphere of the scene itself, I was painfully aware of a further change in Amberville— a change that was an actual alienation. His recent mood, whatever it was, had strengthened upon him enormously: he had gone deeper into its morbid twilight, and was lost to the blithe and sanguine personality I had known. It was as if an incipient madness had seized him; and the possibility of this terrified me.

In a slow, somnambulistic manner, without giving me a second glance, he began to work at his painting, and I watched him for a while, hardly knowing what to do or say. For long intervals he would stop and peer with dreamy intentness at some feature of the landscape. I conceived the bizarre idea of a growing kinship, a mysterious *rapport* between Amberville and the meadow. In some intangible way, it seemed as if the place had taken something from his very soul—and had given something of itself in exchange. He wore the air of one who participates in some unholy secret, who has become the acolyte of an unhuman knowledge. In a flash of horrible definitude, I saw the place as an actual vampire, and Amberville as its willing victim.

How long I remained there, I can not say. Finally I stepped over to him and shook him roughly by the shoulder.

"You're working too hard," I said. "Take my advice, and lay off for a day or two."

He turned to me with the dazed look of one who is lost in some narcotic dream. This, very slowly, gave place to a sullen, evil anger.

"Oh, go to hell!" he snarled. "Can't you see that I'm busy?"

I left him then, for there seemed nothing else to do under the circumstances. The mad and spectral nature of the whole affair was enough to make me doubt my own reason. My impressions of the meadow—and of Amberville—were tainted with an insidious horror such as I had never before felt in any moment of waking life and normal consciousness.

At the bottom of the slope of yellow pine, I turned back with repugnant curiosity for a parting glance. The painter had not moved, he was still confronting the malignant scene like a charmed bird that faces a lethal serpent. Whether or not the impression was a double optic image, I have never been sure: but at that instant I seemed to discern a faint, unholy aura, neither light nor mist, that flowed and wavered about the meadow, preserving the outlines of the willow, the alders, the reeds, the pool. Stealthily it appeared to lengthen, reaching toward Amberville like ghostly arms. The whole image was extremely tenuous, and may well have been an illusion; but it sent me shuddering into the shelter of the tall, benignant pines.

The remainder of that day, and the evening that followed, were tinged with the shadowy horror I had found in Chapman's meadow. I believe that I spent most of the time in arguing vainly with myself, in trying to convince the rational part of my mind that all I had seen and felt was utterly preposterous. I could arrive at no conclusion, other than a conviction that Amberville's mental health was endangered by the damnable thing, whatever it was, that inhered in the meadow. The malign personality of the place, the impalpable terror, mystery and lure, were like webs that had been woven upon my brain, and which I could not dissipate by any amount of conscious effort.

I made two resolves, however: one was, that I should write immediately to Amberville's fiancée, Miss Avis Olcott, and invite her to visit me as a fellow-guest of the artist during the remainder of his stay at Bowman. Her influence, I thought, might help to counteract whatever was affecting him so perniciously. Since I knew her fairly well, the invitation would not seem out of the way. I decided to say nothing about it to Amberville: the element of surprise, I hoped, would be especially beneficial.

My second resolve was, that I should not again visit the meadow myself, if I could avoid it. Indirectly—for I knew the folly of trying to combat a mental obsession openly—I should also try to discourage the painter's interest in the place, and divert his attention to other themes. Trips and entertainments, too, could be devised, at the minor cost of delaying my own work.

The smoky autumn twilight overtook me in such meditations as these; but Amberville did not return. Horrible premonitions, without coherent shape or name, began to torment me as I waited for him. The night darkened; and dinner grew cold on the table. At last, about nine o'clock, when I was nerving myself to go out and hunt for him, he came in hurriedly. He was pale, dishevelled, out of breath; and his eyes held a painful glare, as if something had frightened him beyond endurance.

He did not apologize for his lateness; nor did he refer to my own visit to the meadow-bottom. Apparently he had forgotten the whole episode—had forgotten his rudeness to me.

"I'm through!" he cried. "I'll never go back again—never take another chance. That place is more hellish at night than in the daytime. I can't tell you what I've seen and felt—I must forget it, if I can. There's an emanation—something that comes out openly in the absence of the sun, but is latent by day. It lured me, it tempted me to remain this evening—and it nearly got me. . . . God! I didn't believe that such things were possible—that abhorrent compound of—" He broke off, and did not finish the sentence. His eyes dilated, as if with the memory of something too awful to be described. At that moment, I recalled the poisonously haunted eyes of old Chapman, whom I had sometimes met about the hamlet. He had not interested me particularly, since I had deemed him a common type of rural character, with a tendency to some obscure and unpleasant aberration. Now, when I saw the same look in the eyes of a sensitive artist, I began to wonder, with a shivering speculation, whether Chapman too had been aware of the weird evil that dwelt in his meadow. Perhaps, in some way that was beyond human comprehension, he had been its victim. . . . He had died there; and his death had not seemed at all mysterious. But perhaps, in the light of all that Amberville and I had perceived, there was more in the matter than any one had suspected.

"Tell me what you saw," I ventured to suggest.

At the question, a veil seemed to fall between us, impalpable but tenebrific. He shook his head morosely and made no reply. The human terror, which perhaps had driven him back toward his normal self, and had made him almost communicative for the nonce, fell away from Amberville. A shadow that was darker than fear, an impenetrable alien umbrage, again submerged him. I felt a sudden chill, of the spirit rather than the flesh; and once more there came to me the outré thought of his growing kinship with the ghoulish meadow. Beside me, in the lamplit room, behind the mask of his humanity, a thing that was not wholly human seemed to sit and wait.

Of the nightmarish days that followed, I shall offer only a summary. It would be impossible to convey the eventless, fantasmal horror in which we dwelt and moved.

I wrote immediately to Miss Olcott, pressing her to pay me a visit during Amberville's stay, and, in order to insure acceptance, I hinted obscurely at my concern for his health and my need of her coadjutation. In the meanwhile, waiting her answer, I tried to divert the artist by suggesting trips to sundry points of scenic interest in the neighborhood. These suggestions he declined, with an aloof curtness, an air that was stony and cryptic rather than deliberately rude. Virtually, he ignored my existence, and made it more than plain that he wished me to leave him to his own devices. This, in despair, I finally decided to do, pending the arrival of Miss Olcott. He went out early each morning, as usual, with his paints and easel, and returned about sunset or a little later. He did not tell me where he had been; and I refrained from asking.

Miss Olcott came on the third day following my letter, in the afternoon. She was young, lissome, ultra-feminine, and was altogether devoted to Amberville. In fact, I think she was a little in awe of him. I told her as much as I dared, and warned her of the morbid change in her fiancé, which I attributed to nervousness and overwork. I simply could not bring myself to mention Chapman's meadow and its baleful influence: the whole thing was too unbelievable, too fantasmagoric, to be offered as an explanation to a modern girl. When I saw the somewhat helpless alarm and bewilderment with which she listened to my story, I began to wish that she were of a more wilful and determined type, and were less submissive toward Amberville than I surmised her to be. A stronger woman might have saved him; but even then I began to doubt whether Avis could do anything to combat the imponderable evil that was engulfing him.

A heavy crescent moon was hanging like a blood-dipped horn in the twilight when he returned. To my immense relief, the presence of Avis appeared to have a highly salutary effect. The very moment that he saw her, Amberville came out of the singular eclipse that had claimed him, as I feared, beyond redemption, and was almost his former affable self. Perhaps it was all make-believe, for an ulterior purpose; but this, at the time, I could not suspect. I began to congratulate myself on having applied a sovereign remedy. The girl, on her part, was plainly relieved; though I saw her eyeing him in a slightly hurt and puzzled way, when he sometimes fell for a short interval into moody abstraction, as if he had temporarily forgotten her. On the whole, however, there was a transformation that appeared no less than magical, in view of his recent gloom and remoteness. After a decent interim, I left the pair together, and retired.

I rose very late the next morning, having overslept. Avis and Amberville I learned, had gone out together, carrying a lunch which my Chinese cook had provided. Plainly he was taking her along on one of his artistic expeditions; and I augured well for his recovery from this. Somehow, it never occurred to me that he had taken her to Chapman's meadow. The tenuous, malignant shadow of the whole affair had begun to lift from my mind; I rejoiced in a lightened sense of responsibility; and, for the first time in a week, was able to concentrate clearly on the ending of my novel.

The two returned at dusk, and I saw immediately that I had been mistaken on more points than one. Amberville had again retired into a sinister, saturnine reserve. The girl, beside his looming height and massive shoulders, looked very small, forlorn—and pitifully bewildered and frightened. It was as if she had encountered something altogether beyond her comprehension, something with which she was humanly powerless to cope.

Very little was said by either of them. They did not tell me where they had been; but, for that matter, it was unnecessary to inquire. Amberville's taciturnity, as usual, seemed due to an absorption in some dark mood or sullen revery. But Avis gave me the impression of a dual constraint—as if, apart from some enthralling terror, she had been forbidden to speak of the day's events and experiences. I knew that they had gone to that accursed meadow; but I was far from sure whether Avis had been personally conscious of the weird and baneful entity of the place, or had merely been frightened by the unwholesome change in her lover beneath its influence. In either case, it was obvious that she was wholly subservient to him. I began to damn myself for a fool in having invited her to Bowman—though the true bitterness of my regret was still to come.

A week went by, with the same daily excursions of the painter and his fiancée—the same baffling, sinister estrangement and secrecy in Amberville—the same terror, helplessness, constraint and submissiveness in the girl. How it would all end, I could not imagine; but I feared, from the ominous alteration of his character, that Amberville was heading for some form of mental alienation, if nothing worse. My offers of entertainment and scenic journeys were rejected by the pair; and several blunt efforts to question Avis were met by a wall of almost hostile evasion which convinced me that Amberville had enjoined her to secrecy—and had perhaps, in some sleightful manner, misrepresented my own attitude toward him.

"You don't understand him," she said, repeatedly. "He is very temperamental."

The whole affair was a maddening mystery, but it seemed more and more that the girl herself was being drawn, either directly or indirectly, into the same fantasmal web that had enmeshed the artist.

I surmised that Amberville had done several new pictures of the meadow; but he did not show them to me, nor even mention them. My own impressions of the place, as time went on, assumed an unaccountable vividness that was almost hallucinatory. The incredible idea of some inherent force or personality, malevolent and even vampirish, became an unavowed conviction against my will. The place haunted me like a fantasm, horrible but seductive. I felt an impelling morbid curiosity, an unwholesome desire to visit it again, and fathom, if possible, its enigma. Often I thought of Amberville's notion about a *Genius Loci* that dwelt in the meadow, and the hints of a human apparition that was somehow associated with the spot. Also, I wondered what it was that the artist had seen on the one occasion when he had lingered in the meadow after nightfall, and had returned to my house in driven terror. It seemed that he had not ventured to repeat the experiment, in spite of his obvious subjection to the unknown lure.

The end came, abruptly and without premonition. Business had taken me to the county seat, one afternoon, and I did not return till late in the evening. A full moon was high above the pine-dark hills. I expected to find Avis and the painter in my drawing-room; but they were not there. Li Sing, my factotum, told me that they had returned at dinnertime. An hour later, Amberville had gone out quietly while the girl was in her room. Coming down a few minutes later, Avis had shown excessive perturbation when she found him absent, and had also left the house, as if to follow him, without telling Li Sing where she was going or when she might return. All this had occurred three hours previously; and neither of the pair had yet reappeared.

A black and subtly chilling intuition of evil seized me as I listened to Li Sing's account. All too well I surmised that Amberville had yielded to the temptation of a second nocturnal visit to that unholy meadow. An occult attraction, somehow, had overcome the horror of his first experience, whatever it had been. Avis, knowing where he was, and perhaps fearful of his sanity—or safety—had gone out to find him. More and more, I felt an imperative conviction of some peril that threatened them both—some hideous and innominable thing to whose power, perhaps, they had already yielded.

Whatever my previous folly and remissness in the matter, I did not delay now. A few minutes of driving at precipitate speed through the mellow moonlight brought me to the piny edge of the Chapman property. There, as on my former visit, I left the car, and plunged headlong through the shadowy forest. Far down, in the hollow, as I went, I heard a single scream, shrill with terror, and abruptly terminated. I felt sure that the voice was that of Avis; but I did not hear it again.

Running desperately, I emerged in the meadow-bottom. Neither Avis nor Amberville was in sight; and it seemed to me, in my hasty scrutiny, that the place was full of mysteriously coiling and moving vapors that permitted only a partial view of the dead willow and the other vegetation. I ran on toward the scummy pool, and nearing it, was arrested by a sudden and twofold horror.

Avis and Amberville were floating together in the shallow pool, with their bodies half hidden by the mantling masses of algae. The girl was clasped tightly in the painter's arms, as if he had carried her with him, against her will, to that noisome death. Her face was covered by the evil, greenish scum; and I could not see the face of Amberville, which was averted against her shoulder. It seemed that there had been a struggle; but both were quiet now, and had yielded supinely to their doom.

It was not this spectacle alone, however, that drove me in mad and shuddering flight from the meadow, without making even the most tentative attempt to retrieve the drowned bodies. The true horror lay in the thing, which, from a little distance, I had taken for the coils of a slowly moving and rising mist. It was *not* vapor, nor anything else that could conceivably exist— that malign, luminous, pallid emanation that enfolded the entire scene before me like a restless and hungrily wavering extension of its outlines—a phantom projection of the pale and deathlike willow, the dying alders, the reeds, the stagnant pool and its suicidal victims. The landscape was visible through it, as through a film; but it seemed to curdle and thicken gradually in places, with some unholy, terrifying activity. Out of these curdlings, as if disgorged by the ambient exhalation, I saw the emergence of three human faces that partook of the same nebulous matter, neither mist nor plasm. One of these faces seemed to detach itself from the bole of the ghostly willow; the second and third swirled upward from the seething of the phantom pool, with their bodies trailing formlessly among the tenuous boughs. The faces were those of old Chapman, of Francis Amberville, and Avis Olcott.

Behind this eery, wraith-like projection of itself, the actual landscape leered with the same infernal and vampirish air which it had worn by day. But it seemed now that the place was no longer still—that it seethed with a malignant secret life— that it reached out toward me with its scummy waters, with the bony fingers of its trees, with the spectral faces it had spewed forth from its lethal deadfall.

Even terror was frozen within me for a moment. I stood watching, while the pale, unhallowed exhalation rose higher above the meadow. The three human faces, through a further agitation of the curdling mass, began to approach each other. Slowly, inexpressibly, they merged in one, becoming an androgynous face, neither young nor old, that melted finally into the lengthening phantom boughs of the willow—the hands of the arboreal death, that were reaching out to enfold me. Then, unable to bear the spectacle any longer, I started to run.

There is little more that need be told, for nothing that I could add to this narrative would lessen the abominable mystery of it all in any degree. The meadow—or the thing that dwells in the meadow—has already claimed three victims . . . and I sometimes wonder if it will have a fourth. I alone, it would seem, among the living, have guessed the secret of Chapman's death, and the death of Avis and Amberville; and no one else, apparently, has felt the malign genius of the meadow. I have not returned there, since the morning when the bodies of the artist and his fiancée were removed from the pool . . . nor have I summoned up the resolution to destroy or otherwise dispose of the four oil paintings and two watercolor drawings of the spot that were made by Amberville. Perhaps . . . in spite of all that deters me . . . I shall visit it again.

1933

ROBERT BLOCH

(1917–1994)

The Cloak

THE sun was dying, and its blood spattered the sky as it crept into a sepulcher behind the hills. The keening wind sent the dry, fallen leaves scurrying toward the west, as though hastening them to the funeral of the sun.

"Nuts!" said Henderson to himself, and stopped thinking.

The sun was setting in a dingy red sky, and a dirty raw wind was kicking up the half-rotten leaves in a filthy gutter. Why should he waste time with cheap imagery?

"Nuts!" said Henderson, again.

It was probably a mood evoked by the day, he mused. After all, this was the sunset of Halloween. Tonight was the dreaded Allhallows Eve, when spirits walked and skulls cried out from their graves beneath the earth.

Either that, or tonight was just another rotten cold fall day. Henderson sighed. There was a time, he reflected, when the coming of this night meant something. A dark Europe, groaning in superstitious fear, dedicated this Eve to the grinning Unknown. A million doors had once been barred against the evil visitants, a million prayers mumbled, a million candles lit. There was something majestic about the idea, Henderson reflected. Life had been an adventure in those times, and men walked in terror of what the next turn of a midnight road might bring. They had lived in a world of demons and ghouls and elementals who sought their souls—and by Heaven, in those days a man's soul meant something. This new skepticism had taken a profound meaning away from life. Men no longer revered their souls.

"Nuts!" said Henderson again, quite automatically. There was something crude and twentieth-century about the coarse expression which always checked his introspective flights of fancy.

The voice in his brain that said "nuts" took the place of humanity to Henderson—common humanity which would

698

echo the same sentiment upon hearing his secret thoughts. So now Henderson uttered the word and endeavored to forget problems and purple patches alike.

He was walking down this street at sunset to buy a costume for the masquerade party tonight, and he had much better concentrate on finding the costumer's before it closed than waste his time daydreaming about Halloween.

His eyes searched the darkening shadows of the dingy buildings lining the narrow thoroughfare. Once again he peered at the address he had scribbled down after finding it in the phone book.

Why the devil didn't they light up the shops when it got dark? He couldn't make out numbers. This was a poor, run-down neighborhood, but after all—

Abruptly, Henderson spied the place across the street and started over. He passed the window and glanced in. The last rays of the sun slanted over the top of the building across the way and fell directly on the window and its display. Henderson drew a sharp intake of breath.

He was staring at a costumer's window—not looking through a fissure into hell. Then why was it all red fire, lighting the grinning visages of fiends?

"Sunset," Henderson muttered aloud. Of course it was, and the faces were merely clever masks such as would be displayed in this sort of place. Still, it gave the imaginative man a start. He opened the door and entered.

The place was dark and still. There was a smell of loneliness in the air—the smell that haunts all places long undisturbed; tombs, and graves in deep woods, and caverns in the earth, and—

"Nuts."

What the devil was wrong with him, anyway? Henderson smiled apologetically at the empty darkness. This was the smell of the costumer's shop, and it carried him back to college days of amateur theatricals. Henderson had known this smell of moth balls, decayed furs, grease paint and oils. He had played amateur Hamlet and in his hands he had held a smirking skull that hid all knowledge in its empty eyes—a skull, from the costumer's.

Well, here he was again, and the skull gave him the idea.

After all, Halloween night it was. Certainly in this mood of his he didn't want to go as a rajah, or a Turk, or a pirate—they all did that. Why not go as a fiend, or a warlock, or a werewolf? He could see Lindstrom's face when he walked into the elegant penthouse wearing rags of some sort. The fellow would have a fit, with his society crowd wearing their expensive Elsa Maxwell take-offs. Henderson didn't greatly care for Lindstrom's sophisticated friends anyway; a gang of amateur Noel Cowards and horsy women wearing harnesses of jewels. Why not carry out the spirit of Halloween and go as a monster?

Henderson stood there in the dusk, waiting for someone to turn on the lights, come out from the back room and serve him. After a minute or so he grew impatient and rapped sharply on the counter.

"Say in there! Service!"

Silence. And a shuffling noise from the rear, then—an unpleasant noise to hear in the gloom. There was a banging from downstairs and then the heavy clump of footsteps. Suddenly Henderson gasped. A black bulk was rising from the floor!

It was, of course, only the opening of the trapdoor from the basement. A man shuffled behind the counter, carrying a lamp. In that light his eyes blinked drowsily.

The man's yellowish face crinkled into a smile.

"I was sleeping, I'm afraid," said the man, softly. "Can I serve you, sir?"

"I was looking for a Halloween costume."

"Oh, yes. And what was it you had in mind?"

The voice was weary, infinitely weary. The eyes continued to blink in the flabby yellow face.

"Nothing usual, I'm afraid. You see, I rather fancied some sort of monster getup for a party—don't suppose you carry anything in that line?"

"I could show you masks."

"No. I meant werewolf outfits, something of the sort. More of the authentic."

"So. The *authentic*."

"Yes." Why did this old dunce stress the word?

"I might—yes. I might have just the. thing for you, sir." The eyes blinked, but the thin mouth pursed in a smile. "Just the thing for Halloween."

"What's that?"

"Have you ever considered the possibility of being a vampire?"

"Like Dracula ?"

"Ah—yes, I suppose—Dracula."

"Not a bad idea. Do you think I'm the type for that, though?"

The man appraised him with that tight smile. "Vampires are of all types, I understand. You would do nicely."

"Hardly a compliment," Henderson chuckled. "But why not? What's the outfit?"

"Outfit? Merely evening clothes, or what you wear. I will furnish you with the authentic cloak."

"Just a cloak—is that all?"

"Just a cloak. But it is worn like a shroud. It *is* shroud-cloth, you know. Wait, I'll get it for you."

The shuffling feet carried the man into the rear of the shop again. Down the trapdoor entrance he went, and Henderson waited. There was more banging, and presently the old man reappeared carrying the cloak. He was shaking dust from it in the darkness.

"Here it is—the genuine cloak."

"Genuine?"

"Allow me to adjust it for you—it will work wonders, I'm sure."

The cold, heavy cloth hung draped about Henderson's shoulders. The faint odor rose mustily in his nostrils as he stepped back and surveyed himself in the mirror. The lamp was poor, but Henderson saw that the cloak effected a striking transformation in his appearance. His long face seemed thinner, his eyes were accentuated in the facial pallor heightened by the somber cloak he wore. It was a big, black shroud.

"Genuine," murmured the old man. He must have come up suddenly, for Henderson hadn't noticed him in the glass.

"I'll take it," Henderson said. "How much?"

"You'll find it quite entertaining, I'm sure."

"How much?"

"Oh. Shall we say five dollars?"

"Here."

The old man took the money, blinking, and drew the cloak

from Henderson's shoulders. When it slid away he felt suddenly warm again. It must be cold in the basement—the cloth
was icy.

The old man wrapped the garment, smiling, and handed it
over.

"I'll have it back tomorrow," Henderson promised.

"No need. You purchased it. It is yours."

"But—"

"I am leaving business shortly. Keep it. You will find more
use for it than I, surely."

"But—"

"A pleasant evening to you."

Henderson made his way to the door in confusion, then
turned to salute the blinking old man in the dimness.

Two eyes were burning at him from across the counter—
two eyes that did not blink.

"Good night," said Henderson, and closed the door quickly.
He wondered if he were going just a trifle mad.

At eight, Henderson nearly called up Lindstrom to tell him
he couldn't make it. The cold chills came the minute he put on
the damned cloak, and when he looked at himself in the mirror his blurred eyes could scarcely make out the reflection.

But after a few drinks he felt better about it. He hadn't eaten,
and the liquor warmed his blood. He paced the floor, attitudi-
nizing with the cloak—sweeping it about him and scowling in
what he thought was a ferocious manner. Damn it, he was
going to be a vampire all right! He called a cab, went down to
the lobby. The driver came in, and Henderson was waiting,
black cloak furled.

"I wish you to drive me," he said in a low voice.

The cabman took one look at him in the cloak and turned
pale.

"Whazzat?"

"I ordered you to come," said Henderson gutturally, while
he quaked with inner mirth. He leered ferociously and swept
the cloak back.

"Yeah, yeah. O.K."

The driver almost ran outside. Henderson stalked after him.

"Where to, boss—I mean, sir?"

The frightened face didn't turn as Henderson intoned the address and sat back.

The cab started with a lurch that set Henderson to chuckling deeply, in character. At the sound of the laughter the driver got panicky and raced his engine up to the limit set by the governor. Henderson laughed loudly, and the impressionable driver fairly quivered in his seat. It was quite a ride, but Henderson was entirely unprepared to open the door and find it slammed after him as the cabman drove hastily away without collecting a fare.

"I must look the part," he thought complacently, as he took the elevator up to the penthouse apartment.

There were three or four others in the elevator; Henderson had seen them before at other affairs Lindstrom had invited him to attend, but nobody seemed to recognize him. It rather pleased him to think how his wearing of an unfamiliar cloak and an unfamiliar scowl seemed to change his entire personality and appearance. Here the other guests had donned elaborate disguises—one woman wore the costume of a Watteau shepherdess, another was attired as a Spanish ballerina, a tall man dressed as Pagliacci, and his companion had donned a toreador outfit. Yet Henderson recognized them all; knew that their expensive habiliments were not truly disguises at all, but merely elaborations calculated to enhance their appearance. Most people at costume parties gave vent to suppressed desires. The women showed off their figures, the men either accentuated their masculinity as the toreador did, or clowned it. Such things were pitiful; these conventional fools eagerly doffing their dismal business suits and rushing off to a lodge, or amateur theatrical, or mask ball in order to satisfy their starving imaginations. Why didn't they dress in garish colors on the street? Henderson often pondered the question.

Surely, these society folk in the elevator were fine-looking men and women in their outfits—so healthy, so red-faced, and full of vitality. They had such robust throats and necks. Henderson looked at the plump arms of the woman next to him. He stared, without realizing it, for a long moment. And then, he saw that the occupants of the car had drawn away from him. They were standing in the corner, as though they feared his cloak and scowl, and his eyes fixed on the woman. Their chatter had ceased abruptly. The woman looked at him, as though she were about to speak, when the elevator doors opened and afforded Henderson a welcome respite.

What the devil was wrong? First the cab driver, then the woman. Had he drunk too much?

Well, no chance to consider that. Here was Marcus Lindstrom, and he was thrusting a glass into Henderson's hand.

"What have we here? Ah, a bogy-man!" It needed no second glance to perceive that Lindstrom, as usual at such affairs, was already quite bottle-dizzy. The fat host was positively swimming in alcohol.

"Have a drink, Henderson, my lad! I'll take mine from the bottle. That outfit of yours gave me a shock. Where'd you get the makeup?"

"Make-up? I'm not wearing any make-up."

"Oh. So you're not. How . . . silly of me."

Henderson wondered if he were crazy. Had Lindstrom really drawn back? Were his eyes actually filled with a certain dismay? Oh, the man was obviously intoxicated.

"I'll . . . I'll see you later," babbled Lindstrom, edging away and quickly turning to the other arrivals. Henderson watched the back of Lindstrom's neck. It was fat and white. It bulged over the collar of his costume and there was a vein in it. A vein in Lindstrom's fat neck. Frightened Lindstrom.

Henderson stood alone in the ante-room. From the parlor beyond came the sound of music and laughter; party noises. Henderson hesitated before entering. He drank from the glass in his hand—Bacardi rum, and powerful. On top of his other drinks it almost made the man reel. But he drank, wondering. What was wrong with him and his costume? Why did he frighten people? Was he unconsciously acting his vampire role? That crack of Lindstrom's about make-up now—

Acting on impulse, Henderson stepped over to the long panel mirror in the hall. He lurched a little, then stood in the harsh light before it. He faced the glass, stared into the mirror, and saw nothing.

He looked at himself in the mirror, and there was no one there!

Henderson began to laugh softly, evilly, deep in his throat.

And as he gazed into the empty, unreflecting glass, his laughter rose in black glee.

"*I'm drunk*," he whispered. "I must be drunk. Mirror in my apartment made me blurred. Now I'm so far gone I can't see straight. Sure I'm drunk. Been acting ridiculously, scaring people. Now I'm seeing hallucinations—or not seeing them, rather. Visions. Angels."

His voice lowered. "Sure, angels. Standing right in back of me, now. Hello, angel."

"Hello."

Henderson whirled. There she stood, in the dark cloak, her hair a shimmering halo above her white, proud face; her eyes celestial blue, and her lips infernal red.

"Are you real?" asked Henderson, gently. "Or am I a fool to believe in miracles?"

"This miracle's name is Sheila Darrly, and it would like to powder its nose if you please."

"Kindly use this mirror through the courtesy of Stephen Henderson," replied the cloaked man, with a grin. He stepped back a ways, eyes intent.

The girl turned her head and favored him with a slow, impish smile. "Haven't you ever seen powder used before?" she asked.

"Didn't know angels indulged in cosmetics," Henderson replied. "But then there's a lot I don't know about angels. From now on I shall make them a special study of mine. There's so much I want to find out. So you'll probably find me following you around with a notebook all evening."

"Notebooks for a vampire?"

"Oh, but I'm a very intelligent vampire—not one of those backwoods Transylvanian types. You'll find me charming, I'm sure."

"Yes, you look like the sure type," the girl mocked. "But an angel and a vampire—that's a queer combination."

"We can reform one another," Henderson pointed out. "Besides, I have a suspicion that there's a bit of the devil in you. That dark cloak over your angel costume; dark angel, you know. Instead of heaven you might hail from my home town."

Henderson was flippant, but underneath his banter cyclonic

thoughts whirled. He recalled discussions in the past; cynical observations he had made and believed.

Once, Henderson had declared that there was no such thing as love at first sight, save in books or plays where such a dramatic device served to speed up action. He asserted that people learned about romance from books and plays and accordingly adopted a belief in love at first sight when all one could possibly feel was desire.

And now this Sheila—this blond angel—had to come along and drive out all thoughts of morbidity, all thoughts of drunkenness and foolish gazings into mirrors, from his mind; had to send him madly plunging into dreams of red lips, ethereal blue eyes and slim white arms.

Something of his feelings had swept into his eyes, and as the girl gazed up at him she felt the truth.

"Well," she breathed, "I hope the inspection pleases."

"A miracle of understatement, that. But there was something I wanted to find out particularly about divinity. Do angels dance?"

"Tactful vampire! The next room?"

Arm in arm they entered the parlor. The merrymakers were in full swing. Liquor had already pitched gaiety at its height, but there was no dancing any longer. Boisterous little grouped couples laughed arm in arm about the room. The usual party gagsters were performing their antics in corners. The superficial atmosphere, which Henderson detested, was fully in evidence.

It was reaction which made Henderson draw himself up to full height and sweep the cloak about his shoulders. Reaction brought the scowl to his pale face, caused him to stalk along in brooding silence. Sheila seemed to regard this as a great joke.

"*Pull* a vampire act on them," she giggled, clutching his arm. Henderson accordingly scowled at the couples, sneered horrendously at the women. And his progress was marked by the turning of heads, the abrupt cessation of chatter. He walked through the long room like Red Death incarnate. Whispers trailed in his wake.

"Who is that man?"

"We came up with him in the elevator, and he—"

"His eyes—"

"Vampire!"

"Hello, Dracula!" It was Marcus Lindstrom and a sullen-looking brunette in Cleopatra costume who lurched toward Henderson. Host Lindstrom could scarcely stand, and his companion in cups was equally at a loss. Henderson liked the man when sober at the club, but his behavior at parties had always irritated him. Lindstrom was particularly objectionable in his present condition—it made him boorish.

"M'dear, I want you t' meet a very dear friend of mind. Yessir, it being Halloween and all, I invited Count Dracula here, t'gether with his daughter. Asked his grandmother, but she's busy tonight at a Black Sabbath—along with Aunt Jemima. Ha! Count, meet my little playmate."

The woman leered up at Henderson.

"Oooh Dracula, what big eyes you have! Oooh, what big teeth you have! Ooooh—"

"Really, Marcus," Henderson protested. But the host had turned and shouted to the room.

"Folks, meet the real goods—only genuine living vampire in captivity! Dracula Henderson, only existing vampire with false teeth."

In any other circumstance Henderson would have given Lindstrom a quick, efficient punch on the jaw. But Sheila was at his side, it was a public gathering; better to humor the man's clumsy jest. Why not be a vampire?

Smiling quickly at the girl, Henderson drew himself erect, faced the crowd, and frowned. His hands brushed the cloak. Funny, it still felt cold. Looking down he noticed for the first time that it was a little dirty at the edges; muddy or dusty. But the cold silk slid through his fingers as he drew it across his breast with one long hand. The feeling seemed to inspire him. He opened his eyes wide and let them blaze. His mouth opened. A sense of dramatic power filled him. And he looked at Marcus Lindstrom's soft, fat neck with the vein standing in the whiteness. He looked at the neck, saw the crowd watching him, and then the impulse seized him. He turned, eyes on that creasy neck—that wabbling, creasy neck of the fat man.

Hands darted out. Lindstrom squeaked like a frightened rat. He was a plump, sleek white rat, bursting with blood. Vampires liked blood. Blood from the rat, from the neck of the rat, from the vein in the neck of the squeaking rat.

"Warm blood."

The deep voice was Henderson's own.

The hands were Henderson's own.

The hands that went around Lindstrom's neck as he spoke, the hands that felt the warmth, that searched out the vein. Henderson's face was bending for the neck, and, as Lindstrom struggled, his grip tightened. Lindstrom's face was turning, turning purple. Blood was rushing to his head. That was good. Blood!

Henderson's mouth opened. He felt the air on his teeth. He bent down toward that fat neck, and then—

"Stop! That's plenty!"

The voice, the cooling voice of Sheila. Her fingers on his arm. Henderson looked up, startled. He released Lindstrom, who sagged with open mouth.

The crowd was staring, and their mouths were all shaped in the instinctive O of amazement.

Sheila whispered, "Bravo! Served him right—but you frightened him!"

Henderson struggled a moment to collect himself. Then he smiled and turned.

"Ladies and gentlemen," he said, "I have just given a slight demonstration to prove to you what our host said of me was entirely correct. I *am* a vampire. Now that you have been given fair warning, I am sure you will be in no further danger. If there is a doctor in the house I can, perhaps, arrange for a blood transfusion."

The O's relaxed and laughter came from startled throats. Hysterical laughter, in part, then genuine. Henderson had carried it off. Marcus Lindstrom alone still stared with eyes that held utter fear. *He* knew.

And then the moment broke, for one of the gagsters ran into the room from the elevator. He had gone downstairs and borrowed the apron and cap of a newsboy. Now he raced through the crowd with a bundle of papers under his arm.

"Extra! Extra! Read all about it! Big Halloween Horror! Extra!"

Laughing guests purchased papers. A woman approached Sheila, and Henderson watched the girl walk away in a daze.

"See you later," she called, and her glance sent fire through his veins. Still, he could not forget the terrible feeling that came over him when he had seized Lindstrom. Why?

Automatically, he accepted a paper from the shouting pseudo-news-boy. "Big Halloween Horror," he had shouted. What was that?

Blurred eyes searched the paper.

Then Henderson reeled back. That headline! It was an *Extra* after all. Henderson scanned the columns with mounting dread.

"Fire in costumer's . . . shortly after 8 p.m. firemen were summoned to the shop of . . . flames beyond control . . . completely demolished . . . damage estimated at . . . peculiarly enough, name of proprietor unknown . . . skeleton found in—"

"No!" gasped Henderson aloud.

He read, reread *that* closely. The skeleton had been found in a box of earth in the cellar beneath the shop. The box was a coffin. There had been two other boxes, empty. The skeleton had been wrapped in a cloak, undamaged by the flames—

And in the hastily penned box at the bottom of the column were eyewitness comments, written up under scareheads of heavy black type. Neighbors had feared the place. Hungarian neighborhood, hints of vampirism, of strangers who entered the shop. One man spoke of a cult believed to have held meetings in the place. Superstition about things sold there—love philters, outlandish charms and weird disguises.

Weird disguises—vampires—cloaks—*his eyes!*

"*This is an authentic cloak.*"

"*I will not be using this much longer. Keep it.*"

Memories of these words screamed through Henderson's brain. He plunged out of the room and rushed to the panel mirror.

A moment, then he flung one arm before his face to shield his eyes from the image that was not there—the missing reflection. *Vampires have no reflections.*

No wonder he looked strange. No wonder arms and necks invited him. He had wanted Lindstrom. Good God!

The cloak had done that, the dark cloak with the stains. The stains of earth, grave-earth. The wearing of the cloak, the cold cloak, had given him the feelings of a true vampire. It was a garment accursed, a thing that had lain on the body of one un-dead. The rusty stain along one sleeve was blood.

Blood. It would be nice to see blood. To taste its warmth, its red life, flowing.

No. That was insane. He was drunk, crazy.

"Ah. My pale friend, the vampire."

It was Sheila again. And above all horror rose the beating of Henderson's heart. As he looked at her shining eyes, her warm mouth shaped in red invitation, Henderson felt a wave of warmth. He looked at her white throat rising above her dark, shimmering cloak, and another kind of warmth rose. Love, de-sire, and a—hunger.

She must have seen it in his eyes, but she did not flinch. In-stead, her own gaze burned in return.

Sheila loved him, too!

With an impulsive gesture, Henderson ripped the cloak from about his throat. The icy weight lifted. He was free. Somehow, he hadn't wanted to take the cloak off, but he had to. It was a cursed thing, and in another minute he might have taken the girl in his arms, taken her for a kiss and remained to—

But he dared not think of that.

"Tired of masquerading?" she asked. With a similar gesture she, too, removed her cloak and stood revealed in the glory of her angel robe. Her blond, statuesque perfection forced a gasp to Henderson's throat.

"Angel," he whispered.

"Devil," she mocked.

And suddenly they were embracing. Henderson had taken her cloak in his arm with his own. They stood with lips seeking rapture until Lindstrom and a group moved noisily into the anteroom.

At the sight of Henderson the fat host recoiled.

"You—" he whispered. "You are—"

"Just leaving," Henderson smiled. Grasping the girl's arm, he drew her toward the empty elevator. The door shut on Lind-strom's pale, fear-filled face.

"Were we leaving?" Sheila whispered, snuggling against his shoulder.

"We were. But not for earth. We do not go down into my realm, but up—into yours."

"The roof garden?"

"Exactly, my angelic one. I want to talk to you against the background of your own heavens, kiss you amidst the clouds, and—"

Her lips found his as the car rose.

"Angel and devil. What a match!"

"I thought so, too," the girl confessed. "Will our children have halos or horns?"

"Both, I'm sure."

They stepped out onto the deserted rooftop. And once again it was Halloween.

Henderson felt it. Downstairs it was Lindstrom and his society friends, in a drunken costume party. Here it was night, silence, gloom. No light, no music, no drinking, no chatter which made one party identical with another; one night like all the rest. This night was individual here.

The sky was not blue, but black. Clouds hung like the gray beards of hovering giants peering at the round orange globe of the moon. A cold wind blew from the sea, and filled the air with tiny murmurings from afar.

This was the sky that witches flew through to their Sabbath. This was the moon of wizardry, the sable silence of black prayers and whispered invocations. The clouds hid monstrous Presences shambling in summons from afar. It was Halloween.

It was also quite cold.

"Give me my cloak," Sheila whispered. Automatically, Henderson extended the garment, and the girl's body swirled under the dark splendor of the cloth. Her eyes burned up at Henderson with a call he could not resist. He kissed her, trembling.

"You're cold," the girl said. "Put on your cloak."

Yes, Henderson, he thought to himself. Put on your cloak while you stare at her throat. Then, the next time you kiss her you will want her throat and she will give it in love and you will take it in—hunger.

"Put it on, darling—I insist," the girl whispered. Her eyes were impatient, burning with an eagerness to match his own.

Henderson trembled.

Put on the cloak of darkness? The cloak of the grave, the cloak of death, the cloak of the vampire? The evil cloak, filled with a cold life of its own that transformed his face, transformed his mind, made his soul instinct with awful hunger?

"Here."

The girl's slim arms were about him, pushing the cloak onto his shoulders. Her fingers brushed his neck, caressingly, as she linked the cloak about his throat.

Henderson shivered.

Then he felt it—through him—that icy coldness turning to a more dreadful heat. He felt himself expand, felt the sneer cross his face. This was Power!

And the girl before him, her eyes taunting, inviting. He saw her ivory neck, her warm slim neck, waiting. It was waiting for him, for his lips.

For his teeth.

No—it couldn't be. He loved her. His love must conquer this madness. Yes, wear the cloak, defy its power, and take her in his arms as a man, not as a fiend. He must. It was the test.

"Sheila." Funny, how his voice deepened.

"Yes, dear."

"Sheila, I must tell you this."

Her eyes—so alluring. It would be easy!

"Sheila, please. You read the paper tonight."

"Yes."

"I . . . I got my cloak there. I can't explain it. You saw how I took Lindstrom. I wanted to go through with it. Do you understand me? I meant to . . . to bite him. Wearing this damnable thing makes me feel like one of those creatures."

Why didn't her stare change? Why didn't she recoil in horror? Such trusting innocence! Didn't she understand? Why didn't she run? Any moment now he might lose control, seize her.

"I love you, Sheila. Believe that. I love you."

"I know." Her eyes gleamed in the moonlight.

"I want to test it. I want to kiss you, wearing this cloak. I want to feel that my love is stronger than this—thing. If I weaken, promise me you'll break away and run, quickly. But don't misunderstand. I must face this feeling and fight it; I want my love for you to be that pure, that secure. Are you afraid?"

"No." Still she stared at him, just as he stared at her throat. If she knew what was in his mind!

"You don't think I'm crazy? I went to this costumer's—he was a horrible little old man—and he gave me the cloak. Actually told me it was a real vampire's. I thought he was joking, but tonight I didn't see myself in the mirror, and I wanted Lindstrom's neck, and I want you. But I must test it."

"You're not crazy. I know. I'm not afraid."

"Then—"

The girl's face mocked. Henderson summoned his strength. He bent forward, his impulses battling. For a moment he stood there under the ghastly orange moon, and his face was twisted in struggle.

And the girl lured.

Her odd, incredibly red lips parted in a silvery, chuckly laugh as her white arms rose from the black cloak she wore to circle his neck gently. "I know—I knew when I looked in the mirror. I knew you had a cloak like mine—got yours where I got mine—"

Queerly, her lips seemed to elude his as he stood frozen for an instant of shock. Then he felt the icy hardness of her sharp little teeth on his throat, a strangely soothing sting, and an engulfing blackness rising over him.

1939

BIOGRAPHICAL NOTES

NOTE ON THE TEXTS

NOTES

Biographical Notes

Conrad Aiken (August 5, 1889–August 17, 1973) b. Conrad Potter Aiken in Savannah, Georgia, first of four children of William Ford Aiken, a doctor, and Anna Aiken Potter. In February 1901, father shot mother and then killed himself; Aiken discovered the bodies moments later. Adopted by an uncle in Cambridge, Massachusetts. Attended Harvard (1907–11), where he formed close friendship with T. S. Eliot. First book of poetry, *Earth Triumphant* (1914), followed by many others including *The Jig of Forslin* (1916), *Senlin: A Biography* (1918), *The House of Dust* (1920), *Priapus and the Pool* (1922), *Preludes for Memnon* (1931), *Brownstone Eclogues* (1942), and *A Letter from Li Po* (1955). The first of his novels, *Blue Voyage*, appeared in 1927. He published his autobiography *Ushant* in 1952. Received Pulitzer Prize for *Selected Poems* (1930); was Poetry Consultant at the Library of Congress in 1950; won National Book Award for *Collected Poems* (1953) and National Medal for Literature in 1969.

Gertrude Atherton (October 30, 1857–June 14, 1948) b. Gertrude Franklin Horn in San Francisco. Raised by her maternal grandfather after parents separated; attended high school in California and college in Kentucky, but contracted tuberculosis and did not complete her studies. At 19, eloped with George H. Bowen Atherton and lived with him at his mother's estate, Valparaiso Park, in San Francisco. Her first book, *Randolph's of Redwood,* was published anonymously in a local newspaper in 1882. After husband's death, moved to New York and began a professional literary career. She subsequently resided for long periods of time in Germany and England. Over the course of her life, she wrote scores of books, many depicting the early history of California, including *What Dreams May Come* (1889), *Before the Gringo Came* (1894), *The Californians* (1898), *The Conqueror* (1902), *The Bell in the Fog and Other Stories* (1905), *Rézanov* (1906), and *The White Morning* (1918). *Black Oxen* (1923), a novel about a woman who undergoes surgery to make herself younger, became a bestseller. Her autobiography, *Adventures of a Novelist,* appeared in 1932.

John Kendrick Bangs (May 27, 1862–January 21, 1922) b. Yonkers, New York. He attended Columbia University, where he edited the literary magazine. Later he was an editor of *Life, Harper's Magazine,* and *Harper's Bazaar*, contributing articles, poems, and humorous stories. In later years he was an editor at *New Metropolitan Magazine* and *Puck* and a popular lecturer. He was a prolific author of satirical and whimsical fantasies, many set in the afterlife. His books included *Tiddledywink Tales* (1891), *Tappleton's Client: or, A Spirit in Exile* (1893), *A House-Boat on the Styx* (1895), *Mr. Bonaparte of Corsica* (1895), *Ghosts I Have Met and Some Others* (1898), *The Enchanted Type-Writer* (1899), and *Olympian Nights* (1902).

Stephen Vincent Benét (July 22, 1889–March 13, 1943) b. Bethlehem, Pennsylvania; siblings were the poets William Rose Benét and Laura Benét. Published his first two collections of poetry while he was at Yale. Received Guggenheim fellowship to write long poem on the Civil War, published as *John Brown's Body* (1928); it became a bestseller and won the Pulitzer Prize. In addition to poetry wrote fiction, radio plays, and film scripts. His fantasy stories included "The Devil and Daniel Webster" (1937), which was adapted into a film in 1941, "By the Waters of Babylon" (1937), and "Johnny Pye and the Fool Killer" (1938). His last book was *Western Star* (1943), intended as the first in a series of narrative poems on the history of the American West.

Ambrose Bierce (June 24, 1842–1914?) b. Ambrose Gwinnett Bierce on farm near Horse Cave Creek, Ohio, one of many children of poor but well-read farm family. Attended Kentucky Military Institute (1859–60) and subsequently enlisted in the 9th Indiana Infantry; fought at Shiloh, Murfreesboro, Chattanooga, Franklin, and was wounded at Kenesaw Mountain. Moved to San Francisco after the war, working at U.S. sub-treasury and beginning career in journalism, writing for *The Californian*, *The Overland Monthly*, and other publications. Lived in England and France before returning in 1875 to San Francisco, where he edited *The Wasp* and later became editor for William Randolph Hearst's *Examiner*. His books included *Tales of Soldiers and Civilians* (1892), *Can Such Things Be?* (1893), *Fantastic Fables* (1899), and *The Cynic's Word Book* (1906, later retitled *The Devil's Dictionary*). He disappeared into Mexico in 1913, writing to a friend: "If you hear of my being stood up against a Mexican stone wall and shot to rags please know that I think it a pretty good way to depart this life." Joined Pancho Villa's forces as an observer and died under circumstances that remain mysterious.

Robert Bloch (April 5, 1917–September 23, 1994) b. Chicago, Illinois, to a bank cashier and a social worker; developed an interest in fantastic stories as a teenager, and began corresponding with H. P.

Lovecraft, whose stories he had read and admired in *Weird Tales*. With Lovecraft's encouragement and guidance, published two stories in *Weird Tales* at 17, and went on to become one of the magazine's most popular contributors. Wrote hundreds of stories, including such frequently anthologized works as "Yours Truly, Jack the Ripper," "The Opener of the Way," and "The Plot Is the Thing," as well as novels including *The Scarf* (1947), *The Kidnapper* (1954), *Spiderweb* (1954), and *Psycho* (1959), which was filmed the following year by Alfred Hitchcock. He also wrote many screenplays and television scripts.

Alice Brown (December 5, 1857–June 21, 1948) b. Hampton Falls, New Hampshire. She worked as a schoolteacher before moving to Boston where she worked for *The Christian Register* and *Youth's Companion* and wrote novels, poems, and plays. She was known for stories of New England life, collected in *Meadow-Grass* (1895) and *Tiverton Tales* (1899). Her many books included *Fools of Nature* (1897), *The Rose of Hope* (1896), *Margaret Warrener* (1902), *The One-Footed Fairy* (1911), *The Wind Between the Worlds* (1920), and *The Mysteries of Anne* (1925). She was a friend of the poet Louise Imogen Guiney, of whom she published a biography in 1921.

Charles Brockden Brown (January 17, 1771–February 22, 1810) b. Philadelphia, son of James Brown, a prosperous merchant, and Miriam Churchman Brown. Classically educated and a precocious student, at an early age he began writing poetry. Studied law; began to publish poems and essays in newspapers and magazines. Helped found Society for the Attainment of Useful Knowledge. Abandoned legal studies and embarked on literary career; read William Godwin, Condorcet, and other social thinkers. In 1798 published *Alcuin*, philosophical dialogue arguing for educational and professional equality for women, and *Wieland; or the Transformation*, novel involving mesmerism, religious obsession, and murder. Subsequent novels included *Ormond; or, the Secret Witness* (1799), *Edgar Huntly; or, Memoirs of a Sleep-Walker* (1799), *Arthur Mervyn; or, Memoirs of the Year 1793* (1799–1800), *Clara Howard* (1801), and *Jane Talbot* (1801). Published journals *The American Review and Literary Journal* (1801–2) and *The Literary Magazine, and American Register* (1803–9). Wrote series of political tracts critical of Jefferson administration. Married Elizabeth Linn in 1804. Died of tuberculosis.

Willa Cather (December 7, 1873–April 28, 1947) b. Back Creek Valley, near Winchester, Virginia. Daughter of Charles Cather, a sheep farmer, and Mary Cather. The family moved to Nebraska in 1877 to

rejoin relatives successfully farming there; lived eventually in Red
Cloud. Cather read extensively from childhood. Attended University
of Nebraska (1891–95), where she began publishing stories, poems,
and criticism in school publications. Moved to Pittsburgh; worked as
editor and journalist; taught high school. Began publishing short
stories in *McClure's Magazine*; moved to New York when offered
editorial position at *McClure's*. Befriended many writers including
Sarah Orne Jewett. Story collection *The Troll Garden* published in
1905. First novel *Alexander's Bridge* (1911) was followed by *O Pioneers!*
(1913), *The Song of the Lark* (1915), and *My Ántonia* (1918). Later
novels included *A Lost Lady* (1923), *The Professor's House* (1925),
Death Comes for the Archbishop (1927), and *Shadows on the Rock*
(1931). Collected works published in 12 volumes by Houghton Mifflin, 1937–38.

Robert W. Chambers (May 26, 1865–December 16, 1933) b. Robert
William Chambers in Brooklyn, New York. Trained as an artist from
a young age, first at the Brooklyn Polytechnic Institute, then the Art
Student's League, where he was a classmate of Charles Dana Gibson.
Studied (1886–93) in Paris at the Ecole des Beaux-Arts and the Julien
Academy. Returned to the United States and published some of his
illustrations in *Life*, *Truth*, and *Vogue* before deciding to pursue a career as a writer. His many popular novels include *In the Quarter*
(1894), *The Red Republic* (1895), *Ashes of Empire* (1898), *Cardigan*
(1901), and *The Fighting Chance* (1906). His collection of linked
stories *The King in Yellow* (1895), revolving around a verse play that
brings madness and tragedy to all who read it, was exceptional in his
output for its fantastic elements.

Kate Chopin (February 8, 1850–August 22, 1904) b. Katherine
O'Flaherty in St. Louis, Missouri, daughter of Thomas O'Flaherty,
an Irish immigrant, and Catherine Reilhe, of an aristocratic but im-
poverished Creole family. Father was killed in a railroad accident
when she was five. Brother, a Confederate soldier, died of typhoid in
1863. Graduated from Sacred Heart Academy in 1868. Married busi-
nessman Oscar Chopin in 1870; couple traveled in Germany, Switzer-
land, and France on their honeymoon, then settled in New Orleans.
Husband participated in white supremacist insurrection of Crescent
City White League in 1874. Following business difficulties, family
moved to small town of Cloutierville in Natchitoches Parish, where
husband died of yellow fever in 1882. Inheriting debt-ridden estate,
Chopin operated husband's general store before moving back to
New Orleans. Began to publish stories and poems in literary magazines; published first novel, *At Fault*, at her own expense in 1890.

Short-story collections *Bayou Folk* (1894) and *A Night in Acadie* (1897) were followed by novel *The Awakening* (1899), widely attacked on moral grounds. Died of a stroke after attending St. Louis World's Fair.

Ralph Adams Cram (December 16, 1863–September 22, 1942) b. Hampton Falls, New Hampshire. He studied architecture in Boston and became a leading designer of buildings in the Gothic style. In 1887, during a stay in Rome, he experienced a religious conversion to Anglo-Catholicism. He married in 1900 and had two children. As an architect he was responsible for buildings at Cornell University, the University of Notre Dame, William College, the United States Military Academy, the University of Southern California, and Rice University. He was supervising architect at Princeton, 1907–29, and was head of the architecture department at M.I.T. He published a number of works on architecture—*Impressions of Japanese Architecture* (1905), *The Substance of Gothic* (1917)—and a volume of weird fiction, *Black Spirits and White: A Book of Ghost Stories* (1895), which was later praised by H. P. Lovecraft for its "subtleties of atmosphere and description."

Stephen Crane (November 1, 1871–June 5, 1900) b. Newark, New Jersey, youngest of 14 children of Mary Helen Peck and the Rev. Jonathan Townely Crane. Studied (1890–91) at Lafayette College and Syracuse University before leaving school to become a writer; wrote journalism, poetry, and stories. His novella *Maggie: A Girl of the Streets* (1893) was praised by Hamlin Garland and William Dean Howells. *The Red Badge of Courage* (1895) became a bestseller. Published other novels and stories, and the poetry collections *The Black Riders and Other Lines* (1895) and *War Is Kind* (1899). In 1896 met Cora Howorth Steward, brothel proprietress in Jacksonville, Florida, who became his lifelong partner. Traveled to Greece to cover Greek-Turkish War; settled in England, where friends included Joseph Conrad, Henry James, Ford Madox Ford, and H. G. Wells. Traveled to Cuba in 1898 to cover the Spanish-American War. Despite declining health continued to write stories collected in *The Open Boat and Other Tales of Adventure* (1898), *The Monster and Other Stories* (1899), and *Whilomville Stories* (1900). Died of tuberculosis at a sanatorium in the Black Forest, Germany.

F. Marion Crawford (August 2, 1854–April 9, 1909) b. Francis Marion Crawford in Bagni di Lucca, Italy. He was the son of the sculptor Thomas Crawford and Louisa Cutler Ward, and nephew of the poet and social activist Julia Ward Howe. He attended Cambridge, the University of Heidelberg, and Harvard; he studied Sanskrit in India, and settled permanently in Italy in 1883. His first novel, *Mr. Isaacs* (1882), was followed by over 40 others, including *A Roman Singer* (1884), *Saracinesca* (1887), *A Cigarette-maker's Romance* (1890), *Khaled: A Tale of Arabia* (1891), and *Don Orsino* (1892). He enjoyed great popularity and also published a number of historical works and a critical study, *The Novel: What It Is* (1893). His supernatural stories include "The Upper Berth" (1886) and "The Screaming Skull (1908).

Emma Francis Dawson (1851–February 6, 1926) A protégé of Ambrose Bierce, who described her as a writer "head and shoulders" above her contemporaries. She wrote for many periodicals in the 1880s and '90s, and was also a poet and translator. Worked at times as a music teacher. She lived reclusively on Russian Hill in San Francisco, caring for her invalid mother. She is said to have starved to death.

August Derleth (February 24, 1909–July 4, 1971) Raised in Sauk City, Wisconsin. Began writing for *Weird Tales* at 16. Was a prolific novelist and writer of short stories, much of his fiction having to do with Midwestern history. A correspondent of H. P. Lovecraft, he founded the press Arkham House in 1939 with Donald Wandrei in order to publish a collection of Lovecraft's fiction. Subsequently the imprint published work by other writers including Derleth. Derleth's fantastic stories are collected in *Someone in the Dark* (1941), *Something Near* (1945), *The Mask of Cthulhu* (1958), *The Trail of Cthulhu* (1962), and other volumes.

Olivia Howard Dunbar (1873–1953) b. West Bridgewater, Massachusetts. She graduated from Smith College in 1894 and subsequently became an editor for the *New York World*. Later she became a prolific contributor to magazines such as *Lippincott's*, *The Century*, *The Critic*, *Putnam's*, and *Scribner's*. She was married to the poet and playwright Ridgely Torrence from 1914 until his death in 1950. In a 1905 article in *The Dial* she called for "a renaissance of the literary ghost" and published many supernatural stories including "The Dream-Baby" (1904), "The Sycamore" (1910), and "The Long Chamber" (1914). She was a strong advocate of woman suffrage and with her husband was part of a social circle that included many poets and writers.

F. Scott Fitzgerald (September 24, 1896–December 21, 1940) b. St. Paul, Minnesota. After failure of father's furniture business, family moved to Buffalo and Syracuse before returning to St. Paul in 1908. Began writing stories and plays at an early age. Attended Princeton (1913–17), where he formed friendships with John Peale Bishop and Edmund Wilson. While undergoing military training, met Zelda Sayre at a country club in Montgomery, Alabama. Moved to New York, where he worked in advertising while publishing stories in *The Smart Set*, *The Saturday Evening Post*, and other magazines. Married Zelda in 1920 after publication of novel *This Side of Paradise*, which became a bestseller. Published story collections *Flappers and Philosophers* (1920) and *Tales of the Jazz Age* (1922) and second novel *The Beautiful and Damned* (1922). Sailed for France with Zelda in 1924 to complete novel published the following year as *The Great Gatsby*. In Paris met Ernest Hemingway, Gertrude Stein, Sylvia Beach, and many other literary figures. Story collection *All the Sad Young Men* appeared in 1926. In following years stayed frequently in Europe; Zelda's mental condition showed signs of deterioration and she attempted suicide in 1930, after which she was diagnosed as schizophrenic and was repeatedly hospitalized. Fitzgerald resided in Montgomery, Alabama, and subsequently Baltimore; novel *Tender Is the Night* published in 1934. Following suicide attempt in 1936, he underwent treatment at Johns Hopkins Hospital. Moved to Los Angeles to work on film scripts; fired by United Artists for drunkenness. Died of heart attack; uncompleted final novel published as *The Last Tycoon* (1941).

Mary E. Wilkins Freeman (October 31, 1852–March 13, 1930) b. Mary Eleanor Wilkins in Randolph, Massachusetts. Briefly attended Mount Holyoke College (1870–71). She began writing stories and verse while in her teens to help support her family. Her early stories of New England life, collected in *A Humble Romance* (1887) and *A New England Nun* (1891), established her as an important figure in the "local color" school of regional realism. Married Dr. Charles Freeman in 1902 and moved to New Jersey. Her more than two dozen books also include the novels *Jane Field* (1893), *Pembroke* (1894), *Jerome, a Poor Man* (1897), and *The Heart's Highway* (1900); the story collections *Silence* (1898) and *The Wind in the Rose-Bush* (1903) contain many of her stories of the supernatural. In April 1926 she was the first recipient of the William Dean Howells Medal for Distinction in Fiction from the American Academy of Arts and Letters.

Charlotte Perkins Gilman (July 3, 1860–August 17, 1935) b. Charlotte Anna Perkins in Hartford, Connecticut. Her father, Frederick Perkins, who was a nephew of Henry Ward Beecher and Harriet

Beecher Stowe, abandoned the family soon after her birth, and
Gilman, with her mother and older brother, lived in near-poverty.
Much of her early life was spent in Providence, Rhode Island. Married Charles Stetson, an artist, in 1884, and gave birth to a daughter,
her only child, the following year. Depression following the birth led
to a breakdown that was treated by Dr. Silas Weir Mitchell's "rest
cure"; the effects of the treatment were fictionalized in "The Yellow
Wall Paper." Separated from her husband in 1888, they were divorced
in 1894. Moved to California where she was active as a writer and
lecturer, and formed friendships with Edwin Markham, Ina Cool-
brith, Joaquin Miller, and other writers; published poetry collection
In This World (1893) and influential treatise *Women and Economics*
(1898). Became prominent in support of women's rights and social
reform. In 1900 married her second cousin George Houghton
Gilman, an attorney, but the two ultimately lived apart. Edited magazine *The Forerunner* (1909–16). Later books include *Concerning
Children* (1900), *Human Work* (1904), and *The Man-Made World*
(1911). Committed suicide in 1935 while suffering from inoperable
cancer. An autobiography, *The Living of Charlotte Perkins Gilman*,
appeared after her death in 1935.

Ellen Glasgow (April 22, 1874–November 21, 1945). b. Ellen Anderson Gholson Glasgow in Richmond, Virginia, to a family of aristocratic heritage. She was sickly in her youth and was educated at
home. Her novels, beginning with *The Descendant* in 1897, were
steeped in Virginia history and traced social change from before the
Civil War to the contemporary era. In her later books she turned in-
creasingly to a vein of satirical comedy. Among her novels were *The
Battle-Ground* (1902), *The Wheel of Life* (1906), *Virginia* (1913), *The
Builders* (1919), *Barren Ground* (1925), *The Romantic Comedians*
(1926), *They Stooped to Folly* (1929), *The Sheltered Life* (1932), and
Vein of Iron (1935). She won the Pulitzer Prize for *In This Our Life*
(1941). Her story collection *The Shadowy Third* appeared in 1923. An
autobiography, *The Woman Within*, was published in 1954.

Bret Harte (August 25, 1836–May 5, 1902) b. Francis Brett Harte in
Albany, New York. After several years in Brooklyn, moved to Oak-
land, California, with his family, in 1853. Gradually made his way to a
small coastal town called Union where he got a job as a printer's
devil and editorial assistant at the local newspaper, *The Northern
Californian*. Forced to leave town after writing an editorial con-
demning the massacre of a group of Wiyots (mostly women and children) living nearby. Moved to San Francisco and began writing
stories and poems for the newspaper *The Californian*. Formed

friendships with Mark Twain and Ambrose Bierce. In 1868, became editor of *The Overland Monthly*, where he published his story "The Luck of Roaring Camp," which (along with his humorous poem "Plain Language from Truthful James") brought him nationwide fame. Early fiction collected in *The Luck of Roaring Camp and Other Sketches* (1870). Relocated to the East in 1871; his later writings found little favor and he struggled against accumulating debts. After the break-up of his marriage, settled in London, where he cultivated literary friendships and continued to publish prolifically. Served in several consular posts in Krefeld, Prussia, and Glasgow, but was dismissed from the latter for inattention to his duties.

Julian Hawthorne (June 22, 1846–1934) b. Boston, son of Nathaniel Hawthorne and Julia Peabody. Attended Harvard sporadically, then transferred to Cambridge's Lawrence Scientific School to study civil engineering; finished his studies in Dresden, where he moved in 1867. Married Mary Amelung and moved to New York in 1870 where he worked for the city as a hydrographic engineer; subsequently returned to Europe to live. His first novel, *Bressant* (1873), published serially in *Appleton's*, was followed by *Idolatry* (1874), *Garth* (1877), *Archibald Malmaison* (1879), and *Sebastian Strome* (1880). In 1882, moved back to the United States and, over the next 30 years, supported his wife and seven children by his successful career as editor, biographer, and journalist. Later books included the novels *The Professor's Sister* (1888), *David Poindexter's Disappearance* (1888), and *Sarah Was Judith* (1920), as well as nonfiction works such as *Nathaniel Hawthorne and His Wife* (1884), and *Hawthorne's History of the United States* (1898). Reported on the Spanish-American War for the *New York Journal*. Indicted in 1913 along with several associates on charges of mail fraud for tricking hundreds of investors into buying fake mining shares; was convicted and served a year in the Atlanta Federal Penitentiary. After his release wrote *The Subterranean Brotherhood* (1914), calling for an end to the incarceration of prisoners. He moved to San Francisco and after the death of his first wife married his long-time companion Edith Garrigues. He was honored on his 85th birthday with a banquet attended by a number of prominent literary and social figures.

Nathaniel Hawthorne (July 4, 1804–May 19, 1864) b. Salem, Massachusetts, second of three children of Nathaniel and Elizabeth Manning Hathorne. Father, a ship's captain, died of fever in Surinam when Hawthorne was four; with mother and sisters, lived with relatives thereafter. Educated at home for a number of years following a schoolyard injury. Attended Bowdoin College (1821–25), where he began first novel, *Fanshawe*. Devoted himself to writing short fiction, eventually collected in *Twice-Told Tales* (1837). Took job at Boston Custom House. Joined utopian community Brook Farm; left after eight months. Married Sophia Peabody in 1842; they settled in Concord, Massachusetts, where he became acquainted with Emerson, Thoreau, and their circle. Story collection *Mosses from an Old Manse* (1846) followed by *The Scarlet Letter* (1850), *The House of the Seven Gables* (1851), and *The Blithedale Romance* (1852). During residence in Lenox, Massachusetts, formed friendship with Herman Melville. Wrote campaign biography for presidential campaign of Bowdoin friend Franklin Pierce; appointed American consul at Liverpool after Pierce's election. Kept extensive notebooks of travels in England, France, and Italy. Last completed novel, *The Marble Faun*, published in 1860. Returned to America in 1860.

Lafcadio Hearn (June 27, 1850–September 26, 1904) b. Patrick Lafcadio Tessima Carlos Hearn on Lefkada, one of the Ionian Islands. His mother, Rosa Antonia Cassimati, was a native of Kythira; his father, Charles Bush Hearn, was an army surgeon of Irish origin. With mother, went to Dublin to live with father, but he soon left family and later had marriage annulled. Mother returned to Greece; Hearn lived with a relative of his father before being sent to school in France. Later attended a Catholic school in Durham, where he was blinded in one eye in a schoolyard accident. Sent to United States to seek help from friends of the family, but ended up penniless; began writing for Cincinnati newspapers. Married Alethea Foley, a former slave; fired from newspaper after marriage revealed; separated from wife and never saw her again. Settled in New Orleans in 1877, writing for *Daily City Item* and other papers; traveled in Louisiana coastal islands and West Indies. Published *Some Chinese Ghosts* (1887), the novels *Chita* (1889) and *Youma* (1890), and travel book *Two Years in the French West Indies* (1890). Traveled to Japan in 1890 and remained there for the remainder of his life. Hired as a teacher in a prefectural school in Matsue; married Koizumi Setsu, daughter of a local samurai family. Later moved to Kumamoto and to Tokyo, where in 1895 he became a professor of English language and literature at Tokyo Imperial University. Became Japanese citizen. Published many books on Japanese culture, society, and folklore, including *Glimpses of Unfamiliar Japan* (1894), *Out of the East* (1895), *Kokoro* (1896), *Gleanings in Buddha-Fields* (1897), *In Ghostly Japan* (1899), and *Japan: An Attempt at Interpretation* (1904). *Kwaidan: Stories and Studies of Strange Things*, containing some of his best-known versions of Japanese supernatural legends, was published posthumously in 1904.

Robert E. Howard (January 22, 1906–June 11, 1936) b. Robert Ervin Howard in Peaster, Texas. The son of an itinerant physician, he lived in many small Texas towns during his early childhood, settling with his parents in Cross Plains in 1919. At 15 he began submitting stories to pulp magazines, eventually becoming a prolific contributor of stories and poems to *Weird Tales, Fight Stories, Cowboy Stories,* and many others. For *Weird Tales* he created the characters King Kull, Bran Mak Morn, Solomon Kane, and, most successfully, Conan the Barbarian, who made his first appearance in "The Phoenix on the Sword" (December 1932). Howard corresponded regularly with H. P. Lovecraft, although the two never met. Howard, who had long suffered from depression, shot himself to death while his dying mother lay in a terminal coma.

Washington Irving (April 3, 1783–November 28, 1859) b. New York City, youngest of eight surviving children of William Irving, a successful merchant, and Sarah Sanders Irving. Studied law in desultory fashion while beginning to contribute sketches to the *Morning Chronicle* under pseudonym "Jonathan Oldstyle, Gent." Traveled to Europe where he befriended painter Washington Allston and met Madame de Staël. With James Kirke Paulding and brother William Irving, wrote *Salmagundi* (1807–8), a collection of comic pieces. *A History of New York* (1809), attributed to fictional author Diedrich Knickerbocker, became an instant success. Edited *Analectic Magazine* (1813–15). Traveled to England, where his brother Peter ran Liverpool office of family mercantile business; due in part to firm's difficulties extended stay for years. Wrote *The Sketch Book of Geoffrey Crayon, Gent.* (1819), including "Rip Van Winkle" and "The Legend of Sleepy Hollow"; book's success made him an international celebrity. Published *Bracebridge Hall* (1822) and *Tales of a Traveller* (1824); traveled to Spain, where in 1826 he became an attaché to the American legation in Madrid. Published *Life and Voyages of Columbus* (1828), *A Chronicle of the Conquest of Granada* (1829), *Voyages and Discoveries of the Companions of Columbus* (1830), and *The Alhambra* (1932). Returned to the United States in 1832 and made a trip west into Indian Territory, described in *A Tour on the Prairie* (1834). Settled in Tarrytown, New York, eventually building residence called Sunnyside. Served as minister to Spain, 1842–45. Later books included *Astoria* (1836), *Adventures of Captain Bonneville* (1837), and multi-volume biographies of Muhammad and George Washington.

Henry James (April 15, 1843–February 28, 1916) b. New York City, the second of five children of Henry James and Mary James; his siblings included the writers William James and Alice James. Family, living on father's inheritance, moved to Europe where father experienced nervous collapse and became proponent of Swedenborgian mysticism. Family moved between America and Europe, settling finally in Newport. James entered Harvard Law School but withdrew and began publishing short fiction and reviews. Toured Europe, 1869–70, returned there 1872–74. Published first novel, *Roderick Hudson* (1875). After brief residence in New York returned to Europe, living in France and publishing journalism; moved to London in 1876. Published novels including *The American* (1877), *The Europeans* (1898), *Washington Square* (1880), and *The Portrait of a Lady* (1881). After a few brief visits to America, settling family affairs, resided chiefly in London and Paris, and traveled extensively in Italy. Published *The Princess Casamassima* (1886), *The Aspern Papers* (1888), *The Tragic Muse* (1890). Made prolonged and unsuccessful attempt to write for the theater, culminating in raucous opening night of his play *Guy Domville* (1895). Settled permanently at Lamb House in Rye in 1897. Later novels included *The Spoils of Poynton* (1897), *What Maisie Knew* (1897), *The Awkward Age* (1899), *The Sacred Fount* (1901), *The Wings of the Dove* (1902), *The Ambassadors* (1903), and *The Golden Bowl* (1904). In 1904 made first trip to America in 20 years; described impressions in *The American Scene* (1907). Published autobiographical volumes *A Small Boy and Others* (1911) and *Notes of a Son and Brother* (1914). After 1914 participated in war relief projects, visiting wounded in hospitals. Became a British citizen in July 1915.

Sarah Orne Jewett (September 3, 1849–June 24, 1909) b. Theodora Sarah Orne Jewett in South Berwick, Maine. Her father was a wealthy physician and professor of medicine. After graduating from Berwick Academy she began to publish short fiction, chiefly about the lives of fishermen and farmers, which won the editorial support of William Dean Howells. Her first story collection, *Deephaven*, appeared in 1877. Following the death of publisher James T. Fields, she became the close companion of his widow, Annie Fields, traveling with her in Europe, Florida, and the Caribbean. Her later books included *A Country Doctor* (1884), *A White Heron* (1886), *Tales of New England* (1890), and *The Country of the Pointed Firs* (1896). She stopped writing after suffering spinal damage in a carriage accident in 1902. In later years she formed a friendship with Willa Cather.

David H. Keller (December 23, 1880–July 13, 1966) b. David Henry Keller in Philadelphia. A graduate from the medical school of the University of Pennsylvania, he worked at a mental institution in

Illinois beginning in 1915, and served as a psychiatrist in both world wars; in World War I he helped pioneer the treatment of shell-shock victims. After writing a number of pieces for college magazines, he published his first pulp story in *Amazing Stories* in February 1928, and thereafter contributed regularly to *Weird Tales, Science Wonder Stories*, and other publications. He also published novels including *The Human Termites* (1929), *The Metal Doom* (1932), *The Devil and the Doctor* (1940), and *The Homunculus* (1949).

H. P. Lovecraft (August 20, 1890–March 10, 1937) b. Howard Phillips Lovecraft in Providence, Rhode Island. Father was committed to an asylum in 1893 and died five years later. Began reading Poe at age eight; wrote story "The Beast in the Cave" at 15. Attended public school in Providence; suffered nervous breakdown and failed to graduate. Began writing astronomy column for *Pawtuxet Valley Gleaner* in 1906. Lived with mother until her death (following mental collapse) in 1921. Contributed to many small magazines and journals; elected editor of United Amateur Press Association in 1920. Began writing stories of fantasy and terror; deeply influenced by Irish fantasy writer Lord Dunsany. After first issue of *Weird Tales* appeared in 1923, submitted several stories, all of which were accepted, including "Dagon" and "The Statement of Randolph Carter"; became a regular contributor to the magazine. Married Sonia Greene, a milliner he had met through the Press Association, in 1924; they settled in Brooklyn; marriage gradually fell apart and the couple were divorced in 1929. Wrote stories including "The Shunned House," "The Horror at Red Hook," "Cool Air," "The Call of Cthulhu," and the novellas "The Dream-Quest of Unknown Kadath" and "The Case of Charles Dexter Ward." "The Colour Out of Space" (later described by Lovecraft as his favorite among his stories) published by *Amazing Stories* in 1927. In the same year published essay "Supernatural Horror in Literature' in *The Recluse*. Traveled extensively, visiting colonial sites in New England and the South. Corresponded extensively with other pulp writers including Robert E. Howard, Clark Ashton Smith, and the young Robert Bloch. Wrote "The Whisperer in Darkness," "The Shadow Over Innsmouth," "The Dreams in the Witch-House," "The Haunter of the Dark," and other stories; novellas "At the Mountains of Madness" and "The Shadow Out of Time." Died at Jane Brown Memorial Hospital in Providence.

Herman Melville (August 1, 1819–September 28, 1891) b. New York City, son of Maria Gansevoort (daughter of American Revolutionary hero General Peter Gansevoort) and Allan Melvill (importer and

merchant). Father's business failed in financial panic of 1830; family forced to move to Albany where father died in 1832. Educated sporadically in New York City and upstate New York; worked as clerk, bookkeeper, and schoolteacher before joining crew of trading ship *St. Lawrence* in 1839, traveling to Liverpool and back. Sailed to South Seas on whaling ship *Acushnet* in 1841; deserted with a shipmate at Nuku Hiva in the Marquesas. After a month in Taipi valley, sailed on Australian whaling ship *Lucy Ann*, but sent ashore in Tahiti as mutineer; escaped, and explored Tahiti; sailed to Hawaii where he worked at various jobs in Honolulu before enlisting in U.S. Navy. Sailed to Boston on frigate *United States*; discharged October 1844. *Typee*, fictionalized account of Marquesas experiences, published to great success in 1846; *Omoo*, a sequel, appeared the following year. Married Elizabeth Shaw, daughter of Massachusetts Chief Justice Lemuel Shaw; they had four children. Published *Mardi* (1849), *Redburn* (1849), and *White-Jacket* (1850). Met Nathaniel Hawthorne, whose work he admired; bought farm Arrowhead near Pittsfield, Massachusetts. *Moby-Dick* was published in 1851; its indifferent reception was followed by the failure of *Pierre, or The Ambiguities* (1852), *Israel Potter* (1855), and *The Piazza Tales* (1856). Made yearlong trip to Europe and the Holy Land with father-in-law's financial help. Last published novel, *The Confidence-Man*, appeared in 1857. Moved with family to New York City in 1863; collection of Civil War poems, *Battle-Pieces and Aspects of the War*, published in 1866. Worked as deputy inspector of customs at port of New York, 1866-85. Son Malcolm died of self-inflicted gunshot wound in 1867. Long poem *Clarel: A Poem and a Pilgrimage* published 1867. Left *Billy Budd, Sailor* in manuscript (first published 1924), along with a number of poems.

W. C. Morrow (July 7, 1854–1923) b. William Chambers Morris in Selma, Alabama. His father was a minister and hotel-keeper, and Morrow graduated from Howard College in Birmingham. Relocating to California, he became a contributor to *The Argonaut* and *The San Francisco Examiner*. His stories were collected in *The Ape, the Idiot, and Other People* (1897). He published a number of novels, including *Blood-Money* (1882) and *Lentala of the South Seas* (1908), as well as *The Art of Writing for Publication* (1901).

Frank Norris (March 5, 1870–October 25, 1902) b. Benjamin Franklin Norris, Jr., in Chicago, to Gertrude Doggett Norris, an actress, and Benjamin Franklin Norris, a successful jewelry wholesaler. Family moved to San Francisco in 1885; Norris showed early interest in painting and in 1887 began studying at Julien Academy in Paris.

Returned to America and enrolled at Berkeley; during his four years there began publishing stories in the *Argonaut, The Overland Monthly*, and other periodicals. Traveled to South Africa to report on Boer War for the *San Francisco Chronicle*; on returning to California became staff writer for *The Wave*. Published novel *Moran of the Lady Letty* (1898); moved to New York to work for Doubleday. Went to Cuba to cover Spanish-American War for *McClure's. McTeague* (1899) was attacked for "lurid" subject matter, but praised by William Dean Howells and others. Published *Vandover and the Brute* (1899), *Blix* (1899), and first two volumes of trilogy "The Epic of the Wheat": *The Octopus* (1901) and *The Pit* (1902). Returned to San Francisco; died of peritonitis before completing trilogy's third volume.

Fitz-James O'Brien (December 31, 1828–April 6, 1862) b. Michael O'Brien in County Cork, Ireland. Educated at the University of Dublin. Changed his name to "Fitz-James" after arriving penniless (having squandered an inheritance) in United States in 1852. He frequented Bohemian circles at Pfaff's Cellar in New York. Began contributing articles, stories, and poems to *Harper's Magazine, New York Saturday Press, Putnam's Magazine, Vanity Fair*, and *Atlantic Monthly*. To *Atlantic* he contributed two of his best-known stories, "The Diamond Lens" (1858), about a man who falls in love with a woman he sees in a drop of water under a microscope, and "The Wonder Smith" (1859), in which fractious toys rebel against their owners. He joined the 7th regiment of the New York National Guard at the outbreak of the Civil War, and after the regiment returned without seeing action, was appointed to the staff of General Frederick W. Lander. O'Brien was wounded in a skirmish in early 1862, and died soon after in Cumberland, Maryland. The critic William Winter, a friend of O'Brien, collected his *Poems and Stories* in 1881.

Edgar Allan Poe (January 19, 1809–October 7, 1849) b. Boston, Massachusetts, second of three children of Elizabeth Arnold and David Poe, traveling actors. Father abandoned family in 1809; mother moved frequently before her death in Richmond, Virginia, in December 1811. Poe was separated from his siblings and taken into the home of Richmond tobacco merchant John Allan and his wife, Frances; they served as foster parents but did not legally adopt him. Accompanying the Allans to Great Britain, attended schools in London (1815–20) before returning with family to Richmond. Entered University of Virginia; lost money while gambling, and Allan refused to honor debts. Moved to Boston; published anonymously first book of verse, *Tamerlane and Other Poems* (1827). Enlisted in U.S. Army; at request of dying foster mother was partially reconciled with Allan, who helped secure appointment to U.S. Military Academy at West Point; he was dismissed from West Point after eight months for neglect of duty. Lived in Baltimore with aunt Maria Clemm and her eight-year-old daughter Virginia; published *Al Aaraaf, Tamerlane and Minor Poems* (1829). Began to publish short fiction in magazines, and in 1833 "Ms. Found in a Bottle" won a competition. Obtained editorial position with the *Southern Literary Messenger*, contributing stories (including "Berenice" and "Morella"), reviews, and poems. Married Virginia (then 13) in 1835. Resigned from *Messenger* after quarreling with editor and moved with Virginia and Mrs. Clemm to New York, then to Philadelphia. Became co-editor of *Burton's Gentleman's Magazine*. In 1838–39 wrote "Ligeia," "The Fall of the House of Usher," and "William Wilson" among other stories. Novel *The Narrative of Arthur Gordon Pym* was published in 1838; story collection *Tales of the Grotesque and Arabesque* appeared in 1839. Became literary editor of *Graham's Magazine* (1841–42), where he published "The Murders in the Rue Morgue" and "The Masque of the Red Death." Moved back to New York in 1844, working for *New-York Evening Mirror* and as editor of *The Broadway Journal*. Achieved fame with publication of "The Raven" in 1845. Later stories included "The Tell-Tale Heart," "The Black Cat," "The Premature Burial," "The Purloined Letter," "The Facts in the Case of M. Valdemar," and "The Cask of Amontillado"; published collections *Prose Romances* (1843) and *Tales* (1845). After years of illness, Virginia died of tuberculosis in 1847. Published metaphysical treatise *Eureka* (1848); returned to Richmond. In October 1849 stopped in Baltimore on the way to New York on literary business; he was found in a delirious condition and died four days later on October 7.

Seabury Quinn (January 1, 1889–December 24, 1969) b. Seabury Grandin Quinn. in Washington, D.C. Attended law school at the National University. Moved to New York after serving in the army during World War I and began writing, editing, and teaching on medical jurisprudence, specializing in mortuary law. Edited the mortuary journal *Casket and Sunnyside*. After publishing several weird stories in various magazines, he wrote "The Horror on the Links," which was published in the October 1925 issue of *Weird Tales* and was the first story to feature the team of Dr. Trowbridge and psychic detective Jules de Grandin. From 1925 to 1951 Quinn wrote 93 such stories, making him the magazine's most prolific contributor.

Clark Ashton Smith (January 13, 1893–August 14, 1961) b. Long Valley, California. Grew up in a small cabin in Auburn, California. Various psychological disorders prevented him from going to high school, but he continued to study on his own, eventually learning French and Spanish. He started writing stories when he was 11 and drew the attention of San Francisco poet George Sterling, who helped him get his first poetry collection, *The Star-Treader*, published; it was followed by *Odes and Sonnets* (1918) and *Ebony and Crystal* (1922), the latter of which elicited a fan letter from H. P. Lovecraft, beginning a life-long correspondence and friendship between the two. From 1926 he began publishing stories regularly in *Weird Tales*, writing more than a hundred during a six-year period, most set in fantasy realms such as Zothique, Hyperborea, and Averoigne. A single collection, *The Double Shadow*, was published privately in 1933. He virtually stopped writing after 1936, living alone and devoting himself to sculpture. He married in 1954.

Harriet Prescott Spofford (April 3, 1835–August 14, 1921) b. Harriet Elizabeth Prescott in Calais, Maine. After graduating from Pinkerton Academy in Derry, New Hampshire, she worked to support her invalid parents through writing; her story "In the Cellar" was highly praised by other writers when published in *Atlantic Monthly* in 1859. The following year she published "The Amber Gods" and "Circumstance." Of the first of these stories, Emily Dickinson remarked that "it is the only thing I ever read in my life that I didn't think I could have imagined myself," and of the second: "It followed me, in the Dark." Published the novels *Sir Rohan's Ghost* (1860) and *Azarian* (1864). Married Richard Spofford, a Boston lawyer, in 1865 and moved with him to Deer Island in Amesbury, Massachusetts. Continued to publish fiction prolifically, but her later work was not as well received. Published a memoir, *A Little Book of Friends*, in 1916.

Francis Stevens (1883–1948) b. Gertrude Mabel Barrows in Minneapolis. Attended school through the eighth grade; later attended night school. After the death of her husband, Stewart Bennett, a British explorer who died on an expedition the year after they were married, she worked as a stenographer to support her daughter and invalid mother. Began to write fantasy and science fiction stories, publishing "The Nightmare," a novella about a shipwreck survivor who finds himself on an island of monsters, in *All Story Weekly* in 1917. "Friend Island" (1918), set in the 22nd century, concerned a world ruled entirely by women. She wrote a number of novels, including *The Citadel of Fear* (1918), *The Heads of Cerberus* (1919), a dystopian fantasy, and *Claimed* (1920), in which an ancient god was summoned to contemporary New Jersey by magical means, and which H. P. Lovecraft praised. In the 1920s, Stevens moved to San Francisco, where she lived until her death in 1948.

Edith Wharton (January 24, 1862–August 11, 1937) b. Edith Newbold Jones in New York City, daughter of George Frederic Jones and Lucretia Stevens Rhinelander, both from socially prominent New York families. As a child, lived with her family in England, Italy, France, and Germany; returning to the United States in 1872, they divided their time between Manhattan and Newport, Rhode Island. Married Edward Wharton in 1885, and they spent several months every year in Europe. Began to publish poems and short stories in *Scribner's, Harper's*, and *Century Magazine*. Published historical novel, *The Valley of Decision* (1902). In 1902 moved into The Mount, a house in Lenox, Massachusetts, which she helped design. Bought an automobile in 1904 and toured in England (with close friend Henry James) and France. Continued to publish fiction, focusing most often on New York society as she had observed it: *The House of Mirth* (1905), *The Fruit of the Tree* (1907), *Ethan Frome* (1911), *The Reef* (1912), and *The Custom of the Country* (1913). In 1908 she began an affair with journalist William Morton Fullerton. The following year her husband admitted to embezzling money from her trust funds, and she was granted a divorce in 1913 on grounds of adultery. During World War I established American Hostels for Refugees and organized the Children of Flanders Rescue Committee. Bought a house near Paris in 1918. Later fiction included *Summer* (1917), *The Age of Innocence* (1920), *The Old Maid* (1921), *The Glimpses of the Moon* (1922), *The Mother's Recompense* (1925), *Hudson River Bracketed* (1929), and *The Gods Arrive* (1932). Her autobiography, *A Backward Glance*, appeared in 1934.

Edward Lucas White (May 11, 1866–March 30, 1934) b. Bergen, New Jersey. Attended Johns Hopkins University in Baltimore, where he lived for the rest of his life. Taught at University School for Boys, 1915–30. Wrote a number of historical novels, including *El Supremo* (1916), *The Unwilling Vestal* (1918), *Andivius Hedulio* (1921), and *Helen* (1926), and fantasy stories, the most famous—"The Nightmare" and "Lukundoo"—based on his own nightmares. He published two story collections, *The Song of the Sirens* (1919) and *Lukundoo and Other Stories* (1927). He killed himself seven years to the day after his wife's death; his last book, *Matrimony* (1932), was a memoir of their marriage.

Henry S. Whitehead (March 5, 1882–November 23, 1932) b. Henry
St. Clair Whitehead in Elizabeth, New Jersey. Graduated from Harvard in 1904. Studied at Berkeley Divinity School in Middleton,
Connecticut, where he was ordained an Episcopal deacon in 1912.
While serving in this capacity in the Virgin Islands (1921–29), gathered
much of the voodoo-related folkloric material he was to use in his
fantastic fiction. Published 25 stories in *Weird Tales*. Became a friend
of H. P. Lovecraft, with whom he collaborated on the story "The
Trap" (1931). His stories were later collected in *Jumbee* (1944) and
West India Lights (1946).

Madeline Yale Wynne (1847–1918). Daughter of Linus Yale, Jr., inventor of the Yale lock. Active in the Arts and Crafts movement.
Studied at the Museum School of the Museum of Fine Arts in
Boston, 1877–78, and at Art Student's League in New York in the
spring of 1880. Moved to Deerfield, Mass., and became president of
Arts and Crafts society; highly regarded as a metalworker. Later
moved to Chicago for the remainder of her life. Her story "The
Little Room" first appeared in *Harper's Magazine* and was frequently anthologized thereafter. *The Little Room and Other Stories*
(1895) was her only published book.

Note on the Texts

This volume contains 44 fantastic tales by American writers originally published between 1805 and 1939 and presents them in the order of their original publication or, in a few instances, of their composition. In the case of stories that were not collected in book form during the author's lifetime, the texts are taken from periodical versions.

The following is a list of the sources of the texts included in this volume, listed in the order of their appearance in this volume.

Charles Brockden Brown: Somnambulism: A Fragment; *Literary Magazine and American Register*, May 1805, pp. 335–47.

Washington Irving: The Adventure of the German Student; *Washington Irving: Bracebridge Hall, Tales of a Traveller, The Alhambra*, ed. Andrew Myers (New York: Library of America, 1991), pp. 418–24; first published in *Tales of a Traveller* (London: John Murray, 1824).

Edgar Allan Poe: Berenice; *Edgar Allan Poe: Poetry and Tales*, ed. Patrick F. Quinn (New York: Library of America, 1984), pp. 225–33. First published in *The Southern Literary Messenger*, March 1835, and collected in revised form in *Tales of the Grotesque and Arabesque* (Philadelphia: Lea and Blanchard, 1840).

Nathaniel Hawthorne: Young Goodman Brown. *Nathaniel Hawthorne: Tales and Sketches*, ed. Roy Harvey Pearce (New York: Library of America, 1982), pp. 276–89; first published in *New-England Magazine*, 1835, and collected in *Mosses from an Old Manse* (New York: Wiley and Putnam, 1846). Copyright © 1974 by the Ohio State University Press. Reprinted by permission of the publisher.

Herman Melville: The Tartarus of Maids; *Herman Melville: Pierre, Israel Potter, The Confidence-Man, Tales & Billy Budd*, ed. Harrison Hayford (New York: Library of America, 1985), pp. 1265–79; first published in *Harper's*, April 1855. Copyright © 1996. Reprinted by permission of the Northwestern University Press and the Newberry Library.

Fitz-James O'Brien: What Was It?; *Harper's Monthly*, March, 1859, pp. 504–9.

Bret Harte: The Legend of Monte del Diablo; *The Writings of Bret Harte, Volume One: The Luck of Roaring Camp and Other Tales*

(Boston and New York: Houghton Mifflin, 1906), pp. 382–97; first published in *The Atlantic Monthly*, September 1863.

Harriet Prescott Spofford: The Moonstone Mass; *Harper's Monthly*, October 1868, pp. 655–61.

W. C. Morrow: His Unconquerable Enemy; *The Ape, the Idiot, and Other People* (Philadelphia: J. B. Lippincott Company, 1910), pp. 48–66; first published (as "The Rajah's Nemesis") in *The Argonaut*, March 11, 1889.

Sarah Orne Jewett: In Dark New England Days; *Strangers and Wayfarers* (Boston: Houghton Mifflin, 1899), pp. 220–56; first published in *The Century*, October 1890.

Charlotte Perkins Gilman: The Yellow Wall Paper; *The Yellow Wall Paper* (Boston: Small, Maynard & Co., 1899); first published in *New England Magazine*, January 1892.

Stephen Crane: The Black Dog; *Stephen Crane: Prose and Poetry*, ed. J. C. Levenson (New York: Library of America, 1984), pp. 501–5; first published in the *New York Tribune*, July 24, 1892.

Kate Chopin: Ma'ame Pélagie; *Kate Chopin: Complete Novels and Stories*, ed. Sandra M. Gilbert (New York: Library of America, 2002), pp. 294–301. First published in *New Orleans Times-Democrat*, December 24, 1893, and collected in *Bayou Folk* (Boston: Houghton Mifflin, 1894).

John Kendrick Bangs: Thurlow's Christmas Story; *Ghosts I Have Met and Some Others* (New York: Harper & Bros., 1898), pp. 109–39. First published in *Harper's Weekly*, December 15, 1894.

Robert W. Chambers: The Repairer of Reputations; *The King in Yellow* (New York: Harper & Bros., 1902), pp. 3–44; first edition 1895 (New York: F. T. Neely).

Ralph Adams Cram: The Dead Valley; *Black Spirits and White: A Book of Ghost Stories* (New York: Stone & Kimball, 1895), pp. 133–50.

Madeline Yale Wynne: The Little Room; *The Little Room and Other Stories* (Chicago: Walter M. Hill, 1895), pp. 7–39; first published in *Harper's*, August 1895.

Gertrude Atherton: The Striding Place; *The Bell in the Fog and Other Stories* (New York: Harper & Bros., 1905), pp. 47–57; first published (as "The Twins") in *The Speaker*, June 20, 1896.

Emma Francis Dawson: An Itinerant House; *An Itinerant House and Other Stories* (San Francisco: William Doxey, 1897), pp. 1–30; first published in *Overland Monthly*, 1897.

Mary Wilkins Freeman: Luella Miller; *The Wind in the Rosebush* (New York: Doubleday, Page & Co., 1903) pp. 75–104; first published in *Everybody's Magazine*, December 1902.

Frank Norris: Grettir at Thorhall-stead; *Everybody's Magazine*, April 1903, pp. 311–19.

Lafcadio Hearn: Yuki-Onna; *Kwaidan* (Boston: Houghton Mifflin, 1904), pp. 111–18.

F. Marion Crawford: For the Blood Is the Life; *Wandering Ghosts* (New York: Macmillan Company, 1911), pp. 167–94; first published in *Collier's*, December 1905.

Ambrose Bierce: The Moonlit Road; *Collected Works of Ambrose Bierce, Volume Three: Can Such Things Be?* (New York & Washington: The Neale Publishing Company, 1910), pp. 62–80; first published in *Cosmopolitan*, January 1907.

Edward Lucas White: Lukundoo; *Lukundoo and Other Stories* (New York: George H. Doran Company, 1927), pp. 9–28; written 1907.

Olivia Howard Dunbar: The Shell of Sense; *Harper's Monthly*, December 1908, pp. 69–74.

Henry James: The Jolly Corner; *Henry James: Complete Stories 1898–1910*, ed. Denis Donoghue (New York: Library of America, 1996), pp. 697–731. First published in *The English Review*, December 1908, and collected in volume 17 of *The Novels and Tales of Henry James* (New York: Scribner's, 1907–9).

Alice Brown: Golden Baby; *Vanishing Points* (New York: Macmillan Company, 1913), pp. 275–95; first published in *Harper's*, March 1910.

Edith Wharton: Afterward; *Edith Wharton: Collected Stories 1891–1910*, ed. Maureen Howard (New York: Library of America, 2001), pp. 830–60. First published in *Century Magazine*, January 1910, and collected in *Tales of Men and Ghosts* (New York: Scribner's, 1910).

Willa Cather: Consequences; *Willa Cather: Stories, Poems and Other Writings*, ed. Sharon O'Brien (New York: Library of America), pp.133–53; first published in *McClure's Magazine*, November 1915.

Ellen Glasgow: The Shadowy Third; *The Shadowy Third and Other Stories* (New York: Doubleday, Page & Co., 1923), pp. 3–43; first published in *Scribner's Magazine*, December 1916.

Julian Hawthorne: Absolute Evil; *All-Story Weekly*, April 13, 1918.

Francis Stevens (Gertrude Mabel Barrows): Unseen—Unfeared; *People's Favorite Magazine*, February 10, 1919, pp. 139–48.

F. Scott Fitzgerald: The Curious Case of Benjamin Button; *F. Scott Fitzgerald: Novels and Stories, 1920–1922*, ed. Jackson R. Bryer (New York: Library of America, 2000), pp. 954–79. First published in *Collier's*, May 27, 1922, and collected in *Tales of the Jazz Age* (New York: Scribner's, 1922).

Seabury Quinn: The Curse of Everard Maundy; *Weird Tales*, July 1927, pp. 49–68.

Stephen Vincent Benét: The King of the Cats; *Thirteen O'Clock: Stories of Several Worlds* (New York: Farrar & Rinehart, Inc., 1937), pp. 48–68; first published in *Harper's Bazaar*, February 1929. Copyright ©1929 by Stephen Vincent Benét; copyright renewed © 1957 by Rosemary Carr Benét. Reprinted by permission of Brandt & Hochman Literary Agents, Inc.

David H. Keller: The Jelly-Fish; *Tales from Underwood* (New York: Published for Arkham House by Pelligrini & Cudahy, 1952), pp. 244–48; first published in *Weird Tales*, January 1929.

Conrad Aiken: Mr. Arcularis; *Among the Lost People* (New York: C. Scribner's Sons, 1934), 12–43; first published in *Harper's*, March 1931. Copyright © Conrad Aiken. Reprinted by permission of Joseph I. Killorin for the Estate of Conrad Aiken.

Robert E. Howard: The Black Stone; *Weird Tales*, November 1931, pp. 500–11.

Henry S. Whitehead: Passing of a God; *Weird Tales*, January, 1931, pp. 98–110.

August Derleth: The Panelled Room; *Someone in the Dark* (Sauk City, WI: Arkham House, 1941), pp. 228–44; first published in *Westminster Magazine*, September 1933. Copyright © 1941 by August Derleth, renewed © 1969, 1997 by Arkham House, Publishers, Inc. Reprinted by permission of Arkham House Publishers, Inc.

H. P. Lovecraft: The Thing on the Doorstep; *Lovecraft: Tales*, Peter Straub, ed. (New York: Library of America, 2005), pp. 692–718; first published in *Weird Tales*, January 1937. Copyright © 1937. Used by permission of Lovecraft Properties, LLC.

Clark Ashton Smith: Genius Loci; *Genius Loci and Other Tales* (Sauk City, WI: Arkham House, 1945), pp. 3–20; first published in *Weird Tales*, June 1933.

Robert Bloch: The Cloak; *The Opener of the Way* (Sauk City, WI: Arkham House, 1945), pp. 3–18; first published in *Unknown*, May 1939. Copyright © 1945 by Robert Bloch. Reprinted by permission of The Estate of Robert Bloch c/o Ralph M. Vicinanza, Ltd.

This volume presents the texts listed here without change except for the correction of typographical errors, but it does not attempt to reproduce features of their typographic design. The following is a list of typographical errors, cited by page and line number: 13.12, de-/cling; 14.4, on?; 190.40, esctasy; 198.39, Yellow'"; 208.3, fire!'; 244.22, 'if,"; 248.4, 'A; 256.37, "l's"; 323.20, Ven; 374.3, A; 374.5, He; 376.36, He; 378.10, girl's; 449.39, see; 458.12, it."; 468.32, Duckworth's; 481.10, transcendant; 530.17, Roscie; 551.34, word; 570.14, are; 598.40, if; 610.21, noblemen; 610.37, Goeffrey; 612.27, aboriginies; 618.25, ecstacy; 623.19, "Have; 695.10, though.

Notes

In the notes below, the reference numbers refer to page and line of this volume (the line count includes titles and headings). Biblical quotations are keyed to the King James Version. Quotations from Shakespeare are keyed to G. Blakemore Evans, ed., *The Riverside Shakespeare* (Boston: Houghton Mifflin, 1974). The editor wishes to thank Stefan Dziemianowicz for his expert and deeply knowledgeable assistance in the preparation of these volumes and the selection of their contents.

21.18   Swedenborg] Emanuel Swedenborg (1688–1772), Swedish mystic.

24.5–6   statue of Henry the Fourth . . . overthrown by the populace] The statue was torn down in 1792 and restored in 1818.

25.12   Goddess of Reason] The worship of reason was promulgated during the French Revolution by Jacques Hébert and others; the Goddess of Reason was personified by Thérèse Momoro in an anti-Christian Festival of Liberty and Reason celebrated at Notre Dame Cathedral in November 1793.

27.4–5   *Dicebant . . . fore levatas.—Ebn Zaiat*] In Poe's translation, from a footnote he later deleted: "My companions told me I might find some little alleviation of my misery, in visiting the grave of my beloved." Ebn Zaiat (or more properly Abou Giafar Mohammed ben Abdalmalek ben Abban) was a poet of Baghdad who died around 218 C.E. The quotation is from a 10th-century poetry anthology, the *Kitab al-Aghani* (*Book of Songs*).

30.26–28   treatise of . . . *"de Carne Christi,"*] The treatise by Curio (1503–1569) was published in 1554; St. Augustine's *City of God* was finished in 426; Tertullian's *On the Flesh of Christ* dates from the early third century.

30.29–31   *Mortuus est . . . impossibile est*] That the Son of God died is to be believed because it is incredible; that He is risen is certain because it is impossible.

33.8   Mad'selle Sallé] Marie Sallé (1714–1756), a dancer.

33.8–9   *"que tous ses pas etaient des sentiments,"*] That all her steps were feelings.

33.9–10   *que tous ses dents etaient des idées*] That all her teeth were ideas.

33.30   preparations for the burial were completed.] In Poe's original version, published in *The Southern Literary Messenger* and collected in *Tales of the Grotesque and Arabesque* (1840), four paragraphs follow which Poe deleted when he reprinted the story in *The Broadway Journal* in 1845:

> With a heart full of grief, yet reluctantly, and oppressed with awe, I made my way to the bed-chamber of the departed. The room was large, and very dark, and at every step within its gloomy precincts I encountered the paraphernalia of the grave. The coffin, so a menial told me, lay surrounded by the curtains of yonder bed, and in that coffin, he whisperingly assured me, was all that remained of Berenice. Who was it asked me would I not look upon the corpse? I had seen the lips of no one move, yet the question had been demanded, and the echo of the syllables still lingered in the room. It was impossible to refuse; and with a sense of suffocation I dragged myself to the side of the bed. Gently I uplifted the draperies of the curtains.
>
> As I let them fall they descended upon my shoulders, and shutting me thus out from the living, enclosed me in the strictest communion with the deceased.
>
> The very atmosphere was redolent of death. The peculiar smell of the coffin sickened me; and I fancied a deleterious odor was already exhaling from the body. I would have given worlds to escape—to fly from the pernicious influence of mortality—to breathe once again the pure air of the eternal heavens. But I had no longer the power to move—my knees tottered beneath me—and I remained rooted to the spot, and gazing upon the frightful length of the rigid body as it lay outstretched in the dark coffin without a lid.
>
> God of heaven!—was it possible? Was it my brain that reeled—or was it indeed the finger of the enshrouded dead that stirred in the white cerement that bound it? Frozen with unutterable awe I slowly raised my eyes to the countenance of the corpse. There had been a band around the jaws, but, I know not how, it was broken asunder. The livid lips were wreathed into a species of smile, and, through the enveloping gloom, once again there glared upon me in too palpable reality, the white and glistening, and ghastly teeth of Berenice. I sprang convulsively from the bed, and, uttering no words, rushed forth a maniac from that apartment of triple horror, and mystery, and death.

37.27   King Philip's war]   Conflict (1675–76) between Native Americans and English settlers in southern New England. Metacom, the leader of the Wampanoag Indians, was known to the English as King Philip.

50.32   pung]   One-horse sleigh.

52.34   Paradise of Bachelors]   "The Paradise of Bachelors" was the companion piece to "The Tartarus of Maids"; the two sketches were published together in *Harper's*, April 1, 1855. The bachelors in question are residents of the Temple Bar in London.

55.9   Actæon] Hunter who in Greek mythology was transformed into a stag and devoured by his own hounds after spying on Diana at her bath.

60.39   Saint Veronica] In Christian tradition, a woman of Jerusalem who took pity on Jesus on his way to Golgotha and wiped his brow with her veil; the cloth thereafter bore a miraculous impression of his face.

65.8–9   Mrs. Crowe's "Night Side of Nature"] Catherine Crowe, *The Night-Side of Nature, or Ghosts and Ghost-Seers* (New York: 1853).

65.18–19   "The Pot of Tulips,"] An earlier story by Fitz-James O'Brien.

66.26   *Rana arborea*] Tree frog.

67.7   Haroun] Haroun al-Raschid, eighth-century caliph of Baghdad who plays a legendary role in *The Thousand and One Nights.*

67.8   afreets] In Arabic mythology, demons or evil spirits.

68.1–2   Brockden Brown's novel of 'Wieland'] In Charles Brockden Brown's *Wieland, or The Transformation* (1798), the protagonist hears disembodied voices created through ventriloquism and mistakes them for divine commands.

68.3   Bulwer's 'Zanoni;'] Novel (1842) involving the achievement of eternal life through occult arts.

68.10   Hoffman] E.T.W. Hoffmann (1776–1822), German writer, composer, and theatrical impresario, whose fantastic tales exerted widespread influence.

74.36–37   Gustave Doré, or Callot, or Tony Johannot] Doré (1832–1883), artist and engraver known for his illustrations of Dante, Rabelais, Milton, and the Bible; Jacques Callot (c. 1592–1635), celebrated printmaker; Johannot (1803–1852), French engraver and illustrator.

74.39   *Un voyage ou il vous plaira*] A trip to wherever you like.

99.10   Jemschid] Or Jamshid; legendary Persian king.

101.36   *Per si muove*] *Eppur si muove*: And yet it moves. The phrase was said to have been muttered by Galileo after his forced recantation in 1633 of the theory of heliocentrism.

136.38–39   Weir Mitchell] Silas Weir Mitchell (1829–1914), physician and author whose works included the novel *Hugh Wynne, Free Quaker* (1897). Gilman underwent his experimental treatment for depression, involving isolation and inactivity, of which "The Yellow Wall Paper" is in part a description.

158.25   "Il ne . . . à Pauline."] We mustn't let Pauline get hurt.

171.16   De La Motte Fouque] Friedrich Heinrich Karl, Baron de la

Motte Fouqué (1777–1843), writer and officer in the Prussian cavalry; best known for his supernatural fantasy *Undine* (1811).

177.23–24 "*Ne raillons . . . la différence.*"] Let us not mock the mad; their madness lasts longer than ours. . . . That is the only difference.

191.25–26 the monstrosity . . . to represent Garibaldi] The statue, by Giovanni Turini, was erected in Washington Square Park in 1888.

201.7 Carcosa] Chambers derived the name Carcosa and many other details of the imaginary play "The King in Yellow" from Ambrose Bierce's story "An Inhabitant of Carcosa" (1886). The story is recounted by a man (later revealed to have already died) as he wanders through an unknown landscape.

235.16–17 Wordsworth's Boy of Egremond] Young Romilly, the heir of a noble family, who drowned in the Strid, as recounted in Wordsworth's poem "The Force of Prayer; or, the Founding of Bolton Priory. A Tradition" (1815). "The story is preserved," according to Wordsworth's later note, "in Dr. Whitaker's History of Craven." "The Boy of Egremond" (1819), a poem on the same subject, was written by Samuel Rogers.

238.4–7 *Eternal longing with eternal pain . . . through some old maze of wrong.*] From "The Wanderer" (1857) by Owen Meredith (pseudonym of Edward Robert Bulwer Lytton, 1831–1891).

238.25 Marryatt] Frederick Marryatt (1792–1848), English naval officer whose popular novels of the sea included *Peter Simple* (1833) and *Mr. Midshipman Easy* (1834).

241.40 'Evil shall not depart from his house.'] Proverbs 17:13: "Whoso rewardeth evil for good, evil shall not depart from his house."

242.25 'The Bells.'] Play (1871) by Leopold Lewis; Sir Henry Irving was celebrated for his portrayal of the conscience-racked murderer Mathias.

243.5–6 'I'll make . . . of you!'] *King Lear*, II.ii.32–33.

243.13–15 Poe's hero . . . and Persepolis, until my very soul has become a ruin.'] In "Ms. Found in a Bottle" (1833).

243.38 'and tell quaint lies'] *The Merchant of Venice*, III.iv.69.

244.5 'Poor Jo's,'] Poor Jo, chimney sweep in Charles Dickens' *Bleak House* (1852–53); he was a principal character in stage adaptations of the novel.

244.7 Io-like] In Greek mythology, Io was loved by Zeus and changed him into a heifer to elude the jealousy of Hera; eventually Hera sent a gadfly to torment her and keep her wandering until she reached Egypt where she was permitted to settle.

244.23–24 Hawthorne's offer . . . exploring expedition] Nathaniel Hawthorne applied unsuccessfully for the position of historian on the Great

Exploring Expedition (1838–42). Under the command of Charles Wilkes, the expedition surveyed areas of Antarctica, the Pacific Ocean, and the northwest coast of America.

244.27 Passavent] Johan Karl Passavant (1790–1857), German theologian and homeopathist, author of *Animul Magnetism* (1821).

244.34–38 VICTOR.—Where is the gentleman? . . . His soul is in Madrid.'] Henry Wadsworth Longfellow, *The Spanish Student* (1843), III.v.

245.15–16 Heine's 'Reisebilder,'] *Pictures of Travel* (1826–27).

246.25 Talma] François-Joseph Talma (1763–1826), actor who dominated the French stage from before the Revolution until after the Bourbon restoration.

246.30 'Court and Stage,'] Play (1854) by Charles Reade, originally titled *The King's Rival*.

247.22–25 'See where he steals . . . in sorrow's knot.'] The lines are from David Garrick's altered version of *Romeo and Juliet* (1750).

248.37–38 "The Wandering Jew,"] A play adapted from Eugène Sue's novel *Le Juif Errant* (1844).

249.1–7 "All in my mind is confused . . . the roar of the limitless sea."] From Owen Meredith, "The Shore" (see note 238.4–7).

249.28 T. A. Trollope's "Artist's Tragedy:"] Thomas Adolphus Trollope's story about Andrea del Sarto appeared in *The Temple Bar Magazine* in 1870.

250.26–29 Macdonald's lover cries . . . when, or where, or how?'] See George MacDonald, *The Portent* (1864).

250.37 Swinburne's queen of panthers] See Algernon Charles Swinburne, "At a Month's End": "But I, who leave my queen of panthers, / As a tired honey-heavy bee / Gilt with sweet dust from gold-grained anthers / Leaves the rose-chalice, what for me?"

251.27 "Chant du Depart."] Revolutionary song written around 1794.

253.19–20 Marquise de Brinvilliers] Marie-Madeleine-Marguerite d'Aubray, marquise de Brinvilliers (b. 1630), was beheaded and burned at the stake for the poisoning of her father, brother, and two sisters; she was also implicated in other poisonings.

269.3 *Grettir*] Outlawed protagonist of the Icelandic *Saga of Grettir the Strong*.

305.29 Remote, unfriended, melancholy, slow.] Oliver Goldsmith, *The Traveller* (1764), line 1.

314.7–8 triumph of Elijah over the prophets of Baal] See 1 Kings 18:21–39.

331.20–21   Shell of sense / So frail, so piteously contrived for pain,]   Cf. William Vaughn Moody, *The Masque of Judgment* (1900): "My heart makes question which were worthier state / For a free soul to choose,—angelic calm, / Angelic vision, ebbless, increscent, / Or earth-life with its reachings and recoils, / Its lewd harsh blood so swift to change and flower / At the least touch of love, its shell of sense / So subtly made to minister them delight, / So frail, so piteously contrived for pain."

346.35   *pour deux sous*]   For two sous.

350.14   *ombres chinoises*]   Shadow-puppets.

371.13–14   Sir Philip Sidney . . . Zutphen]   Sidney was killed in 1586 while leading an attack on a Spanish convoy near Zutphen in the Netherlands.

371.22   William Morris]   British artist, designer, and author (1834–1896). As an artist he was associated with the Pre-Raphaelites.

372.31   'came to the making of man']   Algernon Charles Swinburne, *Atalanta in Calydon* (1865): "Before the beginning of years / There came to the making of man / Time with a gift of tears; / Grief with a glass that ran . . ."

375.29   George Osborne]   Self-indulgent character in Thackeray's *Vanity Fair* (1847–48), a military officer who dies at the battle of Waterloo.

379.26   Sylvia]   Ballet (1876) with music by Léo Delibes.

426.6   *forestieri*]   Tourists.

463.13   Spencer . . . doth the body make,']   Edmund Spenser, "A Hymn in Honour of Beauty" (1596), line 133.

464.16–17   'The bridal of the earth . . . Herbert]   George Herbert, "Virtue": "Sweet day, so cool, so calm, so bright, / The bridal of the earth and sky, / The dew shall weep thy fall tonight; / For thou must die."

489.24   Actæon]   See note 55.9.

489.37   I invited my soul]   See Walt Whitman, "Song of Myself": "I loafe and invite my soul, / I lean and loafe at my ease observing a spear of summer grass."

489.37–38   *à outrance*]   Excessively.

527.6   charge up San Juan Hill]   On July 1, 1898, American troops assaulted and captured the San Juan heights east of Santiago, Cuba.

538.34–35   Haggard's *The Wanderer's Necklace*]   Short adventure novel (1914) by Sir Henry Rider Haggard, recounted by the English reincarnation of a Norse warrior.

552.9   Kipling . . . 'that is another story.']   "But that is another story" became a catchphrase in the 1890's due to Rudyard Kipling's frequent use of it in his early fiction.

563.17–33   Rossetti . . . *Eden Bowers* . . . Glittering sons and radiant daughters] See Dante Gabriel Rossetti, "Eden's Bower" (1868).

573.4   "Iphigenie in Aulis"] *Iphigénie en Aulide* (1774), opera by Christoph Willibald Gluck.

577.36   Monk Lewis] Matthew Gregory Lewis (1775–1818), author of the Gothic novel *The Monk* (1796).

590.34   "But let there be no moaning,"] See Alfred Tennyson, "Crossing the Bar," first stanza: "Sunset and evening star, / And one clear call for me! / And may there be no moaning of the bar, / When I put out to sea."

592.7–8   Melozzo da Forli] Umbrian fresco painter (c. 1438–1494).

594.9   *Empress of Ireland*] Canadian ocean liner that was sunk in the St. Lawrence River in 1914 after colliding with a coal freighter; over a thousand lives were lost.

598.25–26   the Hound of Heaven] God, as personified in the poem by Francis Thompson (1859–1907).

601.29–30   "The Roast Beef of Old England"] Patriotic ballad from Henry Fielding's *The Grub-Street Opera* (1731); the musical setting by Richard Leveridge was widely performed to introduce or close theatrical performances.

605.20   'On such a night as this—'] See *The Merchant of Venice*, V.i.1–22.

655.23   the notorious . . . Justin Geoffrey] From Robert E. Howard's "The Black Stone," pages 607–24 in this volume.

657.11   Plattsburg] A training camp for army officers was established at Plattsburg, New York, during World War I.

678.13   lich] Corpse.

684.35   Sorolla] Joaquín Sorolla y Bastide (1863–1923), Spanish painter.

700.6–7   Elsa Maxwell] Gossip columnist and society hostess (1883–1963).

THE LIBRARY OF AMERICA SERIES

The Library of America fosters appreciation and pride in America's literary heritage by publishing, and keeping permanently in print, authoritative editions of America's best and most significant writing. An independent nonprofit organization, it was founded in 1979 with seed money from the National Endowment for the Humanities and the Ford Foundation.

To subscribe to the series or to order individual copies,
please visit www.loa.org or call (800) 964.5778.

*This book is set in 10 point Linotron Galliard,
a face designed for photocomposition by Matthew Carter
and based on the sixteenth-century face Granjon. The paper
is acid-free lightweight opaque and meets the requirements
for permanence of the American National Standards Institute.
The binding material is Brillianta, a woven rayon cloth made
by Van Heek-Scholco Textielfabrieken, Holland. Composition by Dedicated Business Services. Printing by
Malloy Incorporated. Binding by Dekker Book-
binding. Designed by Bruce Campbell.*